Ilene Prusher was a staff writer for the *Christian Science Monitor* from 2000 to 2010, serving as bureau chief in Tokyo, Istanbul, and Jerusalem and covering the wars in Iraq and Afghanistan. She is now an independent journalist based in Jerusalem, and also teaches Reporting Conflict for NYU-Tel Aviv.

After graduating from the Columbia University Graduate School of Journalism in 1993, Ilene started her career as a reporter at *The Philadelphia Inquirer*, later freelancing from the Middle East for *Newsday*, *The New Republic*, the *Financial Times*, the *Guardian* and the *Observer*.

Raised in New York, she now lives in Jerusalem with her husband and two children. *Baghdad Fixer* is her first novel.

"…a compelling account of the first few weeks following the collapse of Saddam Hussein's regime told through the eyes of a fascinating and gracefully drawn Iraqi everyman… Ms Prusher draws us into his story as he is sometimes unwittingly lured deeper and deeper into the world of war journalism, watching with horror as his country descends into chaos."

Borzou Daragahi, Middle East and N Africa correspondent for the *Financial Times*

"A unique novel, *Baghdad Fixer*'s compelling plot is combined with poignant and difficult insights into the life and tragedies of ordinary Iraqis during the war. This is not just a wonderful read, it is an important book for helping us, too, to begin to understand the Other."

Tania Hershman, *My Mother Was An Upright Piano*

Baghdad Fixer

Ilene Prusher

HALBAN
LONDON

First Published in Great Britain by
Halban Publishers Ltd.
22 Golden Square
London W1F 9JW
2012

www.halbanpublishers.com

A CIP catalogue record for this book is available from the
British Library.

ISBN 978 1 905559 47 3

Typeset by Spectra Titles, Norfolk
Printed in Great Britain by
MPG Books Ltd, Bodmin, Cornwall

To my parents,
to the teachers who parented me some more
and to the Fixer who told me this story

1

Moving

MY MOTHER SAYS that I am an extraordinarily good catch – handsome, smart, employed. My father doesn't say anything. And though the timing would seem preposterous to some, we Iraqis have done stranger things in the middle of a war than agree to go on a date.

These dates, if you could call them that, given that we have both sets of parents present, would seem bizarre to a Westerner. But my parents, modern as they are in many respects, are always arranging them: meetings at the homes of well-heeled acquaintances, of my father's colleagues from the hospital, of second and third cousins I've never met. They all have something my parents want: an unmarried daughter in need of a husband.

The women bear common characteristics. I know her profile before I've met her. She is in her mid-twenties, even occasionally over twenty-five, attractive enough, and decently educated. She is younger than I am, but is considered to be getting old for this game; with each passing month she is less marriageable. She has never lived anywhere but under her father's roof. She's never had a boyfriend, or so her family says.

Noor is not much different, although she is working on a master's degree in psychology, which is commendable. Unlike me, she's never had any international experience. I doubt she speaks English, German or French, but she's considered to be quite clever, Mum says, and rather pretty. It's not like I didn't notice that, which is why I agreed to a second "date", the first having been a cup of tea with her – and her brother Adnan – at an upmarket café next to the University of Baghdad. The air raid sirens went off, so we had to cut it short.

Most importantly, I know my parents would be very happy to have the family of Dr Mahmoud al-Bakri, Baba's old friend from medical school, as our in-laws. And so it can't hurt to agree to a second date.

That's where my tale ought to begin, for those of you who are joining me now, in this, the twenty-eighth year of my life, on the eighth day of the month of April in the year 2003, on the fifth day of Safar in the year 1424. You'll find me here in the Hurriyah neighbourhood in the city of Baghdad, my beloved birthplace, ill-at-ease and feeling foolish, sitting on this sky-blue sofa with my parents. We're facing a matching sofa, upon which Noor al-Bakri and her parents sit. I sip tea from their good porcelain cups and hope to avoid eating yet another stuffed date biscuit made by Noor's mother with great care. If the mother knows how to bake a good *kalijeh*, we assume the daughter will, too.

Should I just say yes? It's as if they've all proposed to me and I've told them I don't yet know. I haven't made up my mind. I'll let you know in the morning.

Noor's mother tries to get me to take one more, and when I decline, she gestures to Noor, then glances in the direction of the fruit on the coffee table that sits between us. Noor rises and then kneels at the table, takes two apples out of the bowl and proceeds to slice them as elegantly as possible. Before I can say no, she lays the pieces out neatly on three small plates. We watch as she cuts into a bright-orange persimmon, and I am thankful when my father breaks our nervous focus on Noor's fruit-fixing skills by asking Dr Mahmoud whether he'd heard that Dr Abdel-Majid did not show up for work today.

"The psychiatric ward will be bouncing off the walls without him," Baba says. Dr Mahmoud's face cracks into a half-smile, the kind a person makes when they're not sure whether it's safe to laugh. Mum elbows Baba gently in the arm. Noor's mother's face goes blank. Apparently, Dr Mahmoud hasn't let her in on the office humour. "Dr Abdel-Majid" is a nickname for Saddam that my father and his doctor friends made up. Many people don't make the connection. The president's full name is Saddam Hussein Abdel-Majid al-Tikriti. We took him on and put him in charge of the lunatic asylum years ago, the doctors joked. It was a bad move.

When you're never sure who is listening, you speak politics in code.

Noor, too, seems unaware of my father's news update: that Saddam has disappeared. Her concentration is locked on attractively arranging the fruit she is expected to serve us. She collects the three plates and rises carefully. Her dark, kohl-lined eyes dart at me, and then back down at the fruit. Her hands are shaking. Despite myself, despite my private conclusion that I cannot marry Noor – and I conclude this within five minutes of meeting most Iraqi women, so at this point I'm only here to indulge my parents' desire to find a wife for me, to assuage their fears and to allow them to feel that they're at least doing something to get me married off – I find myself feeling softened by Noor's deep eyes and her jittery hands, wondering if I should

3

just say yes. She's earning a masters degree in psychology, after all. But at this moment, her marriage prospects will be reduced to her beauty and to how gracefully she serves us tea and fruit, and it all seems horribly unfair. She does have a pretty face, even if only in an ordinary Iraqi sort of way. She comes from a good family. She'll make a perfectly decent wife, I'm sure.

Noor's face freezes and she looks as if she will scream. She pulls in a gulp of air with a sharp squeak but never pushes it back out. Her mouth is locked in a small "o", her dark eyes scrunch in on themselves like she's heard a story she doesn't believe. My mind rewinds to replay the sounds of the moment before, when I was lost in my deliberations, and this time I catch it: the distant pops, the whizzing noise, the fast plink of glass being broken. The echo and bounce and shatter. The eerie calm before the panic.

By the time I catch up to now, Noor has collapsed at our feet, making choking sounds. The red is seeping through the neckline of her *crème*-coloured blouse. For a second, or an eternity, there is an absence of sound. Fruit and bone-china and blood scatter across the floor, on my lap. A sliver of persimmon clings to Baba's shirt. Noor's mother screaming.

"*Rahmet-Allah!*"

"Where did it come from?"

"Get an ambulance!"

"Goddamn Americans!"

"Where did it go in?"

An air raid siren wails like an injured beast, but it's dull compared to the shrieking. Her mother's, my mother's, Noor's younger sister's, conflating with the commotion of a few neighbours bursting into the living room, including Noor's brother Adnan, who lives next door with his wife. Dr Mahmoud's mouth keeps opening but no sound comes out, as if he – rather than his daughter – was struck by something in the back of the head.

Baba is already in motion, has long since run and grabbed a towel from their guest bathroom and is pressing it to the back of Noor's neck. "*Y'alla*," he yells, "has someone called the ambulance?" He shakes his head. "*Maku faida*," he says under his breath. No way. No point. No chance it can end well. I don't know if that's Baba's diagnosis, or just disbelief.

Noor's mother is in the kitchen, pressing frantically at the telephone. I look in on her and she lets the receiver fall to the floor. Her lips tremble and she begins to bawl. "There's no dial tone!"

"Leave it," Baba calls out. "We've got to get her into surgery. We'll take her ourselves. Nabil? Nabil, for God's sake, are you with me?"

I start ordering anyone in the house who is coherent to help me get Noor into our car. Of course there's no dial tone; most phones have been dead for a fortnight. And what are the chances of getting an ambulance here in time? The city has been under bombardment for more than three weeks. Bombs are shattering buildings to bones, aircraft are strafing entire neighbourhoods, shells are picking away at the very flesh of the riverfront. Who's going to send out an ambulance to save one girl?

Adnan and Baba and I carry Noor into my father's car and lay her down on the back seat. Baba tells Noor's mother to stay at home with her younger daughter, who is convulsing with hysterics, and to cover poor Dr Mahmoud with a blanket. There lies on the floor Baba's old school friend, the oncologist, a fast-ageing man who has become accustomed to the slow, manageable death of strangers. Not the shooting of his daughter through the window of his own living room.

Baba gives Adnan his keys, assigns me the front passenger seat, and takes the back seat, where he holds Noor's head in his lap. As we drive, I watch him put one hand against her neck while his other hand periodically feels her wrist for signs of life. Her small, limp hand is stark against her long, red fingernails. The hand my parents suggested I take in marriage, is now pale and clamped between my father's thick fingers.

We speed through the darkened streets of a neighbourhood I've known my whole life, through intersections which have never seemed as empty as they do now. And then on to the main road, with a few frenetic cars rushing by, gunning to get somewhere. Who goes out in the middle of an air raid? It's silly that my parents were so keen to sit with Noor and her parents in the first place, in the middle of this. But I knew it was their mark of *sumud*, their own form of steadfastness. Defiance through denial, by continuing life as normal.

Closer to the hospital, I now see who does go out. Even from a block away, we are stuck behind a queue of cars funnelling towards the entrance.

"To hell with it. Just go around them, up the kerb," Baba orders.

Adnan hesitates.

"It's *my* bloody hospital! I'm not going to wait in line while she dies in my lap!"

Adnan veers on to the pavement and accelerates, passing fifteen, maybe twenty cars. There are no tears in his eyes, only fear. I hear Noor make a small gasp for air, and I want Baba to be doing something more to save her life. More than twenty years as a doctor, and it comes down to this? Taking a pulse? Giving driving directions? My father, one of the best cardiologists in Baghdad, unable to do anything? At this minute he must be ticking off Noor's vital signs in his mind, assessing her chances of survival, and not sharing them with us.

I say nothing, only speaking to God in my mind, asking that He take care of Noor. And we are overtaking all the other cars as if we have a different passport, a special licence that indicates to the world that we don't need to wait in line. Mercedes beats Toyota, Subaru, Fiat. People stare their stares of anger and shock and brokenness, but no one tries to stop us, and so I turn away from searching their faces for responses. My stomach feels like it is contracting from the rest of my insides, trying to hide, trying not to face all the other people pushing get to the hospital in their battered cars, trying to save someone else's life. I wonder how many more Noors there are out there at this very moment, with families praying for them, with mothers sobbing and fathers speechless, with holes in their windows. We all wanted to believe that this war might blow over us like a sandstorm, a force of nature that cannot hurt you if you just seal up the windows properly and stay inside. If only you refuse to go out there and meet it face to face – exactly the opposite of what Saddam told us to do.

The entrance to the emergency room is a communal nightmare, a realization that a hundred other people are all having the exact same bad dream. There are lot of people who don't look right, wandering around in search of doctors, desperate for information about what is happening with their loved ones, men shouting and women crying. One heavy-set woman covered in a billowing abaya stands wailing like a black ghost near the admissions desk, hitting her forehead with her open palms again and again, and I wonder where her family is and why no one is waiting with her and trying to comfort her. A boy in a corner is screeching and rocking himself back and forth and I don't even know where we're supposed to go. I've been to this hospital many times and yet it feels like a place I have never been before, because it's so much more crowded and messy and it looks like they've been bringing injured people in for days and not cleaning up afterwards. Instead of that clean, antiseptic smell that's always in the air, there is a stench of burnt flesh and blood. I see a family carry in a man whose lower half seems to have been completely crushed but he's still shouting and my head is too hot and spinning and—

It takes a while for my eyes to focus, to come back. I am cold and the sound is weird, like a stuffed-up buzzing in my ears. My hands grope for something familiar. I'm lying on a plastic-upholstered sofa, I now realize, in one of the doctor's offices down the corridor from the emergency room.

"You're all right. Don't worry." Baba's voice. "You just passed out again." He puts his hand against my cheek and holds my face for a moment, then messes my hair like he is sending a small child away.

2

Sending

AGAIN. I HATE *again*, but I'm relieved to know what's happened. What am I doing lying down when all of these sick and broken people are heaving in that bloody room down the corridor, now a comfortable distance from me, where I can hear them but can't smell them the way I did before? I wonder, if my father weren't a doctor here, would I be lying on this sofa, or would I have been left out there with all the screaming, reeling families?

It has been several years since I've passed out. Baba behaves as if it happened only yesterday.

"Drink," he says, handing me a glass of water. I wonder whose office this is. Baba would normally be in cardiology, on the fifth floor. I feel the rip of cleaning chemicals in my nose, an odour I have hated since I was a child – the smell of coming to visit my father at work. I passed out a few times then, too, until Baba decided to stop bringing me to see him at the hospital. I sensed disappointment in his decision, which seemed like a punishment. I feel a tinge of it now, just a few little particles of it floating in the air, invisible but irritating, like the chemicals.

When I try to sit up, he holds my shoulder and pushes me gently back down to the sofa. "Lie a little longer."

I look up at him. He seems older, so much older, the dark lines under his eyes turned from ashes to charcoal.

"Where's Noor?" I ask.

My father breathes in and purses his heavy lips to one side. "She's in the operating theatre now. They will try, Nabil. But we need to be realistic. I…" he pauses. "I just don't think so."

"Don't think so?"

"I don't think you should have too much hope."

I close my eyes again, trying to say a prayer for the sick, in my mind, on Noor's behalf. I am ashamed. I cannot remember the words.

When I open my eyes, my father is gone. I stare at the ceiling for a few minutes, at the cheap, corky tiles that were once white but are now a crusty grey, with a film like the kind that accumulates on unwashed cars. I used to love to write on dirty car windows when I was a child. I always loved to use words I wouldn't be held responsible for later.

The building shakes from something that must have landed nearby, and somehow all I want to do is close my eyes once more. It is only when I hear a woman speaking English that I finally sit up and listen. Her voice grows louder and she sounds upset, like she wants someone to answer her, and she's shouting now because no one has. But there are not, I would imagine, too many people in this hospital who can understand English well, and now the woman's voice becomes more pronounced, as if she thinks that by speaking slowly and loudly, yelling even, people will begin to understand.

"My friend, Jonah Bonn was brought here. JO-nah Bonn. We think he was brought here. Please, check your lists for him. Can you check that for us? Do you understand me?"

I walk into the middle of the corridor and see her standing there, the foreign woman talking so loudly, and even if I had not heard her it would be clear that she wasn't an Iraqi because her hair is almost lit by the colour of fire, a strange red I have never seen before and am sure does not occur in this part of the world. She is with another foreign woman who looks Chinese or Japanese, and a tall, freckle-faced man stands behind them. His face is half-covered by his hair, and he looks like he has not slept in weeks and needs to exert great effort to hold up his eyelids. His eyeballs bulge bigger and then recede as the woman speaks, and then he shuts his eyes tight and winces. He leans against the wall next to him. I can't help but wonder, why is he letting the women engage in all the talking?

The red-haired woman looks at the nurse she has cornered and tilts her head to one side. She makes a face like she's about to cry and then is suddenly in control again.

"He was making a film," she says. Shouts, really. "TV film? You know, camera, film for TV? Like CNN? Al-Jazeera?" She makes a gesture of holding up an old-fashioned camera, peering through a hole in her clenched left fist and cranking her right.

"No, no, no," the hospital nurse says. "No film here. You need take permission. Go, ministry...take permission."

The red-headed woman drops her forehead into her upturned hand. "Oh God, please! We don't want to film. What I'm trying to tell you is that we're looking for our friend, our colleague. A reporter, you know, journalist? *Sahafi*? Jonah Bonn. Maybe you have him here?"

The nurse shakes her head and shrugs, looking to me.

"He was working with a man with a big camera and then he disappeared," the foreign woman pleads, moving her hands with the words, as if they will do the interpreting. "He worked for... he *works* for...oh, Jesus." She speaks very slowly now. "We believe...he, Jonah, here," she says, jabbing her two pointer-fingers towards the floor. She leaves out the verb, which annoys me, as if speaking English loudly and poorly is going to make the nurse understand. The foreign woman's face is starting to turn a shade of red that white people sometimes get when they are angry.

She puts a thumb and forefinger in the inner corners of her eyes. The freckled man behind her places his hand on her back and moves it across her shoulder blades. "This is useless, Sam. Forget it." He moves in front of her and hunches down to put his face in front of hers, his hands tucked into his armpits. "Let's go ask at the Red Cross or something. We can try Yarmouk Hospital."

I rush to catch the nurse, who had said "sorry, sorry", several times and begun to walk away, and ask her to wait just one moment more.

"Excuse me," I say calmly, as though they are just lost tourists seeking directions. "Can I help you with something?"

The red-headed woman looks up at me and before I can say more, she begins to cry. And then she turns her crying into a laugh that I think is meant to cover up the crying.

"I'm losing it. Oh Lord," she says, looking up at the ceiling and releasing a few tears that roll towards her hairline. She wipes her eyes with the sleeve of her shirt. Her friend, the small Asian lady, puts her hand on the woman's shoulder.

"Sam...Sam, don't worry. We'll find him." The Asian woman's English sounds perfect and American, and I realize that I am surprised. She turns to me. "Look, we're here covering this war and our friend's been missing for three days and we heard he might have been brought here." She says those words, "covering this war" as if we started it.

The red-haired one, I guess she's called Sam, though that sounds like a name for a man, dabs at her face. All that's left is an afterglow on her cheeks and some runaway smudges of mascara under her eyes. She turns to me. "Please," she says, lowering her voice from the tone she had taken a minute earlier. "Can you help us?"

"Yes, of course, please. I would be more than happy to help you," I say. I hate my choice of words. Awkward, formal. Maybe I'm out of practice. *Happy?* "Are you all right?" I ask her. "Can I get you something to drink?"

Her eyes roll over me with suspicion. They are eyes of a strange colour that I've never seen before, sort of a golden sand or straw instead of a regular brown or blue or green.

"No, thanks," she says. "I'm fine. We just want to find my friend. He's about five-foot-eleven and we know he was near the Rashid Hotel and he was wearing…" And I don't entirely hear everything she is saying because I wonder why a woman like this is not somewhere in America, safe at home with her family, why she's standing in a corridor in my father's hospital, talking at me with those strange eyes, almost the colour of the marmalade I loved when we lived in England. It had a kind of sweetness and a bitterness at the same time.

"Jonah Bonn," I repeat to the nurse on the admissions desk. "Please, these people are guests in our country and it's really important that we find their friend."

"What nationality?"

"American."

The nurse raises her chin and her eyes narrow a little bit and I know she's saying she doesn't really care if there's a dead American in the hospital.

"Listen, I'm Dr al-Amari's son and I, we, would really appreciate it if you would check." I want to sound like she should listen to me, like she should feel she has no choice, but I still sound like I'm asking.

"Here," she says, handing me a stack of paper attached to a clipboard. "See if he's there." The only foreign names I can find are of two Frenchmen.

"Come with me," I say, and the three of them follow me towards the lift at the end of the corridor.

"Pretty modern hospital. Not bad," says the freckled man, and I realize I do not even know their names.

"Sorry," I turn to them when we reach the elevator, pressing the button more times than necessary. "I've forgotten my manners. My name is Nabil al-Amari."

"June Park," says the Asian woman. She's small and lithe and, some men would argue, just as pretty as the other one, but terribly thin for my liking.

"Samara Katchens," says the woman with the fiery hair. She offers her hand. It feels warm and soft in my palm, so much softer than I would have expected from a woman with such strong bones in her face, and such a loud voice. "You can call me Sam," she says. Her teeth are bright white and I realize now that maybe it's true what they say about the Americans, how you can spot them from their perfect smiles, because when people smiled in Birmingham they never looked like this.

The freckled man holds out his hand for more of a slap than

a shake, then presents me his closed fist of knuckles, which I belatedly realize I'm meant to meet with mine. "Raphael," he says. I smile and press the button a few more times.

The doors part, presenting Dr Hamza, one of Baba's colleagues. He walks out and, on recognizing me, his eyebrows form an arc of pity, a well-traced shape I am sure he's honed over the years of working here.

He grabs hold of me to kiss me on both cheeks and behind him, as I tilt my head from this side to that, I see that we are missing the lift. "I am praying hard for your Noor, and *Inshallah*, we'll do our best."

I gaze at him and don't know what to say in return except *Inshallah* again. God-willing. *My* Noor? Why not Dr Mahmoud's Noor?

I tell him I need to help these foreigners find a friend, and with another arc, which feels more artificial than the first, he points us in the direction of the morgue.

I hear Baba's admonitions replay in my head. "Don't tell me *Inshallah*," he used to say when we were children, "tell me you're going to do it. *Inshallah* is a euphemism for abdicating responsibility."

I am worried that I will not be able to tolerate the smell and the sight of the bodies, so I implore the nurse to search for us. And while she is explaining that she is too busy, I fish around in my pockets and take out a wad of cash - at least 50,000 dinars - and even though this is probably half a month's salary for her, it's worth it for me. When I place the money in her hand and call her *uhti*, my sister, and say please, please, help these nice foreign people who are suffering alongside us in such a time as this, she nods and says *tab'an*, of course. I remind her that I am Dr al-Amari's son and that we will be in the fifth-floor reception area.

Raphael, who trails behind the women taking notes, comes forwards.

"Hey, wait, this doesn't make sense. That nurse isn't going to know what Jonah looks like. I mean, Sam, not that he's there. What are the chances? But still, if they don't even have a name ID on him…someone's got to…I'll go down with her."

Sam turns towards Raphael and wraps her arms around his shoulders and gives him a hug. I look around to see if anyone's watching, though I'm not sure why. "That's a good idea," she says after she lets go. "If you can't find us, just meet us—"

"On the fifth floor," I interrupt. "We'll be on the fifth floor."

Raphael nods and leaves, loping down the hall in the direction in which the nurse disappeared.

In the lift, the women smile politely at me but then talk only to each other. They run through the places they've checked for their friend. The places they've yet to check. The time it will take to get back to the hotel in order to "file a story". A story. Is that the same as an article for the newspaper? Isn't "story" the word one uses when it's made up?

We walk down the hallway towards the cardiology unit, but when I open the door nothing is as I expect it to be. The waiting room has been turned into an overflow space for patients, and there are about fifteen of them in various states of injury, a patchwork of flesh in disrepair. Nothing is as it is supposed to be, the machines are beeping too loudly in their cacophony of life-support and there's no fresh air. I feel a sense of relief when I see my father walk out of one of the consulting rooms. He smiles as though he is surprised to see these foreign women alongside me.

"I thought you were resting," he says.

I try to focus on his eyes, to avoid seeing the dried blood on his shirt which I know is Noor's. Just as the splatters of blood on my shirt are Noor's. I am glad that the foreign women cannot understand Arabic, and that they probably won't detect my father's less-than-enthusiastic reception.

"These are foreign journalists who got lost looking for a missing friend," I say to him in English.

My father turns to them and introduces himself, and I find myself wishing that his words could sound perfectly English like mine, instead of his rolling Arab accent that reminds me of being ten years old in Birmingham and suddenly feeling conscious of the way my mother sounded when we went round the shops.

Baba walks the three of us to his office, down the hall past the labs. The small office feels familiar: the worn-out medical textbooks, the picture of the five of us on holiday in Dubai, a poster illustrating the chambers of the heart, which always made me nauseous if I looked at it for too long, all arteries and ventricles ending so abruptly in mid-air, as if they could be cut off from their natural attachments just like that. There is the same shiny black sofa, the one I can remember jumping on to as a boy, but which now seems tiny. My father points politely to it and says, please, please, you are welcome. Sam almost falls into the chair rather than carefully placing herself into it like a lady, like an Arab lady would have done.

"Baba, have they said anything yet about Noor?"

He looks at me and shakes his head, then turns to the foreigners. "You are most welcome to wait here. I wish I could be more help to you, but I'm afraid I'm needed right now in the operating theatre. I leave my good son to you," he says to them in his oddly lilting English. And then to me, "I'll be back." And he leaves, and I don't know what shaking his head means. No, they haven't said anything? No, she isn't going to make it?

June Park plucks a small notebook from the bag on her lap and starts flipping through it, circling things. "I've gotta file soon, Sam," she says, not looking up from the page.

Sam runs a long finger beneath her nose and sniffs. "Let's just see what turns up. We have to at least rule things out."

June Park turns away from Sam and me, as if she wishes we weren't here, and sinks into a mumbling trance. She takes a set of headphones, places them over her ears, and lets her hand rest on the metal gadget sticking out of the top of her bag.

"June does radio." Sam's face bends into an apologetic smile.

"I beg your pardon?" I ask.

"She's a radio reporter, for NPR."

"NPR. Is that a television station?"

"No. National Public Radio."

"Also from America?"

"Yep. Based in Washington." Sam interlocks one hand with the other in her lap. Her hands appear unusually strong, but her fingers are elegant, the nails painted with a light-brown polish.

"She's also American?"

Sam smiles. "But don't hold it against us."

"But, if you don't mind my asking, where is she from, before America? From China or Japan?"

June lifts the headphones off her ears and turns towards me. "I'm Korean."

"Oh, I see, you are from Korea."

"No, I'm from New York and my parents are from Korea." She looks at Sam with widened eyes, and I sense I have said something irksome. She pulls the headphones back on to her ears.

"I, I'm sorry," I say. "I hope I haven't said something...I just didn't think she looked American." June again glances at Sam, then at a manly watch on her wrist, and turns away. "I mean, of course some Americans come from somewhere else, I assume. But I mean, the real American looks, I mean, well. June Park. Such a beautiful name. Like poetry."

Sam laughs and shakes her head. "It is, but I guess you're thinking of June, like the month. Joon spells it J-O-O-N. It's a Korean name."

"It's...so they spell the names of the months differently there?"

She rolls her eyes. "Forget it. But you know, I like people who ask questions. That's how you learn things. It has nothing to do with the month of June." She is looking me over now, and remembering that my clothes are blood-stained I suddenly feel ashamed. But she doesn't seem to be focusing on what I'm wearing. She smiles at me and says, "How come your English is so good?"

"I lived in Birmingham, England for about a year and a half. My father worked there as a hospital registrar when we were children."

"Nice." And then there is a crash somewhere to the south, like half a neighbourhood collapsing, and as it meets the ground the floor trembles and the windows rattle. We all look at each other.

Sam stands and peers out of my father's office window. "Do you know where that came from?"

"Maybe near Baghdad University, or Jazair, or Al-Dura. South of here."

"Yes, well, of course from the south." Her eyes flash at me, as if to warn me that she doesn't need help telling east from west.

"I do know the city a bit."

"I see. Did you come in with the American army, then?" We heard that the Americans have women in their tanks, which seems odd to us. Would they make their women fight the war with the men? Some people say the American tanks and soldiers are already inside Baghdad, but I haven't seen either yet. It was reported on the radio, the bit about the women, as a way of showing the Iraqi people how immoral the Americans are. Infidel invaders, the radio announcer called them.

"Oh no. I'm not an embed, thank God. We're unilaterals." She pronounces the word, which I have never heard used in the noun form, in a funny accent, drawing out the *u*. "According to the army anyway. And you? You and your father both work here at the hospital?"

I see her looking at my shirt and realize that, with the dried blood on it, she's probably mistaken me for a doctor or other hospital employee. "Oh no," I say. "I don't work here. I'm a teacher of English language and literature. At the Mansour High School, which is considered to be one of the best in Baghdad. But this, well, this friend of our family was shot tonight just before the air raid. Or during the air raid. We're waiting to hear... something." If I were working here, wouldn't I be off trying to save someone's life?

Her sharp cheekbones fall a little soft and her mouth opens. Her eyes search me and my shirt.

"I, oh, I didn't know. I misunderstood why you...I'm so sorry. I hope he'll be okay."

"She. We hope she will survive."

Raphael appears in the doorway, slightly out of breath. "Well, thank you, Raphael, for saving us the trip to hell and back," he says in a high-pitched voice. He puts his hand on the wall and heaves. "Sorry for the sarcasm. They say it's a normal reaction to nasty shit. Good news is, Jonah's not there. Gave 'em some more cash, too, so that they'll keep his name on a priority list." No one moves. Raphael leans over and snaps two fingers close to the headphone-covered ears of Joon Park. "Come on, ladies, let's get out of here."

Joon stands and begins to pack up her things without saying a word. Sam and I look at each other for a moment, and then we both get up too. She holds out her right hand and I take it, probably for longer than I should.

"I really hope your friend will be all right," she says.

I take back my hand and put it across my chest. "You're very kind."

"Sam, let's hit it," Raphael says. He stands in the doorway of my father's office and raises his hand in the air, looking at me. "Hey thanks, Nabil. Thanks for your help. Shukran." He mispronounces it, with too much stress on the first syllable. SHOOK-raan. Joon nods and forces a grin in my direction, tossing silky black hair out of her face. Sam reaches into her bag, pushes things around with a frown, then pulls out a notebook. She writes her name on a blank page, and beneath it, Al-Hamra Hotel, Room 323. She rips the paper from its spine and holds it out towards me.

"Maybe we can be in touch," she says.

"Oh? Thank you very much."

"Don't thank us," she replies. "We should be thanking you."

"Your friend, have you thought of checking Abu Ghraib for him?"

"The prison?" The others, walking at the double, turn the corner on the way to the lift, but Sam stops in the middle of the corridor.

"Yes," I say. "When people go missing it often means they've been arrested, and I've heard that there are people there who can provide information from inside. You'd do well to offer tips when you look for him."

"*Baksheesh*?" Sam grins, presumably trying to show off whatever Arabic she's picked up.

"You can call it that. No one likes to work for free, to take risks, especially now in this situation. People are afraid. Otherwise, I mean, normally, we are generous people. Anyone would like to help you. We want everyone, even Americans, to feel welcome in our country." I am surprised by this commentary tripping off my lips, by my sudden keenness to promote Iraqi hospitality.

Sam nods. She moves to walk away, then turns back. "I can see that," she says. And she blinks at me again with both eyes, in a nice way that feels almost like a wink, and then heads towards the lift.

I stand there and wait, and listen to the people and the machines, and decide I will ask around downstairs for an imam or some other religious person who will know which prayer to say for Noor. I think it should be *Ya Latif*, which one is supposed to recite in situations of great distress, or when praying for someone who is gravely ill. I think it's also supposed to be repeated more than a hundred times. Could that be? But then my father turns the corner, and I see his face and stand still. He gestures for me to go back into his office, but I'm stuck here with the corridor narrowing on me, the floor moving all on its own.

3

Narrowing

WE ARE BURYING Noor in the cemetery in Sheikh Maroof, not far from her family's house in Hurriyah. The sun is still low, a time of the morning when I would normally be teaching my first class of the day, watching the usual stragglers trying to slip towards their seats without my noticing that they're late. Only a few of Noor's relatives and friends, the ones who live nearby, have arrived. Her family wasn't able to call people to let them know. Some relatives who did get word sent food and apologized for their absence. No one who lives on the other side of the river, in Karada, is here – they say it's impossible to cross any of the bridges. Baba says it isn't safe to go out now at all, when it isn't a life or death reason. That includes a funeral, doesn't it?

Many people, honest people, are afraid to go out, because other people are on the streets, taking and destroying everything, even killing each other over things, things that are supposed to be valuable but are really nothing. *Hawasim*, people are whispering at Noor's funeral. Everywhere there is *hawasim*. Looting, that's the word one uses in English.

Around me, some faces are contorted, some sad, some blank. But most are dry-eyed. In Arabic, we have our own phrase for keeping a stiff upper lip. *Jamra fil qalb wala dama fil ayn*. A fire in the heart but no tear in the eye. Dr Mahmoud, when he was lucid enough to speak, made a decision that the women in the family should stay at home, as if home were any safer than anywhere else. Home, where Noor got hit by a stray bullet.

Now and then, Dr Mahmoud tries to say something but very little sound actually comes out, his voice stripped with shock. He stands at the edge of the grave, his arms held by other men, and slips to his knees before they pull him up again. "Why?" he moans. "Why did you take my beautiful little girl?" I wonder if he means the Americans or God.

I find myself imagining how Noor would have looked in a white gown as my bride and everything feels wrong, because even if I didn't love her, I might have learned to love her. She seemed marriageable enough. The truth is, just in that moment when she was serving the tea and fruit, I found her quite elegant. She only wanted to help people – she was studying psychology. And she was quite pretty, really, with her dark, cat-like eyes that dominated her round face.

Instead of an *urs*, a wedding, a *genaze*, a funeral.

I listen to the sound of the soil falling over Noor's white sheath mixing with the clatter of helicopters coming from the south of the city and the rapid gunfire, which could be coming from anywhere.

We fold ourselves back into the car, Baba and myself and two of my cousins from around the block who agreed to come along with us, because they are young and look intimidating in comparison to us. The graveyard where we left Noor gets smaller, until its new damp mounds, each brown knoll a mark of someone else who has just been buried without warning, without time to prepare, are like little molehills.

We turn towards the 14th of Ramadan Street, a shopping high street, because we are going to pick up Mum and Amal before going back to Noor's neighbourhood. But as we move closer we see a world convulsing. Waves of people running, stealing, destroying. They are shouting and laughing and carrying outside things that belong inside, moving about a whole animal kingdom of stolen goods. We see them circling wider like a slow-moving swarm, fleeing as beasts of burden in different directions, and when we realize the scope of what is happening, Baba curses and says we have to turn around. While he makes the U-turn, through the rear window the rest of us watch an airborne bazaar – men with televisions and stereos and ovens and typewriters and pots, moving through the atmosphere as though it were perfectly natural. Air conditioners are hoisted high with their wires trailing like tails. Coloured office chairs fly down the street like fish in a stream. Filing cabinets spit out fluttering papers like the feathers of a dying chicken. Clusters of men are carrying desks and water coolers, refrigerators and vases, computer screens and paintings. A man falls as the crowd passes him by without anyone stopping to help him.

Cousin Khaled is twisting and lurching in his seat and he says we should go back to see what's happening, but Baba clucks no so Khaled says, "Just to watch!" And then my father slams on his brakes and pulls over and turns around and asks Khaled if he wants to get out. And Munib, who is two years older, which puts him at about twenty and who has been silent the whole morning, glares at his younger brother like he might smack him and says, *Y'alla*, go ahead, get out and get yourself something. And Khaled says no, forget it, and turns his head away from us, either ashamed or annoyed.

*

At Noor's house, Baba pulls up and parks behind the other cars waiting outside. One of the neighbours points to Adnan's house next door, indicating that the mourners are gathered there. I suppose Adnan's house might be bigger but it just now occurs to me that this might be purposeful, an attempt at relief. To sit in the place where we sat only yesterday? I'm not sure how they can ever have a normal day in their own home again.

I look at Baba, overweight and close to sixty, a time in his life when things should be getting easier. He sits behind the steering wheel with eyes shut. He puts his hand over his glasses as if to shield his sight, although we're not even in the sun.

Baba rubs his eyes beneath his glasses. "She might have been our daughter-in-law, right, Nabil? She might have been the mother of your children. What a waste."

I open the car door without answering him.

We settle in to mourn with Noor's family, and there is a lot of food on the tables put out by the women, though no one eats it. Soon after we arrive, my mother and Amal walk in, and my father is a little bit angry with them for taking a chance and travelling by taxi. My mother shakes her head at him and hisses, "What else could we do? Sit at home because you didn't come back for us? We came for Noor, *Allah yarhamha*."

I sit on the floor of the salon with all the other men while the women sit in an inner room behind us, closer to the kitchen. I listen to the crying and I know it would be good if I could cry, too. It would please Noor's family to see me cry, offer a tearful tribute to my would-be bride. But inside I feel only sad waves of verse, a poem that I am writing in my head. No matter how sad I look, I can feel Dr Mahmoud sneaking glances at me, to check if I am upset the way a man who lost his love would be. He says nothing, but I can read the words in his eyes, running like subtitles in a foreign film. *Why didn't you agree to marry her straight away? What was taking so long?* As if it's my fault. As if that would stop a war, or a bullet. As if, had I already said yes and married her, she would be alive now and ready to present him with a grandchild.

Still, I should be ashamed. If I knew I didn't want to marry her, what business did I have allowing my parents to drag me to a second meeting with her and her parents? If I hadn't agreed to the date, maybe Noor would have been lying in bed reading a book. Lying, not standing at the front window. Maybe she would have been here at her brother Adnan's house, close to the floor, playing with his baby son, her nephew. Maybe she would have been safe.

The recording of an imam bleats through the house, churning out *hadith*, holy sayings of the Prophet. *Al-mu'minuna fi kulli halin bi-kheir.* Believers are blessed in all circumstances. Is that meant to be comforting? But the gloomy melodies sound beautiful, a lilt so melancholy they might help me cry, help me prove that even if I failed to love Noor, I can still mourn for her.

I go through the motions, the bowing and the turning and the mouthing of words, with a feeling of emptiness. I try to say a *qunut* for her in my own words, to wish her peace in the next world, but I cannot take to heart what I am saying. From the corner of my eye, I see her photograph on the wall, a professional picture taken when she was graduating from university. Her hair looks carefully styled, a lush swirl of black against the photographer's red backdrop, and she is wearing too much makeup.

One of the neighbourhood elders, presumably a sheikh judging from his long black robe, rises to offer traditional words of sympathy before leaving. *Inna lil-lahi wa inna il-lahi raji'oon*, he intones. We belong to God, and to Him we return. However trite, these are the only comforting words I have heard in the last twenty-four hours. When he has gone, one of Noor's young cousins wants to turn on the radio to hear the news about the chaos and the Americans, the things people are whispering about in corners but never mentioning aloud. Dr Mahmoud signals no. It would be disrespectful, I suppose. And so we sit and listen to the mourning verses on the portable tape recorder, Adnan flipping the same cassette over and over until I have the urge to grab the tape and rip the dark ribbon to shreds.

The young boys of the family periodically go out to open the door for new visitors and show them inside. So naturally, I'm expecting a few more neighbours when I look up and see the boys standing with a heavily bearded man, most likely from the south, and *her*. Her fire-hair stands out in the room full of dark-haired men, like a burning ember amid black coals, and I can't even remember her name.

"Nabil," she says, and produces a smile that manages to convey sympathy. Hearing her voice helps me remember. Sam. Samara Katchens.

"This is my driver, Rizgar. We wanted to come to offer our condolences." So I am wrong about the bearded man, because Rizgar is a Kurdish name and not an Arab one, and therefore he's probably from the north, not the south. I offer my hand to him and he takes it and he draws me to him and kisses my cheek several times and says *Ila Rahmetu Allah*, God's mercy be upon her. And then he adds another: God avenge her blood. The words make me shudder. But I know that it's an appropriate thing to say, and that it will please Noor's relatives.

Rizgar asks me which one is Noor's father and I signal to Dr Mahmoud, and Rizgar offers more of the same. *Allah yarhamha.* God protect her soul. Dr Mahmoud nods and opens a hand in the direction of an empty chair.

But what to do with this woman? This Sam, who does not belong in this room full of men but will not manage with the women, because she won't find anyone there who can speak English.

Sam smiles uncomfortably, apparently noticing that there are no other women in the room. She holds up a large basket of food, what appears to be fruit and vegetables and canned goods, plus boxes of biscuits and chocolates. "This is something for your family from the three of us. We are so sorry for your loss. We wanted to thank you for your help yesterday."

At another time, this gift could have been awkward. Neither Noor's family nor mine is poor, *Al-Hamdulilah.* Thank God. We are not the type of people who have to go to the UN offices in search of handouts. But since the war started, it's been getting more dangerous to go out for food. These days, there isn't a family who would not appreciate such a delivery.

Noor's grandfather picks up the carved cane at his side and thumps it on the floor. He looks ancient and wears a black sheikh's robe, even though I'm sure he's not a sheikh. He repeatedly clears his throat with great effort, and I can see his fleshy throat flapping as he grumbles to the man next to him. "Nabil," Baba says. "Perhaps you should tell your new friend to bring the gift to Noor's mother in the next room."

My new friend. *In the feminine form,* because in Arabic we

have no choice but to distinguish male friends and female friends. What could sound worse? I stand with my eyes on the floor. "Come, please," I say in English.

"Nabil," Baba repeats my name, as if I'm a small boy who's just learning his manners. "Why don't you first tell them who she is." I introduce her to the room full of men, Noor's relatives, other men who are friends of the family or who have come from the neighbourhood. When I say her name, without realizing, I pronounce it like the city in our country, Samarra, with a *shadda* on the r, which acts like the damper pedal on a piano. Even though this is different from the way I've heard Sam pronounce her name, I can already feel that this is a good thing, and that maybe I have even done it deliberately. They'll say, oh, yes, Samarra, beautiful name, good Sunni tribes there. Maybe they'll behave like she isn't a foreigner and an occupier after all, isn't a brash American woman who can't speak a word of Arabic who has rudely dropped in on a house of mourning.

"*Salaam aleikum,*" she says to them, pronouncing the greeting perfectly.

"*W-aleikum is-salaam,*" they answer and nod. The older men look away, but the young cousins stare as if a film star has arrived. I take the heavy basket from her and gesture for her to come with me to the women's room, as if she would not have already known where it was from the weeping.

I lead the way into the corridor and turn right to bring her to Noor's mother, wondering what on earth the women are going to think of me for bringing an attractive American woman into the house of mourning. Sam touches my elbow, and it makes all the muscles in my back lock.

"Sorry, Nabil, I won't stay long," she whispers. "I hope it was okay for me to come. I need to talk to you." I turn back to her with my mouth open, but no words come out.

Aunts and sisters and girlfriends fall silent and gaze at me with confusion when I enter with the big basket in my arms and this Sam standing next to me. A little girl of four or five points with a chubby finger. "Like my Ginny doll!" she says, and they start to laugh a bit, and note that it's true, this woman looks a bit like a bootleg Barbie women buy for their girls. Sam smiles with them but I can tell she doesn't know why. I explain that Sam is a foreign journalist who was at the hospital last night looking for a friend while we were praying for Noor, and that Sam prayed for her too, and that she came here today to express her condolences. The women smile and say Sam must sit down and have tea with them, except for Noor's mother, who sways with her eyes closed and says nothing.

A young woman rises to her feet, patting her chest. "This is Shireen. I can very well English. I can to help her, please." She takes Sam's hand, and though I suspect Shireen's English isn't going to get anyone through a real conversation, it's a better solution than any other.

Sam stares at me, and her eyes seem to grow wider, like the child's. "I'll be fine," she says, and so I leave, only turning back to tell her she can come and find me when she is ready to go.

It may be fifteen minutes or forty-five; I can't tell how much time passes while I wait for her to emerge. I am only happy that the men are not asking questions about her.

And then she is standing there, her eyes fixed on the floor near my feet. "Please tell everyone that I am so, so sorry for your loss," she says.

My father translates this into Arabic. Noor's father looks at

Sam and nods once. Baba stands. "Are you sure you don't want to stay for lunch?"

My stomach zigzags. I'm afraid Sam won't know this is only a formality.

"Oh, thank you so much," she says. "But I really must get back to the hotel."

I can read the thoughts surely filtering through the minds of the men who caught the word "hotel". Such a pretty foreign lady, living in a hotel. Doesn't she have a husband? Is she a prostitute?

"Well, thank you for coming, Miss Samara," Baba says cordially. "You must come to visit us again sometime."

Rizgar takes a brisk look around and gets up.

I try to pretend they're not watching our every step as the three of us walk towards the door. The moment I close the front door behind me, Sam speaks quickly.

"I hope it's all right I came and I'm so sorry if this is the wrong time to be asking this, but the truth is, I need someone. I mean, I would really like *you* to work with me." She turns to Rizgar. "Can you start the car?" Her hand turns an imaginary ignition key. "I'll be there in a minute." The Kurdish man turns silently, then looks back at me and mumbles a word of goodbye. We stop at the front gate.

"You want me to work with you?"

"You'd be perfect for the job."

"But I'm not a journalist. Or an interpreter. I'm an English teacher."

"That's why I'd really like you to work with me. You'd make a fantastic translator. Where did you learn your English? Oh, right, in England, you said."

She puts her arm deep into her bag, then brings out a small

leather case. She snaps it open and takes out a white card. I run my finger over the raised letters. *Samara B. Katchens. Paris Bureau Chief.* Under her name, she has written in a curling script the name of her hotel and the room number which she had passed to me in the hospital. "This is what I meant to give you yesterday, but I couldn't find it."

"Paris? You live in France? Not in America?"

"I'm based in Paris. Doesn't mean I actually live much of my life there." She peers in the car window and smiles. Perhaps towards Rizgar, or perhaps at her own reflection. "Can you come by tomorrow? Make it the next day. Maybe you need time with your family."

"I don't know, Miss Samara…"

"Call me Sam."

"Sam, yes. Well, you know, I have no training in your line of work. Or in interpreting."

"Who said you need any training? It's innate. Some people have it, some people don't." She lifts a shoulder. "I can see you're one of those people who do. Please, just come. Okay?"

"I can't promise you," I hear myself say. "And forgive me for asking, but how did you find me?"

"Oh, that was easy. I went back to the hospital and asked where your dad lives. They gave me the name of the neighbourhood, and there they said to come here, that you'd be at your friend's funeral," Sam explains matter-of-factly. And then, with some contrition: "It's sad. I hope you weren't close with her."

"You asked for me in Yarmouk?"

"Yeah." She smiles, clearly proud of herself, and clearly oblivious of what that might mean for me. "I usually find what I'm looking for."

"How about your friend?"

Her eyes lose focus and her nostrils widen. "Still missing."

I see Sam to the door of the huge car, which says Cherokee Jeep on the back. Only when she opens the door can I see Rizgar waiting behind the wheel. She waves and I wave back to her, my mind tumbling with what my neighbours are already saying.

4

Tumbling

IN OUR LIVING room my father flicks the light switch, but there is no light. He switches it back and forth, curses and lifts the end table with the lamp on it and slams it down again. "Bastards! How are we supposed to live without any light?" The lamp falls over but lands on the carpeted floor. Amal is standing behind me and I can hear the break in her throat and she starts to cry. My mother announces that they are going to bed.

With dim light trickling in from outside, I watch her walk Amal to her room. In a few minutes, my mother comes back with an old torch from the kitchen.

She hands it to Baba. "We'll buy an oil lamp tomorrow," she says. Baba switches the torch on and off. "Excellent," he says. "Maybe the next day we will trade in our car for a donkey! Would you like that?"

I worry that my mother might start to cry, too, but instead she exhales a brusque retort through her nostrils. "Don't you start, Amjad. And don't stay up too late."

Baba sits in his favourite armchair in the dark, and I sit on the sofa across from him. It's quiet except for the ticking of the antique mantle clock on the shelf above the dining table. My father bought it when we visited London during our time in

Birmingham, despite my mother's objections. Mum said she'd never be able to read the Roman numerals. To him this was already a compromise; he'd wanted a grandfather clock that was taller than a person, but acknowledged it would be difficult to get it back to Baghdad. In tense moments, the ticking reminds me of a children's book we read in England, *Through the Looking Glass*. The clock isn't saying tick tock, but saying *tsk, tsk*.

My father switches the torch off and on again, and shines it in my face. "Where were you on the night of the eighth?" he growls in a perfect Tikriti accent, just like a real guy from the *mukhabarat*. Saddam's men usually have that countryside drawl.

"Start talking," he orders, and we both laugh a little.

He flashes it on and off again, and I realize now why Americans call this a flashlight. I suddenly remember the game my brother and I used to play with the torch as children, when we were off school and would stay up late, making each other dance in the strobe light that we'd create by toggling the torch switch as fast as we could. The jumpy movements, the light that came and went, made the dancing person look like he was in an old black-and-white film. If I reminded Ziad of this now, he'd say he didn't remember. Ziad, my brother, a doctor like Baba, is living comfortably with his young family in Marseille, France. He is my parents' success story.

Baba stops his light show and places the torch on the wooden side table, leaving the beam of light to shine on the ceiling. Its white disc is like a small, full moon above, providing some relief from the darkness.

"I still can't believe Mahmoud's daughter is gone," Baba says. "She was so young."

My father has never liked to deal with emotional

complications. Medical crises are much more manageable. There is either a cure or there isn't.

"There is no justice in this world," he adds. "Even if every imam up and down the Tigris tells you it is God's will that innocent martyrs die in this war, don't believe them." He stares at me in the dark. For a moment, his eyes seem brighter than the torch. "Would God let an innocent girl like Noor die? And the whole Alusi family?" The Alusis were a family of five who died last week, when the Americans tried to get Saddam while he was out at lunch with his sons in Mansour; Baba had once mended a hole in their twelve-year-old daughter's heart.

I nod and say nothing. Tonight is not the night to challenge my father's absence of faith. He reaches over and puts his hand on mine, clutches it to the sofa's armrest. I want to feel thankful for the gesture. But another part of me feels trapped. Pinned, not consoled.

He sits back. "It's a nightmare, isn't it? The evening started like a dream and it turned into a nightmare."

I cannot remember my father ever speaking in such terms. Since when did he ask after my dreams? The clock clucks slowly, marking our silences.

"Nabil, you know it was one of ours, right?"

"What was?" I ask.

"The bullet that hit her. It was Saddam's *fadayoon* shooting at the American helicopters. Can you imagine? Bullets at helicopters. So we have our own brilliant defenders to thank."

"For...Noor's death?"

Baba sighs. I think he's still afraid to say anything directly, even in our own home.

"I think I'll go to bed." I lean forwards to stand.

"You didn't seem sad when that foreign woman came in." I lean further and turn my head from him, glad it's dark.

"No, Baba, I was just – surprised. I didn't expect her to come."

"You were very keen to help her at the hospital. You were practically flirting with her."

"She was desperate for help! I was only trying to help. Her, and her friends. She wasn't alone." I hate sounding like I'm trying to justify myself, but it's too late.

This is one of my father's oldest tricks: a brush at being understanding, an opening, followed by censure. It's a boxing match that's been fixed: I will always lose. But now it's pointless for me to hide the real reason she came.

"She wants me to work with her."

"With an American lady? In the middle of this?"

"What should I do? Sit around at home all day? What are we going to live off? Who will pay the salaries at a government hospital when there is no government?"

"Keep your voice down."

"And school, Baba. When do you think it's starting again? Did you hear what they did to my school today? There isn't a window left intact. All the books are gone. Burned, stolen, I don't even know. Gone! They looted almost every desk, every chair."

His face is full of disbelief. "It's true," I say. "It's to be expected. It was seen as a school for the elite – everyone knows that it's mostly for wealthy Sunnis. What am I going to do until they repair the school? It will be next September if we're lucky!"

"It's only what? April." My father squints at his beloved clock, as if to figure out the month, and maybe the year as well. "What about all the boys who need to finish the school year?"

"None of the schools are going back until the autumn, only some universities."

My father breathes in deeply, and lets out a full belly of air. He takes the torch off the table and slaps it into the palm of his left hand, sending a whir of light against the wall. "Who did you say she works for?"

"I don't remember. The *Tribune*?"

"In London?"

I consider lying. "No, in America."

My father puts two fingers on each eye and rubs his eyelids in and out, like he might be able to erase something from sight. "What will your mother say?"

I lie in bed with her card, bending it back and forth, listening to its small snap. I flick the torch on and off and look at her name lit up, and then catch its afterglow in my vision in the dark of the room.

Samara B. Katchens. Paris Bureau Chief. On the flip side of the card, the same thing, with the job title in French. The paper is much thicker than other business cards I've seen. The edge is sharp enough to slice skin.

There is a quiet knock, then a creaking of the door opening. My sister is in her nightgown, her eyes open as if she has not slept. The clock says 1:20 a.m.

"You're still awake, too?"

"Go to sleep, Amal. You shouldn't be up."

"But you're playing with the torch. I can see the light beneath my door."

She comes over to the edge of my bed and sits down. I put my arm around her and kiss the back of her head. I want to say

39

something to her that will sound wise, something that will make her feel strong. Maybe I'm only searching for something to say because I want her to keep looking up to me, the way I looked up to Ziad.

"Noor lived a good life," I tell Amal. "She was happy before she died. She won't have to suffer through this like the rest of us."

Amal looks at me. Her eyebrows contract. They are almost as thick as a man's: she has yet to be corrupted by Baghdad's beauty salons, which like to strip eyebrows like hers into thin, doll-like arches. Her eyes are like our grandmother's, deep-set and wide, like they have eyeliner on them when they don't. Mine are similar. In junior high school, other boys teased me and said my eyes were pretty, like a girl's. Baba once told me, somewhat disparagingly, that my eyelashes were as long as a woman's.

"You really believe that?" Amal fixes me with a look and I have to turn away. Every so often it feels like she is fourteen going on forty. She has none of the impressionability I would want in a daughter of her age. Amal has always been like this. My father says it comes from being a late-in-life child, as he calls it. When Amal was born, I was fourteen and Ziad was sixteen. Amal was always in a rush to grow up, to catch up with us. Amal says she just has an old soul.

"Are you going to work with the American woman?" she asks.

"Who said anything about that?"

"Don't think I'm stupid, Nabil. I know why she came to the house today."

"Sometimes I wish you were stupid. Just a little."

Amal grimaces and tucks her hair behind her ears. Her hair is perfectly straight and black, almost like Joon Park's. "I think you should do it. You'll learn loads and make good money. You'll get to find out what's really happening and then you'll come back and tell us stories every night."

I already know I want to work with Sam. What I didn't expect is for Amal to encourage me.

She bends her knees and clasps her arms around them. "I know you're sad about Noor," she says, "but she wasn't the one. You could never love her."

If I kept a diary, like they do in England, I'm sure my sister would read it. Instead, she reads my mind, turning pages in a book I cannot keep closed to her, unlocking secrets she appears to know better than I do.

"Amal, you don't know what you're talking about. Don't say things like that."

"Why? Is she going to come back and haunt us?" I admire my sister's way of flaunting superstition, her utter fearlessness, but it worries me. I see my mother's courage and my father's irreverence, and I'm not sure it will always be a good combination.

"I liked her," I shrug. "You never know what could have happened."

Amal takes my chin and looks at me like she's the older sibling, like she knows best. She lowers her voice, and pulls back her shoulders as if to remind me she is more adult than child. "*Nabi*," she says softly. She is the only person in the family who calls me by a nickname, and I like the way she pronounces it, because it almost sounds like the word we have in Arabic for prophet, *nebi*. "You have to live your own life. You shouldn't make yourself miserable because you're not living the one Baba wanted you to."

5

Living

ON THE DRIVE over, I find myself thinking about Amal and her precocious advice. Beneath her sympathy is her own self-interest, and rightly so. She's not sympathetic to arranged marriages – nor to parents choosing our professions. Her hope is that if I can escape all of this, she can as well. Ziad married a woman he met at university in France, but no one even likes the thought of her. This is the only blemish on Ziad's record. But my parents blame her, not him, for the fact that he's stayed in Europe without having returned in over three years. They disregard Ziad's explanation: he's afraid if he comes back for a visit, he won't be allowed to leave again. Only his job at a hospital there keeps him in good stead with Baba. That, and a grandson.

The car park outside the Hamra Hotel is full of cars of a sort I've rarely seen in Baghdad. A lot of them are luxurious-looking vans and big jeeps with wheels almost as high as my waist, and they have signs taped to the windows that say "TV" or "Press". I wonder if the commanders tell the reporters where to stay, or if the reporters decide on their own, because just yesterday my neighbour Imad told me that the new foreign journalists in Baghdad, the ones who weren't here before the war began, are actually part of the American army. I wonder if that's true. Would

Samara Katchens have come in with the army, but not have told me so?

The hotel's front entrance is blocked by a line of cheaply set bricks, and the drivers outside tell me to go around the back, towards the service entrance. After asking two other people which way to go, I finally find my way inside. The lobby is dimly lit and small, but something about it seems posh to me. There's a gift shop selling carpets and ancient jewellery that the women I know would never wear, because it looks old-fashioned and tribal, and is made of silver rather than gold. Each of the windows and doors has an "X" taped over them, like surrender signs. I think that's why Baba didn't tape up our windows at home; it would be an acknowledgement that we're afraid. The X-ing, the boarding, the bricking, all of these are an admission that the Americans are more powerful than we are. That they are going to beat us, that we can only try to minimize the damage.

Small clusters of men are standing around, and it's easy to tell who's who. Young Iraqis dressed in trousers and short-sleeved shirts. Foreigners, largely white-skinned and taller, carrying bags, cameras and bottles of water. The latter remind me of the way football players stand on the sidelines before they rush into the game. Just like the footballers I watched from the stands with Baba when I was twelve, supporting Birmingham City against Manchester United. Back then, I wished that we would stay in Britain forever, become English, be just like a regular family going to see the footie on a Saturday.

All the other Iraqis are dressed informally. When I got dressed earlier this morning my mother had insisted I wear a suit, and now I am beginning to think that maybe I'd have done better not to listen to her.

I walk to the reception desk and tell the man I have come to see an American woman. I put my hand into my jacket pocket to pick out her business card.

"Miss Samara Katchens from the *Tribune*," I pronounce.

The man frowns at me like I am bothering him. Behind him I can see that the wooden honeycomb of boxes for the room keys is almost empty, with only one or two dangling from their nests.

The man asks me to repeat her name, and looks at the business card I have shed from my palm. He checks his list.

"Your name?" he asks.

"Nabil al-Amari."

His nostrils flinch and he jots something down. "The second tower," he says, lifting his chin towards his left.

Sunk into the centre of the courtyard is a vast swimming pool, the likes of which I can't remember ever seeing in Baghdad. The water looks dirty, coloured to a light brown that gets to be almost coffee at the bottom. But the hotel staff are working on it, standing near the edge in their white shirts and black bowties as they run two underwater vacuums across the water with great concentration.

A sun-reddened foreigner with a shaved head directs me towards the second tower, and even though it is right in front of me, somehow I still need it pointed out. A shift of nausea rises in my stomach. How utterly strange to be asking a visitor in my own country for directions.

The entrance to the second tower is brighter and more lush, with plants and oil paintings lining the atrium that leads to another reception counter. The man behind the desk picks up the phone, punches in some numbers and hands the receiver over to me. Beneath his moustache a smile is gaining ground.

"Nabil!" Over the phone her voice sounds strong, less demure than it did when we were at Noor's house. "I'm *so* glad you came. Do you want to come up?" Her voice moves something inside me and subsequently no answer comes out.

"Uh, yes, or…do you prefer to meet down here?" I manage.

She is quiet for a second and then says, sure, she'll be down in a minute, and I think I can hear a tiny ripple of amusement in her voice when she says it.

The ridges in my yellow tie are still crisp from never being worn, and I consider taking it off. I will roll it tightly and stuff it in my pocket. But what will the man behind the reception desk think?

He continues to look me up and down and I pretend not to notice because I don't want to have to answer questions, to admit that I'm about to take a job I wouldn't have been offered if that bullet hadn't come through Noor's window three days ago.

"Visiting United Nations' teams used to stay here, including the weapons inspectors," he says, answering a question buzzing in my head. "I guess they won't be back to bother us for a while!" He laughs like a motor, mechanical and a little too loud. I force myself to laugh, too.

"Are you going to be Miss Samara's new translator?" He has very bad skin, as if someone had taken a fork and poked holes, the way my mother does before she bakes potatoes.

"Perhaps. Did she have one before me?"

"Sure she did. Most of them need an Iraqi or they can't work."

Sam comes down the stairs in multiples and then lands near the reception desk with a clap of sandals on tile. "Rafik!" She beams a wide grin at the man behind the reception desk. "*Sabah el-khair.*"

The pock-faced man looks like the happiest person I have seen in months, and he smiles back at her with a sheepish countenance. "*Sabah en-noor,* Miss Samara."

After they say their good mornings, I step out to greet her. I hold out my right hand and she takes it firmly. Then she extends her left as well and clasps my hand between both of hers. Her hair, so full of that orange fire the other two times I met her, seems darker now, and I realize that's because it's wet. The smell of a shampoo or maybe a powder runs invisible circles around her, carrying the scent of some flower that grows somewhere else in the world, but not here. In Iraq, a woman would never come to a meeting with her hair like this, as if she's just stepped out of the shower.

"You found me," she says, though she doesn't look at all surprised to see me. "I'm glad you held on to that." She points at her business card, which I'm still holding in my hand, having bent it back and forth so often that my sweat has nearly worn it to tissue. On those two occasions I met Sam, she was dressed in clothing that resembled what I might have worn when I was a teenager – loose khaki trousers and a button-down shirt. There was nothing particularly ladylike about it, although the way she moved in her boyish clothes seemed feminine. Today, however, she's wearing blue jeans that are tighter, like the way the women dress in music videos. She's wearing a white T-shirt with a deep V along the collar. I haven't seen a woman dressed like this, in person that is, since our time in England, when Mum used to nudge me in the shopping centre and whisper to me about how inappropriately the young women were dressed. I try to block out her voice grating somewhere between my ears.

And then I realize that Sam has already been telling me what she's been doing since I last saw her, and I haven't heard a word she's said.

"Anyway," she looks at me and blinks twice, then stretches out a hand much the way the merchants do when they want you to look at their fruit. "Why don't we have a coffee out by the pool?"

I follow her out of the atrium to the courtyard, towards the big murky mass of the swimming pool. She doesn't wait for me to open the door, and when I try to hold it open while it's already in mid-swing, she exhales a small laugh.

We sit on the white plastic chairs at a table in the sun, and I wonder why she would choose a table without an umbrella, without shade. I remember that on the rare sunny days in Birmingham, young people with white skin would sit in the park, their faces turned skywards. In England, even a slight suntan was a source of pride. Here, of course, it is frowned upon. Only labourers who must work out-of-doors get suntanned, my grandmother once said, and women especially want to be lighter, not darker.

Sam plonks her notebook on the table, and this seems to define the way she touches things around her. She does not place objects, but lets go of them and allows them to fall – her bag on to the chair next to her, her sandals on to the concrete ground. She looks at her watch and raises her hand to catch a waiter's eye. "Wow, it's almost ten," she says. "We've got an interview at twelve with the INC."

"We…we have an interview? Today?" I am embarrassed by how slow I must sound, but I am confused. "I thought you wanted to tell me more about the position first."

"Oh, right." Her mouth drops open, her lips coated by something shiny. "We forgot to talk money, didn't we? Would a hundred dollars a day be okay?"

"A hundred dollars a day?"

"Well, I could maybe go up to $125, but that's really the most I can do." Sam reaches into her bag and pulls out a thin electronic gadget that is the same size as the grocer's receipt book which tracks my family's monthly bill. She puts the tip of her fingernail to the screen, I expect, in order to clean off the dust. But instead, I see she is curving her index finger in different directions, creating tiny black letters on the screen.

"You write on it with your finger?"

"Well," she smiles without looking up at me. "You're supposed to use a stylus, but God knows where I left mine." I focus on the grey screen and I think I can make out the words, though upside down: *ask M about money*. And then she presses the green button and the words disappear. "I can't remember anything if I don't put it into my palm," she says.

I nod. If I were to write anything at this moment, I'd make calculations about what my savings might look like a month from now, because in one day of working for Samara Katchens, I can make more than what I earn in a month of teaching at Mansour High School.

"Sorry, what is the INC?"

"Oh." She looks surprised. "The Iraqi National Congress. Ahmad Chalabi's group?"

"Yes, yes of course," I say, though there isn't any reason I would have known the name Ahmad Chalabi, had my father not mentioned it recently. "I just didn't recognize the translation to English."

There's a strange jingling coming from her bag, and she pokes around in it and comes out with a black phone about the size of a large spectacles case.

"Damn. Nabil, I'm sorry. I need to get this. Can you wait a minute?" And I wonder where Sam could think I need to be going in such a hurry that I'd have trouble waiting a minute for her, or five, or twenty. "Of course," I say, but I feel that she has hardly heard me, because she is already putting the phone to her ear and bellowing into it. "Wait, I can't hear you. The reception here sucks." And she walks away, moving to the other end of the pool while holding the phone out straight in front of her, like it could be one of those falcons the men in the Gulf States train to fly and return home again, landing dutifully on its master's arm.

She then raises the phone to her ear and turns her back towards me, leaving the fat antenna pointed in my direction. I can still hear her from across the pool.

"Hi Miles. Sorry. Can't always get good reception at the hotel because of the tall buildings." Sam is quiet for a minute. "Jonah? Yeah, he's all right. Well, some of Saddam's security guys actually arrested him while he was filming somewhere without permission and took him to Abu Ghraib. You know, where they torture people for fun. No, I think they just roughed him up. He's very lucky."

She drags a plastic chair from a nearby table and sits down. "Well, yeah, everyone was worried. After we heard that report about the bodies of two European-looking men lying near Haifa Street, and they said one looked like him and all…"

She looks back at me, rolls her eyes, and mouths: "Sorry." She's nodding, issuing several "uh-huhs." She lunges to one side and then the other, like a football player stretching out. "He'll be all right. No, no. I'm definitely staying."

A waiter comes to ask me if I want to order anything, and I decline, not wanting to miss what she's saying.

"Axelrod's big story? Yeah, I read it. Quite the scoop." She hesitates. "Well, to tell you the truth, I don't know how he gets his stories. But yeah, good for him. I mean, good for us."

Sam turns and looks at me again. Her lips have the look of sucking on something sour.

"Of course, Miles, I know we need more of that. I've got a few things cooking here on the INC that could be really good. Just give me some time. Sorry, Miles? I really have to go. You got me in the middle of trying to hire a new fixer."

Trying?

She seems frustrated and her expression is very different from the one she wore when she leapt down the stairs.

"Sorry. My editor. Nagging me for investigative stories at two o'clock in the bloody morning. For him, I mean." She stands the black phone up on the table. Across the top in Arabic and English, it reads *Thuraya*.

"You can get a mobile phone that works in Iraq?"

She smiles as though I've said something silly. "It's a satellite phone. It connects to a satellite somewhere over the Indian Ocean. You haven't seen one yet?"

I have to admit that I haven't, and I wonder, should I have? Our phones have been out of order for weeks. The government said it was because of the US bombing our stations, but now there are rumours that the government itself shut down the lines to prevent the Americans from listening in on any of Saddam's advisors and figuring out their strategies. Even when we did have service, we couldn't call overseas. But we could get calls from abroad, and there were only two types of those. A short call from Ziad every month, and a yearly call from one of my father's old colleagues in England, wishing us a happy Christmas and a jolly good New Year.

"Samara, I must tell you, nobody in our country is allowed to have these kinds of things, not even a satellite dish to watch television," I explain. "The only person who could have a phone like this would be *mukhabarat*, you know, the secret police. Maybe some other people working directly for Saddam."

"Yeah, I know," she says. She picks up the coffee the waiter brought while she was on the phone and blows on it with puckered lips. "And please, call me Sam."

"Even though your given name is Samara? It's a beautiful name."

"Thanks. But I prefer Sam."

"Samara almost sounds like an Arabic name. We even have a city by this name, but we say it a little differently."

She grins at me and sips the coffee, placing it a bit lazily back into the saucer, so that a milky film spills over into it. I hate this kind of coffee, with the hot milk and too much sugar, but I assume that the hotel makes it because this is the way foreigners like it.

"I know," she says. "I passed it on my way to Baghdad."

I feel embarrassed again, because she is new in my country and has already been to places I hardly know. Samarra is less than two hours to the northwest, but I only remember going there once, when I was a boy and our parents took us on a holiday up north.

"Where else did you go? Did you go to Tikrit?"

"Yeah," she says, gazing into the distance, as if remembering the view of it. "We were covering the war from the north and went everywhere we could on the way down, essentially wherever the lines were retreating – from Suleimaniye and Irbil down to Kirkuk, and then Tikrit, through Samarra and then here."

"And you did all of that without an interpreter?"

Sam makes a face like I have just posed the most preposterous question in the world. "Oh, no. That's never an option. We had a translator until Tikrit. And then he, well, decided to give up and go home. So I teamed up with Jonah for a while and shared a fixer with him."

"A fixer?"

"Fixer, translator, same thing. More or less."

"And so your friend Jonah is okay."

"Yes," she smiles, her chest falling with relief – or exasperation. "You heard?" She wags a finger at me. "You were eavesdropping."

"You were not speaking quietly."

She picks up her coffee cup again and puts it to her mouth, all the while with her eyes set on me. "Also, Rizgar's been my driver all along. I mean, since Suli."

After a moment I realize she means Suleimaniye, and I feel a rising distaste over the idea that Sam and her colleagues have already given abbreviations to Iraqi cities I have never seen, as if they are old friends, on intimate terms.

"What happened to the last interpreter?" I suddenly realize that it is as if I'm interviewing Samara, not the other way around, and now I regret my words. I certainly don't want her to find me cheeky or rude.

She grins close-mouthed, her lips spread wide. "I like you, Nabil. I like people who aren't afraid to ask questions." She drinks her coffee again, watching me across the rim of her cup. "My last translator was Saman. Kurdish, of course. He and Rizgar started with me in Suli. They were a good team. But Saman's Arabic was weak and he had an accent when he spoke it, and so when we got to Tikrit he had a hard time."

"What happened?"

Sam lifts her cup higher this time, and I can hear the rest of its contents draining into her throat. When she's done, she shrugs. "Someone said something nasty or something, then, when we were trying to leave, they threw things at the car. It was just...it scared him a bit and he decided not to come to Baghdad with us. Hopped a ride back to Irbil, where he's from."

"I see." Most of the people I know think that the Kurds are part of the cause of the American invasion. One of Baba's friends who came for a visit a while back said the Kurds have been selling their souls for years, begging for Washington to overthrow Saddam. Baba nodded, and though we were sitting in the garden speaking quietly, I felt his discomfort with any political talk in our house. Most people I know don't like the Kurds, especially the nationalist ones from the north. A Kurd from Irbil probably *would* have a bad time in Baghdad.

"I was thinking, Sam, that many of the interpreters for the Ministry of Information are professionally trained. Maybe you would prefer to work with one of them."

Her nose crumples as if smelling something bad. "Someone who used to be a minder? That's the last person I want to hire."

I have never heard of a "minder" before, but I can use my imagination.

"You know, they're basically government lackeys who happen to speak some English. Kinda like a low-grade spy. There's no way I'd voluntarily work with one of them." She raises her hand and waves it until a skinny waiter in a bowtie, the ends of it drooping like a frown, heads over to our table.

"Nabil, listen. Your English is essentially perfect, and that's why I want you to work with me, but I also think this is a good opportunity for you. You'll get to find out what's really going on and meet people you'd never meet, and you'll help me get the right information out there in the public eye. That's never happened in Iraq before. Do you know how important that is?" She looks up at the waiter and offers a tart smile. "I'm starving," she says to me. "Have you had breakfast yet?"

I look at my watch. It is nearly 10:15 a.m. I ate almost three hours ago, and I didn't feel hungry then, either. "Please, not for me."

She turns back to the waiter. "Do you think you could make me a cheese omelette? With toast?" She seems uncertain about this request. Does she think that Baghdad is such an Arab backwater, that we have nothing but *fuul* and *hummos* for breakfast?

She stares at me hard now and when that strange gold-brown light in her eyes hits mine, I have to avert my eyes for a moment.

"Let's try this," she says. "Work with me for a week at $100 and see how it goes. You have nothing to lose because school's not in session anyway, right? If things go well, I'll ask my editor about bumping you up to $125 a day. If it's not your thing, fine, no commitment, we go our own ways, *shukran* and *maa-salaama*."

I raise my eyes involuntarily, surprised at her Arabic.

54

"Deal?" Sam holds out her right hand.

I am about to give it to her, but am suddenly aware of the waiter rushing back to the table, looking apologetic. "I'm sorry, Misses Samara, but no eggs. No eggs today. But toast. We make the toast."

Sam grins and drops her hand.

"Deal." I have the urge to take her no-longer-on-offer hand, to feel her skin against mine for a moment longer than a handshake. Then I remember Noor and instead my hand curls in on itself. I feel my nails digging into my palm, almost hard enough to break the skin.

6

Digging

SAM LEAVES ME at the pool and says she's going upstairs for a minute to change. When she comes back fifteen minutes later, she has swapped her snug jeans and T-shirt for a pair of flowing black trousers and a loose, white blouse with long sleeves. It has blue embroidery around the collar, sort of like a peasant dress converted into a modern lady's shirt.

As she is on her way over to me, a young man with blond, curly hair shouts her name from the far side of the pool, waving both arms in the air.

Sam beams. "Oh my God," she squeals. "I can't believe it!" They rush towards each other, the man more quickly towards Sam, and when they meet they embrace with their bodies locked tightly against each other for a moment.

"When did you get in?" Sam asks when he finally lets go.

"Yesterday," he replies, "but Jesus, it feels like a week." His accent sounds like an American one I have heard in a film, maybe one of those John Wayne Westerns we used to get at the video stall with all the illegal copies of old films. "Came in with the Fourth Infantry. How 'bout you?"

"About five days ago," Sam says, "but we've been in the north with the Kurds since the start of March."

"Sammy-baby, what a trooper! You're my idol, man."

The man's clothes look so informal next to mine: faded blue jeans and a long-sleeved undershirt with an adventurer's waistcoat over it. I look down at my tie, my best trousers my mother pressed to make sure I would be presentable, and I begin to feel ridiculous.

The man smiles widely at Sam and scans her up and down, as though checking to see her own dress code. "You staying here?" he asks.

"Sweet, huh? They're getting the pool cleaned up and everything." She turns to me and gives me a hand gesture to come join them.

"Sunbathing in Baghdad. Nice," the man says. "We're living in tents in the yard of one of the palaces. Can you believe that? We're like campin' on Saddam's lawn. The generals are in one of his living rooms. But I'm hoping to get out of this embed soon and then maybe I'll be able to check in somewhere a bit more plush, like this."

Sam cups a hand over her forehead, shielding her eyes from the sun creeping higher in the sky.

"By the way," he says, "CNN's having a big barbecue on Friday. You should come."

"Oh, yeah," she answers. "I heard that. I'll try to make it."

"You look great, Sam. I think war agrees with you. You always manage to look ever so fetching in the middle of a shithole."

Sam smirks, otherwise ignoring the comment, and then takes my elbow to move me closer to them. "Oh, Mark, this is Nabil. Nabil, Marcus Baker of the *New York Times*."

I hold out my hand and he grabs it roughly, squeezing it so hard I feel that all the bones in my hand ought to have been fractured. "Gooda meet'cha, Nabil." He says my name with a long *Nah* to start, NAH-bil, placing the accent in the wrong place. It's wrong, but not worth correcting. I see that Marcus Baker has the same weird phone as Samara. They read off numbers and jab at their keypads. They smile and hug once more.

"Shall we?" She raises her eyebrows at me. "*Y'alla.*"

I follow her out of the pool area towards the first tower lobby, pondering whether I should tell her that this use of *y'alla* is too colloquial, to the point of being rude, as a way of telling someone to move along, unless you know them quite well. We walk around to the hotel entrance, and the drivers loitering near their cars stare at her, then at me, and then pretend not to notice us. Sam lifts her hand to her brow and moves her head from left to right, scanning. "There he is," she says, and I see Rizgar, the driver who came with her to Noor's house, stand up and raise his hand.

Rizgar is not driving the shiny black 4x4 jeep he had two days ago, but an old blue Impala that is as long as a living room. He holds the back and front doors open for us and sweeps a hand to show us in. "You remember Rizgar, don't you?" It seems a strange question. Does she think there were many foreign women with their own drivers who showed up at Noor's funeral? But perhaps this is her way of reintroducing us.

I feel unsure of where I should sit. Ought not a guest, especially a woman, feel more respected, and more protected, by sitting in the back? But Sam hops into the front seat without a word. The car's interior is dusty, and I can feel the particles in the air starting to tickle my nose. Most importantly, I feel relief. I am glad to find that Sam is no longer travelling around in that fancy new jeep with a sign that says TV on it.

Rizgar smiles at me in his rearview mirror.

"New car!" I say. "Very nice."

"The jeep is good for the north, because the roads are difficult," he says in Arabic. "But here, if you drive big, new cars you look like an American government official or CIA. Those are the cars getting attacked. In a car like this," he says, patting the dashboard, "we look just like regular Iraqis."

"Hey, what are you guys talking about? Don't go leaving me out the first day on the job," Sam says.

"He says that you are safer in this car than in the jeep," I explain.

"Ah, yes, that's true. I always trust Rizgar's judgement. He got us through the war in one piece, didn't you, Rizgar?"

Rizgar peers at me again in the rearview mirror with a serious face. But then he smiles, revealing a gold eye-tooth, and forms a thumbs-up sign and we laugh. The thought that the war is *through*, that Sam – and therefore America – sees it in the past tense, is filling me with the brightest sensation I have had for weeks.

7

Filling

WE DRIVE TOWARDS the centre of town, through Karkh, and suddenly it feels like we're in a film, because all down Rashid Street there are American tanks, big rolling monsters in dark green, and other military vehicles with heavy artillery mounted on them. Nothing here has ever looked like this before. I see a few American soldiers, not many, and I cannot understand why. Where are all the soldiers? Shouldn't they be marching in the streets? In the front seat, Sam is scribbling things into her notebook. Rizgar shakes a box of cigarettes, down to its last lonely occupants, and ejects one into his mouth.

I keep searching for the soldiers who belong with the tanks, expecting to see hundreds, maybe thousands of them, and instead I only catch sight of three or four. I remember one time, when I was about fourteen, we saw a parade of Republican Guards marching by our high school. We all ran to the window to watch, mesmerized by the syncopated stomp of their red boots, ignoring the teacher's reprimand to go back to our seats. Was I expecting the Americans to appear like that, advancing into Baghdad in a perfect phalanx?

"I'm surprised the Americans have not put up any of their

flags around the city," I say, feeling as if I am talking to no one, because neither Sam nor Rizgar react.

I can hear her pen come to rest, and then she turns and looks over her shoulder at me, her hair full of bright light from outside. It occurs to me that for modesty's sake, she should tie her hair back or otherwise put it into place, the way the female professors did at university if they didn't wear *hejab*.

"Well," Sam purses her lips, "they did put that huge flag up on the Saddam statue. You saw *that*, didn't you?"

I peer out of the window and take in the Ministry of Information, which seems to be moving past us in slow motion. A massive hole cuts through three floors, around the fifth, sixth and seventh storeys and the building looks as though it has been hit by a wrecking ball. Twists of mangled metal emerge and wind in odd directions.

I owe Samara an answer. "Uh, no. I didn't see it."

"Oh God, it was all over the news. When they got into Baghdad on Tuesday these soldiers climbed up that big statue of Saddam in Firdos Square and hung an American flag over his face! I mean, before they toppled the thing with the help of a tank. The Bushies are getting a lot of flak for it back home. People here *must* be talking about it." Sam stretches her neck further over her shoulder and smiles again, and in her face I see an expression that says, *And where have you been?*

"They didn't mention it on Iraq Radio," I say.

Everywhere there were stores, everything is either gated up or gone. Or burned. Or wrecked. Alarms are wailing, buildings are smoking, people are hurrying rather than walking. Almost every large building is damaged in some way. Several government ministries look like they have been hit by small airplanes. Maybe that is what this war is about: revenge for what happened a year-and-a-half ago, on September the 11th. But why punish us? Weren't the hijackers from Saudi Arabia and Egypt? If Saddam were a little smarter, we could have been friends with America, just like them.

Sam notices me staring out of the window in awe. "Haven't you seen this part of town yet?"

"No." I am mesmerized by the sight of the Ministry of Transportation and Communication, whose tower is twisted at the top into fine, curly filaments.

Something feels wrong about this, this sense that she knows the city better than I do.

"You know, nobody was going out since the war started unless they had to, to get food or something," I explain. "Everybody was avoiding this part of town, especially this area where the palaces and a lot of ministry buildings are, because we knew that's what would get hit the most."

No one was going out, I think. Unless, of course, they had a date. For many Iraqis, getting your son or daughter married off is its own kind of emergency.

She jots something into her notebook and for a moment I wonder if she could be taking down notes about me, about what I do or don't know. Perhaps she will write up an evaluation of me at the end of the day. She'll send it to her editor and he will decide whether I am good enough to work for the newspaper. Or, maybe Sam isn't a newspaper journalist at all, but a spy working for an international agency. Perhaps even her name is made up. She'll just use me to gather information and later on I'll be held responsible for collaborating with the enemy.

She points out the Ministry of Education on our left, the whole side of it stripped open and exposed. I can see office chairs and desks and cabinets as high as the eighth floor, blackened by fire, sitting in the open air as if in an acrid conversation with the sky. It all seems unreal, seeing our national offices burnt black, left exposed for all to see. Baghdad is like a violated woman.

"Damn! See what they did to that one. Amazing."

I am glad that there are some things that are new to Sam. *They*, she says. Look at what *they* did. Aren't they her own people? Her government?

Rizgar tries to get on to the highway near the 14th of July Bridge, but as we pull close to the ramp, we see three tanks lined up across the road. A soldier's top half emerges from the turret, his page-white hands firmly on the trigger. Behind him, a black soldier puts one hand up towards the traffic and waves it back and forth, the other holding fast to the enormous rifle across his chest. The driver from the car two cars in front of us yells that he needs to get on the bridge.

"Closed! Closed!" the soldier on the ground shouts back at him. He throws his arms forwards in a gesture that seems quite rude. The soldier in the turret puts his face behind his rifle scope and aims at the driver, and then rotates the gun in a wider arc to include all the drivers behind him, some of whom are getting out of their cars.

"Go back! Move *the fuck* back! Now!" Both the soldiers are shouting and a nervous Rizgar turns the car around quickly, grabbing the wheel in short, quick yanks.

Sam shakes her head. "Jeez," she says with more air than sound.

"No worry. No worry," Rizgar says. He appears calmer once

we are on our way, speeding in the opposite direction, towards Abu Nuwas Street. "Many many ways to go."

I keep thinking about the soldiers bellowing from their tanks. "Sam? Don't any of your soldiers speak Arabic?"

Sam looks at me with an apologetic shrug. "Some. But not too many of them. They're usually not the brightest candles on the cake."

I watch through the back window as we drive away and I can see the soldier, his rifle still raised, shouting and enraged, or maybe just frightened, pointing the barrel directly at a man who had got out of his car to talk to him. The soldier is gazing through a large eyepiece on the gun, one of the most sophisticated rifles I have ever seen, and not at the man himself. The figure grows smaller and I wonder whether he will be shot.

"I think they will have a difficult time in Baghdad if they cannot communicate basic things in Arabic," I say. "They cannot expect a simple driver like that to understand English."

"You're right, Nabil." She turns to Rizgar. "But we need to get to the INC. Today. Can you get us to the Hunting Club some other way?"

"Yes, Misses Samara, but is maybe more dangerous way, no highway. Bad places with many stealing." Rizgar uses each hand to indicate one shooting the other. Then he smiles an uncomfortable smile, and I find myself wondering why anyone covers a bad tooth with gold.

"Oh, it'll be fine, won't it? Just be careful." There is no police anymore, no one in control. And so there is nothing to stop a man from simply approaching you at the wheel of your car with a gun and telling you to get out. There are more and more incidents like this every day. You're lucky if they take just your car.

Sam opens the sun visor in front of her, which has a mirror clipped to it, and puckers her lips. She then produces a blue plastic container and with this she runs a clear balm over her lips, drawing them in on each other. Her mouth seems softer now, and a bit more pink. She closes the visor and then flips it open again, this time bending it to an angle through which she can see me.

"Oh, and Nabil? Don't call them *my* soldiers." She appears to be dead serious, but then she smiles in a way that almost seems playful. "I didn't want this war either."

She begins to tap the gadget I saw her use back in the hotel. It emits a little squeak each time she pokes it.

"It's called a Palm Pilot. See?" She must have noticed me studying it. "They'll probably open a store here by Christmas… This is my life, right here in this little slab of electronic memory. I can try to bring one back for you next time I go to America."

"So you will go back to America and then come to Iraq again?"

She puffs out her cheeks and lets them deflate slowly, like air from a balloon. "Probably. I have no idea. Usually we are on an assignment like this for a month or two. That's about all a person can take." She grins. "But I mean, this *is* the story. I can't see leaving anytime soon."

"I see," I say, even though I'm not sure I do.

"Which is why Jonah is more than a little pissed off at me."

"Your friend who was in Abu Ghraib?" I notice my palms are sweaty, and rub them on my trousers which don't absorb a thing.

"Yeah. He's decided he's had it with the story and wanted to leave, which is understandable. But he wants me to go with him, which is not going to happen."

"Why would—"

"Actually," she says, raising a hand, not so unlike the way the soldier had, "let's not get into it now."

8

Raising

I FIND IT strange, this term Sam keeps using, "looter family". We must find a looter family. Does she expect to find an entire family in which everyone is participating in the looting – men, women and children? Or does she mean a larger family, a whole *hamule*, which translates as clan, though that doesn't sound quite right to me. Certainly, one can find extended families like that, where crime or smuggling or being in the *mukhabarat* seems to be a family inheritance, but does that mean now that looting could be arranged along family lines? It would seem odd, and yet this is the myth of what the looting actually is. Sam says that President Bush in Washington is being criticized for it back home because the looting is getting out of hand, doing almost as much damage as the war itself. Maybe more.

Sam says there are reports that the Baghdad Museum of Art is half empty. I tell her that my cousin heard a rumour that the American soldiers stood there and let it happen, even held the doors open as all of Iraq's treasures, our pre-Islamic artifacts and even Babylonian antiquities, were carted away. I find it hard to believe.

What concerns me at the moment is that Sam doesn't seem to realize that it is actually a very small part of the population which is doing all of this stealing. Apparently, the American Defense Secretary, Mr Rumsfeld, said yesterday that it is understandable for the Iraqi people to want to release some of their frustrations. "Free people are free to make mistakes and commit crimes and do bad things," Rumsfeld said, according to Sam, who read the quote to me from a story her editor sent her. The comment made me furious. Do they view us as a nation of criminals?

We have also heard that many institutions are simply disintegrating and people are walking free: patients from psychiatric institutions, criminals from prisons. My father says that his hospital has organized its own round-the-clock security system to prevent the looting that has occurred at other hospitals.

We are driving towards Saddam City and as we get closer I can see that vandals have blotted Saddam's name from the sign and changed it to Sadr City. It is spray-painted neatly, although it is obvious that it is not the real thing, nothing official. Or perhaps they will do this, take Baghdad's largest Shi'ite area and name it for Sadr, one of the most important Shi'ite clerical dynasties in modern Iraqi history. Ayatollah Mohammad Sadeq al-Sadr was killed by Saddam, and his son Moqtada is now becoming the hero of all young Shi'ites. Except me. But then, I'm a half-breed. I don't count for much. And if I had to choose between being Shi'ite or Sunni, I'd just as soon as leave for Europe or America, like Ziad did.

There is an enormous mural of Saddam to the right of the sign, the one with him wearing a black fedora and holding a hunting rifle. The vandals have turned the hat into a woman's *hejab*, added earrings, and painted on false eyelashes. They have also turned his moustache and smile into a pair of fat, red lips, like a woman's. They've made the rifle into a sword and depicted blood – with the same colour red as they used for his lips – dripping down and trailing off the board. Saddam's titles have been crossed out. "The Leader, The Saviour", now reads "Il-Qassab, Il Kadthab" – The Butcher, The Liar.

"Whoah, check out that one." Sam rolls down her window with jerky cranks of the handle. "Rizgar, can you slow down for a minute? I want to shoot that one." As Sam puts the camera to her face, it becomes clear to me what she means by shoot and this strikes me as funny, because I have never heard the word used this way before. It seems noteworthy that the two things Americans shoot in Iraq are either a gun or a camera. Bullets, or photographs.

What's happening to Saddam's image is surreal. I cannot remember a time in my life when it was not around, and so I hardly noticed it. But now that his image is being defaced, he's everywhere. Sometimes it seems funny, and at others, humiliating. His image is becoming a national embarrassment for us in front of all the other Arab countries, in front of the entire world, watching and filming. Shooting. I could tell Sam all of this, but she wouldn't understand.

Rizgar turns back towards me and asks me where we should go. How should I know? I've only been to Saddam City once in my whole life when I was a teenager. Back then, it was called Thawra, meaning revolution. There were troubles here after the war with Kuwait and America and the residents are quite poor. It was a place that you stayed away from, unless you had some reason to go.

"What part do you want to visit?" I ask Sam, searching for

clues. I don't want to linger here without some direction. But she is still taking photographs and she leans out of the window to capture a small statue, presumably of Saddam, lying on the ground. It is nothing like the one in Firdos Square, but still large enough to look like a fallen giant.

The bronze body is splattered with the same red paint that was on the mural, and some small boys are using it like a jungle gym, leaping over its backside, climbing over its shoulders. One boy jumps gleefully on its head, while another uses his shoe to bat it in the face.

Sam leans on the open window. Click click. Click. She puts the camera down and turns back to me. "Oh, anywhere. We need to find a looter family."

I hesitate. "What does it mean, 'looter family?'"

"You know, a family where one of the brothers or sons, one of the men of the house, has been out doing the looting. I want to see them in their house and just get a sense of what they're thinking. I mean, it's not that they're just after stuff, right? It's about getting back at the regime."

This seems simple enough, and yet completely ridiculous. Do you stop a thief in the middle of the act and ask him why he's doing it? Maybe it is different in America, or in France. Maybe in those countries, criminals agree to be interviewed.

"I hope you don't mind my saying so," I begin, "but I think it will be very hard to find someone who will admit that they are stealing."

"Really? Lots of papers have started to run stories like that. Someone's talking."

Rizgar drives deeper into a neighbourhood I don't know. The houses become denser, without any spaces between them, without any green in the gardens. And soon there are no gardens, only dwellings, cluttered and compressed into a warped grid of concrete and pipes and washing lines.

"So any family will do?" I ask. "Anyone who's stolen something since the looting began?"

"Yeah, anyone. Anyone who took things of value. Not just rusty old office equipment."

We enter an area with a string of shops and I get out of the car. I notice a dairy which has a steel gate pulled across it, and even though it's closed, there's a man inside, and I can see that he must still be open for business because a woman just went in looking for milk and I saw him pass it to her through the metal lattice. I walk up to the gate and I see the man, perhaps in his early forties, inside. His face twists in my direction; I appear to have startled him. I hold up my hands, perhaps on instinct to show him that I am unarmed, and begin to explain what I need. And he says to go to Rimal Street and ask for his brother, Hatem.

I thank him over and over, and he looks at me as if he doesn't know why. He wipes his hands on his trousers. "We're not ashamed," he says. "We are only taking back what the government stole from us. Everybody I know took only from the government offices and police stations, not from private stores. Not the real Iraqis. Go to see Hatem. Tell him Adel sent you. He will help you. I'll try to come and join you in a bit, after I close up here."

My mind is racing now with an energy that I forgot I had, like the feeling I used to have when I ran relays in school. I try to hide the breathlessness in my voice. "It's good," I announce. "We have an address of someone who will talk."

Hatem is wearing a thin T-shirt and blue trousers that are

fraying around the bottoms, as if they might have been washed and hung out to dry in the sun a hundred times. He looks very young, but has grown a heavy beard that makes him look more mature. Behind him, two small children are wrestling with each other. The bigger boy has the upper hand and he bangs the slightly smaller boy's head on to the floor. The shrieking swells, and then a woman who is fully covered, I presume she is Hatem's wife, rushes to pick up the crying boy. She slaps the bigger boy lightly on the back of his head, and drags him by the shirt until the noisy mess of them disappears from sight.

Hatem is tall and slim and has a facial structure so sharply defined you can follow its angles beneath his beard. But his height is a slouching height, not a proud one, and I notice my shoulders receding to meet his, as if to assume a stance of solidarity.

Their sitting room is simple: floor cushions, marked and ripping in places, placed in a U-shape around the room. On the wall there is a picture of Moqtada in a cheap plastic frame. But I soon find myself counting up all the things that don't belong. A typewriter, much newer than the model I have at home, sits in the corner, next to a mound of shimmering white glass that sparkles like diamonds in the sunlight from outside. Hatem has noticed me eyeing it. "Do you want to see the other things that we have reclaimed?" he asks.

"Reclaimed?"

"Well, this isn't theft, you know. We are taking back the things the regime stole from us. This is like blood money that can never be claimed."

Sam points to the glittering glass. "Did they take that chandelier from one of the palaces?"

Hatem lifts his gaze to me and his eyebrows move closer together. It's clear he doesn't understand much English, nor does he know why the woman speaking it is standing in his home, and so I begin to explain that she is a journalist, and he says from where, and I don't know why, but I say France, and after all, doesn't her card say she lives in France? And he says *Ahlan w-sahlan*, you are welcome as if family, and that if Adel sent us, we must be okay. And I think of stopping right there, explaining that we only met his brother ten minutes ago by chance, but instead I smile and say thank you.

"First, come," Hatem says, and he leads us into the family room behind the sitting room, the place to which, in many houses of the religious, a stranger wouldn't often be invited.

There are many chairs and sofas and lamps, and everything is in an antique-looking European style, with velvet fabrics and fancy wooden carvings along the edges, some painted with gold. There are also some wooden side tables and a few Syrian folding chairs with inlaid mother-of-pearl. The furniture is packed in so tightly, it looks like a dealer's warehouse.

"Christ," Sam mutters to me. "This is amazing. Did he loot a whole palace living room?"

I ask Hatem the same question, in more polite form of course, and he clicks his tongue against the top of his mouth. "No, not a palace. A villa. One of the minister's homes."

"Really? Which one?"

Hatem hesitates. "Chemical Ali. He has many homes in Iraq, two in Baghdad. My brothers and our relatives decided we would target these homes."

"*Mashallah*," I say, and I am, in fact, impressed. Everyone knows that Chemical Ali, whose real name is Ali Hassan al-

Majid, is said to have killed thousands of Kurds as well as Shi'ites, many by chemical warfare. When Saddam has a problem, I once heard someone say, Chemical Ali has the solution.

Sam is not as impressed as I expected.

"Which house?" she asks. "Where was it?"

Hatem smirks, staring at her but speaking to me. "Ask around. Anyone can tell you where the house is."

Sam walks up to one of the chairs and runs her hands along the rich trim. "Can I photograph him with all of his loot?"

I cannot think of a way to interpret these words without insulting him. I certainly cannot use *hawasim*, since he doesn't view this as looting. The only words I can think of are stolen things, or other words that have *sariqa* in them, which can only mean theft. So for now I won't translate the question at all.

Hatem asks me to ask Sam if she knows who Chemical Ali is.

Sam strokes the green velvet on one of the sofas. "Sure I know."

"Well," says Hatem, "he is responsible for the murder of at least thirty of my relatives."

When I tell Sam that, she looks at Hatem with eyes that seem determined at looking sad. "I'm very sorry," she says. "That's awful."

Hatem nods. "Why don't you come back into the sitting room. Coffee or tea?"

And so we go back into the front room and settle into the cushions, and Hatem begins to tell us about all the relatives who have been jailed or killed in the past fifteen years – or who have simply disappeared.

Sam is fidgeting with the camera inside her bag. "But what

about the rest of the city? The looters are picking Baghdad to pieces. People are getting killed in the street."

Hatem raises his right hand as if shielding himself from something. "That is not our people. Those are others. Maybe the criminals who escaped from Abu Ghraib when the regime fell. Maybe Kurds from the North. They are coming down here and committing the real crimes."

I feel my face tense at the thought: Rizgar. Did Hatem notice him pull up? Is he still out by the car?

"Tell her this," Hatem says to me. "Explain to her that in Islam, there is a difference between stealing and making reparations. The Prophet Mohammed, peace be upon Him, said that stealing is so despised by God that the thief's hand should be cut off. But it also says in the Holy Koran that when an injury is done by one party, he must fix what he has broken or pay the damages. There must be a *sulha*."

"Nabil," Sam turns to me. "Can you translate what he's saying?"

"Wait one minute. I need to understand first what he's trying to say."

"Well, I'd prefer you translate sentence by sentence, or you'll forget what he said."

"No, yes…please continue."

"But in our culture, please explain to her, we have a concept of the *sulha*, in which the families of the two parties get together to reconcile the differences. The elders negotiate and decide what is fair."

Sam's hand cuts the air. "Nabil, just stop him and tell him you need to translate."

"But in this case, Saddam has disappeared and we may never

hear from him again. Maybe he is already in another country. And so, how will we get our *ta'wid*?" he says, using the term for reparations. "Who will give me the blood money for my other brother, for all my cousins who are dead and missing? The United Nations? George Bush? I don't think so."

I turn to Sam. "He is saying that he doesn't believe they will be compensated for their losses."

Sam's shoulders fall and she tilts her head, petulant. "He said a lot more than that. It was at least a few sentences, wasn't it? I need to hear the whole story."

"Okay, I'll tell you after."

"No, not after."

"Just one minute—"

Hatem keeps talking, eyeing Sam like she is interrupting. "In a true Islamic society, if the families cannot solve the problem then they go to a *mahkameh*, to a religious court, and the judge there can decide who is wrong, and will award damages to the injured party. But since a fair court based on sharia doesn't yet exist anywhere in Iraq—"

Sam is shifting noisily now, and I give her a hand signal to wait just one more moment.

"…so then we must act as if we are the judges and must compensate ourselves for what Saddam took from us. We hope in the future we will have a true Islamic society based on sharia, and then we will never again see a situation such as this. Moreover, you must know that all of what we are seeing is presaged in the Holy Koran. You should read sura 15:47. 'We shall strip away all rancour that is in their breasts.' I can show you the place. It means that the belongings of a decadent regime must be stripped away. When there is a war against a corrupt ruler or an infidel regime, this is what we are called upon to do."

"I understand. One moment? Let me explain to the lady." And I start to summarize his points for Sam, but she is sitting with her arms crossed and looking annoyed. "You don't want to write this down?" I ask.

She picks up the notebook she had placed on her lap and grimaces. "Yeah. Go ahead and tell me again."

I give her a summation of everything he has said, focusing on the most important points. Sam shakes her head.

She lowers her voices and tries to sound gentle. "Nabil, this isn't working. I need exact quotes, not summaries. Ask him to run through his day yesterday and tell me what he did. Where he went, what he stole. How he got it home. How did he get all of this stuff into his living room?"

"...and so you can explain to this lady that when we have a true Islamic government that works in concert with the *ummah*," and I cannot think of how to translate this, "we can reconcile any disputes over this process. The Prophet Mohammed, peace be upon Him, said to care for the poor. And we will make sure that the proceeds of what we reclaim are evenly distributed to the poor."

I do not know how to get him to slow down, or how to translate half of what he is saying. His arguments do not even make complete sense to me.

I nod emphatically. "Sorry, sorry? She wants to know where you went for these items."

"Where we went?"

"Yes, where everything is from."

And so he explains that most of these things came from one

of Uday Hussein's homes, and from a government office that was run by him, and I tell Sam all of this, but she still does not look happy.

Hatem excuses himself and leaves the room. "He says that he has at least seven family members who have disappeared in the past decade. He is going to show us pictures."

"Nabil, could you try getting into his voice when you translate? Say, I did this or that."

"I should say I did this?"

"Yes, don't say, 'He says he has more than seven family members.' Say, '*I* have more than seven family members.' First-person. Know what I mean by that? Pretend you are speaking for him."

Of course I know what first-person is. But I didn't understand until now that Sam would want me to speak like that, and I didn't expect that she would be constantly correcting and interrupting while I interpret for her.

Hatem comes back with a stack of pictures. The edges are tatty, and their faded colour betrays their age. Young men in their twenties and thirties with thick moustaches, some resembling Hatem, stare back at us. Hatem names each one and the time he disappeared. Many of them were picked up after March 1991, he says, after the war with Kuwait and America.

"On Monday we are going to go to Al-Mahawil to look for them," Hatem tells me. "The people are digging up the mass graves there and I think this is where they might be buried. We must give them a proper Islamic burial."

"He says he may go to the south to look for them when they excavate the area," I tell Sam. "I mean, sorry. '*We* are going to the south to look for them. The people will dig up mass graves there.'"

"Hmm. Wow, that'd be an amazing story. Nabil, ask him if he minds letting me get a shot of him holding these photographs."

"You want him to stand in front of the looted items while you take the picture?"

Sam seems doubtful, then dismissive. "Nah, I don't want to pose the picture that much, you know?"

I can't imagine how the photograph wouldn't seem posed. If posed means that the people arrange themselves in such a way that they know the picture is being taken, and they try to look appropriate for the photographer, then isn't it posed? Hatem calls his sons over and the smallest boy, fully recovered from his brother's pouncing, comes running to his father's knees. Hatem pulls him on to his lap, and then splays out the family photos like a fan.

"Okay," he says, "now I am ready."

"You can take the picture," I tell her.

"I already did," she says. But this time I didn't hear the click, so I am wondering how that could be.

"Take down all of their names," Hatem says, setting his son, who seems disappointed at the brevity of his father's affection, back on to the floor. "Put them all in the newspaper. Saddam has killed millions of Shi'ites. Millions. Now the future of the country belongs to us, and we will rebuild it in their name," he says, smiling at his boy. "Tell her that."

"He is saying that Saddam was very bad to the Shi'ites and killed a lot of them. But all the Shi'ites say this. We don't know if it is true but many people have been saying this."

Hatem interrupts me. "She's American, no? Maybe if America had come sooner, my cousins would be here with us now. One of them had his tongue cut out." He looks at her. "You had a chance to get Saddam twelve years ago, and then you come now. Why? Why so long?"

"What is he saying?"

"He is saying he is glad the Americans are here now."

"Is that what he said?" Sam gives him a face of pleasant surprise, which looks feigned. "Really? Are you happy the Americans are here?"

"Yez, habby. Now habby." Hatem answers in the shreds of English he must have learned in school, his "p" coming out as a "b". I wonder, is this the kind of English my students will speak one day, long after they have finished my class?

A ringing tone emerges from Sam's bag. She scrambles to find the phone and, pulling it out, looks at the screen. "This is my editor again. Do you have a balcony?" I check with Hatem, and he shakes his head.

"What about a window facing southeast?" Sam stands with a posture that says it's urgent. Hatem leads her through the back of the apartment, towards his bedroom. His wife and smallest son stand at the entrance to the kitchen, confused, but Sam hardly takes notice. She opens the window, fumbles to put an extension into the end of the phone and sticks her arm out with the phone pointed towards the sky. Then she dips an earpiece at the end of a little black cord inside her ear.

"Miles?! Miles?" Sam glances at us and pats the air in our direction to say that it is all right. "Hold on. Can you guys give me a minute? I just need to take this call."

We return to the salon.

Hatem searches my eyes. "She's an American?"

"Yes, she is."

"But you said France."

"I said…she lives in France. I thought you meant that you wanted to know where she was coming from now, before she came to Iraq."

Hatem's face is still. "How do you know she isn't working for the government? Most of the journalists are working for the government. Who else could have such a phone?"

Hatem's wavy beard fascinates me. Though I think he must be my age, and certainly not more than thirty, there is a marbling of grey in it that makes him seem like he could be a decade older. I find myself making assumptions about his life. A childhood of urban poverty in a large family, a brief education. How much could he know about freedom of expression in the West? About a media outlet which isn't owned and operated by the government?

"In America, the media and the government are separate," I explain.

Hatem's mouth twitches with disagreement. He takes a set of *sebha* from his pocket, a string of jade beads with gold dividers. I know that this quality of prayer beads is very expensive, and I wonder if it, too, was looted. He twirls it around his fingers, clockwise and counterclockwise.

"How do you know she's not a spy?"

The thought, however preposterous, has crossed my mind. I want to ask him which kind of spy he would prefer she be, CIA or Mossad. But he looks too serious to think it is as funny as I do.

"Believe me, I know. She's just a young woman travelling with other journalists. I know the newspaper she is writing for. It's famous. I can show it to you."

"How long have you known her?"

"More than a year. She came here to report before the war."

I don't know what shifted, what made me make up another lie. I want people to trust Sam, and for her to trust me.

I feel her pacing back towards us, the squeak of her sandals across the cheap linoleum. "I'm sorry," she says. "I think we should go. There's another story breaking and my editors want me to file on something else."

I stand and Hatem stands, too. I try to explain why we are leaving so quickly, but I don't think he understands. He seems to feel we've only just arrived, and should stay for a meal.

"Thank you so much for your time, Mr— oh! Wait," she says, flipping back over her last two pages of notes. "I didn't get your name."

"I have it," I tell her. "I will give it to you in the car."

"But I need to make sure the spelling is right. Some people have a preference for how to write it in English."

"Hatem Mohammed," Hatem says.

"Mohammed? That's his last name?"

"Badr. Hatem Mohammed Badr." His eyes are locked on Sam's forehead as she writes down the name, but she seems oblivious.

"Do you use b-a-d-r, or b-a-d-e-r?"

He looks to me for an answer. His features expand, a map of his suspicions occupying more territory across his face.

"Put b-a-d-r. No 'e,'" I say. I am afraid that with the "e," Sam's readers will see the name and think "badder." Even though I know there is no such word, it is the way people will see it, and this troubles me. On the radio, I've heard the way Bush pronounces our president's name. He makes it sound like "sad" and "damn".

Sam peeks around the corner towards the kitchen to say goodbye to Hatem's wife. She is reticent but smiles broadly, and then hurries to Sam and kisses her on both cheeks.

Nearing the door, I remember how we got here. "Oh, your brother Adel never came by. He said he was going to join us. Please thank him."

"How do you know Adel?"

"We met—" Lie again? "We met him just today."

"Oh, I see." Hatem nodded, as if ticking off mental notes for himself. "You know, Adel is not really my brother."

And now I feel daft, because when I think about it, the two men do not look at all alike. Adel was fat and fair to the point of coming across as foreign, while Hatem is like any other working-class guy on the streets of Saddam City, gaunt and brown-skinned.

"But you can say he is something like a brother." He runs his hand over his beard and winces.

Sam stands in the hallway, snapping her bag shut. "You'll tell me about this conversation in the car, I take it?"

"Our brotherhood is something the Shi'ites have that I'm not sure you can understand," Hatem says. "Just like it is difficult for you to believe the evil things Saddam did, perhaps because he is one of yours."

"Actually, I'm also Shi'ite," I say. "I mean, sort of – I am both. I am Sunni and Shi'ite."

"*Sedog*?" He smiles and slaps my back as a good friend might, rubbing where his hand has landed. "The two sides of the Iraqi heart. Maybe you are the Mahdi, like the messiah, coming to bring peace!" He laughs deeply, and I try to laugh along with him. "Seriously, it must be hard for you to decide which side you are on."

"Nabil?" Sam is holding on to the rail above the staircase.

"When you choose, if you choose well, you are always welcome to come back and visit us." He puts his hand on my shoulders and draws me to him, kissing alternating sides, three times, or maybe more, because already I am finding it difficult to keep track of how many times things have happened and how much time has passed. He lets me go and Sam is tapping her foot and a waking dream suddenly shoots through my mind: Noor's bullet zooming in the window and me flying up to catch it, my cupped, glowing hands saving the world from disaster.

9

Saving

SAM'S EDITOR, IT seems, wanted her to go to the Museum of Art. He read on the newswire – this is a new word for me – that the museum's ancient art is being carried away by what they called "professional" looters. But we cannot get anywhere near the building. There are American military vehicles cordoning off the area, sending people back.

"Maybe we can come back later," I offer. "What can you do? One can't argue with a tank."

"That's not a tank," Sam says. "It's a Bradley Fighting Vehicle. See? There're no treads on it. It's just a scary-ass Humvee with big guns mounted on it. Okay, Rizgar. To the Hunting Club."

"Now Hunt Club? Again?" I am impressed with Rizgar's Arabic, given that many Kurds from the north do not speak so well. But his English is so nominal that I wonder how he and Sam manage to communicate.

"Yes." She turns towards me, and as she does so, I hear the vertebrae in her back clicking against each other, and then a sigh, maybe of pain and maybe of relief, passing her lips. "We need to see if we can get that interview for tomorrow."

*

Once we get past the checkpoint, where a few American soldiers are posted, we drive into the Hunting Club. The grounds are green and spacious, and from here it seems that we are no longer in Baghdad. There are many types of beautiful shrubs and trees and everything is well-manicured. Rizgar stops the car outside the main building and Sam hops out and I step out, too. "You can walk me up, but I don't think you'll need to come in with me. These guys speak English better than I do." She rolls her eyes, which I've come to realize means that I shouldn't take what she just said seriously.

"I will be happy to escort you anyway."

"No, seriously, these INC folks have been spending so much time in Washington, they ought to be naturalized citizens by now. They probably prefer not to have an unknown Iraqi in the room."

"Oh. Of course," I say, feeling foolish.

We walk into the wide-doored, white building and I follow Sam to the reception area. There are dark, rectangular spots along the walls where pictures must have been removed, the area around them bleached lighter from the sun. I can imagine the line of photographs of Saddam and his sons – dressed in equestrian uniforms or riding atop their favourite horses – which must have been removed only in the last day or two. These photographs of Saddam doing sportsman-like things were often published in the newspapers.

The man behind the desk says that we can stay where we are until the press spokesman comes to collect us.

"Oh, he's just waiting with me," Sam says, gesturing in my direction.

The room has large wooden chairs, upholstered with red

leather seats. Sam runs her fingers down one of the carved arms and sits, and I take the chair next to her.

"It's like Saddam tried to make it look like a real English hunting club, smack in the middle of Baghdad." She points up at the mountings above the window. There are wooden plaques with hooks that were obviously a display for old rifles, judging from the shape of the faded spots, but the guns are absent.

"Look at this place." Sam leans in towards me and lowers her voice. "The lap of luxury when people were supposedly starving due to the sanctions." She gets up and inspects a massive vase, painted blue and white in a Chinese motif, sitting next to the end table. "This one might be an antique." She tilts her head back and uses her eyes to direct me to the huge chandelier, glittering like a sun shower above our heads. She sits down again and crosses her legs, letting the upper bounce against the lower. "Just like the palaces. You'd think people would have wanted to tear the place apart."

The receptionist slides open the glass panel covering the window that he sits behind. He sticks his head through and says to me, "Dr Marufi says he can see her in ten minutes."

"He says ten minutes more," I tell Sam.

"I got that."

I hadn't considered the possibility that Sam would know more than how to say hello and thank you. "Do you speak some Arabic?"

"Not really. Dribs and drabs. I learned a bit from a phrasebook, but the numbers and minutes are among the few things that stuck. I wish I'd done Arabic in college."

"So you went to college? Not to university."

Sam takes out her notebook and flips to a blank page. She

begins making a list. I feel she is speaking to me one moment and then ignoring me the next. But now I realize that she must be making a list of important questions to ask in her interview. She stops after five lines. "I know in England college means something less than university, which is probably what you're thinking of."

"Yes. I have friends who studied there and they say it was very important to get accepted to university."

"Right." Sam shuts the notebook and taps on it with her pen. "You know, Nabil, I think we're having little misunderstandings about a lot of things."

I can feel a muscle in my throat go tight, like a bicycle chain when the gears are changed too quickly.

"I need you to work a little harder to be on the ball for me when we're doing interviews. I wasn't, well, entirely happy about the way things went earlier."

"I…did you find that I was not on the ball?" I know I should listen to her first, but I thought that the expression "on the ball" means to be alert. Was I not alert?

"I mean, we need to be on the same page with how this works. I need you to translate sentence by sentence. Word for word. You can't listen for five minutes and then translate. You'll forget what the guy said and then—"

"Oh, but I won't forget. I have a great memory. Also, he didn't want to stop for me to translate. He wanted to tell me everything, and then for me to explain it to you."

She shakes her head, her eyes squinting as if to see something far off in the distance. "It doesn't matter what he wants, or what anyone we're talking to *wants*. You have to find a way to slow them down or stop them when they're speaking. They'll get used to it, everybody does. Just do something like this," she says, tilting the palm of her hand up at a forty-five-degree angle, "and say, 'wait, I have to translate.'"

"But that would be interrupting him. It might appear impolite. We were guests in his house."

"Oh, I wouldn't worry about that. You'll get used to it. It's already an unusual kind of conversation. Guy's talking with a foreigner and half of the conversation is taking place in a language he doesn't understand." She pauses. "Also, I feel like you're not translating exactly what the guy is saying. I need to have it in their words – as close to their words as possible." She turns to me and lifts her eyebrows, and now the wrinkles that were in hiding are visible.

"I understand that," I say. "That's what I am trying to do."

"But a lot of the time you were letting that man speak for a while and I know he would have said five or ten sentences, and you're coming back to me with just one. I may not know much Arabic, but I can just feel that in my bones."

Sam's right. I wasn't giving her every sentence. I was trying to leave out the parts that seemed extraneous or confusing.

"I see."

Or maybe embarrassing.

"I need to hear everything, even if *you* don't think it would be important."

"Everything? Every single thing he says, like the name of every relative he says Saddam killed? Or how he might go to Al-Hilla in the morning to look for his cousins' remains?"

"Wait, he said he was going to Al-Hilla?"

"He said he was going to go to Al-Hilla to search for his cousins who he thinks were buried in a mass grave there, which is now being exposed."

"Exhumed. And?"

"Or maybe he said Al-Mahawil. I think both, maybe. He said he'd go tomorrow, or on Monday."

Sam expels a long breath. I can smell the coffee in it when it hits my face.

"Nabil, you never mentioned either of those places. You just said the south."

"They are in the south."

"Yes, but the fact that it's Al-Hilla or Al-Mahawil makes a big difference. Specifics. Specifics are the heart of journalism. There were reports this morning that Iraqis are flocking down there and trying to dig up these mass graves with their bare hands. If I had known what he was planning I might have asked him about that. Maybe we could have followed his family there and spent the day with them. That would have been a great story."

"But I'm telling you about it now."

"It doesn't matter now. I can't ask him questions *now*. Unless we go back," she says, looking at her watch, "which I don't think we have enough time to do."

I can't understand why Sam is making such a fuss over one man with looted goods and dead relatives. We can probably find a thousand men who will tell us the same story.

"Do you want to go back?"

"No, not really. That's not the point. I just want you to know that I need to hear these things *while* we're in the middle of the interview so I can ask follow-up questions." She lifts her fire-eyebrows towards me. "Do you know what I mean? I need specific details, all the time."

"Yes, yes I see. I'm sorry. I thought these small details were insignificant."

"Sometimes small details make big stories. Let me be the judge of what's significant or not." She uncrosses her legs and stands up. With her back to me, she leans her weight into a bent knee while the other leg is straight – lunging left and then right, for the second time today. I hear a pop emerge from somewhere in the vicinity of her hips. I wonder how old Sam is. She looks like she is in her late twenties, but sometimes she moves like she might be younger. Like a teenager who cannot sit still.

She spins back around towards me. "Don't get me wrong, Nabil. You're doing a fantastic job. Your English is *beautiful*," she says, pinching her thumb and a few fingers together near her lips, and then releasing them with a tiny kiss. "You just need to learn how it all works." She parts her feet and then doubles over, placing her hands flat to the floor.

Her face is reddish-brown when she comes up. "Sorry," she says. "My body is so sore. The chairs at that hotel are shit, and I was up late last night working. My editor lives in a fantasy world where a good reporter should be able break some big, earth-shattering story within a week of coming to Baghdad."

I almost forgot that some people might have reason to stay up late at night. Since the war began, we rarely have electricity past 8 p.m.

She looks at her watch again. "Oh, and remember to speak in first-person. Don't say, 'he says so and so.' Just say what the guy says as if you're him."

"Sam, excuse me. But is it, 'you are him?' Or, 'you are he?'"

Sam's lips curve into a slight frown of incredulity. "Brilliant," she breathes. "You're right. It is 'you are he.' I think. Do they teach this kind of stuff in school here?"

"Not really. But I studied the grammar on my own to make sure I understood all the rules."

"You like following rules, huh?" She stands and bends towards the glass window, which has no one sitting behind it now.

"It just makes understanding the language easier."

"Jeez, these guys are taking forever. There's also supposed to be another press conference with the army later, but I don't think I'm going to go." She locks her fingers together, then presses them out so they crack at nearly the same moment, sounding almost musical.

A round of automatic gunfire splinters into the air and continues for half a minute. It could be a mile away, or two. Another round comes, with a slightly different rattle, angled to answer the first. They seem like the call of birds in the trees, one speaking to the other.

Sam rolls her eyes at me. "Afternoon target practice. I guess you're used to it."

"No. Really not. We never used to hear this before the war."

"Well, yeah, I guess they killed people in prisons and basements, not out on the street."

I don't know where I could begin to explain, but somehow I want her to know that Baghdad was not a city with a lot of violence and crime. It is true that we all feared Saddam and his men, but we didn't fear getting killed or robbed by each other, the way people do in the West.

"Baghdad can be a very beautiful city," I tell her. "I wish you could see it when everything is calm."

I suddenly feel terribly thirsty and I realize that for April, it has turned into a much hotter day than usual. My shirt has gone damp around the armpits and my face is sweaty. I forgot to bring a handkerchief so instead I wipe my face with my hand and notice that my upper lip feels wet, where my moustache once was, and maybe that's what a moustache is there for. Sam doesn't seem hot at all. And then I realize she is still talking to me about how she wants me to behave in interviews.

"…so even though I've seen some translators take notes, I think it slows down the interview, so I'd really rather you not do that. You just need to listen and let it flow."

The door of the reception office opens. "Dr Marufi will be out for you in just one minute," the man says. Sam gathers her bag and notebook and rises.

I stand as well. "Can't you change things afterwards to make it right?"

"What do you mean?"

"If I say, '*He* says he supports the American invasion,' can't you change it afterwards to say, '*I* support the American invasion?'"

Sam's eyes roll up and down my body, as if somewhere on it is the key to my inability to see things as she does. "No, it's different. You're not supposed to change quotes too much. What if you were just estimating and I make the guy sound like he said something definitive that he didn't actually say?"

"Either this way or that, he said the same thing."

Her chest rises and falls. "No, Nabil. A good journalist never changes the quote if she can help it. I need to get as close to the exact words as possible. And that's where you come in."

The door swings open, and a man wearing a dark blue business suit steps out. It's a much more expensive suit than mine – I have now discarded the jacket – but I am glad that

I am no longer the most overdressed person Sam has met today.

"Ms Katchens! Such a pleasure to see you again." He is a tall, greying man in perhaps his mid-forties. He extends one hand to shake hers and puts the other, for a brief moment, on her upper arm, as if he knows her well. "I've been looking forward to seeing you. Come in."

"Dr Marufi, so nice to see you again. Actually, I had just wanted to confirm the interview for tomorrow, and of course, to say hello to you."

"Yes, well, why don't you come in for a few minutes and we'll talk."

"That'd be great. Oh, Dr Marufi. This is Nabil. Nabil, Dr Marufi from the INC. Nabil is working with us now," she smiles at Dr Marufi, and I find myself wondering, doctor of what?

"A pleasure," he says when he offers me his hand. "Will you be joining us?"

Sam's eyes dart in my direction, and I know the answer.

"No, sorry. If you'll excuse me, I have some things to do." I shake his hand and notice that Sam has a pleased expression on her face.

As I near the Impala, Rizgar grins at me. He tilts his head to his right, indicating that I should join him in the front seat. Inside, he has the air conditioning on full blast, which seems like a recipe for running through an awful lot of petrol in a day.

"Aanisa Samara went into her meeting?" Rizgar asks.

I glance at him sideways.

"Yes, she said just a few minutes."

"That means at least a half hour. It's always longer than she says it will be," Rizgar says, shifting his belly. Well-proportioned elsewhere, he has a hefty stomach that seems to compete for space with the steering wheel. His skin is doughy, with early signs of jowliness in his cheeks. He looks very much as I imagine the Kurds up north to look: meatier than us, rounder, and largely fairer. But he does not behave in the manner we have been told to expect from them. Mainly, he is not aggressive, and he does not seem wily or manipulative.

"So you'll work with Aanisa Samara from now on?"

"I think I'll try it out."

"Oh, I think she is trying *you* out." He laughs, and the rolling depth of it catches me in the stomach and makes me laugh, too.

"Calling her aanisa all the time, isn't that a little bit old-fashioned?"

He shrugs. "I'm a lot older than you. I'm forty-five. I could be your father."

"I don't think so," I offer. But it's true. If he'd had me at seventeen, which isn't so unheard of in the countryside, I could be his son. "How long have you worked with her?"

Rizgar shrugs. "About four weeks. Since she came to Suleimaniye, before the war. It seems longer. We don't take many days off, even Fridays."

I wonder if Rizgar is religious. Then again, it might just mean that he wants to have a day of rest.

"What was the other translator like?"

"Luqman? Oh, he was a nice young fellow, like you. I liked him very much."

"Not anymore?"

"No, no, I don't mean that." Rizgar reaches into the box next to the gearstick, a compartment that separates driver from passenger, and retrieves a pack of cigarettes. I am surprised that he is smoking an American Brand, Lucky Strike, for surely this is much more expensive than our Iraqi brands. He flips open the box and holds it out to me, but I wave my hand and say no thank you.

"Good boy." He taps the filter-end of a cigarette on the dashboard. "Your father is a doctor, so you must know better." The lighter, which I hadn't noticed him push in, pops out. He puts the cigarette in his mouth and mashes the end of it against the glowing circles, much like the target on the cigarette box.

"Luqman was a decent guy, bright. But he was not brave enough for covering war. He was always afraid we were going to get hurt, or that he would get hurt and there would be no one to take care of his family. And his Arabic wasn't very good because he was young and had only studied in Suleimaniye. You know, after '91, they stopped teaching Arabic in a lot of the schools in the north. Only Kurdish. And a little bit of English or German."

"Samara told me he had a hard time in Tikrit."

"Well, yes, they shot at him while he was getting into the car when we were trying to leave, and it scared him so much that he decided to quit the job."

"Was he hit?"

"No. But it was very close." Rizgar makes a gesture with his finger, indicating a bullet whizzing over one's head. "He was fine. He just got scared. But he was scared of other things, too."

Rizgar takes deep pulls from the cigarette. Opens the window just enough to blow the smoke out into the hot afternoon, then closes it again. He takes another drag and says in a smoke-choked voice, "He was falling for her."

"For Sam?"

"Of course. He told me he was in love with her and that he would try to make Samara his second wife, though he'd only been married for five years. Hah! The guy knew he was going to either wind up dead or with a broken heart. So he quit."

An explosion somewhere makes the car shudder. Rizgar sneers and flicks the burning end of his butt in a tumbling arc out of the window. He presses on the accelerator. "*Walla*, I was wrong. *Al-Amira* is back, much more quickly than I thought," he says. I realize that he means Sam and wonder whether he intends this as a compliment, calling her the princess, or if there is a part of him which has started to resent her.

She is still writing in her notebook as she walks over to the car. Rizgar flicks the remains of his cigarette out of the window. "You're not married, are you?"

"*Inshallah*," I reply. In my mind, I picture my father's irritated gaze.

They threw something at him, Sam had said. Not shot. *A good journalist never changes—*

She opens the door and her scent enters before she does: I think it makes her smell sweeter than she otherwise would. My mind's overactive easel paints a picture of a handsome young man. He has my eyes but a shock of wavy red hair. He's wearing an American military uniform and is sitting in a tank near the Tigris, turning people away from the bridge. That's what my son would look like if I married her. A red-haired soldier. An occupier. No, I cannot imagine ever loving Samara Katchens.

10

Loving

I FOLLOW SAM into the pool courtyard between the buildings. A cluster of foreigners turns when she strides past the white tables and one woman waves, while another man with yellowish-blond hair and no shirt calls out Sam's name. I see Joon Park is with them and I nod and smile at her but she doesn't respond – perhaps her eyesight is not very good.

"Hello," Sam chants back to them. "You guys still going to catch dinner at the Flowerland?"

"After seven," the shirtless man says. His T-shirt is tucked into his trouser pocket like a rag, "just after my Q&A." His chest is firm and muscular in a way I would expect a professional athlete's to be, and it has no hair on it. He seems half-man and half-boy.

"Well," Sam pulls the door of the first tower open again and gestures for me to walk ahead, "I may be a little late." And I think I catch a gesture, a nod in my direction. Late, because of me?

"Samara, my love, we wouldn't dream of dining without you," the blond man says sounding affectionate but artificial. "We'll wait for you."

"It'll give you time to work on that tan," she says, and lifts her sunglasses with a quick flash that borders on flirty.

She lets the door fall shut behind her and walks to the entrance on our right. We enter the hotel café, all done in orange and white, the futuristic-looking white chairs reminiscent of the 1970s. The café is empty except for three men sitting behind the counter. The oldest among them, maybe in his early fifties, rises to his feet.

"*Maftouh?*" she asks. Open?

"*Aiy, tfaddali.*" Yes, please, says the man. He points to the unoccupied tables near the window overlooking the pool, which seems surprisingly clear and blue compared to how it looked earlier.

Sam faces me. "Why don't we sit here and have a coffee before we call it a day?"

I wait for her to choose a table, and find myself relieved when she chooses the one furthest from the men behind the counter, who are looking me over with some interest.

"Two coffees," she says, holding up a V-sign with her fingers. "Do you want something to eat?"

In truth, I am getting hungry, but I just shrug as if to say anything will do, and Sam takes this for a no.

"We had a really good start today," she says. "But we also had some problems we're going to have to work on." She leans her right elbow and her hand rests for a moment in the hollows of her cheeks. "You know, sometimes I forget that the translation thing isn't always so intuitive."

I move to respond, but then stop myself.

"I mean, your English is wonderful so I assumed it wouldn't be a problem, but I don't think fluency is the issue here. You just need to learn to get into the right rhythm for, you know, for the interview process to work."

Sam flicks up her wrist and peeks at her watch with a hint of a frown. "I should call the desk. Anyway," she smiles at me with her chin slightly lifting, mouth closed. "They can wait. So, what I was saying is, I think that you just need to get into the right rhythm of translating. I ask the question, you translate it, and when the person starts talking, you stop him every two or three sentences to translate. And I mean, two sentences *max*. If he gets to three, you just gotta cut 'em off. And don't forget to use the first-person."

I can feel my palms start to grow damp, as if tiny springs in them have just now decided to release their dammed up waters, and the same sweatiness is growing between my legs. If she tells me once more to use the first-person, I just might tell her she can find herself another interpreter.

"I want to understand correctly," I begin. "Is the problem that you would prefer to have me write down whatever it is the person says and then translate it to you?"

"No," Sam says, looking perplexed. "I didn't say anything about writing."

"But you've been saying that you want me to translate, and as far as I understand the word, to translate is to work in written form. To translate is to take a written document and then to change the material into a written document in another language."

Sam's eyes grow narrow.

"If one moves from a spoken language to another spoken language, that is interpretation," I say. "The other is translation, is it not?"

"What are you—? Oh, you mean interpretation as distinct from translation?" Her eyes ride upwards, as if reviewing a registry of terms embedded in her frontal lobe. "That's probably a British thing. We don't really make that distinction in America. Or you might be spending too much time memorizing the dictionary." She laughs in a way that sounds like a sneeze that has stopped midway. "Just kidding," she says. She tilts her head to one side and smiles slightly, as if to apologize.

"Do you not distinguish between translating and interpreting, then?"

"Hmm. No, actually. I mean, I might say you were my translator or my fixer, but I wouldn't say interpreter. That sounds a little too, I don't know, formal, like one of those funny little guys sitting in a glass box at a UN meeting, you know what I mean?"

The waiter appears at the edge of our table with our coffees, and a plateful of green and black olives.

"Thanks," Sam says, without actually looking up at the waiter. She throws a bunch of her hair, which had been hanging just above the table, behind her shoulder and plucks a large black olive off the dish. She puts it in her mouth and begins to work it, and suddenly I feel aware of her tongue and her teeth, sucking salty bits of flesh from the perimeter of the pit.

"Why fixer?"

She lifts her long fingers to collect a pit, and then she puts another olive in her mouth and begins again. "You know, a person who fixes things – appointments, travel, whatever. A fixer's the guy who makes it all happen when a visiting reporter comes to town. Anyway, I'm not interested in the semantics of the whole thing," she says. She smacks her lips together, the sound of a kiss, and pushes the olives towards me. "Have some."

These olives look like they've come from a can, but I take one anyway. "That's no problem at all," I say. "In future, I will interpret it just as you require."

"You know, I don't even like the word interpret. Interpret suggests that you're going to filter what you're hearing through your own opinions, and that you might pepper in your own analysis and understanding of the situation. You know, like trying to give a forecast, like interpreting the future or something."

"Right."

"Right," she smiles quickly. "That's exactly what I don't want. I mean, I'm really curious to hear your opinions, but not in the middle of the interview. For example, telling me you're not sure whether Saddam really killed as many Shi'ites as people say he did, that's also the kind of thing that, well," she sits straighter and pats down the air with her right hand, "...better to leave that out." She picks up her coffee cup and takes a short sip. "Okay?"

"Okay. But you might want to know that, right? I mean, you would want to know if someone's lying to you, would you not?"

"Well, sure, but I don't need my fixer telling me that in the middle of an interview. I mean, you can't read someone's mind. No one can. Half the things that Hatem character said might have been lies. But what can you do? You can't run a polygraph test on him while he's speaking." She pauses. "Think of it like being a two-way radio," she says, sitting up, excited by her analogy. "You know how important a radio is in a time of war? Crucial. Just crucial. But the radio never interjects. It's the means of communication. And that's what you need to be, I mean, once the interview is underway. Sort of like a human radio."

I nod and glance quickly at my watch. It's almost seven o'clock.

Sam reaches for the satellite phone, pushes a few buttons on it, and looks surprised. "Oh, wow. My editors have been chasing me for the past hour. I really have to run upstairs and call the desk. How about you meet me up there in fifteen minutes so we can finish the conversation?"

And with that she is on her feet, telling the men at the counter to charge it all – and anything else I might order – to room 323, leaving me at the table with nothing to do but to sip lukewarm coffee and eat bitter olives and watch two foreigners diving into the pool on the other side of the glass.

Rafik is still working the front desk when I walk into building two. His face seems heavier than it did this morning, as if he'd gained a bit of weight over the course of the day. He brightens when he sees me. "Miss Samara said you can go right up," he says, gesturing to the lift. "Third floor."

I wonder if what is going through my mind is going through his. Loose woman. Prostitute. Only a prostitute would allow a strange man to come up to her hotel room. Especially in the evening. If my sister ever did a thing like that…

"You only need to press it once," Rafik says.

"Right, sorry." I stand there waiting, resisting the urge to make an excuse as to why it's okay to go up to her room. When I can't stand it anymore, and the lift still hasn't arrived, I ask if I can take the stairs instead.

"It's a free country now, my friend," Rafik answers. "You can do whatever you want."

I'm almost out of breath when I reach the third floor and wishing I got more exercise. As I walk along the corridor, I see a handsome man with Mediterranean features and hair down to his chin, pulling the door of room 323 shut. We have to turn sideways in the hallway to let each other get by, and he gives me a small "hey" as he does, not quite looking me in the eye, and I watch him disappear down the stairwell. He could almost be a European-Arab, perhaps Lebanese but certainly not Iraqi, because I don't know any Iraqis who wear their hair long like that. I notice it, in particular, because it's wet.

I stare for a moment at Sam's door. My fingers hesitate, and then knock. When there's no reply, I rap harder. The door creaks open, and when Sam sees it's me, she swings it wide and holds it open.

"Hi Nabil. Look, I want to apologize. I'm under a lot of stress. I didn't mean to give you such a hard time on your first day."

She moves a few inches back, behind the line that separates the room from the hallway, her from me. She smiles at me and says, "Well? *Ahlan w-sahlan*. Welcome to my humble abode."

Inside, to my surprise, is a small kitchen area and a modern lounge which looks very Western with two small sofas, a coffee table between them, a large cabinet with glasses, and a white formica desk with a small computer sitting on it, open. There are at least a dozen wires running around the computer and on to the floor, leading towards the sliding glass door that might lead to some kind of balcony. Whatever is out there is blocked by a line of eggshell-coloured curtains. If Sam sleeps, it is not here – or not in this room.

"You're still on board, I hope?"

"Me? Of course. You don't need to apologize."

"Good," she says, gesturing towards the sofa against the wall, and seating herself in the other one. "Because I've just realized I'm already having an astonishingly shitty day."

"Sorry?"

"No, I'm the one who should apologize for my bad manners. I know that's important around here. Can I get you a drink? Orange juice? Pepsi?" Out of the corner of my eye, I notice there's a bottle of what looks like vodka on the cabinet.

"You're quick, Nabil," she says. "But that one's not mine."

"Oh, no, I didn't mean to suggest that—" I glance at the Timex watch my parents gave me as a graduation gift. It's 7:15 p.m. "I probably should go soon anyway. My family will start to wonder…and I think there's a military curfew at eight."

"Nine," she says. "But no worries. You should get going soon."

"Was it that bad a day?"

"Oh that," she says, rising and going to the kitchen. She takes a jug of orange juice out of the fridge, pours two small glasses and then slams the refrigerator door shut. "I tend to exaggerate. But not in my copy," she says, raising a finger. "Never in print."

She brings the glasses to the coffee table and sits down. "My editor, Miles, wants me to drop everything and focus on some clean-up story."

"You mean from the oil spill? I heard on the radio this morning that someone blew up the pipeline from Kirkuk to Baghdad."

Sam shakes her head. "Not that kind of clean-up. Though that *would* be a good story. In fact, that's a story I'd be glad to do right now. What I mean is that they need to clean up the mess from another reporter, and they want *me* to do it. Can you believe that? It's practically a fact-checking job. Something you'd give an intern. I don't know what to say. It'll totally take us off news features for a while. I won't get a damn thing in the paper, all because of having to clean up after some schmuck."

Sam shakes her head in disbelief. Funny, that word. *Us.*

"The best part of it is, this morning, which was last night for him, East Coast time? Miles was using Harris Axelrod's stories as an example, suggesting that I should be trying harder to get good scoops like that. Hah! And now it turns out Harris is in hot water, and the paper is trying to decide whether to bail him out."

"A scoop, that's a good story?"

"Hell, at this point, I'd settle for a good story that isn't exactly a scoop. That's where I need your help. Anything that might give an indication as to where Saddam's weapons facilities are. Or, in fact, if there are any. Any story that gives clear evidence of life under Saddam. Witnesses to a massacre, people who say they've been tortured. We had a big story in the paper yesterday about people who had their tongues cut out for criticizing the regime. Made the front page," she says, focusing somewhere in the vicinity of my chest. "That's what my editors want. Any time you get a good story that no one else has, it's a scoop. Or an exclusive."

"Why do you call it a scoop?"

"I don't know. Maybe because it usually means we're digging up the dirt on somebody. When you dig up something," she says, her hands holding an imaginary shovel, "it's a scoop. But we don't always use the dirt when we have it. Sometimes it's more trouble than it's worth. You have to save things for a rainy day. For example, do you know why the Hunting Club isn't being looted, even though every other symbol of Saddam's regime is? Did you notice that it was hardly touched?"

I hadn't given the contrast much consideration. "Perhaps the people don't really know it's there," I say. "It's hidden away, not like the other buildings right on the main roads. Ordinary people wouldn't be aware of it."

"No, no." Sam is shaking her head. "That's not why. It's because Chalabi wanted it for a base, or at least one of his bases, and his folks went straight there with the protection of the Pentagon. Rumsfeld had a nice gaggle of Marines sent over to guard the place so the riffraff wouldn't come in and Chalabi could slide right into his new headquarters. Or at least one of them, because I've already seen another huge villa that he's taken over. How's that for planning?"

One of several phones on the desk rings. She rises, still watching me, and picks it up. "Hello?" A smile spreads across her face. "Hey, surfer boy. Did you have a nice swim?" I soon realize, during the part of the conversation that I can't hear, that this is an internal hotel telephone. "Wait for me. I'm coming down for dinner right now."

When she hangs up, she remains standing. "How about we wrap this up. I'll explain the rest of it tomorrow, okay? Come, say, 8:30?"

As I make my way out, my own head is swimming with questions, about the Marines, Chalabi, the Hunting Club…

"You be careful going home at this hour, all right?"

This "surfer boy", presumably the blond fellow I saw earlier, is he Sam's boyfriend? And what about the one I saw leaving as I arrived?

"Of course I will," I say.

"Don't get in the path of any of those looters."

"Sam, if the Marines could guard that Hunting Club for Chalabi, like you say, or any of the other buildings, why couldn't they manage to guard the other buildings from looting? The Art Museum. Or the hospitals."

Sam jiggles the doorknob for a moment, then shrugs. "No

idea. Understaffed, I guess. They're picking and choosing their battles. Just like we have to pick ours. At the moment, mine is getting you out the door so I can get a decent dinner in my stomach." She gives me a wide smile and so I smile along with her, though I'm not sure if this comment is funny or insulting. "*Bukra, Inshallah,*" she says. Tomorrow, God willing.

I suppose these are the kinds of sayings a foreigner would pick up in a few days, but still, the sound of her words in Arabic moves something in me, and I'm not sure if it's attraction or disdain. I want to compliment her on her pronunciation, but she is already releasing the door, allowing it to close behind me.

11

Allowing

I DEVOUR THE *baamya* and rice my mother has saved for me, one
of my favourites, meat with okra. But since they've already eaten,
they seat themselves around the table and use the opportunity
to pepper me with questions.

Baba: So what did you do for so many hours?

Mum: Didn't she give you a lunch break? You haven't eaten
all day!

Baba: Did you interview anyone important?

Amal: What's she like? Was she nice?

Baba: How much does the job pay?

I feign being hungrier than I am so I don't have to answer,
buying time. And when I get to the fruit for dessert, I allow my
eyes to flutter as if I'm about to fall asleep on them. *Bukra*, I
promise. Tomorrow I will tell them more. Tonight, I'm too
exhausted to speak.

But later, in my room, I'm wide awake. I want to tell
someone, anyone, everything. But there's no point – it will only
confuse them and worry them. Or maybe I want to tell Sam.
Maybe. So I take my old typewriter out of the cupboard. I've
hardly touched it in the past year, and am relieved to find that
the ribbon is still good. The surprising thing is that I don't have

an urge to write about what happened today. Instead, I feel the need to write about what happened leading up to today, about things that happened a long time ago. Things I would like to tell Sam, assuming she would want to listen.

I didn't lie to Hatem, not about myself, anyway. My mother is a Shi'ite and my father is a Sunni. When I tell people this, which isn't often, they sound surprised. But it's not so uncommon. Sam was impressed when I told her. Westerners assume that all Sunnis hate all Shi'ites and vice versa. But it doesn't work that way. It's all much more complex than that.

In our neighbourhood, there are other mixed families like us, though no one really talks about it. Still, it's considered a Sunni neighbourhood, and that meant it always felt relatively safe and calm – that is, up until now. In university, I met friends who were real Shi'ites and I came to realize that they had suffered more harassment, more late-night visits by the *mukhabarat*, than the rest of us.

My mother's family was willing to accept the marriage because she was marrying up, as they call it in the West. Although she was in university when she met my father, her parents had not had a higher education and they were, therefore, very impressed with him. His father was a doctor, and he was going to be a doctor, too. It promised moderate wealth, but also prestige and security, which were more important.

With my father's family, it was a little different. They wouldn't have been keen on their son marrying a Shi'ite girl, Grandma Zahra once told me in her later years. But there were several mitigating factors. First, my father's father, had once treated one of my mother's cousins when he was very ill. Thereafter, my mother's cousin sent presents every year at the end of Ramadan.

And so, my father's family knew that my mother came from a good family. Even if they were working class – my mother's father was a welder – they had dignity, pride, good manners. Second, they were impressed that a working-class family would send their daughter to university, and that my mother, unlike her mother, did not wear a veil, which they viewed as a sign of backwardness.

Finally, my mother was beautiful. As beautiful as any model in Paris or London, Grandma Zahra said. I knew she'd never left Iraq, and I wondered how she could know what women in Europe looked like. Later I realized it was just an expression, a way of saying that our beauty was as good as their beauty.

The typical path in our part of the world is for the woman to adopt the man's sect or religion. And so, the idea was that even though my mother was Shi'ite, by marrying my father, she would follow Sunni ways, and adopt the Sunni style of prayer.

The only problem with that was that my father was probably the last person on earth to teach a person how to pray.

When I was small, and then after we came home from England, Mum would take me to the Imam Khadum shrine on Fridays, or to a small *husseiniye*, a Shi'ite mosque, in the neighbourhood. I was fascinated with the men who knew the Koran by heart. Oh, to have the labyrinth of all those poetic words imprinted in one's mind! I didn't know what they meant, but I loved the way they sounded. I came home one afternoon declaring that I wanted to learn the Koran by heart and become a *hafiz*. Baba gave Mum a talk and said she should stop taking me to prayers so much.

We've never even had any framed calligraphy with Koranic verses on the wall, like many Iraqis do, with the exception of a small ceramic plate my mother has hanging over the kitchen sink that simply says "Allah" on it. Baba didn't like such displays of religiosity, and considered them closer to superstition than divinity. He didn't like for Mum to put up pictures of Ali, as many Shi'ites do, but I'd seen the one she kept in her handbag, and another one she kept tucked inside the Holy Koran that sits by itself in a drawer in the lounge. When I was about fourteen, I asked why some of my friends' homes had these religious items displayed and we didn't. Mum told me that I should have a sign on the inside: in my heart and in my mind.

I was in my first year of high school when the Gulf War broke out. After Saddam pulled our defeated army out of Kuwait, all of the Shi'ites in the south tried to launch a war against him. We knew it was going to fail, but somehow the people in the south didn't see that. My father said it was because America encouraged the Shi'ites to overthrow Saddam and made them think they could do it, but then did nothing to back them up when Saddam began to slaughter them.

I remember some of the boys in the school playground chanting slogans against the Shi'ites. Bassem Azabi started a chant, calling Shi'ites dirty infidels and collaborators with

Bush. I was stupid enough to challenge him, trying to get everyone on my side in the name of Muslim unity. No one bought it. After class, Bassem and two of his friends jumped on me and started laying in to me, and all the other kids gathered around us in a circle, shouting. I don't think they were for or against Saddam, because most of them didn't know anything. They were just boys excited to see a fight. The headmaster came out after a minute or two and pulled them off me. By then, I had given up trying to fight back and was curled up like a snail on the asphalt. I don't know what was more embarrassing, having the headmaster rescue me, or the fact that no one had jumped in to defend me. The friends I had were disparate parts who did not constitute a whole, and individually, they were no match for Bassem and his boys.

That evening, at home, my father saw my puffy left eye and my red face, patches of it swollen like I had been stung by a bee. I would have preferred that to having my father know I got beaten up at school.

"But you haven't been in a fight since you were ten years old." My father looked at me like he was looking at somebody else's child, as if he preferred to trade me for the real son I must have been switched with at the hospital, the son who had his strength, his bulky arms instead of my skinny ones. The son who would be a doctor by the time he was twenty-five, just like my brother; the son who was popular in school. The son who never got pushed around.

I told my father what they had been saying in the school playground that day about the Shi'ites. He sat down on the edge of my bed and ran his fingers over the black stubble emerging from the pores of his chin. He sucked at something in his teeth.

"Did you tell them that your mother is a Shi'ite?" I was sitting at my desk and just wanted to go back to my books, where everything was resolved in the end, where my father and Bassem's boys would never find me. I thought for a minute about running away, tracking down my mother's simple relatives in Al-Kut and spending the rest of my life with them.

"No, I didn't tell them, that wasn't the point. I just didn't think it was right."

"Of course it's not right," he said. "But you don't need trouble at school. You don't need to talk about your family with boys like that. No one needs to know your business. You just do your work. Don't get mixed up in politics. You'll be sorry you did."

"I am *not* mixed up in politics." As usual, my father failed to understand what I was saying, to even try to understand. It was amazing that he could care so much and listen so little.

"Tell your mother you got hit in the face with a ball," he said, beginning to stand up.

"She already knows," I said, turning away from him and back to my book. He stood where he was and when I looked up at him, he was studying me. Behind the pity, behind the disappointment, was something that told me I had failed an even bigger test. What was it? Failing to protect the women from everything that went wrong? Refusing to reassure my parents that there were no complications to being half-Sunni, half-Shi'ite?

And after all, few people really see me as half-anything. You always take the religion of your father. My mother had to know that when she married my father, Grandma Zahra reminded me.

But my mother was the only one in the house who ever mentioned God, the only one who seemed to turn to something greater when she was upset, and the only one who had any interest in taking me to the mosque on the occasional Friday.

My father never went because he saw religious people as a bit common and naive, and the mosque as an intellectual backwater. He could appreciate the culture, the architecture, the liturgy, the literature, the history, but never the belief that required submission of thought. He didn't like the idea of there being one truth, he said, when I asked him to explain it further. My father wore his Sunni identity like a pedigree that signalled grooming, a tick-box in his profile that gave him privilege. It had little or nothing to do with religion, except that he was proud that Sunnis don't beat their own backs the way Shi'ites do on Ashura, to commemorate the martyrdom of Hussein, the Prophet Mohammed's grandson.

It was my mother who sometimes got me dressed on a Friday and announced that we were going to the mosque, usually the Imam Ali Shrine in Khadamiyah. My father would smile, his lips closed and faintly callous, and say *zein*. Good. Very nice. Good, fine, repeatedly, like he was trying to convince himself. *Zein, zein.* Please enjoy yourselves and put in a nice word for me.

When my father wasn't around, my mother seemed

freer. Freer with her piousness, freer with her lips. She used them to place kisses on everything she saw: on the shrine's weathered doors, on the larger-than-life pictures of Imam Ali, on the tombs of the great departed martyrs, on the laminated picture she carried of the faceless twelfth Imam. Even on the prayer *turba* she brought with her, that little square of pottery, so that when she put her head to the ground she would be in touch with God's own earth.

In summertime, everything grew so hot I was afraid she would burn her lips kissing the walls as they baked in the sun's open kiln. I've heard it can happen. But I came to the conclusion that my mother's lips must have had a holy salve of protection over them, a special lip balm from God. Before letting me head off to the men's side, she kissed my forehead, wishing me Allah's *baraka*, His blessing. *Allah ma'ak. Allah bi-kheir.* God be with you. God has good plans in mind for you. After, she met me in the courtyard with her palms radiating bright orange from henna, as if God had placed a portion of his best light right in her hands.

12

Radiating

WHEN I STEP up to the desk in the morning, Rafik hardly bothers to mumble *sabah en-noor* after I say *sabah el-khair*. He presses the numbers for Sam's room and hands me the house phone. His mouth is pulled down at the corners, almost into a frown.

"Hello?" Sam told me 8:30, but her voice sounds groggy, as if she has just woken up.

"Good morning," I say. "Shall I wait for you here in the lobby?"

"No, why don't you come upstairs? I really need you to help me plan out what we're going to do next. I don't want to do it in the car."

I hang up the phone and notice Rafik watching me. I wonder if he understands a lot of English or only a little. "She says to meet her upstairs," I say, as if he is some male relative in charge of her safety, and I must ask permission. I still feel as if Rafik is keeping an eye on me on Sam's behalf, whether she realizes it or not.

The stairs seem less onerous now that I know my way. I stare for a moment at her door. There's a new sign on it. *For main Tribune office, go to the first tower, Room 520.* Perhaps she hopes this will deter people from bothering her. I press hard on the buzzer until my fingernail goes white. Sam's voice skips towards the door. "Come in! Door's open."

She is in the kitchenette, lighting the stove. She sets the kettle over the flames and turns around. Her hair is wet, and damp indentations around her shoulders make the straps of her bra more visible.

I keep my gaze on the stove, away from her body, trying not to stare. Sam crosses her arms and looks at me. "I know Iraqis start early, so that's why I said 8:30, but this isn't my best hour of the day. I hope you don't mind talking to me before my mind's fully functional. And I need some coffee first. You?"

"Me?"

"Do you drink coffee?"

The kettle moans softy, growing gradually more audible, like the morning *muezzin*.

"Real coffee or Nescafé?"

"Nescafé." She opens the cabinet and pulls down the jar, adorned by a picture of an attractive, European-looking man with his nose happily close to his cup. "That's all we've got. If you want that rocket fuel you guys drink, just order it from downstairs."

"I'm fine. I already drank some this morning." It isn't true, I had tea. But I will not drink her artificial coffee after she has put down our own.

Sam sits and blows across the surface of the milky-brown liquid. As she puts the mug on the coffee table a spill runs over the rim of her cup. "Uch, klutz!" She picks a few tissues out of the box on her desk to her left, pink then yellow then blue, dabs them over the spill and then pushes the soggy, coloured pile away from her.

"All right." She takes a big breath and then exhales with a flourish, almost as if, had she puckered her lips properly, she might whistle. "So here's the deal. A few days ago, the paper ran a story by a stringer named Harris Axelrod, and now—"

"The stringer is the writer?"

"Yeah. It's a freelancer who gets paid by the piece. Anyhow, Harris is a very high-profile freelancer because he also writes for all of these vanity magazines, uh, how I can explain that? They're very glossy magazines that cost a lot and pay a lot, and if you write political stories in them, you get a lot of attention. This guy is really a known name in journalism, even if most people out in the field have been saying for a few years that he's bad news. Sketchy. There aren't so many rules in journalism, but there are a few, and he doesn't play by any of them. Okay? So this guy, Harris, files a story saying that a very controversial black politician in America named Billy Jackson took millions of dollars from Saddam to oppose the war, to oppose the sanctions, everything. And in fact, this politician – he's a congressman from New Jersey – he's been one of the lone, national voices against the invasion of Iraq. He was totally critical of Bush's policy on Iraq from start to finish. I mean, this guy was one of only a handful of congressmen to oppose the use of force. So news that he was on the take from Saddam Hussein, and we know that Saddam was probably paying lots of his buddies in various countries, hey, that's a pretty sexy story. You with me?" She lifts her coffee. "You sure you don't want a cup?"

"No. Yes. I'm following. Thank you."

"So you do want instant?"

"No. By thank you I meant, no, thank you," I say, watching her take a few gulps of hers.

Her eyebrows dip. "So, why don't you just say that?" She exhales. "Where was I? Look, a very sexy story…*if* it's true. Harris said the whole thing was solid, and my editors believed him. Two days after Baghdad falls and he has this story, based on documents he says were found in one of the vacated government buildings, and then provided to him by a reliable source. You know, this Harris always has some big scoop that no one else has, and you'd have to wonder why that is. But you know how editors can be. They just assume some people are 'charmed,'" she says, wiggling her fingers at the last word. "And if we don't run with it quick, maybe someone else will get wind of it and beat us to it. And Harris convinces them, like he does every time, that it's all air-tight. Stop me if I'm going too fast."

"Not at all. I understand," I lie. I wish I could take notes. My fingers are getting itchy to do so, virtually air-typing against my will.

"Okay, so he calls the desk, says he has documents to back it up. He photographs and e-mails a copy of the documents to the editors, and the paper goes and runs it. And that's it. Presto, scandal of the century. Or the month, anyway. The paper gets to break the story and no one else has it, and everyone on the foreign desk feels very good about themselves."

"If you break the story, it's good, right?"

"Yeah, that's the point. When someone breaks a story, it means they were the first ones to report it. If you have it and no one else does, you're golden."

For years we've had newspapers like *Babil* and *Al-Zawra* and *Jumhuriyye,* and also magazines like *Al-Musawwar Al-Arabi* and *Alef Bah.* Baba dutifully picked them up and left them near his reading chair. But they always had the same stupid stories flattering Saddam, often with almost-identical wording and photographs, and they never seemed to be worth reading. It now occurs to me that in Western countries, newspapers compete to get stories that other newspapers don't have. Here, an editor who did such a thing would probably be sent to jail.

"Nabil, you with me?"

"I don't think we break stories here."

"Not yet. Listen, so my editors run this story, thanks to Harris, and it made a big splash. Actually, more like an earthquake. We're talking about a liberal, African-American congressman who some people think has a very bright future. And now his whole career is in question. But here's where it gets even better. As of last night, it turns out, we're getting sued. And for quite a lot, I might add. This congressman, he said from the start that the story was patently false and that he'd clear his name. Well, turns out his lawyers think he has a strong case and they filed a huge libel suit against the newspaper yesterday." She stops and smacks her lips, and leans forwards to take the coffee again. "You know what a libel suit is, right?"

"Sure," I say. In truth, what I know is the definitions of the words "libel" and "suit", but I don't actually know what happens when they combine, though I can guess.

"In America, for someone whose livelihood depends on his reputation, if he can prove he was defamed, he could be awarded millions of dollars in damages. And, Jeez, I don't have to tell you this, but my editors are *flipping* out. Not only that, but given that this congressman is black, it makes the whole thing even more explosive. People in his camp are making charges of racism."

I don't want Sam to feel I don't understand things first time round, so I nod occasionally, and try to look alert.

"I mean, no paper in America wants to have the African-American community looking at them like they went and smeared one of their most esteemed, promising politicians, and in some ways, an important one, even if he's really not someone with a hell of a lot of power in Washington."

"But…I'm not sure I understand. Is he important or not?"

"Well, he's important to his constituents in New Jersey. He's important to a lot of people in the black community, and he's often the first one to make noise when there's a whiff of racism, even when there isn't. He knows how to make news. Actually, I think he genuinely tries to represent his voters' needs in Congress. But look, he's a Democrat who opposed the war, which means he's out of fashion on two fronts. He was one of very few people in Congress who voted against the use of force in Iraq. What does that tell you? He's obviously persona non grata with most of the establishment in Washington." Sam searches my face. "Didn't the papers here cover his visits? I think he came to Baghdad twice, maybe three times in the past year or so."

"Perhaps." I consider trying to hide the truth from Sam, and then realize there's no point. She'll probably wring it out of me eventually, and I'll be ashamed for having tried to pretend. "I don't really know because I didn't read the papers very much in the last few years," I admit. "I read them when I was in high school and university, but the quality of the writing was so poor that I thought it was actually very bad for me."

Sam looks amused. "*Bad* for you? What, like drugs? Like drinking too much coffee and not getting enough sleep?"

"Are you asking about my health or yours?"

She laughs into her cup and sips her coffee. "This could be huge," she finally says. "Or, it could be a total wild goose chase."

"I don't," I start again. "I don't think I understand what you're supposed to do. What's your assignment?"

"Miles, my editor? He wants me to track down the person who gave Harris the documents. And meanwhile, this reporter, Harris? He wants to do it himself."

"So why doesn't he?"

"Well, that's exactly what I said. Apparently he's down in Basra on an assignment for some magazine. He wants to come back to Baghdad to clear this up, but the paper wants him off the story at this point, and won't let him come anywhere near it. They're pulling him off the story, which is like getting dumped in public. Miles says they're not sure they trust the guy at this point."

I feather my fingers through my hair, wondering how anyone in journalism trusts anyone. Why do Sam's editors trust her? Should I? The access to my scalp seems much more immediate than it did a few months ago, with loose, baby-hair tufts that seem to float rather than stay combed in place.

Sam is now seated in front of her computer and is tapping on the long space bar. "Let me look at my notes from last night."

She types in a word. "All right, here it is." She reads through the page quickly, mumbling a litany of words that I cannot distinguish, like the murmurings of men at prayer.

"All right. Our story said Billy Jackson took at least $25 million dollars since the Gulf War. The story ran on April 10th. Harris said he got the documents from a former Iraqi general. Akram. That's his name. Miles says, 'We also want to know if Harris paid for the documents. We asked him flat-out and he says that he didn't, but we're starting to wonder,'" Sam says. "Hah! *Starting* to."

Sam mumbles again, reading but not really pronouncing her words, which I guess is her way of skim-reading out loud.

"So," she looks at me. "That's the crazy part of it. They want me to track down the source of these documents that implicate Jackson, and they want to know if Harris paid for them. Essentially, they're asking me to play policeman on Harris. It's just a little – *ick*. Not very collegial," she says with a grimace that drains some of the prettiness from her face.

She gets up, strides into the kitchen, opens the refrigerator door, and shuts it. On a wooden rack above the stove, next to salt and pepper cruets and a box of matches, is a packet of cigarettes – a brand I haven't seen before – with a blue emblem on it. Sam picks it up and shakes it, stares at it a second longer, and puts it back in its place. "That's just what I need now, Carlos, for you to leave your cigarettes around."

"Who's Carlos?"

"Oh, he's my roommate. Sort of. The suites here have two bedrooms. So this guy who's a photographer for the *Tribune*, I'm sharing with him."

"A bloke with rather long hair?"

"Yeah. Why, do you know him?"

"I think I saw him leaving here yesterday."

"Probably. But he's not around much, so as a roommate he'll do."

She returns to the screen and reads, "'Harris is not being so co-operative, but he did give the name of one fixer he worked with on the story. Subhi el-Jasra, a student at Mustansiriyah University.' That's it. Can you believe it? A story like that, and all Harris is giving up is the friggin' fixer's name?" I stand behind her. She is still scrolling down to the bottom of the document file, and on her screen, I can see she is on page three.

"You wrote all of that, just from having a phone call with your editor?"

She shrugs. "It's just I think better when I'm moving my fingers."

Me too. So why did I stop writing?

"And it helps to keep a record of things. As a journalist you need to back things up. If you don't, you wind up like Harris Axelrod, who after an illustrious career, finally appears to be up Shit's Creek." She glances at me with the eyes of an apologetic child. "I'm sorry. I'm not always this crude."

"You don't have to—"

"You know, part of me is pissed off because I'm also under the gun. I'm being taken off news, and therefore off the front page, and all anyone in Washington will notice, if anything, is that my byline has disappeared. It doesn't look good for me. If this produces a great story and we get to hitch a ride on it, great. But if not, it'll be for nothing and my byline count will suffer." She stares at me. "You probably have no idea what I'm talking about."

I open my mouth, but she continues before I can answer.

"They count up our bylines at the end of the year to judge our performance. The number of articles we write. If I end up spending weeks on this, I'm not going to be doing other stories, and I'll have fewer bylines at the end of the year. That's going to kill me in my year-end review."

She snaps her laptop shut hard, almost as if, were it a door, she'd be a hair shy of slamming it. Noor's face flashes in my mind. *That's going to kill me.* How Americans exaggerate.

"Maybe it's a test," she says, packing up her bag. "Or they

dumped it on me because I'm the youngest *Tribune* reporter here."

It's as good a moment as any to ask. "How old are you, if I can—"

"Thirty-three." There's nothing between us but an imperceptible sprinkle of dust in the air. I thought she looked thirty at most, except when she looks either annoyed or happy, and then the lines she's growing around her eyes and mouth become visible. Five years between us.

She sets her bag diagonally, across her chest, the strap drawing a division between her breasts. "So Mustansiriyah, and then Abu Ghraib."

"Abu Ghraib? The prison?"

"Well, that was my plan for the day, and I'd like to stick with it. Perhaps we can have our cake and eat it too. On the way there, we'll go and see if we can find this fixer Harris worked with."

She gestures for me to head for the door, and she follows after me. I have to grip the knob two or three times before I manage to turn it. To my surprise, my hands are soaking wet with sweat.

13

Soaking

In the car downstairs I explain things to Rizgar as briefly as possible. We are going to Abu Ghraib, the prison whose name Baghdadis usually say in a fearful whisper. But first we'll head for Mustansiriyah University to find a young man named Subhi.

Rizgar frowns at me. "But all the universities are closed," he says in his funny-accented Arabic. His meaty hands grip the wheel to pull out of the Hamra Hotel parking lot.

"Oh, right…the universities are closed," Sam says, turning to me. "Why didn't you say so?" I wonder how she gets this when she doesn't, apparently, speak Arabic. "Well, whatever. Rizgar, we go anyway. There'll be someone around."

During the drive, I ask Sam more questions, but she only gives me vague three-word answers: "I don't know." "We'll find out." "Not sure yet."

And so I stop asking.

The campus is a collection of angular, plain buildings, lacking the distinguishing features of the University of Baghdad. Most of the windows are broken, and the glass on the ground sparkles in the sun. Sam stays in the car with Rizgar and I walk up towards the main entrance alone. Drawing closer, I see that the painting of Saddam's face on the wide pathway has been vandalized. Someone, perhaps a group of students, must have dipped their feet in red paint and then danced on his face. His eyes have been blacked out, making him look as evil as I have ever seen him.

A bearded guard with a Kalashnikov slung over his right shoulder moves the weapon in front of him as I approach. I hold up my hands and tell him I'm just hoping to see one of their students. He says there is no one here, the students aren't around. But I plead with him, explain that I'm trying to find someone very important. When he asks who, I blank for a minute and then say Subhi, Subhi el-Jasra. He asks, Subhi el-Jasra, is he a friend of mine? And in that split second I can only think to pretend, and I say yes, Subhi is my friend. The guard tells me that he doesn't know him personally, but indicates that Subhi is one of the five young men in charge of the Hawza Committee. And I say, yes, my friend is on the Hawza Committee. He then announces that they are working on the security arrangements to open up the university again in a week, and I say of course, I know that, and he asks whether I want to see the head of the Hawza Committee so he can put me in touch with Subhi, and I say it would be very helpful. He makes tiny circles with his finger to ask if I have a pen, and I give him the one in my pocket and my notepad, and he writes: Mahmoud al-Tarabi, near the Showja Market. And then he says that Mahmoud's father, Iyad al-Tarabi, is the head of security for the market there. And I say thank you, he has been such a help to me, and he says I am welcome, and I look him in the eye and then down at his right hand, to see if it is discreetly held out, motioning to receive something from me. But his hand is only holding the pen and depressing the plunger in it a few times, and he nods towards it to indicate it's a nice one. I ask him if he could use it and he nods that he can, and I tell him to keep it, I've got another one in the car, which isn't true. His beard is a young beard, full and yet not fully grown, and there is something about its unkempt edges that tells me that he is a religious man, and that he would not appreciate being offered money in this particular circumstance. But a nice pen is a tiny gift, not a bribe. And so I thank him again and he says God be with you, and I say, And with you, and I am back in the car so quickly I almost feel as if I have flown.

"We're in luck," I tell Sam. "Apparently he's a well-known student here, or maybe more than that. The guard knew him."

Sam looks up from the magazine she was skimming. "What do you mean, more than a student?"

"Well, he says Subhi is on some security committee. Hawza security, he said."

"House security?"

"No, HAW-za," I say, pronouncing it so she can hear the word clearly. "Hawza is the religious establishment in Najaf. I mean, not the establishment, but where the establishment get their—" I search for a word, but have a hard time finding the right one. "Their intellectual ideas."

Sam's eyebrows form a sceptical arch. "Intellectual ideas? Really? I thought the purpose of being a fundamentalist was to shun all things intellectual. It's all about the man upstairs, right?" She points her finger upwards. "Nothing too complicated about that."

Sam must notice something in my face that betrays my discomfort with her generalization. It occurs to me that she and my father would get on well. Her eyes narrow. "I'm being facetious, Nabil."

"Well, there is some truth in what you say. But maybe not the full truth. But the men in the Hawza study holy Islamic books all the time, and they try to come up with decisions on all of the social questions of the day."

"Like issuing fatwas?"

"Yes, like *fatawa*," I say. "This is the plural of fatwa." I can't help but feel that it sounds strange when English speakers take an Arabic noun and simply add an "s" to it. In fact, this is one of my translation peeves.

Sam takes a black clip and snaps most of her hair into it. It's so thick that it doesn't all fit. "Do you take those seriously?"

"What? The *fatawa*? It depends." It's beginning to irritate me, the way Sam uses words like facetious. And all sorts of slang. What if I were just a regular Iraqi with decent English? Most people wouldn't know words like that.

She turns in her seat, with the bottom of one foot, free of a sandal, against the inside of her thigh. "Whadd'he say?"

"He said we could go to see this man in Aadhamiye who's the head of the Hawza's security committee, and that maybe he would tell us how we can find Subhi."

"Cool. Shall we go now?"

I look towards Rizgar, hoping he will chime in with some advice about driving to Aadhamiye. But he says nothing, flicking his cigarette into the hot wind through a crack in his window. I keep expecting direction from him, as if simply by virtue of being older and wiser, he must have a better idea of what to do. And then I remember that he only knows about twenty-five words of English, and so he often isn't listening. I'm the Baghdadi, not him.

But that does not mean he isn't thinking.

It didn't take long to track down Mahmoud al-Tarabi. I went to the Showja Market and said I was looking for Iyad al-Tarabi. The smell of the spice-stalls there infused me with energy, and I asked a few merchants and one thing led to another and I was pointed towards a line of homes facing the market, ones that didn't look run down compared to others nearby. Mahmoud came to the door right away, a young man with a light-brown beard that was destined to become bigger and eyes that made me suspect that I had woken him from a nap. When I said I was looking for Subhi, he asked who I was. Right there I decided that Sam's story was too long and complicated and so I told him I was from the University of Baghdad and we wanted to talk to Subhi to co-ordinate setting up a similar student-run security committee there. He nodded and said he'd have helped me but he was busy now although if he could help some other time he would. But he gave me the address I was after. As I walked back to the car I bought some fresh cardamom, always my favourite spice because it gives coffee – real coffee – just the right flavour, and I wondered if this was Saddam's legacy to us: the sense that if you just co-operate a little and tell people what they want to hear, you make your life easier.

We stand in Subhi el-Jasra's doorway. He doesn't look happy that his friend Mahmoud was so co-operative. He smiles only the most feeble of smiles, as if a ventriloquist from above has yanked the corners of his mouth into the most perfunctory crescent a mouth can make. And then his smile collapses, but he turns away from me so fast I hardly see it.

It could be the heat. Today feels less like late spring and more like midsummer, when no one goes out in the middle of the day if they can avoid it.

"Do you want to sit?" He points to a shabby blue sofa. A film of cigarette ash covers its fabric like a grey, carcinogenic dew. As we move into the room, I notice another young man, about the same age, engrossed in a newspaper. He looks up to acknowledge us, but doesn't say hello.

We sit but Subhi remains standing, clearing newspapers off the other sofa. With better light here than we had in the doorway, I can see that he has traces of a black eye, a dark arc that throws his face off balance. Perhaps I didn't introduce ourselves properly, because Subhi doesn't seem impressed.

"So, I am Nabil and I'm finishing my doctorate at Baghdad University, and this is Samara Katchens, from the *Tribune* newspaper." I clear my throat, waiting for the "Ah, yes." It does not come. It is true, I have been saying for several years that I'm going to do my doctorate, though I've done nothing to forward this goal, save some graduate courses.

Subhi sniffs at the air as if trying to sniff us out. Or maybe all the smoke hanging around him has clogged his sinuses.

"So what do you want from me? I mean, what kind of information are you after?"

His manners are not usual for our part of the world. He has not said "welcome" yet and he has not offered us anything to drink, and I'm wondering whether I was wrong to accept his offer to sit.

"I want to find the general you introduced to a colleague of this fine lady-journalist here from America. This general, or maybe he was a former general, gave some documents to another reporter, Harris Axelrod."

"Harrees?" Subhi turns to his friend, who has his head buried in a newspaper in the corner. "Do you remember a Harrees?"

"Harris," I repeat. "Harris Axelrod." *Aks-el-rad,* I pronounce it, as this is the closest pronunciation when you put it into Arabic. "He says you were the one who led him to General Akram," I offer. "He said you were a part-time translator for him."

"Oh, him. The big American guy, yes? Green eyes, very tall. Yes, I remember. I wasn't a translator for him. I worked for him maybe three days. I'm still a student at the university."

There are papers all over the floor and we could be in the sort of flat a young bachelor would keep. But I don't know many students who live on their own. In Iraq, a decent son lives with his family until he gets married, which is why I am still living at home.

Unless, that is, the young man is estranged from his family, or makes an awful lot of money.

"I'm just trying to understand how you got some of the documents Harris had. We need to find the general who gave him these documents."

Subhi turns to his friend. "Munir," he calls, "do you remember anything about this Harris having some help from a general?"

Remember. As if I were asking about an event that happened years ago. Munir gives an indifferent blink. "Can't say I do."

"Me neither," Subhi says, eyeing Sam out of the corner of his eye. "Like I said, I didn't work with him for long. But you should go find Adeeb. He was the one Harris worked with most of the time."

"Adeeb? And where would I find him?"

"Adeeb. Adeeb Maher. Or Malaki. He has a pharmacy in Mustansiriyah. You can look for him there."

"Can I tell him you suggested I find him?"

Subhi watches me with a distrust crouching in the hollows of his cheeks. He is about twenty-one and in his presence, sluggish as I am and with a bit of a paunch, I feel much more than seven years older than him. He takes a pen out of his breast pocket. "I have to leave to meet someone, but I'll try to explain how to get there."

We stand and he shows us to his front door. He raises his chin, and now the fading purple bruise seems more prominent, like a border indicating where the cheekbone ends and the eye socket begins. "Do you have some paper in that notebook?"

I had forgotten the small pad tucked into my breast pocket and tear off a blank page. Subhi takes it and scribbles in an almost-legible script: Adeeb Maher/Maliki – Mustansiriyah Pharmacy. "There you go. So you won't forget. He's about five streets away from the university." I hold out my hand and he compresses it slightly in his, and then nods at Sam without offering his hand. "Good luck," he says in English.

We head down the exposed stairs. From the car I see Subhi still standing there in his doorway, watching us, lifting a hand to his sandpaper beard and stroking the hairs in the wrong direction.

14

Stroking

IT TURNS OUT that the cells of Abu Ghraib are empty. Just before Saddam disappeared last week, he set the remaining prisoners free. Some former prisoners are going there now to tell their stories to foreign reporters, and ordinary people are arriving to listen, to look, to check if there's anything left to loot.

That's how we find people to interview. Somehow I thought that this work of being a real journalist would have more logic to it, but what I'm discovering is that most of it is random and unplanned. The business of "reporting" resembles hungry shoppers scooping up bargains in the last hours of a flea market more than it does a method of research.

Anyone who feels bad about his life should spend an hour interviewing someone who's been held in Abu Ghraib. Some were tortured for actually being opponents of Saddam, and some simply for being suspected as such. Some for being overheard saying the wrong thing, and others for getting on the wrong side of someone. Sometimes, there was no reason. Some of the stories are so horrific – one actually involved a meat grinder – that I find myself ashamed to relay the details to Sam. But whenever I leave something out, she notices and insists that I translate everything. A few times I notice her wince at the thought of what I have told her. But she asks more questions. It's as if her protection from being truly disturbed by such gruesome details is to ask for more. And to take down every detail. "How long did they beat you that day? With what? How did you feel? And then?"

I don't know how she can tell when I leave something out. She listens even when she doesn't understand. More than once, I've found myself entertaining suspicions of her being an American spy who actually speaks fluent Arabic, and who is gathering information to be used against us. When she works the two of us into a rhythmic dance of conversation with the person she's interviewing, she's just like a musician playing a piece of music. That makes me the instrument, and if I miss a note, she notices. She just senses things.

Our Abu Ghraib visit leads us to the home of the Sarraf family in Khadamiyeh to interview one of their sons, who was held over the last two years. Mohammed Sarraf was active in a religious Shi'ite group with support from Iran, he readily admits, and that's why Saddam had him thrown into prison and tortured. Sam steps into her usual interview mode, and makes pained faces when Mohammed Sarraf describes his torture or shows the marks on his back. I even start wondering if perhaps this is exactly the kind of "story" the American government wants the rest of the world to hear. The more their reporters describe the bad things that happened under Saddam, the more they're able to justify taking over our country.

I try to push these thoughts out of my head. But the work of interpretation is becoming more natural, almost automatic: I am becoming the two-way radio Sam wanted me to be. But that leaves the creative corner of my mind yearning to keep itself occupied while the translation part of my brain does its job of moving sentences. They flow in through my ears, pass back and forth between the Arabic-English membrane in my mind, and exit my mouth.

As we wind down the interview, a woman of about twenty-five comes into the room with her gaze towards the floor. She asks if she can tell her story, too. This is Mohammed's younger sister, he explains, Malika. Mohammed and his father – a sunken-faced man who has been sitting in the corner saying absolutely nothing for the past hour – look at each other and agree.

Malika has moist, dark eyes that seem girlishly large, and she is carrying a baby boy in her arms. She sits with him and begins to tell the story of her husband, who was arrested in the middle of the night about a year ago. She has gone to Abu Ghraib, she tells us, and all the other prisons, searching for him in vain. Her family, she says, has reached the conclusion that he must have been killed, and has even brought her some report that her husband was probably buried, along with many other young men he was arrested with last year, in a mass grave near Baqubah. Malika doesn't want to believe it.

"My husband must come home," she announces slowly, in English. "He has never seen his son!" And then she is in tears, which are quickly turning to sobs. "What America will do for me now?" Malika demands of Sam, pleading with her a bit louder and rocking the child, who has also begun to cry. "America will bring back my husband? America will pay support for my son with no father? Every child must have father!" The words come tumbling out of her mouth, and she looks at me, and then back at Sam, as if expecting one of us to say something.

Malika wails louder. Her father whispers her name and clicks his tongue to hush her, but it seems her family's sympathy is spent, spread in too many places over too many days. Mohammed stares at the blank television set, studying his exhausted reflection in the curved glass. He picks up the remote control and presses it, shrugs, and tells me that even in Abu Ghraib they had electricity.

Sam keeps writing. When Malika calms down a little, Sam begins to ask more questions, and we get some answers. What his name is. What he believed in. Finally, Sam sighs. Asks me to tell them she's sorry for their troubles and that she hopes things get better. She rises from the chair.

"Can I take a picture of Malika holding a photograph of her husband?"

Mohammed shakes his head. "It isn't nice for Iraqi women to be photographed for Western men to see."

Sam appears to understand the "no" without any translation from me, says she is very sorry again, and closes her bag.

Outside, the hot afternoon haze hovers over us, prickling my skin. We walk towards Rizgar's idling car, and the most appealing thought is the air conditioning inside. Sam tugs at the handle several times. Rizgar has locked the door and is dozing, open-mouthed, against his headrest. Sam bangs on the window and Rizgar sits up, momentarily confused, and then clicks the lock open. She tucks herself into the front seat and I climb in the back, as I've become accustomed to doing.

"Where go, Miss Samara?"

She rests her head against the window, then pulls it back, bringing her hand to the bridge of her nose and holding it there.

"Where do you want to go now?" I ask.

"Give me a minute," she says, turning to look out of the window. I can see her back rise, almost as if she were about to retch. When the rise subsides, there's a tear clearing a path down her cheek.

"Are you all right?" But Sam is my boss now. Is it even appropriate to ask the boss if she's all right? I never imagined a boss being a she.

She uses the edge of her hand to wipe her face. "I'm fine."

Is Sam really crying for this woman? It must be about something else. Although it *is* an awful story.

"You wanted to go and meet another guy who was tortured in Abu Ghraib, right?" I take the paper out of my breast pocket, the one on which I've written the names of four other men who have terrible stories to tell.

"Fine. Let's do that." But her fingers are still holding the upper part of her nose. She moves her hand up, taps on the space between her eyebrows. "You know what? I've had enough for today. I've got what I need here. Let's head back."

No one says anything all the way home. The unreal blur of Baghdad passes us in silence. The river, the buildings, the trees, the bridges, the mosques, all of these are the same, except for the damage to the bigger buildings. And yet, nothing looks like it once did, because now you can really see that the American military is everywhere, and that the Iraqi government is nowhere. Unlike last week, there are no people out stealing and looting in the street. The summer heat is crashing in, luring us inside, slowing us down. We have conceded.

As I walk Sam to the reception desk in the second tower, she thanks me and says I'm doing well. Doing a much better job, she says. Really excellent, in fact.

She stands with her back to the stairs as if I shouldn't pass, as if she wants to say goodbye to me right here. But then she says, "Why don't you come up for a moment?"

I follow her, watching the sway of her body as she takes the steps, one and then two, one and then two. Outside her room she exhales heavily and pushes the key into the door. When it swings open, a man sitting at the desk looks up, one elbow leaning over the back of the chair. It's the same man with the Mediterranean features and the long hair, now pulled back into a ponytail.

"Carlos!" Sam looks surprised.

Carlos is wearing a tight-fitting, sleeveless undershirt, showing off arms with tightly braided muscles. He looks like one of those young Lebanese heart-throbs my sister tapes up on her wall.

"Hey, Sam," he smiles somewhat guiltily, as if he might have done something wrong, but he's not yet sure. He grins at me and then looks back at Sam. "Hope you don't mind. Just using your computer to file some pictures to Washington. My sat phone's busted."

"No worries," Sam says. "Oh, Carlos, this is my new translator, Nabil." She gestures between us, and I hold out my hand. He rises lazily so he can extend one of his athletic arms to meet mine.

"Carlos is a star photographer with the paper," she says. She smiles at him in a way that suggests she's holding back a joke I wouldn't understand. "One of the best up-and-coming shooters around."

"Nabil, was it?" Carlos looks me over and puts those arms, which look pumped for a fight, on his hips. "Do you know you're working with one of the hottest young talents in journalism?"

"Oh, right." Sam rolls her eyes and gives him a playful push in the arm. "Actually, Nabil and I have some things to talk about for tomorrow, so I was just dropping this off," she says, dumping her bag onto one of the sofas. "Be back soon."

She walks to the door and holds it for me with a flash of petulance in her eyes. "Come up to the roof," she says. "There's a good view of the whole neighbourhood up there."

We walk across the roof's funny white surface, which is almost as I'd imagine the moon to be – bumpy, crusty, pocked. There is a sprinkling of small satellite dishes. Some of them look like inverted mushrooms, and others, like solar panels.

Sam's right. From here, the pool looks quite beautiful, and already surprisingly clear compared to its green-and-brown appearance of a few days ago. I wonder what kind of chemicals they put in it to make all the dark, corroded stuff go away.

She puts her back to the rail and leans her elbow over it, sending a wave of worry through my bones. What if a gust of wind were to push her off? What if there was another stray bullet?

"You're sure it's safe by the edge?"

"Why?" She shrugs. "I don't see any soldiers around here that anyone's trying to hit."

From below, there's a commotion of splashing, and then laughing. Sam watches the swimmers. "I guess the pool is open for the season," she says. "Looks pretty nice, actually." She faces me again and crosses her arms. "I can't believe I got upset today. It's not like me to get all teary like that in the middle of work. I mean, I'm not a big crier."

"That's okay," I offer. "We were already in the car."

"It's just that, I don't know…that one really hit me somehow."

"The men being tortured, you mean?"

Sam sinks towards the floor, and I join her, sitting at a respectable distance.

"Well, hmm. Where to start? When I was twenty, I lost someone very close to me," she says. She drags a finger across the roof's pasty white surface, and then rubs it against her thumb to make the fine powder disappear. "We were together throughout school. I thought I was going to marry him."

"Your boyfriend," I finally force out the word. A relationship forbidden in our culture, but normal, I know, in hers.

"Yeah, Jack. Jacob Sorenson," she says, closing her eyes. "We always thought we would get married."

I try to imagine it, and find it easy. He's blond, handsome, wealthy. Together, they raise happy white children with cheeks that glow like summer tomatoes. They live in a big American house where there's no danger and nothing ever goes wrong. Samara Sorenson. It even sounds better.

"He died in a car accident, just after sophomore year. He got caught in a rainstorm on a very slippery road."

Better than what?

Her face tightens. I hear her swallow old tears.

"He was really my best friend," she says. "We had the same kind of…background." She runs her fingers into the mess of locks near her forehead and pulls some of them into a bunch. She ties this section above her head into a twisted knot, which splays itself up against the white wall behind her like a spill of orange juice. Like this, she looks more girl and less woman. "I guess that story, Malika losing her husband, reminded me of Jack. It's still hard sometimes." She shakes her head. "I'll never find anyone like him."

Sam appears to be watching a replay of some other moment in time. I wonder if Noor dying is anything like that. Can you grieve for someone you didn't actually love?

"You can understand, yeah?" She searches my eyes, her own seem out of focus. I consider telling her about Noor, but decide against it.

"And with Jonah going missing, that gave me a big scare. But he's fine. I was running nightmare scenarios in my head."

"Jonah is your boyfriend?"

"Sort of." She picks at a white bubble on the roof's surface, and I keep it in mind to warn her to wash her hands afterwards, that we might be sitting on a blanket of asbestos. "He was, for a while. It's probably coming to an end. He's a little ticked off with me."

She tilts her wristwatch into the weakening light. "Ooh, is that the time? I really have to get writing," she says. She moves to get up and I do, too, but then she is back down again, as if something heavy is pulling her back towards the lunar surface of the roof. She's laughing at herself, and as I'm already up, she holds out her hand for me to help her.

15

Laughing

I, TOO, HAD wanted to be a writer. Not a journalist, though. The journalists told everything from Saddam's point of view. They pretended to ask questions, but only the questions they were allowed to ask. If you were smart enough, I thought, you should be a real writer, which meant being able to criticize the regime in a way that was so obscure, so intricate in design that no one in government would realize it. I wanted to write the *Animal Farm* of Iraq. No one who mattered would be clever enough to know you were taking the piss out of them.

Yes, some Iraqis read books.

I should cut back on the British slang. I learned most of my colloquial English when I was in year six. All the kids made fun of my accent, and I hated them for it. For a while, I even hated my parents for bringing us to Birmingham, which was so lacking in local pride that people didn't seem to have the energy to pronounce the city's name, so they called it "Brum." No one does that to Baghdad, abbreviate it like that. I think making a nickname out of your hometown shows a lack of respect.

But there were other things about the English that I

loved. One of them was all the funny nicknames they made up for things, and the way people would say, *'ello, love*, which reminded us of the way Baba would call Mum *hayati*. My life. It was then that we stopped calling my mother Mama and began calling her Mum. Ziad liked it and began using it mostly because it made us laugh, saying it just like the English school kids when they whined for their mothers to buy them something in the shops. When we returned to Iraq, we kept on calling her Mum because we thought it made us sound posh.

I learned more English in that year and-a-half, I expect, than at any point in my life. My brain was like a dry sponge, soaking up the new words and then dribbling them out in some inappropriate place. I still worry about saying the wrong thing.

For a so-called immigrant – they didn't know from where so sometimes they just called us Pakis – I got excellent marks in English Lit. I read anything ten times if I had to, looked up all the words I didn't know. Just as I had begun to master the language, my parents announced that it was time to go back to Baghdad. I didn't want to go.

In fact, I wanted to stay in England. And then, angry at my parents for making us leave, I felt the urge to write. By the time I was fourteen, my fingers were constantly twitching and typing out sentences in the air as I walked around. It drove my father crazy. I told him that I had learned to type in school and that I wanted my own typewriter. He said typing was for girls who wanted to grow up to be secretaries, not for boys who would grow up to be doctors.

When I was sixteen and nearly failing biology, my father finally bought me a typewriter. By then, I'd got used to Iraq again. I started forgetting some things about how Birmingham looked. I had high marks in Arabic literature, English and history. My teachers once nominated my essay on the greatness of "Our Beloved Leader, Saddam" for student essay of the year, and it came first. At the awards ceremony, the headmaster led the kids in the audience in singing odes to Saddam, written by Daoud al-Qaysi and other famous Iraqi singers whose songs we had to memorize. One song compared Saddam to the sun and the moon. What a bloody joke. I wonder if, at the time, I believed any of it. I only remember that I liked it when the teacher said I excelled at writing.

Unlike Ziad, I would not follow in Baba's footsteps. When I was fourteen, in fact, the doctors diagnosed with me vasovagal syncope, which is a medical term for an extraordinary tendency to pass out. They said it was not a disease so much as a syndrome, and that a fainting episode or "attack" might be triggered by situations of extreme stress or dehydration, or something as simple as a blood test. It might go away as I matured, they said. I was happy to be excused from having to dissect any more animals.

My head was wired for words. I typed out poems in the air when I was walking around during the day, and tried to get them down on paper at night. They never came out as well as the air-typed ones.

"Ah, the poet is home," my father would say when I was still in middle school. "Recite a poem for us." The more he asked me to read something I had written, embarrassing me in front of relatives when they were over for a meal, the less I wanted to write anything at all.

I decided it made more sense to study other people's writing, and to become an expert in English. My twitchy fingers got me as far as the English department at Baghdad University, where I did my Bachelor's degree before finding a teaching position. It's only now, years later, that I'm trying to write again. Sam would surely laugh if she saw my typewriter, a pale-blue, manual machine by Remington that comes in its own portable case. It is probably thirty-five years old, but it still works well, except for the "o" key bending in towards the "p." Sam and the other journalists all have small, thin computers that they carry around with them everywhere, as though it were as natural as carrying your wallet or your spectacles. Before the war, I had never ever seen a laptop, though we'd heard about them. The only computer I've used, the one at the university, is the size of a small refrigerator.

As much as I envy them, Sam's friends and their laptops, I like this old typewriter. I love the clack of keys against paper, the feeling of my fingers rising and falling with deliberate force, the inability to erase things so easily and make them prettier, without any trace of what went before.

That's what the Americans seem to expect of us. We are a country of typewriters that will always leave the mark of corrections – a line through the words, a bumpy streak of liquid white paint over the mistakes. The Americans want us to be computers. With computers, it's very easy to delete a few lines you don't like. But this, I believe, has spoiled the

147

Americans' expectations, because this isn't the way human beings work. The Americans believe they can erase our corrupted files and make everything right with the world in just one click.

By the sound of her knuckles, I know it's Amal at the door.

I rip the paper out of the typewriter. "Just a minute."

The door creaks open, she peeks in with one eye, and then walks in anyway. I turn the pages upside down on my desk.

"What are you working on?"

"Nothing much."

"Come on, you've been banging away at that thing for an hour." She crosses her arms. "Last night you did the same. I thought you were going to tell me about what you're working on every day. That was the agreement."

"What agreement?" I stand and cross my arms back at her. "Amal, I'm just messing around, writing myself some notes. I'm too tired for this."

"But you're always tired," she whines. "It's not fair. I was the one who encouraged you to take the job and you're not telling me a thing!" Her face morphs into a look of happy intrigue. "Are you writing reports for her?"

"Not even close. Isn't it your bedtime?"

"Mum," she calls as she leaves my room. "Nabil's writing secret reports for the Americans!" She looks back at me from the hallway with a giggling smile, but I don't smile back. "Oh, Nabil. Stop worrying. They never take me seriously."

16

Worrying

WE ASKED AROUND for long enough and people told us to try this small commercial street between Aadhamiye and Maghreb, and sure enough, we found Adeeb's barber's shop. It looks like it ought to be closed because the blinds are pulled tight and there doesn't appear to be anyone inside. But I knock a few times and then I see two of the dusty white slats part, slowly, like an eye opening after a deep sleep.

He yells at the locked glass door. "What do you want? Who are you looking for?"

Sam shrugs, indicating that she hasn't thought up a back-up story for us to use to work our way inside. And after all, what could we possibly say? That I'm an Iraqi man who happens to be going to get a haircut with his foreign girlfriend?

"We're looking for a Mr Adeeb? Subhi sent us. Subhi el-Jasra. He said you might be able to help us." I try to appear as innocent as possible. But, judging from my reflection in the glass, I mostly look sweaty and nervous.

The man, a rather short and wan-looking fellow with a wispy moustache and a high forehead, stares into my eyes for a moment, as if waiting for me to flinch or reach for a weapon, and then he shifts his gaze back and forth between Sam and me.

He pulls away from the window and I hear the sound of the lock turning, and thank God he's going to let us in after all.

"*Ahlan w-sahlan*," he says. He has sharp, narrow scissors in his hand, and strands of hair on his hands and tee-shirt, which covers a roundness in his belly that seems almost maternal. "Subhi sent you?"

"*Ahlan fi-kum*. Yes. He said that you would be able to help us. I am sorry if we are disturbing you at work."

"No, no. It is I who must apologize for my behaviour. I would have let you in sooner, but you must understand, there have been several attacks on barber shops recently. I don't know – they think we have money or something. Do you think a barber makes so much money? I only make enough to feed my children."

"What's he say?" Sam demands, pushing for a translation.

"He apologizes for not letting us in straight away, but he says a lot of barber shops like his have been attacked in days past."

"Really? You know, I heard that there have been a few attacks on beauty parlours because fundamentalists don't want women getting all dolled up anymore."

"Dolled up?"

"I mean, made up. You know, with a lot of makeup," she says. "Great story."

I ask Adeeb if this is the case, and he says yes, he knows of several beauty parlours that have been robbed and even had their clients kidnapped in the past two weeks. He says it's not a religious thing, but rather, people know that the lady clients usually come from families with money. "Even though we don't do women's hair, we are worried that they will *think* we do and so they will target us, too."

The heavy-set middle-aged man sitting in the barber's chair turns his head slowly over his shoulder, like a person who has been in an accident, and frowns at Adeeb. His hair is greying but thick and wavy, and I imagine it would be interesting to cut. Adeeb notices his disapproving gaze.

"Would you be so kind as to sit and wait for me for a few minutes while I finish with this good man, one of my most esteemed customers?" The man smiles with a parting of his heavy lips, and I point Sam towards the bench at the back of the room.

An adolescent boy, probably Adeeb's assistant or apprentice, watches us carefully, his eyes almost locked on Sam. Adeeb resumes trimming, eliciting a strangely comforting noise, like the chirp of early birds before dawn. The big customer sighs and leans back a little deeper into his chair, and these soothing sounds, along with an old-time Ustaz al-Gubbenchi ballad wafting from a staticky radio perched above the basin, is almost enough to put me to sleep. *Hubb o-hikam*...love and wisdom.

But Sam is wired, and though others probably wouldn't see it, I notice it in the way she is bobbing her head to the beat, a little out-of-time with the music, trying to appear entertained in the vacancy of time when there is nothing to do but sit and wait.

"Is it real?"

The boy, having swept up as much hair as he could until the burly customer is done, has his skinny legs crossed and his head turned to me.

"Is it real?" He asks again, lifting his chin, in a failed attempt to seem discreet, towards Sam. "The hair colour. And all the curls. Does she put something on it to make it look like that?"

"He wants to know if your hair is real or not."

Sam glances at me and then at him, and then sniggers. The young man laughs back. Adeeb glances at us as though he's unsure whether he likes the idea of having us joke around while there are important customers in his shop.

"Tell him you can buy it at Wal-Mart."

"What?"

Sam smiles widely. "I'm just kidding. Sure it's real."

"I wasn't asking it, he was."

"I know, Nabil. Just being silly." Adeeb glares at us.

"So what is Wal-Mart?"

Sam lets out a sigh, the sound of a flat musical note. "Just a store."

The fat man propels himself out of the swivel chair, leaning back first and then using the momentum to hurl himself forwards, leaving the chair in a spin behind him.

"Only 7,000 dinars today," Adeeb says. "Special post-war price." The man plucks a wad out of his wallet, hands Adeeb what looks like twice that amount, and when he whispers a thank-you in Adeeb's direction I realize it is because he is out of breath from getting himself upright.

He nods at all of us, and walks out slowly with the side-to-side gait of overweight people. When he is gone, Adeeb's expression changes to one of happiness that we have come. I look at Sam, who seems to be trying hard not to interfere with the pace of my introductions. She is studying the pictures on the wall, mostly photographs of Iraqi actors and singers, with great interest.

"Subhi said you could help us," I say. "We wanted to talk to you about a reporter named Harris Axelrod."

He smiles and my eyes follow his to the floor, where greying hair lies scattered around the chair vacated by the fat man. I have a fleeting thought of how Sam's red curls would look if they mingled among the snippings. Like sparks of fire amid the ashes. Adeeb signals to the boy to come and sweep.

"Harris," I repeat. "Harris like Fares."

"Yes, yes, Harris," he says. "I am surprised that Subhi would send you to me if you are looking for information about Harris."

"Really, why is that?"

"Well you know…Hakim!" he calls out. "Would you please sweep up here so I can give you your million dinars and we can all go home?" Until now, the young teenager had been sitting behind the last basin, watching Sam and emitting an occasional plume of smoke from his cigarette. He swaggers out with his broom, smirking, and begins to push it brusquely across the floor.

"Beautiful, thank you!" Adeeb says. We watch in silence as Hakim finishes his sweeping.

Adeeb takes out his salary, and out of the corner of my eyes I can see him count out 30,000 dinars, or about $10, which is too much for someone doing Hakim's job, at his age.

Hakim thanks Adeeb, bids me goodbye, and stretches his neck to try to bid farewell to Sam, too, but having lost interest in the photographs, she appears to be unaware of him as she studies the combs and scissors in the blue fluid, and occasionally, herself in the mirrors.

Hakim slams shut the door and it rattles the whole barber shop. Adeeb shudders as the swaying blinds come to rest.

"You see, you can't talk anywhere here. You couldn't talk in public with Saddam, and even now you can't talk because you have to worry about other people! Do you know him?"

I turn to the door, as if the boy still stands among us. "This Hakim, your helper?"

"No! The big guy. He was an operator in the Ba'ath party. We had to pay him to stay out of trouble. I give him cheap haircuts because I'm still afraid of what he could do." He wrinkles his nose as if he smells something bad. "But I think they will get him soon enough."

"Who will?"

"I don't know," he shrugs. "Either the Americans, or the revenge mob. In fact it isn't entirely a mob. They have a hit list with all the people on it they plan to get, and one by one," he says, methodically picking stray hairs off his shirt, "they will get them." He smiles at me. "Or so they say."

A sprinkling of sweat has sprouted on Adeeb's forehead, as if he were the one who'd swept the floor.

"Which people are you worried about?" I ask.

"If you say you don't know, maybe you're one of them!" He laughs with his mouth wide open and almost nothing but a wheeze coming out, but he so appears to be enjoying himself that it makes me laugh with him.

Sam gets out of the barber's chair in which she had been swivelling. "Hey," she says, stopping herself with her toe. "Did you tell him what we're looking for?"

"I think he knows."

"I know many thing."

"Oh, you speak English?" she asks.

He squeezes a thumb and forefinger together to suggest only a little.

"But your English is very good," Sam says excitedly.

"I prefer...no." He struggles for a word, behaving as if he is very close to finding it, like a person riffling for a lost file. He turns back to me and continues in Arabic. "It's better if you come to my house and I will explain. Come to us tonight after dinner, about 8 o'clock. My wife will be thrilled to serve the foreign lady tea and practise her English." He takes out a pen and scribbles his address across the back of a receipt pad. It's in Shamasiya, not far from here. Adeeb whispers to me, as if Sam could understand were he not speaking in undertones, that it would be good if she could come in a long dress with her hair covered, so the neighbours wouldn't easily notice a foreign woman coming to visit.

I coax Sam out of the door and indicate that we'll see Adeeb later, and she seems content with this and thanks him.

"Ah, and also," he says, "I almost forgot. If you see Subhi again, tell him when you came by the shop was closed, okay?"

I agree, wondering why I'd have any reason to see Subhi again anyway. Sam says *shukran*, stretching the vowel out as so many foreigners do until it sounds like *shuuukran*. He repeats his quasi-English niceties, mechanical as the talking doll Amal had when she was small. "You are most welcome. Please. Hallo. You are most welcome," he says, his hand waving like a child's.

17

Waving

"This car's an oven." Sam turns to Rizgar. "No air condition?"

Rizgar turns it up higher so she'll feel it.

"Let's go to Fallujah," she says.

"Fallujah? Why? You know it's far," I say. "And maybe not so safe."

"I spoke to a colleague last night who says he knows a sheikh there who might be able to tell us more about General Akram." She shrugs. "It's worth a try."

"Who? What sheikh?"

She glances in her notebook. "Uh, Duleimy. *Yalla*, let's go".

Rizgar seems concerned. "Tell her she should go in the back seat and you should be in the front." He looks at me in his rearview mirror. "We don't want to announce that we are driving a foreign woman around when we're near Fallujah."

"Rizgar suggests that you sit in the back seat whilst we drive into Fallujah and that I take the front. For your safety."

Sam smiles at Rizgar with a half-open mouth. "Really? Is that what he said?"

Rizgar nods with his eyes cast downwards and laughs a little. He turns to her and smiles gently. "For you safe," he says.

"Well, then, no problem," she says, and hops out. She climbs into the back seat and I take her front seat, which is warm and a bit sunken in where she sat. A flash of a thought: how warm her body must be to heat the seat like this.

We head south until we get to the Qadisiya Expressway. Sam yawns and lays across the back seat. "I didn't realize how nice it was back here," she says, putting her hands behind her head. "I think I'm going to close my eyes for just a few minutes. I was up too late last night. But wake me if anything good happens."

Rizgar asks if he could put in a tape of his music, and Sam and I readily agree. I immediately regret it: he has put in Zakaria, a Kurdish singer from the north who is liked even by many Arabs here in Baghdad. But I have also heard he is a separatist and very nationalistic, and that makes me wonder about Rizgar. Mostly, I don't much care for Zakaria because his music is mournful and even if I can't understand the words, there is something about the longing in his voice that I don't really want to hear just now.

At the entrance to Fallujah, there are several American tanks in the centre of the line that divides traffic going in and out of town. On the right, the police station appears to have been looted and vandalized, and then taken over by American soldiers. Next to that, a building carries a banner with a handmade sign in Arabic and poorly written English: Democritic Fallujah Counsell. Otherwise, most of the buildings are intact.

"Just keep going straight," Sam says, "and then when you get to the large mosque with the nice blue tiles on it, you go left."

She directs us to the northern edge of town, where the houses become larger and are spaced further and further apart. Suddenly we are no longer in the city, but in a semi-rural area with farmland; Sam points the way to a marshy terrain and then up to a long white house so large, it looks more like an institution or a *madrase*, an Islamic school.

A man in a *thob* opens the door, and we ask when Sheikh Duleimy is expected.

"Soon, *Inshallah*. Soon time," the aide answers in English. "But you can please to wait for him, he says, and leads us into one of the most beautiful sitting rooms I have seen in Iraq, with brocaded fabric, opulent floor to ceiling curtains, and two sparkling chandeliers that scream wealth. The aide indicates a choice between Western and Eastern sitting areas, and Sam immediately opts for the floor cushions. "We can wait," she says.

In minutes, I'm bored with waiting.

"Sam, what was it like growing up in America? Where did you grow up?"

She seems pleasantly surprised, and a little embarrassed. "Good ole Phoenixville, Pennsylvania."

"Is that a small city?"

"No," she laughs. "Actually it was more like a village! But, not like here. In America, village doesn't necessarily imply rural. Phoenixville probably has 20,000 residents. It's about an hour from Philadelphia, which is a big city."

"I know about Philadelphia. It is supposed to be the city of freedom and I know much of American history begins there. But in terms of history," – a fly is now circling over Sam's cup, and she flaps her wrist to chase it away, paying more attention to it than to me – "in terms of history, the original Philadelphia is actually here."

"What do you mean, here?"

"I mean, not here exactly, but in the Middle East. Amman

was once called Philadelphia, and so was a city in Turkey. Americans didn't invent brothery love."

Sam pouts her lips in that shape that tells me she isn't sure she believes what she's heard. "Really? Didn't know that."

"So what's it like in Phoenixville? Is it beautiful?"

"No! It's ugly as sin. Well, that's not totally fair. It has its charms. These cool old colonial houses with big porches. Ours was kind of nice. But essentially, the place was a steel town, so it's pretty much dead. It's falling apart at the seams. Or it was when I was growing up there."

I try to picture a dead town, but I imagine Halapca, in northern Iraq. There are rumours that Saddam killed the entire village. But things like that don't happen in America.

Sam's eyes run back and forth across the blank wall across from us, like she's viewing an old film that only she can see.

"Why do you say that the village is dead?"

Sam holds up a finger. "A borough! We were actually a borough. Whatever that means. The borough of Phoenixville. Like the mythical Phoenix? And ville, like a little city. P-h-o-e-n-i-x-v-i-l-l-e."

I don't mind her spelling it out. Otherwise, the names are hard to grasp. I might have spelled it fee-necks-fill.

"Do you think it is anything like Birmingham, England?"

"Never been there. But I doubt it. That part of Pennsylvania, it has its own feel to it. It's basically, well, in a way I guess it's very American. It grew up around the whole Industrial Revolution." Sam draws her index finger down through the air, meandering this way and that. "There's a river that runs through that area and basically, industry sprung up around that, so they used hydropower for the steel mill. For years it was a sort of boomtown for immigrants from poor countries in Europe. Almost no one lived in Phoenixville without being connected to the steel industry in some way. My father grew up in Philadelphia but he moved to Phoenixville after he finished school to be an electrical engineer at the Steel Works."

I had never given much thought to what Sam's father might be, but I assumed him to be better educated than mine. More privileged, and more successful.

"He worked there for over twenty-five years and then one day in 1985, they closed the plant. Just like that," she snaps her fingers. "It simply devastated him and he hasn't worked since. If it weren't for my mother's work, I don't know how they would even survive."

"What does she do?"

"Teaches piano. Nearly every kid in Chester County – which goes far beyond Phoenixville – who knows how to play learned from her." Sam nods several times. "She was considered really talented when she was younger. She studied music at the University of the Arts, which was regarded as very prestigious." There is something in her face that looks wistful on her mother's behalf.

"Do you play as well, then?"

"Of course!" She wiggles her fingers with a dexterity that suddenly makes it very easy to imagine her at the keyboard. "How do you think I learned to type so fast?" She moves them more quickly now, as if she has a more upbeat tune to play. I can picture her fingers moving effortlessly from black to white.

I'd imagined every American's life to be perfect. Perfect houses, roads, cars. Perfect skin and perfect teeth. Nothing ever rotting, nothing corrupt, nothing, anyway, that one can see.

Certainly Sam – with her beautiful face and her important job, everything about her seeming smart – could not have had anything but a perfect existence until she arrived in Baghdad.

A tall man towers over us, and his size startles me. I stand, and Sam, taking my cue, follows suit. He smiles widely and says, "How do you do," in perfect English. He holds out his hand. "Sheikh Faddel el-Duleimy."

"Oh, hello. I'm Samara Katchens from the *Tribune*, and this is Nabil al-Amari, who works with me." I notice that this is the phrase she often uses when she introduces me. Not translator or interpreter. A verb but not a noun. Nabil, who works with me. *Works*, do they wonder, doing what?

He holds out his hand to suggest we sit back down. "Please, please, make yourselves most comfortable."

"You speak English so beautifully," Sam says, with a look that mixes curiosity with flirtation. "Better than most Americans I know."

He laughs. "Even in Iraq we have many well-educated people," he says. "I wonder if most Americans realize that."

It is hard to place his age, due to the fact that he has a lean, handsome face, and a physique that seems equally young and trim. Only the wisps of grey near his temples make him seem any older than forty.

"I studied for several years at a boarding school in Switzerland. We had all our classes in English," he says.

"Oh," Sam replies, "did you enjoy it there?"

He pulls his arms in on each other and shudders. "I suffered from the cold. It was a good place to learn, but not to live," he says. He calls out to the coffee boy in the adjacent room. "Will you have a coffee? Tea?"

Sam's eyes brighten. "Yes, coffee please." He looks to me, and I nod that I will have the same.

He sits and spreads the extra material of his *bisht,* a black robe with fine gold embroidery at the edges, over the cushions.

"What can I help you with today?"

"Well, my friend, Jonah Bonn sent me. He spoke very highly of you and said it would be helpful to get your opinion of the current situation in Iraq."

Funny, I thought we were here for information on General Akram.

"What would you like to speak about?" he asks.

"Well, I've heard that several sheikhs are working out a co-operation deal with the Americans so that there won't be any resistance to them in this area."

He smiles and closes his eyes a moment. "Do you think that will work? They can sign, but it's only the beginning of what is going to be a very brutal fight."

"Really?" Sam sounds amused but interested. "I keep hearing that these are just little pockets of resistance, of Saddam loyalists and hangers-on that the Americans just have to shake out, and then it's done." Sam looks at me and then back at him, waiting for one of us to offer some agreement. "To be honest, I don't think there's much they can do at this point to put even a dent in the American military."

"I think you might be wrong there," Sheikh Faddel says. "I think maybe you are being influenced by the hopeful propaganda of your own government."

Sam opens her notebook to a new page. "Do you mind if I take notes?"

"That's fine," he says. "Look, the Americans are doing everything wrong."

"Such as?"

"Not getting a grip on the lawlessness. Everyone here is starting to think the Americans want this lawlessness. And then it will be an excuse for them to stay here longer, and longer, and they will say it is never the right time to leave. And by that time, they will have full control over all our oil resources."

"Not if these stupid saboteurs keep bursting pipelines all over the place."

"Yes, that's true."

"Kind of self-injury, isn't it?"

"Excuse me?"

"I mean, you're only hurting yourselves by attacking your pipelines. They're *your* natural resources."

"It nice to hear an American say so." He reaches for the small coffee that has been left in front of him. I was so mesmerized by his odd charm that I had not even noticed that it had arrived.

Sam smiles and takes hers, too. She holds it up to her curled lips and blows.

"I am just joking with you, Miss, please tell me your name again?"

"Samara Katchens. People call me Sam."

"Is that not a name for a man?"

"Sometimes."

"Interesting for a very beautiful woman to have a man's name."

Sam grimaces slightly and looks at her notebook.

"I'm sorry," he says. "I hope I haven't embarrassed you."

She gives him what I know is an artificial smile. "Not at all."

"We're not used to seeing foreign women like you in our country. It's a surreal situation, is it not, Nabil?"

I open my mouth to respond, but nod instead.

"Let me tell you why the Americans are failing here. From the very first day that Saddam disappeared and no one knew where he was, the Americans should have taken control of the city and made sure that it was secure. But instead, they let everything collapse into chaos and turned a blind eye while the criminals started looting all of the offices and villas and museums. And the banks. How are you going to stabilize a country if you can't get its financial resources under control? That was their first mistake."

When he stops to take a breath he notices that Sam, who has been taking notes at a quick clip, has stopped doing so. He says, "Please, write this down. The second mistake is you let this chaos continue for a long time, despite the fact that you are the most powerful country in the world and you have the best army. You just proved it. We are the most dangerous country in the Middle East and now you have conquered us. And it only took a matter of weeks! So what does that make the Iraqi people think? It makes us think that maybe the Americans do not want what's best for us. Maybe you want us to suffer, to make us appear backwards and in need of a foreign occupier to take charge of us, because we are so out of control.

"In the meantime, you give us no indication of turning over any control of the country to a new Iraqi leader – even a temporary one! You say it's too early. And then, in the meantime, your most senior official comes here and says that he is dissolving the entire army. No more Iraqi army. Bye-bye," he says, kissing his hand and then sending it away.

"And then," he continues, "all the Iraqi people should have to give up their weapons. We should have no defence at all. I wonder, can I ask you, what would happen if we tried to do that in your country? What would happen if a foreign army came to America and tried to take everyone's gun away?" He lowers his face to try to get her to focus on his. "Well?"

Sam stops writing and looks up. "It wouldn't go over well."

"No. No, it wouldn't. The problem, unfortunately for the Americans, is that they can't win."

Sam is trying to maintain a neutral stare, the one she gives people when she wants to refrain from reacting. "What can't they win?" she asks. "I mean, they have won, right? President Bush said yesterday that major combat operations are over."

Sheikh Faddel watches her for a moment. "It is very easy for them to win the war against a country like us. We are no match for American firepower. But they will never win the peace. Because the problem we have in Iraq is that we have never really been at peace unless one very strong party is in power and is, what do you call it, is dictating to the others what to do. The British realized that when they drew up the map of Iraq, and they knew we were the best candidates for being the bully, so they put us in charge."

He laughs and shakes his head, goading me to laugh with him. "Ah, Nabil? Am I right? Look, this is only the beginning. Sunnis from other Arab countries will come and fight alongside us and say it's a war to defend Islam. Shi'ites will come and say this is a chance to spread the revolution, to finish what began in Iran in 1979. Soon we'll be fighting each other as much as the Americans. I'm not talking about me," he says, patting his right hand hard on his chest. "I'm only trying to tell you how our people think. How do most people in the world behave when they stand to lose power?"

Sam isn't writing anymore, just blinking, listening, twirling the pen in her hand.

"But I'm sure you have some other questions for me."

"Well, this is all fascinating," she perks up, "but yes I do. Do you know a man named General Akram?"

"Akram, of course. He was one of Saddam's top military advisors, but he turned on the president after the Gulf War. Became convinced he could overthrow Saddam under the auspices of the Americans who ultimately did absolutely nothing to ensure the rebels' success. That was in the early 1990s."

"And today?" she asks.

"He was in jail for a long time, but then I heard he was released a while back. Not sure why Saddam didn't kill him; that's what usually happened to rebels. Whatever he's up to, he's got to be dancing a *dabka* now."

I hesitate to interject, but then I do. "A *dabka* is a dance, Sam."

"Smart man," says Sheikh Faddel. "But then again, not so smart that he knew how not to get caught."

The aide from earlier appears followed by three older *shiyukh* in black robes. He approaches Sheikh Faddel and then stops half-way across the room to kindly suggest that he should prepare to leave with the others. All of the *shiyukh* will be meeting a very important American military official at another house.

"May I take a few minutes to finish my discussion with the American lady?"

"As you wish. But we have been warned that the Americans like to start on time."

I whisper this translation to Sam as they're having the

conversation. She seems very excited, but is trying to remain calm so that the others won't notice.

"That's pretty interesting," she comments. "What...who? Can we come?"

"I don't think so," I say quietly, clearing my throat as I do. "They are not suggesting that."

"Yeah, I know. But suggest it to them. Tell them we'd like to come."

"But I don't think—"

"Nabil, just *ask*." And I can see Sam trying to catch their eyes right now and smiling, as if to warm them to the idea even before they hear it.

One of them suggests that the Americans may not allow it. Another says he's not sure if a woman will be welcome because the Americans are meeting a group of tribal elders.

I translate these points for Sam who stares back at me bug-eyed, indicating that she is both challenged and entertained.

"Well, it's the American way for reporters to have access to government meetings. That's what happens in a democracy. And I'm sure the Americans will have women with them, too." She smiles at them widely now, and then back at me. "If it's a problem, of course, I'll leave."

"No, no," says one of the wrinkled men, who has the most exquisite tribal robe, the gold trimming along the black fabric as intricate as a fine necklace. "No problem. Welcome. Welcome."

We file out briskly and pile back into Rizgar's car and tell him to follow the other vehicles. I watch Sheikh Faddel's convoy as they lead us past well-kept compounds divided by large patches of grassland and crops. In a few minutes, we're on a narrow road that's walled on both sides and suddenly Rizgar twists his head, quick and twitchy, and hisses, "What's this? Where are they taking us?"

Rizgar's instincts are surely what's got Sam through Iraq safely, perhaps with the help of God, but if Rizgar is worried then I am, too. Can Sheikh Faddel be trusted? But then we crest over a slight incline and I see there are many other cars, including some rather fancy ones, and a lot of men in the same long black cloaks, and suddenly it seems perfectly clear that we've come upon a tribal meeting, and I can see the light fill Sam's face like a child outside a sweet shop.

"*Whoa!*" she whispers. "Our boys are definitely up to something here." Rizgar continues to follow the convoy towards the clearing, next to the long white building where dozens of cars are already parked. "Maybe they're trying to do a buy-out of some of the Sunni tribesmen, to stop their resistance," says Sam. "I heard they were doing that a lot around here."

Sheikh Faddel signals to us and we follow him. He is in the midst of a cluster of other *shiyukh* just up ahead, walking into a hall with wooden double doors large enough to be the entrance to a moderate palace. He turns back and gives us another sign, with a crick of his neck, to follow him. We mill closer. And then I'm suddenly aware that there is an unusually tall and broad-shouldered man standing in our way.

"Uh, sorry, ma'am?" He is wearing crisp, tan trousers and a light blue shirt. "You from the press?"

"Yeah. Hi." Sam holds out her hand. "Sam Katchens from the *Tribune.*"

He holds his hand out in return but doesn't seem to shake it the way I've seen other Americans do, and doesn't smile. "Look, sorry, but you'll need to leave now," he says, glancing at her and then scanning the horizon beyond us. I notice he has a translucent piece of plastic hanging over the rim of his ear and curling into the middle of the ear itself.

"Me?" Sam points to herself like she's not sure the man is talking to her. To me, it's clear he is. "Well, who gets to decide whether it's open to the press?"

"I do. And it's closed. I suggest you leave now."

"I'm sorry, but we've been invited by these people here to attend the meeting, and it's *their* country." Sam looks at his waistline. Is she searching for a gun? "Who are you, exactly?"

"It's not important. We're in charge of this area and I suggest you go right now."

"Is this some kind of a, uh, *agency* event or something?"

He leans in a little closer to her and speaks close to her face. "Ma'am, please take your little crew, get in your car and save yourself some trouble. If you want to be covering these areas, you gotta get yourself embedded with the military."

Sam gives him a hard stare, her lips slightly parted, her eyes darting back and forth across his face. Then she smiles. "Wow. You guys really are charming. No wonder you're off to such a good start here."

He stands staring back at her, his nose widening. I can feel a rattling in Sam's breathing.

"In fact," Sam continues, "I'm really proud of the example you just set for all these Iraqis of what American democracy is all about. Threatening a journalist and barring her from attending a big public meeting. Now *that's* not the kind of thing that happened under Saddam, is it?"

The bulk in his upper arms tenses and he places his hands on his hips. Only then do I notice it, the pistol at his left side, the furthest from me, sitting in a holster connected to his belt.

"Ma'am, I did not threaten you."

"Oh?" There is a shaking in Sam's voice, but she keeps turning it into something that sounds more aggressive than scared. "Then perhaps I'll just stay."

"Look, all I'm saying is that if I were you, I'd want to move on. You can't stay here, that's all. There's no authorization for press to be at this meeting."

"That's funny, because every Iraqi I talk to says there's no authority anywhere, which is why the whole place is pretty much falling apart." She stands straight, pulling her shoulders higher and wider, and he says nothing, his chest heaving up and down, a sign that he is growing angrier by the moment. "Good luck with your meeting," she says.

Sam walks unhurriedly back to Rizgar's car and I follow her. She ignores our agreement that she sit in the back, hops in the front and slams the door hard.

"The fucking nerve! Can you believe it, talking to us like that?"

Actually, he spoke only to Sam, and completely ignored me, but this is probably not a point worth making just now.

"These guys come in here and act like they own the place. Probably got here yesterday and already, he's the man."

We start driving west, towards Baghdad. It's quiet in the car. Sam puts her feet up on the dashboard. Anyone who sees would know in a second that she is not an Iraqi woman, and might find this behaviour insulting. I wait for Rizgar to say something, or to tell her to move into the back seat, but he's silent, which I take to be a sign that he doesn't push Sam when she's angry.

A few minutes later, to my relief, she takes her feet down.

"That was stupid," she says.

"What?"

"My reacting like that. I shouldn't have let that schmuck get me upset. Just a stupid spook."

"A spook is a spy, right?"

"Yeah, basically. I mean, not much of a spy, really. He wasn't exactly undercover. But he had to be CIA. He could have asked me to just keep it all off the record." She tsks, shakes her head. "I lost my cool. I'm not used to having some American official trying to stop me from doing a story in a place like this. Usually it's a local person, and then I can sweet talk my way through." She turns around and smiles with a closed, mischievous mouth. "Usually I find a way to get people to let me in on anything."

We are passing a column of tanks, which puts a chill in my neck.

"How do you convince them?"

Sam shrugs. "I try to play according to their rules," she says. "Guilt's always helpful," she says matter-of-factly. "You appeal to their sense of duty or national pride. You give them the sense that it would look bad if they didn't talk to you."

"Look bad for them?"

"Not necessarily them. The family, the company, the country. It doesn't really matter. At heart, people generally want to please. In this part of the world, especially, it seems that people want to please foreigners. They want to seem hospitable at all costs."

I think of the time when, as a kid, my parents found out that Ziad had stolen another boy's bicycle. *Aib*, was all my father had to say. *Aib alek*. Shame on you. My brother returned the bike immediately.

"Is a schmuck also a spy?"

Sam is on the verge of a laugh, and she looks away. "Sometimes. Sometimes a schmuck is also a spy. But in general, a schmuck is a jerk."

"Like a wanker?"

"Yeah, exactly. Like a wanker."

The checkpoint comes out of nowhere. Sam sticks her arm out of the window, clutching her American passport and a plastic card that says PRESS in large letters. An American soldier with hair lighter than hers, thick but cut close to his head like a carpet, is holding his gun with both hands while he approaches the car.

He takes her passport and opens it, turns a page and hands it back to her.

"What about them?" he asks.

"My driver, my translator," she says, using her two index fingers to indicate Rizgar and then me, like windshield wipers on a car.

"Do they have IDs?"

"They're Iraqis," Sam says. "What kind of ID do you want them to have?"

"We need to see some ID. Driver's licence, passport, something with a picture on it. I can't let you pass otherwise. This area's under surveillance."

I explain to Rizgar what they're looking for, and he pulls his driver's licence from his back trouser pocket. I open up my wallet to find that all I have with me is my expired university identification card.

"Wait here for a minute," the soldier says, walking off with our IDs. He walks back to the small encampment set up beyond the road, surrounded by piled-up sandbags and topped with swatches of sandy-toned, netted fabric that reminds me of an animal's lair. There, another soldier is speaking into a black device that looks a bit like Sam's Thuraya, only bigger.

Sam lets out an agitated sigh. "As if these guys can even read an ID in Arabic."

I shrug. "Maybe they have pictures of wanted men," I say.

Rizgar's foot is tapping nervously on the car floor. He reaches for the gearstick as if he is tempted to just throw it into first and go. Sam looks at him, and he sits back and sighs.

"Isn't there anything you wouldn't do to get a story?" I ask.

"Lots of things. First of all, I don't lie."

"No?"

"Well, I try not to. Not unless it's a really dangerous situation. It's mostly about convincing. You don't break rules, you bend them."

Rizgar points. The soldier is coming back. He taps on Sam's window and she rolls it down. "Here y'go," he says with a pleasant tone. He stoops a bit to address her. "You can go 'head, but if I's you I'd be careful out there."

"Thanks!" she calls, and begins to crank the window back up. It gets stuck, as usual, near the top of the frame. She puts her hand against the glass to help it up, adding, "And if I were you, I would have gotten posted to Guantanamo Bay."

18

Adding

ADEEB'S HOUSE IS situated in a way my mother would have never tolerated: directly above a small grocery store and a butcher. In Birmingham, these stores were mostly run by Muslim immigrants, and although she would shop there for the halal meat, she looked down her nose at the people – mostly Pakistanis or Afghanis – who ran them. She thought there was something unclean about living above a place that sold food, as if untold numbers of filthy creatures would be living in the walls and pipes as a result.

But inside, Adeeb's house is nicer than I would have expected for a barber. The only thing that gives away the slight unseemliness of the location is the neon sign outside the window. Despite his wife's apparent efforts to dull it with a curtain, it shines a reddish light into the room, bathing his children's faces in an unnatural cherry glow.

They are four boys, and they sit in order of age next to Adeeb, who has the comfortable spot in the corner. Each child looks uncannily similar to the next, each a more tender version of the one before him. They remind me of one of those famous Russian dolls, the kind my father once bought Amal for her birthday, where each is a little smaller than the last.

Adeeb offers Sam and me seats covered in bright red carpets on the opposite side of the wide room. When he calls his wife in to meet Sam, a thin, pretty figure rushes in. Sam stands up and Adeeb's wife kisses her on both cheeks. Sam seems charmed. Adeeb doesn't say what his wife's name is.

"She doesn't speak any Arabic, right?"

"Very little," I reply.

"Arabic no?" he says, looking at Sam.

She smiles as if a little embarrassed. "*Inshallah.*" She cocks her head in my direction. "Nabil here promises to teach me, but he's not doing such a good job so far."

I translate this and everybody laughs.

"I'm sorry to make you come at night. People are watching me during the day, and may be listening as well. If anyone saw you, they'll think you're only relatives or friends."

"No problem," I say.

I am surprised to hear Adeeb's wife speak up. "Is she a Muslim?" Her voice is genteel, almost delicate, as if she knows that this could be an inappropriate question.

"She wants to know if you're Muslim."

Sam is expressionless.

"No," I say. "She's Christian."

"I thought so," his wife says. "So she doesn't have to wear the scarf. Please tell her she is free to take it off if she likes."

I pass this on to Sam and she touches the black silky scarf that draws a dark border around her hairline. Against it, her skin seems fairer than usual. "I don't mind it, actually," she says. "It's very comfortable."

I tell this to Adeeb's wife and she smiles, pleased with Sam's answer. She must start getting the children to bed, she says, and begins by whisking the smallest one away, eliciting a cry of protest.

Adeeb pulls a short string of beads out of his pocket and leans back into the cushions. "How did you get to Subhi?"

"Subhi? We got to Subhi because…" I must ask Sam. I don't know how much to reveal. "How did we get to Subhi?" I ask her.

"To Subhi? Harris gave us his name."

"Aah. Yes, Harris," Adeeb says in English. "Very good man."

Sam nods. She doesn't mention that she has never met him, or that her editors have begun to think that maybe he is not so good.

"I…want help…you…" Adeeb shakes his head, starts again in Arabic. "I wanted to help him more but he didn't have so much time for me."

I tell Sam this, and she looks puzzled. "But wasn't Adeeb his fixer?"

"Were you not translating for him? Working for him?"

Adeeb nods. "Yes, I was working only for him, but he had others. At least four, I think."

"Four fixers?" Sam asks. "At the same time? Who could afford that?"

Adeeb shrugs. "He had a lot of money. But we didn't get paid every day. We got paid only on the days when we got some good information for him."

"They were paid for providing him with information, Sam."

"How's that work? No information, no pay?"

"He met us in the morning at the Palestine Hotel, gave us ideas, and said if we came to him at the end of the day with something good, he will pay for it. We were all competing with each other for the information so we can be paid. And for me I think this wasn't a good way for working, but otherwise I think Harris is a good man and if you—"

"Nabil, can you translate?"

They're both talking at the same time and it's starting to make me frustrated. I tell Sam I want to speak to him for a minute so that I can get it right. And she says fine, and leans forwards to take the tiny porcelain cup of tea Adeeb's wife has left on the table in front of her.

"So, many of you were working for Harris?" I ask.

"I think so," Adeeb says. "At least four that I know of."

"And he paid you whenever you could get him information?"

"Exactly. Fifty dollars a day."

"And if you didn't get any information that day?"

"He would give me about 30,000 dinars, just for the transportation."

I reach into my shirt pocket and take out my tiny notebook. "And so what kind of information did you get for him?" I assume this is the question Sam would ask, although I am not entirely sure.

"Small things. The day-by-day news. Anything I could find on Saddam and his sons. He said he needed me to be his eyes and ears because he couldn't be everywhere."

"And that's it?"

"Subhi said he had important information and documents that would help Harris get a big story that would prove that Saddam was very corrupt. So Harris was very happy with that. At the end, he owed me for a day of work that he hadn't paid, but he told me that he was out of money and would pay me back some other time. I guess it was because he had to pay a lot to General Akram for the documents."

"He paid? I mean, he paid General Akram for the documents?"

Adeeb looks at me as if I have asked a silly question. "Of course he paid. This is how it works for everyone who wants documents. Akram collected reams of documents. And a lot of beautiful furniture. You'll see."

"Everyone paid…you mean there were others?" I make a few notes and he seems unsure he likes the fact that I am writing down what he says.

"Are you writing about me?"

"You? No, no." I turn to Sam. "Are you hoping to write about him in the story?"

"I doubt it," she says. "But at this point, I have no bloody idea what the story is. If we even *have* a story."

"She says no. You can trust her." I proceed to give Sam the highlights of what Adeeb said. I can see in her eyes that she's a little frustrated again with my translation, but I think she's also realizing that sometimes she needs to let me figure out how to go about things. And I see that Adeeb is unsure whether to believe me, and that maybe trust is not the reason he's trying to help us.

I start again. "May I ask you something on a different subject?"

He opens his hands wide and shuts them.

"Who was the young man working in your barber shop?"

He smiles and raises his eyes, as if I've passed a test that shows I'm smart.

"He's a son of the most powerful criminal family in the neighbourhood. I have to pay money to them to keep my shop open and not have anyone attack it. On top of that, the head of this family made me take in one of his sons as an employee. They said they want him to work, to learn a trade. But I'm sure they sent him to watch me and listen."

"So you agreed?"

"Do you think I could say no?" His voice carries resignation in it, as if he didn't even bother to resist. "I come from a very small family. Even if we have enough money, thank God, it doesn't help. In fact, it makes it worse, because they think we are rich and so they target us. What do we have? A barber shop and a few grocery stores. Do you think it makes a man rich? Do you see a Mercedes parked outside?"

"Nabil?" Sam is smiling calmly.

"Excuse me, let me translate this for her."

"It's not necessary," he says. "You want to know about General Akram."

"That's true."

"What else do you need to know?"

"Let me check with her, if you don't mind."

I quickly give Sam a rundown of everything he's said, and she begins to fire off questions.

"How did you meet Harris?"

"Someone introduced me to him at the Palestine Hotel."

"If you don't speak much English, how did you and Harris communicate?"

Adeeb smiles, as if he's acknowledging her for catching on to something out of the ordinary. "Deutsch. We spoke in German."

"How do you know German?"

"I lived in Germany for three years when I was younger. I have some cousins there who run a restaurant in Cologne. Harris spoke German very well."

"What stories did you work on with Harris?"

"We didn't work on any stories together. He asked me to get him information and to bring it to him. And he wanted documents."

"What kind of documents?"

"Any documents. Anything we could find that was coming from Saddam's offices but he said it had to be something useful that could prove something."

"What do you think he wanted to prove?"

Adeeb shrugs. "That Saddam has big bombs that he could use to destroy America and Israel. Or that he was working with Al-Qaeda. But it was difficult. Everything was a mess. Papers everywhere, everybody fighting to take a box of what he could and run away. People would kill you for a box of paperwork."

"How did General Akram come into the picture?"

He stares blankly. "I can't remember. I only remember that Harris had heard about him and had wanted to see him." He holds out his hand to Sam to indicate he would like a piece of paper. "I can give you his address. Why don't you just go to General Akram and speak to him yourself?"

Sam tears a page out of her notebook and hands it over to him. Adeeb's wife breezes in to pick up the second-to-last son, who starts to yell that he doesn't want to go. She enlists the oldest son, who is probably eight or nine, to help carry him away. "But I want to hear," he cries. "I want to hear them speak the infidel language!" He really called it that, using the word *kafir* and all. I'll have to tell this to Sam later on, just because it's so amusing.

"Do you know how much Harris paid to Akram?"

Adeeb shakes his head. "Thousands of dollars."

"Thousands of dollars? Are you sure? That's a lot of money for a journalist."

"Maybe it was one thousand. I don't remember." He looks at Sam. "Why can't you ask Harris? He is your colleague, right?" I translate this for Sam, and I see the hesitation, the look of uncertainty when, in a moment, you must decide: to lie or not to lie? Adeeb probably doesn't realize that Harris is in trouble. He couldn't know that if Sam's editors confirm their suspicions that Harris paid for the documents, this will be even worse for Harris.

"Yes, of course," says Sam. "We just can't get in contact with him because communication is so bad right now. I can't reach him."

Adeeb nods several times. The room is quiet for a moment, and then our silence is punctured by the sound of one of the boys whimpering in his bed.

"I remember now," Adeeb says.

"What do you remember?" I ask.

"How Harris learned about General Akram. But you must swear that you will not tell anyone I told you. No one."

"*Bismillah.* In the name of God. I swear." On Sam's behalf, too, like her legal and spiritual representative.

"It was an odd chap named Suleiman. Suleiman Mutanabi. He was one of the fixers. He came to Harris at the Palestine Hotel and said he could put him in contact with a man who has good information. Lots of documents. So Suleiman took Harris there the first time."

"Do you have any idea where this Suleiman is now?"

"No idea. He was from Syria originally, so people also call him Suleiman es-Surie. Just go and speak to General Akram himself."

He wipes his forehead, grown damp even this late into the evening, and then dries his hand on his trousers so he can write.

"Go and see him, and if I can help you any more, please do come and visit me again."

His pen scribbles across the paper, twice piercing a hole in it. Just as he finishes I notice a squarish blue blur on his hand. It looks like he had something tattooed on the skin between his thumb and forefinger, and then later tried, somewhat unsuccessfully, to have it removed. He must have noticed me staring, because he lifts his hand to eye level, turns it out, and smiles.

"It was a cross," he says. "I was a Christian but I decided to become Muslim." He gives the paper to Sam and retakes his beads, moving his fingers through them rapidly. His eyes roll over the perimeter of her body, looking while trying to look away. "Do you have any tattoos?"

I translate this for Sam. "He wants to know if I have tattoos?" She is amused.

"Yes."

"The answer is no."

"This very good," Adeeb says, switching back to his spotty English. "Then you can marry fancy city man like this," he smiles, putting a forearm on my shoulder and squeezing it roughly. "And to become Muslim should be very much easy for you, like for me."

Sam's laugh emerges short and sharp, like the honk of a horn. Embarrassed, she lifts her hand, quickly covering her mouth, and one of Adeeb's little boys begins to cry again.

19

Covering

IT MADE SENSE to stop at a restaurant with Rizgar and Sam for dinner, but it's also made me late. When I walk into the house, my parents and my sister are sitting around the radio. They are lit by two kerosene lamps, which gives them a strange yellow glow. My mother jumps up and puts her arms around me, and then takes my face in her hands. "*Al-Hamdulilah,*" she says. "Thank God you came back."

"Of course I came back," I tell her and kiss her cheek. I unbutton my damp shirt and walk towards my room.

"There's dinner waiting for you in the kitchen," my mother says. "Don't you want?"

"Maybe later," I say. "I want to have a shower first."

"Don't open your mouth when you're showering," Amal calls as I near the hallway. "And don't let it get in your eyes. The water was coming out brown today and it smells funny. Baba says there's a bacteria in it."

Lately, when I come home at night, our house is like this – almost dark, without electricity. I think of Sam's room at the Hamra, of all the foreigners who mill around the pool into the late hours, of the lights that are in the very pool itself, making it possible to swim at night. They just arrived and they have all the light in the world, while we, the native inhabitants, are sitting in the dark.

It is amazing the things you can manage to do without much light, when you are in a place that you know so well that you don't really need to see. Amal calls out and asks if I want a torch, but I tell her no. If the water is brown, I'd rather not see it anyway.

The water is warm and it washes away layers of the day, and in my mind I can imagine how the dirt and dust look as they stream towards my feet and down the drain. I inhale deeply, but cannot detect the smell my sister is on about. Poor Amal. She has nothing to do these days but roam around the house and notice what's wrong.

After, I lay in bed and fiddle with my own small radio, searching for a station that doesn't have news. I'm forced to settle on Oum Kalthoum, whom I like but have never loved. She's one of my father's favourites, and to say you don't like her is considered unpatriotic to the Arab cause. Nearly every song sounds like an elegy; every love ballad could easily be mistaken for a dirge. But it happens I like this one, *Il Atlal*, The Ruins, because the words were written by Ibrahim Nagi, who was a very talented Egyptian poet. Baba told me that after the Six Day War, *An-Naksah* (The Setback), this was played on the radio all the time – an ode to our losses.

A rapping on the door, and then the creaking of it opening. Baba stands in the doorway with a raised arm leaning on the frame. In the other, he holds a small gas lantern, one of the new ones he purchased in the past week.

"Can we talk for a bit? Are you feeling okay?"

"I'm fine," I say. "I'm just tired."

He walks in and takes the chair from my desk, dragging it

closer to my bed. He turns it around, with its back towards me. The chair emits a groan of protest.

"Why don't you eat what your mother made?"

I sit up and straighten out my back. "I ate in a restaurant with Sam on the way home. She was…we were hungry so we ate dinner at a restaurant on Arasat Street," I say. "I can't eat again."

"Do you realize how hard your mother is working to try to keep things going around here? Do you know how difficult it is just to get fresh food now?"

"Of course I know. That's why if I have a chance to eat with Sam, I will. It saves us a little."

"No, it doesn't," Baba says. "Your mother will make food for you because she'll always assume you're coming home for dinner. Until you get married…"

"If there were a way to call you, I would." I roll the ridges of the tuner beneath my forefinger and thumb, trying to get clearer reception.

"Ah, Oum Kalthoum. I thought you didn't like her."

"I don't. What else am I going to listen to? I can't get another station. When I save up enough money from working with Sam, we can buy our own generator. That's what they have at all the hotels, so that they can have electricity all the time. Then we can do what we want in the house, and maybe we'll even get a satellite like I promised for Amal so she can watch all the TV channels."

"Yes, terribly important," he says, which could be either serious or sarcastic, and I'm not sure which. He rests one arm across the back of the chair and in the light from his lamp, I see the wiriness of the hair on his arms and knuckles.

"We were in Fallujah all day and we didn't have lunch. Everyone was hungry and she wanted me to eat with her.

Actually, a very nice restaurant called Lathakiya. You know it?"

"I don't like Syrian food," he says. "Why would you go to Fallujah? I thought you were supposed to work as her translator in Baghdad."

"Well, mostly Baghdad."

"I don't like you going to Fallujah."

"It was fine. We didn't have any problems. In fact, we were received very well by one of the tribal leaders."

I like the picture I am presenting for my father. There is a thread of truth running through it, just like it is when the journalists write their stories. They choose a string of events and some words that were said, but they never present the full picture of all that transpired. Sam let me read her Abu Ghraib story the other day, and it had only a fraction of all that we saw and heard, stitched together like embroidery, so that you couldn't tell what was missing.

Baba leans over and plucks the radio from the table. His thick thumb moves the volume louder for a minute, then back in the other direction, clicking it off.

"Mr Mubasher came to visit today."

"From school?" Moin Mubasher is the headmaster of the Mansour Boys School. My other boss.

"Yes. He says that they are going to try re-opening the school next week. They want the boys to be able to finish the school year. He says they only expect about half the students, or maybe even a third, to show up. But they will fix some of the windows and bring new chairs. He would like you to come."

"To teach? Now?" It had never occurred to me that any school in Baghdad would try to re-open before September, which is five months away.

"Sure. He says some of the boys need to take tests to move up into the next year's class, or to university. He doesn't want them to have to repeat a grade, to have a whole year of work go to waste."

"And what about the girls?"

Baba shifts in the chair. "What do you mean? It's a boys' school."

"I mean what about the girls finishing out the year? Doesn't that matter? If Amal's school were going back into session, would you send her now?"

He doesn't respond but I know the answer. No one is sending any daughter to school right now because of the chaos, because of the rumours of kidnappings.

"That's not the point," Baba says.

"Did he say that there were other teachers who were willing to come?"

Baba shrugs, nods without looking at me. "A few."

"So let them teach."

"Nabil, you have a job to do."

"I have a new job now. I'm working in journalism. It's much more important."

"More important than education? More important than the future of the best students in Iraq? I don't think even you believe what you're saying." Baba stands up and I feel his bulky body breathing heavily, hanging over me. "Think about it. You could tell your lady friend that your family insisted."

"She's not my lady friend." I gape at the air, searching for a word. "She's my employer."

"But what about the Iraqi employer you've had for, what is it, five years now? And what happens after the Americans leave?"

I roll out of bed. I'm too far from sleep now, and I want to be on his level. I lean against the window. If my father pushes any harder, maybe I can just escape from here, fly out on a carpet like they do in the fairytales. "I'm not quitting," I say. "Definitely not."

In the distance, a crackling of gunfire fills the air. It is a gentle popping, so benign it may as well be the sound of boys bursting balloons at a birthday party. Then a bigger bang, followed by a feeling of a sound wave moving through my flesh, the sensation of something tingling down the length of my arms and across my back.

What makes Baba think the Americans are leaving? Who says it would be any better if they left now?

"You'll do what's right," he says. He turns and lumbers towards my door. Across the floor, even his footsteps feel weighty. Then the sound of the door opening, the heft of my father standing in it. "My boys always do well. Eventually, they always do well."

He moves to close the door but then opens it wide again. "Your mother made a *tabeet*. That chicken is bursting with raisins and apricots and cardamom, the way you like it. She must have been in the kitchen all day. If you don't eat some, then maybe you really have lost your mind."

"Tell her to save it for me and I'll eat it tomorrow, Baba."

"There's no electricity, remember? So there's no refrigerator," he says.

"Well then, I'll get up in a bit and eat some," I say, but he's already shut the door.

I am alone again, and there is a small happiness that derives from the quiet of having no one here, no one talking to me or

through me. But the joy of this feeling passes quickly, and I begin
to think of how good it would be to be here with Sam. How, if I
could be honest with her, I could tell her how hard it is to let my
father down. How complicated she has made everything. She and
the army she brought with her.

My mind fails to enjoy the stillness. Instead, it circles like the
thrilling rides at those little amusement parks Baba took us to
when we were young, before Amal was born. I go to the section
on my bookshelf with a collection of my favourite Iraqi poets.
As I read I translate aloud, as if for Sam, to make her understand.
This one is by Muzaffar al-Nawwab, who spoke most of his
poetry in live performances.

I whisper to my imaginary Sam, who lies with her head on
my pillow, listening intently.

I have been shining so radiantly for this moment,
while the letters of passion on my lower lip lay sleeping.

I read more to her, and she is mesmerized by the cadence of
our poetry, the music inherent in its rhythm. It loses little of its
beauty in translation. Soon her eyes begin to flutter. I want to
tell her about Noor, that *Noor* means light, and that for the rest
of my life, each time I see the word for light I'll have to think of
her and how she died trying to marry me. And then I will read
more Muzaffar to Sam, until she is asleep.

Who are you? And what is the story of your soul?
What of the known world and its days have you lost?
And who have you come to visit?"

*

I think I was sleeping but I heard something crash and Baba shouting. I race out to the living room, sure we've been attacked. But it's only Baba, who in the darkness tripped over the propane fuel stove he bought and the glass lantern that was next to it. He is cursing and limping and my mother is up with a candle already in her hand and I try to help them clean up, but it's hard with the lamp broken and just my mother's candle lighting up the living room and a bit of moonlight from outside.

I find the torch and more candles and we sweep it all up and my mother says she's amazed that Amal didn't wake with all this commotion and that she's going back to bed.

I hold my watch close to my face. Not yet midnight. I can remember a time when we would all have been up watching an old Egyptian film on a warm night like tonight. Now, with nothing to do in the dark and no electricity for television, everyone goes to bed early.

"Do you want to have a drink?"

"Sure, Baba. I can make some tea."

"Not that kind of drink." He takes the torch off the table and walks into the kitchen. From the cabinet above the refrigerator, so high Baba needs to stand on a chair to reach it, he retrieves one of the bottles which were only of interest to me when I was fourteen or fifteen, and fascinated with the idea that Baba was drinking alcohol despite the religious prohibitions. I was also aware that he seemed to drink more often after we came back from England than he did when we were actually there.

He retrieves his bottle of Glenmorangie and pours a little into two glasses, his golden line a bit higher than mine. Still limping a bit, he hands me a glass, puts his on the table and relaxes into his favourite armchair.

"Are you all right?"

"Couldn't be better," he says. "Just bashed my foot against that damned gas cylinder. Can you remember that we didn't always have that in the centre of the living room?"

"I remember."

He holds his glass out to mine and says "cheers" like he is pretending to be British, and clinks my glass. "No," he says, "still doesn't work for me. *Sahtak*." To your health. To clinking Baba's glass again. He sips and I sip and I tell myself that this time, I'll drink it like a man and it's not going to make me shudder. Baba sighs, as if a little air has been let out of an over-pumped tyre.

"It seems you're keeping yourself very busy with this journalist friend," he says. "But don't you think it's dangerous?"

"Isn't it dangerous wherever you go now?"

"If you were teaching it wouldn't be as dangerous."

I taste some more, let it burn the insides of my mouth. The whisky goes down hot, like sweet soup. It makes me shudder, against my best efforts to sit steady, like Baba. I still cannot see what makes people find this so pleasurable. But somehow I'm glad for a moment like this with Baba.

"Ziad got through on the phone today," he says.

"Oh, is the phone working again? How are they? Are they going to come for a visit?"

"Not for a while."

I knew the answer. Maybe I asked the question because it's a subtle way of making Ziad look bad, of reminding Baba that his beloved Ziad left, and that I'm still here.

"I told him what you were out doing," says Baba. "He says he's afraid you'll be accused of being a collaborator. He said if he were me, he'd demand you quit immediately. 'He shouldn't be working with some American whore,'" Baba quotes in a sardonic tone.

"It's not like that, Baba. Not at all."

He swirls the whisky in his glass and puts his nose down into it, inhaling slowly. "But he's got a point. And if the school wants you—"

I say nothing.

"I didn't think you'd agree," he says. "If she weren't beautiful, would you quit?"

"That's not what this is about."

"I hope not." Baba puts two fingers on his temples and rubs in circles. He sniffs, tips his glass back a bit more, and after a minute, tosses back the rest. "So what are you doing out there? Are you reporting on what the Americans are up to?"

"Sometimes."

"Are they going to rebuild things soon? All the damaged buildings?"

"I don't really know."

"They have to take control and stop all the chaos and the crime. They should go back and arrest all the criminals they let out of Abu Ghraib."

"Saddam let them out, Baba." I breathe in the whisky, enjoying the scent of fermented alcohol, though I can't stand to drink another drop.

"So what's the Americans' game plan? Did you find out when they're going to appoint a new Iraqi president? I guess it'll be like Karzai in Afghanistan, where they just put their favourite man in charge. Or do you think there'll be elections first?"

"No one really knows." I wish I liked alcohol. Maybe it would make it easier to talk to Baba. "There's a new American being sent out to Iraq and he's saying maybe by next year, or something like that."

"So what are you really working on? You must be spending all those hours working on something, and it's not the things I'm asking about."

What harm could be done? If I can't trust Baba, then who?

He sits watching me, waiting.

"Actually, we're doing an investigative story."

"Isn't that what a journalist is supposed to be doing all the time?"

"This is different. We're spending a lot of time trying to get the answers to one big story that seems very important to her editors."

"And?"

"It's about Saddam paying millions of dollars to a politician in America so he would have a supporter there who would be critical of President Bush. The newspaper has documents to prove it. But now they don't know if the documents are real or fake."

"That's what you're working on?"

"Yes."

"I thought you were just making basic little reports about what the Americans are doing here and there."

"No. More than that." Suddenly I long to be back in bed, to have not been woken up by Baba's fall. Maybe it's stupid of me to be telling him any of this. Maybe it will only make them more worried for me.

My father picks up my glass. "You're not going to finish this, are you?"

"You have it."

Baba holds the glass up and makes a small circle with it. He puts it up to his lips, but then puts it down again. "It's amazing that two sons from the same family can be so different."

Here it is, that thing my father does, thinking he's saying something so revealing for the very first time, when in fact, he's said it a hundred times before.

"*Leil o-nhar*. Night and day, you and your brother. It's okay. You don't have to like the things I like."

What things, I want to say. *What things?* Hospitals? Drinking? Does it occur to Baba that, by all accounts, life in France has made Ziad more religious, not less, and that he probably hasn't tasted alcohol in years?

"I have a suggestion for you. Go to see your cousin Saleh in Amiriya."

"Why?" Saleh and I only see each other at big family events: weddings and funerals.

"Yes, as soon as possible. Go and see him."

"He was just some manager in a UN office under Saddam, Baba. I doubt he knows a thing about what's going on now."

"You may be surprised. He had very good relations with Saddam and all sorts of international officials through the UN. Maybe he can help you. He's really well-connected."

I say yes, perhaps I'll go soon, because what else can I say? But I won't go. I won't go because we have too many other things to do, and this story to report. Surely, if I told Sam she would say it was a waste of time. I move to pick up the glasses so I can take them into the kitchen, but Baba puts his hand over the one that's not empty, with fingers that say, *I'm not finished*. He will stay here. I say goodnight, and he says, yes, goodnight. And soon I'm back in bed and in my head I see Baba's hand with its wiry hair across the knuckles, holding fast to his glass like someone might take it from him.

20

Holding

I AWOKE FROM a strange dream about Sam. We were in the back of the Impala, holding each other, as it swerved on a wide-open highway. I realized we were both in the back and no one was at the wheel. Sam started to scream and I woke up, swimming in sweat.

Something about the dream is nagging me, making me feel like listening to my father's advice for a change. Last night, I went to sleep sure that Baba's suggestion was nonsensical. This morning it seems like the most logical thing in the world.

And so after a short cab ride, I find myself at Saleh's front door, where a guard or servant of some sort answers. Saleh soon appears, well-dressed for work in a tailored suit. He is angular and distinguished-looking despite his short height, almost like Hashemite royalty. He has a compactness and a darkness that might, on a less graceful man, be judged by some Iraqis to indicate a lower-class status. I would never like to admit to Sam or another foreigner that skin tone matters to us so much, but it does, although this contradicts the teachings of Islam. The swarthier you are, the more likely it is for people to assume you come from *fellahin*, farm people. Peasant stock, they called that in England. Skin-lightening cream is a popular product among Iraqi women.

The only thing that looks different about Saleh since last I saw him two years ago is that he has grown a short beard, and it makes him seem older than his age, which is somewhere around forty.

The moment I tell him I'm on my way to the Hamra Hotel, where the journalist I'm working with is staying, he insists on driving me there – apparently so he can bend my ear far away from his home as he proceeds to confide in me about his troubles. His wife, Ashtar, has been seeking advice from a mystic sheikh because in their more than eight years of marriage, they have not had any children. This mystic, who calls himself Ibn Suhrawardi after a famous Sufi master who died in the thirteenth century, is advising Ashtar that the couple must return to Islam.

"I didn't know we left it," Saleh jokes, pounding on his horn for a slow driver to move faster.

"Ashtar's been haranguing me to grow my facial hair, especially now that it is much more acceptable, now that Ba'athists are out and beards are in." He reaches over and rubs his knuckles teasingly against my close shave.

"Ashtar also says Ibn Suhrawardi has advised her to adopt a new Muslim name, Aisha, because Ashtar is a pre-Islamic name from the *Jahiliye*, the period of ignorance before the Holy Koran was revealed, and perhaps that has angered God," Saleh continues. "Or, he says, it might have attracted a *jinn* who's now following her and cursing her womb. If she changes her name, it will be as if she is a new person, and the *jinn* will become confused and go away."

He waits for my reaction.

"*Yaani*, she's driving me a little crazy," he groans as he drives towards Karada, the annoyingly long way around, since the 14th of July Bridge is still closed by the US military.

"I love the woman, so I'm trying to indulge her. I only allowed her to start making visits to the mystic when she began having nightmares. She had always had vivid dreams. Now she was waking up in a terror, saying that she dreamt that the UN building where I work was blown up, killing everyone inside." Saleh brakes, the rush hour traffic up ahead coagulating into a jam. "What do you make of that?"

I shrug. It sounds like utter nonsense to me, but then of course the dream I had last night was what pushed me to come to Saleh today.

"Such dreams are just the unhappy imaginings of a woman who'd be content if she had children," he says. "At the same time, I have a friend who joined some group of guys planning attacks on big targets. Anything international, anything *Western*, is considered fair game. Moreover, I'm hearing that most people who worked at the UN liaison office during Saddam's time will soon be fired anyway. The Bush administration is demanding a purge of all Iraqi employees connected in any way to the Ba'ath Party. Don't they realize that anyone who wanted a job dealing with any issue of import had no choice but to join?"

I clear my throat. "I've heard that."

"At any rate, I've got decent English. I need to get some work with foreign journalists, like you did. Maybe you can set me up? It'll probably pay much better than this UN job anyway. Then maybe we can afford a trip abroad, to Europe or America, so Ashtar can see a fertility specialist."

He parks in front of the Mustapha Hotel across the street. "I know too many people who work at the Hamra, and if they see me, I'll have to go in and say hello. After all, the UN delegations used to stay here."

He turns to look at me. "Wait, I thought you were a schoolteacher."

"I was. I mean, I am. But this is more interesting."

"How much does it pay?"

How much to tell him? Not just about my salary, but about Sam, about Akram, about the documents. "It depends."

"Look, Nabil, why don't you come by this evening so we can continue," he says.

"That would be wonderful. Thanks for the lift."

"Anytime, brother, you're my flesh and blood." He gives me a pattering of small kisses on the cheek, and as I kiss back, I feel the edge of his beard against my shaven face and realize how fortunate I am to come from a good family, and wonder why I was reluctant to visit Saleh in the first place.

At the reception desk, Rafik rings Sam and she says to come right up. But it's a shirtless Carlos, not Sam, who opens the door. Sam appears a moment later, looking more striking than usual. A flowing white scarf is wrapped around her neck, one end hanging delicately in front of her, the other crossed over her shoulder and draped behind. She looks like a 1920s baroness in a photograph I once saw. I have a hard time imagining the scarf being transformed into something modest and Islamic.

Sam notices my disconcerted look.

"This okay? Don't you think there's a chance that Akram could be religious, and that I'll want to put it on?" She demonstrates, draping it over her head.

Carlos picks up one of his cameras sitting on the sofa and

says, "Let me photograph that and send it to National Geographic."

Sam makes a playful frown at him.

"Seriously, that'd be about the sexiest *hejab* in Baghdad. Nabil, is that kosher?"

She grabs my elbow and pulls me towards the door. "Don't listen to him, Nabil. My friends will only corrupt you."

On the way down to the car, she turns serious again, giving me a rundown of her latest conversation with Miles, on how they want her to dedicate herself entirely to this Jackson story, on what we should ask Akram. She does so in an undertone that's almost a whisper, eliciting a stare or two from the hotel staff.

It may be a bit of a ride to get to the Jihad neighbourhood, where Akram lives, and so Rizgar slips a Kurdish tape into the player. He glances at me and smiles and then turns the volume low. I've already told him I'm getting tired of his music – it sounds like one long nationalist lament. *Ismaa, ismaa,* he pleads, listen. Murad Kaveh. The best Kurdish music ever made.

"Sam?"

"Hmm?" She underlines something in her notebook, draws a hasty star next to it, and turns the page.

"Sam, I have a favour to ask."

"Yeah?" Now she looks at me, but only for a brief moment before returning to her notes.

"Do you think you could get my cousin Saleh a job?"

"Do I know your cousin Saleh?"

"No, you don't, but he's very smart and his English is also good. He worked for the UN and now his wife doesn't want him to go back there. She says she's sure they're going to get bombed soon."

Sam shakes her head, then juts out her chin – her questioning posture. "Uh, so why would he want to work with the foreign press?"

"It's different. It's not like sitting around all day in a building that's going to be a target."

"Nabil, I'm not an employment agency."

I look out of the window. The flatness of the Jazeera plains to our left is filled by the intermittent green blur of the date palms.

"I know," I say. "Of course not. He'll find something." I crack my knuckles without realizing how loud it will sound, an aggressive snap across the quiet car. Murad Kaveh croons from the speakers, singing the same lyrics again and again, none of it making any sense to me.

"I didn't mean it that way," Sam says. "It's just that I don't have the power to hire a whole bunch of people. We have a budget for one translator and one driver per correspondent."

"I understand."

I think she's sorry she was so hasty in her reply. It's something Sam does often. She is quick to spout out some reaction, something clever, and then regrets it.

"I guess I could ask around for you at the Hamra," she says. "Maybe someone there needs a translator."

"Also, Sam, it's more than that. Saleh could be very helpful to us. He has a lot of contacts."

"Yeah?"

"Of course. That's how he got to be working for the UN in Baghdad. The regime allowed him to have that job. Uday had to approve everyone who worked with foreigners, especially the UN. Saleh knows people."

"So why does he need a job with some journalist?" Sam's

mind seems to be in a constant cycle of dissection. I feel she is constantly trying to figure out if people are lying to her – including me.

"Sam, do you trust me?"

She turns around, her eyes compressed, concerned. "What, about your cousin?"

"No, I mean in general. Do you trust me?"

"Nabil, of course I trust you. I asked because you have to wonder about a person's motives. That's what I do. I ask questions. Doesn't mean I don't trust you."

"Do you always trust the people you work with?"

She closes her notebook, and reaches into her bag to retrieve a Turkish chocolate bar labelled Metro. "Have some, Nabil. It's a Turkish knock-off of a Mars," she says. She offers each of us a piece, but we both refuse. The idea of chocolate first thing in the morning disgusts me.

"Do I trust people I work with? That's the question? Absolutely," she says while she chews. "Otherwise I wouldn't work with them."

"How did you know to trust me?"

"You? Oh, you're easy," she smirks, "you have an honest face."

I peer into the rearview mirror, notice my eyebrows a bit askew, the beads of sweat on my forehead. "Do I?"

"I saw it that first night in the emergency room. Those big puppy-dog eyes. Sometimes you just have a feeling about someone."

Sam puts the chocolate wrapper in the ashtray. Rizgar removes it and throws it out of the window.

"Rizgar! Don't do that!" She rolls her eyes at me. "Tell him not to do that."

"It doesn't matter," I shrug. "It's fine."

"Don't just litter like that. You could be fined $500 in my country for doing things like that."

"Five hundred dollars!" I say. "That's bollocks."

"Bollocks?"

"Bollocks. Bullshit. Do you not say bollocks?"

Sam grinds out a guffaw that never quite leaves her throat. "Well, we don't say that in America, but Jonah grew up in England. I've heard him say it."

The car goes quiet. Jonah's name has a way of shutting me up. I'm starting to hate the sound of it. Why didn't he stay here with her? If he loved her, he'd have asked her to marry him by now.

"It's good you trust me, Sam. In our culture, it's very important. It's everything."

"Uh-huh. You think it's not important for us in the West?"

"I don't know. Maybe it is. Not in the same way. I've heard that in America, people break their promises a lot and then they sue each other to get things sorted out. Just like Mr Jackson, suing your newspaper."

"Right," says Sam. "Because if it had been Iraq, all he would have had to do is put a bullet in the editor's head."

I cover my mouth with my hand, pretending to ponder this, when it's really to stop my urge to say something more.

21

Pretending

JIHAD ALWAYS SEEMED a nice enough West Baghdad address to me, with sprawling houses and mostly Sunni families. I knew some boys from school who lived here. But as we drive down the streets, following the path that Adeeb explained to me and I have explained to Rizgar, I feel a sense of cold dread. It must be the air-conditioning; Rizgar has been keeping it turned up to full freeze.

"Sam?"

"Hmm?"

"I think this could be dangerous," I say, trying to sound more authoritative than scared. "What if General Akram knows we are trying to catch him?"

"We're not trying to catch anybody, Nabil. Except maybe Harris Axelrod in a big bloody lie. If Akram's documents are real, then he'll want to sell something to us. And if his documents are fake, then he'll *still* want to sell them to us because he thinks he can make a good profit from it. It's win-win."

"What if he knows what we're doing?" I feel embarrassed that I'm the one who seems so nervous. I'm only the fixer, right? But I have the sense that Sam doesn't appreciate how dodgy this could be. That's a word I haven't heard since I was at Alston

Primary School in Birmingham. *Hey, Amari! What kind of dodgy lunch you got there today?*

"Why should he know what we're doing? A friend told me that CBC was just here two days ago and that Fox is in the market to buy something, too. So obviously a lot of people are shopping around for documents. He has no reason to suspect us in particular." Sam exhales a tight chestful of air. She's not as relaxed as she claims to be. She opens the visor in front of her and, after only a flash of light from the mirror, snaps it closed again. She pulls open the glove compartment, pushes some paperwork aside and comes out with two black devices that are like her Thuraya satellite phones, but smaller, and without any number pads. She turns each one on, and moves a small dial to No. 5. It emits a static buzz, a little like the scrambled radio stations.

"Keep this on at all times," she tells Rizgar as she hands it to him. "Just stay in front of the house and don't leave." She reaches into the big styrofoam container in the seat next to me. "There are drinks in here so there's no need to go anywhere."

A few days ago, Rizgar wasn't waiting for us when we came out of an interview. He said he was hot and had gone to get a drink. As it happened, some insurgents hit a passing American convoy with a mortar and the area turned into a shooting gallery in a matter of seconds. Sam and I had to crouch in an alleyway while the gunfire whistled and ricocheted in the air above our heads. Rizgar agreed later that it was a bad idea to leave, and that he wouldn't do it again. Since then, Sam has kept what she calls a cooler, filled with water and Coca-Cola, in the car at all times.

"I have this one with me in case we need you," she says, holding up the other antennaed gadget. She laughs with a rawness that sounds like it is caught deep in her throat. Rizgar looks confused by her swing from gravity to levity. But this seems to be her way – pretending she's amused when she's actually scared.

"Do you know why it's funny?"

Our silence answers.

"Because I had a set of these when I was about nine years old," she says. "We used to use them at night in the summer on treasure hunts. And now I'm thirty-three and I'm still on some crazy treasure hunt. Except now I'm depending on a piece-of-shit walkie-talkie to save my life!"

"This safe, Miss Samara," Rizgar says, standing the device on the arm rest, right next to his cigarettes. "No problem. Problem? Call. Say, 'Rizgar, problem!' No problem."

Sam flashes a wide smile at him and pulls back the door handle. "*Y'alla*. Let's go."

We are both standing on the driveway and for a moment, we are too close to each other. The guard directs Rizgar to reverse out of the driveway and wait on the other side of the street.

"Are you sure you want to do this?" I hope she knows I am only concerned for her safety.

"Definitely," she says, as the door to the house opens, and a young man waves us inside.

"No appointment?" he asks. "Usually you must take an appointment, but I'll check to see if the general can see you now."

The man appears to be in his mid-twenties, with a belly that protrudes a bit too much for someone of his age and physique. Otherwise, he looks like a body-builder, with large shoulders and a fat, muscular neck. His heft seems to warp the way he walks. He holds out an arm, a heavy, hairy block emerging from a short sleeve, and points us into the salon.

Everything around us is blue and gold, everything matching, everything looking like it should be in a palace or a museum. In fact, it fits what Adeeb told me about the looting Akram has done, whether personally or through his proxies. The room is full of too-fancy furniture, which looks out of place in his otherwise middle-class home. The sofas and armchairs are padded with a plush blue velvet, and the ornately carved ridges of the furniture are painted with gold trim. It must have come from some palace or Saddam-family home somewhere, and that knowledge makes me wonder if the furniture trim might have real gold in it, for it shines as bright as a set of dowry bracelets. The room is also well-lit – I can hear the hum of Akram's generator, presumably tucked into the garden, powering the house.

"Have a seat," the brawny man says, and disappears.

But Sam doesn't, and neither do I, because we are both too fascinated by the room and its incongruent objects. Sam is studying a massive Chinese vase as if appraising it.

"Please, sit!" The man says to our backs. "The general will be with you in a moment!"

I hope he didn't notice Sam's startled response but I did. She picks the most ornate of the sofas, the one facing the entrance to the salon, and I take a seat next to her. She runs her hands down the velvet and back again, towards her bag, which is sitting open, the notebook on top.

"Can you believe this?" Her voice is a hard whisper, like the winter stormwinds from Turkey. "It's like Louis Quatorze meets Qatar. On crack."

I shake my head. More of her American slang. In fact, I do not think I have ever seen a home like this. Everything is co-ordinated with the opulent blue velvet furniture. There are waste-paper baskets and tissue boxes and flower vases made to match the furnishings. There are also, let me count, at least one, two, three, four, five pieces of Japanese artwork, and painted folding screens that also look like they come from the Far East. Several carpets are rolled up in a corner, in addition to the enormous silk rug, which must be from Isfahan, under our feet. I have the urge to suggest we take our shoes off rather than dirty this carpet, but I think Sam would find that strange. She writes quickly in her notebook.

A man enters the room and instinctively, we stand. General Akram has an extraordinarily thick head of hair which is greying, but coarse and full as a broom. His face is just on the verge of getting jowly below the moustache, drooping in such a way that makes me think he must be my father's contemporary. But Akram's body is harder, without my father's paunch and rolls. He is wearing a tan suit that is in perfect condition – considering that it was probably made over twenty years ago, judging from the style.

I reach for my handkerchief to mop the sweat on my forehead. But I've forgotten it again, so instead I use my hand, and I have to stop myself from playing with the thinning hairs on my head out of nervousness.

He holds out his hand to motion to us to sit back down, and he takes his place in a large armchair, with a beautiful marble coffee table creating a barrier in between. He is at a comfortable distance, but it suddenly feels as if he is breathing in my face.

Sam seems for a moment to have lost her words. "So…so, so please tell him I say thank you for agreeing to see us." I translate this and he nods, saying that we are welcome anytime.

"Just go ahead," I say. "I'll translate everything just the way you say it."

"Well," Sam begins, "I'm an American reporter working here in Baghdad. I understand that you have been providing important documents to some of my colleagues." I translate it just like she said, without any embellishments or commentaries. Just like she taught me to do. Don't pad things unless I tell you, she said. Don't *candycoat*. Most importantly, I did not say exactly *who* Sam is – or who I am. I have never seen her start off an interview this way before. She also hasn't presented her business card.

"Yes," Akram clears his throat. "This is true. I have many documents that are in demand with the foreign media, and with the Americans and the British. Maybe I can help you." He crosses one leg over the other and leans on his left elbow, sinking into it comfortably. He is taking in Sam with an ogling stare, and then converts his gaze into an artificial smile.

"Oh?" Sam lifts. "Are you working with the Americans? Officials, you mean?"

"Yes, of course. Ah, but wouldn't you like some tea?" Sam understands this much, I know, but I translate it anyway, and Sam says yes and he yells out to the hallway for three glasses of tea.

"I was in touch with the Americans before the war and as they were coming to Baghdad," Akram continues. "I was known to them as an opponent of the regime. You see, many members of my family were killed by Saddam, and even I was almost killed on many occasions. So, we helped the Americans by showing them our information about the palaces and the villas of Uday and Qusay. We gave the Americans information about their positions. Two days before the fall of Baghdad, we found the place where Uday and his staff were hiding. We raided it and killed fourteen Ba'athists hiding there. We missed Uday, but we'll get him."

Sam's pen bounces across the page like a car in a hurry on an unpaved road.

"We all suffered from Saddam's regime, so we formed a commando unit, all of us former military people," Akram says. He leans towards the end table perched to the right of his chair, a scaled-down version of the expansive coffee table, and picks up several files. "This one shows that Saddam had planned to have me executed," he says, holding up a folder. He takes a page out and hands it to me. "Read it," he says.

It does have his name on it and several words are highlighted, including "death sentence for treason". Sam's eyes switch from Akram to the pile of files on the table next to him. "Who's in this group?" she asks. "I mean, the commando unit?"

"We are a group of thirty members. Some of us are relatives."

"So how did you get out of being executed?"

"When I was in prison in 1991, Saddam's brother-in-law came to my brothers and asked if they wanted a pardon for me. They asked for 200 million dinars, and my brothers paid. We had money back then. I come from a very established family, thank God. I was released and discovered that my own family was finished: my wife and my two daughters were killed. When I came home, I asked the neighbours where they went and the people said, 'After you were arrested, they took your family.' They never came home again."

Akram puts a hand over his eyes and shakes his head. "*Ya Allah al-Muntaqim,*" he says, invoking one of God's divine names

– the Avenger – sometimes called out by one whose loved one has been murdered. "Do you see how evil this man was?"

Akram gets up and walks out of the room, and Sam is about to say something to me but already he is back, holding another folder of documents. He sits down again in his chair. "This is the intelligence file on me. They were trying to prove I was a traitor and that I had a link with the monarchy in Amman. They accused me of trying to bring back the Iraqi monarchy, because my father once worked for the king."

I'm surprised by this information, because I was under the impression that most of the senior people who worked for the monarchy left Iraq in 1958, right after King Faisal II was dragged through the streets of Baghdad. But Sam is copying everything he says without any indication that she doubts a word of it.

"My father also had Jewish friends who left Iraq in the 1950s, and he corresponded with one of them. After he died they found the letters and accused me of conspiracy with the Zionists, and for this I was held in prison and tortured for five years. Five years! From 1995 to 2000, I was held in a secret prison by the intelligence services. I, an Iraqi general. You understand, I was a general in the Iran-Iraq war. You should know how much we have suffered. I'm lucky to be alive. When they thought I was totally broken – and my brothers were able to pay the ransom – they decided to let me go."

Sam nods, pulls in her lips the way she does when she wants to show sympathy. "How awful. This country's history is – tragic." She lets a few moments of quiet pass. "So, may I ask you, when did you start helping the Americans?"

"Two weeks before the war. Some undercover agents were sent from Kuwait to see me and they asked me for the location of key regime members. They were with an Iraqi who had left Baghdad many years ago. He said, 'We need your help.' I agreed. The Americans wanted Saddam and his sons, dead or alive. But the man I wanted was the man who took my daughters and my wife and killed them – and he was one of Uday's aides. He was in charge of thousands, maybe tens of thousands of executions." Akram sighs. "And that's why I was after Uday's house, and along with that, I came into possession of these documents."

"Where was this house?"

"Behind the As-Sa'a restaurant," he says, pointing over his shoulder. "Near the Embassy of Oman."

Sam shakes her pen, and draws blank circles on her page, pressing harder until the paper emits the brusque sound of a tear. She begins searching in her bag. Akram reaches into his breast pocket and pulls out a green felt-tip pen. He leans forwards and offers it to her with a graceful turn of wrist. "*Tfaddli*," he says.

"*Shukran.*"

"Do you speak Arabic?" he asks her slowly.

"*Shwaiy shwaiy,*" Sam grins, signalling very little.

Akram sits back in his chair. "I have a lot of information that would be of interest to you. For example, some of the documents show that one of your important politicians, Mr Billy Jackson, took millions of dollars from Saddam."

Akram opens another folder and pulls out a page with a light-blue background. There is an Iraqi government crest in the centre of the page, and some kind of stamp at the bottom. He holds the document on the table, facing us. "Look here," he points. "Here is Jackson's signature." The document looks like some kind of an order to a finance department manager, ordering that Billy Jackson receive $1 million in cash. The document is signed and dated the 15th of January, 2003. Akram lays out another dated the 23rd of June, 2001. Then he reads off the dates of numerous other payments, stretching back to 1995.

While I am translating this for Sam, Akram sips his tea. Then he pulls out yet another folder. He reads that so-and-so is ordered to give a $1 million gift from Saddam to…Jacques Chirac for his support of the Iraqi people…signed by Uday Hussein and Abdel Rahman Mansouri, treasury department.

"Down here," Akram says, "you have the signature of Jean-Marc DuBois, who is an assistant to Mr Chirac. Most importantly, they are all signed by Uday, who ran the finances, as I am sure you are well aware. And Mansouri, he was Uday's money man. He held the keys to the vault, which of course, they raided before they disappeared."

Akram reaches into the pocket of his trousers and pulls out his wallet. He opens it and takes out a 10,000-dinar note, spreading it out on the table. "Look," he says, tapping on the bottom left corner of the note. "Show her. You can compare Uday's signature on the documents to the one on the bill. They are exactly the same."

"Amazing," she says. "But why would an American congressman or someone in Mr Chirac's cabinet agree to sign something like that? Wouldn't they be afraid to leave a trail?"

Akram's eyebrows crash in a small ditch above his nose. "Afraid? No, they weren't afraid. This regime was in place for thirty-five years. No one could touch it. No one thought it would fall, so who would know?" He pauses. "You understand what these men have in common, don't you?"

Sam shrugs. "I'm not sure."

Akram's lips spread flat and wide. "They were opposed to the

Bush campaign to overthrow Saddam! All along, they were supporting Saddam and trying to prevent the world from sanctioning this war against him. Ah! Also Kofi Annan."

Sam's eyes open wider. "The head of the UN?"

"Yes, we can show you documents that demonstrate that Kofi Annan was also receiving money from Saddam Hussein. In return, he fought very hard to allow Saddam to sell oil when they said the restrictions on the Iraqi people were too tough."

Sam corrects my translation. "Or sanctions? You mean the Oil-for-Food programme?"

"Yes, yes," General Akram says in English before returning to Arabic. "Exactly. Saddam was allowed to sell oil again, so he gave Mr Annan a very nice tip for his help. About $3 million. What's important is to expose all of these people who made Saddam a leader with continued legitimacy. It's their fault he stayed in power as long as he did."

"I see." Sam nods. She breathes in and exhales, then lets the tip of Akram's pen fall on to her notebook, leaving bleeding green dots wherever it lands. "I want to talk more about Billy Jackson—"

"Yes, Mr Jackson," Akram interrupts. "I know personally that he received about $15 million since the early 1990s. I know a driver named Karim al-Azzawi. He was in charge of driving Mr Jackson from Iraq back to Jordan. He was told that if he didn't get Jackson safely to Jordan with the money, he'd be executed. Then they deposited the money in a bank there."

Sam tilts her head to one side. With much of her hair covered by the white scarf, which she chose to wear after all, she looks younger. Simple and curious. "How do you know all this?"

"If you want to verify what I say, I can arrange for you to

interview him. This is how all the money transfers were done. There was no other way to get such a large sum of money out of Iraq. It's not as if Saddam could wire it to New York or Paris," he laughs.

A young teenage boy comes into the room with a plateful of diamond-shaped *baklawa*, a bottle of orange soda and three glasses. Akram thanks him and pats him on the back. Sam accepts the orange soda Akram pours for her, and takes a bird-like sip. I drain my glass in one shot; the translating is wringing me dry. The general pours me another glass.

She turns to me. Her eyes seem to search mine for cues, but she gives up and looks back at Akram. "You know, this is all really fascinating. But we got right down to talking about the documents and in fact, I wanted to ask you more about one of my colleagues."

Akram nods, sorting through his files as she speaks, looking up only when I am giving my translation.

"Now, I have this colleague named Harris, Harris Axelrod, and I believe he wrote about these documents for my newspaper I'm not positive, but I think," she pauses and looks at me, "I *think* that Harris has written about these very same documents for the same paper I write for. And I believe he told my editors that he got these documents from you."

After I translate this, Akram rises and goes to an armoire in the far corner of the room. He lifts a key from his jacket, unlocks the cabinet door, and pulls out a small cardboard box. He carries it back over to his chair and sets the box beside his feet. Inside, it seems, is another batch of documents.

"My goodness!" says Sam. "How many documents did you get when the regime fell?"

"Many. Many, many documents."

"Could you estimate?"

"About twenty sacks. We put them in sacks because we were in a rush. Saddam and his sons took some of the most important documents from the presidential palace and put them in these villas for safe keeping."

"But didn't the INC take most of the documents?" Sam asks. "That's what was reported."

"No," he replies. His tongue seems to be shifting back and forth inside his mouth, as though he is growing annoyed but knows he shouldn't show it. "I gave them a lot of documents from the Republican Palace, just to be helpful."

"You mean, you had documents from there, too?"

"We have access to whatever documents we need." Akram bends to pick through the files in the box at his feet. "There are others here you may want to see." His voice is muffled. When he comes up, his face looks flushed, almost burnt.

"So, do you remember Harris?"

The general smiles leisurely. "Of course I remember him. I met him many times. He told me he lives in Beirut."

"Yes, that's right. Didn't he get these very same documents from you, these ones on Billy Jackson?" Sam holds up the papers he handed her a minute ago. "Isn't this exactly what you gave Harris?"

The general signals for Sam to hand them back, and she promptly does so. "These are not the same documents," he says. "You must be confused. Harris took the documents about the weapons facilities, not these."

Sam sits up straight. "You also gave him information about weapons sites?"

"That's right."

"Did he buy those?"

The general coughs, and reaches for a tissue. With a screeching hack that makes my ears hurt, he expectorates something from his lungs, crumples the tissue and puts it into the waste-paper basket beneath the end table. He tilts forwards to take his tea then looks up at me. "Smoke?"

"No, I'm sorry."

"Don't be sorry. It's better. I would have been tempted to ask you for a cigarette. My wife made me quit."

"Your wife?" I ask.

"Yes." He looks at his knees. "I remarried only last year. It has taken me many years to get over the death of my first wife."

"*Allah yarhamha,*" I say. God's mercy be upon her.

"Thank you."

Sam turns to me. "Did he say if—?"

"No. I'll ask again." And I pose the question, once more, if Harris paid for the documents about the weapons sites.

"Yes. But he didn't pay for them in full. He paid a small amount and then he said, 'I'll come back and pay for the rest of the documents.' He's an honest person, I'm sure, so even if he's late, I'm sure he'll be back."

"And the documents on Jackson? Did Harris pay you for those?"

"No, I told you, I didn't give Harris those documents. I have them right here with me." He shifts. "When will our friend Harris come back to Baghdad?"

"I'm not sure. So how much did Harris pay for these documents about the weapons sites?"

Akram sits back in his seat. "You know, I'm just one man.

Many of the people in this unit, the people who are the caretakers of these documents now, were made very poor by this regime. Saddam took away everything we had. We lost our income and we suffered greatly. That's why the money is necessary. It gets distributed to many families."

"I see. How much did Harris pay?"

"Harris paid, it was around $10,000 or $12,000. I think he was expecting to get a lot of money for this information, from other people he could provide it to."

I'm beginning to wonder where Akram is lying and where he's telling the truth, if anywhere at all. I wonder why Sam doesn't tape-record the conversation.

"Also, we have documents on the meetings between Saddam Hussein and Osama bin Laden. We have a set of about fifty documents that show the training of seven members of Al-Qaeda in Iraq. The documents show how they were trained to fly planes and to do those attacks in America. We have an American television station coming tomorrow to take these documents."

"Really? So when was this meeting between Saddam Hussein and Osama bin Laden?" Sam is sounding breathless.

"In 1999. That was when Saddam accepted seven members of Al-Qaeda to train inside Iraq, learning to fly aircraft and to use chemical weapons. These are the same people who hit the World Trade Center." He hands a few documents to me and says *fahim-ha; fahim-ha*. Make her understand.

"You're saying seven of the nineteen hijackers were trained in Iraq?"

"Yes. Then they participated in the attack on the World Trade Center."

"And how much will these TV people pay?"

"They agreed on $20,000."

Sam makes an "o" with her lips. She blinks at Akram. "That's quite a lot of money."

The general nods. "But very important for the Americans to know."

I read Sam the names on the list. "Nawaf Alhazmi… Mohammed Atta…Ayman al-Zawahiri…"

"Wait, Ayman al-Zawahiri is Bin Laden's number two. He was not one of the hijackers."

"Yes, correct," Akram says. "Six were hijackers, but the seventh was Zawahiri. He was also trained here in Iraq, but he was not a hijacker. They trained for one year in Iraq in 2000. See the signature here," Akram says, pointing vehemently to the scribble on one of the pages.

"Hmm. It's a lot of money," Sam says. "But also a very compelling story."

Compelling? Should I say that? She's behaving as if she, too, might be interested in buying documents. Was that what she'd planned?

"The money you collect for these documents," Sam continues, "to whom does it go?"

"Our group, as I told you. We're about thirty people. Many have been through desperate times. Their families didn't even get food-ration cards during the sanctions because they were enemies of Saddam. Imagine, people from educated families who have had their lives ruined, people who believe in freedom and democracy." Akram shakes his head to convey his dismay, and then smoothes his jacket.

Sam turns to a new page, and draws two lines across the top.

"If you'll forgive me," she says, "I want to go over this again. Harris *didn't* take documents from you on Congressman Billy Jackson?"

Akram shakes his head. "He only wrote down the information. You know, the money is secondary. I want people in America to know what Jackson did."

"Why does that matter to you?"

Akram frowns at Sam. "He gave Saddam legitimacy. You see, the aim is not the money, but to expose all the world politicians who kept trying to prop up Saddam. And as we punish them for this, we will aid our suffering people in the process."

"Right, I can understand that," Sam says. "But you know," she taps the pen against the notebook, then grasps it tightly. "What I don't understand is, I think that my editors told me that Harris e-mailed copies of these documents to my newspaper headquarters, and then sent them the originals you gave him. Now, how can that be?"

"It's impossible," he says. "Harris is lying. Or, he's confused."

"But that's what my editors have, copies that look just like these."

Akram's eyes narrow, drawing out rivulets of wrinkles around them. He waits. Waves a finger back and forth. "Oh, *now* I remember. We put the documents on the table and Harris photographed them. I didn't know that in this way he could try to avoid having to buy them." He begins to laugh. "If I had known, I wouldn't have let him do that."

"And he didn't pay anything to do that?"

"Well, Harris gave $1,000 the first time he met the men in the unit. I took him to one of their houses and he couldn't believe how poor these former generals were, so Harris asked if he could give them money to help them."

"He volunteered to give it?"

"He considered the information they gave to him a great benefit, so he gave the money as a compensation for the information."

"Wait, I'm a little confused. You're saying that Harris paid you $10,000 or $12,000 for documents on the weapons sites, and another $1,000 to compensate the men in the unit?"

General Akram pauses. "No, the $1,000 was part of the $12,000. That's why I said ten or twelve. It was $10,000, plus the $1,000 that he paid separately, and then some extra money, around $1,000, to get all the documents translated. So that's $12,000 in total."

Sam is running out of room in her notebook. I can see that she only has a page or two left, and that her handwriting is getting smaller than normal.

"My job is to publicize the truth about all those people who made Saddam into an angel. And I'm already succeeding because our stories are in the newspapers."

A *muezzin* releases his sombre voice into the air, inviting the faithful to midday prayers.

"Sam? It's my prayer time," I say. "I think we should go soon." I turn to Akram. "I hope you'll excuse me, but I must pray *dhuhr*."

"Of course," he says. "You can come back later after you decide."

Sam sets her notebook on the sofa between the two of us. She interlaces her fingers like a net and rests them on her knees. "You know, I've really appreciated the time to talk to you. But in terms of anything more, moving forwards, I will have to speak to my editors. I don't know what they'll want."

She is being purposefully vague. And the only way I can think to say this is to say that she is speaking *an il mustaqbal il qaribe*, regarding the near future. From this, I fear he'll think we're coming back to buy something from him.

Akram nods. "Which of the documents are you most interested in?"

"Oh, I'm really not sure," she says. "They're all very interesting. But paying for documents is a complicated matter. It's usually not allowed."

"I understand," he says.

"You know what?" Sam sits up, looking happy again, her scarf slipping off her head. She reaches to put it back on.

"It's okay," Akram says, patting the air. "We are not fundamentalists here. This isn't Iran, despite Tehran's efforts."

Sam laughs before I can translate. She runs her fingertips through her hair playfully, like she's out joking with friends. I find myself wishing she would put the scarf back on immediately, but what does it matter now? Once it's on, I should have told her, you can't suddenly take it off, right in the middle of things.

"I like to take pictures of everyone I meet, everywhere in the world," Sam says coquettishly. "It's just what I like to do. Can I photograph you?"

Akram stiffens, and I can see the muscles in his throat at work. He shrugs. He coughs again, reaching for another tissue. Sam is already reaching into her bag for her camera. "Just one or two?" he inquires.

"Yes, just a few," she says, and she is already twisting herself beyond the coffee table, fingers manipulating buttons and dials, closing in on Akram's face. He folds his arms. His mien is stern.

Sam is snapping away, her finger pumping on the button, the fake shutter-sound of her digital camera fluttering against the silence. "Keep 'im talking," Sam mutters to me. I wish she would tell me what to keep talking about. Continue the interview, perhaps the most intense we've ever done, or try to get him talking about something else?

"It must have been amazing to be in Uday's house the night the Americans arrived in Baghdad," I say. "What did his house look like?"

Akram turns away from Sam and towards me with a deliberate and controlled stare that conveys he's taking me in fully, watching me.

"He lived like a king. Pure opulence," he answered, drawing his hands out in a circle to suggest how big. Sam clicks furiously while he's in mid swing, the rattle of picture-taking popping like a distant spray of gunfire. His gaze shifts back towards hers, the left side of his mouth twitching, making his moustache dance.

The beefy man who had led us in enters the room, followed by one wearing an eager smile. Akram stands, holding his hands out in greeting. The man embraces Akram and then puts his lips close to his right cheek, kissing it sideways three, four, five times. He exchanges warm words and then turns to Sam and me. I stand up, and Sam follows, putting her camera on the sofa.

"I'm Suleiman," he says, holding out his hand to me. Sam extends hers as well and he takes it, smiling at her with what seems like too many teeth. His eyes are an unusual pale blue. I offer my name and introduce "Miss Samara." He turns back to Akram.

"Oh General Akram! If only a man like myself could have such distinguished guests as you always do."

Akram laughs with an air of self-deprecation, and this Suleiman laughs with him. Something about his accent is different. Something of the Levant, either Syrian or Lebanese.

"I am glad for your gracious visit," Akram says. I can see his attention flitting from Suleiman to us.

"And I'm honoured to be in the presence of such great beauty," he says, indicating Sam but bowing his head slightly towards me, as if asking my permission to say so. It has to be. It has to be Suleiman es-Surie, or al Mutanabi, or whatever his name is, the man Adeeb mentioned among the web of fixers Harris worked with.

Sam turns to me and raises her eyebrows gently. "I think we'd better be going," she says. "I don't want to be responsible for you missing prayers. Please offer our deepest thanks for all his time."

I translate this and I see Akram's jaw tense. His eyes shift to Sam and then come back to mine.

"What about the documents?" Akram asks. "Which of the documents did you say you were interested in?"

"He wants to know which ones we want."

Sam puts her camera back into her bag. Closes her notebook and wears her enigmatic smile, her lips tight against one another. A little bit kind, a little bit condescending. "I really need to check with my editor first to see what they want. I won't know until I speak to them." Her wording is ambiguous and it probably feels quite comfortable to her – walking the thin line between hiding the truth and telling outright lies. Could Akram be so daft that he hasn't figured out by now that he *is* the story?

"How much would they pay for documents on the biological

and chemical weapons production facility?" Akram asks. "We can give you information on the ones in Al-Kut and Al-Diwaniyah. That is a very important story that hasn't been reported yet."

What else can I do but just feed it to her straight? Like she said – a two-way radio, no static blocking the airwaves.

"Well," Sam says. "That is very interesting. I will have to think about that and see what my editors say. I don't know if – how much they would pay for that."

We stand there uncomfortably, everyone waiting for the next move. "He's very reliable," says Suleiman, raising a tiny *tut* from Akram, a diplomatic signal to shut his mouth. Akram follows Sam's motions, the bag over her shoulder, the hand held out to say goodbye to the two of them, and he escorts us to the door. He is still asking questions.

"He wants to know how he can be in touch with you about this," I tell her.

"Just, uh," her upturned hand suggests a shrug, "just tell him now that we know where to find him, we can come back when we have some kind of answer."

"He wants to know where you stay."

"Oh. Well, the Sheraton."

Akram is trying to smile, but the twitching side of his mouth pulls his face into more of a scowl. "Come in here with me," he signals to us to step through the hallway and into an inner room, the one that visitors are usually not invited to enter. "Come and let me show you something." I tell this to Sam and she says fine. My heart speeds up as I consider the possibilities.

He shows us in, indicating that I should go first, with Sam following, and he comes in after us. It is dimly lit and mustier than the big room with the fancy furniture. I can see a corridor leading to the kitchen, a dining table. A glimpse of the back of a woman retreating as we enter the room.

"Come here," he says, leading us towards the right, where the sofa faces a television set with wavy lines moving across it. "Here," he says, and flicks on the lightswitch near the wall.

I hear Sam suck in a quick breath: on the carpet is a mound of weapons, piled on top of each other like worms: bazookas, RPG launchers, ammunition belts, Kalashnikovs and, I think, AK-47s. Maybe mortars too? Many of the guns are old, and one has a knife attached to the end of it.

"What the — is he running a militia too?"

Akram crosses his arms. "They're the weapons we used to raid Uday Hussein's house. The night I told you about, when we killed Uday's men and took these boxes of documents." He leans against the wall, seemingly pleased with himself. "Do you want a picture of these, too?"

"No," I answer for Sam without consulting her. "I don't think that will be necessary."

"Whose weapons are these?" Sam is drinking in the cache. Her eyes are skipping over every inch of it and back to Akram. Now he's at ease and she seems nervous.

"Our men. We're a very reliable group of friends, very loyal men." He begins to move towards the door now, and I can see his guard brooding in the corridor. "I only wanted to show you some of what we used that night to break into Uday's house. So you…" he says, pauses. "So the good lady will see how we helped the Americans when they came to Baghdad. And so she will understand, and so she can tell her boss in America how we were able to obtain such important documents."

I thank Akram several times and promise that we will be in

touch. Sam says a short *shukran* and puts her hand across her chest and nods, an appropriate gesture when men and women don't want to touch. But even at that moment, and as we walk out of the door, I can see that the same trigger finger that kept pumping shots from the camera is still shuddering.

In the car, I feel out of breath, as if I've been running, my lungs heaving, my feet pulsing. Sam is simply shaking her head back and forth. When we're safely down the block, she begins to shout. "Oh my God!" She lets out a squeal and begins to laugh. "Can you believe this guy? What a piece of work!"

Rizgar looks curious to know what happened.

I roll my eyes at him and hold up a finger, telling him that I will explain later. "Yes, he was lying a lot, wasn't he?"

"Lying a lot?" Sam turns her back to the dashboard to face me. "Uh, ya think? For a guy who deals in forgery, he's a pretty shitty liar. It's too bad his story isn't as seamless as his documents."

"You think he makes the documents himself?"

"Who knows? I'm not even up to that yet. First we need to figure out what the hell this guy's really up to." Sam looks excited, her eyes lit and jumpy. "I mean, if he's stupid enough to try to sell me the same set of documents he sold to Harris and claim that they're originals, and he's trotting out this whole round of other bogus stuff like it's a friggin' flea market, how was it not obvious to Harris that *something* was up?"

Rizgar says that the neighbourhood feels creepy and he wants out, quick. Does he have our permission to speed up?

"Problem? No problem," Sam says lightly but Rizgar is serious. He steps hard on the accelerator and we are sucked backwards in our seats. I didn't realize an old Impala could go so fast.

"He must know that we have him figured out, though, no? He is not that stupid," I say. "You kind of trapped him in his own lies. Don't you think he realized that?"

"Look, he's not regular stupid. I mean that special kind of stupid," Sam says, "when someone is smart enough to think of a really clever crime, but stupid enough to get greedy about it and want more. He tries to mass produce to expand his profit margin and ends messing up. That's often a criminal's downfall. They never get enough."

"So all these people, Sam. Chirac, Kofi Annan. You don't think they could have been receiving money from Saddam to support him, like Akram said?"

Sam rolls her eyes at me. "I really doubt it, Nabil."

My stomach feels queasy from Rizgar's sudden speed and fast turns. Sam picks up his packet of cigarettes, and shakes it, listening to the rattle. Then she flips open the box, runs it under her nose and inhales. "Why do you have to have these lying around?"

He laughs. "Sorry, Miss Samara."

"Look, if he knows we've already got his game, then why was he telling me about all the other news organizations he's servicing? We could end up derailing his big deals to come."

"Maybe he's trying to establish his reputation – to show us all the important clients he has."

"Ah-ha," Sam says, "that he's in demand. But you don't think he's worried that we'll put him out of business?"

"Actually, I do think…maybe. I think you have to be careful. Did you see all the guns he had?"

"Yeah, that was quite a collection."

"I think it's a subtle way of threatening you. Us."

"The thought crossed my mind." She picks up the cigarette packet again and takes one out. Rizgar smiles at her. She holds the cigarette between her fingers like a person who is smoking, but makes no attempt to light up. "You're not going to start giving me guilt about it, are you?" she asks me sheepishly.

"Me? I don't care. It doesn't bother me." I do and it does, but what business is it of mine?

"It's this country of yours that's driving me to it," she says, putting the cigarette in her mouth for a minute, then taking it out. "Okay, here's my theory. He wants to be the it-boy for documents. So when we walk in, he readily admits they're for sale, and gives me a sample. Thinks I'm the next customer in line, right? It just happens to be a sampling that the *Tribune* has already tasted. But when he begins to realize that he's shopping me a story that the paper's already run – and how could he have known that – he goes and denies that Harris got the Jackson documents from him. And he says instead he sold Harris stuff on weapons, because he knows that's definitely a hot commodity. Whether you want to uncover weapons facilities or smear unsavoury politicians – come one, come all! There's lots to go around, and everyone wants a story."

I can follow most of Sam's reasoning, and if she's right, I'm thinking that there should have been some other way to go about it. She should have met Akram without making him feel as if we were trying to buy something. And then after all that, putting him on the spot with the truth. Photographing him. Or, on the other hand, maybe he was confused. Maybe he thought Sam was just asking a lot of annoying questions, as reporters do, trying to make sure no other journalist had the same story. Maybe for him, all that matters is that we came shopping in his personal market. He will make us a final price, and then he will expect to collect.

"So?" she asks. "Do you agree?"

I think for a moment. "What's an it-boy?"

"Usually it's an it-*girl*. A model or an actress. Someone who everyone wants, you know, mindlessly." She's twirling the long, white cigarette between the fingers of her right hand. "Just like I want this cigarette."

22

Twirling

"Excuse, me, Miss Samara," Rizgar says. "You like eat ice cream?"

Sam's eyes light up. "Really? Do they have good ice cream here?" Rizgar points out the Al-Ballout ice cream shop.

"That'll keep me off nicotine a little longer," she says. "It's actually open?"

"Al-Faqma is better," I offer. Rizgar's eyes flash at me. But it's the truth; I can't pretend otherwise.

Sam looks to me and then to Rizgar. "Well, where's Al-Faqma?"

"It's by the next round-about," I say. "The ice cream there is famous. Ten times better than Al-Ballout."

By now Rizgar has stopped the car outside Al-Ballout, with those crude, cartoony pictures of children and animal figures painted on the wall. He gives me a look that makes it clear he's annoyed, but when he realizes I've registered his discontent, he forces up a conciliatory smile.

"It's much better," I insist. "Nobody would go to Al-Ballout if they can go to Al-Faqma."

Rizgar sniffs and shoots back into the traffic. No one says a word. Sam shifts uncomfortably, sensing Rizgar's frustration and probably wondering whether she should have sided with him.

He may have been working for her longer, may even be better loved: I can tell that Sam avoids the possibility of slighting him in any way. But no Kurd from the north is going to tell me he knows a better place to get ice cream in Baghdad than I do.

She tries to put our disagreement aside with a declaration. "We're a team now, and in America, when the team wins the game they go out and celebrate with ice cream. Or beer, of course."

She's disappointed there's no chocolate, but consoled by another favourite flavour, raspberry. Rizgar and I pick out ours but are more focused on arguing over the bill; he all but armwrestles me into letting him pay. We take a seat at one of the outdoor tables in the shade.

Sam runs the overturned spoon across her tongue and closes her eyes. "Umm. Not bad." I haven't been eating mine quickly enough, and in this heat, it's already becoming like *chorba* – soup. "Did you think it would be bad?"

"No, Nabil," she drops her jaw a bit, and as she does, I can see that her tongue has gone magenta-pink. "I meant, it's really good. I had ice cream in Turkey once and it was, I don't know, kind of weird and gluey. I thought maybe it was going to be like that."

I mix my colours together – green for pistachio and orange for peach – until it starts to become a brownish, unappealing mess. I should have picked out the flavour Sam did, which suddenly looks very appealing. Her lips are now stained red, and they look a little pouty, almost swollen.

"This is definitely the best ice cream in Baghdad," says Sam. "In fact, one of the best I've had anywhere in the world."

"You don't have to exaggerate." I make myself take another spoonful.

Sam scrapes at the bottom of her cup, finishing off the last spoonful. "It's a funny name, Al-Faqma." She smiles at me with closed lips, coloured like a doll's mouth. "Al FAQ-ma." She says it like a foreigner who doesn't know the difference between the letters qaf and kaf.

"It means 'the seal'," I say.

"Oh?" Sam reaches over to the corroding silver canister on the table for a napkin. "What is this, wax paper?" She dabs the corners of her mouth and crumples the stiff paper into a ball. "Like a seal on an envelope?"

"No. Like this," I say, and proceed to demonstrate, clapping and making the appropriate sounds.

Sam laughs a bit and shakes her head. "You're too cute, Nabil. You crack me up."

If I don't say something soon, it might be obvious that I feel embarrassed.

Rizgar, sucking on the banana shake he chose instead of an ice cream, probably with some intent to demonstrate that my choice of parlour was not the best, makes a short whistling sound. When I look over at him, he signals for us to get in the car. Something in his eyes says *now*.

"Let's go, Sam."

Without saying more, we make our way back to the car and not until we're pulling away do I ask Rizgar why he wanted us to leave so quickly.

"Yeah…*shaku maku*?" she asks.

"*Shaku maku?*" We both repeat, laughing. "*Shaku maku!*" It would be as if someone who hardly knows any English ran about saying, "What's up, dude?"

"Where did you learn that?" I ask.

"Oh, you know. I'm picking up a little lingo here and there. It's not rocket science. So what was the deal? Did you see someone suspicious?"

Rizgar shrugs, says he just had a feeling it was time to leave.

"Good. I'm all for going on hunches," she says. "Ach, Nabil!" She touches the back of my shoulder, then quickly pulls her hand away. "Miles is going to hit the roof when he hears the whole run-down about what Harris did. How is it that Harris's bullshit detector didn't start screeching when he met Akram? I mean, how could anyone meet that guy and not walk away feeling like you'd just met a used-car salesman?"

We're close to the Hamra now, just passing the Karma Hotel. But instead of turning in as he usually would, Rizgar keeps going straight. He then turns off to the left, in the wrong direction, and speeds up, quickly taking a right and then a left, in a direction we've never taken before. Sam seems not to notice, and Rizgar glances at me in a way that says not to ask.

"Hey," Sam interjects from the backseat. "I know we're almost at the Hamra, but I want to go to the press conference at the Convention Centre. Rizgar, sorry, can you turn around?" His smile tells me he's perfectly happy to take her there rather than back to the hotel.

As we approach the Convention Centre, soldiers stop Rizgar and tell him he can't go any further. "New security regulations," is all they say. But it's at least a mile's walk to the spot where the press conferences are, which is a place I'm curious to see. I offer to walk Sam there. "Sure," she says, slipping on her round sunglasses. I never can tell if such a terse response belies reluctance, but I hop out of the car to follow her anyway.

Sam, despite being a head shorter than I, always seems a pace ahead. "Sam," I ask, a little out of breath in the heat, "if your editors say they want you to just focus on Akram, why bother going to these press conferences?"

"Oh, for the fun of it. And to get you in shape. It's a good workout, isn't it?" We both laugh. "They'll say they want you to focus on one story, but the truth is that they'll still be thrilled to have other stuff coming in. And what if nothing pans out with this Akram angle?"

"Do you think that could happen, after what we just saw today?"

"Actually, no. But it's only just after 7 a.m. in Washington, which means Miles isn't in yet. He's probably just getting up, if that. So what else do I have to do at three in the afternoon? And besides, it's good for keeping up with sources."

I can think of lots of things to do, in the old Baghdad. Take her to one of the riverside cafés. Or browse in the bookshops on Mutanabi Street.

"What time does it start?" I ask her when we reach the entrance.

"Three-thirty."

"Well it's only three-fifteen now. Can we sit here for a minute?"

Sam shrugs and smiles. "Yeah, sure. We can watch the camels go by." This doesn't strike me as funny and when I don't smile back, she gives my upper arm a push. "Kidding, Nabil."

One never sees a camel in Baghdad, only out in the tribal lands. But I know this is the image Westerners have of us. In Birmingham some kid called me a camel-jockey, and I went home that day and punched a stuffed animal, pretending it was him.

We seat ourselves on the stone bench, which is very warm but tolerable, since it's in the shade.

"I still can't believe what happened back there," Sam says. "I almost feel ashamed to give my editors the run-down on what we learned about Akram. That man is slimy!" She shudders. "I can't wait to have a shower."

"Why ashamed?"

"Between you and me, and this is really not to go beyond this bench, I feel like I'm ratting out a fellow reporter, even if it's not someone I particularly like. I had sort of hoped Harris's story would hold up. But this – buying documents from this Akram – it's outrageous."

"I see." I hesitate, thinking of the way she's begun to touch me at times, like she did in the car earlier. "Would you mind if I asked you something personal?"

"Ask me anything," she says.

"Are you with Carlos, or with Jonah?"

Sam looks at me with confusion, her mouth half-open.

"That day at the hospital, when you were looking for Jonah, you were so upset. And you said he's sort of your boyfriend, and obviously you must be speaking to him all the time because he told you to go to see Sheikh Duleimy. But Carlos is living with you and he seems very…close to you."

"Nabil, Carlos is just a friend and colleague. You know that there are two bedrooms in the suite. So there's room for other reporters. You understand that, right?"

"Yes, but as a woman, they would have to respect your need to have your own room. Because to anyone who would see it…"

"What?" Sam seems angry. "I don't have to justify my living arrangements to you!"

"I'm sorry. I didn't mean – I was just trying to understand."

Sam shakes her head in disbelief. "Nabil, if a colleague who's a good friend needs a place to stay for the night, and we've got an empty room here with no one in it, and there're no vacancies in the hotel, of course I'm going to offer it to him. I even let Marcus stay one night last week so he could have a hot shower and a good meal. The man's been living in a tent, for God's sake. Most of the time, Carlos is off somewhere in Najaf or Karbala or some God-forsaken place." She pauses a moment. "I understand this co-ed dorming thing isn't so popular with you guys, but you have to realize, it just isn't an issue for *us*. And right now, it's really more of a practicality than anything else."

"If one of my cousins did that, her brothers would kill her." I was thinking of our distant relatives, of my cousin Raed.

"God. I just don't get that."

"*I'm* not that way. Neither is my brother. But many people are, and they are from good families. The threat itself is a sign of love and respect."

Sam sneers. "That makes no sense whatsoever."

"It does make sense. If you really love someone, you want to protect them."

"Uh-huh. So much that you end up killing them? That's sweet."

"I'm just trying to explain to you how people here think. People protect their family as a whole, not just the individual. It's not simply about what one person wants." I can feel that I'm speaking a little too forcefully now. My heart is banging in my chest. Sometimes Sam's statements are so outrageous I cannot even find the words to tell her how far away she is from understanding our culture. Calling our holy cities God-forsaken!

I have heard her meet someone new and say *tsharafna*, or "how do you do", which means, literally, we are honoured. But perhaps she does not actually understand what the word *sharaf* means.

"Nabil? I don't even want to be having this conversation now." She glances at her watch. "Hey, I have enormous respect for Arab culture. But when an innocent woman gets killed for loving someone, I have to draw the line on my cultural relativism. So let's just drop this, okay?"

I look up to find Joon Park walking over to us, and others trailing behind. Her translator, Daoud, waves to me. Joon, who looks mildly annoyed, calls out, "Hey, Sam. Press conference is cancelled."

"Really? Well I'm so glad I've been wasting time sitting here. Couldn't they have sent a text to our phones?"

Joon and Sam start walking back to the cars, and Daoud and I follow them, walking one step behind and saying very little to each other. Twice I've tried to start a conversation with him around the hotel, and both times I found it impossible. Either he has no personality, or he mistrusts me. Perhaps Joon told him that she doesn't like me.

When we reach the cars the women give each other a quick kiss on the cheek, and Sam bounds back into the front seat, pulling the door shut with a bang.

After a few minutes' silence, I try to clear the air. "I was just asking, Sam, for your own safety."

Rizgar sees her glares at me. He can't understand enough English to get the conversation, but our bodies speak a language which needs no translation.

"I just didn't understand, that's all," I say, attempting an explanation. "In our culture if you were staying in the same room with a man, then it would be clear that these two people," and I fumble for words that won't sound crude, "that these two people are, you know, not just friends."

"Nabil, we are not sleeping in the same room."

"But he was staying in the same big room."

"It's a *suite*. That means it's more than one room. Have you noticed that the suite has two bedrooms?"

"But then they should have you share with a female reporter."

"I can't believe we're having this discussion." She scowls at me. "I told you about Jonah, and that's it." A line of Bradley Fighting Vehicles is cutting in front of us, making scores of cars wait. "And Nabil, with all due respect, it's really none of your business."

I feel myself gulping for words. Suddenly all my English has been drained from me, and I'm drowning in a sea of Arabic. Waters in which Sam will never learn to swim.

No one says another word until I can't stand it anymore.

"You're right," I say. "I apologize. I think I misspoke." No reply. "Sam?"

She leans her head on the window. Her heated sigh makes the glass fog.

"It's only because," I blurt out, and then I stop myself. And what can I say? That every Iraqi in the hotel will just assume she's sleeping with Carlos if she's living with him, suite or no? And that they'll notice there's no ring on her finger? And that sometimes the handsome blond reporter flirts with her, and that she flirts back? Is Sam even going to care? Can I convince her that she should?

"Let's just leave it, okay?"

When we reach her hotel, she gets out of the car without a word, and I follow. "Should I come up?" I ask.

"I guess so."

We walk across the courtyard, through the atrium, to the stairs of the second tower, the tension between us like an electric field. Closer, further, closer. When I was a kid, I had a trick magnet toy like that. The two pieces were attracted to each other and then, once they were up against each other, each repelled the other's force.

In her room she goes straight to her computer. Should I leave? Wait in the car?

"Sam, it was only that…" I stop and then try to start again. "I only want to help you, to protect you from having the men here see you like they see the other foreign women."

Sam looks in the refrigerator. "Damn. No milk for coffee. Carlos probably…" She leans on the counter and crosses her arms. "Nabil, I am a foreign woman. Here, anyway. Who do you think you're kidding? What, and if I don't have a male guest for the night, they'll see me as…maybe, what? A nice Muslim girl who'll make a good wife? And what the hell would the point of *that* be? Am I trying to win some kind of popularity contest around here or get my job done?" Sam puts a hand over one of her eyes like it hurts and breathes in deeply.

I feel ridiculous. I should have stayed in the car.

"I'm sorry. I didn't mean to raise my voice." She looks me up and down, like she's never seen me wear these particular clothes before.

"Out there, out there in Iraq, I'll play by your rules. But in here, inside this little hotel, it's a totally different world, and a woman can do whatever she wants. That's the deal, right? Jeez, don't you see the women swimming out there every night in the pool? If this place were such a fundamentalist stronghold, how could you have that going on?"

"People talk about it."

"About what?"

"About the women who wear their bikinis around the pool, how they're almost naked. How the culture of the West is shameful and we have to resist it. Their words, Sam, not mine. Maybe, maybe these journalists think it's safe, but it's really not."

"That's why I came to Iraq, because I thought it would be nice and safe."

I can see from the way Sam's wrist is twisting, the way her chest is rising and falling too quickly, that she is furious with me.

"So why did you come?"

"What?"

"Why did you come to Iraq?"

"Oh, Nabil, please. Enough! You know, I'm going to stop over at the AP for a while. I need to visit a friend there and check a few things out. We can continue another time. Actually," she looks at me and nods rhythmically, "I think we're done with this conversation."

"Do you want me to wait downstairs?"

She swings the door open and it creaks in a way that almost sounds like an animal's cry. The way she's holding it, it's clear she's waiting for me to leave. "No, let's get a fresh start tomorrow," she says as she lets the door go.

Rizgar offers to drive me home, which he doesn't usually do. He stays with relatives on the northern edge of town, beyond Qahira, and I'm not exactly on the way.

I'm happy for the free ride, but then I realize it too has a price.

"What did you say back there that got her so angry?"

"Nothing," I say. "I don't know." He glances at me and sucks air through his teeth.

"Why were you in such a rush to leave the ice cream shop?"

"Nothing," he says. "I don't know," almost mimicking me, and we both begin to laugh.

"I think you think we were being followed."

"I think you think too much. And I think you're falling for her."

23

Falling

WALKING INTO SALEH'S family room in Amiriya is like walking back in time, to at least the 1970s, when being a member of the Ba'ath party was as stylish as wide collars and bell bottoms. People in the West might think we didn't have such a thing as fashion in Iraq, but we did. Saleh's father, Zaki, was a university professor and a well-known Ba'athist until he died a few years ago. Saleh has left his father's pictures up as a sort of shrine to his memory, primarily black-and-white photographs from his glory days, and the wall is full of awards and honorary doctorates from universities in the former USSR, and plaques recognizing his services as a professor of history at the University of Baghdad.

Saleh appears in the high-arched doorway between the salon and the rest of the house. "Nabil, my brother," he says warmly, and presents me with a tight, quick embrace. "I'm so glad you came back."

He sits down on an orange velvet sofa with fancy wooden arms, its cushions letting off a sigh as he releases his weight into them. He points to its matching armchair, a beautiful, wide-seated piece which I'm sure was his father's seat of honour, and invites me to sit in it.

The room is full of elite-looking European furniture of

decades past, a testament to the days when we thought there was nothing more sophisticated than disliking Westerners, all the while trying to think, behave and set up home just like them.

Saleh coughs loudly, emitting the kind of croupy sounds you usually hear from a child's lungs in winter. "You heard the news this evening?"

The truth is, I haven't. I tucked into a respectable amount of everything Mum laid out – we never turn the radio on during dinner – and then excused myself and popped out to meet Rizgar, who had agreed to drive me to Saleh's for a spot of extra cash. In the car we listened to a cassette of Munir Bashir, the great oud player, who has a way of soothing a man's nerves.

"Another forty people were killed by a car bomb, just outside Saddam City," he says. "Or I should say, Sadr City. That's what they're calling it now, right? Maybe fifty or so injured."

"Oh God," I say. "*Allah yarhamhum.*" May God have mercy on them.

"It's a nightmare what's happening here, Nabil. Did you know that in exchange for the Kurds fighting with the Americans up there, President Bush promised them their own state? They're going to carve up the whole country and take as much oil as they can. America is destroying us, day by day."

I find myself sinking into the chair. I push myself to sit straighter. "Well, they're not setting off car bombs."

He smirks in the manner of someone who has just discovered your secret.

"You're glad the Americans are here." He says it as a statement, rather than a question.

"Glad? No, no. Not glad. I just think…maybe we should give things a chance. Better democracy than dictatorship, no?"

Saleh shakes his head. "Your American friends have already brainwashed you," he says. He stands and moves closer to me, taking my head between his hands and moving it in circles, making a whooshing sound. "See, I can still hear the water in there," he says, making both of us laugh.

Saleh's laugh turns into another bout of coughing. "You know," he says after he catches his breath, "I actually can't stand this room. Mother thinks that we should receive all visitors here because it's so impressive. Respectful of Baba's wishes. But I hate it. Let's go inside."

I follow him down a hallway with more pictures of his father's glory days. My eyes linger on a photograph of Zaki shaking hands with Saddam.

"It was just an award," he says. "My father got an award for best professor of the year and Saddam came to congratulate him at the ceremony. He wasn't a real Ba'athist."

"Oh," I say, "I didn't think—"

"Didn't you? I suppose anybody would. Everyone assumes that any successful professor on good terms with the government must have been a Ba'athist. But it isn't true. I think certain kinds of people, like my father, like your father, certain kinds of other professionals, and I might even include myself in this, find ways to rise above the politics of the day and stay true to their art, or to academia, or to medicine, or what have you. Without compromising on their principles."

He holds out his hand for me to take a place in their sitting room, a much more comfortable-looking space than their *ghorfat al khotar*, their guest room with its impressive European furniture, and I settle on one of the long cushions along the wall. Closer to the floor, and closer to Saleh. We don't have a room like this in our house, though I've often wished we did.

"How is your father, by the way?" he asks, and before I can answer: "Why didn't you go into medicine, like him?"

"Oh, it wasn't for me...being around all that blood."

He coughs and takes a tissue from the Syrian tea-table in front of us, spitting something into it. "Well, never mind. That's not why you came here tonight, is it?"

"Yes, well, I thought it would be good to talk."

"Nabil," he says, placing his hand on my thigh. "If something's troubling you and you need some help, you don't have to be shy about it. That's what family's for."

Ashtar enters the room. She offers a modest, understated greeting to me from the doorway, but does not approach as I would expect. I wonder if her spiritual advisor has convinced her to start behaving like a pious woman, who wouldn't touch a man other than her husband, not even a relative, not even to shake hands. Ashtar asks Saleh questions. "Are you all right? Did you take your medicine?" Though she has a scarf on, it only covers the crown of her head and I can see her hair is dyed a copper-blondish colour with black roots showing through. Her pretty, sad eyes are unusually elongated, almost tiger-like, and are lined with black to accentuate this fact. Though there is something artificial about her, perhaps it is the coloured hair, she's quite an attractive woman.

"*Eiy, Ayouni.*" Yes, he says, calling her "my eyes", a term of endearment that my father used to use for my mother. "Can you just bring us some tea?"

I hate to admit to this, but in most homes, it would be seen as shameful for the woman of the house not to have offered to prepare tea straight way. Ashtar turns on her heels and leaves the room.

"Where were we? Ah, so tell me about your job working with this reporter. What's his name?"

"*Her* name. Katchens. Samara Katchens."

"Oh, a woman," he grins. "I see."

"No, not like that. She's – much older. And married." Another unplanned lie, two in fact. Unnecessary, but probably in everyone's best interest. And too hard to take back once it's out of my mouth.

"Good," he says. "So you've got some kind of situation on your hands with this lady reporter, but you don't have the kind of problems I have…yet," he smiles. "Lucky you. But it's about time you got married, isn't it?"

"Well, yes. After the war, *Inshallah*. So right now we're just… doing some research." I don't know how much to leave in and what to leave out. I never discussed any of this with Sam. But a few basic facts can't do any harm. "At this point," I continue cautiously, "we're researching some documents that might be fake, some documents that are getting all kinds of people into trouble."

Ashtar re-enters silently, putting two glasses of tea, small and steaming in the warm air, on the little table next to Saleh. And then a plate of *kalijeh*, stuffed with walnuts and pistachios, one of my favourites. She moves the table carefully so it is within my reach as well. *"A'shet ideik,"* I say, May God bless your hands. It's a religious way to show appreciation when you are served. She leaves again without responding.

Saleh takes his tea glass and blows on it. "That wouldn't surprise me," he says. "At the moment, there are probably more artificial documents swimming around this town than there are fish in the Tigris."

"Ever heard of a guy called Akram? General Akram?" I take my tea and sip it.

"Can't say I have," Saleh says.

"Says he was a general in the Iran-Iraq war."

"Could be," he shrugs. "In those days I was busy doing my doctorate in economics, keeping my head down so I could avoid getting drafted. And?"

"We went to see him. He's offering documents to journalists, documents that make it look bad for all kinds of people, including your boss."

"My boss?"

"Kofi Annan? The UN chief."

He snickers. "The documents make it look like Kofi Annan took money from Saddam?"

"Something like that," I say. "How did you know? Is that true?"

Saleh shakes his head. "I don't think it's true. But I heard there were some reports about this surfacing in the British press, about British politicians doing the same. It's been around for a few days. I think it's a game people are playing. People for Saddam, people against Saddam. With the Americans, their whole justification for invading Iraq was built on bogus information. Don't you know what Chalabi and his friends did?"

Rather than admit I hardly knew he existed until Sam showed up, I sip my tea and wait for his explanation.

"Chalabi had all sorts of information cooked up to look as if we were well on our way to having a nuclear bomb. He found the best forgery artists available, which happen to be some of the very same ones Saddam used, and paid them to come up with elaborate documents and import lists and fake photographs, which made it look like Saddam had completely built up our ability to arm weapons with biological, chemical and even nuclear warheads. Which of course, was physically impossible given the UN sanctions and those arrogant weapons inspectors who were here nearly every week, soaking up our nice Arab hospitality."

Saleh leans back and takes his tea, but something about the tightness of his small body doesn't look relaxed. "Did you know about the yellowcake issue?"

Instead of answering, I reach for a dark-brown biscuit.

"Well, you should know. President Bush's foreign secretary, Colin Powell, presented a big report to the UN in February, accusing Iraq of trying to buy yellowcake from Niger, and it was the same thing Bush talked about the month before when he made his big State of the Union address." Saleh takes a *kalijeh* as well, but instead of eating it uses it to gesture, as a professor might a pen. "But it was all false, all of it! Of course, at the time, that didn't matter, because if the Americans say something is true, the rest of the world must agree or they will be accused of supporting terrorism. You see, when you have the most power and the most money, it doesn't even matter if you're right. So if—," he breaks off and begins to wheeze, putting down the biscuit and patting his chest with an open palm. Then he takes an inhaler out of his breast pocket, and puts it to his mouth. The sound is of air being sucked out rather than rushed in.

"I didn't know you had asthma."

He shakes his head as he inhales. "I don't," he says, and breathes out. "I had a bad lung infection a few months ago, during the damp months. My doctor says it should dry up soon, now that summer's coming. It had better, because these damn things are getting hard to buy. Some of the pharmacies are barely stocked because the shipping trucks coming across from Jordan keep getting attacked by bloody bandits." When he is finished, he puts the inhaler back into his shirt pocket. "Where was I?"

"Yellowcake. Africa. I didn't entirely follow."

"Of course. Of course you didn't. How would you know? Before, you were what, a teacher? I mean, a very noble profession," he smiles. "Yellowcake is a form of uranium, and it can be used in a nuclear reactor or a nuclear weapon."

"Of course," I say.

"You know what it is, then?"

"Sure," I say. "Chemicals for making weapons."

"Yes, but bigger than that. Yellowcake is a mixture of uranium oxides and other uranium compounds, and if Saddam were trying to buy it from Niger, it would prove that he was trying to build a bomb of the worst kind. But you see, I know from people who know that this uranium report was a fabrication. When Saddam was around, we only suspected that it was a hoax. Now we know for sure. So that means someone dreamed it up, and then came up with a bunch of documents to prove it. Someone paid a lot of money to have that done, and have it done well enough to be convincing to the Americans." He shrugs. "Which is probably not so difficult to do."

I feel I should be writing this down, the way Sam does when the conversation gets interesting. Because now he's beginning to make references I don't catch, to dates and deals and different inspectors, and I see that there are so many things that I just don't know. Before you were what, a teacher? *Qabil*, before. In that other life, before the fall. Saleh continues to talk and wheeze and cough, filling the air between us with chemicals and dates and people, with motives and counter-motives, with his medicine-scented breath. After much rambling on, he asks whether this was what I wanted to know.

"Well," I start. "We're investigating a story about an American politician who is suing her newspaper, the *Tribune*. But I can only tell you this in absolute confidence, just as you have spoken to me."

"Nabil." He reaches to touch my shoulder and shakes it, making my tea swirl in its cup. "We're family! I wouldn't have told you all of this if I wasn't sure I could trust *you*."

I finish the tea to give myself a moment to think. "It's like this," I say. "The *Tribune* published a story about a week ago which accused an American politician, someone who visited Iraq several times, of taking millions of dollars from Saddam Hussein in order to defend him in the West."

"Jackson."

"You know him?"

"Nabil, I know the name of every politician who came to visit Iraq in the past ten years. Doesn't mean he was taking money from Saddam. Who else would they accuse? He's black and he opposed the war. Perfect target."

Saleh coughs into a tissue, and I can sense a glob of something thick having landed in it before he crumples it and sticks it on the table.

"You think that Chalabi could be part of this as well? Would he have been trying to retaliate against influential people who were too friendly towards Saddam? Or who opposed the Americans coming?"

Saleh runs his hand over his small beard. "You know, that's a very interesting theory. But the truth is, I would imagine it's just that. Interesting. I think Mr Chalabi has more important concerns to attend to. He is dealing with the Bush administration and the CIA, and MI5, and probably the Mossad, too." He laughs again, leaving his mouth hanging open in a smile that is both boyish and hungry. "Then again…let me think about it. I can ask around."

"But you can't tell anyone," I say. "*Yaani*, off the record." Funny that those words would come out of my mouth – I only learned the expression the other day, when Sam told me about how it works when someone talks to you "off the record". As she spoke I daydreamed of the turntable Grandma Zahra used to have in the living room, where she'd play the records of Salima Pasha and spin her wrists to the languid melodies. Now I know "the record" means something else, some kind of holy boundary between what you are free to write about and what you are not, and that if you violate this unwritten rule of journalism, it's as good as committing blasphemy.

"I can't find anything out for you if I can't give away some details." His voice has an authoritative tone. "I won't tell anyone I don't really trust."

"Well, then you should be very, very vague. Don't mention Sam, Samara that is, or her newspaper or the lawsuit."

He pretends to zip his lip. "I never even heard her name. And Akram?"

"Well, other journalists seem to know about him, so I guess that's fine."

Saleh looks at his watch. "Curfew starts in twenty minutes. So unless you have a special military pass from your American friend—"

"I don't."

"Then you'd better get going. But look, I need you to help me, too." His throat clicks a few times, as if trying to swallow an insistent wad of phlegm. "I really need a new job. My family name is associated with the Ba'athists, mostly because of my father. I'm not going to be able to keep my job with the UN now that the Americans are demanding they fire all Ba'athists, and it's going to happen soon. I need a job like yours, in the news with foreigners. Or even with a foreign aid organization. I don't care where. Just not the army. I avoided the damn Iraqi military, I'm not going to work for the Americans. You know my English is excellent. Maybe not like yours, *ustaz*, but more than decent."

I smile at his compliment, calling me something akin to professor. It's a way of saying you really respect someone who is a teacher of any sort. But this is the second time he's asking me, and given Sam's reaction, the conversation makes me uncomfortable.

"Not even a job, Nabil, just introductions. You know how it works. Foreigners are afraid of us and they don't know who they can trust. But a recommendation from people they know, that's what gets a man a job." He looks into my eyes, hard but intimate. "You know that, don't you?"

"Sure."

"So just try. Try for me and I'll try for you. If you can't, if the woman you're working for says no, then it's not a problem. I have other contacts. But the truth is, I need the money. We are looking into going to a private doctor in Europe to see about our problem, you know," and he falls into a whisper, his head so low it's as if he's talking to his belt buckle, "about why we haven't had a baby yet. These doctors cost a lot of money. Can you believe, in the middle of a war, the country being invaded, people stealing and kidnapping and killing each other in the street."

He looks towards the door, then back at me. "All that," he mouths almost soundlessly, "and all my wife can talk about is wanting to have a baby! That, and this bloody dream about the UN being blown up with me in it!"

He dismisses his tea cup towards its saucer, but it slips from his hand and fails to regain its composure, spilling its speckled brown contents on to the table.

24

Spilling

It's close to the 9 p.m. curfew when Rizgar drops me off, grumbling about how he'll hardly make it home in time, how he should have let me take a taxi. A few days ago, I began to ask him to drop me at least two blocks from my house, because after all, there's no need for everyone to see me getting dropped off each evening in a chauffeur-driven car. People will wonder why I never came home in this fashion before. Baba warned me not to tell anyone who doesn't already know that I'm working with Sam.

The neighbourhood is dark and silent. It used to be that everyone would have their televisions on at this hour, but there is no electricity tonight, like the night before. I guess people are cooking on gas stoves or talking quietly near their propane lamps or making love by candlelight or telling stories to their children. We are doing many things at home in the evening these days, but watching television is not one of them.

I walk towards our house, open the front gate and close it quietly behind me. I hope that Baba bought a small generator like he said he would so we can watch television again and hook up the new satellite dish I bought with my first week's salary and do something else at night, something other than just sitting by the dim candles and listening to the radio.

And just as I'm passing the car park, I have a feeling that something isn't right but now it's too late because I hit a pole, except there's no pole here, and I haven't hit anything but something has hit me. And then I realize that it's a man's hand that's slammed across my mouth and his other arm is across my chest and I start to squirm but then I feel the cold metal pressing into my temple and am conscious that there's another man with him and the sound of the safety lock being released is like a deafening rush in my head that smothers my ability to breathe, to think, to do anything at all.

"Don't move," the man with the gun against my head says, and he could never know that my real fear is that I will faint and he'll think that I moved and that will be the end of it. "If you say a word we're going to distribute your brains all over your baba's nice big Mercedes over there." The gun is cool against my head, like ice on hot skin on a sweaty day, and I feel oddly thankful for the low resting temperature of metal because it may be the only thing saving me from melting.

"Listen, Amari." It is another man now, and though I cannot see him I can suddenly picture him: one of the thug-boys from middle school, grown fatter and thicker. "We suggest you stop working with all foreigners. Particularly the Americans."

I'm coming to hate this label – the Americans. As if Sam represents the Americans as a whole, as if she is the same as the soldiers who dropped bombs on our homes and rode into our cities on their tanks. I think I could bite the man's clammy hand and hurt him, but I realize the futility of this, as the gun presses even harder against my temple.

"Do you understand?" The man with the gun hisses in my ear. Then the other man lifts his hand from my mouth and pushes me up against the car park wall. Unlike the gun, the concrete is surprisingly warm against my face, as though exhaling all the heat it has reluctantly accepted throughout the day. "If you turn around in the next sixty seconds, we'll shoot you in the head and you'll be gone so quickly, even doctor-baba won't be able to help you."

I hear clicks again and I wish I knew something about guns, to at least know for sure whether he is switching the safety lock on or off, or maybe rotating the revolver a few times just to scare me.

I hear the man who is holding my hands mutter something in the other's man's ear. "Yes, and your friend," the man with the gun says, poking the barrel hard against my temple before pulling it back a bit. "We'll get her, too. She'll go back to America in a pretty coffin with a red, white and blue flag draped on it. Would you like that?"

I feel a quiver in my neck but *stop it*, I will stop it from swelling into a flinch, a palpable shudder. The thought of something happening to Sam feels worse than something happening to me. And then, the second man rearranges his grip to hold me at my elbows, which sends a bolt of pain through my shoulders, and then he pins my hands in the small of my back and finally lets go. I can now feel the gun against the back of my head.

"They are just innocent journalists," I say. "They don't agree with their government." Sam told me this is true, that most of the American journalists here don't even agree with their government's policy, and that most of them didn't vote for Mr Bush. But neither did we vote for Saddam, and did that make the Americans think we were innocent? I have been fighting the urge to struggle against the clamp of their arms holding my arms, their hands stronger than my hands. But once they let go, I have to fight my instinct to twist and run. But to where? To my father, inside the house? I am practically inside my house. They know where I live.

"No! Not just journalists." It is the man who slammed his hand into my mouth, the one without the gun. Between my tongue and my lips I taste blood, sweet and salty, and I draw my mouth in on itself and hope the bleeding will stop before the thought of it starts to make me nauseous. "They're Americans. We in the neighbourhood resistance committee have ruled that no one here should work with Americans. Do you understand, Amari?"

I wonder if they even know my first name and if they know Sam's name or whether they just heard something about me or about her, a picture not quite complete, and as I'm thinking this, the man with the gun puts the barrel into the hollow of my right cheek and pushes harder.

"The infidels are only here to occupy our country and exploit it. They're here to steal our oil and defile our women. No collaborators will be tolerated."

It is pointless for me to say another word. The one without the gun has a sandpaper voice, and he leans in towards me, hangs an elbow on my shoulder and puts his mouth up to my ear. "Do you understand?"

"Yes," I murmur.

"You know, you might think of joining the resistance, too," he says. "We could use English-speakers like you. Think about it."

I can feel the heavier one, the one who first jumped on me

and clamped my mouth, moving away and heading for our gate, whispering for his friend to hurry up. I can sense the gun being tucked into the front of the man's trousers, and the sound of a half-laugh, as though amused by my compliance, waiting there for the next order.

"Sixty seconds," says the man at the gate, the gunman. "Start counting." I hear a small explosion somewhere to the south and it makes me feel insignificant. Somewhere in Baghdad, someone else's house or car or store or Bradley Fighting Vehicle is getting blown up. Why would anybody care if there's a man holding a gun to my head just outside my doorstep?

"Count!"

And I do, and I can hear them run for the gate, leap over it without using the door. When I get to twenty-five and can't hear them anymore, I stop counting and rush to the gate, where I can see the soles of their trainers rising and falling, growing faint somewhere at the end of my street.

25

Growing

SAM'S DOOR FLIES open with such a rush that it fans my face and forces my eyes shut. "*Gooood* morning!" she says to my closed lids. She sounds artificially cheery, like one of the radio anchors back in Birmingham. She looks surprised to see me. "You're early. It's not yet 9."

"I couldn't sleep last night, and got up early. But I can wait downstairs."

"Wait, before you do," she says, and indicates for me to come inside. Once the door is closed, she talks quickly, and in a lowered voice. "Can we go to Tikrit today?"

"Tikrit? Well, I guess so. Why?"

"Miles asked me to. He wants me to verify the signatures on the documents. Even one man who knows Uday or the other signers and can vouch for a signature."

"Who, you mean, Uday's signature? That's…we can't do that."

"Nabil, you never know what you can or can't do until you try." She takes some milk from the refrigerator and stirs it into the coffee she was making. "Do you want a cup?"

I ponder the container of instant coffee on the counter, deciding to say yes, but not quickly enough.

"Oh, right, you hate my coffee. Picky, picky," she says. "So yeah, why don't you go wait downstairs in the lobby and I'll be down in ten minutes. I'm not quite ready to go. Oh, wait in the main lobby, not in the one downstairs. Lately that Rafik gives me the creeps. I don't want him picking your brain while you wait for me. And don't tell him what we're working on."

I make for the door, but pause before I open it. "Sam, you do know it could be dangerous, going to Tikrit now? And to get someone to look at a signature and say it's real or not real? And how can we trust *that* person? What difference would it make?"

"All the difference in the world," she says. "In Miles's mind anyway." She puts her hand on the wall and leans into it.

"Isn't it already clear from what we saw yesterday that Akram's documents are fake?"

Sam shakes her head. "No, Nabil. It's not enough that something looks clear. It has to *be* clear. That's why people like Harris Axelrod get into trouble. You can't run a story on a hunch. We need concrete proof," she says.

I nod and she looks at me with a little bit of embarrassment in her eyes. "Nabil, I'm sorry about last night. I think I overreacted to your questions."

"No, I should—"

"No, it's me. It's your country and I want to understand your culture. I'm learning a lot from you." She drops her hand from the wall and clasps it in the other one. "I told you I like people who ask a lot of questions. That's why I hired you. I guess I'm just not as good a sport when the subject of the questions is me."

Is I, I think. The subject is I. Though I can't be sure, because certainly her English must be better than mine. Or maybe in America it's different? I think about the strangeness not just of the American language, but of the American mind. Concrete proof. As if truth were so hard in that way, like rocks and cement. In Iraq it is rarely so.

"Sam, I—" What happened last night is on the tip of my tongue, but why bother? It'll only worry her, and what can she do? Either I want to keep working with her, or I don't. "I'll just wait for you downstairs."

I take a chair next to the youngest man in the lobby. He is well-dressed and has what I think of as a stylish haircut which makes me think he's not from here, though otherwise he certainly looks Arab. His legs are crossed, the top one playfully kicking in the air.

When I check my watch, I notice that a full two minutes have gone by.

What is it about sitting in a hotel lobby that is so awkward? Even, dare I say it, humiliating? Everyone knowing that you're waiting for someone, and that they have kept you waiting. For ten minutes, or for an hour? No one around you knows exactly. And yet, we're all waiting here, for one of them, *il aganib,* the foreigners. Our bosses. Our big salaries. I can see it in their faces.

The young man turns to me and to my surprise opens in perfectly clear British English, almost like mine, but with a regional accent I cannot place.

"Are you enjoying it?"

"Enjoying what?"

"Being her fixer."

"I'm her interpreter," I say. "*Mutargim.*"

"You don't need to translate for me, mate," he says, and switches to Arabic. "*Mutargim* sounds nice, when you say it in

Arabic. But when you're not around, she'll say you're her fixer, just like the rest of them."

I shrug, wishing I had a newspaper with me. "What's the difference?"

"Well, an interpreter, out in the real world, is someone who gets paid by senior government or business people and is expected to do the work of interpreting their conversations. For example, I know someone who worked for the United Nations, and there he was treated with dignity. Here, with the journalists, they pay you more, but they don't treat you with respect."

I can think of many moments where Sam and I have had difficult conversations, where we have disagreed, and where she has been perhaps a little too direct. Even too demanding or lacking in patience. But I wouldn't say she ever treated me with disrespect.

"A fixer is a fixer because they want us to fix everything for them, from start to finish. They don't want us to just interpret what's said in the interviews. They want us to arrange their meetings, get their money changed, go and fetch food and supplies for them, go ahead of them to check on the situation to see if it's safe enough for them to go. My fellow sat down to send his story yesterday after I'd been chasing about with him all day, and while he sat there in his comfortable, air-conditioned office, he asked me to go out and buy him a case of bottled water to drink, and some chocolates. Hands a little stack of dinars to me, doesn't even look me in the eye when he does it. Doesn't say please or thank you. Then looks at me while I'm standing there and says, "Do you think you need more?" And then as I'm leaving he asks me to stop by the INC headquarters and see if we can get an interview with Chalabi."

"You, too? Sam is trying to get an interview with him. We haven't succeeded yet."

"What am I? An errand boy? The illiterate man around the office who makes the coffee? I am expected to translate these interviews, but also to pick up food and fuel and other supplies? And when I come back, if I've spent too much, I have to explain why I didn't get a better price!"

He spits into the standing ashtray, about as high as his waist, to his right. A puff of grey particles go flying. "They treat us like they own us. That's what a fixer is to them. Someone you own. Someone who will do anything you say. And we do it, because we have no choice. Just like the old days. Still living with a dictator, just a different kind."

As he gives vent to his anger, I notice the sad lines running from the bottom rim of his eyelashes towards the arms of his bookish spectacles. He is lean and extraordinarily muscular, as I could be if I had some way to get exercise. I wonder if Sam could get me permission to swim laps in the pool.

"Sorry," I clear my throat. "I don't think I caught your name."

He holds out his hand. "Taher al-Zubeidy."

"Nabil al-Amari."

"I know."

"Sorry?"

"I just mean that I know your name because I'm often sitting here in the lobby waiting for my bloody journalist, and so I made friends with one of the guys behind the desk. He mentioned your name."

I glance over to the desk and notice that the man from the first day, the one who gave me nasty looks, is not around. I glance at my watch; the face is more scratched than I'd noticed before.

She said just a few minutes.

"What did you do before?" I ask Taher.

"Me?" he points to himself, as if I had struck up a conversation with *him* out of the blue.

I nod. He takes off his glasses and rubs the inner corners of his eyes. "I was living in London," he says.

"Oh? I lived in Birmingham for a year and a half."

He raises his eyebrows and looks away, seeming less than impressed, and already bored with me. "Yeah, well, we've been there for ten years. My parents convinced me to come back to witness the supposed liberation and to test whether it was safe for them to return. In truth, they wanted me to check on our house and our relatives. Well, our house has long since been taken over by people I don't know, with more guns than I have ever seen in my life. My relatives are destitute, and they think my parents should have sent over more money with me to give *them*. I didn't have a job in London anyway, but I had just been accepted on a post-graduate course."

"Doing what?"

"Architecture and urban planning."

"*Wallahi*, that's very impressive." I search for things to say. Should I ask him what kind of structures he hopes to build? He seems so miserable. I wonder what I would be like if we had stayed in Britain. "We'll need good architects when the war is over," I offer. "You can be the new Harun al-Rashid, directing the great reconstruction like in the Abbasid Dynasty."

He gives a sceptical frown. "The war's not ending anytime soon. And this itself is going to be the big business for the foreseeable future. Not building – destroying. And just because I speak English, I can sit here and take part in capturing the destruction, so people back in England can say, 'Oh my, oh dear, dreadful, isn't it?' And then go back to their tea and crumpets and wish Mohammed at the chip shop well and go on with their nice, middle-class lives."

I wish Sam would come. "So why did you stay?"

"What choice did I have? I was here and I went into the Sheraton Hotel to see if I could make an international phone call, and I met a journalist from Sky News. When they found out I was a native Iraqi with perfect English, they offered me a job. Starting at $150 a day, and they give me work every single day. I don't take any days off and they're very happy with that. Do you think I could make $4,500 a month in Britain right now, without anything more than a university degree? And do you know how hard it is to get a job when you have an Arab name? England sucks. It sucks here, and it sucks there, too. So may as well stay here."

I glance at my watch again with a slight tilt of my wrist. In five more minutes I will use the internal hotel phone to check on Sam. Tell her that Rizgar says that if we're going to Tikrit, we'd better get going.

"How old are you?" I ask flatly, hoping it will sound neutral.

"Twenty-one." I had already begun to suspect he was young, but not that young. His body is fit, but the lines around his cheekbones make him look like he could be almost ten years older. "You?"

"I'm twenty-eight. Almost 29." I imagine that sounds old to him. When I entered my twenties, people who were leaving them were, unlike me, actual adults.

"Married, then?"

"No." I can picture Noor, and then Noor falling to the floor, and so I stand up quickly. "Really? Handsome bloke like you? Isn't everybody here usually married by the time they're twenty-five?"

"Not everybody. You know, not all of the foreigners lack respect. Some do, but the woman I work with is really an excellent journalist."

"Yeah?" He laughs with a glaze in his eyes. "I'm sure she thinks you're an excellent fixer!"

I offer him my hand, and he rises quickly and shakes it in both of his. "Oh, I'm sorry. I hope I haven't said anything to offend."

"Of course not. It's just that I need to go back to confer with her now."

"Aah. I see. She wants you in on the decision-making, does she?" He waves out a hand in an effeminate way. "Off you go!" His voice is raised an octave, making him sound like one of the schoolteachers in England, sending us out to play at breaktime. "Come back in an hour!" He looks around, as if speaking to someone just beyond me. "'Would someone send the fixer out and tell him to come back in an hour?'"

I wait for him to stop, hoping that no one is listening.

"Hey, Nabil. Sorry. Just taking the piss. Passing the time."

"That's all right. But I do need to go. You take care now."

At the desk, I ask the man to dial Sam's room. She picks up immediately, and before I even say a word, she knows it's me. "Ten seconds!" she says, almost shouting. "I'll be down in ten seconds."

26

Shouting

FAISAL HAMDANI. As we drive, my fingers repeat his name on my invisible typewriter. Sam's editors say that's the man whose relatives we want to find today. Faisal Hamdani. Or, according to some places where his full name is written out, Faisal Mohammed Hamdani al-Tikriti. His name is on each of the Jackson documents. He's a distant cousin of Saddam's, but judging from the description, looks nothing like him. He's slighter, fairer, and rather nice-looking, to the point of appearing more Italian than Arab. His eyes are greenish-brown and he's a good dresser. Same big moustache, though.

This according to a source, "a friend of a friend", but Sam won't tell me who, who's said he's seen Hamdani on several occasions. Hamdani, the source says, may or may not be in Tikrit, and if he is, he's probably in hiding. Several of his family members, however, would certainly be there. Perhaps one of them could verify the signature. I try to press her for more, working to convince her that at this point, it might be better if I know everything she knows. She says she got the info on Hamdani from a well-informed American source. "More than that, it's better you don't know," she says, and I don't know how I'm supposed to interpret that.

On our way to Tikrit, we pass the detritus of the old regime: buildings that have wilted like flowers past their season, burned-out Iraqi military equipment left like crushed aluminium cans on the roadside. Even the fertile green areas seem to be yielding a crop of rubbish and ripped plastic bags. There's something about the landscape that I don't recognize.

Faisal Hamdani. Should I have known this name? I don't, but Sam does. She says if you read any of the books written about Iraq in recent years, you can find mention of him. As we drive north, she begins to fill me in on what she's read and heard. Faisal Hamdani is considered deeply loyal, not particularly political, and financially astute. Most importantly, he was one of the only three people entrusted with keeping tabs on Saddam's cash.

Cousin Faisal. A blood relative, a member of the clan, probably a player in Saddam's inner circle. Most likely, a man of substantial wealth and the means to maintain a small militia to protect himself. If any of these things are accurate, we should probably turn the car around and head back to Baghdad. The more I think about it, I cannot believe Sam's editors have compelled her to go into Tikrit searching for such people. Even more unbelievable is that I haven't really tried to stop her. We are barrelling up the highway at 130 kilometres an hour, the villages beside the road a haze of muddy brown and palm green. Rizgar makes an emergency stop and the abruptness of it throws us forwards, a feeling that our bodies and the car are at cross-purposes.

"Shit!" Sam is pushing, involuntarily, on the back of my seat; she had agreed to let me sit in the front in the interest of safety in the countryside. Neither of us had noticed the line of cars up ahead, which we might easily have crashed into at that speed. At the end of the queue are two tanks, various military vehicles, and soldiers in clothes the same colour as the desert.

Rizgar turns around. "Sorry, Miss Samara."

"Okay, okay," Sam says. "But I don't want to get stuck waiting at some checkpoint. Just drive up to the front of the line."

"Do you think we should?" I ask. "There are a lot of people waiting. If we skip the line it will be very obvious and then people will know that we are foreigners."

Sam stares out of the window to her right and I follow her gaze. A framed and encased photograph of Saddam, perhaps twenty feet tall, emerges from the grassy garden just to the side of the road. In it, he wears his full military regalia and a smile that is almost that of a roguish youth. In the picture, he looks trim and almost dashing – it must have been taken twenty-five years ago.

"They haven't touched it," Sam says with wonderment. "Not even a dot of graffiti."

Rizgar chuckles quietly; from the corner of my eye, I can see his belly shake. "*Tadhkar!*" he says. Souvenirs. "Tell her! It's a good souvenir. Maybe we can get one for her to bring home."

I translate this for Sam and she grins and doesn't answer, but has already slipped her camera out of her bag and is holding it to the window. She winds down her window and I hear her camera devour a few images. And then there is someone in my face, in front of the windscreen, and another guy knocking on my window near the front passenger seat.

His knuckles rap the glass louder, and I look at Rizgar and then roll the window down.

"*Salaam Aleikum,*" I say to the young man, whose eyes glitter with agitation.

"No photographs. You tell her not to photograph here or we will make sure you don't leave Tikrit. No more American pictures for laughing at!"

"Sam, put the camera away," I say, trying not to stare at the pistol on the other guy's waist.

Sam takes the lens away from her face and squints. "Is that what this guy's on about?"

"Just put the camera away and don't make eye contact with him."

She complies and looks in the other direction. The line moves up by a centimetre and the man who threatened us, accompanied by two friends, disappears down a sidestreet.

"Well," says Sam. "So much for trying not to make it obvious that we're here."

My head screeches with a thousand retorts for everything Sam has said and done in the past week. I don't know how I will contain them any longer. She doesn't consult me enough.

"Maybe you shouldn't take pictures when we come to a place like this."

Sam sighs. "That's fine. Just tell me ahead of time. I can't read your mind."

I tell Rizgar we should make for the front of the line after all.

"What?" Sam grabs on to the handle on the ceiling. "I thought you said you didn't want to go making a scene by getting in as foreigners!"

"Yes, but it's too late now. Those men already saw you taking pictures. Do you think there are many Iraqi women holding thousand-dollar digital cameras out of the window when they are entering Tikrit?"

Sam puts up her hand like a stop sign. "Fine, I get the point.

Just *tell* me when you want me not to do something I would normally do, like taking pictures. That's part of what I do, remember?"

Rizgar lurches to the front of the line so that we're only two cars from the inspection point. Some of the drivers behind us are honking their horns, though no one gets out of his car. A soldier, fattened by his gear, his hands positioned to shoot the M16 hanging around his chest, rushes to Rizgar's side and kicks his bumper. "What the fuck do you think you're doing?" He shouts, glaring at Rizgar. The soldier's face is red and his pupils are as tiny as *nuktateen*, two little dots that hover above certain letters in our alphabet.

Rizgar's face flushes. He moves to open the car door.

"Don't, Rizgar!" Sam is lowering her window on the other side. "Let me." She leans her arm and head out of the window. "Sir? Officer? I'm sorry. I didn't mean to make problems for him. He's my driver and I asked him to skip to the front of the line. We're journalists. I'm with the *Tribune*?" She smiles widely at him, and although I know her well enough by now to see something around the edges of her lips that is entirely artificial, she is, none the less, suddenly all the more comely for it. "Sam Katchens from the *Tribune*." She holds a business card out of the window, and with the other hand a plastic badge that says "PRESS" on it.

"Yeah? I see," he says, taking the card in the hand that is not on the trigger. His lips move as he reads the name. "Ma'am, I'm sorry, but there's no more preferential access for media."

"What? Really?" Sam is speaking a little more sweetly than she normally would, and more slowly. "I was here twice since Tikrit was captured, and they always let us go through."

"Well, orders have changed. You'll have to wait in line."

"Really? But…oh sorry, what's your name, sir?"

"Specialist Gavin Johnston."

"Specialist Johnston, please, do you think you could just let us through this time?" She smiles and lowers her head a little, so that she's looking up at him with a wide-eyed, flirtatious face. "It's just that it's not very safe around here and I'm kind of scared. Two guys just threatened us while we were in line."

"Well, if that's your feeling, maybe you shouldn't come to Tikrit."

"But we have to. We just need to get in and get out. We're only looking to find one guy for a report that I absolutely have to do. Please?"

He lingers, looking at her with his mouth half-open. "All right, then. But you better tell your driver he should never do that again. We have orders to shoot anyone who refuses to stop at a checkpoint." He waves to a soldier next to the crossing bar and yells something to him, but the car in front of us has yet to move. Specialist Johnston – and what kind of title is that? – repositions his rifle to his side. He leans back in towards Sam, resting an arm over the window where she sits.

"How's things in Baghdad?" he asks. His pupils seem fuller now and less agitated, and the irises around them more blue.

"A mess," she answers. "But otherwise, quite a kick."

"Must be more interesting than here. We're bored out of our skulls. When we're not gettin' shot at." He looks around to see if the other soldiers are listening. "I hear that you guys got like, parties and stuff down at the big hotels. Is'sat true?"

"Sometimes," Sam emits a silent laugh, and her eyes flutter suggestively. "You'll have to try to get sent out on a visit and see."

The car in front of us begins rolling.

"Which place d'ya stay at?"

Sam winks at him and begins raising her window. "Top secret. But thanks, Specialist Johnston."

I feel angry at Sam, but the truth is, I know I have no right to be. For what could I blame her? Talking our way through the checkpoint? Pacifying a volatile soldier?

We turn towards the centre of town, and come to a sort of square where there remains the only untouched statue of Saddam Hussein I have seen. In years, I want to say, in years, but in fact, it has only been days. In the statue, made of what appears to be a darkened bronze, Saddam cuts a trim military figure on horseback, forever poised to be our hero.

Sam says Rizgar should do a quick detour so I can see the Tikrit Museum. He drives straight to the museum car park, though I tell Sam it's not really so important for me to see it. She says it doesn't matter, we're already here, and we are. The museum is more like a small palace actually, one that has been stomped on by a mythic monster, a destroyer who is larger than life. The ends of the building are intact, while the centre is nearly flattened. The brokenness in the middle makes a fascinating valley that I follow with my eyes many times over. Why does one part get spared and another destroyed?

"Amazing, huh? When we came here, all the local folks were saying it's a sign of America's attempts to wipe out Iraqi culture. But the Americans say it was just a big propaganda house for Saddam. Apparently it wasn't really a Tikrit Museum but a museum dedicated to Saddam. They're trying to wipe out all the personality cult."

Sam again, calling the Americans *them,* when it's about

things *they've* destroyed. She only makes the Americans *we* when it is something she finds easy to defend, such as American journalistic ethics.

We turn back to the main road, each lamppost carrying its own photograph of Saddam in the different stages of his life, some of them in black-and-white, each in a different costume. A more recent one, the one in his hunting hat, pointing a shotgun into the air with one hand, makes me want to laugh. How ridiculous it now seems, the very notion of Iraq with a strong military. Our Kalashnikovs against their F16 fighter jets. Our trucks against their tanks. Precision bombs versus pathetic bullets, which are liable to tumble through the atmosphere and land up in the belly of a girl like Noor.

I have the urge to tell this to Rizgar, but thinking twice, I don't. Sometimes I can forget for a while that he is a Kurd from the north. He has his *peshmerga*, his Talabani and Barzani tribes to protect him. His people have their defences intact. He is not among the defeated.

Rizgar asks me where to go next. Sam says that she was told to make for the northern part of the town, towards the river, where the grander houses are.

I turn around and face her. "You just want to ask random people when we get there?"

"I don't know. Not so ideal, huh? We could ask to see a sheikh or something."

"I thought you had some kind of lead from your friend."

"What friend?"

"Your CIA friend."

"Jeez! Don't say that out loud! I don't know for certain if he's CIA. What do I know? I'm just a little reporter here who's got an

274

intelligence source, but I wouldn't put a name on it yet. Don't tell *anyone* we might even know a soul in the CIA. Do you know how royally fucked we'd be? Let's just not say those initials again, okay?"

"What, CIA?"

"Nabil, I'm serious. Do you think this is a game?"

I feel my front teeth cutting into my tongue. No, Sam, it's not a game, but you're acting like it is. It's only the three of us in the car, so what does it matter? If I don't lose my hair by the time this war is over, I will have made myself buck-toothed instead.

"You are the one playing with fire."

"Me? I'm the one?" Sam leans into the space between Rizgar and me. I realize now that I prefer having her in front. With her in the back seat, I feel she is hanging on to me, pushing the hair on my neck in the wrong direction.

"Being here is dangerous. And if you want to be discreet about it, you don't stick your camera out of the window just to take some fun pictures."

"Fine! I was wrong." The sound of a page being ripped out of her notebook triggers a nerve inside my eardrums. "But you need to be careful about what you say to people. For everyone's sake. Would you have gone and thrown the word *mukhabarat* around when Saddam was still running the show?" Sam folds the paper she ripped out into a square, and shoves it into her pocket. I hear her exhale with force, as though she is trying to push aside bad air.

Rizgar's eyes are checking me out, as though he's wondering what I did wrong. After a moment, Sam starts again.

"Nabil, this is getting out of hand. I don't mean to overreact. Should we do this, or not?"

Should? I don't know what that means anymore. But I do know the answer she wants to hear. "We'll be fine. We're already here. I'm just afraid they will think you are some kind of American spy and if we ask about anyone related to Saddam, they will think we're looking for him, and then I don't know what will happen." Rizgar pushes in the cigarette lighter, and after a few seconds with no sound but the wheeze of the air conditioning, it pops out. He brings the burning hot circle up to a cigarette dangling from his lips, and for the first time, I envy his habit – an activity to fill the void and stifle the stress.

Sam's head tilts back on her shoulders and her eyes ride up. She seems focused on the ceiling of Rizgar's Impala, as though she's never noticed it before. She puts her finger into a hole in the fabric and pulls it out, ripping it a little wider. He glares at her in the rearview mirror. "Sorry," she says.

"I have an idea," I offer. "I will go to a few houses on foot. You stay here in the car with Rizgar. Keep your sunglasses on. And cover up your face more, so that only your eyes are showing." I pull my hand across my face to demonstrate what I mean.

"You're joking."

"I'm not. Welcome to Iraq."

The door slams. I'm out. The two of them soundless inside and me outside, my head hit by the buzz and heat. I wish I hadn't shut the door as forcefully as I did. I re-open it.

"What did your friend say?"

"He said to try near the homes close to the riverfront and to ask for Abu Wahid, because that's how people know Hamdani here, so—"

The door closes hard again, as if something else, a wind perhaps, is controlling it.

I head towards the houses, each one a comfortable distance from the next. When I look back I can see that Sam's face has half disappeared beneath a white scarf, and from this distance anyway she no longer stands out as a foreigner.

This cannot be so hard. I'll ask people for Abu Wahid and someone will know. Tikrit is a small place. If he was important to Saddam, people will know him. What people? There isn't a soul on the street. I approach a small house on my right. I knock and they say yes, and I say I'm looking for Abu Wahid, and they don't answer. At the second house, a man comes to the door, and I ask about Abu Wahid and he stares at me and says he doesn't know him. The next two houses are shuttered and no one answers at all. As I move on, someone behind me calls out and I spin around, more quickly than I would have liked.

"Are you looking for someone?" Two ageing men, probably in their sixties, are sitting in the shaded doorway of a house, playing *tawli*, which is our version of backgammon. I always thought it funny that there is such an English name for a game that was invented right here in Iraq, a few millennia ago. One of them is shaking the dice in his hand and smiling at me.

"Yes, that's very kind of you." I step over to their side of the road and stop at the gate, which isn't locked. "May I?"

"*Tfaddal, ibni.*" Welcome my son, he says, and lets the dice tumble against the wooden side of the playing board. The metal gate creaks as I push it open, and whines behind me as it closes. I take a few steps closer. "I'm looking for Abu Wahid. Or even some of his family." I'm not sure how that sounds, but it's been said.

The other man, who has barely looked at me, takes his turn with the dice. When he is happy with his roll, he laughs and smacks his hands together, quickly rearranging the configuration of the board. He laughs again and leaves his jaw open, revealing only a sparse attendance of teeth. There are small stains on his *dishdasha*. He is older than I first thought.

"Why do you want him?" The other man, the slightly younger one, takes the dice and jiggles them rhythmically in his hand.

"Well, I need to ask him something. I, I think someone may have tried to use his signature improperly and I want to find out so I can clear his name."

He yawns and tosses the dice again. "Oh, is he in trouble?"

"I don't know. I'm just – do you know where I can find him?"

"You still haven't told us who you are."

"I'm a teacher from Baghdad. My name is Nabil. Nabil Amari," I hold out my hand, and the younger of the two grasps it for a moment, after which his eyes fall back to the board. "I am doing some work, some work for a journalist who wants to disprove some of the lies that have been said in the West about President Saddam." I can feel my pulse pounding in my neck, that banging in my chest like the feeling I get each year when I walk into a classroom for the first time. Why did I say *that*?

"Oh? What kind of journalist? Where from?"

"Ireland." If someone passed Sam on the street, wouldn't they think she was Irish? Many of the Irish kids I met in Britain had red hair.

"Ireland," the older man spoke up, sending spittle onto the younger fellow's hand. "Did Ireland help the Americans occupy the country?"

"I don't know," the junior player says. "Nabil, did the Irish help the Americans invade Iraq?"

"No, no. Ireland was very much against." I have no idea how Ireland behaved, or if Ireland had any say at all. Isn't Irish policy whatever Britain says it should be?

"Really? That's good." He pulls out the white plastic chair, its seat half baked to powder by sun, and drags it next to him. "Do you want to sit? Drink some tea."

"Oh, really, I would like that, but there are some people waiting for me and this matter is very important, so I must keep moving until I can find Abu Wahid."

"Well," the man says, resting his arm onto the back of the chair. "I don't think you'll find him. He's probably gone by now. But I do know some family members you could talk to." He reaches for the remains of the tea glass on the table. He swirls the grainy liquid with interest, frowns and puts the cup down. "I would like to help you, but I think they might be very angry if they knew I was helping some outsiders locate them. You know, the situation around here these days is very bad. Raids all the time, the Americans breaking into our houses and arresting people in the middle of the night, or while we're having dinner with our families. They come in and look at the women." He meets my eyes. "The financial situation is especially bad."

"I understand."

"Really, it's terrible. The Americans are blocking us from going anywhere, no one can work. A man needs to feed his family."

"I wish there was something I could do to help."

"Yes. Perhaps there is. I'm sure there are at least fifty people in Tikrit who would like to kill me simply for sitting here talking to you, if you're working with foreigners." He returns to the game, and the other man does the same.

I take the tiny notebook out of my back pocket, and then reach into my right front pocket, where I keep a little bit of cash. I pull out a wad of dinars, worth about $30, and fold it between the pages of the notebook, letting the crisp blue edges stand out. I place the notebook on the table next to the older man's hand. "Could you write me some directions to the place I'm looking for? I don't really know my way around this area."

The man takes the notebook, and the bills disappear under his sleeve. Sam probably wouldn't like it, but there is no other way. Using my pen, he scribbles a quick script in the notebook, then hands it back. "Suad al-Hamdani, in Al-Tamer neighbourhood, just south of here, in Ad-Dawr." He looks up at me. "That's Faisal's sister. She should be around."

I offer my thanks. He says I should be as quiet about his identity as he will be about mine.

"Actually, *hajj*, I didn't get your name."

"That's fine," he answers, happy that I have bestowed this honorific on him, which is appropriate for a man of his age, regardless of whether he's made the pilgrimage to Mecca. "I don't remember yours either. Nizzam was it?" He grins wider, almost towards a laugh, and stands up to shake my hand. He is much taller than he appeared to be when he was seated, almost a full head above me. His hand feels like worn leather, but the grip is strong.

The older man looks up at me and nods. "Be careful, now. There are a lot of crazy people out there." I nod in agreement and wish them well. I rush off down the street, forcing myself to slow down to a walk. Sam will be thrilled we have names and a location. And what would Sam say if I tell her I paid for it? She's been clear – we needed to come here to get something done. And look, I'm getting it done. How else could I have done it? It's an investment in getting the story. If she were an Iraqi, she would understand that sometimes there is no other way.

And if she were an Iraqi, she would never be doing the job she's doing now. She'd never have been my boss.

I hurry towards the corner where they left me, but Rizgar's car isn't there. I scan up and down the main road but I can't see them anywhere. Why would they leave? Didn't they say they would wait for me there? Why didn't I take the phone?

The sun is beating on me like a *masghouf* fish baking in the oven. I walk towards the shade of a few palm trees along the road. Where are they? What if someone noticed Sam and tried to kidnap them? What if she gets killed and the Americans hold me responsible? What if her family thinks it's my fault?

What if someone tries to kill Rizgar and rape Sam?

I can feel the sweat slipping down my back, the urge to pace. Suddenly I remember something my grandmother used to say. *Al ajala min as-shaytan watta'anni min ar-rahman.* Haste is the devil's work and patience is from the Merciful One. Just be patient, Nabil. But working with Sam has not taught me patience. And there is nothing, as far as I can see, that is patient about the process of journalism.

A few men in passing cars stare at me as they go by. Where *are* they?

I crouch closer to the earth, the way the day labourers do when they're waiting for a lift. Like this, maybe I'll pass for a farmhand. And if I wind up passing out in the sun, I won't have far to fall.

Finally I see the low-lying hood of Rizgar's Impala round the corner down the street. The car slowly pulls up next to me with the passenger-side window down. I suppose my face must give away my mood.

"What's wrong?" Sam, now in the front, looks baffled. "Is everything all right?"

I jump in and shut the door. "It's fine. I just thought you were going to wait for me here."

"We were," says Sam. "But there were some people watching us so we decided to beat it and keep driving around. We drove by one of the palaces. I was dying to go inside to check it out but we wanted to get back here to you of course."

"I have some names of Hamdani's relatives. I think we should just go quickly and find them and then return to Baghdad."

She looks over her shoulder at me. "Realistically? There's about a million troops in control of this town?"

Does Sam make her equations that way? If there are a lot of American troops, then we're safe? What if it's the other way around? The more of them that are here, the less safe we are. People who drive by us seem to stare into our car for too long.

"Why are you so worried, Nabil? Everyone says Tikrit is totally safe now. Last time we were here, it was fine. Right, Rizgar?"

Fine, except that last time they were here, Luqman, Sam's last fixer, was shot at. Why does she never mention that?

Rizgar shrugs, reminds me that Sam's the boss.

I shake my head. "Let's go to Ad-Dawr now and try to find some of these people and then head back to Baghdad."

Sam relents and we head towards Ad-Dawr. Going out is much easier than it was coming in and I'm not sure why the soldiers are so much more concerned about one direction of traffic than the other. Soon we're at the edge of Tikrit again and the big houses turn into mud huts and shacks. In minutes everything and everyone seems much poorer, as if we were in another country altogether.

I roll down my window to ask someone on the street for the Al-Hamdani family. As we follow his directions, we start rocking over an unpaved road with the Tigris visible at the end of it, dreary and brown.

"What palace did you go to last time?" I ask.

She looks surprised at the question. "Oh, we saw the Zulfakker Palace. It had these enormous carved wooden doors on the front and a sign outside that said the palace was built in defiance of UN sanctions. Isn't that a trip?"

I suddenly feel a well of jealousy against Sam. I would have liked to see Saddam's palaces. Now that he's gone, they're *our* palaces. She continues to explain how it looks, and I'm only half listening. A local person should explain his country to a foreigner, not the other way around. How strange that I'm always seeing Iraq through her eyes, virtually touching it with her hands.

27

Touching

WE KNOCK ON several doors, all locked. Until we get to this one, which isn't even fully closed. After tapping on it a few times, I push it open. And then I have the feeling that maybe it would be a terrible idea to just walk in like that and so I step back, just as a voice calls out. "Marwan? Marwan is it you?"

"No, no. Uh, no, it's – I'm sorry, I was looking for someone from the Hamdani family." A woman appears from the hallway and looks frightened when she sees me, but after she notices Sam she seems more confused than anything else.

"I was just, pardon me, I was just looking for the Hamdani family and I thought that – is this the right place?"

She stiffens. Her fingers are arthritic, bent at unusual angles that look uncomfortable. "Who are you looking for?" Her clawish fingers grab for each other as if for solace. "Who are you?"

"I'm Nabil al-Amari, from Baghdad. This is Miss Samara. She's a Western journalist I work with."

Sam, hearing her name, bows her head slightly and smiles.

"We wanted to find some of the relatives of Abu Wahid," I say. "Faisal al-Hamdani?"

"You're looking for Abu Wahid?"

"Well, yes, it would be a pleasure to meet Abu Wahid. But we understand that he's probably not here."

She looks at me with hurt in her eyes and I can see that her hands are now trembling.

"Are you his relative then?"

"I'm his sister."

"Ah, I see, it is such a great pleasure to meet you. Such a pleasure to meet someone from such an esteemed family."

She smoothes her houserobe a bit, attempts to stand up straight, become taller, and smiles almost without moving her lips.

"We're very concerned about Abu Wahid's welfare," I say.

She eyes us standing in the doorway, as if trying to decide whether she should invite us in or tell us she cannot be of help. "Please," she says at last. "You must come in and have tea."

"That would be lovely, Sayida Suad. Pardon me, but you are Suad then, yes?" She nods and holds a craggy hand out to invite us inside. "We won't stay too long," I say. "We're just passing through town."

She leads us into a room of middle-class size, but which is wrapped in an upper-class veneer, and points to places for us to sit. The floor is covered with a red Persian carpet that I know costs at least $2,000 in the market, and the cushions are covered in a velvet fabric. An air of abandonment mopes about the room. Suad leaves us, shuffling off to make tea.

Sam refuses to sit, and takes herself for a tour, ogling the art on the walls. There are two cheap paintings of Saddam, and many family photographs, all well-framed.

"Don't ask any funny questions about Saddam," I whisper. "I made it sound like we're on their side."

Sam views me with a shot of scepticism.

"It was the only way I could think of to get her to let us in. So, if you can, play along."

Sam sits, reluctantly, and leans back into the cushion against the wall. She takes a breath that sounds like a sigh in reverse. A young man in his early twenties appears at the door, his eyes open so wide it seems as if he's in a state of shock.

I rise to shake his hand and exchange greetings. Sam stands up, her hands clasped. He must be Suad's son. I search his face for signs of Saddam, marks of the same genes as our great leader, murderous and missing. I see none, other than meaty skin with big pores. Saddam's skin always looked like sandpaper, as if even a lover who brushed his face would be chafed by it.

The young man takes a seat opposite us, taking interest only in watching us and stroking the scant beard growing around the perimeter of his chin. I try to make small talk with him, but he hardly responds, offering a guttural motion to wait for his mother. Maybe he has some sort of speech problem.

Suad comes in with a tray of orange-coloured drinks that appear to have a bit of juice mixed in and sets them down before us. I'm feeling a bit guilty that she has had to bother, when all I want is to have her look at the signatures on the documents, recognize them or not, and then leave. She sits down next to Sam, rather than next to her son, which somehow surprises me.

Suad hadn't been wearing a scarf when we walked in, but now she's draped a white one over her head. She has what my father calls country features – a wider nose, thicker lips, a fleshy face.

She waits for Sam to sip the juice and when she does, the rest of us follow suit. "Why are you looking for my brother?" she asks.

"Do you work for the Americans?"

"No, no," I say. "We work for a newspaper."

"From what country?"

"Oh, Germany. An important newspaper in Germany."

"Is that German you were speaking to each other? With the lady?"

"Yes." Something churns in my stomach. Maybe the water mixed in with the juice is bad. What if the son isn't as stupid as he looks?

"We think maybe your brother will be accused by the Americans of doing things he didn't do. They'll look for him and they'll try to accuse him of war crimes, along with Saddam. Abu Wahid never hurt anyone, did he? I mean, he didn't kill people."

"Of course not!" Her face is indignant, her skin a spider's web of lines that weren't visible a moment ago. "My brother is an honest man. Only because he was smart and had an important job, he has these problems now."

"Of course," I say. "I imagined so."

Her eyes scan mine for a minute and then she looks to her son, who is staring at Sam. When I catch him, he averts his gaze. I motion to Sam to pass me her bag, and from the main pocket, I pull out the folder. "Would you know your brother's signature if you saw it?"

"His signature?"

"What he would sign, I mean, on a letter or a cheque, or a document. Anything like that. Would you know his handwriting?"

She nods. "I think so. We were only a year apart in school. He is only eighteen months older than me so I used to use his books." She purses her lips together, the skin around them lost in wrinkles. "Actually, I stopped going when I was sixteen because my father wanted me to get married and have a family."

"And this is your son?"

She laughs heartily. "He's my grandson. One of twelve. They left him to take care of me. But instead I think I mostly take care of him."

The young man emits a grunting sound like something hurts, and gets up and walks out.

"Where is your brother now?" It's probably not what Sam would have wanted me to ask, at least not so directly, but that's how it came out.

Her eyes begin to brim with tears. "Everything is the wrong way round now," she says, letting two tears go, and then wiping them with the back of her hand. "We have no one coming here but the American soldiers. No one to protect us. No electricity most of the time. Shooting every night." Her cry is like a near-silent wheeze, her voice suddenly hoarse. "I don't even know where my husband is," she wails. "He said he was only leaving for a few days. That's who I thought you were when I heard you come in."

Sam reaches into her bag and pulls out a packet of tissues. She hands one to Suad who thanks her and dabs at her eyes, leaving a few white shreds beneath her stubby eyelashes. I wait for a moment, until her crying subsides, and then open the folder.

"It would be really helpful if you could look at this." I take out one of the papers and put it on the coffee table in front of Suad. Just tell me if the signature looks like it could be your brother's."

She picks up the paper and puts it in her lap. A teardrop falls on to the paper, and she uses the tissue to blot it. She sighs and blows her nose in the same tissue. I feel an urge to grab the paper back, afraid she'll drip and wipe and ruin it, somehow.

"Nabil, maybe she's too upset to do this. I don't want to force her to talk when she's—"

"No, I think she's fine. She's just sad, but she wants to help."

She examines the paper closely. "Muwafeq?" she calls. "Can you bring me my glasses? Muwafeq! They are just sitting on the table in the kitchen."

The sound of thumping, Muwafeq's slippers slapping over the tiles. The pace of his feet seems syncopated with the beating of my heart, which is pumping just a little too fast. He hands the glasses to his grandmother, then, without looking at anyone, reclaims the seat he had before, cross-armed and sulky.

"Where?" Suad asks.

"Here." I lean over and point to a signature on the sheet. "See, it says in print that it's the signature of Faisal al-Hamdani, and then, here, a signature." I tap on the page. "Is this your brother's signature?"

"This? This is someone writing my brother's name, but it cannot be my brother's signature."

"Are you sure? Sam, she says it's not his signature."

"Really?" Sam leans forwards a bit. "How good do you think her eyesight is?"

"You don't want me to ask *that*, do you?"

"He had very wide letters. Fat and large. Which is funny because he's quite slim. But they say people like to write their names the way they want the world to see them."

"And this?" I indicate for her to look at the second page. "You're sure it can't be his signature?"

"That? No. I'm sure. His signature would be plump and round, like a big man, like watermelons. These are date palms. Too tall. See, this is too angled and neat. I'm sure my brother didn't write this."

"Are you positive?"

"*Taban*," she says, of course. "Why do you keep asking?"

I want to tear out of the house right now, now that we have our answer, now that we're through with what we need here. But the very thought pushes a wave of guilt over me. I'm thinking just like Sam did, that first day I worked with her. Give me what I want, give it to me now. And now that I have it, I'm through with you. Through. Like a lemon that you squeeze for all its juice, and then let go.

"Sayida Suad, you've been so helpful," I say. "Is there anything we can do for you? Anything you need?"

She looks at me and then at Sam, and then her eyes go misty again. "I just want my family back. I want the soldiers to leave us alone. But you can't do anything about that."

I have nothing comforting to offer, except to keep listening.

"Why is somebody imitating my brother's signature? Just to steal? Is it just money?"

"Maybe. Or maybe more than that."

"But what do these documents say?" The question surprises me; she's had them in her hand for a few minutes now.

"Can you read them?"

She scans over them. "I see it's about paying something. I can't tell more than that."

"The reason, I think, is that there are people who want to make everyone who worked with Saddam look bad," I explain. "And they can use papers like these to prove it."

Sam's Thuraya phone is ringing in her bag, which means she must go outside to take the incoming call.

"What's that?" Muwafeq's voice is sluggish. I had begun to think he was unable to speak.

"A phone," I say. "A special phone."

"Let me see it."

"It doesn't work inside," I say. "And actually, we really need to go because there are some people we have to meet later this afternoon in Baghdad. I'm terribly sorry we can't stay longer. You've been so hospitable to us," I tell Suad.

"But I didn't serve you anything yet. I was just heating up a soup for you."

"Oh, well, that is so kind of you, but we really do have to be there—"

"Maybe you're spies," Muwafeq says.

"Muwafeq! Stop it. Don't say such terrible things to guests."

I rise slowly and Sam follows my cue. Suad nods with a tight-lipped grin and says we are welcome anytime. I keep thinking I should give her money but I'm sure Sam will be very angry if she sees me offer it, and all the way back to Baghdad she'll tell me it's as bad as what Harris did and didn't I see by now that it is unethical for me to pay someone for information? I'm not sure Sam could see the difference between buying and giving. Sometimes I just want to give.

Our legs carry us to the door and as we open it I see Rizgar waiting in the courtyard, his eyes peeled. I turn to thank Suad, and she is suddenly a little too close to my face.

"*Man hafara hufratan li-akhihi waq'a fiha.*"

"Sorry?"

"You're such a smart young man," she says. "Do you not

know this saying? It is my favourite. I think everything that is happening in Iraq today can be explained by this." I have to think of how to translate this for Sam.

He who digs a hole for his brother will fall into it.

"I will think about that. Thank you so much, Sayida Suad. Please stay well and safe."

Suad brings her gnarled hands together in front of her, suddenly looking so disfigured that some of the fingers seem broken. As we leave her, she holds one knotty hand up, as if waving goodbye, or to ask a question, or to tell us to stop right there.

28

Waving

NONE OF US says a word as we drive south from Ad-Dawr, not to comment on our relief at getting out of there alive, nor on our various deceptions to get the information we wanted. It's quiet in the car until we reach the outskirts of Samarra.

"Look," I say. "Your namesake city. Funny, isn't it?"

"What, that I'm named after an Arab city?" She grins back at me with an oversized smile, the kind where you can see both the top and bottom rows of teeth.

"You're not, are you?"

"What do you think?"

"So why did your parents name you Samara?"

"Guess they just liked it. Sounded exotic to them. And better than naming me Sarah."

"Why Sarah? I mean, what's wrong with Sarah?"

"Nothing. Just a little boring. It was my grandmother's name. She died a year before I was born so they wanted something with an S."

From the highway, I can see the top of the Malwiya minaret. I remember climbing up the amazing spiral staircase on the outside when I was a child, and the thrill of its grandeur.

"Look, Sam, there is the the Malwiya tower. Maybe we

can stop for a moment so you can see it. You really should."

"Hmm, that is such a nice thought, Nabil. But I think we need to hoof it back to Baghdad. I need to write up some notes for Miles and the other editors. You know, they wanted answers yesterday, and they're turning up the heat on me to get them."

"But everything from Akram yesterday, doesn't that answer things for them?"

Sam has since picked up her digital camera and is fiddling with it, studying the photographs she took earlier. "Actually, it's only the beginning of an answer. What we have at this point is a very blurry picture. Just like this one," she says, and holds the camera out for me to see the shot. In the little screen, I see the shot she was trying to get: the portrait of Saddam. The arm of one of the angry goons cuts a skin-coloured smudge right through the middle of it.

"You can't believe how big a mess this is turning into back home," she says. "Now that Billy Jackson has filed suit, which means he must think he has a decent case, a lot of African-American groups are starting to write letters to the editor and are going on TV, saying that the *Tribune* is racist. And then the lefties who opposed the war are saying that the *Tribune* and all the other mainstream papers are in bed with the Bush administration, so of course they went and ran a story like this. A bunch of conspiracy theories, if you ask me. But the bottom line is there's a lot of pressure to set the record straight."

When we pull up at the Hamra, Sam sends Rizgar off but says she needs me for just a little while longer, to figure out what comes next. In her room, she orders us "lunch" on the phone, even though it's 4 p.m., and I wonder what this means about when she intends to have dinner.

To me, it is impossible to eat a meal and work at the same time. I would rather fast as if it were Ramadan and wait for a proper dinner in the evening. But Sam eats with one hand while racing through her notes with a pen in the other, sometimes letting a drop of hummus fall on to her notebook, a few crumbs on to the keyboard. I have never seen anything like it. In Iraq, we don't eat and work at the same time. To do so shows a lack of appreciation for the food, as well as the person who made it. After all, how many things in life do we really do that cannot wait a half-hour or an hour before being completed? A person shouldn't be expected to take in and put out at the same time. Maybe Americans don't see it that way.

If eating and writing at the same time is not enough, Sam also moves to pick up the telephone when it rings. I offer to answer for her, but she holds the fork in her hand and waves it, which I take to mean "no". Instead, she puts the call on speaker-phone, grabs a tissue on the desk and spits what she was chewing into it.

"Hello, Sam. It's Axelrod."

"Harris!" Her voice bursts as one would when hearing from an old friend after many years. "How are you?"

"Good, Sam. Never been better. Just got back from hanging out with some fishermen in Basra. How's Baggers treatin' ya?"

Sam clears her throat. I can see that she is nervous from the way her eyes search the void in front of her. She quickly opens a file and begins typing. Her fingers are moving much more lightly over the keys than they usually do, like tiptoeing. I suppose she doesn't want Harris to know she is taking the conversation down, word for word.

"Oh, you know, the usual. A few soldiers getting picked off

every morning. America is in the throes of firing the entire Iraqi military, and some of these disgruntled guys are starting up their own militia. So I'm working on a story about that."

"Really?" The tone in Harris's voice sounds pushy, almost bullying. "Now, I thought you were working on a story about me."

"About you?" Sam laughs in a way that impresses me. It is casual, as if she's just having a good joke. "Well, Harris, unless you're planning to start your own militia." She laughs again, and this time, it sounds a bit more forced. She drives her highlighter pen into her notebook, letting the bright-pink ink bleed into a wider splotch.

"Let's cut the bullshit, Sam. We both know what story you're on. I know Miles asked you to check up on my story about Billy Jackson."

"Oh, is *that* what you mean? Well, yeah, of course I'm working on that as well. I wouldn't say that's a story about you. I'm just trying to figure out where those documents really come from."

"What do you mean, really come from? Okay, let me explain it to you again like I explained it to Miles. I got them from General Akram, who got them from Uday Hussein's house. What's so complicated about that? I mean, what are you guys trying to do here?" Something about his voice is condescending, rather like the way a bad teacher belittles a poor student.

"Harris, look. I didn't even want to do this story. But the fact is that we're getting sued by Congressman Jackson, and Miles and everyone in Washington has laid it on me to help figure this out. At this point, we're just checking facts."

Sometimes when I watch Sam, I am entertained by the effort I have to exert to figure out which things are half-truths, which of them white lies, and which of them pure manipulation. She did tell me she wished the paper would send Harris to clean up his own mess – but that was days ago. Lately, she acts as if the story matters as much as anything else in the world. She no longer seems unhappy that they assigned it to her.

"Well, they're refusing to let me work on the story anymore at this point, and they won't even pay my expenses to send me back to Baghdad to clear things up." Harris says. "But I might come back, on a gig with *Harpers* or *Vanity Fair*. They're both quite interested. And with you guys taking this story away from me, it becomes a prime example of how the *Tribune* mishandles things and screws its own reporters. Typical."

"Really," says Sam. "Well, that'd be something." Sam looks at me and her mouth drops open.

"Sam, I heard from Miles last night that General Akram told you I paid him $3,000 for those documents."

She stands up and sits again. Her top teeth bite into her lower lip.

"Sam, it's bullshit. Don't believe a word of it. I didn't pay a thin fucking dime for those documents. I just paid $1,000 to have them translated."

"A thousand dollars to translate documents in Baghdad? That's like, more than a year's salary for most people here."

"C'mon, Sam. You know how it is. You need something done in that town, you gotta pay for it. I was in a rush. Look, I didn't do anything wrong – nothing different than any other reporter would have done. Everybody was shelling out cash for papers. You know it."

"I knew people who gave $50-dollar tips to get into guarded buildings. Not $3,000."

"Jesus. What did I just tell you? I didn't pay $3,000! Shit, I guess I *am* going to have to come to Baghdad, because obviously you're not getting it."

Sam cracks her knuckles softly, plucking each finger out with a snap that I almost feel in my own joints.

"You know how good my reputation is. I've got a book deal on the way. Do you think I'd have gotten this far if I didn't know what I was doing? If I went around buying documents in Baghdad?"

"Harris, I'm telling you, I resisted taking on this story, but they said I had no choice. So I can't do anything about it. I think you have to discuss this with Miles, not me."

"The man hardly has the time of day for me now! He says I should put all further correspondence on the matter in writing. Their fucking lawyers are vetting everything."

"Harris, I wish I could help you more. But I'm actually on deadline so I ought to go."

"Sam! *Sam*, don't you hang up on me. My career is on the line. You're besmirching my reputation. You know, I also could sue *you*. Especially if this is turning into character assassination."

"Hmm. Okay, Harris, I think I've had enough. I'm going to go now."

"Yeah, well, you tell your little translator pal there I say *dir balak*. You just—"

As my finger presses the red END button, I imagine what it would be like to poke my finger in Harris Axelrod's eye. I wonder whether Sam even knows that when someone tells you to "watch out" like that, it usually means they're planning to hurt you. Or at least, wishing something evil happens to you. It's a kind of curse. Sam doesn't seem to mind that I hung up the phone on her behalf, or that I'm standing over her now, so close that I could let myself fall all over her and cover her up and be a shield to protect her. I could wrap her up in me and be her blanket and her bodyguard all in one.

She shakes her head and says, "Smart, Nabil, very smart." She drops her head down and lets her eyebrows rest on the hard, lower edge of her palms. "Why didn't I think of doing that five minutes ago?"

29

Doing

WHILE WE SIT here waiting, I find my mind reviewing everything we did yesterday in Tikrit. That, and all Saleh told me this morning after he arrived at my house at 8 a.m., kissed my parents hello, and then offered me a lift to the Hamra. He pretended it was on his way, but I know it wasn't. As he drove, I listened and took notes. Jotted down places where high-quality forgeries have been known to be done.

Why we'd ever need to go to such lengths, I don't know. There can't be much doubt now that the Jackson documents are forgeries. What more could Miles want?

Plenty, says Sam, starting with Fayez Aloomi from the INC. Aloomi has been a source for other *Tribune* reporters in Washington, and now he's in charge, among other things, of examining and categorizing regime documents that will later be used to build the case against Saddam, if and when the Americans ever find him.

If Aloomi's people say he's going to be back soon, Sam says, we'll gladly wait outside for him. I said that seems menacing – only *mukhabarat* or some other official planning to drag you off for interrogation would do something like that. She laughed and said that was the old Iraq. The new Iraq will be like America. In

America, it's normal for journalists to wait around for hours if they really want to see someone. Especially if he's someone important. Sam said it's called door-stepping; others would call it a stake-out. I told her I thought that was a barbeque. She chuckled again and said that was a cook-out. When she wasn't looking, I changed the spelling in my notebook. Stake, not steak.

We've been waiting in the car for almost an hour, but it feels longer.

"Sam, I was wondering. What do you know about Harris?"

She turns completely around in her seat, so that her back is resting on the dashboard and her legs are folded in the style of an Indian guru.

"I mean, the *Tribune* is an excellent newspaper," I say, "so they would hire only writers with an excellent reputation, isn't that so?"

"Yeah, that's the way it's supposed to work." She coughs. "Please, Rizgar, blow that smoke out the window or you'll get me started again."

Rizgar smiles, puts his half-smoked cigarette between his lips, and steps out of the car.

"Harris was never hired. He's a freelancer who began overseas," Sam says, holding on to the neckrest of the seat and repositioning her own neck from left to right, eliciting a vertebral snap. "So they view him differently than they view a staff writer. But they shouldn't. Most freelancers are great. What's important is that every reporter in the foreign press corps thinks the guy's a sensationalist who makes shit up and cuts major ethical corners."

"So, if Harris had been hired in America, it would be better, but because he has international experience, he is frowned upon?"

"He *is* frowned upon, not because he has international experience, but because as far as we know, he had no local reporting experience. Never covered the cops, the school boards, the local crap every reporter is expected to cover. That's how you learn the ropes. But Harris never did it. He's been war-zone hopping since he graduated college, and he started to make a big name for himself out of it. So who the hell knows what his reporting habits are like. Before Iraq it was Afghanistan, Rwanda, the Balkans. I think he started to make a name for himself there, with a big piece in *Harpers* or *The Atlantic*." She turned her head to one side. "Or maybe it was *The New Yorker*. Whatever. These are the most important magazines in America. Every editor is reading them." She still seems to be struggling to find a comfortable position. "My back is killing me like this. Come sit up here."

Just then, Rizgar swings open the car door and sits down.

"Oh, forget it, I'll come sit in the back." She steps out and shuts the door as quickly as she opens the other. Rizgar shrugs. She slides in next to me and grins with only half of her mouth. She has her left knee on the seat, bent towards me. "Riz, can you turn up the air conditioning? Please. Too hot." She fans her face to demonstrate.

"He doesn't function like a regular journalist," Sam continues. "He goes around rustling up tipsters whom he pays for information. A normal journalist comes to a country and hires one fixer. Harris might hire five or more."

"Like Subhi and Adeeb. But how can he afford that?"

"Well, I don't know. But what I heard from another reporter I really do trust is that when Harris got to Afghanistan, he had a whole gaggle of fixers and tipsters coming to his room every day.

He told each one of them that if they came back with a good scoop on Osama or the Talibs at the end of the day, Harris would pay them $100. And if they don't come back with something, they don't get paid." Sam lets out something of a snort.

I consider this information for a moment. "Does he make that much on a story to cover his expenses?"

"Probably. But forget about the money for a minute." Sam looks at me with her head slightly lowered, so that her eyes glare up at me. "Maybe it was only $50 a day. That's not the point. The point is that you can't just throw money around like that to get information. You can't tell people, 'I'll pay you if you produce some information for me,' because inevitably they'll manage to come up with exactly the information you want, even if it means completely manufacturing it."

"But that's assuming everyone's a liar."

"I'm not assuming everyone's a liar. I'm just telling you it's something you're not supposed to do. You don't go creating a market for information. If you go out there shouting that you have a demand for something and you're just jumping to pay for it, you can bet your bottom dollar someone is going to come around and supply it. That's not even journalistic ethics. It's basic economics. And what you get in return will be tainted by the fact that it was manufactured for the buyer, which in this case, is probably going to translate into being fed a lot of absolute bogus."

Sam takes a ballpoint pen and picks the blue stopper from the top of the plastic shaft. Then she pulls out the tube of ink, and puts the clear shell of the pen in her mouth, inhaling deeply on her substitute cigarette. "All right, this is getting ridiculous," she says, looking at her watch.

"What if it's just gossip?"

"Come on." Deep grooves appear where her smiling lines should be. "That much shit doesn't follow someone around for no reason."

"But what if it's just...*namime*. That's what we call it. Like, in English, I guess you would say chatter. Gossip. It's very bad. We've seen it happen a lot of times when the old ladies start talking about some beautiful young girl whom they think is going out with boys, maybe because they've seen her out with one of them. They start to make up stories about how they saw her with so-and-so, and next thing you know, she winds up dead. They usually say it's a suicide, but everyone knows it's really because a family member has killed her."

Sam suddenly seems fascinated by what I have to say. She is searching my face the way I have seen her do to people she is interviewing.

"But despite what I said the other day, I think it's wrong to call it an honour killing, because most of the time, it's a gossip killing," I say. "Gossip is usually what kills these girls. And often it's the women who are perpetrating the entire thing."

Sam rubs her tired-looking eyes and exhales make-believe smoke. "Do you think we could do a story about that at some point? I think readers would find that fascinating."

"Sure we could." A month ago, that would have sounded preposterous to me. But now, anything seems possible.

"I mean, not now. Not until we figure out this documents thing." And she stops rubbing, but leaves two fingers at the inner corners of her eyes, as if her hand could save her, if only for a moment, from seeing us for who we are.

*

And then it happens, near dark. An assistant approaches the car to tell us we can come in, that Mr Aloomi will see us now. I can't help but wonder, was he here all along, and they were just making a show of him having "arrived"? Wouldn't we have seen a car pull up?

Fayez Aloomi looks younger than I would have expected, a handsome and tanned mid-forties, and he is dressed in the kind of suit I would surely buy if I were to visit England now.

"Thanks a lot for seeing us on short notice," Sam chimes, holding her hand across a desk piled high with paperwork. "I know you must be very busy these days. I really don't want to take up a lot of your time but I came to you because I know you've been really helpful with our reporters in the past. Some people in our Washington bureau are big fans of yours. Joe McClintock in particular sends regards."

"Oh, Joe. He's a fine reporter. I think he did a very thorough job on all of the WMD coverage before the war. He was one of the few reporters who was able to demonstrate how dangerous Saddam really was. In fact, he was the first one to report the uranium story, when it was discovered that Saddam was about to buy yellowcake from Niger. Do you remember?"

"Of course," Sam says. Her eyebrows lift knowingly, almost like a barrier holding back more than she is letting on. "I spend a lot of time in Washington."

"Oh?" He shifts forwards and picks up the card she had put on his desk. "I didn't realize. Your card says Paris Bureau Chief."

"Yes, actually, I'm ending my posting there and taking up a Pentagon posting back in Washington, so I've been in DC a lot in the past year to get a feel for the job." Sam never mentioned that, and I'm wondering if it's true. "By the way, this is Nabil al-Amari, my translator."

He meets my eyes and nods with a quiet, slurred *salaam aleikum*. "Miss Katchens – Samara," he says, picking up her card from his desk. "What a lovely name. Very interesting. Can I call you Samara?"

"Of course."

"Samara, I would appreciate it if this were totally off the record."

"No problem," she says, though I can see the petulance in her face.

"You know," Aloomi says, "I served as an advisor to the Iraq office at the Pentagon. I know what government documents look like and I helped the Americans with them for years, while I was doing my PhD in Virginia." He signals to see the folder, and Sam pulls it out of her bag and presents it to him. He leafs through the copies of the documents Harris sent Miles via e-mail when the story first ran. The other day, Miles e-mailed them to Sam, and she printed them out at the Hamra's business centre, which actually has a working printer.

Aloomi looks up. "It's obvious these documents are copies of the real thing."

"They are?" Sam hesitates, draws in a breath. "How can you tell?"

"The insignia. Do you see?" He points to the calligraphy at the top. The letters fold in on each other in a way that makes it a little difficult to read, like the old signature of the Ottoman Empire. "I don't know if you'd know the difference, but...you, Nabil." He shifts the page towards me. "Do you see the way the 'qaf' here becomes the 'rah' here?" He points to a dip in the

Arabic "q" at the end of Iraq to the "r" in *jumhuriyye*, or republic. "It's obvious right here. And here," he says, pointing to ties in between other letters, where the same stroke for ending one is used to start another. "This insignia is difficult to imitate. Impossible."

None of what he's saying makes a solid argument, but I nod anyway and say I see.

"If your editors think that these documents are fakes," he says, pushing the folder back towards Sam, "you should tell them, what was that saying you have in America? They are barking at the wrong tree."

"Up," says Sam.

"Pardon?"

"Barking *up* the wrong tree."

Aloomi suddenly stands, pushes his tie again over his middle. "I wish I could help you but I really don't think there's any point in expending any more energy here."

Sam stands up slowly, and I follow.

"Are you sure you can't try to find some other documents for us with Uday's signature? That couldn't be too difficult, with all the boxes of documents you have here. I'm sure everyone back in Washington would really appreciate your help with this." Sam smiles, seeming sweet – and yet threatening.

He looks through her, not at her. "I'll have to check with some other people at our headquarters to see if there's any way we can help you." He walks to his door and holds the knob. "But honestly?"

Sam and I walk towards the door. I have a feeling of being dismissed. Sam looks at him, indicates she's waiting for him to finish.

"With all due respect, I wouldn't bother wasting time on this, if I were you," he says. "You should just be glad that the *Tribune* was first to report the story of Mr Jackson's corruption. Unfortunately, that's the way the world works. Corrupt politicians in the free world and brutal dictators in the Third: they make great friends." He smiles broadly. "You must know that."

Sam places a hand on her hip. "How will we know if you do have something for us?"

"If I have something that can help," he says, pacing the three steps back to his desk and then picking up her card, "I'll call you. Or drop something off for you." He studies the card. "Did you write your Thuraya number on this?" He flips it over, where Sam has written a long line of numbers. "Ah, so you did." He looks at me and back to her. "Well, anyway, I can always find you at the Hamra Hotel, I presume?"

Sam glares.

"I have been hearing that all of the top journalists are staying at the Hamra now because it's considered the popular place to be," he says. "And you have that lovely swimming pool, too."

"Yes, it is something. I go there sometimes to see some of my colleagues. But I don't stay there. I'm at the Sheraton."

"I see. Also a good choice." Once again he makes for the door and opens it as if welcoming us in, though he's showing us out. He holds out his hand to Sam and she takes it stiffly, as if she's unsure whether she wants her skin to meet his. And then his hand reaches mine, squeezing the bones a little too hard.

30

Squeezing

SAM IS DIPPING chunks of bread into the hummus, but she hasn't touched the kebab. I ask her why, and she says she doesn't like red meat. I consider telling her that it's quite brown now, but it would sound too cheeky. She insists she is not a vegetarian because she occasionally eats chicken. But if you don't eat meat, as far as I can see, you're not really eating a normal diet.

"You should come back in the winter and have my mother's *kubbeh* soup."

"Oh yeah?" She is eating the vegetables and the pickles, and occasionally a french fry. It's a treat to be eating again at Lathakiya, but she's missing the best part. "What's that?"

"*Kubbeh?* It's a very famous Iraqi dish. It's like a, what do you call that? A dumping? Sorry, a dumpling! A dumpling with meat inside it, except that the outside is better than a dumpling."

She gulps her Coke, draining the glass. I'm amazed how she could stay away from red meat but is happy to fill up on this. "But I don't eat meat."

"It's just little bits of meat. Not really like a big piece of meat. Mincemeat, that's what they call it. It's very delicious – it's the best thing on a cold winter day. You have to come to my house and try it. Mum makes the best."

Sam shapes her lips in a way that suggests she doesn't fancy the sound of it at all. "Maybe she'll make me a veggie one? As I said, I don't eat meat. Only chicken."

Realizing she isn't going to budge, I reach for the last kebab, although I've probably had one too many already, as my stomach is pressing against my belt. I consider loosening it a notch, then decide against it.

"Sam, that thing that Aloomi was going on about, the yellowcake issue, about how Saddam tried to buy it from Niger?"

"Uh-huh."

"Well, my cousin Saleh says that report was totally fake. And he says Chalabi, or someone at the INC, made it all up. A total fake."

Sam wipes her mouth, leaving a lipgloss afterglow on her napkin. "Really? Saleh who wants a job? How would he know?"

I shrug. "He knows. I guess from working at the UN liaison office here. I've been meaning to tell you more about it. I mean, I wasn't totally sure I believed him. Though now that I saw Aloomi act the way he did, it's starting to make more sense."

"Start over. Tell me again about Saleh."

I stab into the last kebab on the table and push it into my mouth, glad for the need to chew, and therefore to think. "He works for the UN, but as I mentioned to you before he wants to get out, and he hopes we can get him a job somewhere."

"Tell him he should check out CARE. I think they're hiring translators."

"Oh, yes? Good." I hand her my small notebook. "Can you write down the names? I mean, of anyone you know there? It would help."

Sam jots down two names as I talk. "And?"

"The night before last, I told him about our story. And then, early this morning, he stopped by and gave me a lift to the Hamra, and in the car, he gave me a lot of information about forgers."

Her eyes narrow. "Wait. What did you tell him?"

"Not the whole thing, of course, just that we were looking for some information – that we are investigating the issue of fake documents, of where they come from."

"The *issue*?" Sam wipes at the dust on the napkin holder. "Nothing specific? I have a hard time believing anyone would be satisfied with that explanation."

"It wasn't really an explanation, Sam. It was just a short visit. I had told him that we could use some help, he said that he wanted to do anything he could."

"Well?" Sam suddenly looks anxious.

"He thinks a lot of the information Chalabi and the INC people gave to the Americans before the war was fake. This morning, he gave me a description of how to find several forgery operations in Sadr City, and he thinks these are the places where such documents were made."

Sam stops picking at the radishes on the table and looks over to the waiters, in case they might be listening. "Really? Can we go?"

I nod. "Maybe I should go first, to check out if it's okay for you."

Sam's mouth twitches, her nostrils widen. "We might not need to go more than once. I think I should just go with you. I'll wear an abaya."

"It isn't just about wearing an abaya. You look too American. And even if you were Iraqi, an Iraqi woman wouldn't be involved in going to these places."

Sam grabs a wad of napkins, more than she needs, and wipes her hands on them. Then she takes a tiny plastic bottle from her bag and spills a gooey clear liquid on her hands, rubbing them together.

"What's that?"

"Oh this?" She turns the bottle around to look at the label. "It's Purell." She reads on. "Instant hand sanitizer. Disinfectant." She turns the logo towards me and smiles. "Makes life a little cleaner."

"Do Americans use this all the time? After every meal?"

"Of course not!" she laughs. "I mean, some people – when you're in a place where it's…where you're travelling." She rubs her hands together, giving off an odour that is a mix of ammonia and menthol. "Want some?"

I shake my head, and mouth to the waiter that we would like tea. Thinking again about how my refusal could be insulting, I hold out my hands.

Sam spills a drop into each palm. It feels like cold glue, but after rubbing it into my hands for a moment, it disappears.

"Actually, you're supposed to use it before you eat so that you're eating with clean hands," she says. "But whatever. Sometimes I do things backwards." She dips her head closer to me. "How does your cousin know about these places? Is he involved in this sort of thing?"

"No!" I probably sound too forceful, but the question is a little off-putting. "No, absolutely not. But he was some kind of management official at the UN liaison office in Baghdad, and of course anyone in those jobs had to be approved first by Saddam. He's a smart guy, my cousin Saleh, and basically innocent – he was doing what he had to do to survive. I don't think he ever really liked Saddam. He's definitely not a Ba'athist, though his father probably was."

Sam nods. "Okay."

"Okay, so, during the oil-for-food programme, and you know, during the years of the embargo against Iraq—"

"The sanctions?"

"Yes, the sanctions. He was one of the people who had to give the UN the reports about the number of children dying from lack of medicine and malnutrition. They had to make the number look very high – to make America look bad. So these experts in documents, I mean, these men who have an expertise in creating documents that look very real, well, Saleh and another guy in his office sometimes had to go to Saddam City, you know, now it's Sadr City, to pick them up. He said that's where the best forgers were. Saleh knows a few names."

"Where?" she asks. "I mean, do you know where exactly? Sadr City is huge."

"One place is Souq Mureidi," I say, my voice so low it is almost a whisper. Across the screen in my mind, I see myself whispering that way right in her ear, her eyes closing, her mouth opening.

Sam stares at me. Her face is still but her sealed lips grow full, pleased with themselves. The tea has arrived, hers first. As the waiter puts mine down a hot splash lands on the back of my hand, making me flinch enough to knock over my water glass. Sam manages to catch it before much can spill.

"So sorry. So sorry." The waiter, a spotty-faced fellow with bushy hair who cannot be more than sixteen or seventeen, keeps apologizing while I dip my napkin in the rescued glass and dab it on my hand. I tell him it's fine, but he still looks concerned and, looking a bit helplessly at me, runs off.

Sam makes the kind of sympathetic face you might for a small child. "Let me see."

I peel the wet napkin away to reveal the red spot across my hand. "It's fine. It hurt for a second, that's all."

Sam turns her head to watch the young waiter rushing back towards us, a plate in hand. "Well, sometimes it pays to exaggerate a little, huh?"

He puts the plate down in front of us. "*Sambusi*, special for you, on the house," he says in English, which I find a bit worrying, because it just proves how obvious it is to everyone around us that Sam is American. "So sorry," he says again.

"That's not necessary," I say.

"Please. Please. On us," he says, and makes for the other side of the restaurant where the other waiters, who are not as young, are smirking at him.

"Have you tried this?"

"No-o," says Sam, interested. "Looks decadent. Bet it's really sweet, yeah?"

"Sweet, but with warm cheese inside. Try it."

She shudders, which tells me this doesn't sound appealing, but places her fork into the triangular pastry none the less and tries to break it in half. I want to tell her she would be better putting the whole thing in her mouth, but I suppose that's not the way a woman, Arab or otherwise, likes to approach the eating of a dessert.

"Mmm," she says, or moans, really. "It's so rich." She closes her eyes as she chews. Something in her shut lids suggests a deep satisfaction, a side of herself she has never shown me.

She opens her eyes again, breathes out through her nostrils. "Sam, are you happy?"

She smiles wryly and takes the half she left behind, more interested in the *sambusi* than my question. She puts the fork down and stops chewing, her eyes rolling across mine like one of those scanning lights in the middle of the night looking for invading ships.

"Oof," she lets out a breath, as if she'd been holding it all this time. "That's crazy sweet. But amazing," she says, nodding, as if to make sure I know she likes it.

"You should taste the ones my mother makes."

Sam smiles, pushes around the second piece of pastry on the plate, and glances at her watch. With Sam, there is rarely a full attention, an awareness that it isn't polite to talk to someone about food while looking at your watch. Everything that I hate in these moments, when her courtesies fail, I can love a minute later, when I remember that it's only about her dedication to the story. My grandmother, Zahra, once told me you could be a *mujahid* your whole life, she said, just in struggling for the truth.

"Am I happy? What kind of question is that?" She stares at the second pastry, pondering, I presume, whether or not she will eat it.

"Oh, I mean, do you like this job you have, being in Iraq, travelling all over the world all the time? Don't you want, well… I guess you must think my life is boring. I have only been to England and Dubai, though that's more than most Iraqis."

"You're not boring," she says. Her eyes leave the plate a second to meet mine, and then go back to the second *sambusi*.

"Why don't you eat it?" she asks.

"I don't want any sweets now," I say. I almost forgot. The

truth is, since Noor was killed, I decided that I would give up eating anything sweet for a year, which is an appropriate period of mourning for a loved one, even if that's not how I see Noor. I want to show that I'm not indulging in sweetness after what happened. But to whom? As if God cares whether I eat sweets. But there aren't many other luxurious things in my life to give up.

"Why not?" Sam says, spreading out the sweet honey sauce that surrounds the pastry. "You sure?"

"Yes. And you can't let good *sambusi* go to waste."

She pushes it across the table, towards me. "You eat it, then."

"What I meant is, maybe you're the happiest woman in the world. All your dreams come true. But in your country, is it not important for a woman to have children? To get married and be a wife?"

She stares at me, and there's something of a hurt look across her face, flaring in her nose. "Sure it's important. But it's not the only thing. I'm not just a body with a womb."

"I-I know. I didn't mean that—" I feel my hands stuttering to defend me.

"No, it's fine." She taps her fork into the *sambusi* she had pushed away. She looks at me to make sure I haven't changed my mind, and when I shake my head, she presses her fork down into the pastry, and watches the cheese ooze out from the sides. She continues to press on what was round and full until it is flat.

"It's fine that you ask," she says. "I do want those things. I know I don't have forever." She licks her lips, a shine on them from the buttery pastry.

"I just think you would make a really wonderful mother."

Sam steals a glance at me, and then out of the window. She

looks like she might cry. But very quickly, whatever tears that had almost been born are aborted. Her eyes wait with a thin gloss, like the one on her lips. "Thanks, Nabil. That's the nicest thing anyone's ever said to me."

"Really? Ever?"

She is quiet for a moment. "Okay, ever since this war began." We both smile and she gives a small nod of her head in the direction of the waiters, which I can read as the sign for me to get the bill. "But look," she says in an undertone. "Before we bring babies into the picture, I need to know who cooked up these documents. So can we get going?" She seems almost embarrassed now, a pinkness in her face that perhaps I brought on without intending it. She folds one hand into another, the right gently turning the left sideways to allow her another quick glance at her watch.

31

Turning

SALEH SAID THIS Khalil was a real professional, one of the best in the business. Long before he got on Saddam's bad side, Khalil made up reams of fake Ministry of Health documents to show inflated numbers of Iraqi children dying due to the sanctions. Had those numbers been correct, more than one in five Iraqi children would have died for lack of food or medicine due to America's insistence on slapping sanctions on the sale of Iraqi oil. After the UN dismissed a whole batch of documents as complete fabrications, somewhere around 1998 or 1999, Saddam had Khalil arrested and dragged over to Abu Ghraib. There, Saleh explained to me, Khalil was tortured for failing to do his job correctly. Several months later, after they let him go, he went to work for the underground opposition, most of them based abroad. His skills, he realized, were in demand from a better-paying clientele who didn't break their suppliers' fingers if the final product flopped.

Given such an introduction, Khalil's appearance isn't at all what I expected. Did I imagine a suit and tie, perhaps a proper receptionist? Little pens and scalpels sticking out of his shirt pocket? Khalil Ibn Khaldoun's office is just a mid-sized *dukkan*, a small convenience store where people get their milk and eggs and biscuits.

He watches us walk in, and makes a noise with his tongue like someone calling a cat. A young man who looks just like him, only taller and less textured by time, joins him behind the counter. As we get closer, I realize that it isn't just lines on Khalil's face, but a patchwork of scars. Moreover, the entire tip of his right ear is missing, curved and scarred into a knobby flap of skin. Of all the things that can happen to a person in Abu Ghraib, I suppose this is like…what did they call that back at school in England? A rap on the knuckles.

The father and son look at each other like their conversation needs no more than a round of eye contact and a lift of Khalil's chin in the direction of the door. Khalil's son walks to the entrance and locks the door, turning a deadlock. He twists a plastic baton that makes the dirty blinds close their eyelids to block out the light.

"For your protection," Khalil says. "You never know what kind of thugs and troublemakers could have seen you come in here with the nice foreign lady."

"*Maluum*." Of course. "*Maluum*," I say again, wishing I had only said it once. I nod to Sam that this is a good idea, but her eyes speak other words to me, just the way Khalil's did with his son: *I don't like it one bit.*

"Please," says Khalil, pointing towards the door at the end of the aisle, near the cash register. "The office in which we do business is downstairs."

Sam seems to hesitate but I smile at her a little and blink slowly, signalling that it's all right. Saleh wouldn't have sent me here if he didn't think it was safe.

Khalil holds the door open and makes a gentlemanly gesture for us to enter ahead of him, and I feel that he must have had a better education than I had thought, because not everybody in my country knows that in the West it is considered polite to let ladies go first. On the contrary, it can be read as a sign of disrespect. By putting a woman in the vulnerable position of entering the room first, one might signal that she does not merit the protection of those accompanying her.

We walk down the concrete steps, dim and mangy around the edges, and then I feel my shoulders fall with relief. The downstairs is clean and has all the trappings of a real office: a fax machine, modern telephones with LCD displays, several filing cabinets with labels on them, and two slanted drawing tables I would expect to see in an architect's studio. Lodged in the wall is a large white air conditioner, continuously exhaling a cool, comforting hiss. I pray that Khalil doesn't notice me exhale, too, as if only now do I trust that nothing terrible awaits us in his basement.

"The lady will have tea?" he asks.

"Sure," she brightens. "Thank you very much."

"*Talata chai!*" He calls out for three glasses of tea, and suddenly I can hear someone rustling in the adjacent room. It irks me that I cannot tell how big the office actually is, or who else is here. He offers us a small black leather sofa that sometimes is called a loveseat.

There is just enough space between us to ensure the appearance of modesty, though I consider switching to the armchair so the thought that Sam could be my girlfriend will not even cross Khalil's mind. But it would be odd to move now, and anyway, sticking close to Sam seems more important.

Khalil excuses himself for a moment, and we sit in silence, knowing there is nothing for us to say, worth the risk of being overheard. From the corner of my eye I watch Sam's profile, the straight, gracious slope of her nose and the fullness of her lips, the silhouette of her eyelashes in the slight shadow she casts on the wall next to her. The lighting is oddly attached by a lamp in the corner as if an afterthought, reminding me that such a basement was never intended for an office. There are no windows, and therefore, no natural light. Sam's eyes dart sideways at me, asking, *Do you think it's okay?* A few purposeful dips of my eyebrows shoot back, *Don't worry.* But Sam does seem worried. Her eyes are somewhere else, as if studying a picture I cannot see.

Khalil comes back into the room, this time with a stocky man with a neck only a little less wide than his back. In his huge hands, he carries a stack of documents as thick as three or four Korans. Khalil nods at the coffee table and his friend puts the files down on it. As he does, I notice the revolver tucked into the back of his trousers, inside his belt. I try to acknowledge him but he does not respond, and Khalil does not bother with introductions.

Instead, Khalil sits down in a large leather chair that matches the other furniture, except that it rolls and swivels. He rotates back and forth for a moment and looks at us. Then he leans back and closes his eyes, as if considering taking a quick nap before our conversation.

He sits up quickly, eyes refreshed.

"So, Mrs Katchens. You are interested in the documents we are making."

Sam smiles with her mouth half open, hesitates, and then answers. "Uh, yes, Mr Khaldoun, we are." I am relieved Sam does not correct Khalil and insist on being called Ms or Miss. Maybe it's better for them to think she's married.

I did not expect Khalil to speak much English at all, although perhaps that was shortsighted of me. I scan the walls of the office. No pictures of any of the new leaders, neither secular nor Islamic. No posters, no paintings, no Kaaba, no Dome of the Rock, no holy men, no calendar. Just one clock, its steely edges oxidizing in the underground humidity, ticking loudly.

"You want to know about the documents of General Akram. Is this to be the correct thing?" He smiles with teeth fighting a losing battle against decay, like coffee steadily overtaking the milk-white. He is directing his words straight at Sam, and that makes me angry. I want him to treat me as her *wasta*, her middle man. Maybe even like her *wali*, like her brother or father, like someone in charge of her safety. I want Khalil Ibn Khaldoun to at least recognize I am here to protect Sam, a young American journalist sitting in the basement of a locked grocery store in Sadr City, and yet he is acting as though I'm hardly here.

"That's right," Sam says.

"Well, this is the kind of information that I could make available to you – for a price. You are willing to pay a price for the information you require?"

Sam hesitates. "I don't know. It would depend on what you're offering."

"I'm offering what you're asking for."

That's the problem, Sam must be thinking. You'll concoct exactly what you think I want. Perhaps that's what happened to Harris.

Khalil runs his hand over the sides of his face, which seem so bumpy that I wonder why he doesn't grow a beard. Perhaps he likes people to see his scars, the way other men like to wear a lot of stripes and medals on their military uniforms. His fingernails are uneven and dark, I assume from working with ink.

"Why don't you give me two days to find out what I can for you," he says. "I will do my research, and you will do yours, so you can be certain of what you need, and how much you need it." He turns to me. "*Wadih?*" he asks. Clear? He sounds the way I used to when I was giving out an assignment to my students. "It is good that you came."

With that Khalil rises, his hand gesturing to the stairs in the manner of a busy waiter seating us at a restaurant.

Outside, Sam exhales as if she's been holding her breath from the moment we walked into Khalil's storefront. She takes deep gulps of air and lets them out, sounding like someone who has just finished running.

"Are you all right?"

"Yeah," she says, pulling at Rizgar's front passenger door. She steps back with a shock. There's a young man sitting in her seat. Rizgar points to the backseat and we get in.

"Sorry, Miss Samara," Rizgar smiles pleadingly. "This cousin mine, Hoshyar."

Rizgar tells me to tell Sam that he just ran into his young cousin and that he needs a ride home, and he hopes she doesn't mind. Sam shrugs and says fine, if he's a cousin after all, and she tugs at her headscarf as we pull away. She looks at me for a hint of disagreement, and though I wonder what his Kurdish cousin just happens to have been doing here, I hold my face in place and simply smile back.

They engage in a low chatter of Kurdish, making sounds which, I am ashamed to say, sound like utter nonsense to me. It's hard to believe so many people in our country speak a language other than Arabic, and that the rest of us cannot understand a word they're saying.

As we leave Sadr City, Sam takes off her headscarf. She shakes her head, beginning to breathe normally again. "That was bad news."

"With Khalil? Yes, I didn't like him either. He doesn't seem honest."

"Not just that." Sam turns to me. "I started feeling like I was going to choke. Did I tell you that I have a bit of claustrophobia?"

"Claustro—no. That's when you are afraid of crowded places, right?"

"Something like that. I used to feel that too, but I got over it. The only thing that I still kind of have a problem with is small, enclosed places where there's not a lot of fresh air, and in particular, no windows. I can't stand to be underground, or in rooms without windows."

"Why didn't you say so? What happens?"

"Nothing. I can deal with it now," she says, making lines through the fog her breath made on the window.

"What about in the lift? You take lifts, don't you?"

"Elevators? Well, yeah, I used to have a problem with that. In fact, they think that's how it started. I once got stuck in an elevator as a kid for a really long time." She opens the ashtray at the back of her seat, now filled by Hoshyar. She snaps it shut a little too hard, and when Hoshyar turns around to look at her, she smiles tartly back at him. "Didn't you notice I always take the stairs if I can? At least there's movement there – vertical space. You know you're probably not going to get stuck."

I nod. Other than the two occasions I've seen her shed tears

– once out of worry for Jonah and then in that moment when she was reminded of Jack – this is the first time I've seen something to indicate that Sam might not be the most invincible woman on earth.

"But I learned this visualization technique. I just stare off into space and imagine I'm standing at the edge of the ocean, looking out at the wide, blue horizon, and then I can get through anything. Sometimes I tap on my forehead and it grounds me. Or sometimes I see myself lying on my favourite old sofa, floating down a river and watching the clouds in the sky."

Such imaginings don't seem at all like Sam. Moreover, a sofa on the river would sink. I'm waiting for her to laugh, but she looks dead serious.

"Does all that really work?" I ask.

"Sure it does!" She seems surprised by my doubt. "But you have to train yourself to do it."

I wonder if, next time I feel I might faint, I can imagine Sam's river and stay afloat. "Can you put a boat in the picture?"

Sam breathes hot air on the window, then draws the crescent and triangle of a stick-figure sailboat. "It's your imagination, Nabil. You get to do whatever you want." She puts her hand flat on the window and drags it down, erasing everything.

32

Erasing

SAM SENT ME off in the late afternoon with some errands to do, told me to take some time for "lunch or dinner or whatever it is you eat this time of day", and asked me to come back at around seven to "check in". I had thought that term referred to one's arrival at a hotel, but now I realize it can mean something else entirely. So it seems that check-in time should probably be an appropriate moment to let Sam know that General Akram appears to be looking for her. I don't know which of today's events felt more uncomfortable: the feeling that we could have been trapped in Khalil's basement, or running into Suleiman es-Surie in the supermarket.

But when I walk into Sam's room, carrying the case of Coke she asked me to pick up while I was out, she appears to be holding three other conversations. One on the satellite phone, where she's on some kind of conference call with several people at the newspaper; one on the hotel phone, where she's pleading with the restaurant to send up the room service she ordered an hour ago; and a third at the computer itself, where her fingers are playing the keyboard with great nimbleness.

She doesn't seem to notice me reading over her shoulder,

watching her sign off. *Things are fine...I just don't have time to talk. Don't worry about me. Love you, Sami.*

I wonder if she is writing to Jonah. Or maybe her mother. She exits out of the screen and swirls around in her chair.

"Nabil! *Shlonik, habibi?*" she chirps. Her Arabic pronunciation, I've noticed, is better than many other Americans. But the few words she knows are often too informal for a newcomer to the language. My boss, the woman who pays my salary, calling me *habibi*, my love. "Give me two minutes."

"You wanted me to come back, right?"

"Yes, of course. I need two, no, ten minutes to finish up here."

"Sam, we need to talk about the story."

"Right now?"

I study her face closely, and the reddened rims of her eyes. I try to imagine what goes on in her head when she is racing towards a deadline or towards some other goal. She's like one of those runners who grab cups of water from anonymous people along the sidelines of a marathon without ever stopping to thank them, to look at their faces in return. I wonder whether in Sam's life, I am like one of those anonymous people passing cups to a tired runner, or whether I will be more like one of those people at the finish line, someone Sam will throw her arms around after the race is over.

"No," I say, "not this very minute."

"Well, look, the editors want some answers from me about what we've found so far. A memo. I mean, they wanted it yesterday. And I need to eat. Can you wait down by the pool for a little while and read a book or something until I finish this memo and get some room service before I faint?"

"Sure, Sam. I'll come back in a bit."

"Wait, Nabil, don't you want to eat, too?"

"I ate. You told me I could get dinner and come back, remember?"

"Oh, right." She looks at her watch, and sees it's after 7:00. "But that was at about 4:30. Can you eat dinner so early after schlepping around in this heat?"

I shrug. The truth is I went to visit Saleh again and had a late lunch with him. Then I stopped to pick up Sam's Coke, and found myself face-to-face with Suleiman es-Surie, who was wondering why we hadn't been back to visit.

Sam pops open a can of Coke and suggests I take one too, but I hold up my hand to say no thank you. In this respect, she has a palate just like I imagined Americans would. I tell her that the owner of the store, who has been profiting from the arrival of so many foreigners, promises they will be getting Diet Coke in a week. She seems to find the prospect thrilling.

"What was that word, shepping?"

"Schlepping. You know, schlepping around?" She sucks in a chuckle. "You haven't heard it?"

"No. I don't think so."

"I guess they don't use that one too much in Birmingham. It means dragging or carrying. Or, you know, like dragging your butt around. Or schlepping a case of Coke?" She smiles as if she knows that it's not something I relished doing. "Anything that's tiring or annoying, really."

"Oh. And what is the etymology of this word?"

Sam shakes her head and goes back to her screen. "You have the sweetest vocabulary. I don't think I've heard that word since college."

328

"Which, etymology? Isn't it a common word?"

Sam gets up and traipses into the kitchenette, taking the block of dates I brought her earlier this week off the shelf. "Agh. I can't wait any longer. I'll waste away before that chicken comes. By the way, I love these." She breaks off the equivalent of five or six dates, which I believe are the best in the entire Middle East, and holds out the block to me. I shake my head and decline.

"So the term schlepping is common, then?"

Sam laughs like she is tired but amused. "In certain circles," she says. She looks at me and does her double-eye blink, which always seems an eyelash short of a wink. "All right, Nabil, I really need to boogie here. Order something down by the pool if you like and charge it to my room. With all you're doing, the newspaper can spring for your dinner."

What Sam doesn't realize is that the days of an Iraqi man seen reading a book in public went out with Nasserism. Up until the late 1950s, it was acceptable. But it wasn't long before the Ba'ath Party made a suspect out of anyone who was too inquisitive, and being labelled an intellectual was almost as bad as being fingered as a royalist.

The fear still has its residue. But I put one of the new Iraqi newspapers under my arm to impress Sam none the less. She seems so convinced that all of these new publications signal a blossoming of free media after Saddam. I am afraid to tell her that the new papers are just as full of lies as the old ones – but now we have a greater variety of liars to whom we can donate a few dinars.

And so I sit down by the pool, at a table in the far corner in the shade, and watch some of Sam's colleagues swimming. Brooke from *Time* is doing laps. Melanie from French TV is enjoying the last of the day and reading a book, while that young blond man with the body-builder physique tries to talk her into a swim. Both women are wearing bikinis. I notice the pool attendants and the hotel waiters staring at them with every free moment they can get, making an entire occupation out of peering at the ample display of foreign flesh. I cringe and think of Sam; I hope that she doesn't dress like this by the pool, too, in the late evenings when I'm not around.

In some of the men's eyes, I can see the awe, the longing for the freedom of a culture that lets its daughters wear what they want, even if it is a swimming costume that doesn't cover very much. On other faces, I see disdain and resentment. Before the Americans came, we never had these foreign women walking around like they were on a beach in California.

I open the *Az-Zaman* paper, which has a sensationalist story about Americans stealing all the army's pension funds from the national reserves. Then again, could it be true? It might explain why one of their first acts after Saddam's disappearance was to dissolve the army.

It occurs to me that the sun is setting, which is a time of day when I'm usually with Sam or with my family, and I decide to slip out to that small gathering room near the car park behind the hotel to pray. *Salat al-maghrib*, the fourth of the daily prayers, should be said now, and I wonder, is it wrong to start here, when I've missed the first three and probably won't do the fifth? I've been wanting to make prayer a habit again, but I don't seem to have the time or the discipline. It was something I had done for a while, back in my teenage years and at university, but then I just stopped. I have no interest in going to the mosque, especially now, because everyone there is anti-something. Everything is political, everyone is a target. And to whose mosque shall I go? So I prefer to pray alone, or just in a roomful of men. Lately, I find myself also wanting to pray for Sam. Sometimes my *sallih* feels wonderful. Sometimes I feel like a fraud. Nabil, a voice in my head sometimes asks, do you really think anyone is listening? I wonder if the voice is Baba's or my own.

I have counted thirty minutes, and so I go back up to the suite to see Sam.

When I knock, she opens the door briskly and mouths "hi", and runs back to her desk to pick up the Thuraya earpiece.

"Yeah. Yeah. Miles, look, someone important just came by and is waiting for me. Can I call you back a little later? 'Kay. Thanks. Bye."

Sam's plate of hummus is swiped almost clean, just a few trails left like tyre tracks in the drying mud. But she hardly dented the chicken they brought for her – she says it's too dry. She is sitting like a swami, one leg folded on top of the other, and she seems calm now, or like she is trying to convince herself she is calmer.

"Sam." I clear my throat and sit on the sofa. "Sam, I ran into one of Akram's guys today and he was asking about you. He was asking me where you live and which newspaper you're working for."

"What? Which guy?"

"That Suleiman character. Suleiman es-Surie. Or Suleiman Mutanabi. Even that's probably not his real name, apparently. He assumed it because it's the name of a famous Iraqi poet, Mutanabi, who was of Syrian origin. And speaking of which, they're not even sure what *your* name is. But they want you to come and talk to them again."

"Wait, go back." The lines between Sam's brows trace themselves deeper. "Where did you see him?"

"I decided not to go home to have dinner. I went to my cousin Saleh's house instead. On the way back, I stopped in to the Al-Wahde Supermarket to pick up the case of Coke for you, and as I was leaving, he came in."

"Wow. *Wow*," she repeats. Do you think he was following you? Or that he followed you here?"

It hadn't occurred to me to check, and so I shake my head no.

"What did you tell him?"

"I told them that your name is Sally and that you work for *The Guardian*. I said I was in a rush and took off."

"Well, that was quick thinking. But I don't think you had to lie outright."

"Sam, didn't he tell us that he and his whole group of mates killed everyone at Uday Hussein's house the night Baghdad fell? Maybe they kill other people, too." I wonder if, in Sam's obsession with Harris's lies and Jackson's lawsuit, she's paid any attention to all the Iraqis who've been killed just in the past week. "Yeah, but what if some woman freelancing for *The Guardian* runs into problems now? You can't do things like that. It's unethical."

"But there's no Sally, and apparently they weren't sure what your name was because you didn't leave a card. He's trying to figure out where you live, and maybe where I do. Why would they need to know that? Doesn't that concern you?"

Sam sighs and follows her feet into the kitchen. There, she tears open a bag of chocolate chip cookies that one of the other reporters just brought in from Jordan.

"You want?" She holds them out in my direction and grumbles something inquisitive, which seems to say "take one", but never quite enunciates itself.

I eat two, waking up some dormant gland in the back of my throat. But when she offers a third, I hold up my hand to say no thanks, suddenly remembering my vow not to eat sweet things. Sam throws another in her mouth, then falls into the seat in front of her desk and taps on a key, bringing her computer back to life. She hands me a copy of the *Ninth of April*, a weekly newspaper, named for the day after Baghdad fell. I tell Sam I've never seen it before. She says I ought to be watching for these new papers springing up everywhere. This one is in its third edition.

I take the paper in my hands and start thumbing through the pages of such cheap newsprint that it is already leaving foggy trails of evidence across my fingers. I can immediately see that the quality of the writing is terrible, just like the newspapers before Saddam. What should I tell Sam – that no one here has figured out how to be a journalist yet? That we are too accustomed to being told what to say?

"Can I talk while you type?" I ask.

Her shoulders droop a little, and then she stops and closes the computer. "The memo will wait." She turns to me. "So you think I should be concerned about Akram."

"I don't know about should be…but I have a question." Seeing her eagerness, I begin again. "What if Harris had paid for the documents and they *weren't* artificial? Everything would have turned out fine, would it not?"

Sam swivels in her chair and studies me with a look of wonderment. The gold in her eyes, usually the colour I'd imagine a lion to be, drains into a shade of straw, as if made lighter from trying to take in a bigger picture of me. She says nothing.

"I mean, is that so bad, paying for some information that's true?"

"Nabil, of course it's bad. As a journalist you shouldn't *buy* information. It prejudices the integrity of what you receive. If there's money involved, maybe they'll just tell you what they think you want to hear."

I listen and nod, as if she might be right. I must try to make her understand.

"But," I say, "I don't think that's the most important thing. In our culture, you pay for things you value. The documents, or any information, that's of value, right? Otherwise, if you don't pay, it's a gift and a gift comes with all kinds of obligations. If I get a gift, I feel obligated until I give a gift in return. And then it never ends. Our grandchildren will be giving each other gifts on every *eid*, bringing food over each Ramadan. But if you pay, the relationship is over. Then you're done. Being obligated, that's much more dangerous. Then they own you."

"Nabil, you're wrong on this, trust me." She stands and leans back on her desk, her arms folded. "We don't pay for documents. It's not allowed. And if Harris took them – what, he'd have been indebted to General Akram for presents at Ramadan? Give me a break."

"No, Sam. Not like that, of course. But in Iraq, you don't want to be in debt to someone like that. And now we are, too."

"What are you talking about?"

"We took his time and his tea. We took that…that picture of him when we visited. We were there for a long time. He'll think we owe him something."

Sam's brows fold into a scowl. She walks towards the sliding glass door to the balcony and reaches for the handle. "I'm going to reposition the sat dish," she says, letting in a steam column bleached with end-of-the-day sun. "The reception lately has been really bad." She turns back to me with a wry half-smile. "Oh, and it's 'det'. When you say it, you don't pronounce the 'b'. It's silent."

I stew with embarrassment at getting something wrong, with irritation at having her correct me. Sam messes around with the machine on the balcony. It's the one that I had thought was a laptop computer at first, and I was shocked to see her leaving it outside, balancing it on the ledge as though it were nothing special. Won't it get damaged sitting out there in the sun and dust, I asked. She laughed and said oh no, Nabil, this one isn't a laptop, this is our new satellite. Later, when she was in the loo, I went out to look at it and realized that this was, in fact, the B-GAN of which she spoke not long ago. What a strange name. She said it cost about $4,000 – all sitting out on the balcony! Maybe it will accidentally slip from Sam's hands and land in the pool below. I air-type a couplet, an ode to its demise.

it began as the B-GAN began to sink
upon me did she at last begin to think

Sam comes back in smacking her hands together, letting dust particles disperse in the air. "It's lost the signal," she says. "Carlos says when that happens you need to shut the whole thing down, give it a couple minutes' rest, and then bring it up to the roof or to some other wide open space again where it can sort of find itself again."

I nod as if it's perfectly clear.

"Do you want to see how to position it?"

"Whatever you prefer."

Sam breathes out hard through her nostrils. "Fine. Wait here and I'll go and do it."

"No, Sam," I say. "I would be happy to come."

In silence, I follow Sam upstairs to the roof. I can see it has filled up with more satellite dishes and other journalists' B-GANs. She sets hers down and says we should leave it for a few minutes to get a GPS coordinate. That means global positioning satellite, she explains. In the meantime, she says, we can sit in the hallway, where it is cooler – the roof feels hot, even at sunset, perhaps due to the little colony of technology taking root here. She drags a plastic chair across the balcony, and I grab the other, a wooden and metal one, which reminds me of a classroom chair.

Sam leans back in her chair and puts her feet up on the edge of the staircase. "I'm sorry I was being all huffy and rude with you before," she says. "There's really no excuse for it." She looks at her shoes – worn black sandals that seem more like a pair for men than any kind of sandals most women here would wear – and then at me.

"Of course, Sam. Don't worry about it."

She rests her hands on her head. "Look, I'm stressed out. But I don't want to go getting all snippy with you. It's not your fault."

"What's not?"

"None of this," she shrugs. She pulls her knees up close to her, wrapping her long arms around them. "You know how I got claustrophobic?"

"No. Do you just get it? Like a disease?"

"Well, no, you don't really *get* it. But they made me figure out when it started, and then I remembered," she says. "You know, when was the first time I remember feeling trapped, how do I feel in small spaces, and then I remembered. My older brother and one of my cousins, when they were about ten and eleven and I must have been four or five, my parents gave us permission to leave my grandmother's place in the city, to go outside to play. But in the elevator, they pressed a whole bunch of buttons – out of order, when I wasn't looking – and then at the ground floor, they ran out and left me inside. Actually, they pushed me back from following them just before the doors closed, and ran off."

Sam winces. There's a tiny, sour smile on her lips. She doesn't look at me.

"And so I was all alone and the elevator just kept going to different floors for the longest time. You know, 8, 12, 3, 6, 10, all over the place. I had no idea where I was! It was terrifying. I just started bawling." She smiles with a kind of embarrassment in her eyes. "At that age, you don't pay attention to things like what floor your grandmother lives on, what your own address is, how you get from one place to the next. People just take you and you don't need to know where you're going. I kept peeking out of the elevator but every floor looked exactly the same, even smelled the same. I was actually sniffing for my grandmother's food. Finally, I just decided to get out, crying, going left to the end of each hallway, to that last door on the left, where I knew her apartment should be, only to see that it wasn't hers. Eventually, some old couple heard me sobbing in the hallway and they asked who my Grandma was, and they just happened to know her, and finally took me back to her place." She lets her legs go and slumps a little in the chair.

I look at her, and she seems sad, or maybe as if she's seeing her grandmother now, and I feel jealous because I want to see her, too. And then Sam comes back to me.

Though I would never say so, I find the story hard to imagine. We don't have many tall apartment buildings like that in Baghdad. I don't know anyone who lives in a building with more than four storeys. And I can't imagine leaving a four or five-year-old Amal somewhere to get lost, even as a joke.

"That's awful, Sam, for such a little girl," I finally say. "It must have been terrifying."

"Yeah," she laughs. She sits up straight again, shakes her head. "They were real pranksters. But I guess because of that I've spent my life keeping track of exactly where I'm going and what my surroundings are." Her hands grip the edges of the chair tightly, as though bracing herself. "I explore all the options, travel everywhere, but make sure I always know my way back. And whenever possible, I stay in big, open spaces where there are other people around. I hate feeling, you know, *stuck*."

I think of Amal again, sitting at home and not going out for weeks on end.

"You know what the hardest part of doing this job is?" Sam stares at me now, her lips parted, waiting. "Learning to trust someone like you. And Rizgar. I have to. But sometimes I feel like I shouldn't trust anyone at all, should just keep my eyes on the buttons and make sure I know exactly where I'm going. Which is a pain-in the-ass in your country, I might add," she says with a half-moon of a smile, "because for starters, there's hardly any street signs."

"You can always trust us. We know the way."

She nods a few times. "Also, there's something else I'll never forget after that day in the elevator."

"What's that?"

"My grandmother lived in 3G."

I laugh and she elbows my arm, then withdraws it.

"What was her name?"

"Her name?"

"Your grandmother's name."

"Sarah."

"Oh, right, you said that. You know this is also a Muslim name? My grandmother's name was Zahra. It almost sounds the same, no?"

"Yeah," she says, "is it?"

"No, Zahra means flower. And she was just like that. Like a stubborn desert flower." I look at Sam. "What was your grandmother like? What was the smell you were looking for?"

"Oh, you know how grandmothers smell."

"No, I mean, what did she cook?"

Sam turns away, looking back to the balcony. "I think the B-GAN's probably ready now."

"Wait, tell me. What do grandmothers in America cook?" I am imagining the *masghouf* that Grandma Zahra made, and also the slightly spicy *kubbeh* from my mother's side, from the Samawa area, and I want to know what real, home-cooked food would taste like in America.

"I hardly remember," she shrugs. "It was so long ago. All I can imagine now is the smell of that chicken tikka I ordered from room service. Remind me not to do that again. *Y'alla*," she says, and is already halfway across the balcony. She gestures for me to come over to her B-GAN, sitting on the roof along with a dozen or so others, half-open to the sky like oysters on a great white beach. "Let me teach you how to turn this puppy on so if the day comes, you'll know what to do with it," she says. She runs her finger over the tiny lights on the panel, clearing a coating of dust from the machine. Two black helicopters, with propellers at either end looking like giant locusts against the darkening sky, whirl overhead. "Children," she pronounces in an artificially deep and authoritative voice, fiddling with the tilt of the satellite receptor with both hands, "don't try this at home."

33

Fiddling

IN THE KITCHENETTE, Sam opens the refrigerator and pulls out what looks like a tall, green can of soda. She holds it up. "Beer?"

"Oh. Uh, no thanks."

"All right then. More Carlsberg for me." She detaches the ring-pull with a *psht* and takes a double-sip. "I think you worry too much, Nabil," she says. "You know, we're getting really close to the bottom of all of this."

"Sam." *She'll think you're a poofter. She'll think you're silly.* "If you want my honest opinion, I think this is all becoming… *majnoun*. You know that word? Crazy. Don't you think your editors would understand that if you explained it to them?"

Sam sits and drops her head back over the top of the sofa. She coughs up a puff of air. "Understand what?"

"That what you're doing is dangerous. Aren't they worried about you?"

She busies herself with drinking the beer, which is not one of the things I picked up for her in the Al-Wahde Supermarket, which has plenty of foreign products. There are small Christian-run liquor shops in town, and I guess the journalists have found their way to them. "Sure," she finally says. "I'm sure they are. But they need this story done. They leave us with a lot of personal autonomy. They just…leave it to us. We can decide whether to say no."

"Did you ever say no?"

Sam looks at me sideways. "No, what?"

"As in, 'no, I won't do that story.' Or, 'no, I won't go there because there's a war going on.'"

She rolls her eyes, and her arms fold in on each other. She seems smaller, yet stronger. "No, I haven't. But that's not the point."

"Sam, everyone in America is supposed to be free to do as he pleases. And you have all your civil rights, rights no one in this country has ever had. So if you're free, why do you have to do things you don't want to do?"

She stares at me for a moment, and then turns her hands out. It reminds me of one of the motions we use when we pray. "I don't. I don't do anything I don't want to do. I chose to do this."

"You mean, you chose to come to Iraq? To cover the war?"

"Well, more or less. They asked me to come, and I said yes."

"Did you have to say yes?"

Sam reaches for the box of Parliament cigarettes sitting on the table. It's probably the same pack that Carlos left behind – the one Sam cursed about the other day. She slides one out, runs it under her nose, inhales and closes her eyes, like the tobacco has jarred something in her memory that makes her feel good. She puts the cigarette in her mouth, sucks on it unlit, then takes it out and breaks it in her fingers over the ashtray. A snowfall of tobacco flakes quietly into the dirty silver dish below.

"You used to smoke."

"I did," she grins, and dismantles the remains of the cigarette without looking up. "I quit a long time ago." I'm glad I didn't meet Sam then. All the Iraqi women who smoke look like they're trying hard, too hard, to look sophisticated and cosmopolitan. Instead, they just look hard.

"Sam, you didn't answer the question."

She laughs like there is a joke she isn't going to let me in on. "Nope. Never said no to a story. That's the question, right? But doesn't mean I wouldn't. Just that I haven't." I can't tell if she is proud or embarrassed.

The satellite phone rings. It has such a strange, metallic jangle, like the sound of a device that has yet to be invented. Sam moans and looks at me. "You're closer to the phone," she says. "Just press the green 'call' button, would you? Then hit speaker phone."

I do what Sam asks, press the buttons, and sit back down.

There's a lot of static, but I already know it's Miles's voice. It's distorted, as usual, by being sent through a satellite somewhere over the Indian Ocean. I wonder what he sounds like in real life.

"Sam?" he asks loudly. "Sam, can you hear me?"

Sam drags herself off the sofa and on to the armchair next to her desk, to get closer to the speaker. "Yeah, Miles, hi. I hear you."

"Sam, we've got news."

"Well, we've got news, too. I was in the middle of writing you a memo about it but I stopped to fix the sat and eat dinner. You wouldn't believe what we've learned in the last twenty-four hours. I think we've almost got it figured out."

"Look, we figured it out at our end. We got the tests back."

"Wh-which tests?" Sam sounds confused.

"Oh. Didn't I tell you? We sent the documents that Harris

343

gave us to an Iraq expert in Washington. He compared the signatures on the documents to Uday's real signature and it's not even close to the real thing. No resemblance at all. Can you believe that?"

Sam blinks in astonishment.

Miles continues. "The letterhead isn't even right. So at the same time, we talked to a private investigator, who said we should send them for ink-ageing analysis, and the guy who did that says the documents are no more than two months old. There's no way the dates on these documents can be right."

"Wait," Sam says. "I thought you only had copies of the documents."

"No, no," Miles says. "Harris sent us the originals via another reporter who left Iraq last week."

"Uh-huh." Sam blinks. "Well, this is what I was about to tell you. We're pretty close to being able to prove that the documents were fabricated here, in Sadr City. I think we're even going to be able to pinpoint where they were made and then maybe we'll even figure out who did it and why. So tomorrow we're going back to find the—"

"Sam," Miles interrupts. "You may not have to bother now. I mean, unless you're certain you can pinpoint in the next twenty-four to forty-eight hours who made these documents and why. If so, great. Otherwise, we just won't even address that in the story at all. We just need to come out and clear the record: they're fake, we made a mistake and we're sorry, that's it. We don't need to go breaking some additional story that increases our risk and keeps this whole thing in the spotlight for a minute more than absolutely necessary."

"Miles. Miles? I don't understand. Three days ago you said

you needed us to figure out who made the documents, to meet Akram, to go all out to verify the signatures." Sam's voice is rising as she speaks, and I can see a wave of disbelief passing over her. She rushes over to the phone and picks up the receiver, so I can no longer hear what Miles is saying so well.

"I want you to know what we've put into this story so far. I've devoted the last week to this alone. I haven't done anything else but chase after these people and these documents, and now you're saying it's all wrapped up?"

Miles's voice crackles from the phone. "...still need a confirmation on the documents...we'll get a second opinion... you know with the front office...the decision is not entirely in my hands...and with such high legal fees..."

Sam nods her head petulantly, making circles with her free hand as if to urge him to finish his point.

"But Miles, why didn't someone tell me about taking this to an ink-ageing analyst? You said something about using contacts at your end, in Washington, and that was the last I heard of that." More Milesmumble, Sam walking the length of her desk a few times and then sitting on the edge of it. "I *am*," she says. "I am happy we've got that now. It's great. It's just that I didn't even know that you were going that route. If I had known you were about to find that out, I wouldn't have been chasing down some of these nasty people we've been chasing down."

She nods with shut eyelids. "Mmm. Um-hmm." She pushes herself further on to her desk and pulls one knee towards her chest. The words she's saying to her editor sound assertive, even forceful. But to look at her, she seems like a little girl trying to protect herself. "No, it's great, it's just that we're poking around in Sadr City and Tikrit and Fallujah and asking for the relatives of these nasty characters to verify these signatures, which is what you said you wanted me to do, right? And that's a little sketchy, according to our local staff, and if we really didn't need to do that, if you were on the verge of getting an answer some other way…uh-huh. But look, we've gone this far. At this point, tell them to wait a few more days. I think we're on the cusp of finding out so much more. I mean, we wanted to know who made these documents and why, right? And finding out that they're fake is only the tip of the iceberg. Why would someone in Iraq make up documents to embarrass Billy Jackson of Newark, New Jersey? I mean, something about this stinks, Miles, and in *such* a bizarro way. What if there's other stuff involved? Maybe the same people who made these documents are the same folks who were drawing up fake documents on WMD! It's possible, isn't it?" Sam looks at me and opens her eyes with exaggeration, like she knows she might be taking this too far. She slides off the desk and leans on the glass door that leads to the balcony. There's still a large X taped across it.

"But Miles, we still need to figure out who made these documents. I mean, there's something fishy there."

The tinny crunch of Miles's voice emanates from the phone. I pretend to get up to get a glass of water, but really I do it so that, on the way back, I can seat myself in the smaller sofa next to her desk, nearer the phone.

"Miles, would you run a crime story and not let the reporter *try* to find out who the perp is? I mean, if you could figure it out…but, but I think we *can* figure it out. We're close. Just wait, Miles. Please don't do anything with the story yet. There are still a lot of gaps to be filled in."

Sam listens. Her lips and nose behave as if they are perpetually in protest at food that's gone off in the fridge. She rubs the pretty bones that her eyebrows lie upon and sighs. "I understand. Just tell them the story really isn't done yet. If they can hold off for just a couple more days, I think we're going to have a much, much better story. Okay? Good. I gotta run, but I'll check in later."

Sam slams down the receiver. "Jesus H. Christ," she says with a voice that would convey rage if the disbelief hadn't sucked the air out of it. She looks at me and her eyes grow big for a moment, so that I can see all the whites around the edges, and then they fall back to their natural state. She turns away from me then, slides open the glass door to the balcony and walks out. She bends over and looks down at the pool below, where I can hear people splashing in the water.

She turns her neck when she notices me standing there, watching her. "You heard all that, right?" It's as if she didn't pay any attention to which part of the conversation was on speaker-phone, and at what point she had picked up the phone, turning their exchange into a monologue.

"Part of it."

"Can you believe that? They didn't even bother to tell me and they've got us chasing after Saddam's best friends. I'm sorry to say this in front of you, Nabil, but that's fucking ridiculous. This is patently, objectively insane." She takes another cigarette out of the packet in her hand and brushes past me, stomping towards the kitchen. She clicks on the gas flame at the stove, lowers her face sideways towards the fire, and turns the cigarette tip bright orange. The smoke curls she lets escape from the sides of her mouth wind up inside her hair and hover there a moment. She seems half-angel, half-Medusa. "I'll be back in a bit," she says, not waiting for a response, and walks out.

I want to chase after Sam straight away, but that seems like something stupid men do in those trite Egyptian tearjerkers. Run after the woman, tell her that everything's going to be fine, then grab her and kiss her when she's most vulnerable. When she *needs* you.

Somehow, I don't think that following Sam the moment she storms out of the room is something she will appreciate.

I wait and pace for several minutes, which pass like hours. I peer over at her computer screen, though I know I shouldn't, and read the subject lines of the messages lined up in a column. There is a message from Miles. *Please call ASAP.* One is, judging from the name, from Sam's mother. *Stay safe!* And one from Jonah: "*Re: Where are you?*" I watch my fingers finding their way to her unfamiliar keys, and somehow, managing to open and read *because the risks you're taking aren't worth it, Sam, and I learned that the hard way. And if you really cared about us, about yourself, you'd consider dropping that story before something* and then I force myself to stop and exit because Sam could walk in at any moment and would be furious.

But she doesn't. And so I scroll down the page with the arrow key, past a dozen or so news headlines that the paper apparently sends Sam every day, to find more messages from Jonah. There are six messages whose subject lines read, *Re: I love you*, and a last one, stating simply, *I love you.* I have never told a woman that I love her, but when I do, I certainly don't want to tell her through a computer.

I have to fight the urge to read more. I recall The Unjust, a sura from the Koran. It tells us that the records of righteousness and sin are not meant for us to know in this world. "It is a sealed book, seen only by the favoured. (83:20)" My mother once taught me that this sura means we should not read other people's mail or pry into their private affairs, even if we suspect them of wrongdoing.

Instead, I grab the cigarettes off the table. I can hardly believe myself. I have hated cigarettes since my father let me see pictures of diseased lungs from the hospital morgue when I was twelve. But it gives me a good excuse to go looking for Sam. I have something to bring her.

I am not surprised to find her on the rooftop. I know Sam likes it up here, because from this height she can watch the two worlds below. Inside the Hamra walls, her colleagues saunter half-naked in their bathing suits, swimming or drinking alcohol. Outside the walls, a claque of women in full-length abayas float past like black spirits, sending bad omens to the foreigners inside. Once inside for the night, the foreigners try to forget the Iraqis outside. The Iraqis never forget.

"I brought you these," I say, and place the box on the ledge in front of her. I smile a little bit, and try to stop myself from imagining a lung going black in Sam's body.

"Thanks." She points to the chairs in the hallway, where we left them. We drag them out to the space she likes, in the front corner where you get a bit of crossbreeze.

I feel we're being accompanied by a quiet orchestra of satellite dishes. Millions of people around the world get their news from this very rooftop. I catch myself fantasizing again about throwing it all over the edge into the pool below, drowning the communications equipment in a watery, chlorinated tomb.

"I never saw you smoke before," I offer.

"That's because I don't," she says, pulling out another cigarette and lighting it with the burning butt of the last one. "I quit five years ago." She drops the remains of the old cigarette on to the white floor, turning it into a black blur with her sandal. I hate that fresh cigarette, and the thought of Sam ruining her health with it, but there is something sensuous about the way her mouth wraps itself around the tip and pulls it in. Her lips seem a little puffy, but perfectly sculpted and pinkish, as though they belong on one of those plastic baby dolls that seem to multiply like mad before the holidays, when people are expected to bring gifts to all the children in their family. There is something about the lines in her lips that is attractive, even if I know that someday, they will be an old lady's lines. Even as a grandmother, she will still be beautiful.

"Five years ago is a long time." I don't know what to say. I don't want to be in a place of giving Sam grief.

"Yeah, well," she says, inhaling deeply, as if she expects half the cigarette to be pulled inside her all at once. "That was when I met Jonah. He got me to quit."

I can feel my chest fall as Sam exhales. "He required you to quit? In order for him to be your boyfriend?"

"Well, something like that. He convinced me. No one *requires* me to do anything." She laughs a little. I watch the smoke make ringlets above her hand, floating up towards her neck before being caught by a hot breeze and carried off somewhere north, towards Sadr City.

"You're disappointed in your editors, yes?"

Nabil al-Amari, master of subtle questions. She doesn't answer and so we don't say anything for a while, and I don't mind that. It is good to just sit here and know that she must be comfortable enough around me not to say anything. I think only people who really trust each other are able to do that.

On her third cigarette, Sam begins to talk again.

"Disappointed isn't the word, Nabil." She takes two drags, one after the other, and then exhales the smoke through her nostrils. It reminds me of a bull in the cartoons, just before it charges. "I'm fucking furious."

I think of the conversation we'd had about cursing, how I had used "fuck" during an interview – as part of my translation, to convey someone's anger – and she scolded me for it afterwards. She said it was too impolite to use, even in an informal interview, around anyone who knows any English at all, because you never know how much they really know.

But now doesn't seem the right time for pinning Sam down on the finer points of when vulgarities are or are not acceptable.

"It's fine," she says, as if trying to convince herself.

"Is it?"

"What's the difference?" Sam takes off one of her sandals and throws it on to an adjacent roof across the slim alley. "After all I've done for them, they go ahead and do this without even telling me! I'm endangering my life in this hellhole and they're playing around with some friggin' Get Smart, Inspector Gadget nerd in Washington. Jesus! The fucking nerve of them!" She annunciates the words in a staccato, as if spitting each one into hot air. She gets up and paces for a moment, limping because of her missing shoe, and then she stops and looks at me.

"You know what?"

"Yes, Sam?"

"The floor's too hot to be walking on barefoot, even at night!" She plonks herself back down into the chair, dropping her bare foot over the sandalled one. "This is pathetic," she hisses at her feet, as if talking to herself. "Why am I here if they want to figure it out from their end? Why *am* I here? What am I *doing* here?"

Quiet. And then the sound of the *izzan* to answer her, called out by a nearby *muezzin*, who is soon joined by a chorus of many more, none quite in sync with the other, sending their melodic dissonance wafting over the rooftops. There is now a sweet quorum in the air, and I want to pray with them, to pray for Sam and for all of us, but I am not about to say prayers with Sam around.

"Why is it so bad, Sam? The information they have, doesn't it back us up? The story is still correct. I mean, it doesn't contradict what we've found."

"Yeah, but they think it's all we need, as if it's the end of the story. They want to run it in the next day or two. Tomorrow if they could. They're impatient. Just like they were when they ran Harris's original story that got the paper into this mess. Just like every damn newspaper in America. And across the free world."

"Does that include Iraq? President Bush says we're free now."

Sam sputters a mouthful of smoke. "Very funny."

"Can't you get them to wait?" I ask. "You're good with negotiating."

"How? Well, I could scream and pout and insist until I'm blue in the face and threaten to quit…"

"Would you?"

"No, I can't go giving them an ultimatum. It's…bad form."

I turn to her and say in my poshest English accent, "Oh! Terribly tawdry!"

She laughs. "You're a trip, Nabil. You crack me up sometimes. Do you know how ridiculous it sounds when that accent comes out of a mouth like yours?"

Even if I'm glad to see her laughing, I'm a little bit insulted. What does it mean, a mouth like yours? Is my mouth so different from an Englishman's? I do not even wear a moustache anymore. But I can see that no matter how good my English is, Sam will always view me as an Arab who, by speaking so well, is a source of amusement.

34

Speaking

Taking the steps two at a time, I fly up the stairs and tap on the door of Sam's room. There is no answer. I try buzzing and knocking, but still no reply. Nearly 9 a.m. She had said to come between 8:45 and 9.

Next door, a young woman in shorts that only cover the start of her thighs shows herself in the doorway. I have noticed her around the pool, usually in a bikini and dark glasses, as if the latter might let her disappear among the other foreigners. I have noticed her because she has a skinny Western figure but a delicate Arab face, almost like a Yemenite, I think.

"You're Sam's fixer, right?"

The fixer: the person who makes it all happen. Will I ever live up to the title? And then Taher, who made it sound sort of insulting, someone's errand-boy.

"I'm her interpreter. Uh, translator."

"She asked me to tell you that she decided to stay overnight at the Sheraton. There was some big party there for all the journos last night, and she didn't want to rush back before the curfew. So you should just wait for her."

When I left at 8:30 p.m., Sam left afterwards and went to a party? From being so angry, she went out to socialize?

"I see." I can feel my Adam's Apple move up and down, a lever gauging my nervousness. I try to avoid letting my eyes fall towards her bare legs. She closes the opening a bit, moving her body further from the door.

"Excuse me," she says, "I just woke up. Had a late deadline."

"Yes, oh, I'm sorry if I disturbed you. I'm Nabil." I consider giving her my hand, but as the opening in the door is so narrow now, I hold it up instead, a frozen, mid-air wave.

"I know. I'm Leila," she smiles, without looking directly at me. "See you soon, then," she says, and shuts the door, leaving me between their two doors in the hallway.

I wander downstairs to the bakery that I must have passed a hundred times since I started working for Sam, but never bothered to enter. I'm surprised by the wide selection of biscuits and cakes, and I feel that the two women working the counters are equally surprised to see me. Perhaps only foreigners staying at the hotel shop here, and very few Iraqis, despite the beautiful delicacies. Can they possibly get enough traffic here to keep such a well-stocked bakery in business?

Caught in the coffee-eyed gaze of a young woman waiting for me to buy something, I order two boxes: Arabic ones for Sam, European-looking puff pastries with coloured icing for my family. Each will be more impressed with something from the other. I will use the opportunity to teach Sam about the different kinds of *baklawa*. It would be a shame if she left Iraq someday and didn't know that much.

Walking out, I realize there are only a few choices. The first is to sit here with Rafik. The second is to go back to the first tower, where I might have to sit with the nasty receptionist, or Taher, or some other translators I don't feel like talking to just now. I'm afraid I'll open my mouth and say something I shouldn't.

A third option is to wait for her in the café with the ugly orange decor and those guys who watch and eavesdrop. Or to wait by the pool, though it's already hot like a *firin* out there. So I may as well wait here in the second tower lobby, with Rafik at his desk.

I open the European pastry box for him. "*Tfaddal.*" Take, please.

"No, no," he says. "It's too early." He grabs at the small tyre around his middle. "And my wife says I must watch this."

We laugh and I sit.

"Miss Samara not in?"

I know he knows she's not in, so why must he ask?

"She had to stay with her friend Melissa at CNN, over at the Sheraton Hotel. She was asked to do a live interview at midnight. That's only four in the afternoon in America." I don't know why I do this, start making up lies to protect Sam. But what will the men in the hotel think of her if they see she doesn't come home at night, off late at parties with men and alcohol? They will assume the worst. It's only for her own good.

Rafik nods, but looks down at his desk. "Want to read a newspaper?"

"Thanks," I say, getting up to take it. It's one I haven't seen before, *Al Sabah Al-Jadida*. The New Morning. *Paul Bremer Arrives in Baghdad Today to Replace Jay Garner, the failed Occupation Chief of President Bush.* In the first paragraph, it says that Mr Bremer is going to dismiss anyone associated with the Ba'ath party and senior and even mid-level officials will be investigated and then banned from government positions. I know that Mr Bremer's real name is L. Paul Bremer III, because I saw it in a story Sam showed me on her computer screen the other day. Otherwise, if I were only reading the Iraqi papers, I might think his name was Bol Breemer, a terrible start because it's too close to *buul*, which means urine. Since we have no "p" in Arabic, most people substitute a "b". When people try to speak English with Sam, they start talking about the Iraqi *beoble*, and that's when I convince them to stick to Arabic and let me translate.

"So we'll have a new American in charge," I offer.

"*Aiy*," says Rafik, nodding. "Things can only improve, yes?"

I wonder if Rafik is testing me, trying to determine whether I actually like the Americans. Who can know whether to trust him? But he is friendly, and does seem to like Sam.

Rafik scans the hallway, where there is no one but us, save a German photographer making his way out of the door. The bank branch across from him is still closed.

I continue reading about what Mr Bremer is expected to do.

"Do you tell the men at the other reception desk what you're doing when you go out every day?"

I look up. "What?"

"Do you tell them? In the first tower," he says, lifting his chin with a quick jab towards the pool and the other building beyond it.

"No, not usually."

"Well you shouldn't tell them at all," he says, coughing into his hand, like he's trying to hide what he just said.

"You don't trust them?"

"I didn't say that. It's just that one of them is mad at you."

"At me?" I sit up. What could I have done?

"At you and Sam. He says his cousin worked with Sam first and that you took his job away."

"But I've been working with Sam since the start!" I feel my back stiffen, my vertebrae acting defensive. "Since Baghdad fell, I mean."

"Didn't she say that she worked with someone before then?"

"No, she said she worked with a Kurdish guy who didn't want to come south of Tikrit."

Rafik nods, but says nothing. "And then after, when she got to Baghdad, she must have worked with someone. None of the foreigners are capable of functioning here alone."

It's true. I don't think there's been any story Sam was able to do without my help – without my fixing. Why didn't I consider that she must have had someone else before I met her at the hospital?

"Anyway, he's the brother of one of the bellboys, and he's got a grudge against you because they think you've wronged his family by taking his brother's job."

I can feel the blood pushing up against my heart. Why didn't he tell me this before? Why didn't Sam?

"There's another thing you should beware of. You and Miss Samara have a staffing problem."

My hands have started to shake, and feel moist against the newspaper. I fold it up so Rafik won't notice. "Really? How is that?"

"You're a Sunni, and your driver is a Kurd. You don't have a Shi'ite working for you."

I shrug. "We don't have a Christian or a communist, either. Maybe we need one of each of them."

"I'm serious," he murmurs. The lift arrives and Joon Park

walks out, smiling slightly for a change. "Oh hey, Nabil. Did Leila tell you that Sam decided to stay late at the party at the Sheraton last night?"

I nod. Joon, the one time she bothers to be friendly with me, ratting on us. But then, maybe Rafik's English isn't so great; I've never heard him say more than hello, goodbye, thank you, and please, as he hands over the keys to the hotel clientele. Maybe he missed it. Otherwise, he'll start thinking that I'm a liar.

Rafik stares at me until Joon is out of the door.

"You should have a Shi'ite on staff, too. To have all of your bases covered."

"Maybe a Yezidi for good measure? The Mandeans are also not well-represented."

Rafik's nostrils flare so much that I can see black tufts of nose hair.

"Sorry, sorry. I was only joking," I say. "It's just, we're a small team. I don't think Sam would want another person."

"You should have a Shi'ite with you," he says in a low voice. "And maybe a bodyguard."

"A guard?" I laugh and look out to the pool, where I can see two sets of peach-white arms emerging from the water at a fast clip, racing each other. The truth is, I have thought of it in recent days. If someone ever tried to hurt Sam, *la-smuh-Alla*, God forbid, what would I do? Talk them out of it?

"You need to be very careful about making enemies around here," Rafik says. "Shi'ites are going to be in control in the future. You have to accept that."

"You know, I'm also Shi'ite."

"What do you mean, also? With a name like Nabil?"

"My mother is Shi'ite and my father is Sunni."

"Oh," he says, motioning for me to come back with the box of sweet pastries. "That's different. But you're still a Sunni. You can't be both."

"I am both," I say, holding the box open. He takes one that looks like a giant chocolate hotdog. I think it's a Napoleon. No, an éclair.

Rafik mumbles a *Bismillah* and sinks his teeth deep, covering at least a third of it. I hadn't taken him for a religious man. As he chews he wiggles his head from side to side, as if he likes the taste. "It's delicious! I have never thought to go in there."

"In the bakery? It's right behind you."

He shrugs. "It's meant for foreigners, you know. It's not priced for Iraqis."

I sit back down, and wait for Rafik to finish. I'd have one myself, but there's my rule on sweets. Noor.

He eagerly devours the last bit. When it's gone, he makes a tiny grunt of pleasure. "You can't be both Sunni and Shi'ite," he declares.

"Why not? Of course you can."

"No," he says. "You cannot. Either you are a supporter of Imam Ali or you are not. Either when you say the *Shahada*, you say there is no god but God and Mohammed is His Prophet *and* Imam Ali is His Successor, or you don't. Either you fast and cry and suffer on *Ashura* or you don't. Either you go to a *husseiniye* instead of a mosque, or you don't. You make pilgrimages to the holy places in Najaf and Karbala, or you don't. This is what it means to be Shi'ite. You can't be both." He smiles, looking at me as if he could go on all morning. "So which is it for you?"

I fold my hands over my stomach, which still seems to be mulling over my breakfast. I am relieved to see Sam at the door, her body swaying backwards as she pulls it open. "I am simply a believer," I say. "I don't believe in making these distinctions. All a Muslim needs is faith in God." I stand, watch Sam stride towards us, her hair still heavy from a shower, her hands swinging.

Beyond the shampoo scent emanating from her hair, as I follow her up the stairs I can smell last night's party on her clothes: drinks and cigarettes. She pushes open the door, and shuts it behind her immediately. "Nabil, I met someone really interesting at this party last night who I think is going to help us get some answers. And you're going to be pretty interested to see who he is."

"So," I say, "I know him?"

"Hang on. Take a seat for a few minutes. Or better yet," she says, eyeing Rafik's paper, which I forgot to hand back to him when I followed Sam up, "translate some headlines for me while I change. I'm curious to know what these new papers are saying."

"How did you know it was new?" I ask, but she is already in her room, the door only slightly ajar, rummaging, I presume, for something else to wear. Something much more conservative than the snug black pants and very-short-sleeved black blouse she wore to last night's party. I wonder why she never mentioned she would be going there when I left yesterday. I feel it is my job now to know about the major things going on in Sam's life, at least her life in Iraq. How can I fix things for her if I don't even know where she is?

She appears in a light-blue blouse and those loose khaki trousers she wears often, striking that serious-but-sporty look the women reporters around the Hamra all seem to have. At first it seemed uniquely Sam, but now that I've seen it on others, it looks like an American uniform.

"How did you get back this morning?"

Sam stops her rearranging of things in her bag and looks at me, watching without blinking, as if she is gauging what to say based on how capable I am of handling the information. "A friend from the BBC drove me home," she says. And then raises her eyebrows. "Anything else, Mom?" She laughs a bit and I make a show of laughing with her. "Hey," she says, eyeing her watch. "We've got to head over to the Green Zone."

"I thought you said your editors didn't want you to do any more daily stories for now."

"They don't. This isn't a press conference," she says. "Um, what's in here?"

I forgot to present her with the box of Arabic sweets; I carried them up in a bag and then set them on the kitchen counter when we walked in. Now she is lifting open the top and discovering them before I had the chance to present them to her. This is Sam; taking what you want to give her anyway. If only she'd be more patient.

"I got them for you to—"

"Wow!" She takes the first box out of the bag and opens the second. "And these, too?"

"I got, well, I bought a box of the Arabic ones for you and the European pastries for my family, because I'd have thought you'd have had enough of that sort of—"

"Oh, Nabil, that's so sweet of you!" She purses her lips like she might, for just a moment, want to kiss me. "Thanks, Nabil. These look great."

"Well, they're just from downstairs. Someday I will take you to Abu Afif. That is the best sweet shop in all of Baghdad. I'm not sure these will be as good."

Sam lifts up a small one, prying it from its tight alignment. It disappears into her mouth, and she closes her eyes, circling her head and pretending to swoon. "Oh my God. That's like a direct injection to the veins."

"Try this." I point to the round ones in the centre. "It's called the bird's nest. See why? The nuts are supposed to be the eggs."

"I see," says Sam, but reaches for an Oum Ali instead, which is much too heavy for this time of day. "So at this party," she continues, holding the pastry up to her mouth and using her teeth to break it in two, depositing the rest on a plate in the sink. "Mm. *So* good. I'll tell you about it on the way." She licks two fingers, then holds her hand under the tap, rinsing the stickiness away.

35

Rinsing

By the time we reach Damascus Street, Sam has filled me in on why we're heading to the Green Zone. Last night at the party, she got invited to a smaller party in someone's suite. She walked in, and among the ten or so people there was that rude American man who had forced us to leave the meeting in Fallujah. Except that he wasn't rude now. He was suddenly very nice to her, and apologetic about how he had acted that day. He took her aside and said he'd love to make it up to her by helping her out, and that she should come to his office today. He's working in an ORHA office for reconstruction projects, ORHA being the name the Americans have given for the office of all the things they're supposed to be doing in Iraq, other than just occupying our country with tanks and soldiers. His name is Franklin Baylor, but we can call him Frank.

Rizgar rolls over the Jumhuriya Bridge, inching behind the other cars which gingerly pass the tanks and Bradleys with men posted behind their guns. To our left, the Ministry of Construction stands like a rotting dinosaur, parts of it bombed out by the Americans in the first days of the war, each window shattered, every part of the frame warped and frayed. I wonder if Frank is going to reconstruct that.

"So he's really not a spook?" I ask.

Sam shrugs. "I'm not so sure about *that*. I think he could be a spook whose cover is that he works on reconstruction."

What really amazes me is that she has forgiven him so quickly for his treatment towards us that day. Or maybe she just thinks he has something she wants.

We wait for the soldiers to check our boot, and then they tell us to get out of the car so they can search the inside. We stand and wait, and I notice that her hair still looks wet, perhaps because she tied it up and didn't give it a chance to dry. The thought of her showering somewhere else, but not being clear where, filters through the part of my mind that feels like shaking her. *Anything else, Mom?* Sam sees me as worrying about her like a mother – not even like a father! – not as being defensive of how staying out all night could affect her reputation. Not as being curious about whose bed she slept in.

The inside of the presidential palace is spacious and confusing, Arabic in style but American in function, bustling with soldiers male and female, and civilian people dressed like they do in the American films about California, many of them in jeans or shorts and colourful, short-sleeved polo shirts. Most spectacular are the elaborate ceilings, high as the grandest mosque, and the intricately tiled floors, beautiful as a Persian carpet. I want to take it all in, but Sam hurries me along. Apparently she knows the way from her previous visits here.

"Nabil!" she whispers, catching me gazing upwards. "Come on! I don't want anyone noticing we came in here without an escort."

Sam doesn't realize how new this is. How we have grown up learning to be afraid. How it is baked into our *samoun*, rolled into our *kubbeh*, stuffed into our *dolma*, filling up the very fibre of who we are. Unless, of course, you are one of the people who makes others afraid.

"In here," Sam beckons, her hand cupping me towards a corridor of offices with paper signs on the doors. Written on them are all our country's problems in need of fixing: sewage, water distribution, health services, road repair, electricity.

The tall, muscular bulk of him rises to shake my hand. He has the same arrogant face that made Sam so angry that day, only now he seems a shred softer. He welcomes me with a laugh in his voice, as if to acknowledge that circumstances were quite different last time we met.

"Nabil al-Amari."

"Franklin Baylor. Pleased to meet you," he smiles, pointing to a chair for me to sit in, and something about the way he smiles makes me realize that he probably was not expecting to see me. Perhaps he thought Sam would come alone.

Baylor sits and folds his hands on the edge of his desk. "So, another reporter who wants to know what the hell's going on with the electricity."

Sam is slow to respond, her eyes sweeping from one side of his face to another. She smiles gently. "Well, yes. I mean, why is it that no one is getting more than a few hours a day? I mean, it's more than a month since the US forces took control of Baghdad and there are parts of the city that have no power at all."

"There are a lot of reasons," he says, rolling his eyes back at her. "I can explain most of them and show you what we're doing to fix it. The administration really wants this problem solved. But I think the best way to explain it to you is when we're looking at a chart of all the grids, for the whole city of Baghdad."

Baylor looks out of the window, then pushes back one of the huge maroon curtains, pendulous with dust. "Come with me down to the utility logistics room and I'll show you what I mean."

"Oh," Sam says, "you don't mind if Nabil comes with us, do you?"

"Well," Baylor sounds hesitant. "We have certain policies on access for Iraqis who haven't been through a security clearance." He scans my face and stares at me for a moment, "But I think we can get around it. You look like an honest one. You can vouch for this guy, right?" Baylor grins, and at one end of his mouth is a tooth that seems sharp enough to open a can of vegetables.

He's off down the hall. And because he's tall and his stride is long, it's an effort keep up with him, especially as I keep getting distracted. Above us there is a soaring ceiling with intricate Syrian wood carvings fitted into it, and a sparkling chandelier more elaborate than anything I have seen in any mosque. Baylor leads us into a grand reception room with windows that look out on to a tropical garden. There are gargantuan columns lining the room and an ocean of rich marble flooring so shiny I feel we could skate our way across it. The sun from the windows bounces off it and glares into my eyes, so that I feel compelled to shield them with my hand.

I try to keep in step with their brisk but breezy-looking pace through the chambers as they change from vast to vascular, leading from one place to another, past offices with computers, men in military uniform and others in shorts and trainers, women dressed like the men or wearing sleeveless tops. Each has a collection of plastic-coated tags hanging around his or her neck, and they trade cheery words as they pass without stopping.

"Heya. How'ya doin'? How's it goin'?" Most of them are young, with the exception of a few middle-aged men with grey hair and wider middles, tugging at their collars in the heat. And the heat is stifling. My shirt is almost soaked. "How could a palace like this not have air conditioning?" I ask Sam.

"No, no," Baylor says. "Apparently, there was always air conditioning here but when our boys bombed the electrical centre during the invasion, we destroyed it and now they can't get it to work again." He smirks at me. "But the official line is that it's the looters fault for stealing all the wiring."

Baylor continues to lead us through the maze of the palace. We descend three flights of stairs from where we started, and as we go the air gets staler, but also, pleasantly cooler.

"See now, Iraqis will tell you that there was full-time electricity under Saddam, but that's a blatant lie," he says. "And in fact, the deal was, Saddam was sending all the juice to his buddies in Baghdad and the Sunni triangle and places like Tikrit, while poor Shi'ites and people in the south weren't getting much of anything at all. See? Let me show you the damage that was done to some of the circuit-breakers," he says. He holds open the door to what I imagine is some kind of control room, but as we step in, it looks little more than a small storage room with a dirty window that gives on to a concrete wall.

He shuts the door behind us. "All right, it's a bit hot and shitty, but it's safe to talk." He offers Sam the only seat, a beaten-up wooden chair against a narrow counter, and leans on the wall. "Sorry," he says to me. "I know it's not the swankiest of places."

"Might we open the door a bit?" I ask. It is already hot in the room; with three of us shut in here, I can imagine the temperature soaring, the air being sucked out, me hitting the floor. But Sam seems fine; she has her window. It's only now that I realize we have something in common: unpredictable syndromes liable to get the better of us.

"Sorry," Baylor says. "But that would defeat the purpose." He goes to the window, undoes the catch and yanks the window up a few inches, releasing a mouldy puff of dust. "That should do it."

"So," Baylor crosses his bulky arms, facing Sam. "You want to know where your problematic story on Congressman Jackson came from, the one that he's suing y'all for in court."

"Right," she says. "Well, actually, at this point it's more than problematic. We can say, pretty much with certainty, that they're fake."

"Yes, and so you'd like to know who cooked them up. Well, I think I can help you with that, and then maybe you'll help me out with something."

"Okay…" Sam says tentatively.

"I don't think you have to look any further than the office of Ahmad Chalabi. I mean, I'm liable to get fired if it comes out that I told you that," Baylor says, looking over at me and then back to Sam, "but I'm sure that's never going to come out, is it?"

Sam nods her slow nod. "So this is just a theory you have. Don't get me wrong. I realize someone went out of his way to stir this thing up. But Ahmad Chalabi? Why would he need to be messing around with domestic American politicians like Jackson? I mean, why should he be dabbling in smear stories when he's got a recently liberated country to run? Chalabi's got the whole Pentagon behind him, the White House, and the CIA. This guy's going to be the next president of Iraq, right?"

Baylor bows his head to one side. "If some people have their way, sure. At least, that was the plan. But I would trim your list of supporters a bit. In fact, I'd lop off the last third."

Sam crosses her legs, pulling the right so far over the left that it's like she's only sitting on one side of her body. "Yeah?"

Baylor squints as if to say of course, that same kind of squint that Sam gives me when I've said something dumb. "Sure. Agency's been warning for a long time not to trust him. In fact, State department folks don't like him either. The guy's wanted in Jordan for bank fraud, for God's sake. But DIA loved him. They and the Pentagon told the White House everything the big chiefs wanted to hear. No one cared if it was true or not. No one went out and said, hey, you think we should do some reference checks on this guy before we hand'im the keys to the castle?"

Sam turns to me. "DIA is Defense Intelligence Agency. You get the difference, right?"

I nod.

Baylor points to me and to Sam and back at me. "So both of you guys are in on *all* of this?"

"Totally," Sam says, sounding emphatic, even defensive. "I couldn't have done any of this without Nabil."

"Okay, so then Nabil needs to be in on the confidentiality agreement, too. You can't tell anyone we had this conversation, and my name can never be mentioned, nor the agency."

"I know," I say. "Off the record." I'm surprised by the way it rolls off my tongue.

"This isn't even off the record," he says with eyes narrowing in my direction. "This is such deep background, it may as well be at the bottom of a mass grave in East-fucking-Baquba. You get my drift?"

"Sure." I still dislike his arrogant tone. But I like that I am getting most of his slang, and that he sees that my English is good enough for him to use it.

"Listen, Ahmad Chalabi is a character and-a-half," Baylor says. "He's now one of the wealthiest, most powerful men in Iraq, and he's done that primarily with taxpayer money. It's amazing this guy was in our good graces as long as he was."

"Was?" Sam interrupts.

"Well, look, there's a lot bubbling now that I can't talk about yet, even on background. But let me tell you this much. Ahmad Chalabi—"

"Do you mind if I take notes?"

"Go ahead. But you're not recording are you?"

"No," Sam says, putting her notebook on the counter. "I hardly ever record."

"Fine. Don't even put my name at the top of your notes there," he says, stretching his neck to see what she just scribbled. It reads: On Chalabi.

Baylor clears his throat. He quickly opens the door a crack and sticks his head out to see if there's someone in the hallway. "Just bear in mind, if you burn me by sourcing any of this back to me or anyone who even smells like me, I will make sure that no one in any agency that matters will ever talk to you again."

Sam holds up two fingers. "Scout's honour."

"Nice, but I think that's a peace sign."

Sam smiles with a hint of embarrassment, drawing the two fingers together.

"Here's what you should know. Since around 1994, when our guys back home really started regretting not taking out Saddam in '91 when they had the chance, the United States has given over a hundred million dollars to Chalabi and the INC. Every month the INC gets about $350,000 from the Department of Defense. And that whole time, it turns out, he was double-dipping: getting funds from the Iranians and cultivating close ties with them. Meanwhile just a couple of years back, after 9/11, Chalabi starts feeding us all kinds of info about how Saddam has resumed his WMD plans and wants to build a bomb. And you know what I think? Not just me. A lot of us. A lot of us think that nearly every piece of information the guy provided to us about Saddam's weapons capabilities was fake. But we wanted it. Oh, you can imagine how hungry Bush's boys were for every tasty tidbit that Chalabi served up. So, let's see, you feed us bogus information, and we pay you handsomely for the privilege of receiving it. Either we're too blind to see you're bullshitting us, or we're pretending we don't see it. Because hey, it makes *such* a good excuse for a war. And a great opportunity to take out a brutal asshole who no one likes anyway."

Sam is scribbling so furiously that her script looks more like unfolding coils of Arabic than English, except for it running from left to right. Her cheeks are flushed. I wish I had a handkerchief with me to wipe the sweat from my face.

"So your guys at the *Tribune* bought bum documents from some guy who professes to have more, and all of these documents seem to incriminate people who were pro-Saddam, or at least anti-invasion. What does it tell us? It's an ideologically motivated forgery ring, not just a financial one. Hey, criminals are people, too, you know – they got a right to a cause. So, if you've got a whole slew of documents and most of them just happen to be incriminating people who were pro-regime or even *looked* pro-regime and who worked their tails off to keep us from knocking out Saddam, you bet'cha bottom dollar that is no coincidence. And if I had to say who was the most likely suspect, as a person who might have the will and the wherewithal to organize such a thing, well, I'd say that that person must be Ahmad Chalabi. See what I mean?"

Sam finishes off another two lines in her notebook and stops, putting it aside. "Wow. Huh! That's pretty incredible. But look, Frank, I can't go on must-be. You can put two and two together, I guess, but maybe there's more than one person who fits the profile of four. Maybe someone else who's smart and corrupt did this. How can we know for sure it's Chalabi?"

"Hey, well, *proving* that Chalabi is behind it, now that's going to be pretty hard. That man's one slippery individual. And clever, too. Did I mention well-connected? You're sure you want to pursue this?"

Sam shakes her head. "It's not a question of wanting."

"Well, then I'll say this. I'm positive that Chalabi is your man. But if you want to trace the whole paper trail, that's going to require a little more work."

"What about your sources? Could any of them help us nail down whether it's Chalabi?"

"Now, Miss Katchens," he says in a sermonizing tone, wagging a finger at her. "I'm happy to give you whatever information I can that will be helpful for your story, if it will help bring out the truth. But not at the expense of some other guy getting his head blown off, which keeps happening around here."

Sam exhales, turns her pen over in her notebook. Point, plunger, point. "So, what's the truth you're after?"

Baylor shifts his back against the wall, blinking. His eyes search blank airspace for a moment, and he stands up straight.

"The truth is that I don't give a shit about Billy Jackson and his political career, and I don't have a particular axe to grind against Chalabi. But I'm going to help you with this Jackson thing, and after that, I think you're going to help me by doing a story about the WMD farce."

Sam squints. "Are you saying there are *no* weapons of mass destruction in Iraq?"

"Not in useable condition. And whatever was useable has probably been carted off elsewhere," he says, using his fingers like little feet running away. "But first things first. Sam, how about you come back to my office upstairs so we can make things look good in terms of you having talked to me about electricity. I can send out a couple of messages from there, maybe get you some leads," he says. "And Nabil, I'm going to send you out with one of our undercover intel guys who can show you areas where a lot of the illegal activities are going on: weapons markets, chop shops, looted goods up for resale. You might find some connections to the forgery operations there, too."

Sam views Baylor with hard eyes. "We don't usually split up." It isn't entirely true, but I like the way she put it. *We.* "And if this guy is intel and knows all this stuff," Sam says, "I'd like to be there, too."

"Afraid not," Baylor says. "Nabil will see where they're at. He could always bring you back there later in your own car. But I don't need you going there on my watch. It's way too dangerous."

"Well then it's dangerous for Nabil."

"Less so for an Iraqi," he says, reaching for the door knob. He looks me over. "I want to send you out for a tour with my guy Louis. He's not really in intel so much as security with a bit of information-gathering thrown in, but don't tell him I said that," he says, giving me a wink. "He can show you a few interesting things around town, and then drop you off at the Hamra."

"Frank," she says. "I need to get out and check these places, too. If I don't do it in one of your bullet-proof bulldozers, when will I?"

"Look, Louis is a quarter Latino and wears a nice big moustache, so he can pass in a crowd. But people would be suspicious of a woman in these places. Am I right, Nabil?"

I look at Sam, knowing that lying might put her in danger. "Yes."

"With that mane, if you don't mind my saying, you're never going to pass for anything but a good-lookin' media chick," says Baylor. "Oh, sorry. Was that politically incorrect?" He smiles widely, pulling the door open and holding out his hand for her to walk first.

36

Holding

Up close, Louis, who makes it clear that I don't need to know anything about him other than not to call him *Lou-ee,* and not Lou either, doesn't look at all like he might be mistaken for an Arab. But he does wear a thick moustache, and from afar, I suppose, I see what Baylor is talking about. He is a touch more brown than most Americans, unlike Baylor or Sam, who have skin somewhere between a peach and an apricot. He could pass for Lebanese, maybe. But not Iraqi.

After a kind but fast hello that says, *don't waste my time with your Arab niceties*, Louis flies off at speeds we haven't driven since before the war, when we weren't worried about the possibility of being mistaken for someone trying to attack a US convoy.

He reaches into his glove compartment, cups a red glass box in his hand, and when he rolls down the window I get a better look at the ruby-coloured charm and only now do I see that it is a siren. He lifts himself out of his seat and, with his left arm out of the window, plonks the siren on top of the car.

The wailing sends a bolt of fear into my neck. It's the knell of heart attacks, strokes, accidents. The sounds of the hospital while I waited in Baba's office after passing out from some terrible sight or another. *Akhir marra.* This is the last time I'm taking you here, Nabil.

But we don't often hear the sirens anymore, unless it is a really big bombing, the kind that shakes the ground and rattles the windows and sends a shudder through your arm-hairs, so that you know that many people, not just one, have just passed from this world, whisked out of the city through the secret doors only God knows. There are fewer sirens now because when it's only a few people dead no one bothers to get the ambulance to come, but instead they take most of the injured to hospital on their own.

We carry our own dead and wounded, in our cars and trucks and trunks, and afterwards in our minds, which brings them back to life just when we least expect it. Recently, I saw a blackened body, or maybe it was an almost-dead man, flung over the seat of a bicycle while his friend, crying, pushed it along from behind. For every Iraqi who has done harm to his fellow man in this war, there are a hundred others who have done good. I've seen them in corners, trying to help, trying to stay honest, trying to live. I've seen them lift torn flesh and blood and put it on human wings and spirit it to places where we try to do the work of God.

Sometimes I wish I had been stronger, like Baba and like Ziad, so that I too could heal people. But I'm doing a different kind of mending, aren't I? Fixing. Without me, the communication between Sam and the rest of Iraq would be broken. Instead of bodies, I stitch together words.

I feel the impact more than the ache; Louis just punched me in the arm. I must have been lost in my thoughts for too long. He grins at me and laughs.

"Look, man. You gotta have some way to get around traffic in this town, because it is fucking deadly. You don't think I'm going to sit here and wait for us to get shot at, do you? I've taken lots of small arms fire, that's nothin'. Do you know what it's like to come under a barrage of mortars and RPGs when you're just trying to get the goddamn boss to work?"

Before I can answer, he turns up the volume on his stereo and veers on to the central reservation, and now he is higher than I am. He overtakes the other cars at speed and he is hooting like a schoolboy and I feel like we could tip over at any second, surely in my direction, and that he would crush me in an instant.

"Yee-hah! Hold on there, Nabel!"

I find myself grasping on to a hook just above the window with one hand, and with the other, the dashboard.

"Is this allowed?"

"Come on, my man. What *isn't* allowed in this hellhole? There're no rules here anymore. This here's make-your-own!"

Off the central reservation and back into traffic, he veers to the right, down a sideroad. "Gotta know the shortcuts, Nabel."

"It's Nabil."

"Nab-eel? Like an 'eel' at the end?"

"I guess so." My stomach has the feeling I get just before I become nauseous, and my heart is thumping like it's trying to escape through one of the spaces in my rib cage. It is embarrassing that I cannot stop thinking this way, that some things are allowed – *masmuh* – and other things are forbidden – *mamnua*. You should always ask. You don't want to make trouble for yourself by breaking the rules. It is a philosophy that has kept my family out of trouble for generations.

"Don't worry, dude!" He slaps a hand on my knee and shakes

it, his left hand still vibrating at the steering wheel. His touch makes me recoil.

He smiles and slows a little. "Just having fun wit'cha. But look, you want to wind up a piece of roadkill just to avoid making cutsies?"

I glance back at the line of people we just blazed past and I remember that night of taking Noor to the hospital. On their faces, that same resentment and resignation.

"What's this?" I ask, watching him pound his head with the music.

"Nirvana, dude." He turns a switch next to the radio, and now the sound of the siren changes. It was long and wailing. Now it's short and staccato.

"Pick a tune, any tune," he says. "Anything to get these schmucks out of the way. Fucking towelheads."

I haven't heard that term since we lived in England. My father said it was very offensive, and that people who use it are ignorant. My father has probably never worn a *ghutra* on his head in his life, thought he does sometimes wear a *dishdasha* around the house, a long men's dress, on his day off, because wearing one is just plain comfortable.

There is no point in me reacting. What could I say? That most of us, in fact, don't wear towels on our heads, and that a *ghutra* does, in fact, provide very good protection from the combination of extreme sun and airborne dust? Or that I had expected more from someone who is working for the US government?

"Oh, by the way, I don't mean you," he says, speeding to the front of another line of traffic, towards a checkpoint. He rolls down his window and thrusts a pass in the face of a young soldier. "When I say towelhead, I only mean these *hajjis* with shit-for-brains who keep targeting our boys. That's all. There's a lot of folks 'round here will shake hands with their right and shoot you with their left."

I nod, as if to indicate that I accept his racist commentary. I wish I could take the nod back.

"No harm done, eh?"

"Of course not."

"So who is it exactly you guys are looking for? I mean, what's your interest in this whole, you know, underground illegal goods market thing?"

I have to think for a minute. What would Sam say if she were here? What are we looking for, exactly? Connections to Akram? Chalabi? Saddam?

"We want to find out how a certain set of documents got made, now that we're pretty sure they were fabricated. And who made them, and why." I guess that's the most I could say, off the record. "It's a bit complex."

He smiles. "Sounds like it."

"Well, they certainly looked quite realistic to the average person, at the start."

"Things always look good at the start, my friend." The car rattles with the invisible backblow of an explosion somewhere, probably to the north, maybe around the neighbourhood of Al-Khansa or even Sab'a Nisan. "Like us coming here, Nabil. Looked good from the start, didn't it? Boy, it was downright brilliant."

I want to tell him that none of it looked good from the start. Not that things were so good with Saddam either, because every day they discover some new mass grave where Saddam and his men dumped a few hundred bodies, and you start wondering, could America have made that up, too? I don't think so.

A phone is ringing, and it occurs to me that we're practically shouting at each other. Louis turns the volume on the music down and reaches for what I thought was a small weapon on his belt. He flips the black, egg-sized gadget open, and answers. A phone, on his belt! I thought Sam's Thuraya phone was the best technology around, but you need to be outside for that to work, and hers is three times the size of Louis's.

"Yeah. Yeah. Yeah," Louis says. "Well, I'm busy doing a little recon work for the desk chief right now." Louis looks at me and winks. "Okay, yeah," he says, looking at his watch. "I'll be back within the hour."

He flips the phone closed and tosses it into a space just below the gearstick. "Hey, sorry about this, but this ride ain't gonna be as long as we planned because I'm being called back to the office by forces more powerful than Mr Baylor, and there ain't many of them, as Baghdad ops go."

"No problem."

"Look," he says. "I'll drive you over to the Souq Mureidi area in Sadr City so you'll know where it is."

"Well, I *know* where that is."

Louis raises his eyebrows. "Oh yeah? And do you know what you'd find in Habibiyeh market versus the one in Chuhader? Or where Baghdadis are going these days for guns?"

"Well…" I could find out such things if I needed to, if I wanted to. "I haven't had much reason to research that."

"Well, truth is, you can get illicit stuff all over the city now." He switches off the siren and turns east on the Dura Expressway, instead of north. "You just need to know where to find things. I wish I could bring you around town to check'em out all afternoon. So maybe instead I'll just show you one of the markets in Zayouna."

"Zayouna? I know Zayouna very well."

"Is that right?" Holding on to the wheel with his left hand, he reaches into his back pocket with his right. He pulls out a packet of chewing gum that says *Big Red* on it. "You want?"

I take a piece and thank him. Inside my mouth, however, it burns so much I'm tempted to spit it out, and then I find myself getting used to it.

Louis frowns. "What do you know about Zayouna?" he asks, shoving two pieces in his mouth.

"Well, I grew up in Baghdad. I had some friends who lived there, and also some distant relatives. It's a good neighbourhood. Very nice people."

"Very nice people who are actively involved in trying to kill my people, who are even nicer. Ha!" He shoots a glance at me. "That was a joke, Nabil. We need a nickname for you. Or maybe a title. 'Nerves-of-Steel Nabil.' Haddya like that? That's a good one to have written on your tombstone."

Louis pulls another red-hot strip from the packet and balls it up into his mouth, working his jaw hard to keep the wad going. "So you got relatives in Zayouna? Maybe a nice cousin you want to introduce me to? Someone cute? Some of these ladies are good-looking if you get them out of their veils, you know what I mean? Except that a lot of them wear too much makeup, man." Louis veers off the highway, taking us towards Baghdad Jadida – not necessarily the shortest route to Zayouna. How could he possibly know all these neighbourhoods, anyway? Still, for someone who hasn't been here long he seems to be very familiar with the city.

Louis pushes his tongue out, blowing air to form a small, sugary bubble. In the pop, a speckling of spit lands on my cheek.

"Some of the ladies here, they're like, all covered and shit, and yet they're wearing an inch-thick coating of makeup. And then the men go around in those man-dresses! Explain that to me."

"It's called a *dishdasha*."

"A dish-whatta? A dishrag?"

He's trying to wind me up, I know. "A *dish-dasha*," I say slowly. "Shall I spell it for you?"

He laughs. "Now you're talkin'. Just trying to see how much shit you're prepared to take. Just bustin' chops, Nabil."

"And sometimes it's a *thob*. That's more a like a robe." At Maisun Square, he turns up Palestine Street, through Muthana. "Maybe I can draw a picture for you so you won't confuse them."

"Hey, now, that would be useful. Maybe you can make up a whole picture-book you can sell to dumb Americans like me. 'The Idiot's Guide to Understanding the National Dress of Iraq.' By Nabil, uh, what's your last name?"

"Al-Amari."

"By Nabil 'Nerves-of-Steel' al-Amari. But those women, with the big dark eyes? I'm down with that."

I listen to Louis yammer on for a while, that sort of polite listening which is only hearing the sound. Suddenly I feel homesick for the days when I had to listen hard to understand English. As a boy in Birmingham when, if I didn't listen carefully, the language was like a hum in the background.

"Have you thought of checking out the Tuesday Market as a place for counterfeiting? That's just up on the right."

"Yes, I know that one. But we're not looking for counterfeited goods, not exactly. That place is purses and watches, no?"

"Hmm. Well, it's just a suggestion. You also have Serai and Safafir. And Shorja."

I feel a laugh surfacing in my throat, and a quick instinct to suppress it. He sounds ridiculous trying to pronounce Iraqi names.

"Just trying to let you know about some places to check out, in case you didn't know," he says. "Baylor said you needed some help in figuring out the black market scene."

"Well, most of those are regular markets." Al-Shorja is one of my old favourites, with all the fresh spices piled high, mounds of orange cardamom next to dark-gold saffron and shrivelled green spices I never could quite place. I used to love going there as a boy.

"Whatever," he says, lowering his window. "But maybe if you rummage around the regular markets, you'll find what you're looking for." Louis brusquely pulls the car over, reaches out and over the roof, and takes back his siren. "No need to look like pigs in this neighbourhood."

"Pigs?"

He glances at me and pulls away again, as quickly as he pulled over. "Pigs. You know, cops? I guess that's slang. They probably don't teach you that when you learn English from the BB fucking C."

"I went to school in England."

"Really? Well then," he says, trying to feign an English accent, but sounding like an Irish brogue instead. "Smashing, I'm sure."

I suppose every culture has some sort of unflattering name for the police. But pigs? I can't think of a more insulting thing to call a human being. But then, maybe Americans don't see pigs in the same way we do. When I came back from England and told my friends at school that kids in England eat pig-meat for breakfast, they didn't believe me. Mum forbade us from eating bacon, but Baba let us have it a few times when he took Ziad and me out to see the football game at the St Andrew's ground.

The wide streets and large houses of Zayouna look pretty much the same as they did when I was last here. What's different is the shops, many of them closed, and the sidestreet checkpoints and homemade roadblocks, which are almost everywhere.

At the mosque, Louis makes a right and then another right, and then heads past a line of large houses, many of them just like the ones in my neighbourhood, only a little bigger.

"Do you see this primary school on the right?" He uses his chin to point.

"Al-Watheq School?"

"I guess that's the name. There's an illegal gun market inside. I'm told you can get a single-action, semi-automatic there for as little as $75."

"There? In the school? I find that hard to believe."

"Well, I'm pretty sure of it. Do you want to go in and check?"

"With you?"

"Nah, I'll just raise suspicions. Despite what that Waspy-assed Baylor says, I don't pass for an Iraqi."

I move my hand towards the door handle, then use it instead to smooth my trousers. "Well, if I go in and there are people there, I'm sure I'd have to spend at least ten minutes shopping around. If I go and leave quickly, they'll be suspicious of *me*."

"Take my word for it. They just want to make sales."

"Well," I say, looking at my watch, "if you do have time…"

"Go already!" he says. "Make it fast."

I'm out, pacing quickly towards the school entrance. I hate it when Americans think everything can be done quickly. There is no sense of appreciation that important things take time. I'm walking faster, and as I do the heat creeps up around me, moving across my skin, beneath my clothes. The lobby door is unlocked.

Two young guys holding Kalashnikovs look up. One of them puts his hands into place on his rifle.

"*Salaam aleikum*," I say.

"*W-aleikum is-salaam*," mumbles the one without his hands ready to shoot.

"I was looking for a place to buy some…defence." Stuck between weapons, *silah*, and defense, *difa'*, the latter sounds more dignified.

"They're not here today. Try coming back tomorrow."

"Not here?"

The quieter man, wearing a stubbly beard that looks like it is based on lethargy more than piety, puts a cigarette in his mouth and lights it. "They went to sell in Aadhamiye today," he says. "They'll be back tomorrow."

"Oh, well maybe I'll come back then," I say.

He takes his cigarette out. "Looking for something in particular?"

"Nothing special. Just something small…maybe a Beretta."

He puts his cigarette back in and leaves it there. "Well, the Zayouna Brotherhood has the best prices. If we're not here, ask for Mazen at the pharmacy across from the mosque. He'll tell you where to find us."

"Thanks a lot."

"*Fi m'Allah*," the smoker says, raising his head in a gesture of goodbye. I nod at the other and take off, back through the courtyard. *Fi m'Allah*. A shortened form of *fi iman Allah* – with faith in God. May God see to it that we see each other again. Though religious people say *fi m'Allah* often, it seems strange coming from them. If you have faith in God, why do you need to rely on weapons? I suddenly remember a line by the Indian poet Kabir: "But when deep inside you there is a loaded gun, how can you have God?"

Louis is not where he dropped me off. What if someone shot him and stole his car? What if they're waiting for me, ready to shoot me for working with the Americans?

The sound of a car horn, and with it, the sight of Louis's car, just down the road, closer to the mosque. When I see him, he blinks his lights at me. I walk over, trying not to look too rushed, too obvious, to people on the street. It's so much better travelling with Rizgar. Even though I often worry about Rizgar looking or sounding Kurdish, at least he is Iraqi.

"So?"

"Just two guys with guns."

"Really?" Louis looks surprised.

"But usually they're there, I guess. It sounds like they took their goods over to Aadhamiye for the day. They might be back tomorrow."

"Aha! So it's a mobile market. Well, that's good to know." Louis puts the car into gear and takes off, making too much noise as he does. For someone who is not supposed to be conspicuous, I feel like we may as well have spray-painted news of our visit across the mosque walls.

"D'you price anything?" Louis puts his chewed red blob into one of the wrappers and dumps it in the ashtray.

"You mean to buy a gun?"

"No, I was hoping you'd buy me a fresh fucking pack of chewing gum."

In the wardrobe in my parents' bedroom, I know there's a small revolver. I was fascinated with this fact when I was a teenager, wondering how Baba could work on saving lives while arming himself for the possibility of taking them as well.

"I wouldn't want to carry a gun." I turn to face him. "If I did, I might end up having to blow the heads off assholes like you."

Louis guffaws. "Ka-ping!" He rasps through the rest of his laugh, which ends in a sigh. "That's the spirit, my man. Can't lose your sense of humour in all this. You won't survive without it."

I can almost feel the cold metal moving into my temple, the pressing of the gun against my head. *We suggest you stop working with all foreigners. Particularly the Americans.*

I'd get one to protect Sam, though. *She'll go back to America in a pretty coffin.*

"So they only cost $75?" I ask. "I mean, for a basic one?"

"About that," he says. "That's what I've heard. Can you afford one?"

Getting $100 a day to work with Sam, I can afford a whole arsenal. But that's not the point. I watch as he turns onto the Khalid bin al-Walid Expressway, reaching again for his removable siren to navigate us through the traffic.

"Don't worry, I'm not turning on the siren for now," he says. "Just us getting ready."

"I'm not worried."

"Sure you are, man. It's been written all over your face from the moment you got in the car!"

I feel the urge to pull the visor down, the way Sam always does when she's sitting in the front in Rizgar's car, to check myself in the mirror. Instead, I weave my fingers together and turn them out, sending out a rip of cracks.

"No problem, dude. I can imagine what it must be like. Our guys don't go out nearly as much as your reporters do. Your people do some crazy shit!"

My people. As in journalists? Or Iraqis?

"So how do you get information if your guys don't go out much?" I ask.

"Well, from people like you, Nerves-of-Steel. Not every Iraqi who can speaka da English is lucky enough to land a job like you did."

Louis turns the siren on again and weaves through the cars that let him pass. The unsettling rise and fall makes my heart accelerate. I let him talk for a while, feeling my coiled spine loosen a little when he turns the siren off again to get back on the local road, leading to the beautiful Masbah, with its huge houses right along the riverfront. We never drove through here before the war because most of it was closed off to the public, protecting the mansions of government ministers and senior Ba'ath party people. It's one of the few things I like better about Baghdad *ba'id* than *qabil* – driving through the Masbah. I can only imagine how much more beautiful it must be from inside the houses, on the balconies, perched high and proud along the Tigris.

A queue to buy petrol winds around the bend on the way to the Hamra. While Louis talks, I count. I'm already up to more than seventy cars waiting in line.

"Hey," Louis says. "When you start scouring the city for stuff in the illegal markets, can you give me a little briefing on what you find? You know, very off the record?"

Maybe Sam would say sure, off the record, and say it's all in the name of cultivating a source. *Cultivating.* She explained that idea at length the other day, as it applies to journalism. I thought it was for gardening.

"I – might be able to help. I think I have to check with Sam first."

"You do that, buddy. I'd appreciate it."

Stop working with the Americans. "I don't want to promise anything, though."

"No sweat. Here you are, Mr al-Amari. Next stop, Hamra Hotel," he says, pulling into the car park. Some of the drivers who recognize me are watching us roll in, staring.

"Thanks a lot, Louis."

"Hey, Nerves of Steel," he says. "I'm sorry if I insulted you before with all of that nasty *hajji*-bashing. I really don't have anything against the Iraqi people or Muslims at all. Just that I lost a good buddy here last week."

"I'm sorry to hear that."

He nods. "Yeah, poor guy was only twenty-eight years old. Got a wife and kid at home."

"That's terrible." I want to ask how and by whom, but instead I wait for him to offer more.

He shakes his head. "Yeah, well. Look, Nerve-man, it's been a real pleasure," he says, thrusting his hand towards me, making me meet it halfway. "Come visit us anytime."

"*Ahlan w-sahlan.* In our country, you must allow us to welcome *you*," I say, still feeling the force of his hand against mine, waiting for him to let go.

37

Waiting

I'VE BEEN SITTING in the ugly orange-and-white café of the first tower lobby for hours, waiting for Sam to come back. I've skimmed through three newspapers and have run out of things to say to the few people hanging around. I'm avoiding Rafik in the second tower, in case he might expect some explanation of where Sam was last night, or resume his lecture about hiring a Shi'ite.

Where is Sam? With Franklin Baylor, a man she hated only a week or so ago. A man who is posing as an expert in electricity, but presumably doesn't know anything about it. A man who is cultivating *her*, a man who has access to information she wants so badly that she doesn't do anything but roll her eyes when he calls her a media chick.

Sam breezes in the door just after 4 p.m. She smiles and makes an exaggerated sigh. "How long have you been waiting?"

"A while now."

"Good stuff?"

"Not really. He got called back right away so we only went to one place."

"Really? Oh, I thought he was going to show you a lot more than that." She scans the lobby, empty except for one fixer-and-driver team who have kept to themselves. "Let's go up and talk."

I follow her past the pool and into the second tower, where Rafik meets our entry with a fake smile. He's on the phone, asking for a room to be cleaned that was somehow overlooked, but as we round our way to the stairs, something about his tone seems artificial – to the point where I wonder if he's pretending.

In the room, Sam goes straight to her computer, taps around a bit. Her hands land on her face. "Oh, Jeez. Don't do this to me. Shit!"

"What?"

"They're telling me now that they want to run the story right away. Listen to this. 'Sam, we feel we have all we need to run the story about the Jackson documents. Your interview with Akram all we needed. The ink-ageing is being confirmed by a second analyst. Call as soon as you get in.' Jesus Christ. I have to call them right now."

"Didn't they want you to find out who made the documents?" I ask. "We already knew that they were fake."

"Well, I thought so," she says, "but apparently they don't know what they want any more. They want the whole story, but they wanted it yesterday." Sam stands and leans her forehead on the sliding glass door, where the view seems blurrier than it did before, as if we're under water.

"What happened to the windows?"

"The security guy coated all the correspondents' offices with mylar," she says matter-of-factly, "in case we get bombed."

"You think the Hamra could get bombed?"

Sam shrugs. "Everything's possible."

"I don't think you need to really worry. It's not so famous like the Palestine or the Sheraton. I didn't even know the Hamra existed until you wrote the name down on your card."

"That feels like ten years ago." She goes back to her desk. "Baghdad years are like dog years."

"Like what?"

"Dog years. Have you ever heard of dog years?"

"I'm not sure."

"They say each year is like seven years for a dog. So if you're here for a month, it's like you've been here seven months."

The maths of that doesn't entirely make sense to me, but I get the idea. Is that good? Maybe it feels like seven months because she already feels at home here. Or maybe it means she is tired of it. Of us.

"We're going to have to really boogey from here on in," says Sam. "I'll ask them to hold off for just another forty-eight hours. I'll explain to them that we're really close."

"What happened today with Baylor?"

"Not that much," she says, waving an invisible fly away. "He gave me some leads."

"What sort of leads?"

"Why don't we talk about it tomorrow? You may as well go now and then tomorrow we can go into the specifics, after I speak to Miles."

"Sam, if you want to get this done, you need to tell me!"

"Nabil, sometimes you just need to cultivate your sources a little. Trust me. If there's something important to tell you, I'll tell you." She taps on the keyboard again.

Should I ask her, or would it be embarrassing?

"Hey Sam? What's nirvana?"

"Nirvana? It's um, you know, a state of peacefulness. But let me get you a fuller definition," she says, tapping a few keys on her computer. "Gotta love dictionary.com. It's a term from

Buddhism and Hinduism: a stage in which one reaches a higher state of harmony and tranquility by disassociating oneself from worldly possessions."

That doesn't sound like Louis. I walk closer to her desk. "Check if there's another definition."

"That's it. It's like, paradise. Why?"

"This Louis had his music on loud in the car, I asked him what it was and he said nirvana."

"Oh! That Nirvana. It's also a rock band. *Here we are now,*" she sings in a sinister slur, "*entertain us...*"

"That's it. That's what he had on."

"Jeez. That's a bit much. I guess you got a good crash-course in American culture, though."

Every day I work with you, Sam. "It was pretty interesting."

"They're depressing. The lead singer killed himself." Sam looks at me with that look, the one that says I'm worried about you. "I'll burn you a CD with some, you know, more chill stuff. I think that'd be more your speed."

"Maybe," I shrug.

"All right," she stands, sending the signal that my invitation to leave is being sent a second time. "Come at, say, around nine tomorrow? Or, wait, you said you might go to check out that other forger in Sadr City without me, the one your cousin Saleh is going to recommend. So why don't you do that first, and come to me around ten. Oh!" She rushes to the refrigerator. "Your desserts, for your family." She hands them to me in a gesture that says take them. "You're not going to leave me with these sugar bombs, are you?"

I take them in my left hand, and make for the door handle with my right.

"So see you in the morning," she says.

"I'm down with that."

Sam leans against the refrigerator. "Picked up some good slang today, eh?"

I point at her with my thumb pointing up, pistol-like. "Ka-ping," I reply. Sam shakes her head and stands, frowning at my hand, in the shape of a gun.

38

Frowning

LIAR. SAM IS a liar. Samara B. Katchens, Paris Bureau Chief who is hardly ever in Paris, has been lying to me. Who in this city is not a liar?

I have the whole walk through Yarmouk and the taxi ride to Karada to review things in my head. Last night, as I was walking out of the hotel towards Rizgar's car, a broad-shouldered young man bumped into me. Then he pushed an envelope into my chest and murmured, "For you."

"For me? What's this—" and halfway through my sentence, he was gone. So I shoved the envelope into my trouser pocket, not wanting to have to read it in front of Rizgar, and got into the car. Then I remembered that I wanted to see Saleh, and decided maybe I shouldn't open it there either, and so I may as well just wait until I get home.

I had Rizgar drop me off in Amiriya, close to Saleh's house. I have started to do that wherever I go. What if Saleh's neighbours don't trust him? What if they see a fancy car they don't recognize stopping at the house? They might suspect he's working with the Americans. I've already heard too many stories of guys getting shot, and neighbours just shrugging and saying that he was working with the Americans, so he deserved it.

Saleh gave me more precise directions on how to get to the office of a guy called Mustapha al-Tamimi. Saleh said I should forget about going back to Khalil Ibn Khaldoun. He does not have the goods, but he will try to pull the same trick on us, in which he'll play Akram and we'll play Harris. Saleh says Khalil will just produce information demonstrating what it is he thinks we want to prove, and then expect us to pay. That's the trouble with people in the forgery business, Saleh said. You rarely get an honest word out of any of them. The guy we really want, Saleh insisted, the guy with a direct line to our documents, that's Mustapha, and Khalil is just one of his competitors.

They insisted I stay for dinner. Ashtar makes an incredible *teman o'morga*. It's just a simple rice stew with vegetables, but I like the way she makes it, with dried mint and sweet peppers.

I started filling up on it, and her homemade *leben*, which is like yogurt. When she saw how good my appetite was, she heated up some *baamya*, a stew of lamb and tomato sauce, which was probably left over from the night before. I sat at the table, pushing it into my mouth and thinking of Louis and his foul, funny mouth, devouring his spicy sticks of gum. Ashtar said I looked tired, and that maybe I hadn't been eating enough. She was thrilled to get the box of European sweets, which looked close to soggy by the time she opened them. My family won't know the difference.

After dinner, Saleh and I went into their garden and smoked some *sheesha*. It was probably the most relaxing hour I've had in weeks. I hate cigarette smoke, but I don't think smoking an occasional nargila could be bad for you. Baba said the people who got lung cancer smoked cigarettes, the best of which are exported from America. But *sheesha*? That never hurt anyone.

I almost smoked myself into nirvana, and then I started talking. First about Sam, then about the thugs outside my house the other night. Who else could I tell? Baba? He would worry too much. Amal? I trust her the most, but she is too young to handle any of this.

Saleh said to be careful. Maybe I should think seriously about getting a gun, he said. Or maybe I should quit my job – the same kind of job he's trying to get. I tried to explain that it wasn't about the money. What else could work be about, he laughed. It's not like you're going to do these things to help some American woman. Unless you're in love with her! I laughed with him and said of course not. He lit another bowl of *sheesha*, this one with cherry-flavoured tobacco, and promised it would be the last.

By the time I got home, just in time for curfew, I felt better than I had in weeks. Citing exhaustion and Ashtar's good cooking, I went straight to my room. And read the letter.

Liar, liar. Liaress. Is that a word?

It is exactly twelve hours later, I notice, as I knock on Sam's door. She opens it, looking surprised. She's still wearing something that approaches night-clothes: sweat-pants, I believe she calls them, and a crumpled tee-shirt.

"I thought you were going over to see the guy in Sadr City first thing," she says, glancing down at her clothes. "Sorry, I didn't expect you until at least ten."

"I was," I say, "but something came up overnight, and I need to discuss it with you first."

"Come in," she says. "Good news. It seems like maybe Miles is on our side now, but the front office guys are impatient and they're ready to run with what they have. Miles is trying to hold them back."

With the air-conditioning and a fan on, the smoke from Sam's cigarette is swirling around the room. It's hard to believe she is now smoking this early in the day.

I wait until she types out her last words. The clicking of the keys finally slows to a stop, and then, the "hmph!" that I've learned to recognize as a sign that whatever she was working on is done.

She turns to me and rolls her eyes. "If only they knew what we're going through for this friggin' story. I need coffee."

"Sam," I start, "I want to talk to you about some important things. Is now okay?"

Her shoulders drop, which tells me she'd rather not talk about anything other than the story, but she says sure, and suggests we go down to the pool.

"Not there," I say.

"Let's at least go outside, then. It's not too hot yet." She stands up and slides open the balcony door, and the heat and buzz from the pool rise up and enter the room with no delay, as if they had been pushing to get in all along. A warm swampiness of chlorine and exhaust goes in; round-the-clock, $75-a-night air-conditioning spills out.

Sam settles into one of the dusty plastic chairs and I take the black one, speckled with tiny white drops that must have been left behind when they last painted. She slips off her sandals and lays her bronzed feet, striped white in the places where the straps lay, up on the ledge of the balcony. The rusty-coloured polish on her toenails has flaked into small bar-graphs of colour.

"Sam, what kind of name is Katchens?"

She looks at me and the rims of her irises, today the colour of honey, seem to grow thinner. "It's a German name."

"What kind of a German name? Does it mean something?"

Her toes curl, and one of them cracks. "It means 'pure'. So my ancestors must have been saintly people, or at least very clean." She faces me for a moment with an artificial grin.

"Sam, someone gave me an envelope in the car park last night, and then just took off."

"Hmm." Sam plucks another cigarette from the pack on her lap and turns to me with it in her mouth, unlit. She takes it out. "I can't believe I'm smoking like this again. Did I tell you that I quit five years ago?"

"Yes, you did."

"So what was in the envelope?"

"Someone doesn't want us to continue with our investigation. And I think it's far beyond Akram."

Sam's face crumples into a wrinkled pout, as if someone has just tried to sell her something for ten times its rightful price. "Nabil, these guys don't have any say-so over what stories were working or not. Don't let them intimidate you. It's a free country. Or it will be anyway."

She rolls a thumb over the orange plastic lighter in hand. She holds a flame to the fresh cigarette and breathes in the glow. I watch her belly rise as she draws it in, holds it somewhere inside, and sends its amorphous grey exhaust into the morning air.

"Inside this envelope was a letter, a typed letter, saying that you're Jewish. It said you are Jewish and your father is Jewish, and that you should avoid interfering in the internal affairs of Iraq, and that you might otherwise find yourself accused of being a Zionist spy."

Sam's eyes bulge. She takes her legs down off the ledge.

"If this is true, Sam, they could make a lot of problems for you. For us."

Sam stares ahead, beyond the pool and the buildings on the horizon, where the date palms stand guard. Of all the buildings we have seen shattered during the war, our *tamr* are the one proud thing on our landscape which stand unscathed. She is quiet, but I see her eyes running back and forth, searching.

She puts the cigarette back into her mouth and drags on it, and then crushes the burning butt against the balcony ledge, sending a spray of embers to the floor. She turns to me, and I see lines in her forehead I don't remember seeing before, arrows pointing towards an axis of stress between her eyes.

"Nabil? I would never lie to you, and I never have. It's true. My father is Jewish. But I'm – I don't know what I am. I'm really not anything. Not in terms of religion, anyway. I'm just an American. I mean, maybe I believe in God, or at least some kind of intelligent design, but that's about the extent of my religious identity."

"Why didn't you tell me?"

"Tell you? There was really nothing to tell. Like I said, only my father's Jewish. My mother's Catholic. Neither of them think it's important. I didn't think there was something worth telling."

"You could have told me anyway. You should have told me."

Sam looks annoyed. "Did you ask me? No. You never asked me."

"I asked you where your family name was from. You should have told me then."

"Oh, please," she says. Sam goes inside and comes back with her sunglasses. "This sun is killing me." She sits back down and lights another cigarette. I wave the discharge of it out of my face.

"Sorry," she says, though I think she's only willing to apologize for the smoke.

I don't answer.

"You think I should have told you."

"Yes, I do."

She pulls one knee up towards her chest, wrapping a hand around her shin. "Well, I didn't think there was anything to tell. I'm telling you right now. My father is Jewish, so that is part of my heritage, but the only –ism I follow is journalism."

"But if your father is Jewish, then you are Jewish."

"No, actually. No, I'm not. That's not how it works. To be Jewish your mother has to be Jewish. At least, that's the way it works if you go by the book."

"But the religion always comes from the father." I can hardly believe my own words. Exactly what religion did I get from my own father?

Sam coughs out her negation, shaking her head. "Well, yes, in the Muslim world it works that way, but for Jews, it's the other way around. Every religion has its own way of discriminating… of deciding who's in and who's out."

The Muslim world. I never thought of there being a Muslim world before. Sam makes it sound like we're on our own planet.

"But still, you are partially Jewish then, right? Like I am half Shi'ite, half Sunni."

It never occurred to me until now that this makes us very much alike. I wonder if she realizes this. I want her to know I don't like her any less for being Jewish, but I'm pissed off at her for lying.

"It would have been fine if you told me," I explain. "I don't have a problem with that. I am open-minded. But Sam…" I search for the right words, and there are none. "I feel very sad." I want to say angry but I don't think I should. "Sad that you would keep that from me. You've asked me so many questions about my life, my family, and I answered everything, everything, as honestly as I can. So why weren't you honest with me? Why did you lie?"

Sam tilts her head to one side, looking sceptical. "I didn't exactly lie to you. I never told you I was something I'm not. I just didn't tell you. It didn't come up."

"But when you spoke about your family, about where you're from, you kept it from me. Not saying what is true can also be a lie."

Sam's shoulders lose their composure. Her face shifts from right to left, arguing "no" without putting out the energy to say it.

"You know why I didn't tell you? Because I had a feeling you'd react like this. You'd make a big deal out of it, and that's exactly what I didn't want to happen. I didn't want it to be an issue. Because frankly, I don't care about religion. I mean, I respect it in you and in other people. But it doesn't mean anything to me." Sam is waving her right hand in circles, like she is digging for words to show she is right. "It's an interesting thing to study, to watch. Especially here. But I don't want it for myself. I never did. I never really had much of it in the first place. And so I'm not going to go around wearing it on my sleeve."

"But you believe in God?"

"Oh, Nabil. I just said I did."

Sam walks back inside, and I follow her. She plants herself on the sofa and puts her thumbs between her eyes, while I remain standing.

"Sam, it's not an issue with me. But of course, with many people it is."

"No, really?"

"Look, I'm not daft," I say. "I know there are a lot of people in my country who don't like the Jews. But that's not the way I am. That's not the way I was raised."

Sam runs her hand through her hair, twirling up a loosening curl. "So then why are you making such a big deal out of it?"

"I'm not! I'm trying to protect you!" I wish I weren't losing my calm. Everything is going the way it wasn't supposed to go.

"Yeah, well, that's not the job you were hired to do. I didn't ask you to be my bodyguard!"

At the top of the small stack of cards in my wallet is the fake press ID we had made up for me so I could have an easier time getting past American checkpoints. I slip it out of its slot, and toss it down on the table in front of her.

My hand is on the doorhandle when she calls me. "Wait. Nabil, I'm sorry. I didn't mean that. Please don't go."

I turn around, lean on the door.

"Nabil." She approaches until she reaches the kitchenette by the door. "I do need you. I do need you to protect me. It's just, for Christ's sake, the whole thing is starting to scare the shit out of me!" And I can hear the break in her voice, and for a moment, in her eyes, too, but she has already turned around and now her back is towards me. And by the time I walk back towards her, she has banished the onset of tears and is focusing on some place in the distance, taking deep breaths.

"Look, Nabil, I want you to know, I really do trust you. If I had thought that it was important to know, I would have told you. In fact, I was thinking that if I told you it might create problems rather than prevent them, so I just never told you. And what difference would it have made?"

In my mind, I take Sam into my arms, hold her close and stroke her hair until she feels safe enough to cry. But in the room, that's not what happens at all.

"What difference does it make? I would have known, so I could have protected you. I would have kept it a secret."

"Yeah, but you knowing or not knowing wouldn't have made the slightest bit of difference. It wouldn't have stopped these goons from somehow figuring out my father is Jewish and then trying to use it against me."

"Why do you never ask me if I would like to drink a beer with you?"

"What?" Sam laughs. "I didn't want to offend you. Isn't that against your religion?"

"You know, you can be a good Muslim and still have a drink once in a while. The point is not to abuse it. I believe that. My father always had a drink at weekends, on Fridays." I smile at the hypocrisy, and I think Sam gets it, because she smiles back. "Besides, I think the Koran is clearer about not drinking wine or spirits. It doesn't say beer, so some people say this isn't really included."

"It's also 9:15 in the morning," she says.

"So?"

"So. Well, desperate times call for desperate measures. Let's have beer for breakfast. It's liquid bread, you know." She gets up and heads to the fridge. I watch her from behind as she removes the top from two greenish bottles. "I just didn't want to corrupt you," she says, and hands me the beer, a Carlsberg, cold and still smoking.

She falls back on to her sofa and holds up her bottle. Before my eyes, it drains into her until it's almost half-gone. She takes the neck of my bottle, my hand still wrapped around the bottom of it, and raises it up. She clinks hers against mine. "So what are we going to do about it now?"

"Sam, you have to tell me about things. If we're working together on this, you need to let me know everything that's happening. You didn't tell me you were Jewish, or half-Jewish, or however it is. You didn't even tell me what happened in your meeting with Baylor yesterday and you were with him for hours!"

"Nabil, we had lunch, and then we stopped over to see some military source whom I thought would be a good contact, but so far, nothing. There wasn't that much to tell."

She tips her bottle back, and I watch the moving lump in her throat as it goes down.

"I don't ask you for a full briefing of everything going on in *your* life. Did we sign some contract in which I've agreed to disclose my entire day's events to you?"

I rise to leave again, though we both know I won't.

"Nabil, wait. Sit. Please. I'm sorry. I'm cranky today, and that was before you walked in."

Back on the sofa I swirl the beer in my bottle.

"You were right about something," she says, staring at her beer. She peels at the label, letting wet, silvery flakes fall into her lap.

"I was?"

"Yeah. The thing you told me about the yellowcake story? That bit your cousin told you?"

"Yes?"

"It's true. That's what Baylor told me yesterday."

"So it wasn't true? I mean, that Saddam was trying to buy this stuff, the yellowcake, from Nigeria so we could make a nuclear weapon?"

"Apparently not." Sam shakes her head.

"And now you want to do that story, too?"

"No, no. Not now, anyway. My editors want Congressman Jackson's suit off of their backs. They're complaining about all the legal fees they're racking up each day. They think that the sooner we clear the record, the better it looks for us, and then Jackson will drop his case or settle quickly."

I try throwing back a bigger gulp of beer, but it simply doesn't go down as quickly as it seems to for Sam. Some of it catches in my nose, and I cough.

"Whoa, partner. Maybe you should stick to orange juice."

"It's not that," I say, wiping my nose. "I think I'm getting a bit sick."

Her eyebrows round in sympathy and she pouts, as if to say, poor Nabil.

"You're right, Sam."

"About what?"

"I'm also keeping things from you."

"Yeah? Good. Let's hear all your dirt." Sam finishes off another long swig and puts the bottle on the table. Her beer looks shabby from having its label pried away.

"A few nights ago, someone came to my house and accosted me."

"They what?"

"Two gunmen grabbed me on the way into my house after work. They knew I was working for an American woman. I don't think they knew who you were. But they accused me of working with the occupation."

Sam sits up, her face contorted. "Are you serious?"

"Yes." I can feel my chest shaking as I tell her, a shiver coursing through my right arm. "They held a gun to my head and they knew who I was, and that my father was a doctor. They threatened me and said that everyone had to stop working with the Americans, and that I should join the resistance."

"Jesus, Nabil! Why didn't you tell me?"

I take another sip, but find myself wishing it were a cold lemonade.

Sam shakes her head. "Does it make you want to quit? I would understand if—"

"Before we're finished with this story? Never."

"What about your family?"

"They don't know. But I am a little bit worried about them, too. I told them to tell everyone who asks that I quit the job with the *Tribune*. I'm going to pretend to go back to my job as a teacher. And I don't have Rizgar drop me off at home anymore. In the morning I will just walk, like I always did when I was teaching, towards Mansour, and then I'll take a cab from Yarmouk Square. That's what I did today. It makes it much harder for anyone to follow me."

Sam nods, but I wonder if she gets the difference, if she knows where my neighbourhood is in relation to the Hamra here in Karada. I'm walking in the opposite direction for fifteen or twenty minutes every morning just so it will look like I'm going to work somewhere else.

"Has anything ever happened like that before, since you started working for me?"

I shrug. "Not really."

"What do you mean, 'not really'?"

"Nothing like that. But Rafik downstairs thinks we need a Shi'ite working for us. He says I'm Sunni and Rizgar is Kurdish and you have no Shi'ite working for you."

Sam's head falls back, her mouth open. "What? Anyway, you said you're both, right?"

"It doesn't matter. He said everyone will see me as Sunni because of being called Nabil, and my father's Sunni. Which is true. That's the way it works."

Sam smirks. "Well, which do you identify with?"

"Both. Sunni history is very important, very proud – it is the history of the Arab people. When we make *hajj*, we go to Mecca, and that's a Sunni country."

What can I tell Sam that she would understand? I suddenly feel guilty for drinking beer and having this conversation in the same sitting.

"But the Shi'a way is more spiritual," I say. "More mystical, perhaps. There are some nice rituals that I like, like visiting the tombs and asking for help from the martyrs and holy men. But then, maybe that's just my mother's influence. What else? I think Shi'ites are more idealistic."

Sam waits, with even her eyes listening.

"Shi'ites believe that the Mahdi will come back and perfect the world. So we are always dreaming of a better time, of peace."

"Which will come when the Mahdi comes," she says. "So maybe that will be hastened by the Mahdi Army?"

I shake my head. "You shouldn't link it with Moqtada al-Sadr. He's a politician. But yes, he took the term from this. Mahdi is like, what is the word in English…"

"Messiah."

"Yes, that's it! So you know."

Sam takes her bottle back, running her finger along its mouth. "I read a lot. And you know, we have Messiahs, too. A Christian one, a Jewish one…"

"I know."

"*So you know*," she says, mimicking me. Beneath the coffee table, I nudge her foot with mine. She laughs. What in the world made me do that?

"I should go and try to find this guy Mustapha in Sadr City," I say.

"I'll come. Give me ten minutes to change."

"You have to let me go alone, at least to check it out first."

"You still want to do that?"

"Yes, it's the best way. That's what everyone says. It's a place where they make forgeries. Women don't go to places like that. It's better if I go without you."

Sam looks reluctant. "How'd you get to this guy?"

"Through my cousin, Saleh, the one you helped. They offered him a job at CARE, you know. He's very happy about it."

"What a credit," she coos. "Maybe I can put that on my resumé someday: Helped find gainful employment for fixer's relatives."

"Just your fixer?"

She nods. "You deserve a fancier title. How about, Fixer Extraordinaire. Or, Interpreter Emeritus?"

If Sam weren't so amusing sometimes, I don't think it would be worth doing any of this.

"How about…my best friend in Baghdad," she says. I hold out my hand, and she slaps hers into it like a playful child, smiling and scowling at the very same moment.

39

Scowling

As I walk through his hallway, I notice Mustapha glance around to see if anyone on the street appears to have been watching me. He spits, sending out a brown teardrop towards the cement.

"You're the guy Iyad sent?"

Iyad, yes, that was the name of the guy Saleh said was the go-between, who sent me here, to Souq Mureidi in Sadr City. Saleh said he was sure that if there was any answer to be had, if there was any confirming who made Akram's documents and why, it would be here.

I nod. "That's right."

I follow him up a set of dirty steps, those grey and black tiled ones that are ugly when you put them in and even uglier when they sit unwashed for ten years, and he pushes a door open for me to walk through. Near the window stands a very stocky, wide-shouldered man with one of the most threatening moustaches I have ever seen. He doesn't smile or greet me, and when I say *salaam aleikum*, he only grunts out a *salaam,* a sort of half response.

Mustapha focuses his eyes unwaveringly on mine, and I notice they are slightly green, a kind of hazel colour, and suddenly I have this sense that maybe he's a good person, the sort of person I should trust. Maybe he's as nervous as I am. Maybe he doesn't even like the scary-looking chap; maybe it's just his security guy, or one of his bosses.

"It's like this," Mustapha says. "There are all sorts of documents that we know how to create. Not we, not *me,* you understand. My friends. I am only a connection for you. Maybe I'll be the *wasta.* Maybe I can help put you in contact. Please, sit," he says, and points to a beaten-up little armchair that looks like it's been covered in carpeting. I do, and he takes a wooden chair from what I presume to be his desk. It has some files on it and things that might seem appropriate for a desk – a holder with pens, a calendar, a thin pile of folders – but nothing that would look like this could be the place where the work of forgery is actually done.

"You have to promise first not to tell anybody about how I helped you or where I send you," he says. Out of the corner of my eye, I notice the machine-gun leaning on the filing cabinet, within the other guy's reach. Brutus, that's who he looks like, just like in the Popeye cartoons they used to show when I was a kid, dubbed into Gulf Arabic. I should give out nicknames, like Louis does, to maintain a sense of humour. He was right about that much. I'm taking everything too seriously.

Brutus must have seen me notice his gun, because he takes a handkerchief out of his pocket and begins cleaning it. Louis, he'd know immediately what kind it was, fully or semi-automatic. I know it's only for show, but my spine aches with fear.

"Of course," I say. "Just between us." I sip the glass of tea that Mustapha has set on the plastic table he dragged up to my shins while I was watching Brutus. It tastes too sweet, as if someone was trying to cover up the poor quality of the leaves by using much more sugar than necessary.

"It's an M-16," Mustapha says.

"I know," I lie. I'm lying more all the time, since the day I met Sam, and realized that she was lying all the time, too, and probably for her own good. Lying to stay alive. That can't be a bad thing, can it?

"It's a nice one. I've been in the market for something like that."

Mustapha breathes in, like he's waiting for me to finish pretending I know something about guns. "Listen, you're here about documents, right?"

"Exactly."

"There are documents on weapons, on imports and exports of security materials, on scientific equipment that can be adapted for alternative uses," he says, ticking these off on his fingers, "to use the phrase the weapons inspectors like. There are documents that show what the accounting looked like when the UN said we could start selling oil again so the Iraqi people wouldn't 'starve,'" he says, crunching two fingers in the air to make a quote, to show me he doesn't believe anyone actually went hungry in those days, at least not because of the sanctions. He, for one, looks as if he has been eating better than most of us, with an expansive middle that spills like an overstuffed ice cream cone over the edge of his belt. "We did all sorts of documents for the UN, for the weapons inspectors. All sorts of accounting records and import documents and even fake affidavits. You would never be able to tell the difference. We have some talented people in this country." He reaches for his cup of tea which, once cupped in his hand, looks miniscule, like a thimble. He sucks it back and drains the rest into his mouth. He crosses his right leg over the left, limbs too lanky for a man of his girth.

"Really," he says, "it is an art, you know, creating an image of something so perfect that it is no longer a fake, because in the act of creating this new thing based on artificial information, you have actually created something real. It is quite beautiful."

"Yes, well, that is a very interesting point," I say unconvincingly.

"Interesting? Not just interesting. Practical!" He corrects me. "That's what this country needs. Practical leadership. In English they have a word you probably haven't heard before. It's called pragmatic." He pronounces it slowly and clearly: *brag-maht-eek*. I sit and listen.

"We need more people who are pragmatic. We don't need ideology. We certainly don't need democracy. You see, at the other end of the spectrum, we deal with very mundane things as well. We can provide licences, permits, travel documents, for people who want to pay top quality, we can even get you a new passport – sometimes, sometimes, we can also arrange to get you a visa to a Western country. At least, we did, before the war. And you?" He pauses, scanning my face, my body, taking in my old shoes worn especially for Sadr City, and returns to my stubble, asking are you planning to become a beard or not? Because if not don't bother me.

"Are you looking for a new passport?"

"Well," I reach for my tea so I will have time to think. "Possibly. I might want to go to France." It doesn't feel like a complete lie. I do want to go to France to visit Ziad and his family.

"Got family there?"

I smile and nod.

"Me, too. Paris?"

"Indeed." Another lie. But why start giving him extra information about my family, telling him that Ziad lives in Marseille?

"Ah. So, for a passport you need to wait about two weeks, or maybe only ten days, and it will probably cost you $800. Can you afford that?"

I feign shock. "God. Seriously? I will have to think about it." It is, in fact, much more than I expected. If I weren't working for Sam, how in the world would I afford it? How would anyone?

"Take your time."

"I was expecting more like $400 or $500."

"Well, we might be able to do that."

I reposition myself, leaning in to him with an elbow on my knees. "And what if I wanted to see some of the documents these people, you know, made up for the weapons inspectors?"

"Ha-hah!" He slaps the side of his thigh. "Brother, forgive me, but if you have trouble getting together a few hundred dollars for a passport, then you're not getting anywhere *near* that. And what would you want with it, anyway?"

"It wouldn't be for me. It's not me, I…I certainly wouldn't have enough money to pay for these things. But I know someone who might. I mean, perhaps I can help bring an important client to you."

"Oh? And who is that?" Mustapha brightens with a long-toothed smile that reminds me of the neighbourhood butcher my mother went to for many years. I dreamt he killed the animals with his teeth; I refused to eat meat for months afterwards.

"I really can't say just now. I have to talk to her."

His eyes shift with curiosity, and I realize I've slipped.

"The *group*, that is," I add, as naturally as possible. "I have to talk to the group." It sounds plausible, since the word group, or *magmua*, is feminine in Arabic.

Mustapha smiles. "That's fine. There's no rush. You can check with this – group."

I study his face for a moment longer, those pleasant greenish eyes like the palm trees in Jadriya, and I realize that maybe there's a reason he looks pleasantly familiar to me. I know his face from somewhere. University? Yes. He was a law student, my year. Mustapha al-Qaeis.

"Didn't you go to the University of Baghdad? Class of 1996?"

"Hah! I thought your face looked familiar. Al-Amari, right?"

"That's right. It took me a while to place you."

"Hey man," he says, holding out his hand in a more brotherly way, and I give him my hand in return, and before I know it he's pulling me in for a hug.

When we're done, he smiles and looks off into the distance for a moment, as if remembering. "It's been some time. Don't think I've seen you since second or third year."

"Yes, that's right. But it feels like longer, no?" Now I know why I didn't recognize him straight away; he's probably gained twenty kilos since then, and has lost most of his hair. In comparison, I have nothing to complain about.

"Yeah, a lifetime ago. Remember there were air strikes that year, before graduation? We got stuck with all that, even after the war with Iran, and then the war with Kuwait and the Americans," he laughs. "I mean, the Americans the first time around."

His eyes search me for a minute, and I wait for him to ask what I've been doing. I want to ask him how he got here, but something in his gaze tells me to wait. "Well it's good to see you, again."

416

"And you," I say. The truth is, we weren't friends, though also not enemies. Nor did Mustapha strike me as very bright. I had the sense that he was one of the many university students who got through school the easy way – paying off professors for a passing grade. It was one of the many reasons I didn't feel like continuing in school for my PhD – the thought of working with all of those professors accepting bribes.

"Wouldn't you like something cold to drink? Here we are giving you tea but it's quite hot already. You'd think it were August."

I swipe at the sweat that sits like drizzled rain on my forehead. "That would be great."

"Nadim," Mustapha says, turning to Brutus, who has said nothing since his monosyllabic recognition of my entry. "Would you mind running out and buying a cold drink for our guest?"

Brutus gets up, and lifts the strap of the weapon on to his shoulder.

"I don't think you need that," says Mustapha, looking up at Brutus, which is a more fitting name for him than a gentle one like Nadim, meaning friend. "We just want a couple of 7-Ups," Mustapha says. Brutus puts the gun back down, his fat lips curling a bit as he does. He leaves, the fabric on his big body swishing as he goes.

"He's good to have around," says Mustapha, cracking a smile once the door is safely shut.

"I'll bet."

"You need a bit of security in this business."

I nod as if to say of course, and then turn over in my mind the events of the past twenty-four hours. Sam being Jewish, not denying it at all. Why don't I get a gun? Can I trust Mustapha, given that Saleh sent me here? Saleh has a law degree, and that makes him an attorney, right? So he must have some respect for the concept of the law, some understanding of it.

"So you're a lawyer now?"

"Indeed," he says. "And you?"

"I had been teaching. Now I'm working with a foreign journalist."

"An American."

Did I not tell Saleh not to tell?

"Don't worry, it's fine. Just tell me what you're trying to do."

Sam would say—

"We're old classmates," he says. "Aren't you from Yarmouk?"

—go with your gut.

"Yeah."

Don't hesitate too much, or it will make you look weak. That's what Ziad told me when he was trying to teach me to fight.

"We need to find out where a certain set of documents came from," I start.

"Sure. Go on."

"Like you said, some of them are almost artwork. These might even be masterpieces. But they're fake."

"And? What do these documents show?"

"Well, I don't know if I can tell you that part just now. But what we want to know is, who made up the documents, and why."

Mustapha runs his hand over the short, grizzled goatee beard he is either growing in or cutting somewhat carelessly. "Well, you have to show me the documents for me to figure out who made them and why. Obviously."

418

"I think I can do that. But I don't have them with me now."

Mustapha lets out a long breath through his nose, and looks at his watch. "Can you at least tell me how you got hold of these documents? I need something to go on if I'm going to help you at all."

We're running out of time, Sam said. The editors think they have all they need to run the story. Why does it have to involve running? Hasn't there been enough rushing into things around here? Now or never.

"A former military official gave them to another reporter for the same newspaper."

"General Akram, then?"

I watch his eyes, that strange green glow, and I can see that he knows he has me. He's proved he knows who he's dealing with, that he knows all the important players, and he knows I need him. But does that mean I should trust him?

"Look, he's not the only big-name seller," Mustapha says, "he's just the only guy who used to be in the military. How much are you prepared to pay if we can help you?"

A lawyer who bribed his way through school. What does a lawyer do in this country anyway? Everything is fixed. Nothing gets solved inside the courtroom.

"I don't know. I didn't really come prepared to answer that question," I say, offering something that is more honest than what I would have said if I had thought it out in advance. "But the truth is, the newspaper this woman works for, well, her editors were angry about the other reporter paying for the documents. So I don't think it would be a simple thing for her to pay again, because that was part of the problem the first time around."

Mustapha takes a writing pad off his desk, and jots some notes into it. "Nothing is simple these days, Nabil," he says, without looking up. "You must know that."

Ya mistarkhis al-lahm, ind al-maraq tindam. A proverb my Grandma Zahra used to use when she cooked. If you buy cheap meat, you will be sorry when you get to the gravy. I think there is a near equivalent in English: you get what you pay for.

"I'm sure things are negotiable," I explain. "I'll have to discuss it with her."

"Oh, so it's a lady journalist. Or is 'she' still this group you're talking about?"

"Well, she, yes, she works for a large group of editors, you know, at a newspaper, so that's why I said that. I'm sorry if I was being a bit cagey."

"I understand completely," he shakes his head earnestly. "You have to be discreet in these things. What hotel does she stay in?"

Fast, Nabil. "The Sumerland Hotel." It's just down the alley from Hamra, after all. Near it, but not it.

"Right. I see. Well, I'll see what I can find out today. When I have information, I'll have a messenger drop off a note at the reception desk there. Room number?" he asks, pen hovering.

"They know her. You don't need a room number. Just ask to leave a note for Miss Samara."

"A very pretty name," he says, writing it down in English capitals. Damn, should have lied about that, too. Since I'll now have to pay a bribe to the receptionist at the Sumerland to pretend that Sam is staying there, rather than having an occasional meal with friends, I could just as easily have made up a fake name and paid the guys to pretend they recognize it. But then, what if Mustapha already knows more than he's admitting?

"So," he says, looking at me. "You know where to find me. If you can get me a copy of the documents you want to have traced, and get it to me right away, all the better."

"Good. That's great," I say, standing up, hoping I don't appear to be rushing off. "It's great to see you after such a long time. It looks like life is treating you well," I say, patting my stomach in reference to his.

"*Al-Hamdulilah.* We have one little boy already, and another one on the way. I added this to make my wife feel better," he says, running a hand over his girth. "How about you?"

"I'm not married yet."

"No? Well, don't lose hope. You'll find the right one," he says, walking me towards the door. "And if not, by the time the Americans leave, this country will have so many widows that there will be a lot of young women in need of husbands. You can get one going around a second time!" He laughs and so I laugh, too.

I pull open the door and find Brutus holding the other side of the knob, two cold cans wrapped in his enormous hand, prompting Mustapha to laugh harder.

40

Prompting

I HURRY INTO the Hamra's second-tower lobby on my way to get Sam, and smile at Rafik. His face, however, is like a graveyard.

"Miss Samara asked me to give you this," he says, pushing a folded page written on her notebook paper across the counter.

I thank him and pick it up quickly, as if it might be read by the wrong person in the interim. I know her handwriting, loping and large, from watching her fill her notebooks. *Nabil, Had to go over to the Sheraton to do an interview with MSNBC. Meet me there, 14th floor.*

"Thanks very much," I say, turning to go.

"Not at all," he answers, looking me over disapprovingly. "You haven't heard about your colleague, Taher?"

"Who?"

"The young fellow. One of you fixers, but with the British, I think," he says. "The Americans opened fire on a taxi trying to pass through a checkpoint in Yarmouk this morning. The car didn't slow down, so the soldiers thought it was an attack. They opened fire and killed all five people inside. Taher was one of them." He shakes his head. "So young."

"*That* Taher? The handsome fellow working with Sky News?

The young guy who sits there in the main lobby sometimes, waiting?"

"That's right. The Americans are saying it's an accident, a misunderstanding. But people are very upset. A lot of the employees from the first tower went to the funeral. I didn't know him, so I didn't go. Very sad."

"That can't be," I say. "He was just – I just saw him yesterday!"

"*Rahimahu Allah,*" Rafik says. God take mercy on his soul.

"Do you know where he lives? Or, I mean, where his family lives?"

"I heard Hayy Riyadh," he says. "But what do I know?"

Taher, dead. I barely knew him. Just awful luck. What was the driver thinking, not stopping at the checkpoint? Or what if that's just a story the soldiers fabricated? I should try to pay a condolence call. Or maybe contact his family in England. I reach Rizgar's car out of breath. "Go. To the Sheraton."

"Where is Miss Samara?"

"She went there for some kind of interview."

He shakes his head. "*Majnouna.*" Crazy woman.

"*Mu majnouna, mashghule,*" I protest. "Not crazy, just busy."

"She shouldn't be getting into other people's cars like that," he says, peeling out to Omar bin Yasir Street. "It's dangerous. She should only travel with me."

"I'm sure she wouldn't go over there if she didn't have a safe way to go."

Rizgar shrugs, reaching for his cigarettes. I see he is now smoking Marlboros, a testament to his improving financial situation. When I first met him, he smoked Sumer, our cheap national brand in the blue packet. Now, it's either Marlboro or

Pall Mall, which seemed a strange name to me at first. According to the dictionary, the most common meanings of pall are something dark and gloomy, and secondly a coffin or a casket. A mall is a place where they sell things. So Pall Mall could be the place where they sell darkness and death. In that case, they would be appropriately named cigarettes.

However, when I shared this amusing fact with Baba, he shot down my theory: Pall Mall is a street in London, he said, named after a ball game no one plays anymore.

"You shouldn't smoke so much," I tell Rizgar as he lets out another column of smoke, much of it hovering over my face.

"You shouldn't separate from Miss Samara," he says. "You should stay with her."

"Miss Samara is smoking again like you. You're being a bad influence on her."

Rizgar takes two deep drags, lowers his window and blows most of it out, saving me from the rest of the exhale. "Miss Samara is a big girl. And you should worry more about keeping her alive in Baghdad when she's thirty than about what will happen to her health when she's sixty."

Thirty-three. You don't even know how old she is, and I do. You don't know half of what I know.

He inhales deeply once more, cups the cigarette in his left hand, and releases the smoke into the whipping wind.

The security around the Sheraton is much more elaborate than at the Hamra, with many layers of guards and a quasi-checkpoint, and most frustrating for Rizgar, a prohibition against parking in front of the building. We look for a space along Abu Nuwas, but the riverfront near the hotel is full, and we end up having to circle back towards Kahramana Square, my favourite in Baghdad, in order to locate a spot. As we drive, I find myself wondering how I keep neglecting to tell Sam Kahramana's story, which comes from *One Thousand and One Nights*. It is the brilliant Kahramana, just a slave-girl, who saves the city from Ali Baba and the forty thieves who were terrorizing people with their crimes. She convinces them to hide from the authorities in a series of jars, and then pours boiling oil on their heads.

The bronze sculpture in the square is a water-fountain that has Kahramana pouring her "oil", in this case water, though lately the fountain hasn't been running at all. Maybe Sam will be like Kahramana, a woman who stops the work of unjust men, a struggler who has to do the difficult job of holding the crooked accountable for their deeds.

The Sheraton lobby is nothing like the Hamra's. It is large, multi-levelled, and bustling with people. Men sit in groups on sofas and armchairs while others stand alone, looking around, hiding between the greenery provided by person-sized plants. I make my way through them and notice the glass lift, saving me from the need to ask anyone how to get up to the fourteenth floor.

Standing at the doors and waiting for the next lift, a man appears next to me, wraps his hand around my forearm, and says my name. My mind goes lopsided to the point of dizziness. Suleiman al-Mutanabi. Suleiman the Syrian. Akram's guy.

"It is so good to see you, my brother. Where have you been?" He pulls me away from the lift. "I have looked for you and Miss Samara many times."

"Oh, I'm sorry you had trouble finding us. We have been so busy with all of the news."

He hasn't let go of my arm yet, and now has his right hand in mine, his left hand on my elbow, pulling me just a little further away from the lift. "You haven't let us know yet what her editors decided about the story. About the documents we showed you." He looks happy to have taken me off guard, and I try to imagine what Sam would do now: sigh, smile, breathe calmly.

"We have been waiting for an answer! Can you believe those ridiculous editors cannot even make up their minds?" It's the best I can do to feign frustration. "Stupid Americans."

"We didn't find you or her here. We looked for you."

"Oh, that's because she had to move to another hotel last week. This one is so expensive. The newspaper is tight on money."

"A big American newspaper doesn't have enough money?" He looks incredulous. "Where does she stay now?"

"The Karma Hotel."

Stupid! Just around the block from the Hamra. Couldn't I have picked something further away? Does he remember that I told him she worked for the *Guardian*? If so, he must know I'm lying about everything.

"How can we get in touch with you?" he asks. "We have some new information that may clear up some of the questions you have. You can come to see it."

"I'll let her know that as soon as I see her," I say.

Suleiman finally lets go of me, and I step an inch away from him, back towards the lift. "You remember where General Akram's house is, don't you?"

"Certainly."

"Well, then. Where is your lovely friend now? Is she in the hotel?"

"Now, no. I'm just doing an errand. But I'll tell her I ran into you and that she needs to make a decision soon. It's not right to be made to wait like that, is it? Foreigners. They don't understand these things."

The *bing* of the lift behind me, and my hand over my heart to offer a non-contact goodbye. "You will hear from us, I am sure." I step in as the people get out, relieved that Suleiman stands there, his arms folded and with an intense expression on his face but making no effort to get in with me.

The lift soars, with only a few stops on the way. On floor fourteen, I rush up and down until I find an MSNBC sign, and am hit by a feeling of relief that there is an armed guard keeping anyone from just walking in, anyone like Suleiman al-Mutanabi. "Sam Katchens," I say, somewhat out of breath, and the guard says he needs to check. I feel my heart racing and my head pounding. What if Suleiman changes his mind? What if he emerges through those lift doors right now and Sam walks out and we look like a couple of liars and Suleiman just shoots us, and the guard, right there? Who could stop him? Who would come after him?

A trim black man pokes his head out of the door behind the guard. His face is distinctively shaped, like I would expect for a man on American television. "You looking for Sam? Nabil, right? She told me to expect you." He holds out his hand. "I'm Wayne. She's up on the roof doing a Q&A live-shot. You can head up there and watch if you want. Just be quiet unless you know the shot's over." When I look confused, he walks me to the stairwell and holds the door open. "There you go, buddy. Up two flights to the roof."

The sun hits me hard in the eyes, making me sneeze. Inside

a tent made of poles and black fabric I can see Sam across from the camera, and she looks beautiful. For the first time since I've known her, she has on makeup, either eyeliner or mascara, and brown lipstick. Her hair is tied up nicely behind her, more controlled. She's wearing a jewel-green blouse that I've never seen her wear before, and it sets off her hair in a way that makes her look simply striking.

Sam is talking but I can't hear the words, the way it sometimes is in a dream. She smiles widely, her lips say thank you, and then she is still, almost frozen. She reaches down the front of her shirt takes out a small wire, presumably a microphone, and hands it back to one of the crewmen. She is chatting with the man behind the camera, and then he points at me.

"Nabil! Glad you got the note."

She indicates that I should come and join them, presumably to introduce me to everyone, but when she sees I'm motioning towards the door, she walks over to me. "Hey, don't you want to see how the TV side of things works?"

"Not today. We need to get out of here. Now."

"What's wrong?"

"Suleiman is here. Akram's guy. Asking after you."

"Shit." She looks back to the tent. "Let me grab my bag."

"Wait." My hand takes her forearm near the wrist. Unintentional, unintentional. But once it's there, I like the warmth of it, the narrowness. "What if he sees us on the way down? Ask those guys if there's another way out of the building."

Sam scuttles back, and as she talks to them, I find my nervousness mitigated by watching how glamorous she looks today. Less natural, but extraordinarily beautiful. Is that the Iraqi in me? Louis said our women wear too much makeup. Perhaps we like it that way.

Sam leads the way, back towards the stairwell. "They said we could walk down to the first floor," she says. "The lobby is actually on three. They told me to try to go through the kitchen and use the exit there, which goes out to the employee parking lot."

"You always prefer the stairs anyway."

"Yeah, well, that elevator is mostly glass so it doesn't bother me." She whips around to face me before she starts the decline. "Are you sure he's still here?"

"*Miyye bil miyye.* Do you know that one?"

"A hundred per cent," she answers. "To the bottom."

She begins the rush down and I follow her, taking the stairs quickly, sometimes skipping one when she does.

"What were you doing here?"

"Got asked to do a Q&A on the situation here. No one else from the paper was available."

"So?"

"So they called and wanted me to do an interview," she says, taking the stairs so quickly that I fear she might fall. I want to tell her that we don't have to go this fast, and that an extra minute won't keep us from bumping into Suleiman again, but once the momentum is going, it isn't easy to stop it.

"Did you know that the army today gave orders to all US soldiers to shoot looters on sight?" Sam asks. "So that's their answer for stopping the looting."

We both are almost running, a *pa-pum* with each two steps we take, but there's a weightlessness to it, a lack of effort due to gravity, and it almost makes me giddy.

"Also, you know, all the political players, the Shi'ites and the Sunnis, they're all up in arms now because it seems like the Bush administration is putting off the whole Iraqi interim-government thing, indefinitely."

"Really?"

"Yeah, so now everyone's thinking it's going to look like more of a long-term occupation and less of a 'let's hand it over to the best Iraqi we can' sort of thing. And now it's seeming that they won't just present the whole thing to Chalabi on a platter, so he's pissed off…"

pa-pum pa-pum

"And all the Shi'ites are pissed off, because they say the Americans are reneging on all their promises…"

pa-pum pa-pum

"…and the whole thing is getting to be a mess because no one's got control of the security situation and it's looking bad for Washington. It's now five weeks since they've been here and the place is still in freefall. I mean, my God!"

pa-pum pa-pum

"So what did you talk about?

Sam stops, her chest heaving. "What did I talk about?"

"The interviewer in America. What answers did you give them about all the problems here?"

"Oh, you don't actually have to give them any answers. They just prompt you with some situation-questions and you talk a bit and then wait for the next question. It's very, you know, basic."

"We don't have to run this fast. Another minute won't make a difference."

"I know," she sighs, taking the steps again, a little more slowly. "But I miss working out. I can't get any exercise in this place."

Only four more flights to go. "Sam, how did you know all these things were happening? You said your editors completely took you off news to do this investigation."

Her eyes open with surprise. "A journalist never totally cuts off from the news, Nabil. Even when I'm not *on* news I'm on top of the news. You can't afford to shut off from what's happening. Not in a place like this."

A place like this. Are there other places like it? This time next year, Sam will simply go to another country, to the seat of some other regime accused of threatening the world, and cover a war like ours, in a place like this, with a guy like me.

"Hurray!" She waves her hands in the air in what looks like a dance move I saw in a music video at my friend Alan's. I think he said it was hip-hop. The name fits our run down the stairs. "Last floor," she sings.

"*Al-Hamdulilah*."

"Yeah, seriously. Thank God." Sam reaches for the door-handle, and stops to catch her breath. "Please, please don't be locked." She turns it, pulls, and the door opens, the fresh air like the sweetest I've felt on my face in years. "I say we just find the kitchen and pound through it. Don't stop for anyone until we get to the exit."

"Yeah, but we should just walk very quickly," I say. "Not run. Running looks suspicious."

"Fine."

We push open the swinging doors into the kitchen, which feels hot and damp. "Go," she whispers, poking me in the back. "I'll follow you."

I hurry past the ovens and the cooks, at least two of them looking at us but the rest are oblivious, past the pots and the smells and the cabinets, Sam close behind me, my suddenly shouting that we're sorry, we need to help a friend with his car out in the car park, and despite what I told Sam about walking I'm almost running anyway, and she follows and I can't decide if it's fear or the fun of escaping with her that's pulling me along, and through the storage room, past bottles and boxes and bags of rice, until I see the exit sign, and we tumble through it, and we're out, and we're free, and we're safe.

"Don't run anymore," I order. "Then we'll really attract attention."

We're both working to get enough air, to regain composure, to save ourselves from making a spectacle. But Sam can't help herself, she's laughing now, and so am I, and I hope not too many people are noticing us, out in the open, because there just isn't such a thing as a couple walking around Baghdad like that, breathing hard, bending over, laughing out loud.

We have the short walk to Kahramana Square to bring ourselves under control. Sam has sweated a bit through her nice shirt, and I through mine.

I take the back seat, and Sam waves me to move over, falling in beside me. Rizgar takes one look at us and says "*Shunu, shunu?*" What? What happened?

"*Maku 'shi,*" I answer. There's nothing, no problem. "Back to the Hamra, right?"

"Yeah," says Sam. "Hi Rizgar. Nabil and I need to have a bit of a conference call."

Rizgar turns to me for a translation.

"We're trying to plan what we will do next," I tell Rizgar. "Does it bother you if we both sit in the back?"

Rizgar looks at me and then Sam and shrugs. "*Tfaddalu.*"

Please, be my guest, he says, in a way that somehow says that's not exactly what he's feeling.

Sam looks at me and shakes her head, smiling, slowing down her still-fast breathing. "This place is crazy."

I nod, wanting to tell her that it wasn't always like this, but the truth is, I realize that it was crazy before, too, just in very different ways.

"Sam, this guy was acting very suspicious of us. He says he's been looking for you and wants an answer. He said he might have new information."

Sam raises her eyebrows at me. "Do you believe that?"

"Not really."

"So forget about it." She notices the blocks-long queue outside the Rafideen Bank.

"What's going on there?" she asks, her head turning as we leave the men, hundreds of them, behind us.

"It's a bank. There's a rumour they might open today. A lot of people haven't been able to get money yet."

"You mean since the war began?"

"Of course." I guess I never told her that it's been my weekly payments from working for her, rather than Baba's hospital salary – which arrives over a month late – that makes it possible for us to live without feeling the strain of the banks being closed, looted or otherwise unable to operate.

A thought flashes through my mind: Mustapha and big Brutus, waiting with the coke cans and their M16. As if I've just had a nanosecond of a nap and met them in my dream.

"We need to get back to the Hamra," I say. "And just so you know, Suleiman thinks you're at the Karma Hotel, and this guy I met this morning, I told him that you're at the Sumerland."

She looks at me with bewilderment. "Wouldn't it be better if we were at least consistent in our lies about where I'm staying?"

At Fateh Square, the traffic slows to the speed of an ant crawling across the pavement. What if Suleiman gets there before we do?

"Do you remember when I asked you if you trust me? You said I have an honest face."

"I remember."

"Well, I think you have to trust me now, even though I haven't been so honest with everyone. I don't know if we can trust either of these guys, so it's better they don't know where you're living."

Sam puts her back against the car door, folding up her left foot into the inside of her right thigh, facing me. "You're right. They don't need to know that." Does she only put on make-up like this when she's going to be on television? Or would she put it on, for example, if she were coming to dinner at my parents' house? To a wedding?

"Maybe it was good thinking," she says. "You gotta go with your gut. So what actually happened today?"

"Well, this guy," I say especially for Sam, because she makes fun of me when I say bloke and chap. "This guy says that he is pretty sure he can help us, but he wants to see the documents we have from Akram. And he knew who Akram was."

"Huh!"

"It seemed like Akram has nothing to do with making the documents, he just sells them. But he's probably one of several who do this. There might be many others."

"Others involved in making these documents?"

"No, other people selling the work of the forgers. It sounds like a competitive business."

Sam's eyes widen with wonder. "Brilliant," she says. "We should do a story about Baghdad's new cottage industry: the forgery factories. So what he was really saying is that Akram is sort of a retailer and marketer, and then there are some middlemen who are wholesalers, and they buy it from one of the producers – and that's who actually draws the thing up."

"I don't know, I suppose." This evening, I'll have to look up all of Sam's business terms.

"And you know what would really kill me? If we could find any indication that some of these forgery artists were at work before the war and were producing made-up documents related to WMD. If we find that," she says with a dreamy smile, "we're golden."

It takes a minute for this to wash over me, both the concepts and the words – that killing in this case is meant to be a positive.

"Excuse me, Miss Samara." Rizgar peers in the rearview mirror. "You want Al-Faqma?"

Sam glances at me. I find myself shaking my head, enjoying the chance to make all the decisions. "We really don't have time, now."

"Sorry, Rizgar. Thank you. Maybe later?"

Rizgar nods, disappointed.

"This guy thinks you're at the Sumerland, so I'm going to go over there and will pay the receptionists something to pretend you live there. He says that he'll get in contact with us there, somehow, later in the day."

"Nabil, you know how I feel about paying bribes to people. It's not the right way to go about getting the truth."

I imagine Sam having a tiny holy book somewhere, the way we have tiny Korans that we, especially religious people, sometimes put on the dashboard. Hers would be a bible of journalism, with rules about the right way to do everything.

"It won't cost a lot, Sam. Something small. It's not like a real bribe. I'll take care of it. If anyone finds out, you can blame it on me and say you didn't know."

She looks at me sympathetically. "That's not the point. It's just not a good idea to get people used to that sort of thing. You know, you end up encouraging these people and raising their expectations so that every time they do something, they expect some kind of kickback, a little *baksheesh*."

Sam speaks like a parent who thinks she can prevent her child from getting accustomed to eating sweets. Maybe she can't help it: it's how America as a whole looks at us. Us in Iraq, us in the Middle East, us in the Muslim world. They know what's good for us, what mix of dictatorship and democracy is acceptable, how many weapons we are allowed to have. What is that word? Patronizing? No…Paternalistic.

I'm tempted to remind her that the favour we're asking involves them lying for her, but it hardly seems to matter now, since I'm the one who made up the lie.

"Also, there's more than that," I explain. "This guy, Mustapha, he is also going to want to be paid. And I don't think we will have a choice in that either, because it will be work for him to get us the answers we need."

Sam tilts her head. "Did you promise this guy you'd pay him?"

"No, of course not." *Negotiable.* How could Sam understand? "But it was very much implied."

"And do you trust this guy? Do you think he's really going to be able to get us definite answers?"

"I went to university with him."

"Oh! So you know him."

"Not really."

"So let me get this straight. This guy you sort of know from college, your cousin sent you to him. He wants to see the documents and he wants to be paid if he can find out for us where the documents come from, who ordered them made, and whether they made other documents that might be even sexier."

"More or less."

Sam rakes her hair around the crown of her head, then unclasps the barrette holding it neatly in place. She shakes the locks out, massaging her scalp as if tying back her hair that way makes her head ache.

"Sam, I found out today that one of the other fixers was killed. Taher, for Sky News."

"Who?"

"This nice young guy named Taher. Handsome-looking? He was often sitting around by the windows in the first tower lobby when we come in. The American army shot him and four others in a car at a checkpoint for no reason. Or they say because the car didn't stop."

Sam shakes her head. "That's awful. Jeez. Why the hell didn't the driver stop?"

Why the hell did they shoot? Why doesn't Sam ask that? Maybe the car was rushing for good reason. I feel a frustration banging in my chest. She doesn't really seem upset about Taher, doesn't realize that an innocent guy, someone just like me, is gone.

And Louis's friend, who was killed last week? Did I feel anything when Louis mentioned him? Some sympathy for Louis, perhaps, but behind it, a malicious voice is keeping score: a lot more of ours have been killed than yours. And you bloody well started it.

We round the corner towards the Hamra car park. Sam gazes down the street in the direction of the Sumerland, where she occasionally meets her friends for dinner, and the Duleimy Hotel, which is reputed to have been a hotel for prostitutes. Now, young freelance reporters on tight budgets stay there.

"Let's go up and talk through things. And maybe eat," she says, putting a hand to her belly. "This is too much running around on an empty stomach."

"I think I should go and talk to someone at the Sumerland first. How about you wait here in the car for a few minutes."

"Fine," Sam says. She goes into her wallet and takes out two fifty-dollar bills, handing them to me. "You shouldn't have to pay for your bribes out-of-pocket."

"No," I hold up my hand towards hers. "I don't need it."

"Take it, Nabil. I'm not going to let you pay for it."

I shake my head, pushing her hand back towards her bag. "Not now," I say. "You'll pay me back some other time. I'm counting on it."

41

Counting

As I WALK into the Sumerland Hotel, I try to suppress the guilty feelings Sam conjured up in me about paying bribes. Some bribes are necessary, no? The only person at the desk is a middle-aged man named Munzer, whom I've noticed once before. *I'm gonna just give you the headlines*, Sam said to me recently, when I asked her for an explanation and she was in a rush. Headlines only.

And so I tell Munzer that I need to protect Sam, that nice foreign lady I work with. The one with the red hair? And he says yes, he's noticed her. And I say that if anyone asks I need him to pretend that she stays here, because for her own honour, we don't want certain people to know where she lives – she's a very important person and we need to keep that information private.

Honour I said, not security, and I think he could understand that, just in the way that some men will never mention their wives' and daughters' names in front of people they don't know well. Women's names are part of the family's honour, and why should a stranger have access to information like that?

Munzer understands, I see, and he takes the small stack of dinars as I pass it behind the counter, which probably came out to somewhere around $30. Munzer smiles, and as this is probably a week's salary for him anyway, I feel like I have a friend for life.

I ask him which room he will pretend she's in, and he says how about 125, and I say that's fine, just make sure it stays the same. And he promises to send a message over to Sam's room at the Hamra if he hears anything, and to be quiet about it. And I tell him he's been very kind and he nods and reaches behind him and sticks a folded white piece of message paper into the box for 125, taping it in as if conjuring up imaginary guests is something he has been doing forever.

Sam and I agree to send Rizgar off for a lunch break, and to have ours inside. In the lobby, my eyes focus on the chair where Taher used to sit while he was waiting. But Sam keeps heading straight for the courtyard and tower two, and after a moment of contemplating his empty seat, I follow.

In the shaded corner, I can see Joon facing us, chatting and nodding. Across from her is a fellow who screams "American" with his big broad shoulders, and as we move a few steps closer I can see the profile of his face: Franklin Baylor.

Sam strides ahead of me, and pretends to be pleasantly surprised.

"Joon, hi!" Sam says as Baylor rises to greet her by holding out his hand.

"Miss Katchens. Nice to see you again."

Sam's mouth is slightly ajar. "Likewise." On the table, we both notice, is Joon's recorder and a mini-microphone, though they don't appear to be turned on.

"You done that electricity story yet?" he asks.

"Not yet," she says, staring at him and forcing a smile. "I've got so many stories on my plate this week."

I glance at Joon, who has a barely perceptible air of annoyance at our arrival.

"Well, you better step on it or this here Joon Park's going to do the story first," he says, sitting himself back down.

Sam smiles at Joon, Joon smiles back. Sam rolls her eyes in a way that almost seems authentic, but not quite. "No problem there," Sam says. "We're not competitors, we're friends."

Joon nods as if she agrees. And then her Thuraya phone, sitting on the table, begins moving with a buzz, and finally begins to ring. She looks at the number of the incoming call and makes a sour face. "Damn. Washington Q&A at the top of the hour. I have to take this. Frank, would you excuse me for a few minutes?" She avoids Sam's gaze and brushes past her, heading to the other side of the pool, where there is reception.

Frank gestures to us to take a seat, but Sam remains standing, although moving closer.

"What are you doing, Frank?" she whispers in a voice that sounds flirty, but also aggressive. "You tipping off every reporter in the Hamra?"

"Easy there. I came here to see you. I tried calling you three times on that Thuraya thing but couldn't get through. And I was on a little errand in the neighbourhood anyway, so I thought I'd stop in."

"And how the hell—"

"Don't forget your friend there was also at that party the other night at the Sheraton, and so she thinks that I'm actually working on electricity. In fact, I've spent the last ten minutes explaining what we're doing to fix it, because apparently everyone and their mother wants to know why Iraqis have been sitting in the dark since we came to town."

"Oh." Sam looks over at Joon, who from the way she's answering questions, loudly and clearly, sounds like she's being interviewed live.

"Listen," he says in a low voice. "Chalabi is not responsible for the documents, but someone with a similar mindset is. And the man who made them, is named Ali al-Yaqubi al-Sadr."

Sam moves to uncap a pen.

"Don't write. Just listen." And then to my surprise, he turns to me, and in perfectly accented Arabic, repeats the man's name and spells it for me, as if to emphasize. *Sad-dall-raa.*

"Related to Moqtada?" I ask.

"Unclear," he says. "But not a bad guess. Either way, I don't suggest you go looking for him further. You're a reporter, not a police force. You have enough to go on now."

"Well," Sam says. "Not exactly—"

"I don't want to tell you how to do your job, but you'd better watch yourself. *Dir Balak*," he says. "Because furthermore—"

Out of the corner of my eye I see Joon heading back in our direction.

"Because furthermore, you have to realize just how much more power we're going to be able to generate from the South Baghdad Power Plant in Dura. That plant will be generating a thousand megawatts a day when our emergency rehabilitation plan is implemented, starting next week." Baylor lifts his eyes to acknowledge Joon's return. "That's going to have this town buzzing with more power than it ever had under Saddam."

On the way up to her room, I begin to ask Sam a question, but from behind I see her shaking her head, telling me to wait. She opens the door and her body jerks as if a little current just went through it. There's a strange man standing at her desk, in front of her computer.

It dawns on me that he must be one of the hotel cleaning staff. He has a rag in one hand and a spraybottle in the other.

"Sorry, madam. Clean your room." He seems startled as well.

Sam lets out a sigh and unloads her bag. "Thanks, that's enough," she says, looking around. "It looks very clean already. Maybe come back tomorrow?"

I start to translate this for him but he seems to get the point before I finish my sentence and moves to leave. I try to explain that she just has a lot of work to do, but he says *maku mushkile, maku mushkile*. No problem. And walks out, closing the door quietly behind him.

Her eyes grow twice their normal size. "I'm starting to suspect everyone," she says. "Not a good sign."

Sam paces a few times, goes to her computer, and taps it awake. She takes the file that's been sitting under her laptop and opens it, and counts the five pages of photocopies of the Jackson documents.

"I think I'm keeping this with me from now on," she says, tucking the folder into her day bag. "Some of these hotel guys give me the creeps."

I take a seat on the sofa. "But don't you trust your own friends?"

Sam closes her laptop gently. "What? You mean Joon?" Her nostrils flair. "It's not that I don't trust her. It's just that you can't share every story you're working on with everybody else. Some things you have to keep quiet. And Jesus, I don't know what to make of Baylor."

I shrug. "He seemed to hold up the electricity expert routine."

"Or not. Maybe he's fooling both of us. Who knows what he's up to." She stands. "Nabil, I'm starving. The Chinese food here is not that bad. Let's order something now, because by the time it gets here, it'll probably be dark."

The knock on the door comes sooner than I would have expected and Sam is up quicker than I am, heading for the door. "That was fast," she says. "Room service is really improving around here."

Sam opens the door to find Joon, who doesn't look happy. But then, I've hardly seen her smile.

"Oh, hey," Sam says. "What's up?"

"Can I come in?" Joon asks as if it's awkward to have to ask.

"Of course," Sam replies. "But I'm kind of on deadline so I can only talk for a few minutes. You want a quick coffee?"

"No," says Joon, who continues to stand despite Sam heading towards the sofa. "Look, Sam, I have to be honest with you. I didn't appreciate the way you acted downstairs."

"What are you talking about?"

"You know exactly what I'm talking about. Frank Baylor? Your, um, electricity source?"

Sam shoots her a blank look.

"Look, you want to be all secret and clandestine about your sources, you go ahead. But don't start acting all pissy and territorial if some of your sources also speak to some of your colleagues. The rest of us have jobs to do, too."

Sam gets up and goes to the kitchen, taking down the coffee jar from the cabinet. "Joon, I'm going to make myself a coffee.

444

You can have a cup with me, or maybe you want to just have a make-believe cup to save yourself the caffeine. Because you seem to have quite an overactive imagination at the moment."

"Don't be ridiculous! I know you're on that Jackson story, everyone in this hotel knows it. So Baylor's a source. So what? Maybe he's a source for me on something else. For your information, I met him before you did. He was in Suleimaniye before Baghdad fell, just before you arrived. And suddenly you're looking at me like you own the guy."

Sam slaps a mug on the counter, almost hard enough to break it. "I don't own anyone. And I don't owe you anything. Look, if you're pissed off because I've been too busy to hang around in the evenings—"

"I'm pissed off because you're acting like I'm moving in on your sources."

"Well maybe you are," Sam shoots back.

"Yeah? Just like you moved in on my boyfriend."

"*What?*"

"Sam, don't pretend you didn't know I was with Jonah last year when you guys hooked up in Kabul. And then after all that you dump the guy."

Sam's mouth drops wide open. "Dump? Jonah? You don't know what you're talking about."

"Well, after he was released from Abu Ghraib with his head inside out, you were pretty damn quick to send him back home to England to let someone else deal with him."

"Just because I wasn't going home with him, doesn't mean I dumped him," Sam says. "The man's been wanting to get out of journalism for years and this was the final straw. If you guys were so tight you should know that."

Joon's eyes are suddenly brimming with tears.

"What do you want me to do," Sam scowls. "Jump on his funeral pyre?"

Joon's face is a wall of outrage. "You make me sick. I can't believe we're having this conversation in front of your *fucking* fixer! What are you two, attached at the hip?"

They both glare at me as if I should say something in my defence, or out of offence. I wish I'd excused myself and left the minute Joon walked in. Sam looks as if she might pick up the mug and ram it into Joon's pale, pretty face.

"I could have asked him to leave if you wanted," Sam says in quiet, forced calm.

"Yeah, I'm sure you have him trained really well."

"Get out, Joon. I have nothing else to say to you."

Joon turns with the grace of an alley cat and grabs the door, slamming it behind her.

42

Slamming

"I THINK I'M going up to the roof to have a scream."

I stare at Sam, wordless.

"But that will probably make the neighbours think someone just got shot. I think I'll have a smoke instead." She opens what looks like a biscuit jar on the kitchen counter and takes out a packet that says Marlboro Lights on it, shaking a cigarette into her hand. In one brisk movement, she lights the gas on the stove and makes the tip of the cigarette in her mouth glow orange.

"Nabil," she exhales. "I'm sure you want to talk about everything that just happened, but you know, at this moment, I really don't want to get into it. Because I've got too much on my plate at the moment to worry about Joon Park's little intrigues. And her jealousy, which is really her downfall."

"I…em…I probably should have left."

She blows out a line of smoke like an exclamation point. "Why? Look, let's leave it for now. Come, sit," she says, and I do.

She is inhaling the cigarette so deeply, it's already half gone. "Smoke bothering you?"

"No," I lie.

"Good. So give me a quiet moment," she says. "The smoke helps me think." Sam closes her eyes and lets the ash grow long.

The hum of the air conditioner fills the void.

"You know, Nabil, I think I'm going to have to leave Iraq as soon as this story is done."

Sam had said nothing about leaving. Not until now, not until we got into this crazy story. I think I imagined that she would soon start giving out a card like the one she gave me on the first day we met. *Samara B. Katchens. Baghdad Bureau Chief.*

"I mean, I was supposed to be leaving soon anyway," Sam says with shoulders jutting uncomfortably high. "I've been in Iraq since March 10th. It's now May 1st? That's nearly two months in Iraq. I need to go home and take a break."

She stubs out the cigarette and stares into the ashtray. Then she reaches for the camera in her bag.

"I can't stay here forever, Nabil. But I'll probably come back, maybe in the fall." Sam takes off the lens cap. "What? Why aren't you saying anything?"

"I think that's the right thing to do. You should leave. I don't want you to leave, of course, but you have to do what is right for you."

"It's not just what's right for—"

"And also for your safety. You're right to be a little bit worried now. I don't know about some of these people. Did I tell you I saw someone shot on a local expressway yesterday, on the way to work in the morning?"

"No. What happened?"

"I saw three men pull another man out of his car and just shoot him. They then got into his car and drove off, along with the rest of the traffic moving at about, I don't know, forty miles an hour. No rush, because there's no one to catch them. No one did anything. What should people do, go and find an American tank and ask the soldiers who don't speak Arabic to come and catch the criminals? This is what's happening, Sam, this is what I can't control. What if Akram's men come over here and try to shoot you in the car park and just drive off?"

"Hold on. Let's not get carried away."

"I'm just trying to tell you that anything could happen. No one's in control here."

"So you think it's good that I'm leaving."

Just like that, moving seamlessly from "I think I'm going to leave" to "I'm leaving".

"Of course. You know you are always welcome in Iraq and I'm happy when you're here, but you have to take care of yourself."

Sam reaches for the camera again and holds it up to her face. "I don't know why I want to take a picture of you here when we could do it out in a pretty place, along the waterfront. Okay, smile," she says.

I do, and she frowns. "Looks artificial. Okay, don't smile," she says, wrapping her hand around the black body of the camera and pressing down on the silver button, releasing the sound of a fake shutter opening and closing.

The plates of Chinese food don't look particularly appetizing to me, but Sam is exactly right: they're not too bad. They have a sweet and spicy taste, and all the sauces have strange colours, like a red that I don't think occurs in nature, and another dish has a sort of electric yellow glow. Everything seems heavily fried and then stewed or soaked in something, and somehow, it's vaguely satisfying. Sam ordered broccoli and beef for me, which she refused to touch, plus several plates of vegetable dishes: eggplant and garlic sauce, chow mein with snowpeas, peanut and peppers. She had been asking over the phone if they could make her a Buddha Delight, which is steamed vegetables, but the guy on the phone didn't get it, and Sam hung up the phone, laughing. I think he thought I was saying "put out the light", she mused.

"Do you eat this a lot at home?"

"It depends on what you mean by home."

"In Paris."

"In Paris there are even more exciting things to eat. In Washington, though, there are a whole bunch of good ethnic restaurants not far from where I live, in this area called Adam's Morgan."

"But which one is home, Sam?"

"I don't know." She picks up a chunk of dripping broccoli with her chopsticks. "Right now, home is room 323 of the Hamra Hotel. That is, when my doppelgänger is not staying at the Sumerland Hotel."

"I never heard it pronounced until now, but I actually know that word."

"See, that's what I like about working with you, Nabil. I wouldn't have used it with just anyone."

I feel full already, despite not having eaten very much. I will keep eating, though, so Sam doesn't feel like she's eating alone. "What kind of food is ethnic food?"

"Oh, you know. In Adam's Morgan there's Korean, Mexican, Japanese. There's even a good Lebanese restaurant. I bet you'd like that. Oh, and there are these fantastic little Ethiopian places—"

"So ethnic is everything but American?"

Sam has one of those laughs that just stays in her throat.

450

"Yeah, basically."

I push the syrupy noodles around my plate with a fork while Sam snaps things up with her skinny chopsticks. I find myself wondering how she learned to eat with them, and where the Hamra Hotel gets such things.

"So we have a name," she says. "Ali something."

"Ali al-Yaqubi al-Sadr."

"Name ring a bell?"

"No. Except that if he's related to Moqtada al-Sadr, well, that might be logical. They also hate the people who tried to stop this war. Even if now their main thing is to complain that the Americans are occupying Iraq illegally and should get out."

"And what about this guy you saw this morning?"

"Mustapha," I say, taking another mouthful of noodles. "My cousin Saleh says he's the right person to be talking to. But he wants to be paid," I say. "Mustapha I mean."

"How much?"

"He didn't say how much. He asked how much we'd be willing to pay."

Sam digs around a little more, fills up her plate again, but then sits back, putting her hands on her slightly distended stomach. "I think I've had enough. So where did you leave things with this Mustapha."

"He wanted to know what we'd be willing to pay."

"You know the paper's policy."

"Sure."

"But we pay other people who provide services. Fixers, for example," Sam says, gesturing in my direction, but looking towards the map of Baghdad she recently taped up on the wall. The place names look funny written out in English, and many neighbourhoods I would consider important are not even on it. Zayouna, for example, where I was yesterday, is nowhere to be found.

"Using fixers," she continues. "Now that's a sort of paying for information, right? Information on how to get to the people who matter so we can interview them."

"Right. So you're saying if he's considered another fixer, like on a short assignment, then it's okay to pay him?"

"I'm not sure. I mean, is this man a fixer, a lawyer…or a forger?" Sam shakes her head. "Paying him and paying you, that's a whole different ball of wax."

"Is that like a kettle of fish?"

"What?"

"The other day you said something was 'a whole other kettle of fish'. Is a ball of wax the same thing?"

Sam looks to the ceiling with scrunched up eyes, as if to check the big reference book in her mind. Or maybe to ask God for patience. "Yeah, I guess so, it's the same idea."

"But why 'ball of wax'? What does it mean? And why a 'kettle of fish'?"

She shrugs. "It's just one of those things people say. I'll look it up for you if you want." Sam's eyes search mine. "You're always working, aren't you?"

"No. What do you mean?"

"On your English. You're constantly trying to learn new words and phrases, so you can do your job better."

"It's not that." My job? And what happens to my job if Sam leaves? The *Tribune* will replace her with another correspondent who will want to work with someone else – some other person to fix things.

"I'm just curious," I explain. "I like to know where sayings come from. I've learned a lot with you, especially the slang."

Sam smiles.

Learned. As if she is already a thing of the past.

"I think I might someday write something in English. If I really worked hard on it."

"What, like a book?"

"Maybe. Or some poems."

"I think you'd be terrific at that Nabil. I've never seen anything you've written, but from the way you speak, from the way you use language, I think it would be really beautiful."

I don't know what to say, but my body feels like it knows what it wants to do – to move over to Sam's sofa, to kiss her and touch her until she begs for me to love the rest of her.

"Excuse me," I stand, pointing to the hallway. "The bathroom's there, right?"

"Uh-huh. Feel free."

I shut the door slowly, trying hard not to seem rushed. Sam Katchens, the only woman to have truly appreciated my love affair with language.

When I come out, she has moved the dishes to the counter near the front door, and is staring down at the Jackson papers laid out on the table.

"Such a big deal over five little pages," she says. "Just words. Looks real to me. Would you have known?"

I look closer. "I don't really know what government documents look like. Except maybe the draft notice from the army."

"You were drafted?"

"I only had to serve for two months," I say. "A lot of the boys from better families, their parents pay bribes so they don't have to serve."

"Oh," she says, and I wonder if it is an oh of understanding or of judgement. Sam puts the pages back into the file.

"This whole thing is becoming just a little too sketchy, Nabil. Harris might be coming back. Suleiman and Akram are looking for me. Some sick person made up this letter to try to scare us. My editors have no clue what I'm going through here."

"You are a brave woman, Sam. I have never known you to be afraid, ever."

"Maybe I just hide it well."

Knocking. First a soft one, and then, two louder ones. "Who is it?" Sam calls. There is no reply, and she jumps up. "Maybe it's the fried rice they forgot to bring up. They always leave something out and then—"

Sam stands at the open door and shifts her weight impatiently. There is no one there, and in the empty space I can feel a kind of nervous energy in the air, left behind by someone who didn't want to wait for an answer.

"Huh!" She moves to close the door. "Oh, hang on," she says, bending to a squat. When she comes up, she's holding an envelope in her hand. She opens it – either the person who wrote it hadn't bothered to seal it, or the person who delivered it decided to have a read for himself.

She unfolds the contents, a letter in Arabic on yellow writing paper. "Special delivery. Apparently it's for you."

Even before I can begin to read, I feel in my bones who it will be from: Mustapha. The beautiful and somewhat bombastic handwriting makes it seem like the kind of letter a lawyer would write. I skim through it and then translate for Sam.

"It's from this lawyer I saw today, Mustapha."

"Yeah? I thought you told him I was staying at the Sumerland."

"I did," I say. "He says, 'Dear Nabil. I am certain I can provide you with the information you require. Come to my office tomorrow morning with the American lady in a regular taxi. I strongly suggest you avoid coming with your usual car and driver. Certain people may be watching and they already know your vehicle. Tell the journalist to come in *hejab* so she won't easily be noticed. I trust that you will use the utmost discretion in this matter. Other news organizations are requesting similar information, and I want to ensure that you have access to it first. With sincere trust. Your friend and classmate, Mustapha.'"

"Jee-sus," she whispers. "Seriously?"

"That's what it says." I wonder why, if Sam is Jewish, even only half-Jewish like I'm half Shi'ite, she says "Jesus" all the time.

"Do you trust this guy?"

My stomach is beginning to hurt, probably from these strange sauces made by someone who is no doubt from Al-Ummal and has no idea how to make Chinese food. Something inside contracts, then relaxes. "I don't know. I didn't know him well at school. But I don't think my cousin Saleh would send me to someone he doesn't trust."

Sam picks up a chopstick from the counter and puts it into her mouth at the same angle she would a cigarette. Unsatisfied with her almost subconscious drag, she eyes the biscuit jar.

I look over the note again. Mustapha did say he'd have a messenger drop off a note.

"Rizgar's not going to like that," she says. "He doesn't like when I do things without him." She chews the chopstick a bit between her molars. "He's very protective of me."

"I know."

"Not that you're not—"

I hold up my hand, trying to make her stop explaining. "I understand what you meant. I'll talk to him."

"Rizgar? Yeah, but I'm not sure he trusts *you*."

"Really? I think we work together well."

"Maybe it's a Kurdish thing. Your guys did kill about a few hundred thousand of theirs, easy."

"My guys? No one in my family worked for—"

"I mean, the half of your guys who are Sunni."

I wonder if Sam even knows about some of the things that Kurds would do to Arabs, given the chance. About the fact that they want to break up Iraq so they can make their own country and take all our oil wealth with them. About the Arabs in the north who have been chased out of their homes at gunpoint in the past few weeks, decades after Saddam moved them there. I've been reading about it in the newspapers.

"Sorry, I'm not being fair," says Sam. "I'm just trying to see it through his eyes." I wonder if, when I'm not there, she tries to see it through mine. "My God," she says. "This place is too complicated. I don't know if we should do this. My editors are happy to just run the story as is, so what am I doing putting my ass on the line? Mine and yours!"

"You don't have to worry about me. I'm ready to do whatever it takes to get the story."

Including getting a gun. I'll go back to Zayouna first thing, pick one out, pay for it, and keep it under my shirt, like everyone else. Protective, like Rizgar.

"We have to finish this, Sam. If we give up on getting to the truth, what was the point of any of the work we've done together? What *are* you doing here?"

She looks at me with a mix of sweetness and pity, like she's sorry she ever gave me all those talks about the truth, about ethics, about what good journalists do and don't do.

A baretta. Or maybe a Smith and Wesson. Louis said that was one of the best.

"He also wanted you to bring the photocopies."

"Maybe Baylor's right. Maybe we hold off a day and see."

"But you need to finish the story as soon as possible, right? I mean, your editors don't want to wait another few days, do they."

"No." Her mouth twitches. "It's now or never."

I come towards her in the kitchen. I have an urge to cover her mouth with mine, to turn that twitch into a kiss. Instead I lean against the wall by the door, on the back of which is a newly placed page of emergency instructions, signed by the Hamra Management.

In case of an attack on the hotel, such as by mortars or shelling, hide under furniture such as desks for protection.

In case of an attack outside the hotel, I'll be Sam's furniture.

"You're a guest in Iraq. Let me do the worrying. Everything will work out the way it's supposed to." I hardly know if I believe that, but when Amal says it, I always like the way it sounds.

Sam puts her fingers on her eyelids and makes slow circles.

"You know what, I *am* worried. And I'm feeling awful about Joon. I've known her for three years and we've never spoken to each other like that."

"Maybe you'll sort things out with her."

"Maybe." She opens her eyes again. "So you'll talk to Rizgar?"

"Yes. I'll explain."

She smiles with crooked lips, not looking up.

43

Looking

EVERY SO OFTEN my mind will work in a very organized way. The plan of action comes out short and clear, like my poems once did. On my way across the lobby, I find my fingers air-typing a list of what I need to do. See Munzer, then Rizgar, prepare for Mustapha. Talk to Saleh once more to check that he doesn't have any doubts about Mustapha. Take money out of my bottom drawer, waiting in an envelope behind my old notebooks, and decide what kind of gun to buy.

I catch Munzer just as he is leaving his shift for the day, on the steps outside the hotel.

"You got the note?" he asks.

"Yes," I say. "I would have come over to get it. I thought you were going to leave it here for me."

"I was leaving soon and I wanted to make sure it got to you. It seemed important."

"You read it?" I didn't mean to sound so accusatory.

"No. You just seemed anxious about it, so I thought whatever you were waiting for must be very important."

"The people who were dropping it off were supposed to believe that Miss Samara lives here, at the Sumerland."

"Okay, so no problem."

"Well, what if they saw you or one of your guys run across the street right afterwards to deliver it to the Hamra?"

He looks at me with eyes that don't seem to have blinked even once. "I don't think so, Mr Nabil. I don't think so at all." He gazes at his watch and takes a step down, away from me. "You don't have to worry. I'll keep our secret. But you must excuse me. I need to pick up my wife from work. She works at the Babel Hotel. Let me know if you need anything else," he says, taking the next three steps towards the street, a car key already in his hand.

Rizgar is asleep behind the wheel, the windows down. I shake the car a little bit until he awakens.

"I'm glad Baghdad is now safe enough that you can have a nap out on the street," I say, teasing. He unlocks the door languidly, letting me in.

"Just closed my eyes for five minutes, that's all. It's so hot, and it's bad for the car to run in the heat all day just so I can sit in the air-conditioning."

"True. Also expensive," I say, as he takes off into Karada. "But you could sit inside the lobby, where it's air-conditioned."

"The lobby is for the translators," he says. "The drivers sit and wait by their cars."

That's right, I think. But not all of them. Some translators go to their journalists' rooms and eat dinner.

I ask Rizgar to take me to my cousin Saleh's house again. It's short, I promise. It's really important.

"I'm her chauffeur," he says. "Not yours."

"Five minutes. Just five."

"Fine," he says, and we drive in silence, me holding back the information that I now have, wanting to wait until I'm ready to jump out of the car to tell him, so I won't have to face him lecture me for too long, or to feel him brooding the whole way.

Instead, I find myself pushing Rizgar towards small talk, asking him questions about his family that I had never asked before. His wife and three children are in Irbil, but he has relatives in Kirkuk and Suleimaniye. His wife's family is from Halapca. He asks me if I know what happened there. I say that I've heard some stories, but I don't know what part of them is true. It's all true, he says, and it's worse than you would think. He says he has a lot of young cousins who keep having children with strange birth defects like bad fingers and missing body parts, or other things in the wrong place, or diseases that kill them before they're old enough to run.

"I'm glad Saddam is gone," I say. I suppose I mean it, too. It can't all have been made up by the Americans, all those stories, those deformed children. If America hadn't come, maybe Saddam would do that to some other place. If Saddam were still here, Sam wouldn't be.

Rizgar nods as if he's ready to believe me but hasn't yet made the decision to do so. He points out that we're on Saleh's street. I'm startled; I had meant to ask him to wait a few blocks away, and now down the street will have to do.

"Can you wait here? It's better you don't park in front of his house."

"*Maku mushkile.*"

Ashtar answers the door. She invites me inside and tells me she will set the table for me to eat. I tell her I had a huge, late lunch, and that I just need to have a quick talk with Saleh. He isn't here, she says; he said he'd probably be staying late at his new job, but why don't I have tea and wait for him? I end up running inside to use the toilet. It's a terrible feeling, knowing that someone else is having to listen to the sound of you throwing up.

Out in the hallway, her face is drawn with concern. Am I all right? Do I want to have a *biriani* – just rice and potatoes this time, not at all spicy? Just tea? Stay and rest, she says. I tell her no, just a glass of water, and that I really should be going home. And in fact, that's all I want just now, because I'm thinking that it might not be the last time tonight I'm going to be sick. "Stay here. Let me call your parents and tell them you weren't feeling well," she says. "You don't have to," I say, "and besides that, the phones still aren't working," and she touches her forehead to show she forgot. Just tell Saleh I came by, and that maybe I'll try to stop by tomorrow before work, and she says he leaves early now, by 7.30. And as I head for the door she rushes back to the kitchen to give me some *dolma* she made for me to deliver to my family.

In the car, Rizgar is waiting, his face still bearing traces of sleepiness.

"Don't you get enough rest at night?" A stupid question on my part. I rarely get more than five hours these days.

"The family that I'm staying with just had a baby girl," he says. "She keeps me up half the night. I'm going to have to find some other place to live."

"Really?" It occurs to me I hadn't asked him much about his living situation. I assumed that he was staying either with relatives, or in a cheap hotel. "Where are they?"

"In Karada." I try to contain my surprise. Karada is a

relatively affluent neighbourhood, right near the Hamra. Did I assume poverty, only because he's Sam's driver? They might be Rizgar's distant relatives, Kurds who'd done well for themselves as businessmen in Baghdad.

"So when you drop me off in my neighbourhood after work, it's totally out of your way," I say.

He bends his head to one side, a kind of humble acknowledgement that he had never let me know that he was sometimes spending an extra half-hour in the car, maybe more on bad days, just to help me get home safely. "It doesn't matter," he says. "It's my duty."

"It's not your duty. Sam probably doesn't know the difference."

He shrugs. "There are a lot of things Sam doesn't know. It's my job to see that you do everything safely."

"Oh, by the way, can you drop me off in Mansour? I'm going to walk from there."

He glances at me with a squint.

"Like you said, there are a lot of things that Sam doesn't know."

He smiles, reaches for a cigarette, and opens the window a crack before he lights it.

"You're very kind."

"Anything for the prince," he says.

"Oh! The prince," I chuckle.

"As I see it, when I'm driving her I have to treat her like the queen. You, you don't exactly qualify as the king, so I decided that you get to be the prince."

"Oh, really. Well, then I'll have to appoint you as the head of royal security!"

He grins and I find myself wishing, just for a minute, that I also smoked, so that I could share that with him, or that I knew some Kurdish.

"How do you say, how are you?"

"What?"

"How are you, in Kurdish."

He blows out the smoke with rounded lips. "It depends on the Kurdish."

"Well, your Kurdish."

"*Choni chaki.*"

"*Choni chaki? Choni Chaki* is *shlonak*?"

He nods as if he knew I would make fun of it.

"And *zorspiz*, this is thank you?"

"*Zor spas,*" he says, correcting me.

"What a great language."

He glares at me with his cigarette dangling from his mouth.

"*Zor spas.*"

"You're welcome."

"*Shei ne nah.*"

"What?"

"That's you're welcome. Or not at all."

"Ya Rizgar, we have to do an interview tomorrow, Sam and me, and we have to go alone."

He gives me one of his looks that says he thinks I'm kidding, like I've suggested maybe we should drive to Mecca tonight, do a mid-year *hajj*.

"We have to go back to that office I went to today, and they want us to come in a taxi."

"What…why?"

"They made it sound like they might recognize your car."

"Who are *they*?"

"I don't know, some people." And I don't, which is the most unsettling feeling of all. "Some people who also have an interest in the story."

"So I'll get another car."

"I think they recognize you, too."

"So I'll get an orange-and-white cab. One of my relatives can get me one if you give me a day."

The traffic on Jinub Street is heavy, forcing us to slow down.

"We don't have another day."

Rizgar seems to be thinking this over, tapping his fingers on the steering wheel as he does.

"You shouldn't do that," he says. "You shouldn't just get into any taxi."

"Why not? I do it all the time."

"You're not American."

"I told her to wear *hejab*. No one will notice."

"And what if you get into trouble and I'm not there with you?"

I start to think of the times we've already slid towards trouble, like the day I thought we might get trapped in Khalil's basement. It seems funny now. I got all nervous for nothing. But what if Khalil had been planning to murder us, or hold us to ransom? What would Rizgar, sitting outside in his comfortable car, have been able to do about it?

"What would you do if you were there and we did get into trouble?"

Rizgar opens the glove compartment, and then I see it. The gleaming silver body of a short-barrelled gun.

"What kind is it?"

"A Remington."

"How much?"

He waves his finger at me and snaps the compartment shut. "You don't need to know."

"I'm thinking I should get one."

He shakes his head. "I don't think so. Not you."

"What do you mean, not me?"

"You're not the type."

"What's the type? You don't need to be a type. I need to protect myself. And Sam."

He sniffs at the air. "What's that smell?"

When I sniff at it too, I feel a bit sick again. "Ah, my aunt's *dolma*. She wanted me to bring some home to my family."

He smiles. "You come from a nice family, Nabil. You don't need a gun. Besides, if you have a gun, it's more likely someone will use a gun against you." He sits waiting for the light to change, looking me over. "Do you know how to use a gun?"

"Not really."

"Well, I can teach you. And after you've learned, then you can decide whether you're ready to go out and spend your money on a piece of equipment meant to kill people." He stops for a red light and looks me over. "But you're not the killing type."

I look at his ashtray, full of dead, twisted butts in their pool of grey ash. "You sure of that?"

"I'm sure, *dostum*," he says. Everyone knows that one – friend. "Where to?"

"There. In front of Mansour High School."

He moves his elbow towards my arm. "Good idea. You should go back to teaching."

I consider convincing Rizgar to give me his gun for the day, but he's probably right. I know nothing about how to use it. I asked my father once about his, but he said that until I'm ready to have my own house – in other words, get married and have children – I didn't have any need for it. I thought he didn't trust me enough, but at the time, I was only seventeen. I never bothered to ask again.

Rizgar pulls up in front of the school. Some of the windows have been repaired, but others are still broken.

"I'm going to follow you tomorrow in a separate car," he says. "You'll go in a taxi, and then I'll follow you in some other car. Not this one. I'll manage to get another and I'll follow a few cars behind." He looks in the mirror, pushing his thick moustache in the direction of his nostrils. "And maybe I'll shave this off. It'll be part of my disguise."

He hums a tune that I think comes from one of the old Egyptian films, played at the moment the villain comes on screen. We both laugh.

"That's what I'm going to do. I'll follow you," he smiles, pleased at his decision. "I must protect Miss Samara. *Zayy uhti, bint hallal.*" Sam is like his sister, he says, a good girl, using a term we usually use to refer to a young, innocent Muslim girl. Not the words I would use to describe Sam, but a great compliment just the same. Almost the total opposite of calling her *majnouna* earlier today.

"You, too. You're like a younger brother," Rizgar says.

I smile to show I feel the same. "If you really don't think it's safe, maybe you should tell her we can't go."

Rizgar shakes his head. "Never."

"Never?"

"I never say she can't go. That's not my job."

"I thought you said it was your job to protect her."

"Yes, but to protect her while she's doing her job. This is her job." Rizgar lowers his window to spit into the street. "You love all those Arabic mottos, Nabil. I always hear you telling them to her. Here is a good one for you. 'What is written on the forehead, the eye must see.' This means that whatever will be, will be. We have this one in Kurdistan, too. There is even a *hadith*, maybe you'd know it, since you're so smart and you must have read a lot. 'Everybody will do according to his destiny.' Do you think if I told her not to go, she will not go? If I won't take her, she'll probably find some other way to go. She'll do what she wants. That's how American women are." He spits again, then smiles at me with his teeth, the one on the side capped with gold, the rest of them growing brown with nicotine and time. "It's different there. You can't make decisions for them. My job is to protect her in whatever decisions she makes, not to make the decisions for her. Understand?"

I nod that I do.

"Don't forget your *dolma*," he says, pointing to the bag at my feet. If I do, it occurs to me, I won't have to give it to my parents, and therefore, won't have to explain why I went to see Saleh a second night in a row.

"Why don't you have it?" I say, handing it to him and opening the car door. "Courtesy of the Sunni-Shi'ite-Kurdish Reconciliation Committee." He takes it with the happiest face I've seen on him yet, like a little boy getting a birthday present. "Mmm," he says, prying the lid open and pushing his nose into the container. "I love that smell."

44

Pushing

I'm late, late, and late. I'm not the kind of man who is late, who likes to be late, who thinks it's fine when other people are late. Of all days to sleep late!

Not that it was without reason. I came home last night and threw up twice more. I got up in the middle of the night, thinking I might be sick again, and instead passed out in the hallway. Apparently it woke up Baba and Amal, whose door I hit on the way down, but not my mother, who slept through the commotion. I told Baba I had eaten something bad. He made me drink a glass of water with sugar and salt in it, which tastes downright strange but always puts me right again, and then put me to bed. Amal must have shut off my alarm clock after I went to sleep.

And now, close to 10 a.m., I am finally heading out to meet Sam, filled with some eggs and fresh *samoun* my mother made me, cursing the fact that I can't call to say I am running late. I promise my parents that I am perfectly fine. I am not sick, I just ate something bad. As I move towards the door, Mum moves in the other direction, heading to my room and the bathroom to do what promises to be an antiseptic cleaning job, as if I had the plague rather than an upset stomach. Amal, seeing that I wasn't going to stay home despite my illness last night, went back to her room, a rather sad place for a fourteen-year-old to be at 10 a.m. on a weekday. But they've already decided that her school, unlike Mansour High School, is not reopening until the autumn.

"I want to ask you something." Baba is sitting in his favourite chair. It seems he took the morning off to check that I was doing all right.

"Yeah, Baba?" My back is to him, and my hand, just a few inches from the knob of the front door.

"Can you come back here so I can ask you?"

"Sure." There's a part of me that would like to tell him I'm not up to it, I'm still not feeling so well, and most importantly, I'm running late. I turn around, a squish of inner cheek caught between my teeth. "They are waiting for me at work, Baba," I say, glancing at the mantle clock.

"We've barely had a conversation all week," he says.

"It's been a busy week."

Suddenly I realize that I sound just like him. All these years, it was Baba who wasn't around because he was busy at the hospital, who couldn't always keep regular hours because there were patients who needed tending. But teaching at school, we always knew that was something that had regular hours. That was controlled. That wasn't about life and death.

I take a seat on the sofa, next to Baba's armchair. He blows on his tea.

"What's going on, Nabil?"

I shake my head. "Just busy. You know, she takes me on many, many interviews. It's tiring, but very interesting. We're still following up on that story I told you about."

"And what? Haven't you found anything yet?"

I look into Baba's tea cup. The amber colour reminds me of Sam's eyes. "Not really."

"No?" Baba sips. "You didn't have any tea this morning. What kind of day can a man expect to have if he hasn't first had his tea?"

"The eggs were enough," I say, putting my hand to my stomach. "I'm glad I managed to eat anything."

"Tea's good after you've been sick."

"I don't want to be late."

"Some delays bring the best rewards," he says, quoting a motto in *fusha*, high literary Arabic.

"I can always have tea somewhere later."

My father clears his throat, and in it, I can hear something disapproving.

"I want to ask you about working with this journalist. This... Samara. What's her family name again?"

"Katchens. She goes by Sam."

"Do you know a lot about her?"

I lift a shoulder, release it. "I know enough. She's a very good journalist. And very serious, very modest. Not like a lot of the Western women at the hotel."

"They aren't modest?"

"Well, they run around the pool in their little swimsuits and it doesn't look very good. The Iraqis who work there think they're practically prostitutes."

My father looks at me hard, swirling the bottom half of the tea in its glass, making a whirlpool. "That's just ignorance. It's different in the West."

"I know. I was there, too, remember?"

He smiles. "It was lovely, there, wasn't it? Maybe we should have stayed in England after all."

"Could we have? Was that an option?"

Baba yawns, covering his mouth as an afterthought. "Not really. Our parents were still alive. They needed us. Besides, we thought that if we stayed, we'd never be able to come back. That's what happens to people who leave. They get stuck, living in exile. Sucking off someone else's economy, living in someone else's culture. It's not for me." He sniffs, curls his lip. "I don't know how your brother does it."

I check my watch. "I really need to go, Baba. We have interviews."

He leans his left elbow on the chair's arm, and lowers his voice as though he's afraid someone might hear. "Tell me," he says, his tea-breath right into my nose and eyes. "Is it true this Samara is Jewish?"

I can feel the floor falling out from under me, the clockhands spinning behind my head. I try to look mildly surprised by the question. "Who told you that?"

Baba unfolds the letter, slightly more crumpled than before. "Found this," he says. "It must have fallen out of your trousers when you got undressed last night."

I stare at the paper until the words blur. "No, I put that letter back in my pocket after I read it. I'm sure of it."

"Well it wound up on the floor somehow."

"I don't believe you. You went through my things while I was in the shower? How could you do that?"

"Drop it, Nabil. It doesn't matter how I found it. The main thing is, it seems that someone is trying to scare you by letting you know she's Jewish."

I focus on my father's face, on the lines in his forehead that are becoming like bars, a checkpoint that keeps anyone from entering. His eyes are searching mine, flitting back and forth as if doing a scan.

"She's not even really Jewish, Baba. Just half, or something like that."

My father stares back at me. Didn't he once tell me that he had a lot of friends growing up who were Jewish? They went to the Frank Eini School together, which was even run by Jews, and was considered one of the best secondary schools in Baghdad. He said he was sad when most of them left, and even sadder when a whole round of those who stayed were hung in 1968. He never said by whom. *Were hung.* Passive construction: the *mu-* form in Arabic. *Muqatil* – was killed. One who receives the action, who has it done to him. It was always safer to speak that way. Then you never had to say who did the hanging.

"It's not that I would mind, Nabil, it's just that it makes it more dangerous for her. And for you."

"But it's not even true, Baba. She's not really Jewish."

"So why are these people saying she is?"

"You know. It's a way to try to threaten her, to scare her away from her work."

"And it's not working?" Baba hands the letter to me, and picks up the *As-Sabah* newspaper from the small table next to his chair. He unfolds a few pages as if he is browsing, though I'm sure he can't be focusing on much. "If you want to go running around town making a new career for yourself as a journalist, maybe you should work for a paper like this. At least work for an Iraqi paper, not an American one."

"What's it matter?"

"If you worked for Iraqis you wouldn't have these problems," he says. "Personally, I don't care if she's Jewish. I always liked the

Jews. Pity they all left. But you know everyone here isn't like me."

But they are, Baba. They're exactly like you. Saying they don't have anything against anyone – the Jews, the Kurds, the Christians, the Americans, the Iranians, the Shi'ites, the Sunnis, the religious, the secular. The Yezidis, the Chaldeans, the bourgeoisie, the *felaheen*. The people who aren't exactly like us. But it's always the same. They are always *they*; they are almost never individuals. I am guilty of the same thing. Everything Sam does that I don't understand, I explain by assuming it must be something Americans do.

Why do I need to lie to my own father like this, keeping half the story from him? This is what Iraq has done to us. Fathers had to lie to their sons to avoid saying something that might get them in trouble with the *mukhabarat*. Sons know what not to tell their fathers.

"I should get going, Baba," I say, rising. "I have a lot to do today."

He closes *As-Sabah*, tossing it into the bin of yesterday's newspapers. "You didn't want to read this, did you?"

"No, I've already read that one."

"I'm just worried that you're not being careful enough," he says. He examines a smear of grey print on his fingertips, rubbing them together with a look of distaste on his face. "If you're going to be a journalist, maybe you can publish your own paper, and then, at least do a decent job of it. These new ones are always dirtying up my hands."

45

Dirtying

LATE, AND STILL later, I keep thinking as I trot up the steps of the Hamra. Too late to see Saleh again. Too late to go out and get a gun of my own. Too late to do anything but hurry over to Mansour and find a taxi, and Sam will be waiting, wondering what in the world took me so long. Too late to stop and buy her a gift, since apparently she is leaving soon.

From Rafik's desk, I call up to Sam's room.

"Is everything all right?" Not where were you and why are you late, though I can hear a tone of those, too.

"Yes," I say. "Sorry I'm late."

"It's fine. I'll be down in five, ten minutes."

"I'll wait for you here." Five, ten minutes. Never right now. No matter how much later I am than I have promised to be, Sam is never ready anyway. Five, ten. Enough time to chat with the Shi'ite taxi driver I asked Rafik to arrange for me – in large part to stop his nagging for us to diversify our cadre of employees – and maybe just enough to find something small in the giftshop.

The taxi, a Dodge that must be more than twenty years old, feels odd, like clothes that don't fit. Perhaps it's only that in all the time I've known Sam, we've never travelled like this, in a regular orange-and-white cab, like two ordinary people. I have this feeling that she's far away, even though she's only in the back seat, like I want to be closer to her, protecting her, to find it easier to look her in the eye.

In my sideview mirror I can see Rizgar, following in a car he borrowed from one of his relatives, a beat-up old maroon Chrysler. Our driver, Ibrahim, seems competent enough. If we are going to go out without our own car, I figured, we can at least be in a taxi with a driver we have some connection to, in some small way.

I introduce him to Sam but I notice that he only smiles and doesn't say it's nice to meet you or anything of the sort. It seems that he doesn't speak a word of English, which is something of a relief. Just in case, I decide to test it out.

"You have the ugliest car I have ever seen," I say to him as we wind through outer Karada, away from the Hamra. He nods, glances in the mirror towards Sam, who has her head wrapped up in a pale-blue scarf I took from my mother's wardrobe. When I asked Sam the other day if she had a headscarf, she said she had two. I asked her to show me, and she modelled each of them: one black and one white. In black, she looked like a member of the Badr Brigade from Iran, which for reasons I don't know, produces people with fair skin and unusual eye colour. In white, she looked like a Sunni from some Eastern European country, like Bosnia. I decided she needed to wear a colour, so that wherever Mustapha was planning to take us, Sam wouldn't be suspected of being pro-Sunni or pro-Shi'ite.

"So have you cleaned this car in the last five years? Or are you just letting the dust pile up to the point where it will feel like sitting on a beach?"

"Nabil," Sam admonishes, pushing at my seat. "Stop it."

I look back at her, hoping she would laugh with me. "It was just a joke. I'm testing to see if he knows any English so we can talk."

"And?"

"Not a word."

"Just *hallo*?"

"*Hallo* is goodbye."

"I know. I've been here for almost two months, remember?"

Once, as I was passing by the pool, I overheard some journalists laughing about how often Iraqis finish a conversation by saying, "hallo", when what they actually mean is "goodbye".

I check in the side-view mirror again, and cannot find Rizgar. I turn around and see that he's a few cars behind, but still there.

It's a hot day and I feel my body growing clammy as we drive with the windows open. I wonder how it is that I convinced Sam to do this, when I should be getting her to reconsider the risks, to resist the urge to follow every lead. Maybe I am just like Rizgar. I don't help her make decisions, I help make her decisions possible.

In Mum's light-blue scarf, then, whom does Sam resemble? A Russian lady? Or maybe one of those Western converts you sometimes see, married to rich Gulfies?

Or maybe a Jewish girl. Would a religious woman wear a scarf like that? Maybe that's what it is about Samara that fascinates me, that makes me want to keep looking at her even after I know I should turn away. The colour of her hair is so foreign, Western, shouting *agnabiyeh*. But something in the shape of her eyes, in her cheekbones and in the length of her nose, seems Eastern, familiar. Semitic.

Ibrahim winds around Al-Wathiq Square, where some of the traditional gift shops are. I've been thinking that if Sam is actually going to leave Iraq, I should find a special souvenir for her. But what would be appropriate? She would probably consider a carpet to be too much. Too expensive, too cumbersome to carry home. We have many great painters, but it is hard to know what she would like. She once joked that she would like to go home with one of those Saddam wristwatches, which I found hard to understand. If the Americans dislike Saddam so much, how could anyone in America wear a watch with his picture on it?

When I turn back to ask her whether this is still what she wants, a totally different question comes to mind.

"Sam? What does Samara mean? I mean, where does the name come from?"

Sam slides towards the centre of the back seat, so she is a little closer to me.

"You really want to know?"

"Of course I do."

"It says a lot about my parents, who they were when they named me."

"So?"

"Samara means guarded by God. In Hebrew," she says, lowering her voice. "Actually, I'm told the Hebrew version of it would be *shamar-ya*. But in Latin," she smiles gently, "it means elm tree."

I turn my body around as much as it can go without seeming too awkward. "Elm tree. In Latin?"

"Yes, well, Latin for my mother. I told you, she was raised Catholic."

I must not have given the appropriate expression of getting it.

"Latin, you know, that's the language of the Catholic mass. It was, well, I guess you can say it still is, the Catholic religious language."

"Oh, right."

"Samara was really my Dad's choice. And my Mom went for it because it meant something nice in Latin, and she liked the way it sounded."

I try to combine this in my mind: a meaning so steeped in God it seems Islamic, and on the other hand, a tree I've never seen. "What does an elm tree look like?"

"An elm?" She shrugs. "I don't even know how to describe it. It's just a regular green, leafy tree you have on nearly every street in America. Or in Pennsylvania, anyway. In fact, a famous peace treaty between William Penn and the local Native Americans was signed under a huge, old elm tree…"

"Samara, is that a popular name?"

"No," she says. "In fact, not at all. I think I've only met one other Samara in my whole life, though I know there are others out there. It's not just a place in Iraq, you know. It's also a city in Russia, and there's a river there called Samara, too. My father's family came from there."

"From Russia? I thought you said Germany."

"I did," she says. "His father's side was from there. But his mother's side was from Russia. That's where I got this." Sam puts her hand to her head with open fingers, as if she expected to run them through her hair. She pats the headscarf instead, fiddling with the edge of it. "My bubbe had the same hair. And of course, my mother's Irish Catholic, so I probably get it from both sides."

"Bobby? Isn't it a boy's name?"

"No, not Bobby. *Bubbe.* Grandma."

"Oh. In Russian or in German?"

She smiles and looks away. "Neither. Yiddish."

"I see." She'll think I won't know what that is, but I do. I've read references to it in books.

"All those funny words you've heard me use, like *schmuck* and *schlepp*? It's not really slang, it's Yiddish. It is, or it was, the Jewish European language. It's almost dead now."

"Why dead?"

"I don't know. I guess people learn Hebrew now instead."

"Did you?"

"No. I never went to religious school or anything like that. It was the deal my parents made with each other. No conversions, no Sunday schools, no rites of passage. Yes to presents on all holidays, and yes to family meals that involve eating or drinking a lot. All in all, not such a bad way to grow up."

A deal. I thought that in the West, marriage was all about love. Deals exist only in the East, where families discuss marriage prospects in very concrete terms, down to who's paying for the furniture and the apartment. I have so many more questions for Sam, but I'm starting to feel nervous, thinking that we should prepare for going to see Mustapha. We're already at the edge of Sadr City.

"Did you bring those photocopies of the documents?"

Sam pats her bag. "Yep. They're right here."

"What about money?"

Sam's mouth flinches, more of a tick than a frown. "I always have some money with me but, I don't know, Nabil," she says, pushing her hand down on her bag. "I'm still not comfortable with paying this guy."

I reach into my pocket to find a handkerchief and wipe my forehead. It feels like the weather is slipping into summer early this year. Maybe God is disappointed by how we have responded to violence with even more violence, and is turning up the heat on us, harsh and ahead of schedule. I heard on the radio that it may get up to 44 degrees today, or about 111 Fahrenheit, which is pretty high for May.

"Sometimes," I say, "it's good to make a deal."

Sam grins with closed lips that say, don't go throwing that back at me.

"Did their parents oppose it, your parents getting married?"

"That? Oh, probably," she says. "But they never really talked much about it. Neither of them is particularly religious and they just didn't think anything should stand in their way."

"But your father chose Samara in part because it means 'protected by God'. So he is a religious man."

"Not exactly. I mean, he probably fancies the idea of God. But he was never really into religion." Sam looks out of the window. "'You can have faith without thinking any one religion has a direct line to the man upstairs.' That's the kind of thing my father used to say."

The man upstairs, as a term for God! If you said that in front of some imams, you could probably be accused of blasphemy. Comparing God to a man!

"And your mother? When you were a little girl, did she take you to church or to the…Jewish shrine—"

"A temple. Or synagogue. Neither. Honestly, they met in the late sixties, free love and all that. They thought you could raise kids on good morals. Just be nice to each other, stop making war, that kind of thing. A whole generation was raised like that. And we turned out okay, didn't we?"

"Except for the making war part," I say, just to make her laugh again.

A memory of Mum taking me to the Imam Ali Shrine flashes through my mind. Where would I be today if at least one parent didn't believe in taking us to pray, in nourishing our souls as well as our bodies and our minds?

Guarded by God. I wonder if a name creates a reality, a sort of personality that is outlined for us before we even begin to be.

"Why do you use 'Sam', then? Samara is very beautiful."

"I like it, Samara. Sam is just, I don't know, easier, catchier. I remind people that it's Samara when they assume it's Samantha and I have to correct them. And after all, it's in my byline."

The housing has become dense, the road bumpier from neglect, the architecture grim and crumbling. I begin to direct Ibrahim towards the address for Mustapha.

"What does Nabil mean?"

I hold up my hand to her, asking her to wait, describing the rest of the way to Ibrahim. "I'll tell you later."

"Here," I say, when we get to the building where Mustapha's office is. "This is it."

I turn back to Sam. "You're ready?'

She snaps shut her bag and looks at me, indicating that she is.

"You know what Samara actually means in Arabic? I mean, the city name?"

Sam shakes her head.

"The name Samarra is derived from the Arabic phrase of

sarre men ra'a which translates to 'A joy for all who see'. And, this is also very fitting for you." I get out and hold the door open for her, my hand feeling the heat of the metal handle that might burn me were it any hotter, and as she leaves the car, I notice that for the first time, I believe I made Samara Katchens blush.

Brutus pulls open the door. Mustapha is at his desk.

"Ah! We've been waiting for you!" he rises to offer a hand towards Sam.

"This is the American journalist I told you about," I say.

"Yes, Misses Samara, right?"

"Yes," she says, putting her hand in his open one. Were Sam a marionette under my control, I might have pulled on the strings just before her hand went into his. The fact that he asked her to come in a *hejab* suggests that he is religious, or at least, the people he plans to arrange for us to meet are.

"I expected you earlier," he says. "We're running a little late."

"Sorry," I say. "We had another commitment. She's a very busy lady. She was being interviewed on television."

"Oh," he says, looking at Sam transformed, wrapped up in her blue scarf, all the red hair tucked away, except for the hints in her eyebrows and around her temples. "Is she a famous correspondent?"

"Of course," I say. "One of the most important in America."

Respect, first and foremost. They must know to treat Sam with respect.

"Well then it's definitely appropriate for her to meet the people to whom I'm going to introduce you." Mustapha turns and switches to English: "It's such a pleasure to meet you."

"And you," she answers, oblivious to everything that has just transpired.

"Please. Have a seat," he says, pointing to the old sofa I sat on yesterday. "Would you drink the tea?"

"Well, if we're running late," I say.

"Nonsenseness," he says, claiming his right to speak English, even if he seems to be creating the language as he goes along. "Always there is time for the tea."

Mustapha seems different today. A change of clothes? A closer shave?

"You are very nice American lady," he says, his eyes coursing over Sam as if she were wearing a skimpy dress rather than her loose trousers, a long-sleeved tunic and a headscarf.

Sam's lack of reaction makes me proud; her expression is pleasant but not pleased.

"I think we can help you very much with your research, but you must trust on me. Can you trust on me?"

Sam glances at me for a moment, and then back to him. "Sure I can trust you."

"Trust is very important to the Iraqi people. If I trust you, I am willing to give you the keys to my own house," he says, picking his own pair from his pocket and dangling them in the air. "Nothing is more important than trust."

Sam nods.

"You don't agree?"

"I do. Trust is important."

"In America, you have a lot of money and the big weapons, so you doesn't need the other countries to trust you. But here, different. We think, important to trust each other."

"Of course. Mr—"

"Call me Mustapha."

"Mustapha, I do trust you. Excuse me for getting down to

business, but can you explain something to me about these documents?"

He looks to me for a moment like he wants me to translate, and then turns back to her. "You understand everything when you getting there."

"Where?" she asks. "I mean, where is this neighbourhood you want to go to?"

"You see. No need for worry about no thing."

We follow Mustapha down the few steps from his office and out of the front door. Sam and I turn right to go back towards the place where Ibrahim is parked, but Mustapha goes left. Brutus stands beside him, twice his width and probably six inches taller.

"It's this way," Mustapha says, switching back into Arabic.

"Well, our car is this way," I say, pointing up the narrow street. "We'll follow you."

"No, no. That's no good. Leave your car and come in my car."

"I thought that was the whole point of not coming in our own car. We came in a taxi."

"Yes, of course. For your own safety. But it is also for your safety that you come in my car because the people we're going to see will know it's me, and you'll be safer."

"Sam, he wants us to go in his car."

"Because?"

"Because he says it's safer that way."

There is a deepening in her eyes, like sand darkened by a rainshower. "Is that…okay with you?"

"Well, it's up to you. It's…whatever you want to do."

"I told you," he says, smiling at Sam with an almost flirtatious face. "Don't worry. You're with me! My goodness, American people, so careful! In Baghdad we trust people, especially our friends." He puts his hand on my shoulder. "Do Nabil tell you that we went to university together?"

"Yes," Sam says. "He did say that."

"See," he says, holding on to my collarbone and shaking it affectionately. "*Ahui*," he says, calling me his brother. "If you study with someone, you're like his brother, always."

"Always," I say, and look at Sam, who looks back at me with the most neutral face possible. "Well, then. Give us a minute to go back and tell the driver to wait here for us."

"Ah. He's still here? Well then, you can send him home. We'll get you other taxi, later, or if I can, maybe I can drop you off."

"Well, how long will we be?" I ask. "Maybe he should just wait here for us while we're gone."

"That the problem," Mustapha says, shaking his head. "We don't know. It no make sense you pay the taxi to wait here for you. Don't worry," he says.

Sam and I make our way past the stores and stalls selling the average sorts of things that people, particularly women, used to come to this part of the market for: frilly nightgowns, handbags, slippers, veils, makeup. Piles of fake blue jeans no woman in her right mind would be caught dead wearing on the street now, unless it were totally hidden under her long *jupeh* or an *abaya*.

"See something you like? Maybe a new handbag?" Sam asks, smiling mischievously.

"I was looking for a present for you. I think maybe you need a nice gown like that," I say, pointing to one of the long, embroidered houserobes usually worn by women my mother's age.

"Beautiful!" she whispers. "Or one like that," pointing to a mannequin dressed in one of those fancy, finely embroidered *abayas* that come from the Gulf countries.

When we are far enough away from Mustapha's building, she moves closer to me. "Do you trust this guy?"

Now we're passing the section with household goods, buckets, cleaning materials, sponges and mops. Things anyone who had a home would want to stop and price, things that are far removed from Sam's reality because someone comes into her room to clean every day.

"Not entirely."

"You don't? Well me neither. He seems like a slimeball to me."

"I know. But sometimes the slimeball people have the good connections. I don't think he would lie about that – about what he can get for us."

"Really?" Sam touches a silk scarf as we pass through the part where the market gets narrow.

"I think he is a crooked man, for sure, but he might be our only way for you to finish the story," I say. "And if Saleh sent us here—"

At the mouth of the market, where the cars are parked, Ibrahim awaits us. Across the street, about four cars away, I see Rizgar, his eyes peeled towards us. "Don't even look at Rizgar," I breathe in Sam's direction, "just in case they are following us."

I open the door to Ibrahim's car, and we hop in. He looks suspicious, like he can feel that there's been a change of plan.

"Nabil, wait," Sam says. "Do you think we should go with this guy or not? I mean, we could have tried to insist on taking our own driver—"

"I don't think so."

"Oh."

"I don't see any other way. I don't know who else to go to get you the answer you need. Maybe we don't go with him and we just say thank you very much and you tell your editor that that's it. We did what we could."

Sam clucks her tongue.

"You said they were ready to run the story without knowing who made the documents and why. You said they would just do a story saying that they were fake and that would be it. So if you want, let them do that, and *khalas*. You did your job."

"No, I didn't. If I let them run it now, it's a totally incomplete story." She pulls at her headscarf around her chin, clearly uncomfortable with the way it frames her face. "How can I just give up and not really get the story?"

I see in her eyes a love that I don't love. A love of the story, whatever that means. But in that love, I see a love I respect: a love of getting to the truth, of a chance to set things right.

"So we go, then." I face Ibrahim and put a small stack of dinars in his hand. "As soon as we re-enter the market, can you go and tell our friend over there in the old Chrysler that we want him to try to follow us? Tell him that we're getting into a car parked at the other end of the market. Just tell him to stay back and follow us, several cars behind, like he did this morning coming here. Got that?"

"Okay," he says, "*Inshallah*." We get out with only the smallest glance in Rizgar's direction, and Ibrahim waves us goodbye, his wrinkled hand held up in a way that almost makes him look like a holy man bestowing blessings on his followers.

46

Bestowing

WE ARE INSIDE Mustapha's 1991 Mercedes 300 SE, black outside, brown leather inside. It is spotless; perhaps he vacuums his car every day and dumps his dust on the floor of Ibrahim's. In Iraq we call this kind of car "the submarine", and everyone knows it was one of Saddam's favourites, in particular, we understood, because it seemed to defy America after they forced their way into the war with Kuwait. In 1991, Saddam bought new luxury cars, started several new palaces, and apparently sent for all sorts of lavish goods from Europe.

Maybe Mustapha has done well as a lawyer. Or maybe he stole the car last month.

With Brutus in the passenger seat, Mustapha drives us towards Ishbiliya and Idris, back towards the centre of town, and as he does, I can feel the tension in my spine drop just a bit, like letting a little bit of the air pressure out of an over-inflated tyre. If we're no longer in Sadr City, where everyone knows bad things happen, where you probably ought not to bring a foreign girl anyway, we must be in less danger. We pass through Saddoun Street, the old theatres, the safe places. I find myself looking at the silver buttons on the doors, noticing that they're unlocked.

If things went terribly wrong, we could jump out. I should write this down for Sam.

I reach for the notebook in my backpocket and then realize I don't have a pen. I make a sign with my thumb and forefinger, asking her for something to write with. She takes a pen out of her bag and hands it to me, but as she does, Mustapha looks over his shoulder and notices what she's doing.

"I just want to check our schedule," I say, unable to think of anything better, drawing a line through some notes in the pad. "Sam, we have to be back in the Green Zone at three for your interview, right?"

"That's right," she says. She lifts her sleeve to look at her watch. "We really can't be late for that."

"Don't worry about no thing." Mustapha says again, which has a way of making a person worry more. What is the worst that can happen anyway? These people are in the business of making fake documents, not killing foreigners. If they kill Sam, *la smah'Alla*, they can't get any money out of her, and that's what they want. *La smah'Alla.* What Mum and Grandma Zahra said for just about anything terrible under the sun that could happen. May God not allow it.

Sam won't mind the lie. She'll know that mentioning the Green Zone wasn't just by chance. It tells Mustapha that we need to meet the Americans later, and that if he doesn't bring us back on time, the Americans will notice. Will come looking, maybe. It's a theory I have: as much as we sneer at the Americans, at their tanks and missiles, as much as we speak of them as if they are strong but stupid, we are terrified of them and what they are capable of doing.

Mustapha raps the backs of his fingernails softly against the window. He bends his head to look past Brutus and then turns to Samara. "You see that big stadium there? You know what stadium?"

"Is that Shaab Stadium?"

"Ah, you know Baghdad very good," he says, sounding impressed. "Too good."

"Somewhat," she says. "Shaab Stadium is famous."

"Maybe you heard about it because here we have our football game. Sometimes the national team plays another country team and Iraqi lose. And then Uday is torturing the players right there in the basement, below the looker room!"

"Locker room," I interject.

"Lucker, lucker! That's what I said. Did you know it?" His tone is aggressive, demanding an answer from Sam. "Did you know that people were being tortured?"

"Well, yes, I mean, there were stories in the paper sometimes about how cruel Saddam was, although I think the Bush administration was more concerned about what kinds of weapons he was acquiring than whether he was beating up on a few athletes."

Mustapha frowns. I'm not sure he is getting the nuances of Sam's language, the hints of sarcasm about her own government. I have the urge to translate what she said.

He suddenly thrusts his hand between us, scaring me to the point where I almost lurch to protect Sam. "Have you ever seen fingers like that?"

Each of the nails on his fingers is dark and disfigured, ridged like a carpet that needs straightening. "That," he says, pulling his hand back again, "they do to me while I was still in high school. One of my uncles was involved in the uprising against Saddam in one-and-ninety and they said I'm not giving them enough information about him. Not being enough helpful. And so they pull out each one, until I convince them I don't know anything about my uncle, my cousin, no one."

Next to me, I see Sam's fingers curl in on themselves. "That's awful," she says.

"Yes, very, very awful. But this is how we live here. And America see and say oh, very bad, Saddam, but wait another twelve years to do anything. So why now?"

Sam doesn't respond.

"I mean, why now? Why come Iraq now?" His voice is louder, and he seems to be struggling for the words. "If America come in one-and-ninety—"

"In ninety-one," I say. "You mean in nineteen ninety-one."

We say *wahad u-tiseen* instead of *tiseen u-wahad*. But Mustapha is clearly furious with me. He doesn't want my corrections, regardless of his mistakes.

"If you want to stop him because of the human rights, then you must stop him in ninety-and-one. American knows Saddam kill many people, and torture them and take my fingers out," he says, becoming more and more agitated, wiggling his hand in the air. "You know what I think? I think that if you, *yaani*, America, were here for our rights, you must come *long* time ago. And if you come for our weapons, then *Ya Allah*, where are they? And why you don't find them and show them! So maybe, just my opinion, maybe you come here for something else."

Brutus turns up Abu Nuwas Street, and the sight of the river comforts me. On it there is a lonely fisherman in a boat as slender as a banana. A flash of jealousy for him burns through me. Living a simple life, barely literate, selling the day's catch to the great fish restaurants along the Tigris. Bringing home the proceeds to a loyal wife and doting children. Far away from the problems of how to play Mustapha and how to protect Sam.

"What do you think America came here for?" Mustapha asks.

I hope Sam doesn't think she can win this argument with Mustapha and his completely incompatible premises. *Saddam was evil. Who are you to take Saddam away from us? You have no right to be here. But what took you so long come?*

"You are the journalist, yes? Maybe this is your job to find out."

No one says anything more, and as we drive north on Abu Nuwas, I watch the array of some of our family's favourite old restaurants along the water, shuttered up or empty of everyone but their owners. When things are better, I will bring Sam there sometime for dinner. Afterwards we'll go strolling, and perhaps I'll hold her hand, even just for a moment.

I must have passed these three-storey brick homes along the waterfront a thousand times in the last few years. There were rumours that after Saddam had these townhouses built, he gave them to senior members of the Republican Guard. The officers received a gift of prime land with one of the best views in town and Saddam received a ready-made line of defence from any attack from the southern side of the river.

The houses stand out from the landscape because something about their neat lines, overly modern and attached like townhouses in some smarter part of Birmingham, is really not the architectural style of Baghdad. They have pointy angles that don't belong here, triangular roofs designed for countries where there is much rain and snow to be managed. It is a European design, imported for prestige purposes. The only thing that is familiar is the colour of the bricks: lighter than mud, darker than tan, something like a mix of camel hair and sandy earth.

It's now, what? More than three weeks since Saddam and the other ministers simply ceased to appear in public, signalling Iraq's surrender to America. People say all of the Republican Guard fled these houses with their families on the very same day, and that hours later, new tenants took over. Whether they are poor squatters or armed militias is anybody's guess.

Brutus stops the car and Mustapha steps out, brisk and confident, and motions for us to move with him. We get out, too, following the *yalla yalla* motions from his hand of unseemly nails, telling us to move quickly. We follow Mustapha up the steps to the front door, Brutus shifting heavily behind us.

Mustapha knocks twice but doesn't wait for an answer, pushing the door open and telling us to follow him inside and up stairs demarcated with a red line of carpeting, as well as one of those plastic runners that make sure you don't trample the carpet into peach fuzz. "Come, come," he says, racing up almost as fast as we raced down yesterday, at the hotel. Why does every yesterday feel like three days ago? Dog years. We run up the stairs, me behind Mustapha, Sam behind me, Brutus behind her. At his size, if he moves as fast as Mustapha he could have a heart attack in the stairwell. And then, perhaps, we can end up back at Al-Kindi hospital, right where we started, Baba rolling his eyes at me.

On the third floor, Mustapha taps on a simple door once and then once more. The door is opened by a man who is built like a goalie, fairly young but with a bald head, which makes the grizzly nature of his beard all the more striking. He looks past Mustapha to take us in, with eyes like those of searchlights that nervously pan the sky at night.

The room is big and sparse, with a large writing desk and some chairs to the left, windows to the right. On the carpet are discoloured, flat spots where the furniture used to sit. There are others: three men. One sitting, two standing in varying forms of repose against the wall, armed with pistols.

Be calm, like the Tigris, flowing out there through the windows, just beyond the void of what was someone's living room. Four of us coming, and they needed to match it with four of them. Perfectly normal for a business meeting: parity.

"Mr Ali," says Mustapha, "this our American friend, Miss Samara, and her translator, Nabil al-Amari."

We smile at him and I move to shake his hand, but he doesn't seem to notice because his eyes are focused on Sam. *The* Ali, as in Ali al-Yaqubi al-Sadr?

"American?" he asks.

Sam nods twice before saying "yes", as if working up to it.

"So you don't need to wear this *hejab* here," he says, pointing to her headscarf. "This is not necessary."

Sam puts a hand to her scarf. "I like wearing it. I have great respect for Muslim tradition."

"Sorry," I say, knowing that I've interrupted, but not wanting to let him begin a treatise on *hejab*. "What was your name?"

"Ali," he says, giving a sideways nod to Mustapha, almost imperceptible. "Some people call me Technical Ali, because they say my work is so good, I'm almost technician." He laughs in a way that is more of a sneeze and then points to the chairs, which put our backs towards the windows. He sits down at the other side of the desk, in a swivel chair unlike the others, facing the river and the sunlight.

"I understand you wanted to know more about the work I

do," he says. "Mustapha here says that you already have done a lot of your own research." He raises his face, which is more Lebanese than Iraqi, sharply angled to the point of being bony, the kind of Arab looks that can pass for Italian or Greek.

"A little bit." Had I arrived earlier this morning, as I should have, I would have gone over things with Sam, discussed every possible direction the day could move in, working out in advance what Sam would want to do so that I wouldn't have to turn to her and have her seen to be making all the decisions on the spot, which might not look good for either of us.

"Ya Mustapha," Ali calls, as if Mustapha and Brutus were standing somewhere far away, instead of near the door, where they stayed even after we sat. Mustapha steps forward.

"Aren't you hungry for lunch?" Ali asks.

Mustapha puts a hand over his belly. "In fact, very."

"In that case," he says, switching into Arabic after having greeted us in English, "you must go over to the Nabil Restaurant on Arasat Street in honour of this young man and pick up lunch for all of us. Our treat, of course."

I feel a wave of fear, but I know I have to let it level out here, inside my head. Mustapha leaving us here?

"Of course," Mustapha says. My body moves to rise, but I press it back down. What would Sam expect?

"Well, really, you're so generous, but that's not at all necessary," I say. "In fact, we really were only expecting to make a short visit and then we're off for some other appointments." I turn to Sam, switching to English. "You have an early deadline today don't you?"

"Yes, that's right," she says, looking at her watch. "I do."

"Do we have time to stay for lunch?"

496

"Oh. That's so kind of you," Sam smiles. "I hate to refuse but—"

"So don't," Mustapha says. He gives a sympathetic but patronizing look that says, *don't fight it.* In Arabic, he says: "Clients and foreign guests always get treated to a meal, Nabil, you know that. It's natural. We'll be back soon."

Natural as the sound of another explosion somewhere, the kind you feel under your feet like a tiny tectonic tremor. Mustapha walks out, and Brutus closes the door behind him.

"Terrible, all of this violence, is it not?" Ali says to Sam, who seems nonchalant about our escorts' departure, or is simply putting on a very good show of it.

"It's horrible."

"Maybe your America government don't send enough of soldiers here to make security. Why not?"

Sam shrugs and shakes her head. "I don't know why. I guess they're trying."

"Trying," he says, giving his "g" an exceptionally strong ring, as if he is trying to imitate Sam.

Ali reaches into the front drawer of the desk and takes out a file. He opens it, and on top is a document that I immediately recognize. It looks exactly like one of the photocopies Sam has in her bag, the order from Saddam to pay $2 million to Congressman Jackson.

He passes it across the table, facing us.

"Is this one of the documents which is interesting you?"

"That's right," I say.

"You have a copy of this document already, I understand."

Naturally he knows by now – Mustapha must have told him. I nod, waiting for him to ask whether we have the documents with us, knowing that they're sitting in Sam's bag.

"So let me ask you, if I may, Mr Ali," says Sam.

"You may call me Ali."

"Okay, thank you." Sam is jumping on Ali's English, which I find myself cursing. It is better – safer, really – when the conversation flows through me, where I can play filter and arbiter. Censor. "Are you the one who made these documents?"

"Yes," he says. "I made them. Are you impressed with my work?" I have been trying to place his accent, trying to figure out where he learned his English. He almost sounds like he'd have learned in Germany or some Scandinavian country.

Sam pulls the page closer to her. It is a much better, clearer copy than the one we have, but obviously not the original, which you can tell from the signatures and the flatness of the government seal. "I am very impressed," Sam says. "You can hardly tell this from the real thing."

"It is the real thing!" His tone startles me. "Maybe I can even show you some more of my works, if this interests you."

"Okay," she says. "But what I'm mostly interested in right now is this set."

Ali blinks at her a few times, the bottom of his face in a sneer.

Sam, I'm proud to say, is calm. "Can you tell me why you made this set? And who asked to have it made?"

Ali looks perturbed. "Why I made them?"

"Yes, I want to know, why make up a document trying to make an American politician look bad?"

"Not make up!" Ali shouts. He oscillates rapidly in his chair. "We don't just make up!"

I want to put my hand on Sam's arm or her back, to tell her to slow down, to not push so hard, but in view of everyone, it would be totally inappropriate.

"We are providing the documentation for the crimes which we already know have been committed. Do you know that? Do you understand the difference?" Ali rises rapidly from his chair. One of the guards moves towards him.

"We are not criminals," Ali says, calmer now. "No. It is your country's fault that you must always think you need to have something on paper to prove that someone is a big criminal, and so we give you that. We give you evidences, because that's what you want," he says, drawing imaginary lines with his finger across his palm. "And you are even liking to pay for it, because otherwise you think it is not real."

Sam takes her notebook and pen out of her bag.

"No!" He shakes a finger towards Sam's face. "No. Not for writing."

She puts the pen back.

"You know, even when I see a woman dress like you do today, I know there is nothing true underneath it because you are not a Muslim inside. You don't have the modesty of a Muslim woman."

Sam stares at him.

"You know, a lot of people are glad you got rid of Saddam, but now they want you to go. Because if you don't, you'll bring here all of your infidel ideas."

Sam lifts her pen towards her notebook again.

"No writing!" He shouts, one hand slashing beneath the other in a motion meant to convey that something is forbidden. *Haram.* He stops, breathing deeply, and I can feel my heart rate accelerating inside my ears. "I think you want to make our society sick, like your society is sick. Isn't it true that a woman in America cannot walk anywhere at night without getting raped?

Or that the men feel they are free to take her because she is all the time dressing like prostitute?" He leans towards her, his eyes wider. "Or maybe the American woman like being treated like that."

Sam's hands hold each other stiffly. The Thuraya phone in her bag starts ringing.

"Tell me," he says, taking in the length of her body and the curve of her breasts, so much so that it's making me nervous. "Is it true? What they say about American women?"

Sam stands. "Would you excuse me? That's an urgent call that I need to take, but I need to be outside to get reception." I rise, too. Three of the men casually walk around the desk, fanning out.

Ali smiles. "Why don't you sit down and stay with us for a while, Miss Katchens?"

It must be part of the act. Saleh trusted Mustapha enough, and Mustapha led us here. It must be just an attempt to scare us.

"I need to go downstairs, or even from the roof—"

"This is your problem, Miss Katchens," he says, sounding entertained. "This is what is wrong with your culture and what will make everything go wrong for your people in Iraq."

"I'm sorry if there's been some misunderstand—"

"You think you make all the decisions. You are guest in our country and you begin to act like you own it. You are one woman among the men here and you think it is for you to decide everything."

"Pardon me," she says, putting her bag on her shoulder, prodding at me to prepare to move. "If you'll forgive me," she says, putting a hand across her heart. "I have a story on deadline and my editors will be wondering—"

The sweep of the gun from the back of his trousers moving into his hand. The sight of the metal there, pointing right at Sam's head. The snap of the latch, like the cracking of a small animal's bones when you accidentally run it over.

His grip is firm around the pistol. The barrel is inches from Sam's head.

Two of the other men with their pistols are turned on me. The third, whom I thought was not armed, trains an AK-47 on us.

"Maybe the deadline is *you*."

Ali lunges closer and grabs Sam's scarf under the chin and yanks it off. What was an almost-scream stops and Sam is speechless, staring at Ali open-mouthed and I am shouting "don't, don't don't, don't hurt her" and "we didn't do anything" and I'm saying everything without knowing what I'm saying at all and another guy comes from behind me and knocks me sharp in the back of my head and barks, "Shut the fuck up!"

I know it will hurt soon, but right now it feels light and numb, like everything in my head spilling out and spreading itself into the air.

And all is silent, just Sam's mouth half-open, and me feeling the heat in my eyes and ears, the way I do sometimes just before I go under, and please God, don't let me go.

But I guess he must have banged me with his fist and not a weapon, because if he had, I would definitely be on the floor by now.

Ali keeps his gun trained on Sam, and with his left hand pulls away the chairs we have been sitting on, dragging them to the middle of the room, facing the windows and the river. "Both of you, shut up and sit down!" Ali shoves me down into one of the chairs, pushing my shoulder and palming my head like a football. "Put your hands out in front and hold them together! *Now!* Don't move or you both become deadline right here! Do you understand?!" He waves his gun from Sam's face to mine and back to Sam's. "Subhi, you have some tape for my friends?"

"Yeah, boss."

Subhi?

"Bring it now!"

I know that in her head Sam is running through a thousand arguments about what to do, what to say, how to proceed. How to get the story, how to get out of the story. Sam always has a plan. She must be coming up with something. Samara Katchens, a beautiful foreign woman, working for an important American newspaper. They will not hurt someone who is pretty and young, someone who is a guest in our country.

Subhi el-Jasra?

I glance sideways at Sam and open my mouth to say something, but Ali grabs my face hard and pushes my jaw so that I'm facing the window straight ahead.

"Face forwards and put your hands out in front of you. Your wrists together."

I'm afraid to turn, afraid to get whacked again. But when he's standing over me, I glance up with no movement of my neck and see that it *is* him, that same Subhi who was our first point of contact in Mustansiriyah, the one and only connection that Harris passed on to us when we first got into this mess.

In Subhi's hands is a roll of heavy duct tape. He catches my eye for a millisecond, then looks away, handing the roll to Ali and taking a pocketknife from his back pocket. Sam is staring straight ahead, not looking at him or anyone at all, as if in a trance. Deep in thought, sorting through her plans to get us out of this.

What if Sam has no plan at all?

Ali starts to bind up my wrists with the tape winding it rapidly six or seven times. On the screen in my mind, I see myself tackle him with it, strangling him. I let him go just as he is on his last breath, choking himself purple. Even in my fantasies I cannot kill. What a pathetic soldier I would be. Ali takes the knife from Subhi and cuts the tape from the roll.

He wraps Sam's hands with the tape and I feel her wince. I want her to tell them that they're doing it too tightly, to plead nicely the way I know she could, but she says nothing. When Ali is done, he walks back to his desk, leaving the others watching us.

"Please," I say. "I think there's been some misunderstanding."

Subhi looks at me again, quietly shaking his head, half-frowning. Ali is back, the roll of duct tape in hand. I close my eyes when I see his hand coming, raising my tied fists a moment too late. The slap stings across my face, reverberating in the near-empty room. "I'll let you know when I want to hear from you," he says.

Ali hands the tape to Subhi, pushing it towards his stomach.

Subhi steps back. "Are we going to tie their feet?"

"I don't think it's necessary. I think they are well-behaved. You will behave here, won't you, Nabil? You will tell your American ladyfriend to behave, won't you? Maybe just their waists, Subhi. Just tie their waists to the back of the chair. We don't want them dancing around the room, do we? You, too, tie them," he says, and one of the guards comes over, looking uncertain. "Ah, I'll do it myself. Lift your arms," Ali says to me, and I do, because what else should I do? Ali and three armed men plus Subhi against Sam and me.

Ali winds the heavy tape around my stomach and the back of the chair, which doesn't hurt, but when I feel the sticky black stripes going around, it makes me think of the pain of a lashing, one strap at a time. I remember once reading an article about someone being given lashes like that in Saudi Arabia or Iran. "You see," Baba always said. "That's another good reason not to let the religious people run the country."

"I think we leave you just as you are, Miss Katchens, don't you think? You won't try anything funny, will you? Not with Abu Ihab in the room." He gestures to the larger guard, the one with the AK-47, standing by the door with his gun across his chest.

Sam says nothing. I hear Ali and Subhi walk behind us and leave the room.

"Sam, you okay?"

The guard with the AK-47 starts, rattling his rifle across his chest. Abu Ihab, I want to say. You seem like a decent man. How did you get caught up working for these people?

No answer from Sam.

"Sam?"

"*Uskut!*" The guard lifts his rifle in my direction. "No talking."

And so we sit, listening to nothing but breathing and the dull buzzing of traffic along Abu Nuwas, named for one of the most famous poets of Baghdad. He was infamously creative, hedonistic, and gay. Most of his poems are irreverent and joyful. If he saw the city now, I think he would write endless, angry lines until his hand hurt. And then, in disgust, I can imagine him tearing them to shreds when he's done.

47

Tearing

His footsteps unnerve me. I can feel them as though he were walking up my own spine. Ali drags over a chair and sits opposite Sam and me. In my neck I can feel Subhi standing in the doorway, out of view.

"Okay, Samara Katchens. This is your name, right?"

"Yes." Sam's voice sounds robotic and flat.

"Samara. Very nice. Almost sounds Arabic. Are you sure that's your real name?"

"Yes."

"Who are you working for?"

"The *Tribune*. An American newspaper."

"Not a spy for the CIA?"

"No."

"Or the Mossad?"

"No."

"Maybe you are MI6."

No answer. The sound of her vocal chords stripping up each other. "You can check my passport," she says. "Look at all the press visas. I'm an American journalist."

"But you also tell people you are a French lady."

"I never told anyone I was French."

I should die, right now. It's my fault. If someone is going to die here, it should be me.

I hear Subhi's voice in the corner. "They saw her with a CIA man. It was a CIA car."

I feel a slicing in the bottom of my stomach, like someone at work on cutting open my lower intestines. I need to go to the loo.

"She's definitely CIA." Subhi. On second thoughts, perhaps I could kill *him*. "*Akid*", Subhi says. For sure.

"She's not CIA," I say. "He was just a source for her story. She was only interviewing him. She's not CIA."

I can feel Sam's eyes stretching in my direction, but she then stares down at her hands. The initials she told me never to mention.

"You can check," I say. "Check on the Internet for her. Do you have an Internet connection yet?"

Ali pushes the pistol up against my head and moves metal between his fingers.

A gasp rocks Sam's body like an electric shock. *"Don't!"*

The room is still. Ali begins to laugh. I can feel the rancid wave of his breath. The others push themselves to laugh with him.

He squeezes my cheeks with one hand, shakes my face a bit, then lets it go. "This girl really likes you," he says. "She's a pretty one, too. Lucky man."

I keep thinking that Sam will start to cry soon, and that maybe this would be good, because then they will take pity on us. But after her outburst, she is silent again. And yet, from the corner of my eye, I can see that her hands are shaking.

Ali laughs again. He puts his pistol back into the waist of his trousers, and leans his forearms on the chair he had been sitting in. "We could do this all day. Or many days. It's not bad for you. You have nice view, right? Saddam built nice houses for the Republicans." He laughs again, motioning with a kind of exaggeration, as if he knows he misspoke. "Oh, sorry, I mean Republican Guards. Special glass, you know." He gestures to the windows behind him. "You can see everything, but no one can see you. Isn't that a great invention? The Americans invented that. They invent many good things. Like this." He whips out the gun again, inspects it, then holds it out towards Sam. "Look at that. Smith and Wesson 520. A .357 Magnum. Lightweight. Shoots seven rounds. And see the beautiful handle. Finger*groove* wood," he says it slowly and clearly, as if he's practised trying to pronounce the word. "And, what it says here? 'Springfield, Massachusetts.'" He stumbles over the words, so that his -field sounds like filed, and Massach-, like massacre. "Is that where you're from, Miss Katchens? Do they make these there?"

Sam shakes her head. "Pennsylvania."

"What?"

"I'm from Phoenixville, Pennsylvania. We used to make steel."

"So, the same. The steel to make the guns and tanks and helicopters. It's nice, all these things your America exports to all the world, all your weapons. We're very grateful. Most beautiful gun I've ever had," he says, bringing it closer to his face and inspecting it with feigned affection. "Thank you."

Sam sniffs.

"I think America likes this very much, to see Arabs killing other Arabs, Muslims fighting Muslims. And you give us the weapons, and we kill each other for you. Right?"

Sam stares straight ahead.

"I'm sorry," I say. "I don't understand. Please tell us why we are being held. We haven't done anything wrong."

"Neither have we," says Ali. "We just wanted to talk to you but your ladyfriend was in such a rush to leave that you force us to give you some benefit to stay."

"Incentive," says Subhi, whom I cannot see, probably because he is avoiding showing his face.

"*In-centeev?* Yes, incentive," Ali repeats.

Ali continues to play with the revolver; he rubs his finger over the wood, as if to dust it off. He drags over another wooden chair and puts the gun down on it, facing Sam. Then he collects his swivel chair and rolls it over with a somewhat violent swing before bringing it to rest in front of us, next to the chair with his gun on it.

"We want to know exactly what you've been doing. Everything. Why have you been asking people about our work?" For the first time since we arrived, Ali is addressing me in Arabic.

I wish Sam had discussed all of the potential scenarios with me in advance. What would she have wanted me to say? "He says he wants to know what we are doing."

"*La-a. Biddun targime.*" Without translation, he says. "You tell me."

"We are just doing research for a story."

"A story? I'll get my son to tell you a story. It's amazing, isn't it? You went hunting around Sadr City and Baghdad Al-Jadida and Showja and Zayouna, looking for people who know how to make good documents. You went to the amateurs when you didn't have to. You should have come straight to the first-class operation." He smiles, gazes dreamily out of the window towards the river. "It's beautiful, isn't it?"

In fact, it used to be more beautiful. Lately, it seems almost still, hardly flowing anywhere. Beyond Ali's right ear I can see a small dinghy with two men in it, pushing themselves away from the bank with their fishing poles. In my mind I can imagine the sound of the oars against the water, that day on the river with Baba and Ziad, when we were visiting our relatives in Basra. I didn't want to wait any longer for the fish. Patience, Baba said, patience. If you wait long enough, they will bite. There is an old Arabic maxim: Haste is the sister of regret.

"Very beautiful," I agree.

"We all have very beautiful things," he says, glancing at Sam. "It's a shame when we don't take care of them. Isn't it a shame the Americans aren't taking better care of Baghdad?"

"Yes. That's true."

"Tell him the truth, Nabil." From the side Sam's eyes look still and clear, like two pieces of amber.

I turn my head towards hers, and then, thinking I might get whacked for it, forwards again.

"Just tell him the truth."

Which truth? The one that may put him out of business? Or is she putting on an act hoping I'll come up with a good cover story. I said I used to like writing poetry. I never said I was a good storyteller. The walls and floor shake, and then I hear it, like a rush moving inside my head. Another bombing, somewhere to the west.

I watch Ali's face. "It is terrible, all this chaos," I say. "Isn't it?"

He crosses one leg over the other and leans on an armrest. "Yes. It is. And you have your American friends to blame."

"They were supposed to free us of Saddam and then leave," I say. "But now they can't leave."

"What do you mean?"

"George Bush promised people that we had dangerous weapons. So now they need to find them. And until they do, they can't leave. So that's what we were trying to do." A lie a minute, Nabil. Just keep it spinning. "We wanted to look into the documents about weapons, the ones Saddam's enemies gave to Bush, and then we could show they were fake, and then the Americans would have to leave because they didn't find any weapons."

Ali looks mildly surprised. "Is that the truth? You think they would?"

"It is. I'm sure," I say, as confidently as is possible for a person taped to a chair.

"But you were working on a story about the documents we did for General Akram. This American man. Jackson."

"That's true. But we were only looking at that as an example of how it all works."

"How *what* works?"

"The document-making business. We wanted to, to understand the market. Maybe it's a legitimate business."

"Of course it's legitimate," he scoffs. "What do you think happens in a place where there's no government? Or when the government is so corrupt is doesn't really govern, it terrorizes. People have to make up their own government. So, for the time being, we act instead of the government."

"I see." I am terribly thirsty. I need the loo. "We also just wanted to find out what these documents cost. We wanted to know what you were paid to do the Jackson documents."

Ali's eyes shift back and forth, like an accountant checking the details of his balance sheet. "Why is it so important to you?"

"It's just how these journalists work, in the West. She just wanted the facts. I don't know, a precise number. We didn't mean to disturb anyone."

Ali crosses his arms, vacillating in the chair's orbit. "Isn't it fair that we should be paid for producing what people need?"

"Of course."

"What do you call that in economics? Supply and demand?" He pushes at the chair leg next to him with his foot. "No?"

"Yes, that's right."

"I also have a family to feed. No one else in my family has a job. No one has been able to take money from the bank in more than a month!" Ali gets up and pushes his swivel chair out of the way.

"We have the same problem," I say.

"Which is why you're working for her."

Sam's eyes look like they are in a dream. Maybe she is in the midst of imagining herself elsewhere. She isn't here, but out there somewhere, on the river.

"It's a good job for you," says Ali. He walks over to Sam and raises his hand. I feel my jaws clench. He could grab her, hurt her, anything, and it would be on my head. Instead, he lays his hand on her hair, running his fingers through the orange-red curls, fascinated. Sam closes her eyes, and I can see her face close down like a drawbridge. Suddenly he withdraws his hand, looking embarrassed – or disgusted. "So maybe you would like to pay for something you want. Such as your freedom. Her safety. Give us five thousand dollars and we will set you free."

"Five thousand? I'm sure we don't have that kind of money with us."

"Oh? What kind do you have?"

"Sam. Sam? He wants to know how much money you have."

I can see Sam's eyelashes flutter, but she says nothing.

"Sam, he wants us to pay him $5,000 to let us go."

Sam swallows. "I have about $800 with me." Her voice sounds like she has just woken up.

"You're a liar!" Ali leans in close to her face. "I know you have more than that."

Sam pulls in her lips and holds them there.

"Subhi? Check her bag."

Subhi doesn't look at either of us. He walks over to Sam and picks up the bag on the floor next to her chair.

"Go ahead. Let's see what's inside."

Subhi crouches and begins to pick things out, putting them down on the floor between Ali and me. One notebook. One folder. One Nikon digital camera. Two tubes of lipgloss. Four pens, none of them the same. The hotel keychain with a small torch with a miniature pocketknife connected to it. Business cards in her holder. A tattered pack of Trident chewing gum. Her wallet and passport.

Ali motions to hand the last two things to him. He opens the small blue book. "Very nice," he says when he sees the picture, switching back to English. He nods and holds it up to show me. "Beautiful photo," he adds. "Let's see. Born Philadelphia, April 5, 1970. You doesn't look thirty-three. And not married? Or this your husband?" He has a hold of a plastic folder of pictures in her wallet.

"It's my fiancé."

"Fiancé? *Yaani, aris? Ya Nabil, haram.*" Sorry, she's taken.

I can feel blood rushing up the side of my neck, that

pounding in my temples just before I pass out. Try to be like Sam. Focus on the horizon.

"And this? This your parents?"

"Yes." Sam's voice is small and far away. I wonder why she never showed me these pictures. I wonder what Mustapha is doing now, and Brutus. It was all a set-up, and we walked right into it. How could Saleh have sent me to him?

"Let's see what we have in here." He opens up the wallet and plucks out what's inside. "*Wahad, tneen, talata, arba, khamis...* there's only five hundred dollars in here."

"The rest is by my knee."

"What?"

"I am wearing the rest on my knee," she says. She uses her chin to point towards her left knee, and raises her leg a bit to make the point. "To protect from theft."

Ali looks amused. "Which knee?"

Sam exhales, closes her eyes for a moment. "The left knee. Inside the kneesock."

Ali looks at her and then looks longer at me. He points right, left and right again, clearly unsure of what he heard in English. Subhi says *is-shmaal*. Ali bends down and takes a hold of the left hem of Sam's trousers. I can feel her recoil and stiffen. Ali carefully lifts the trouser leg, never touching her skin. Beneath it, her knee is wrapped in what looks like a sports-sock for an athlete who's had an injury.

"Empty it out," Ali orders.

Sam doesn't react.

"Empty it out!"

"With my hands tied?"

"You can. You try."

Sam moves her tied wrists out of her lap and towards her knees. She twists them to the left and begins to pick at the inside lining, revealing a pocket. Her hands are shaking more than they were before. I blink, and a rivulet of sweat that had been held up on my forehead is set loose, stinging on my cheeks and putting a saltiness in my mouth.

Sam's back curves into a C, the way it sometimes does when she is doing her stretches. She finally gets her fingers into the sock, making her shoulder push her right hand deeper. After some pinching, stopping, and then pinching around again, her tied hands finally come out, holding a small fold of money between two fingers. Ali bends forwards and grabs it. The bills whisk through his hands like a counting machine.

"It's only $300!"

"I told you I had $800."

"What about the rest? No foreigner comes to Iraq with just $800."

"It's back at the Ha-…hotel. I keep it in a safe there." Sam lowers her eyes again.

"Don't worry. We know exactly where you stay. And if not, so we are finding you at the Sheraton or the Palestine anyway. For the foreigner, Baghdad is not big city." Ali ducks his neck so he can force Sam to look him in the eye. "I don't think my friends are going to be happy with $800, Miss Samara Katchens. Why don't you think about whether you have some more for us, right here with you, so we won't have to search in places where maybe you put the rest of your money." He gets up and stands in front of us.

"Anyway," Ali backs away, "you can just wait here for a while until we decide what to do with you." He picks up Sam's bag and hands it to Subhi, and then, approaching me from behind touches my backside, making me jump in my seat. "Just looking for your wallet, Nabil," he says calmly. He yanks at it a few times, until it pops out of my pocket with the slight sound of a rip. "You won't be needing this for the time being, will you?" He begins to walk out, and gives the guard instructions that we may speak but not move, not even to scratch.

"Wait, Ali?"

Sam looks at me like one of us has already gone mad.

"Could I just go to the bathroom, please?"

"After all the trouble we took to sit you down? No, unfortunately, you may not."

I listen to the sound of her breathing, and although it still sounds somewhat laboured, there is something about Sam's rhythm that calms me.

And what if I'm deluding myself? What if they plan to take Sam's money and then kill us anyway?

Ali comes back into the room. He is carrying two bottles of Coca-Cola, already opened. "Drinks for our guests," he announces, and puts them on the chair where his gun had been. "*Tfaddali,*" he says, holding one out to Sam, and then laughing to himself. "Oh, here, let me," he says, holding it up to her lips.

She turns her head to the side. "No, thank you," she says.

Ali straightens his back. "Well, at least no one can accuse us of having bad manners. Nabil?" He holds out the bottle in my direction. Although I am terribly thirsty, drinking something, especially Coca-Cola, will only make it harder to hold myself. I shake my head to indicate I'll pass as well.

"What? Would you go without food or water in your last

hours?" He laughs and keels forwards. "Ah, just for laughs. It's good to have laughing in times like these, no?"

He takes his gun out again, sits down and rests the pistol on his thigh. "Of course, we could always kill you later, if you don't go the right way. The right way, I mean, is you pay us for the trouble you made for us. So maybe we can give you chance to do that. How much in the hotel?"

Ali picks up his gun and points it at Sam. "I'm asking you question."

Sam looks dazed, and simply stares.

"How much?!"

"About two thousand dollars," Sam says. Her voice is lifeless, almost another woman's.

"Just this? Not more? I don't believe you. *So* much more. The journalists have so much more than that. Your colleague, Mr Axelrod, he spend at least this amount for our documents."

"Really?" Sam is half-alive again.

"Really," he responds.

"Well," she says, watching Ali, "I wasn't looking to buy documents right now. I was planning on leaving soon, so it didn't matter that I was almost out of money."

"Well, that's nice. I'm sorry you leave Iraq so soon. Maybe you stay longer."

Sam does not answer, and stares again at the Tigris beyond the windows.

"Or maybe we can make arrangement for you to give us the money before you leave Baghdad, so we can make sure you get out safely. *Very* safely. And you know it is hard to leave Baghdad safely. How will you go? To Kuwait or to Jordan?"

Sam's lips stay shut for several blinks. "Jordan."

"Yes. But be careful. The road there is dangerous."

Sam swallows, and the dryness of the roll in her throat makes me want the Coke all the more, so much that I cannot resist it any longer.

"Could I drink some, please?"

"Ya Nabil, of course!" He puts his gun back on the chair and leans in towards me, quickly lifting the bottle to my mouth, banging it against my front teeth. "Oh, sorry. There you are," he says, yanking my head back slightly by my hair. It's sweet and cool and fast, so fast that it's soon running out of the sides of my mouth when I can't swallow it all, foaming over my face, and when he pulls the bottle away I'm grateful that he didn't just force me to choke and drown in it altogether. "Ah, special from America." He stands over me, smiling. "So much easier to get Coca-Cola now, isn't it? Think of the benefits. Right, Subhi?"

Subhi gives off a guttural noise that means yes.

He turns towards Sam. "For you?" She shakes her head no.

"As you like. You can be thirsty," he says. He shoves the gun back into his trousers. Does he have the safety lock on or off? "In fact," he says, his voice behind us and towards the door, out of sight, "you just might have to go thirsty all night. You think about it."

Ali orders Abu Ihab to make sure we don't move from our chairs.

All night? It cannot be later than three in the afternoon. Do they not plan to release us? Will they actually hold us here overnight? My mind rushes with images of American soldiers breaking in to rescue Sam, then thanking me for helping to see her through. Or maybe they would blame me for it all, painting me as the bad fixer who led her into the hands of the worst possible people.

48

Painting

It is like waiting for an injection, a discomfort that you know you have no choice but to tolerate. When I look over at Sam, I am frightened by the sight of her. Her eyes are closed and she is doing that same deep breathing, but I see from the rate of her stomach rising and falling that she isn't really so calm at all. Inside the tape her fingers are twitching.

"Sam?"

No answer.

"Sam?"

Abu Ihad arranges himself in his chair by the door, sneers at me, and says nothing.

"Sam, I'm sorry I brought you here. It's my fault."

Sam's eyes open again, and I watch her eyelashes flutter against each other.

"I made a horrible mistake."

"It's not your fault," she says, her voice a monotone. "Either it's my fault, or it's no one's fault."

"Sam, what do you want to do? Is that all the money you have?"

She is quiet for a moment, hesitant to answer. "Yeah."

"Could you get the newspaper to pay them more?"

She shakes her head. "I don't know."

"Maybe you can offer to pay them more."

She turns towards me for the first time in nearly an hour. Her eyes look dull, almost veiled by something cloudy. "I just want to get out of here."

"That's what I'm trying to do – to get us out of here. We have to have a plan. If we promise them more money, then maybe they will release us."

Sam focuses her eyes again on the water and says nothing. I feel I am losing her, as if she may as well be as distant as the river.

"Promise them you won't write the story. And then for certain they will let us go safely. Sam?"

Nothing. Only the ebb and flow of her breath, the occasional shivering of her hands.

"What do you want to do?" I whisper. But an angry voice in my head is stirring. Where is my Sam with a plan? Sam who always has directions for me about how to approach everything we do? Sam with her philosophy of journalism and her ethical guidelines to every problem that might arise?

"Sam!"

Abu Ihad sniggers, then rolls his eyes back as if bored by my nervous natterings in a language he doesn't understand.

"I don't know," she finally says. "Just wait, I guess."

The minutes become eternities, each one a desert of dunes that undulate as far as the eye can see, so that if you are walking through it, you cannot tell if you've walked for ten kilometres or ten days. *Dog days.* In this wilderness, my thirst is my desperation for a sign from Sam, some indication that she knows how to get us out of this. Or is she really just leaving it all to chance? Or worse, to me?

Lunch and Mustapha never arrived, though I should have given up hope in him long ago. Was that even really his office? Ali and Subhi have only been back to check on us once, letting us sip some orange soda, when Sam finally relented and drank. It must be close to 6:30 p.m. now because the sky is no longer blanched to a washed-out blue, but has begun to welcome the emergence of pink and grey. I can occasionally hear voices in the other room, the sounds of Abu Ihad and other guards shifting in their seats or handling their weapons.

Sam and I have not spoken for hours and I think if we remain in silence any longer I will break down and cry. It isn't only the silence, I need a distraction. I might have to finally go in my trousers, and then I will cry, from humiliation.

"Sam, are you okay?"

"Yes," she says. "I'm all right."

"When they come back I'll promise them we won't write the story."

"Most of it's probably written. I don't know if we can—"

"But I can tell them that anyway."

Sam sighs a shallow breath. Shrugs in a small shudder. "Okay."

"Sam?"

"Yeah."

"Do you think about getting married?"

The exhale in her nose is like a whistle, nearly musical. "Yes."

"Do you want to have children someday?"

She turns her head to me slowly, with soft eyes that seem for the first time like they might allow themselves to cry. But I can see the controller inside Samara Katchens' head, holding back the tears.

She switches back to the river. "Yes."

"Would you marry Jonah? Do you see your future with him?"

She hesitates. "No."

"Do you love him?"

Sam doesn't answer. Her hands shift and make the tape squeak. I look at her, the profile I've traced a thousand times, the hair that lit up darkened rooms. Her cheek is streaked with the tracks of tears she must have shed when I wasn't looking. I would give my life at this moment to press my lips against that cheek, have her drop her jaw with an unexpected sigh of joy.

"Sam?"

"What."

"Did I ever tell you that the night I met you, I was actually on a date? And that I was possibly going to marry her? Her name is Noor. Was. I mean, my parents were hoping I'd marry her."

Sam turns to me, her rounded brows pulled down into a tense, flat line. "Noor?"

"The daughter of my father's friend. My parents were hoping, I mean, my mother – that night, at the hospital, when you were—"

"You were going to marry someone your parents introduced you to? Like in an *arranged* marriage?"

"Maybe. They wanted me to."

Sam closes her eyes and squints, as if trying to picture something and having a hard time summoning the image. Or not liking what she sees.

"Sam?" She does not answer. I do not ask again.

It's been quiet for some time, until now. They came suddenly, the sound of Sam's near-silent sobs, her crying like a gasping, nothing but the breaths of a person breaking down, the release of misery unaccompanied by words. I look at her, but she lifts her arms to block her face, or perhaps to mop up the tears. The guard in the corner gazes nervously at me with a slight smile, and looks away.

"It's my fault, Nabil."

"What?"

"I shouldn't have jumped up to leave. I got nervous. He pushed the wrong buttons for me and I couldn't handle it. I should have stayed calm, and—"

"Sam."

"What?"

"You haven't done anything wrong. It's very likely that even if you hadn't jumped up to leave, we'd be here anyway."

Sam shrugs and sniffles. She lifts her tied hands to wipe her nose somewhere along the sleeve of her upper arm. "Maybe I should have told you," and she hesitates a moment, "everything about me. Maybe I was wrong."

"About? That doesn't matter now. Unless you think they might—"

"I have no idea."

"So just forget it."

"Where do you think Rizgar is?"

"I'm sure he's fine," I say, sounding surprisingly calm. "We'll get out of this."

I have to sound positive, even if I don't believe a word of what

I say. Rizgar was supposed to follow us and wait. If he was outside all this time, wouldn't he have made an effort to come in and get us? And with whom? With a pack of Kurdish *peshmerga* gunmen he's going to hire for a few hours?

Sam struggles in her chair a moment. "I'm worried about him," she whispers.

"I could piss an entire bloody ocean."

"*Tfaddal*," she says. Be my guest.

But I can't disgrace myself like that. My mind is in control, not my body.

The hours pass, the whole world slow and tedious. This is my life, and this is the life of Iraq. Maybe this is how it has always been. Maybe I'll be here forever, tied down and trapped. I only know we have been here this long because the sky grew dark, first to navy and then to ink. It must be close to 9 p.m. I've listened to Sam's stomach growl, to my own breath rattle when my imagination was seized by some worse-case scenario, to the guards changing positions, to the muezzins move their prayer-call across the rooftops. From one of the back rooms, I've heard occasional chatter, the sound of Ali and Subhi and the others arguing.

What if we *don't* get out of here? If Sam dies, it will be my fault. I should have told her that we should stop our investigation and let her editors do whatever they want.

But didn't I? Didn't I tell her?

What if Ali is a rapist? I don't like the way he looked at Sam, the way he talked to her, touched her hair. Maybe Rizgar was wrong. Maybe I should have made the decision for her.

*

I think I actually may have drifted off for a moment, because I feel a bit confused and dizzy. The alarm of Ali standing over me, my chin in his hand. He gives my cheek a light slap and sits back in the chair across from us. The three armed men are standing behind him, scrubby faces and bulky bodies. He indicates for them to move behind us instead.

"Okay, then. Are you listening? I'm glad you've been having a nice little dream."

I can't believe I could have fallen asleep. Is that possible? But then I realize I must have. I was in Babylon with Sam. She was standing next to one of the old columns and I was taking pictures of her and when I got close enough to kiss her, I realized that her hands were tied behind the column and someone's hands had reached for her throat, as if to strangle her.

I look over at Sam, who is staring straight ahead, her eyes like a zombie's. I am relieved when I see her blink.

Ali watches me and then sits in his swivel chair. He crosses one leg over the other and takes his gun out of his trousers and examines it again. Points it at Sam. Pulls the trigger.

Pip. Nothing but a scary, metallic click. "Oh, my God. Did I forget to load my favourite gun? My goodness." He points it towards his own temple, frowns facetiously. "Where is my head?" The voices behind us laugh. Someone's hand pushes the back of my head. "Just a joke. We wouldn't want to do away with your beautiful friend without getting something first."

"Oh, now," says Ali. "Poor little girl."

I turn slightly to look at Sam. Tears spill down her cheeks, quickly replenished by more which seem to emerge from deep inside her.

I keep thinking how good it would feel to ram my knee into

Ali's head now. How, if I had him against an alley wall the way those thugs had me against the wall, I would bash everything in, slamming until he stopped moving.

Sam stares up at the ceiling. The tears leave marks running over her jawline and down her neck.

Ali reaches into his shirt pocket and picks out a cartridge, shoves it into the gun, releases what I assume to be the safety. Points it at her, then me, back at her again. Rests his elbow on his bent knee so that the barrel hovers in the space between us. "I've decided to be really kind with you. You're lucky that I'm such a merciful man." He calls one of the men over, a thin, tall man, and hands him the gun. Ali reaches out to someone behind us and returns with Sam's large bag. Out of it, he takes the folder and opens it up. Holds up the documents we've been carrying around with us, day and night, as if they were the Holy Koran itself. I have seen them so many times, studied them, I can probably draw them blindfolded.

"This," Ali says, displaying the pages as if they were an animal's intestines being offered for inspection at the butcher's before the meat is deemed acceptable, "this stays with me. And this camera," Ali adds, holding up Sam's Nikon. She once told me it cost about $1,500. "This very nice camera stays with me."

He flips a small latch open, pulls out the little square disc that Sam had told me was like film. I had never seen a digital camera before. "It is really nice of you to leave this for me as a present, too." He laughs again. In my mind, I'm imagining all the important pictures saved, somehow, inside that small piece of plastic. Pictures from our first day of working together. Pictures of Akram. The picture Rizgar took of Sam and me, when we stopped by the river that day on the way back from Tikrit. Irreplaceable images.

"It's very simple from here," Ali says, tucking the disc into his shirt pocket. "We'll let you go tonight, but we'll hold on to these documents, these pictures and the camera. After all, you know so much by now that you don't need these." Ali stands up, points his gun at Sam and me, and winds a counter-clockwise circle around us. He walks deliberately, his dress shoes tapping against the tiles. After a full revolution, he stops in front of us.

"You'll give us $10,000 for having inconvenienced us and we will be through."

"Ten thousand dollars? I am sure she cannot have that kind of money with her in Iraq. That can't possibly—"

"*Shut UP!*" Ali bellows at me. I can smell his odour, a mix of cigarettes and roast chicken and I think even beer, a scent that makes me want to throw up. He is closer now, the gun pointed at me. If he slips, my head will be a blur on the wall behind me.

"You just *listen*, Nabil," Ali says. "She can easily get us $10,000 and you know it. We will bring you back to Al-Hamra tonight. If you want to live and you want your very pretty ladyfriend to live, and to leave Iraq walking instead of being carried away, you'll do exactly what I tell you to do. You will meet us tomorrow night with the money and then you will have our assurance that you'll be protected from now on. No one in Baghdad will ever bother you again. I can assure you of that." He looks at the men behind us and smiles with a smug, closed mouth.

"You get that, Miss Katchens? Only $10,000. You getting off easy." He bends a bit to put his face parallel to Sam's, purses his lips for a minute as if he might kiss her. I have never before been so close to a gun and felt I had the capacity to blow out someone's brains with it.

"Ah," Ali says, straightening up again. "The other price for your release, of course, is that you must never write or say anything about us. You don't print anything in newspaper." He rests the hand with the gun in it along his waist. With his free hand, he pretends to pull the trigger in the direction of Sam's forehead, then mine. He blows the imaginary smoke off his index finger. "No story in newspaper," he says in his broken English. "Or maybe say, Jews-paper? This newspaper, the reporters are most of them Jewish, no?"

Sam stares at him blankly, her lips slightly parted. Her face gives away nothing.

"Is it not?"

She clears her throat. "Sorry?"

"I asked you if many of the reporters at your newspaper are Jews. We were told that your newspaper is loving the war because they are Jews, and this war make good for Israel."

Sam shrugs as if the man at the hotel asked her whether she'd like tea or coffee. "I don't know if there are many Jews at the newspaper. In America we don't usually ask people what their religion is in order to be hired for a job."

Ali looks at me, as though he's not sure he got what she said. I repeat it in Arabic, trying to sound as even as Sam did, but my voice is trembling.

Ali lifts his chin towards the men behind us. "Wrap them up." My spine stiffens when I feel it: the blindfold being wrapped around my eyes, twice, and then tied in the back. Next to me I can feel that Sam is getting the same treatment. I feel another rush of anger. *Don't touch her.*

It's darker now, but I can still see a glow of light. And then, a cold ring against my face. The barrel of Ali's gun, pressed up against my cheek. "I'm dead serious, Amari," he says into my ear. "You don't know how lucky you are. We're taking a chance, letting you go." He takes the gun away, lifts me briskly out of my chair by my tied hands, so that a rip of pain tears through the lower part of my back. "If you don't get us the money, or if you publish a story about us, you can be sure that your beloved boss will not leave Iraq in one piece."

And then a bag over my head, burlap perhaps, the smell of dye, or maybe potatoes. Have they done that to her too? At least two sets of hands, maybe three, are leading us out of the door, down the stairs. After the first few steps, I trip like a blind man walking for the first time. The men catch me and laugh.

"Sam?"

"Hmm." Her voice is muffled, distant.

"You're okay?"

"I'm okay."

A too-hard tap on my skull. "Keep quiet, Amari." Subhi's voice, though I haven't seen his face for hours.

We are pushed outside, into the muggy night air. The door opening, the feel of my body against the car, my head being pushed down, shoulders shoved inside, and the strange excitement, suddenly, of my thigh colliding with Sam's. Now I surely will explode.

"I'm sorry, would you mind letting me out to just relieve myself?"

"Amari, good lord," Ali says. "Some guys just can't hold it, can they?" The other men in the car laugh. "Ah well, let no one say I was as cruel as Saddam." He yanks me out and pulls me back towards the building. He stands me up against a wall. "Go ahead," he says.

I stand there for a moment, waiting in the dark with my taped hands in front of me. "I can't undo my trousers."

"Oh, still a bit tied up, aren't we? Subhi, undo his trousers."

"Don't!" I twitch, surprised by my own reaction. "Forget it, I'll wait until I get home."

Ali drags me back in the direction of the car. "These professors' kids. So god-damned spoiled."

As we drive, Ali issues an order from the front seat. Meet him tomorrow, 8 p.m. Just under the Sarafiya Bridge, on the east side. No Americans are posted in the vicinity.

"This time, come in your driver's Impala so we'll know it's you," he says. "Don't come in a taxi. If there is anyone in that car but you and your driver, we will kill you on the spot. And if you don't come, we will kill you before you can get out of Iraq." I feel nauseous from the motion. The turns are fast and numerous. We stop abruptly, the car rocking us forwards and then back. Then the unsettling sound of flick knives being opened. One knife works on my bonds, and another, on Sam's. Oh please, God. All I need now is for one of these mindless men to miss and slit one of my wrists, or hers.

But the bonds break, bloodlessly, and someone yanks the covering off my head. The blindfold beneath it comes off as well.

"*Yalla*," Ali orders. "Go on. You're free to go." The guards sitting on either side of us get out, pulling us out with them, much less roughly than they had pushed us into the car. Ali grabs both my shoulders and looks me in the eye. "It will be easy to find you," he says in English. "If you miss your appointment with us tomorrow, you will soon be regretting it."

49

Regretting

SAM STANDS THERE at the intersection, not moving. I can feel the exhaust of Ali's car filling my lungs, turning them black like in those pictures Baba showed me so I wouldn't smoke. The car is gone, but the exhaust shadow it spurted out still hangs over us on the street where it idled a second ago. Did anyone see us get dropped off? I look at my watch. It's already 11.00 p.m. Well past the 9.30 p.m. curfew. Who else would be out at this hour? Anyone who might try to kidnap us again.

"Sam, let's go!" I start to run across the street, but she isn't following. Maybe she's in shock. I read about that once, when I was going through one of my father's medical textbooks, trying to understand what it was that was making me faint. "Sam!"

I run back and put my arm around her. She shakes me off and starts walking.

"I'm fine," she says. She walks briskly across the road, tearing at the remnants of tape on her wrists, and I follow after her.

"Wait here," I say, pointing to a darkened corner at the edge of an alleyway. A few paces away, I let rip the piss of a lifetime, trying not to cry out in relief as I do. It sends a river down the pavement and a stinky steam rising up in my face.

I zip up and turn round, but she's not there.

"Sam? Sam!"

She's left the alley and gone back to the main road, walking.

"Sam, wait!" I've caught up with her, but she doesn't acknowledge it. Doesn't look at me.

"I'm fine." She's moving so fast now that I almost need to jog to keep up.

"Let's first…Sam?" I leap ahead and stand in front of her. Her mouth opens and I hear a gasp for air, as if I've scared her. "Maybe we should go back to my house instead. Not the hotel."

She steps aside and keeps walking. "Now? With the curfew? Don't be ridiculous. I have to go back to the hotel anyway. I have all my things there."

"Do you even know if you're walking in the right direction?" I say in a half-yell, half-whisper.

"Aren't I? Look," she points up. "There's the Hamra sign right there." And indeed the red neon Al-Hamra Suites sign is lit up against the night sky, indicating it's just blocks away.

She swings her arms as she walks, almost runs, and I reach for one like a brake, to get her to slow down. Even someone from a block away would notice from the way she's walking, even from her silhouette, that she's not Iraqi. Maybe one of the neighbourhood watch committees, the ones formed to prevent night-time looting, will see us and be suspicious.

"Stop it," she says. "I'm fine. I just want to get back to the hotel room so I can figure things out. I should call Miles and tell him what happened."

She is already ten steps ahead, and we're on the block next to the Hamra, so it really doesn't matter anymore. With her arms swinging that way, she reminds me of a small bird, trying – but not quite managing – to fly.

We say nothing as we move through the hotel, past the front desk, and then out into the courtyard which is virtually empty, now that most reporters have turned in for the night.

But across the pool I see them – Sam's friends. Two of them, Joon and Marcus rise from a table which has more bottles of beer scattered across it than there are people around it.

"Sam!" Joon cries. "'My God." She rushes over, leaving Marcus standing there, the three others with their heads fixed on us. "We were worried sick about you, for Chrissake. Are you all right?"

No answer. Sam still moving towards the door, coming home like any other day. Me following behind, unsure what to say.

"We were close to calling AP to put out a story on you," Joon says, almost accusingly. She approaches Sam, but something in Sam's distance holds Joon a few feet away, waiting.

Marcus sizes her up, looking to me for a split second before focusing again on Sam. "I never thought I'd say this, Katchens, but you look like shit. What happened?"

"I'm fine." Sam's voice, hoarse but emotionless, as if every time she speaks, she is adding *of course*. Of course I'm fine. Of course.

"Did you…" Joon stares like she knows something is wrong, but doesn't want to force the issue – to demand what Sam isn't offering. She takes hold of one of Sam's wrists. "What the—? Are you guys all right? Where *were* you?" Despite Joon's professed concern, it looks to me like she has been for a swim. I can see the skinny black straps straddling her neck beneath her shirt, like puppet strings to move her shoulders.

Sam unhinges her arm from Joon's hold. "What the fuck would you care? Wasn't it only yesterday you accused me of hoarding sources and stealing boyfriends?"

"Sam, I'm sorry about that," Joon pleads. "I was way out of line."

Sam stares at her blankly.

"I said I'm sorry. What more do you want?"

"I don't want anything, Joon. I appreciate your concern, but I'm just a little too exhausted to be standing on my own two feet right now, or to speak another word."

"Really, Sam," Marcus approaches. "What's going on? Everyone wants to know—"

"Don't they always," she says, and starts for the atrium door. I avoid their stares and follow her.

"*Sa*-am," Joon pushes in. "Wait, can we please talk?"

Sam pauses, her right hand on the handle. Her hair has an electrified frizz running through it, as if fully aware of the harrowing hours in Ali's townhouse on the Tigris.

Joon's face is a sneer. "You could have at least called or texted one of us to tell us you were all right!"

"No," says Sam, calm and quiet. As in no, I don't want sugar in my coffee. "I couldn't."

Sam drags the door open as if she needs to pull the weight of her body in the opposite direction to do it. Her eyes train on mine and swing upwards. The night guard has already replaced Rafik, which somehow feels like a great relief. What would he think if he saw me following Sam up to her room at this late hour?

I know Sam usually likes to walk up, but the lift is here, open and waiting for us. Her eyes say it all: I'm too tired to take the stairs. She enters and I follow. Her back is to the wall, and mine to the doors closing behind me.

I can see her watching the numbers change above my head.

With her eyes lifted that way, the amber colour looks even more beautiful. But the whites are reddened, as if she hasn't slept in days.

She catches me staring at her. Neither of us breathes. The lift doors part.

Sam is already holding the key to her room, though I can see she is having a hard time steadying her hand enough to get it into the lock. From behind her, I feel myself inches away from putting myself around her, making her be still, just holding her. The clicking turns three times and pricks at the vertebrae between my shoulders. The sound of Ali's gun at Sam's head.

Sam pushes the door open and I hear her exhale, a lungful she had been holding, at the sight of her familiar suite. Sam's things fall off her – her shoes, her bag – and I feel any second her clothes will follow.

She stands with her back to me and I can feel her thinking, collapse on the sofa? Send Nabil away and go to bed?

"I need a shower."

"Do you want me to stay here?"

Her eyes lift, rounding towards me like the second hand on a clock. "Yes."

She walks towards her bedroom, and I am frozen here. She turns back to me. "You…you could have a drink or something. Why don't you make yourself something? There's some, I don't know, some stuff in there," she says, lifting her chin towards the cabinet with the television on it, the one that has never worked, as far as I know.

The sprinkling of the shower carries into the living room almost like rain on the roof in winter – a sound I used to love. Will I be around next time it rains in Baghdad? Will Sam? I can feel myself stirring. I'm ashamed to even think of these things now, after what happened to us today. But it's true. I can feel myself burning with it. There isn't anything I want more right now than to walk in and make love to her right there, with the water falling over us, helping us wash it all away.

A love poem by Nizar Kabbani comes to me, and I air-type it for him, in his memory.

Undress yourself.
For centuries
There have been no miracles,
I am mute,
And your body knows all languages.

Inside the cabinet, below the television, I see what Sam meant. A bottle of Bombay Sapphire, a bottle of red wine that looks to me to be very old, and a bottle of Glenmorangie, the stuff my father likes. I lift out the bottle, only half full, and hold it up to the light. Clear and warm, almost amber, almost the colour of Sam's eyes. With the uncapped bottle under my nose, my chest shudders. One of the many Western things that appear better than they taste. No point in forcing it. I'll make tea.

I stand over the kettle while it builds to a boil, pretending the steam clouds will provide our escape, enjoying how they look when they ride through my outstretched fingers, until my own skin is hot and moist, almost puckered, the way Sam's must be by now. When it's done, I hear her water stop, too.

I choose two bags from the fancy box of assorted British teas she picked up at the store the other day, the one offering imported goods to foreigners at four or five times the normal price. Chamomile. Didn't Sam once say she liked that one? I steep them and seat myself.

She comes out, her hair drenching wet so that it looks more smooth than curly, a white towel in one hand as she tries to squeeze out the water. She is wearing a dark green robe, and she is so striking she looks like a piece of jewellery, an emerald topped with rubies.

When she sees me sitting on the sofa with two steaming mugs on the table, she laughs a little, then collapses into the space next to me, brushing against me as she hits the seat. She has never sat next to me like this. Always on the sofa which is at right-angles to this one, or at her desk.

She leans her head back against the sofa. I can feel the wetness of her hair, the smell of her shampoo. Her eyes are closed. "After all that," she says in a low voice, "you're only having tea?"

I sit up to move. "Did you…I can get you something else. I saw there is whisky and maybe vodka, and—"

"I know what we have. Tea's good." She pulls her mug towards her, leans her face over it, her elbows on her knees. "Mmm. Chamomile, right?" I thought she had leaned her head that way to feel the aromatic steam on her face. But I hear the air in her throat break. Sam is crying out loud now, streams running over her cheeks and towards her tea.

I hesitate, wanting to stop her, to stop myself. Didn't she sit here rather than there? My arm is around her. Across her back, my hand wrapped around her shoulders.

She's crying harder now, in a way I've never heard her. Quiet, deep sobs, like she can't stop it, like something invisible is rocking her, snatching away bits of breath.

I wait for her to pull away, to get up and head for the bathroom, to come back pretending nothing has happened. Nothing has gone wrong. *I'm fine.* Instead she lets her shoulders go, drops them, and falls towards me, shaking without a sound, just contractions of her stomach.

My hands, in that red hair, holding that head, smoothing out the wet curves like ripples in a pond. "Shh…" I whisper in her ear, rocking her a little, so much more slowly than her sobs. "Shh…it's okay now. We're okay now." And there is a rasp in Sam's throat, the sound of gears moving in different directions, a heave of her chest as if she might be sick. I hold her a little more closely, a little more tightly, her knees curled up almost into my lap. What do you think you're doing, Nabil? "Shh…" a rocking like a boat on the river, swaying just a little the way the fishing dinghies do when the weather gets windy, and then I can feel it, her cheek against mine, my lips against her cheek, tasting all of that saltiness, almost repelled and yet pulled closer by the taste of her tears, taking in the curve of the damp bone that rounds up to her eye, wanting to soothe everything, every part of her, to quiet her, and then I feel them: Sam's lips stuttering near mine, and I take them and meet them and kiss them to stop their quavering, kiss them harder than I should. And she's kissing back. *She's kissing back.*

She puts her hand around my neck and she's stopped crying now, but I can feel that her face is still wet and so I kiss her again and try to wipe away those tears with the palm of my hand, and she kisses me harder for a moment and my head is flying with a thousand thoughts of my life about to begin right now, restarting at this very moment. Me with Sam. Sam and me, making love. Me in Sam and Sam in me. And I move my arms around her back to hold her better, to comfort her, to love her, I will love her like no one's ever been loved before, or at least like I've never loved anyone, like I could never have loved Noor, and just then I feel myself deeper into Sam, closer than I ever have been before. Ever. Ever. And the taste of Sam's tongue against mine is so salty and sweet and soft that I can't ever have been happier, ever, ever, and it stops. Sam's tongue slows, her mouth freezes. She pulls away.

She stares at me with bleary eyes, confused as a girl awoken from a dream. Her mouth strains towards an "o", a stretch to ask why. Or maybe to say *oh-no*. I stare back at her, and her eyes study me, taking me in.

"Na, Nabil, I…I don't know what just happened here." Silence. A sniffling, an exhalation. "We can't do this."

You want to do this. You put your lips next to mine. You didn't pull away – not straight away, anyway.

"You, you know we can't do this, right? You understand, don't you?"

You let me kiss you. You kissed back.

Her eyes fill up again, searching mine. They look like they will spill over again, but just build up at the edge of her bottom lids, holding. I watch her, unable to string together a reply. She takes one of my hands in both of hers, lets her eyes close, sets free the waterfall. Her tongue reaches out to catch one without her knowing. She breathes in quick and breathes out slow. "I know you understand. I know you know why this can't be." And she rises, leaving my hand alone in mid-air, only a moment ago held in hers.

50

Leaving

SAM TOLD ME she needed to sleep for a few hours. Four, to be exact. That nothing could be done, no decisions could be made, no discussing why we can or can't do anything, until she had four solid hours of sleep. She read somewhere that sleep experts have discovered that we sleep in four-hour cycles which are in sync with our dream sequences, and therefore, give us enough time for deep sleep and rapid-eye movement. So if you can't sleep eight hours, the study found, better to sleep four. To sleep five or six would only frustrate the mind's internal clock, which would know that it was being woken up in the middle of a four-hour cycle. With that, she left me here, on the sofa with my shirt still spotted from her tears, and went to bed. I reminded her that I thought we should leave the hotel as soon as possible, and that we should do it at night, when no one would be watching. And she reminded me that she needed to pay the Hamra for her last month of hotel bills, and that the main reception desk wouldn't be open until five. She promised to wake up in four hours, at 4.45 a.m., and pack up her essentials. Then she further reminded me that if we violate the curfew without a special permit – something Technical Ali apparently has no problem attaining –

we might wind up dead anyway. And who would drive us? No sign of Rizgar or his car.

It's been more than an hour that I've been lying here in the dark, in the spare room across the hall from hers, the one where Carlos sleeps whenever he is here, the one where Marcus slept at least once, and where other men might sleep in the future.

I get up and turn on the light. Maybe I'll try to read one of her books, because there is no way I'll be able to sleep. How can Sam?

I walk through the suite to get a glass of water from the kitchen, and stop at her door on the return trip. Put my ear against it, wince when I hear it creak. Stillness. Soundlessness. Not even the heavy breathing of a troubled sleep.

Lying on my back again, I go through the selected pieces of the story I will feed my family when I bring Sam home tomorrow. Today, rather. *I will bring Sam home today.* I feel the rush of blood around my chest, the pounding in the pulse points in my neck, wired like Frankenstein in the old black-and-white film, rising from the dead, feigning health and happiness. I close my eyes, and Ali's face fills them. *Maybe the deadline is you.* Open. Better open. I will simply lie here, eyes open, and wait. Wait for the light to come. Keep myself from slipping into that crazy corner of my mind, the one that thought I could fill Sam up with me, instead of words and stories.

A trio of beeps, sounding four or five times, and then the click that brings it to an end. Sam is stirring just as she promised, using the bathroom and letting the door slam, rattling mine.

I go into the kitchen to make coffee, the real one that takes time. The *dallah*, the pot for making real coffee, was in the cabinet all along, next to the other basic crockery the hotel leaves for its guests. I suppose Sam never thought to use it.

I stand and stir, watching the dark foam rise and fall and rise again. Make it sweet, but not too sweet. By the time it is done, I turn to find Sam pulling along a large black suitcase, made of hard plastic and rounded at the edges, into the main room. Manipulating the handle, she wheels the upright case next to her desk and sits down in her chair. She looks at the laptop, dark and idle, and taps twice on the space key.

"I made some coffee."

"I have to call Miles."

"Now? I think we should leave here before people wake up. Before everyone sees us leave. You can stick a note under Joon's door and tell her you're all right. Or leave a note for Carlos and ask him—"

"I need to tell Miles what happened. I should have called him the minute we got home. I should at least e-mail them."

"Sam?" She doesn't turn, starts typing away at the computer. "Sam! Would you listen to me?" I take the coffee off the stove, pour it into two porcelain cups. I bang the *dulluh* back down harder than I should.

"Don't start getting angry at me, Nabil. That's the last thing I need right now."

"It's not a matter of angry!" In my head I imagine myself taking the coffees and sending them across the room, letting them fly past Sam's head, just close enough to shock her, before landing on the sliding glass door, a crash of black and brokenness. Instead I leave them on the counter, and move towards the sofa that separates us. She watches my approach and then stands, moving incrementally, her arms crossed in front of her.

"I want you to understand. It's not anger. I'm just trying to help you. Not just you. I have my family to think about. These people already know you're here. Maybe they know where I live."

Sam claps the computer shut and pulls out the plug.

"Listen to me for a minute!"

"I *am* listening. I'm listening while I pack. You want me to pack, right? This stuff has to come too. If they know where you live, then let's not go to your house."

"Actually, I don't think they know where I live. Ali called me a professor's kid. Which means he doesn't know who my father is, I don't think."

"But what about those guys who grabbed you? They knew."

"Outside my house? Just small-time neighbourhood thugs. I doubt they have anything to do with these guys."

"Nabil," she says. "I'm worried about Rizgar."

"Me too," I say, but in fact, I'm even more worried about what I tried to do on the sofa a few hours ago. Right here, on this sofa, us kissing, only hours ago. "Rizgar probably just went home after a while. He wouldn't stay out after curfew."

Sam reaches to pull plugs out of the power strip, quickly winding them up.

"We need to get you out of the Hamra, and then we need to discuss how to get you out of Iraq altogether. I mean, I presume that's what you want."

Sam leans on the desk space where the computer was. "I have seven thousand dollars."

"And?"

"I'm just telling you."

"Are you saying you want to pay them? Maybe you think you can bargain with them, like in the market?"

Sam shrugs. "No. I don't know what I'm saying. I'm just

telling you so you know. I just want you to know the truth about everything."

"You want me to go back to these schmucks who held us hostage and offer them two-thirds and see if they'll be satisfied? Buy them off, just like Harris buying the documents?"

"What?" Sam's face falls with disbelief. "That's not what I'm saying at all. I'm just telling you facts so that you know what our options are. I thought you might like to know, okay? Because I'm not a walking bank. I only have seven grand. That's what I have left, anyway, not that I couldn't get more if I borrowed from someone, like Joon or Marcus…"

I can see she's not thinking clearly. She can't be. Can she really be thinking of paying our own ransom, after we've been set free, and after all her lessons to me about the ethics of paying for things? Then again, it would be the only way for Sam to keep working in Baghdad. Maybe she can send in an invoice to her editors, along with the handwritten receipts she's been making each time she pays me or Rizgar. Mark it $10,000: This week's price of doing business in Baghdad.

"Get this: the paper is running the story tomorrow. It's going through final edits now. They'll send me a draft before it runs."

"What?"

She looks at me and nods, demonstrating a mix of incredulity and matter-of-factness. "I just saw it in my e-mail now. They said they're ready to run the story tomorrow. They think they have everything they need, now that there's no doubt Harris's story was based on fake documents. They said they'll send me a copy of the story later today."

"But, I thought—" I stop and swallow, wondering if my surprise will only make her feel worse. Sam, my boss, in charge of me perhaps, but not her own story. "You mean, you're not even going to get to write it?"

Sam has a resigned expression on her face that reminds me of certain students of mine, those who barely passed but to whom I kept giving second, third and fourth chances. "Apparently not," she says. "They're just taking whatever information I can give them, and then writing it in Washington."

"Oh," I say. "Did you know they would do that?"

"Nope."

I go to the counter to get the coffees, which aren't giving off the steam they were only minutes ago. I stretch my hand across the coffee table, holding a cup towards Sam. "What about the people who decided to have the fake documents made? What about the people who just created these things to, to blame this guy, this Congressman Jackson, and to make money? Didn't your editors also want to know who did that?"

She takes the small cup, holds it under her nose, shuts her eyes while she breathes in deeply. She sips, then rolls her eyes at me. "They did last week. They don't seem to want it now. They think the story's done."

"But what if the newspaper runs the story and Ali finds out? And you're still in Iraq?" *She's a pretty one, too. Lucky man.*

"That's possible. Then again, maybe he wouldn't find out for a few days. I mean, how would the average Iraqi know what's written in the *Tribune*?"

"Maybe Ali is not the average Iraqi," I say. "We have to leave in three minutes. Drink your coffee."

She lifts the cup to her lips, sighing with exhaustion into the small black sea.

51

Sighing

THE EARLY MORNING is a nervous blur of packing bags and paying bills, of negotiating for a new taxi driver who, I suspect, is an informant for someone, of simple tasks constantly disrupted by a feeling in my blood that we are not safe. That Ali will jump out and recapture us at any moment, that he will drive our taxi off the road and shoot the driver and stuff us in the boot. The screen in my mind keeps replaying the moment when he held the gun to Sam's head, the others also pointing theirs. As the taxi makes its way over the Jadriya Bridge, I make up a new rule. When I catch myself re-living episodes like this, as if it's all before me, I will turn my watch upside down, which will be the equivalent of shutting down the screen in my mind, simply lowering the curtain and closing the theatre doors. When I need to know the time, I'll take the watch off and check to see if I've succeeded, even for a few minutes, in putting it out of my mind.

I join Sam in looking at the view of the water and the early fishing boats floating serenely, as if this morning were the same as any a thousand years ago, when the fishermen, I imagine, were equally oblivious to the political upheaval of the day, the overthrow of the Muslim caliphate in Baghdad. I wonder if Sam knows anything about that time when we were the very heart and mind of the Islamic world. I wonder if the Americans know that they didn't invent regime change for us, because we've already had it for aeons.

Traffic is only now beginning to thicken, and we drive through Mansour, not far from the school where I once taught. *Qabil.* Before. Before the whole city became my classroom, in which I am no longer a teacher but a new student.

Sam, who had seemed deeply uninterested in conversation, turns to me.

"I'm glad you told me what you told me last night."

I look at her and wait. My teeth catch a sliver of the inside of my cheek.

"About you and Noor, I mean. I'm glad you told me that. I understand so much more now."

"About what?" I say, and lean forward to point out the next few turns to the driver. "The antiquated ways of the Arab peoples?"

"No, Nabil." She sounds hurt. "About you."

Without allowing them to, my lips insist on rounding into a slight smile of appreciation. We are only a few blocks from my house, and I don't want everything to feel tense when we go inside.

Sam turns her left wrist over in her right hand, inspecting the marks. "Remember the accident that I told you about? How Jack died?"

"Yes."

"Well." She puts her hands down and stares out of the window again. "I never told you that I was in the car. Somehow I got away with nothing more than a broken pelvis and a few scratches. That's why I'm always stretching out my back. It still aches sometimes."

I try to meet Sam's eyes to offer something of my sympathy, which at this point I don't think needs to be put into words. But for that I need her face. And she won't look at me.

"Who was driving?"

"He was." She blows hot air on the window and then lifts her finger to draw on it: a quick "o" for a face, two dots for the eyes, and a long, flat dash for the mouth.

My family does not ask all the questions they want to, at least not right away. They can sense, I know, from the minute we walk in the door together, that something has gone terribly wrong. Mum sends Amal back to her room, and with a whimper she goes, eased by the fact that it's not yet 7 a.m. Given that she has nowhere to be and no school to attend, she's become used to sleeping late every day.

Mum is very hospitable, and very uncomfortable. Her English is too rusty to make conversation with Sam. But she slips into a welcoming mode straight away, rushing to make up Ziad's room for Sam, who looks more shattered than she did last night. Sam offers her thanks, using the wall to hold her up, and Mum keeps saying things like, "You please home here." Baba, who has been standing around, not quite knowing what to do, goes back to the table, where his breakfast is half-eaten, and tells me that he'll leave for the hospital a little late today so we can talk. "Assuming," he says, dipping his bread into his tea, an odd ritual he maintains, "you want to tell me what's going on."

I've had to wait a long time for Sam to wake up. I poked my head in and checked on her several times, but she was still asleep. It's funny, cracking open Ziad's door like that, the way I did when I was fourteen, to see if he had come home. He was often out late with friends, of which he had many more than I.

This time, I find her wide awake, sitting at Ziad's desk, writing. When I come in, she closes the cover of the book. It's one I haven't seen before – not a notebook, but a hardcover with a maroon fabric binding.

"Am I bothering you, Sam? Do you still want to have some rest?"

"No, it's fine," she says, dropping the book into her bag on the floor. "It's already afternoon, isn't it?"

"Yes. It's after two. My mother is worried that you haven't eaten. Do you want to have some lunch?"

She shrugs. "In a while, maybe. I'm not so hungry now." She picks up a pink plastic bottle on the desk, about half-full of liquid, and shakes it back and forth. "Your sister gave me this."

"I'm sorry. Has she been pestering you?" I take the edge of the bed.

Sam smiles and closes her eyes, then re-opens them slowly. "No, not at all. She's lovely. She's just so curious. I always wanted a little sister like her."

I notice that things have grown a coat of dust in Ziad's old room: a small, golden trophy he won in high school, when he played centre-forward, and a football signed by the French player Zidane. Ziad took the air out and had it shipped home to us. We were shocked that it arrived, when far less valuable packages never did. I bet the primary thing troubling Mum at this moment is that she didn't get to give Ziad's room a good cleaning before I showed up with Sam.

"We need to make a plan, Sam."

"I know," she says. "I just talked to Miles as he was waking up, in fact I think I woke him up. I told him what happened. He agreed that I should leave, if that's my instinct."

"That's what he said? And what about the money Ali's demanding?"

"Well, he said I could lie to management and say it was stolen from me. But I can't just hand it over to them like some kind of gift and expect the newspaper to cover it."

"And the story?"

"I tried to convince him. But he claims he's powerless, it's not up to him," she says. The look in her eyes says she doubts it. "The story with an apology to Jackson is running tomorrow, after the lawyers vet it this afternoon. All Miles can promise me is that they'll send me a copy overnight to read. But at that point, we'll probably be on the road anyway." Sam is shaking her head no, no, no. "First they took the story away from Harris, and now they're taking it away from me. I mean, my byline is going to be on it, along with some bigshot investigative reporter in the Washington bureau, but I won't have written a word of it myself, and I'm not sure I'll get to read it before it goes to print. Can you believe that?"

I see the Thuraya sitting on the windowsill, the reception-bars flashing in the upper-right-hand corner. "You got a satellite signal here?"

"Not a good one. Just enough for a staticky call before it cut off. The best part is that when I tried to tell him to take my byline off the story, for my own safety, he said he'd 'run that up the flagpole' but wasn't sure the higher-ups would go for it!"

"Did you tell Miles *everything* that happened?"

Sam wavers. "Most of it. Not the rough parts. He says if I want to do a profile exposing 'the man called Technical Ali' after

I leave, if I have enough to go on, I can do that and they'll run it afterwards."

"You didn't tell him that he tied us up and threated to kill us? Wouldn't your editor want to know that?"

"Look, if I can do the story about him later, after I'm out, that's probably the best I can get at this point. I don't want to make it sound like a personal vendetta."

"So it's still about the story and not about your life. Or my life."

Sam glares at me. She picks up the bottle, which I now realize is nail-varnish remover. In the middle of all of this, she is planning to paint her toes?

"Sam, listen. Everything I know now makes me think that it was a setting from the start."

"You mean a set-up."

"I said that."

"You said setting."

"I meant set-up. Just listen, okay?"

She shakes the bottle back and forth.

"Sam, I think it was all arranged and co-ordinated, from the moment we stepped into Subhi's apartment until the moment Ali dropped us off by the Hamra. Ali was always in charge, working for Chalabi, working for Muqtada al-Sadr, who's probably his cousin, working for anyone who will hire him – other than the Americans. Ali runs this big forgery ring and makes a lot of money off of it, and he doesn't really care from whom or for what. In fact, maybe he has no politics at all, and that way, he can sell to everyone! Mustapha is nothing but a big fat fascist, just some middleman, despite my cousin Saleh telling me all this time that he was a good guy. What did he know?

Maybe Saleh was fooled. Maybe *he* was set-up. Or maybe no one he knows in that world could possibly be honest, because to get mixed up in that, you've got to be a crooked kind of bloke from the start."

"Nabil?"

"I think even Adeeb was part of it. Subhi sent us to him to stall for time, so they could get ready for our visit to Akram, and Adeeb is so scared of all of them he does whatever they say. He's just a lackey for them and—"

"No, Nabil." Sam is shaking her head.

"—and Khalil, that forger guy, probably is corrupt too and warned Mustapha we were coming. And of course, General Akram was just a salesman! Ali and his friends made him the front man because he looks good and has a name and a title, and thought they could use him and that story of his, his brave little revenge brigade as the alibi for how they captured these documents. Akram would send word back to Ali of what was in demand and what would sell, and Ali would produce it, and who cares if it was about hijackers or yellowcake or some congressman from New Jersey! Who cared if even one word of it was true?"

"Listen. Calm down. There's no way we can be sure they're all connected," Sam says, waving her hand at me. I notice it is shaking, though it isn't at all cold in here. "What if we got shunted from one slimeball to the next and just got unlucky? Or lucky, because we're still here. Don't jump to conclusions."

"I'm not jumping. I'm saying it's obvious!"

"What's obvious?" She purses her lips together and unscrews the little bottle, then tips it over into a wad of tissues, shaking it several times. Everything is clear to me now, and

Sam doesn't see it. She thinks you need to prove things with facts in order to know. I could talk about it with God Almighty until *Yawm id-Din*, Judgement Day. But I don't need to. I just know.

"Don't you see, Sam?"

"See what? What I see is a trail of events that led us from one corrupt fixer or thug or forger to another. I don't know if they connect. It could all be random."

"How can you not see it? Really, how?" Afraid my family will hear, my voice falls into a whisper. I feel myself on the brink of exasperation. If she pushes me more, I will shout. Or maybe break. "Believe me, Sam."

"No. I don't always believe you. Not every little Middle East conspiracy theory you come up with holds water. You guys just love to think the forces of evil are aligning in perfect formation to rule the world. Like it all fits together so easily. Not every crazy event happens for a—"

"What do you mean, 'you guys'?"

"Nothing. Forget it."

"No, what is 'you guys'? All Iraqis? Maybe all Arabs?"

"No!"

"All Muslims. maybe?"

"Nabil, stop it!" She looks close to tears. "I said I didn't mean it that way. Sometimes I say stupid things, okay? I'm not always as eloquent as you."

The smell of the nail-varnish remover fills the air between us, accosting my nose. How I hate the odour of acetone, which reminds me of that horrible cleaning fluid at the hospital. Did scientists invent this putrid substance solely for the purpose of removing ladies' nail colour? But this is not, I see, why Sam asked for it. She ignores her toenails and begins to work at the tape-marks on her wrists.

A shock wave through my head: the terror of that first moment of Ali pulling out the gun, the shouting, the lack of control, the room spinning. I find my own hands in fists. Next time someone tries something to hurt me or Sam, I will hurt them first. I will be prepared.

"I just mean that I don't always think there's a perfect order to everything," Sam says, rubbing at the gummy grey ring around her wrists. "Sometimes things just don't make sense. People die here every day for no reason."

Maybe I'll be one of them. Maybe there isn't anything at all I can do to prepare. But I don't believe things happen for no reason at all. Right now, maybe I shouldn't be reasoning anyway. I'm so exhausted my eyes are starting to burn.

The fight was fixed, is what I should have said. That's something she might understand. In England, the boys at school were always talking about fights and footie and cricket matches and tennis tournaments – being fixed. Fixed as unfair, without a fighting chance. Like the comments that some of the boys said years later about my fight with Hamed al-Alami. It was "fixed", they said, because my older brother Ziad was much stronger than his older brother, and it would become a blood feud if Hamed didn't let me win. There was no truth to that rumour, but that didn't stop people from believing it.

"…and just because we got to Z, we can't assume we know what X and Y are."

"Sam, you said forget it. So let's just forget it."

"Let's. Let's forget everything," she says. Her eyes twitch, and then she closes them. She shakes her head gently, as if in disagreement with herself. "I'm sorry, Nabil. I'm really sorry."

I should tell her there's no reason to be sorry, but finally, I'm out of words. Sam takes a fresh wad of tissues from the box on Ziad's desk and tips more acetone on to them. She's almost scrubbing now, working to wipe away the evidence of yesterday. But the gluey residue still marks both of us, a cuff at the end of each forearm that I'm keen to erase, like Adeeb did to his tattoo. How much did he know, about Subhi, about Ali? He seemed so honest.

I think I'll leave my marks right where they are, wide grey stains around the rim of each hand, until they start fading away all on their own.

52

Fading

AMAL DASHES OUT to open the front gate. It is one of her only chances to get out of the house, this business of occasionally answering the door, and she rushes to the job at every opportunity.

But when she sees it's someone we don't know, she asks him for his name, and scurries back to the front door where Baba is standing, with me next to him, peering out of the window. From his face, the familiar shape of the jaw, the cut of his moustache and a certain sadness around his eyes, I already know exactly who it is, and I give Amal the okay to let him inside. When she opens the gate, I see the car parked outside: Rizgar's Cherokee jeep, which I haven't seen since the day of Noor's funeral.

His name is Safin Barzani, Amal announces, and he is a relative of Rizgar's. Sam, sitting at the dining table, where only moments ago she was eating the *leben* and *baamya* Mum proudly put out for us, rises at the sound of his name.

"Rizgar?" she asks, a hue of hope on her face.

I fall short of speech, putting my lips together but failing to form the right shapes for English. I turn away from her and look back to the man walking up our path, knowing the answer. *No, Sam. Not Rizgar. Rizgar's relative.* Don't you know it by now?

Didn't you think it when there was no trace of him at the Hamra last night? What are the chances that he's just sick or injured somewhere?

Baba greets the man kindly and I do as well, offering him Baba's armchair, the best in our house, which I know Baba usually gives away when we have an important guest. He takes in the lot of us, and then lingers on Sam.

"This is Miss Samara," I say, introducing her. "Sam this is one of Rizgar's relatives." Her face pulls itself into a trembling smile.

"*Choni chaki*," she says, offering her hand and the Kurdish "how are you" she learned from Rizgar.

He takes her hand, smiles a little at the gesture, and nods without answering.

"Amal," Baba says, "go to the kitchen and make us some tea."

"But Baba, I was going to—"

My father's frown is powerful enough to make the Euphrates run upstream instead of down.

"Come," Mum says, putting her hand around Amal's shoulder. "I'll help you," she says, and then whispers something in her ear.

It's not as if our living room has any sort of real privacy from the kitchen: what's said in one is generally heard in the other. But there is something in Safin's brow that is obvious to everybody, and it would be inappropriate to have a young girl sitting with us, listening to the details.

Safin, I think, as I offer him a seat: one of those names which remind me what a mystery the Kurdish language is to me. His face is out of the same mould as Rizgar's, a similar meatiness, wide and less than a decade away from turning jowly.

"Rizgar's been living with us since he came to Baghdad with

556

Miss Samara," he begins. "Our people are from up north, but we've been here in the city for over thirty years."

"He says Rizgar has been living with them since he came to Baghdad with you. They're relatives from the north."

Sam blinks and then her eyes widen. By now she knows what's coming.

"You can translate for her after," Baba says. "Let the man finish."

"That's not the way we work, Baba," I say flatly, and then return to Safin. "Please, continue. Forgive me for stopping to explain to her."

Baba hates to be contradicted. But Safin seems not to notice, or to care. "I understand. That's your job," he says. "Rizgar told us about you and about Miss Samara."

"He told them all about us," I say.

Sam nods. I see her clenching her hands.

"This morning someone came and asked us to identify him," he offers quietly, as if a softer voice might make it easier. "They found his body in Saydiyeh, on the riverbank." He sucks in a quick breath that he holds for a moment. The sound of it lingers.

Safin continues. "It seems that they took him while he was waiting in the car, drove it to Saydiyeh, shot him there and then kept the car. The Chrysler, I mean. My car."

I turn to Sam, but she is already shivering, like an old person with a tremor. She stares at me with disbelief, though it's what I've believed since this time yesterday, when Rizgar, who would have done anything to save us, to save Sam, did not make an appearance.

"He's dead?"

Safin nods.

Sam puts her hand over her mouth and lets out a muffled cry. Then her hand covers her eyes for a minute and she shakes her head again. "Oh, God. I, I have to, excuse me for a minute." She gets up and rushes down our hall to the bathroom, storming through our house likes she's lived here all her life, nearly slamming the door behind her. I can hear her turn on the tap, trying to make noise so we won't hear her cries.

"*Allah yarhamo*," I say, and my father repeats after me. Safin closes his eyes and moves his head left and down, a sort of acceptance of our condolences. When he opens his eyes they fix on his shoes, a dilapidated pair of brown loafers. "I'm ready to work in his place," he says. "It will help make money so I can send it to his wife and children in Irbil."

"But she's leaving," I say. "She is going to leave the country soon, probably tomorrow, or maybe tonight," I blurt, wishing I could take it back. What if he isn't who he says he is, and I've just given him our entire plan?

"How will you go?" he asks.

I hesitate. "We're not sure yet."

Amal draws up a small table in front of Safin and lays out tea and biscuits on it. Sam returns, her face shiny in that way that faces can be, from either washing or crying or both.

She squints into a column of sunlight pouring in through the window. "I am so sorry," Sam says. "Rizgar was like a big brother to me, like a father. He took care of me."

I translate it the way Sam always wanted me to, in first-person, as if I am standing in her shoes. "*Rizgar kan zayy akh il-kbir illi, takriban zayy abu.*"

He smiles. "*W-inti illo, zayy uhto, ow binto.*" And you were like a sister or a daughter to him.

"I want to help in any way I can," she says. "Can you tell me how I can help?"

"Sam, he says he wants to drive for us now."

She exhales, and in her eyes, I see all the pain and guilt, the list of complications and ramifications of taking Rizgar's cousin with us on a journey in which we might well be targets. And me, I can't get past the small doubt in my head, despite everything about Safin that checks out. What if he's part of the set-up, too? Maybe they just found some Kurdish guy to stand in for a relative, and sent him to gather information? Another man could easily resemble Rizgar.

I encourage Safin to take his tea, and he does, offering blessings to the one who made it.

"Do you have anything of his, his identity card?" I ask. "Did they recover anything?"

Safin looks at me like he wonders why I'm asking. Like he wants to believe it's nothing but caring, but isn't sure. "Nothing from the car. At home, though, in the guest room where he stayed, he had just a few things: his clothes, a small Koran, photographs of his family. There's also a painted tile."

When I translate this for Sam, she brightens for a moment, but falls back into sadness. "The tiles we took on the way down from Tikrit."

"Tiles," I ask. "Like, floor tiles?"

"No, there was a big mural of Saddam along the highway," Sam says, wiping away the tear that just escaped from her eye, stopping it before it could go far. "It was kind of like a huge mosaic, of Saddam in a fedora. These young guys were picking it apart with crowbars and screwdrivers, I don't know what. So we stopped to get some of it. Rizgar got a piece of Saddam's throat. He got me a reddish one that made up part of his mouth. I still have it."

"*You* were looting?"

Sam lips crinkle and immediately I want to take the words back. "Not really *looting*, Nabil. It was, you know, little souvenirs of the regime. Not like taking money or something valuable."

I explain the bit about the tiles to Safin and he nods as if he already knows. I'm probably becoming paranoid: how could I suspect this poor man?

"It's probably safest if you go through the north," he says. "Cars on the desert road to Jordan get atttacked every day. If you go through the north, I'll take you. I know my way very well."

"Sam, he wants to drive us through the north."

Her eyes are puffy from lack of sleep, or from crying. She shrugs. "Is that what you think is best?"

"I don't know." My watch says it's almost 3.30 in the afternoon. "Maybe we should just leave now."

"No, no," Baba says. "If you leave now you will be driving through Tikrit at night. It's not a good idea. Everybody will be suspicious of you. Wait until morning. Wait until you plan."

Safin nods deferentially at Baba. "Your father is right. Driving around Tikrit is not safe. Especially after dark." Especially, we are all thinking – except for Sam, who is oblivious to this conversation – if you are a Kurd.

"Sam, give us a minute to figure this out, OK?"

She nods. Amal moves behind her and runs a hand through Sam's hair. Sam closes her eyes and smiles at Amal's affectionate gesture, encouraging her to carry on. My sister's hands move delicately through the fire-curls.

I turn to Safin. "You're driving the car Rizgar used to drive."

560

"It's one of the best cars you can get," Safin says.

"How well do you know the road?" Baba asks. "Do you know people up there?"

Safin turns out his hands. "Of course. I only came to Baghdad to study engineering, when I was eighteen. I grew up there. All of my family connections are still there."

"Good," Baba says. "Do a favour for me. Write out a map of the route you will take so I'll be able to know where they are going. I'll be worried about them."

"Sure," Safin replies. "I'll bring it tomorrow."

"You should leave as early as possible tomorrow," Baba says. "But it has to be after the curfew."

"No later than 6.15, then?" I search Safin's face. In it, there is a kind of flatness, a look of being beaten down.

"I will come at 6.15," he says, rising slowly.

"You don't want to stay for dinner?" Mum asks, which seems like a stupid question. It's so rare we have a guest these days that I suppose she is acting more on instinct than sense.

"Thank you," says Safin. "But I really must get home to my family."

"Wait!" My mother hurries to the kitchen, and comes back bearing a glass-topped pot of biriani – food she had been making for our dinner. "Take it to your family."

"Oh, thank you, but no—"

"I insist," says Mum. "You must take it. You can bring the pot back tomorrow." And it is true, he must take it, because mourners must always accept gifts of food from their guests, everyone knows that, and in these extraordinary times, when it isn't sensible to go out when it's not urgent, he must appreciate that this is as good as a condolence call.

Safin takes the food with two hands and offers humble words of appreciation, carrying the pot like you would any heavy burden, as Baba and I walk him to the door.

53

Carrying

AMAL IS SITTING at the dining table next to Sam. I take the chair across from her, while Baba sits between us at the head of the table.

Sam's eyes are full of tears, and she shakes silently, as if something inside her is rattling.

Amal puts a comforting hand on her back, and Mum brings a box of tissues to the table and puts them in front of Sam. "Rizgar die, no you fault," Mum says, but that only makes Sam shake more.

Her face is distorted. "I can't believe this is happening," she says, burying her eyes in a tissue.

I want to reach across the table and take her hand, to push my mother and my sister away so I can give her all the comforting she needs. Sam kissing me back. Sam pulling away.

"We don't really know why Rizgar was killed, Sam. There's no way of knowing whether the people who killed him had anything to do with your – with our story." Our story. The least I can do for her now is to share ownership of it, to make it ours, and not just hers. *Our* fault, because whatever anyone says right now, there's no way Sam isn't wondering if it's her fault.

"People are getting killed here all the time, for all sorts of reasons," I add. "Or for no reason at all."

"You know, I think I need some time alone," she says. "Would you mind?"

"Of course not," I say. Sam stands and so I stand too. She turns around and finds my mother there, and Sam moves towards her and gives her a hug. Then Amal joins them, and the three of them hold each other in an embrace, and of course I want to join them, but instead I stand here, waiting, Baba looking at me.

When they finally let go, I see Sam's chest fall, and it's as if she has to work hard to make sure her whole body doesn't fall right along with it. She straightens out her shirt, and looks around at my family. "Thank you. I'm fine. I just need some time." She reaches her hand out to lift a stack of tissues from the box before making her way to Ziad's room.

My family is staring at me in a way that makes me feel like they think something here is my fault. But perhaps it's only worry.

"They're killers, these men," Mum says. "You can't go with her or they'll get you, too."

"They might already know where we live," says Baba. He shakes his head at me. "You should probably leave as soon as possible."

"Well if they know where we live, we're not safe either!" Mum is wringing her hands hard enough to dislocate fingers. "We can go to my relatives in Al-Kut."

"Absolutely not," Baba says. "We're not going anywhere. This isn't a family that runs away from their home."

"I want to leave with Sam!" Amal can't be serious, though

she certainly acts like she is. "I do! I hate it here. I want to go live with Ziad."

"I think you want to go to your room," Baba says.

"All I do is sit in my room!" Amal whines. "I'm tired of it. I'm tired of everything here!"

"Amal, stop," Mum pleads. "Come to the kitchen and we'll make a batch of that date jam you love. We can send some along with Sam."

"I'm tired of making food, too! Is that all a girl is good for now, making food? Doing chores? No school, no going out, just working like a maid?"

"Quiet down," Baba bristles. "Think of our guest. She is suffering because her friend has died and you're making a fuss."

Now Amal is on the verge of tears, too. "It's not fair! How come Nabil gets to do everything and I'm always stuck here?"

"You want to go out and get shot like their driver?"

"Baba!" In my frustration, an image flashes across the screen: me tied up, Baba as my captor. I start to turn my watch over. "Hey, Amal. How about later on you and Sam and I can spend some time together? I'll send out for ice cream and we'll eat it up on the roof. Okay?"

She looks reluctant to admit she likes the idea. "Okay," she mumbles. Her shoulders drop, her head tilts with a roll of resignation. "But I am *not* spending any more time in the kitchen today," she announces, and goes to her room. In America teenage girls rebel by doing drugs or getting pregnant. But this is all Amal has. Refusing to make jam.

I sit back down at the table, and hold my hand out towards the chair where Baba had been sitting. Part of me wants to give him a lesson in dealing with Amal, in the futility of meeting her frustrations with anger and impatience. My parents, like any good parents of a fourteen-year-old girl, have hardly let her go out since before the war began. Amal is a prisoner of war, held hostage by parents whose only way to protect her is to keep her virtually locked up at home.

I nod at the seat and Baba drops his hefty weight into it.

"You know, all of this is hard on Amal, too," I say.

Baba tilts his head back and forth, vaguely acknowledging my argument. "But she shouldn't behave like that. She has to start acting like a grown-up."

"She's already pretty grown up," I say, rubbing my eyes. They ache with exhaustion, and at the same time, I can feel a slow panic behind them: they have seen too much on too little rest.

"Do you trust him?" I ask. Definitions of Baba course through my fingertips: brooding, brilliant, a big bully. Also an excellent judge of character.

"That man, Safin? Of course. He's Rizgar's cousin, isn't he?"

I nod. "Relative."

"Whatever. You said Sam really liked Rizgar. She's obviously very upset. So why wouldn't you trust him?"

"I don't know." *I don't think he would lie.* How stupid I was, believing Mustapha. Maybe I was wrong to believe Saleh, my own cousin. Or maybe Saleh just had no idea. Someone tricked him.

My father lowers his head, forcing me to look him in the eye. "Nabil." He lowers his voice, too. "What happened last night? It wasn't because of the curfew that you didn't come home."

I stare at the table. How much of it to tell? Everything? Nothing?

"It's a long story."

"I'm sure it is. Act like a journalist. Give me the headlines."

"We were held captive by the men who made those documents. It was…pretty awful. Now they want $10,000."

"What, they held you and then let you go, and now they want you to pay the ransom once they gave you your freedom?"

"Well, something like that."

"That's the craziest thing I've ever heard. Usually they go to the captives' relatives to demand the money."

"I know. But in this case, I guess they didn't know who my relatives are. They thought you were some professor. Maybe they're figuring that a big newspaper owned by rich Americans will come up with the money – sort of like protection money so she can continue to work here." I thought of Adeeb. "That's not unheard of, right?"

Baba thinks for a minute. "They sound like amateurs to me."

"Do they?"

"Yeah. They're not going to come and find you. There are seven million people in this city. Thousands of people named al-Amari." He clucks his tongue. "They're just trying to scare you."

I shrug. "That's all there is, Baba. It was after eleven and I had no way to call because the phones still don't work." Only now I can look at him again: "I thought you would figure that's what happened. I didn't mean to make you worry." My tongue swipes the inside of my mouth, trying to wash the lies off my teeth.

Baba knows it's not the real story, or the whole story anyway, but says nothing, and for that I love him and hate him all at once. "You don't trust him?"

"I don't know who I trust anymore."

"Then I don't think you should go with him. If you have a bad feeling about him, go with it." My father, the atheist-scientist, the man who treats the heart as a machine, turned reader of omens and premonitions.

"It's not just that," I say. "I'm sure he's a good man. But going out of the city in that big jeep. Only foreigners and Kurds drive those big jeeps, or people working with the Americans."

Baba's head bounces in agreement. "True." His eyes look a lot like mine, plus thirty years, and yet, they are somehow stronger. "You should take my car. Take my car and go without him."

He shows no signs of doubt or any hint of desire to have his offer refused. "Really, Baba? Are you sure?"

"Of course. You shouldn't go with that jeep, and you shouldn't go on a trip like this with someone you don't know, don't trust one-hundred-percent. Maybe Rizgar was trustworthy," he raises his eyebrows. "Maybe his cousin isn't. You can't be sure. So don't go with him."

I am surprised by Baba's insistence, if only because it means he's putting all his trust in me – to drive his car half-way across Iraq, to get Sam safely out of the country, to bring back his prized Mercedes in one piece.

"But he knows the way, Baba. His people are from there."

"You can figure it out. I already asked him to write out a map, or some notes, right? So there you have it. Finished." With that *khalas*, my father runs his hand across the barrel of his stomach. It seems somewhat smaller than it did a month ago. "People are looking for you, aren't they." He poses it as more of a statement than a question.

I shift, hearing most of all an accusation. "Well, probably, yeah."

"Are they the same people who killed Rizgar?"

"I don't know. Actually, they told me to come back to them

tonight with money, and to come in his old Impala. But if his car's gone, maybe they have nothing to do with it."

Baba studies this fact, blinking. "If the people looking for you are not the same people who killed Rizgar, then they will be looking for three people, right? Including a very foreign-looking lady in the backseat. So if you travel as a couple, you have a better, well, disguise." He smiles at me, perhaps waiting to see how I will react to *couple*. "If it's just you two and she's in *hejab*, you'll just be a young couple."

"We're *not* a couple."

Baba lifts his hand again to speak. "I have an even better idea. You can load up the rack with boxes of junk and blankets. You will just look like refugees going back up north after the war."

"Why would refugees come south to Baghdad during the war? It was worse here than it was there. The traffic went in the other direction. People left Baghdad."

"I don't know! You'll make something up. You're the poet. Think of all those poor Sunnis who Saddam stuck in the north, who started getting chased out by the Kurds as soon as the government collapsed. Some of them are going back up north to their homes now."

"That's the worst thing they could think. The people up north hate those Arabs, Baba. They came barging in and got all kinds of benefits from the government that the local people didn't."

His face hardens. I suspect he dislikes hearing me speaking about Sunnis as they, rather than we. "Oh, I don't know, you can pretend to be from Mosul or something. You'll figure it out." Baba gets up, moaning *Allah* as he does, and motions for me to follow him to the storage room upstairs, on the way to the roof.

He leads and we climb up in silence. I find myself wondering what Sam is doing now. Crying? Sleeping? Writing?

Baba pulls open the door and unleashes the dust trapped inside, sending out musty air that smells a hundred years old. I follow him inside, taking short breaths through my mouth. There are all sorts of things that should be tossed out: tattered furniture, old bedding, mouldy boxes. Baba picks up two blankets. He tugs at an ancient mattress, signalling with his eyebrows, and I drag it to the door.

"Do you really think a family who drives a Mercedes would be sleeping on an old mattress like that?"

A laugh bursts from Baba's mouth, and then he kicks at a plastic set of crates at his feet. "Come on," he says. "Be serious now. It's not exactly the newest or the fanciest Mercedes on the market. I was hoping to buy a new one."

I step deeper into the collection of used and useless things. I put a floor-cushion under my arm and he passes me a crate to take in the other, and I know that every hope my father had is now a *was hoping*. Was hoping to buy a new car, was hoping to send Amal to the best preparatory school for university. Was hoping to make a wedding this year. The *was* lingers there as a statement of the past. Is it a hope that continued for a period of time and might one day resume its activities? Or a hope that has already run its course?

We line up some of our booty in the hallway, and then go back in for more. Baba points out two old suitcases in the far-right corner. While I'm there, I yank open the window, blinking to stop the dirt from assaulting my eyes.

"Don't bother," says Baba. "It'll just fill the room with more dust."

"Don't you think this room needs a little fresh air?"

"Nothing's going to freshen up this junkyard."

While passing Baba one of the suitcases, I spot some refuse from our happy past. A blue-and-white football banner for Birmingham City. I think it was from that game Baba took me to when they won; they usually got slaughtered. I pick it up and wave it with a cheer, sending another sprinkling of dust into the air.

"Goal!" Baba calls.

I turn the banner around and there is the emblem of the Birmingham City Football Club, founded in 1875. The ribbons wrap around two spheres: one a football, the other, the world. My connection between the two, when Baba bought me the banner after I begged him mercilessly during the game, was quite uncomplicated. If you were a great player, you could see the whole world. I decided to apply myself harder on the field, which quickly turned out to be a losing proposition: I was fast but completely unco-ordinated.

"You wish we'd stayed in Birmingham, don't you? With all that nice English you have—"

"No, Baba. I'm glad we came back." I put down the banner and pick up the last suitcase.

He smiles and nods like he's finally, for a moment, extraordinarily proud of me. "A man should know where his home is. If you leave home because it's not easy, you'll wind up without one. Come," he says, lifting up the blankets and a suitcase to take downstairs.

It is a good thing we have neighbours we trust – several of them are related to us. But just in case, Baba moved his car behind the house, driving over the fuzz that hardly passes for grass, to park in such a way that it isn't easy for a passerby to see. Here we have spent the last hour or more placing what should appear to be the contents of one's home, in a haphazard enough way to look authentic. I think Baba is enjoying himself, using rope to weave and tie everything into place. Perhaps it is relaxing for him to use his mind for stitching up something other than flesh and blood.

He steps back, surveying our masterpiece. "That's the most beautiful refugee car I've ever seen," he says, laughing and putting his hand on my head to mess what's left of my hair.

"Let's get in," he says, pulling open the passenger door, leaving the driver's side to me. Inside, he hands me the keys and instructs me to turn on the air conditioning. Even though the windows have been left open a crack, the car is an oven.

Baba runs through all the things I could possibly need to know about his car and I listen as well as I can. In the middle of his lecture, he jabs me in the arm.

"Are you going to fall asleep like that tomorrow and crash my car?"

"Sorry, Baba. I'm so exhausted."

"I can see. So, are you going to tell me what really happened last night?"

And then, with the air conditioning breathing its sweet breeze over my forehead, I spill everything. Not quite *everything*. Not the parts about Sam and me. But the brutal basics of the story, Mustapha and Technical Ali. Being held at gunpoint and tied up, being threatened, being let go. Being told to pay our own ransom.

When I have finished, I sit holding the steering wheel,

moving it slightly as if pretending to drive, like a little boy. My chest heaves with that kind of feeling that comes before you cry, and I feel enormous relief when it washes away. "You go and rest," Baba says, laying his hand gently on my back, "and I'll go and see if I can get Wa'el next door to pick up your ice cream."

54

Laying

PISTACHIO, STRAWBERRY, BANANA-DATE. Some kind of a rainbow mix. These are the flavours Wa'el brought to us, which we promptly put in the icebox and saved until after dinner. I think he chose well. But Sam lifts each of the containers and gives something of a girlish frown. "No chocolate?"

The three of us are sitting in a row on the cushions we lined up against the wall on the roof, with Sam in the middle.

"What is it with foreigners and chocolate?" I ask. I pass Sam the pistachio, which I think is one of the best they make. "You don't like this one? It's very healthy. Look at all the nuts."

She takes it and lifts a spoonful into her bowl. "Yes, I'm sure all the green food-colouring is full of nutrients." Amal looks at her like she doesn't get it. Sam takes some and, probably realizing that she may have appeared to be impolite, offers up a sound of enjoyment. "It's good."

Amal is mixing all of the flavours together in her bowl, which is a surefire way not to be able to truly enjoy any of them. She is clearly more interested in Sam than the ice cream. "Chocolate isn't such a favourite here," I explain. "It's not so common to find it, even. But the banana-date is good! Did you try it? Made from the best Iraqi dates." She nods and takes a spoonful of it. Maybe our tastes are just different, like our mentalities. Our mouths start out the same but then get introduced to flavours predominant in our own corners of the world, eating our own spices and delicacies, shaping the words of our own languages, until we can never agree on what's truly best. Not in our governments, not on our tongues.

"When you come to America someday, I'll take you out for rocky road," Sam declares. "That's the best."

"Rocky road," Amal repeats. "The best," she says, parroting Sam.

"Yeah, it's great," Sam says. "It's this super-chocolatey mess with chunks of real chocolate and nuts. Oh, and marshmallows. It's fabulous."

Amal smiles. "This is favourite American ice cream?"

Sam gently swirls Amal's silky ponytail. "It's *this* American's favourite ice cream!"

"Tell more things about America," Amal implores.

"First eat your ice cream," I say, pointing out that it's melting. If Amal's not going to eat it, I'd rather give it to Mum and Baba. They professed not to want any, which I think was a way of letting us enjoy ourselves on our own up on the roof. Before, this was a popular way for Baghdadis to spend a hot summer evening, when the houses refuse to cool down, even after dark. Now, many people are afraid to spend time up on the roof, not knowing what might be flying through the air, or who might try to shoot at you. But as far as I see it, and I think Baba tends to agree, it makes no difference. If you are so unfortunate as to have a bullet with your name on it, it's going to get you even if you're in your own living room.

"Why's it called rocky road?" I ask.

Sam shrugs. "Never thought about it. But I guess the chocolate ice cream is the road, and all the lumpy things are like the rocks in it."

"That's a saying, right? As in, 'It'll definitely be a rocky road towards Iraq's reconstruction.'"

Sam looks bemused, her lips like the wavy hieroglyphic for water.

"I heard you say it once on the phone. I think you were being interviewed by a radio station in America."

"Oh." She smiles at me in a way that makes me think she must find me terribly strange, committing things to memory the way I do. I cannot help it. Even when I'm not air-typing, the keyboard in my mind often keeps going, like one of those eerie player-pianos I've seen in old films. The keys rise and fall all on their own.

"How the life in America?" Amal pleads.

"What's life like?" Sam smiles, looking uncertain how to answer. "It depends on where you live. Some beautiful areas, some terrible areas – sort of like Iraq. It's a huge country."

Amal's face portends a thousand more questions. "America is very free, yes? You do, you say…whatever you like."

"Something like that, but you still have to follow the law and pay your taxes."

"Are you happy America coming to Iraq?"

"She means are you—"

"I know," Sam sighs. "It's a tough question. I don't know. It wasn't my idea to come here, but now that we're here, I hope Iraq will be better off. I mean, you have to believe that, or…" Sam stops mid-sentence and stares towards the south, where there's a dark smoke column rising against the sky, black-on-blue.

576

"Right now, it's not looking so good, is it?"

Amal shakes her head no, it isn't.

"But I bet you're glad Saddam is gone, no?"

Amal pushes out her lower lip. "Nabil says he was too bad. But me, Amal? My life was not bad before. I went to school, saw my friends, go shopping with Mum, no problem. Now, everything problem."

Sam smiles like something hurts.

"I'm going to take the rest down to Mum before it melts," I tell them, collecting the ice cream containers.

"I thought you said they didn't want any," Sam says.

"An Iraqi trying to be a good hostess says a lot of things she doesn't mean."

Back on the roof again, I find Sam sitting behind Amal, plaiting her hair. Amal looks like she is in heaven. Nirvana, even.

I sit next to Sam. "Trading beauty secrets?"

"I wish I were as beautiful as this one," Sam says, and I see Amal's smile spread fast and wide. This is what she probably dreams of – having a big sister, instead of big brothers who are never around.

Sam finishes her work and presents the end to Amal. "Grab it," Sam says. "You need to tie it with something, or it will fall apart."

Amal pats the back of her head with her free hand, obviously impressed by the feel of the intricate pattern Sam has woven. "Sam made a Frenchy braid, Nabil!"

"I see. Beautiful."

Amal jumps up to get an elastic-band. "We'll meet you downstairs," I call after her. But I don't think she heard me, and I don't think she wants to.

Sam looks enchanted. "She's a darling."

"I know. Very smart, too, but you probably couldn't tell from the way she acted tonight."

"No, I could tell," says Sam, leaning her back up against the wall.

"You hardly ate the ice cream."

"It was good," she says unconvincingly. "Maybe I wasn't in the mood."

"You liked it better last time, when we went to Al-Faqma. Wa'el said it was closed so he went to Al-Ballout."

The lines between Sam's eyes emerge like fresh stitches. I want to eat my words. I put my hand on her forearm, near the elbow.

"Rizgar liked Al-Ballout."

"I know," I say.

"I still can't believe it. I keep thinking it must be a mistake."

"I know."

"He's going to come back any moment and just tell me he had to wait on some crazy line for gasoline, or went on a long drive to buy cigarettes where they're cheaper." Sam lets her eyes close, to stop the need to say more. And then suddenly, unexpectedly, she leans her head on my shoulder.

I am the happiest man in the world at this minute. It sounds terrible to say, because it ignores everyone's pain and loss, hers and mine and Rizgar's family's, but that's just what I feel. Stop everything, stay here. My hand in her hair the way I had dreamed, its thickness a deep, dense forest, an easy place to get lost.

She pulls away and sits up. "Are you sure we can't go to visit his family here in the morning before we leave? At least to pay a condolence call."

I sit forwards, too. I cannot concentrate on such radically different emotions at the same time. For Sam, they appear to be all tied up, one in the other.

"I don't think so, Sam. Maybe we could try to find his family on our way through the north."

"Really?" Sam looks hopeful, then washed over by a wave of fear. What would happen, I wonder, if word hadn't got to Rizgar's family yet. If we were the ones to have to tell them?

"Is that what you want? You want to see his family, even if it means taking another day to get to the border?"

Sam touches her own hair now, stretching out a coil. Were her hair straight, it seems, it would be twice as long. Many things about Sam are only half-visible.

"I guess I should just get out. But Rizgar—" she shakes her head and sniffles. "I don't even know what's right anymore."

We sit for a while without speaking, listening to the crickets and to the last teenagers playing football down the street.

Amal returns, as I expected she would, showing off the bow she found for the end of the plait. Sam ties it on for her. "Gorgeous," says Sam. "You're a movie star." With this, Amal beams like a shy girl being romanced.

"Amal, can you leave us here to talk for a while?"

She tuts, her face predictably heartbroken. "I thought—"

"We need to talk about our trip tomorrow. Maybe you can make sure Sam's bed is made up nicely?" I already know it is, but better to give her a job to do, something that makes her feel connected to our guest.

Amal takes her leave, giving Sam a peck on her cheek to say thank you for doing her hair. Sam seems genuinely charmed.

When Amal disappears, I try to explain. "She doesn't know, and I think Mum doesn't. But Baba does."

"Know what?"

"About what happened to us – with Mustapha and Ali and all."

"Oh," Sam says, as if I've just wrecked her efforts to expunge the events of yesterday from her mind. "Okay."

"He doesn't want us to go with Safin, and I agreed. We'll go alone."

Sam tenses, as if waiting for an elaborate defence. "That's the sort of decision I would want to weigh in on."

I stare out towards the palm trees, their towering trunks swaying in the hot evening breeze. I've had fantasies recently about marrying Sam. I daydreamed we would have a girl and name her Lena. It's perfect. I know they have that name in the West. In Arabic it means small palm tree. She'd be like her mother, named after a tree.

"Please trust me with this, Sam. We discussed it round and round and we decided it was the absolute safest way to go. We don't think it's safe to go with him."

"The jeep?"

"That's only skirting the surface."

Sam exhales a laugh through her stuffy nose. "Skimming the surface."

"What?"

"You skim the surface. Or scratch it. You skirt an issue."

If I spent my life with Sam, she would probably drive me crazy.

She is keen to make it up to me. "I do trust you. I do. If you say it's safer, I trust you."

"Good."

"What about the story? Miles says they're definitely running it tomorrow, remember?"

The possibilities spin through my mind. What if Ali reads the story and we're still in reach? What happens when I don't show up to give him the money?

"Is it going to mention Ali? Or Akram?"

"I don't even know, I haven't had a chance to read the thing yet."

"Why can't you tell Miles that the story should be published only when you're out of Iraq?"

"Miles says he doesn't have any choice. They're afraid of how it will look later if it seems that we had the information and sat on it. It's all mixed up with legal stuff, you know, the damage to Jackson's reputation. But mostly, it's about money. Every day the paper doesn't settle this is a day they've got expensive lawyers on retainer. They're incurring more and more legal fees." She breathes in deeply, like it's her first fresh lungful of air all evening. "It's essentially a financial decision, not a journalistic one."

We know where you live. Ali said so. But does he? There's no clear indication that the others – the package, the thugs of the so-called Neighbourhood Resistance Committee – have any connection to Ali. If they do, we're all dead. And the alternative? Pick up the whole family and flee? Baba would never hear of it.

While I'm contemplating these options, like tree diagrams planting deeper and deeper roots in my head, we both grow quiet. The air is damp with humidity, carrying its own language in the form of things that hover: insects, dust, galaxies. "Look at the stars," I say, gazing up at the night sky.

"Wow," she sighs, her head leaning against the wall. "It's

amazing you can see so many stars in such a big city. In Paris or New York, you'd never see a sky like this."

"Really?"

"Really."

"Maybe because in those cities everyone has their lights on at night."

Sam turns to me. "You're right. It's an electricity thing."

I can't help it, my lips meeting hers, my hand back in her fiery hair, my other holding the silky curve where her neck meets her jaw. I hear the shock in her chest, almost like a contraction in her stomach that could be excitement or repulsion and how can I know which? And she kisses me back, and then she freezes, and in the stillness of her mouth I know that everything is not all right, and that there's nothing to do but stop.

I still have her head in my hands, wanting to hold it with care, and when I pull my face away from hers, I can see her eyes are again full of tears. She lets me hold her as she cries soundlessly, and then she is done. I try to wipe her face with my sleeve, but she squirms for me to stop.

"Nabil, we can't do this."

I don't answer.

"We can't. This has to stop."

"Because of Jonah?"

"Jonah? He has nothing to do with this."

"Because I'm Muslim and you're Jewish?"

"Nabil." She shuts her eyes tight, as if she might cry again, or maybe because she wants me to go away. "We just – we can't. We can't be together. I can't be your lover."

"Your lover? You think I just want to *use* you like that?" I feel tears, oh I can hardly believe it, my own real tears, and I blink them back.

I wait a moment, until I know I can speak without my voice breaking. "Sam, I would spend my life with you if you would let me."

She doesn't respond. I can feel how much she wants to lean on my shoulder again, to let me hold her. She shakes her head, looking towards the date palms. "Nabil, I think we work together incredibly well, professionally, and I, I've learned so much from you."

I watch her and feel myself growing angry: a little at her and a little more at myself. I want to make her shut up, to stop her from explaining why she doesn't want me.

"I do care about you. But you know it can't work. It can't work because…" She stops herself and sniffles into the edge of her shirt, and pushes the wetness of her face into the hair beyond her cheekbones. "It just can't work. We're too different. And you know, this is really, what we have is a professional relationship that started to become an important friendship as well. I'm sorry if I made you think I wanted more than that. In another world, I would have loved…look, why do this? I'm leaving Baghdad tomorrow, right? I don't even know when I'm coming back. If I'm coming back. I'm leaving, Nabil. You don't want to be with someone who's leaving." She wraps her hand around my hand and kisses me softly in the crook of my cheekbone, just beyond the corner of my left eye. And then she stands to leave, bending over to pick up the empty ice cream containers.

55

Bending

I PACK MY overnight bag. I lay down and try to sleep, but my eyes stay wide open, sore but alert. I imagine Sam and myself travelling together in Istanbul, taking pictures by the famous mosques, the royal-blue waters of the Bosphorus stretching out behind us, just like in the photograph of my parents on their honeymoon. And then I kiss her and she falls into me, a warm wrap around my chest.

But I'm not going to Turkey with her. I feel the invisible, internal tears starting to shake me again, that shuddering in my chest. I'm living on my own fault-line, weathering small tremors that might one day burst wide open, split the ground beneath my feet, swallow me whole.

It's my mother's tap on my door – I know it from the weight of her fingertips, thicker and sturdier than Amal's. She opens the door. There is a saffron light coming into my room at an angle that tells me it's very early. "Nabil, it's 5.30," Mum calls softly. "You said you wanted me to wake you now."

I sit up. "Let me go and wake Sam." My throat is like a plant on the terrace that hasn't had a watering for weeks, my voice hoarse.

"She's already up. She has been arranging her things and she went to have a shower. I'll put out some breakfast for you."

"I don't know if we have time."

My mother glares at me from the doorway. She appears to have grown new lines beneath her eyes in the past few weeks, and the ones leading from the middle of her lip to her nostrils have cut themselves deeper into her skin.

I squint at my watch and reach for my glasses. "You're right. There's time."

I have to lean towards the edge of the bed to gather enough energy to stand on my feet. Faced with falling, I will rise. My mother points to the glass of water she left on my desk. When its contents disappear into my body, I feel a little closer to being able to speak and to get dressed.

I hold my hand up to knock on the door that was once Ziad's. How is it that we can feel nostalgia even for the parts of our childhood we hated most? He was my older brother, but in my young adolescent years, I saw Ziad as more of a warlord – a dictator to call my own. I was far more frightened of him than I ever was of Saddam. Among other things, Ziad wanted me to knock on his door and receive permission before entering. He, on the other hand, could strut into my room at any time he wanted and push me around.

I tap lightly on the door and hear Sam's voice call out quietly. I nudge the door. "Sam?"

"Come in," she says. She's sitting on the edge of Ziad's bed. Her body is lost in the black *jupeh* Mum lent her. Around her neck is the white scarf, hanging over her chest instead of covering her hair. With the white on black, she looks something like a judge.

I sit down next to her, a respectable distance away. "Did you sleep?"

"A little. Probably five hours, but not much more. You?"

"Same."

I have the urge to put my hand into Sam's damp curls, not wet but just a bit moist from the shower, to touch them just once more. Instead, I reach into my pocket to take out the box I have been holding on to for three days now, ever since I picked out a gift for her from the souvenir seller in the lobby of the Hamra Hotel. I hold it out to her.

Sam's face lights up and she opens the box quickly. She pulls the watch out, and from the look on her face, I can see she almost wants to giggle, but the urge to do so is overwhelmed by the need to be gracious. But now, in her eyes, I see a shimmer of it – a sense of delight.

"Oh…my goodness." She holds up the watch to the light. She turns it over, looking for what, I wonder. A designer label?

She turns it back, and examines the face. "It's beautiful. Is that…is that supposed to be Babylon?"

"Yes. It was this one, or the one with a picture of Saddam on it. But I wasn't sure if you were serious about wanting one like that."

She smiles, her mouth open enough for me to see the pink of her tongue. "No! I mean, those are funny, for a joke, but this is just adorable. I mean, it's beautiful."

I look at her put the watch on her left wrist and carefully fasten the buckle. It perfectly encircles the flesh and bone that is her hand, once bound and now free. Free to wave goodbye to me in a day or two. Had we gone to Babylon, she'd have been so dazzled, she would have fallen in love with everything here – including me.

She turns her wrist to look again at the watch, already set to the right time. Nearly a quarter to six. Not fully light yet, and the best time to leave.

"Does it really still look like that?" she asks. "Or is that some kind of idealized version?"

I stand, holding out my hand to pull her up off Ziad's low-lying bed. "You'll have to come back some time and find out."

Sam and I force ourselves to eat the eggs and *gemar* cream and *samoun* Mum laid out for us, more than either of us would want. Amal helps Sam pin her headscarf so that she looks authentic. In the past, whenever Sam wanted to look local, she would just wrap the scarf lightly and let it slip backwards on her head, which didn't achieve much. But Amal picked out her favourite *dambab*, a scarf pin that I think was Grandma Zahra's, and placed it perfectly along the right side of Sam's face. Now that she is done, Sam almost looks like she could pass unnoticed.

Then we wait, ready to go, feeling impatient. Safin isn't on time. We discuss the possibility of leaving now, leaving it to Baba to explain to Safin, and then decide against it. We hover near the window, watching out for the jeep.

Mum sighs. "You could have gone to the Imam Kadhum shrine for prayers by now."

"Stop that," Baba orders. He then looks at her sympathetically, like he wishes he hadn't answered by trying to shut her up so quickly. He puts his hand on her back. "*Ayouni,*" he says more softly. "They'll leave soon."

"Maybe you'll go to the shrines in Samarra," Mum says. "She'll like that. You can go to the al-Askari Shrine and then take her to the Malwiya Minaret. Yes!" She talks excitedly, tapping my shoulder. "You must!"

"Zeinab, this isn't a honeymoon trip!" When Baba says that, I feel my heart sink, and I avoid Amal's stare.

"What's your Mom saying?"

I turn to Sam, who is beginning to look like a fundamentalist's wife, and find myself unable to hold in a laugh.

"She says I should give you a tour of Samarra."

Sam smiles at Mum. "I certainly would have loved that."

I turn back to the window. "So let's do it. A quick stop for you to take pictures," I say, without turning around to look at her. "It's kind of a religious thing. People make pilgrimages there."

"Tell her that if you pay a visit to the Hidden Imam, he will protect you," Mum says.

Baba exhales loudly, losing patience with Mum's otherworldly beliefs, and goes to check on the car again.

"Mum thinks visiting there can protect us."

"Oh really?" Sam tucks an invisible hair into the scarf; it's clear the snugness of it makes her uncomfortable. "Why?"

"I'll tell you on the way," I say. I look at Sam, so much more conservatively dressed than my mother or Amal, sitting in their sleeveless housedresses, and am struck by the oddness of it all. Me escaping from my own city with a red-headed American girl.

56

Escaping

When Safin pulls up outside our house close to 6.45, he immediately begins to apologize for arriving later than he should have done. The jeep looks more conspicuous than ever, gleaming in the early morning sun. He must have had it washed for the trip.

Baba invites him inside, treating him with a certain warmth – with arm around the back, words of welcome in his mouth.

"Your family has been so helpful to my son and Miss Samara. Rizgar worked so hard to protect them," Baba says.

Safin looks worried, as if he knows bad news is coming. He swallows and shifts his glance from my father to me.

Baba smiles. "But this is the situation. Some things you can't control." My father sighs, and I feel as if I am breathing in what he's exhaled, taking in some of his confidence. "Safin, brother, they must go without you. You know it will be safer for them. And you."

Safin's cheeks elongate with surprise. "Will it?"

"Well, of course. We really don't know *who* killed Rizgar, *Allah yarhamo*. Maybe these awful people Nabil and Miss Samara got mixed up with are still looking for three people: an Arab man and a foreign lady – with their Kurdish driver."

Safin's head lolls to one side, a motion that acknowledges Baba has a point. He nods without looking at us.

"Also, that car you're driving," Baba says. "It is a car only foreigners or VIPs would have."

Safin's eyes dip with some hint of agreement. "I see," he says. "But what happens when they get to Kurdistan?"

"*Habib*," my father smiles, putting his arm on Safin's, "that's where you can help them." Perhaps you could write them a letter saying they are under the special protection of some tribe which nobody will want to have to contend with later. Maybe your tribe?"

"Baba," I look at my watch. "It's late." Yesterday he had suggested we leave as soon as the curfew lifts, at 6.00 a.m. In that case, we should have left three-quarters of an hour ago.

Baba glares at me. In our eyes a whole argument erupts without a word being spoken.

This is holding us up, Baba.

Don't question me on this, Nabil.

You said you didn't trust him.

I said wait.

"Nabil?" I can hear a nervous vibration in Sam's voice. "What's going on?"

"My father wants Safin to write us a letter to protect us when we drive up north."

Sam's arms are crossed. "Uh-huh. Okay."

"Please," Baba says, gesturing for Safin to follow him. My father goes to the old wooden chest and slides open a drawer in which I know he keeps better paper for formal letters, as well as small gifts in case of a last-minute occasion.

He comes to the table with a fine sheet of paper, and offers a seat to Safin. Baba sighs and makes a writing motion with an almost pleading look in his eyes. Safin nods, sits down, and reaches inside his jacket pocket, retrieving a ball-point pen.

"I will mention the Barzani family and the Dizayee family," he says. "That should help."

Baba nods. "I'm sure. I'm sure it will." Baba stands over him and watches, while we wait at the other end of the table. I feel slightly uncomfortable with this whole scenario, this gentle yet explicit forcing of Safin to do what we ask. To write a letter on our behalf, like a couple of fugitives trying to gain entry to some ancient kingdom.

To produce for us a largely false document.

"So...which tribe is your family from?"

Safin answers my question with a glare.

"Just in case we get asked by someone."

"You don't need to mention me directly. That won't do you any good," Safin says, "But since you ask, Barzani. And the Dizayee are also our friends – almost as good as brothers."

When Safin is finished with the letter, he puts a second sheet of paper behind it, folds it in three and hands it to Baba. Realizing his mistake, Safin smiles and hands the letter to me.

"Thank you," I say. "I am so sorry that we couldn't travel together, but I do hope we will have a chance to meet again, or to work together some other time."

"Indeed," Baba says. "You must come back to visit us."

"Of course," he says, blinking fast, as though still trying to absorb whether we are genuine, whether he had any choice but to give in to our modified plans.

Sam lifts a finger as if to excuse her interruption. "Uh, did... did you get the map he made?"

"The map!" I exclaim. Baba's eyes close. In all our worrying about how we would break the news to Safin, we completely forgot.

Safin excuses himself and runs out to his car.

Mum has stuffed enough food for three days into shopping bags, unnecessary since I know Sam will want to eat in restaurants, and she places them by the door. "Tell her to remember all the food's here," Mum says. "Don't forget."

"I wouldn't dream of it."

Safin rushes back inside and spreads a hand-drawn map on the table, plus a list of directions. "It's very easy," he says. "You take the highway past Al-Kadhumiya all the way north. When it breaks off to the west, you drive on until you get to Samarra. It should be quiet there, so make a stop there if you need a bathroom or water or anything."

"We have enough provisions to last us a week," I say. I wink at Mum, who smiles back.

"Fine. So then you continue on to Tikrit – don't stop there – and then to Al Baygi, and after that you want to turn right towards Kirkuk to avoid Mosul, because it's very dangerous there. And so maybe it's a bit longer, but I say go to Kirkuk, then Irbil, and stay in Irbil overnight if you like, where it's safe, and where my family is."

"He says we should stay overnight in Irbil. You said you liked it there, right?"

"Yeah," Sam brightens. "Irbil's great. There are some good hotels there, too."

"Okay," says Safin, pulling the conversation back to Arabic. "From there you can drive to Dahuk, and that's also a very safe place to stay overnight, if necessary. And then from there it's only another hour or so to Zakho, where the border crossing is."

I wonder if Baba is thinking what I'm thinking. Mosul is dangerous to a Kurd, but not for an Arab. The itinerary he has outlined could add a whole extra day to our trip.

More time to be with Sam. More time for someone to catch up with us.

Sam pulls up the too-long sleeve of the *jupeh* to glance at her new watch. "Do you know it's nearly seven now?"

"Yes," I say. "We really should—"

"I will leave you, then," Safin says, moving away from the table and glancing from face to face.

"Wait," Sam says. She reaches into her bag and pulls out an envelope. She takes it in two hands and presents it to Safin, a curtain of sincerity pulled across her pale face. "Please take this."

"What?" He looks at me and Baba. "What's this?"

"She wants you to have it," I say.

"It's what I would have paid you for the trip up north, plus something extra that I would like you to give to Rizgar's family."

"I can't accept it," Safin tells me. "I can't be paid for work I didn't do."

Sam gazes at Safin like she thinks he's a hero. Perhaps he is, but I feel that this is a predictable response – the way any man of dignity would answer without thinking.

"Please," she says. "Give it to his family then. And could you write down their address for us, too? Or telephone number, or some other way we can contact them?"

Safin scribbles out the information on one of the remaining sheets. He hands it to Sam, and she takes it and folds it, then holds it close to her heart. "Please," she says, her eyes glossy again.

"Please tell them how sorry I am – how sad I am about Rizgar. He was one of the most wonderful people I ever worked with."

Safin nods as I translate this for him, and he offers a response in kind.

"He says Rizgar said the same about you. He said 'the most'. Not one of the most."

Sam smiles a sad smile, and looks at Safin with such warmth in her eyes that I almost think she will embrace him but of course she realizes this would be inappropriate, so she wraps her arms around herself instead.

As soon as Safin is gone, Baba and I open the letter to read it. It makes specific reference to Sam being an American journalist who is travelling through Kurdistan in expectation of writing articles in support of the cause of an independent Kurdish homeland in Iraq. The letter asks the reader to facilitate Sam's passage so as to ease the process of decentralized power, leading to permanent Kurdish national and political rights.

When he's done skimming, Baba's eyes bulge.

"You asked him to write the letter," I say.

"I didn't know he'd write a letter like that."

"Is there a problem?" Sam asks. She always seems to know when something is wrong.

"It's fine," I say. "We should go."

"Wait," Sam says. "The letter's in Arabic?"

"Of course," I say.

"Why of course? The letter's written from one Kurd to another, intended for Kurdish officials in Kurdistan. Why wouldn't he write it in Kurdish?"

Baba shrugs. "There are many different Kurdish," he says in his broken English. "Maybe he speak one and the other man speak the another. Arabic is the language that unites all Iraqis," says my didactic father. "It does not matter if you are Arab, Kurdish, Sunni, Shi'ite, Christian or Jew."

Sam smiles at him widely. He smiles back and holds out his hand for her to shake. When she puts her hand in it, he pulls her closer and gives her small kisses on each cheek, the way you would a relative. "You are like a daughter now," he says. "So you must take good care of our Nabil."

Sam laughs out loud. "He usually insists on taking care of me."

Mum approaches and treats her like someone we've known for a hundred years, putting her lips on Sam's cheeks so many times that I think she has spent more time kissing Sam than I have. And then it is Amal's turn. She approaches Sam and quickly throws her arms around her. In her hand is a gift the size of a book. When they let go of each other, Amal presents it to Sam, and suddenly I recognize it: a box of fancy stationery that Ziad gave Amal, part of a big package of presents he sent last Ramadan. It was delivered by a Baghdadi friend of his also living in France, who'd come back to visit.

Sam opens it up and holds up a page trimmed in pretty blue flowers that tell of a simpler life elsewhere, where people binge on rich food and wine all day and then *tsk* about how terrible it is in places like this. "It's beautiful," Sam nearly sings. "Thank you."

"So you will write me from America. You will tell me about all the things there and about your life and the movie stars."

"Amal." Mum's face admonishes her not to pressure Sam to write.

They walk us to the car and Sam gets in. I turn to her and

notice she looks like a real *bint hallal*, innocent and proper as a religious teenager still under her father's roof.

"Now you look like a Samira," I say.

Sam smirks at herself in the rearview mirror. "Good. You can call me that."

I put the car in gear and inch forwards. Amal stands on the path while Baba pulls open the metal gate for us. Mum hurries up to my window and pokes her head inside. She whispers a prayer in my ear, and then part of a sura from the Koran, I think from *Al-Nisa*: the part that pertains to women. "God bids you to deliver all that you have been entrusted with to those who are entitled to receive it." My translation: get Sam home safely to the people who love her. Even if now, we love her too.

"*Fi m'Allah,*" Mum says, kissing my cheek in little pecks. "*Ayouni! Fi m'Allah.* Bye-bye, Sam," Mum calls in funny staccato syllables, as if even these simple words force her to stretch facial muscles she has not exercised in a long time. We drive out and pass the three of them, each smiling. When I glance at them again in the rearview mirror, the smile is gone from my father's face and my mother is waving eagerly, the palm of her hand stained bright by the orange-red henna from Friday's visit to the mosque. The image of that holy sunburst in her hand is still in front of me as we start rolling down the street.

57

Rolling

BY THE TIME we're really on the road, it's much later than we had planned last night, when Baba and I worked out the final details.

"Your parents are so sweet," Sam says as we are passing by Mustansiriyah. Thoughts of Subhi, of the eager young Shi'ites doing the Hawza's bidding, of Ibrahim something-or-other over at the Showja Market. All of that seems a whole epoch ago, before all of the trouble started. Before Akram and Mustapha and Ali, back when the most threatening people in Baghdad were faceless looters and criminals and over-eager American soldiers. Back when all I had to worry about was getting the words right. Interpreting – fixing, maybe – but not protecting. Certainly not escaping.

"Your sister, especially. She has such grace for a young girl. I think she gets it from your Mom." She pauses. "Your Dad's a total charmer, too." Sam opens the mirror on the visor in front of her and looks at her face, drawn into a purposeful and serious pose. "You'd probably pass me on the street and think I was Iraqi, wouldn't you?"

I grin. "Probably." I wonder if she has any idea how worried my parents are. How, underneath all their impeccable hospitality, they have probably come to resent her. If she had never walked into my father's hospital, into Noor's mourning house, into all our lives, I would be safe at home with them now, waiting to go back to my quiet little teaching job.

"They like you very much," I say, and after all, it's true. Amal and Mum were obviously quite enamoured with Sam. But in my father's face, I saw a duty to be kind, a sense of being impressed and sceptical at the same time. I wonder, would he have had this ambivalence before he knew she was Jewish? Or half-Jewish, or Jewish by virtue of her father, which according to Sam isn't actually Jewish? But wasn't Baba a bit cool towards Sam and her friends long before he knew anything about them, that first day, in the cardiology unit?

"What was that thing she kept saying?"

Damn. Three humvees just turned onto the road ahead, and everyone has suddenly slowed down. "What?"

"That thing, that word your mom kept saying as she was saying goodbye to you. Something with 'Allah' in it."

"Allah? Oh. *Fi m'Allah*. It's an abbreviation we use. What you're really saying is *fi iman Allah*."

"And...what's that?"

"With faith in God. It's like saying, with faith in God, we will see each other again."

"Hmm." Sam touches her hand to her scarf with an awkwardness, as though this were the moment when she'd like to feel the thickness of her hair, and now cannot. "That's lovely," she says.

The northern neighbourhoods grow more similar by the mile, spreading out like stones on a riverbed, grey-white and endless. The stretches of drab, sand-coloured settlement are separated by litter-filled roads and ageing cars.

My father's car doesn't look like it is from here. If we get stopped I will have to have a good story ready. If it's a Shi'ite, I'll tell him about the man we met in Sadr City. What was his name? It seems ages ago now. Hamid. No, Hatem. If it's a Sunni, well then, can't I just be myself? My father's son? And why do I always need to work harder to pass as a Shi'ite anyway? Is it my size, physically bigger, or my skin, currently tan but hardly dark? Something about the way you carry yourself. That's what one of my friends at university said.

"You're quiet."

"Just thinking," I say. "I want to concentrate on the road to make sure I don't take the one towards Baquba by mistake."

"Right," Sam replies, her attention trailing off to some horrible apartment blocks on her side of the road. They look as if the highway exhaust of the last half-century has never once been wiped away.

"Some of them might be nice inside," I offer. "It's usually the outside that looks worse."

"Um-hmm."

We're hardly out of Baghdad and already there's a checkpoint ahead with four young Sunnis manning it. They have propped a silver pole across two old oil drums. Sam's eyes search the horizon, then me.

"I think you should put the scarf on even more."

"More?"

I take the small lock that is jutting out from under the cloth around her left temple and push it into the scarf. Moments later I'm embarrassed for having touched her again. But she only smiles at me with her lips and eyes closed, and then looks back at the road. Her skin seems warmer than it should, given that we're sitting in an air-conditioned car.

"If they ask, don't say anything. We'll pretend you're a mute."

"Fine."

We are one car away and my mind is racing. What will I say if they ask us where we're going?

The man at the window holds a Kalashnikov in both hands. I roll down the window and the smell of his oil-drum checkpoint comes in. He has probably been out here since last night.

"Where are you going?" he asks.

"Samarra." I say it as if I had intended to say it all along. Although, for more reasons than one, it is the most logical answer.

"There's been a lot of looting around this neighbourhood. And also, a lot of people giving tips to the Americans. Anyone who does either of these things will be killed on the spot."

"We're going to see relatives."

"Which family?" The man asking is young, but has teeth like an old man, yellowish brown, with the gums retreating.

"Duleimy."

"Which branch?"

"If you wish to know," I say, stalling for time and speaking in the syncopated, proud tones I remember hearing the upper-class *shiyukh* west of Baghdad use. "I'm from the family of Sheikh Faddel of Fallujah. We're a rather large and established family, as I'm sure you know."

The man repositions his grip on his gun and says nothing.

"I'm quite sure that your people are on very good terms with mine, and neither of them would want to have any problems in the future, which sometimes has been happening when people are held up at checkpoints."

He looks over at Sam, who stares out straight ahead. The other two gunmen are staring at her. She runs her hand over her belly, which suddenly seems plump and rounded, the way a pregnant woman's would be. She winces and shifts.

"Fine sir, please." He waves at the others and they lift the barrier. "May you and your family have a safe trip, God-willing."

We drive away and when they are well out of sight, Sam's giggle spills into something like a cackle.

"What is *that*? How did—"

"It's just a little pillow," she laughs, and reaches into her neck-to-floor *jupeh* to take it out. "Your sister gave it to me."

"She did?"

"Yeah. She's one smart cookie, that Amal." She says my sister's name like the word for labourer, *amil*, rather than hope, which is what Amal's name means. "Maybe in Baghdad I should have gone around like that all the time," she says. "Think of all the things we could get away with. We could just pretend we're perpetually on our way to a doctor's appointment."

With her long dress and her hair covered up, not only does she look like an entirely different woman, she looks like a woman who really could be married to me.

"Well, put it back in there!" I grab the pillow from the space between the seats and throw it into her lap. "Who knows if we'll get stopped again."

She puts the pillow back under her robe and her giggling starts again, and then it subsides and we are both quiet. The traffic keeps moving, pulling us from the city like liquid out of a narrow-necked bottle, and the further away we are from the northern slums, the more relaxed I feel. The worst is behind us. All I have to do is get Sam safely to Dohuk, where she can get a taxi to the border with Turkey. Or maybe I will take her to the border myself, if that's possible, and then everything will be fine.

Except that then Sam will be gone.

"Actually, we pronounce it 'Amal'."

"What?"

"My sister's name. You pronounce it *ah-MAHL*. You want me to help you with your pronunciation in Arabic, right?"

"Definitely," she says, looking at me with a mysterious face which I think says, *where did that come from?* "I wish you would teach me more," she says. "What does Amal mean?"

"It means hope."

"Hope? That's beautiful."

"It can also be a verb. *Ani at'amal inno y-kun salaam.* I hope that there will be peace."

"*Ani*…hold on, hold on. Too fast. One word at a time."

"Maybe we'll leave it with '*amal*'. When you come back to Iraq, I'll teach you the rest."

"Deal. What's this area called?"

"This? *Hajj* Sallum. Why?"

Sam shrugs. "I just like to know the names of places. It's when you pass through this part that the architecture changes. You really feel like you're leaving the city for something more, I don't know, traditional…pastoral."

"You mean when there are more mud buildings?"

"Yeah," she says. "It's kind of pretty."

I nod. Pretty to foreigners, poverty to us.

"What does Nabil mean?"

"Didn't I tell you?"

"No, I told you what Samara means, but you didn't tell me what Nabil means."

"Maybe you didn't ask." I glance at her, her honey-and-sand eyes more arresting than ever, with all her hair hidden away. "It has two meanings. The main one is noble."

"Noble," Sam smiles. "How appropriate. That's really you."

I find myself feeling hot. Perhaps it is Sam's words, though she looks warm, too. I put my hand in front of the vent for the air-conditioning. "Is it cool enough in here?"

"Well, it's a little stuffy to me, but I'm not used to wearing this thing," she says, pulling at the *jupeh*.

"I'm sorry about that."

"Nabil, you don't need to apologize. I don't mind at all. In fact, part of me likes it."

"Really?"

"Yeah. It reminds me of being a little girl and playing dress up. Usually I'm so, well, kind of noticeable here. Wearing this, I feel like I can blend in. Sort of lose myself and just disappear."

We are safely out of Baghdad, and I don't see nearly as many illegal checkpoints as we expected. Mostly, I think, they're just attempts by people to protect their neighbourhoods. Baba probably worried too much. Still, I'm glad not to have to make meaningless conversation with Safin. Glad to be alone with Sam. I wonder if I could take her for a visit to Samarra – a beautiful picture to leave her with, to wash out all the ugly ones we saw in Baghdad.

"Ah. So what was the other meaning?"

"Oh. Nabil also means sublime."

"Sublime? Ooh. That's pretty heavy...I mean, deep. Sublime!" We both laugh at the same time. "What an amazing name, Nabil. Is there any connection to the word noble in English?"

"You know, I thought this was very likely, and I still think it. But when I checked in a dictionary of etymology at the university, it said that noble was from Old French or Latin. But I think they are wrong. Arabic has been around much longer than those languages, you know."

Sam nods. I probably sound like I'm trying to hold an originality contest between East and West, which wasn't my intention.

The traffic slows down now, the two-lane highway quite congested, in part with other cars heading north. Baba was smart to have us pack up the car like this; we've probably seen ten others just like it. Occasionally we pass humvees and Bradleys. Painted in their desert beiges and faded browns, they are starting to become an unwanted but familiar part of our landscape, like a piece of furniture in your parents' home that you never liked, but wouldn't dare ask to be removed.

"We will pass through Samarra soon."

Sam reaches back for a bottle of water, twists the cap off, and throws back her head to swig it down.

"You know, if we are in any place where there are people around, you mustn't do that."

"Do what?"

"Drink the water that way."

"What, from the bottle? Don't Iraqis get thirsty?"

"Yes, but they will never drink from a bottle in public. Especially not a woman, and not people of a certain class. You will never find a lady driving in a Mercedes and drinking straight from a bottle."

"So what happens when you're thirsty?"

"You must always pour it into a glass first. If you search

around in the bags there, I'm sure you'll find that Mum has packed at least one."

"Oh-kay-ay!" She drags out her syllables just like that, in a way that says she finds this lesson in Iraqi manners amusing, but won't bother to argue.

"So, you know, Samarra is very beautiful. The city, I mean!" Sam looks at her knees, smiling at my clarification. "Well, not the city itself, but the shrines and the Malwiya minaret. "When you came to Baghdad in April, did you see them?"

"No," she says. "Baghdad was falling. We didn't exactly have time for tourism."

"When we went to Tikrit, I thought to take you then, but we also didn't have time to spare. But it is very special, Samarra, and I haven't been in a very long time."

I glance in my rearview mirror, the way I have countless times in the past hour. *Al-Hamdulilah*, there is no one following us. "I would love to take you there now. To stop just for a little while and see the shrines. I want you to see the view from the top of the Malwiya minaret."

Sam doesn't answer. But the movement in her face defies her quiet: the widening of her nostrils, the suddenly rapid fluttering of her eyelashes.

"You don't want to."

"It's not that I don't want to," she says. Her eyes softening in that arc of pity, that same look I had trouble facing yesterday on the roof. "I just don't want to take any more stupid chances. I want to get as far away from Baghdad as possible. What if someone is following us?"

"No one is following us."

"The people who know how to follow someone *know* how

to make it look like no one is following us. We really have no idea what could—" Her voice breaks up.

"I'm sorry, Sam."

"I can't believe Rizgar is gone."

"I know."

"I still keep expecting to find out it's a mistake. When I woke up at your house this morning, I thought I was at the Hamra. I'll just get dressed, go downstairs and meet Rizgar. That's what I thought."

"I know what you mean."

"You do?" Sam reaches into her bag and pulls out the tail end of a roll of toilet paper, rips some off and blows into it. "I always felt like maybe you two didn't like each other so much."

It takes me a moment to answer her truthfully.

"I know because of Noor. I didn't really want to marry her. But I didn't want her to die, either. It's still a shock. It's still a horrible thing. Just because I didn't want her to be my wife, it doesn't mean I'm not sad for her. And bloody angry, too. Somebody made a totally innocent girl die. And that happens here every day."

She places a hand on my upper arm and squeezes gently. "I'm sorry."

What do Americans say now? Thanks for feeling sorry? It seems better our way. *Allah yarhamha.* God keep her. Then again, that's all about the one for whom we grieve, and not at all about the one who does the grieving.

Sam waits a few minutes to see if I have anything more to say, and then finally asks: "Do you want to tell me about Noor?"

"Not really, Sam. Not right now. I think I'd better concentrate on where we're going."

Sam lets out a quick sigh of acquiescence. "Well, tell me more about Samarra. It's a Sunni area, isn't it?"

I consider telling her I don't feel like talking at all. But in a few days, when she's gone from Iraq, I might regret it.

"In terms of population, yes, it's Sunni," I say, "but this is where it gets interesting. One of the most important sites for Shi'ites anywhere in the world is there. Shi'ites will come from all over to make pilgrimages to the shrines there."

"You mean the Malwiya minaret?"

"The Malwiya is something totally different. The Malwiya, you've seen pictures of it? It's the huge spiral minaret with steps going up the sides, so that you climb to the top on the outside."

"I saw the top of it from the road. How old is it?"

"Well, that's the funny thing. It's built like one of the famous ziggurats of Mesopotamia, but in fact, it is much newer than that. A Caliph, that's the ruler, named Al-Mutawakil began building it in the middle of the ninth century, when Samarra was the capital, during the period of the Abbasids. Oh, but you asked me about Samarra. So, yes, it's Sunni, and the Al-Mutawakil Mosque – I mean, the old one connected to the Malwiya, which isn't really functioning any more as a mosque – that's considered a Sunni site. But also in Samarra you have the graves of two of the Shi'ite imams, the Tenth and the Eleventh, plus the, I don't know what you would call that in English, the spirit, I guess, of the Twelfth Imam, who is known as the Hidden Imam. Shi'ites believe he will return again at the end of days."

"This is why some of the Shi'ites are called Twelvers, right?"

"Exactly. Most, in fact, are twelvers. It sounds funny to me, but that's it. We call it *it'naashariya*, but it's the same thing. Have you heard of the Mahdi?"

"He's like the messiah, right?"

"Sort of. So, in Samarra there's one shrine with a beautiful golden dome, the Al-Askari Shrine, where Imam Ali al-Naqi, who was the Tenth Imam, is buried, along with his son Hasan al-Askari, who is the Eleventh. And the second shrine has very beautiful blue tiles, and downstairs is the place where the Imam al-Mahdi went into concealment. Whether he disappeared or is hidden, we don't know. But people view him as if he is still alive and will come back again to bring peace and justice to the world. Something like what Christians and Jews think too, no?"

Sam's head wavers from side to side. "Something like that."

"In fact, many Muslims believe the Mahdi will come along with Jesus."

"A double-messiah day!" she says. "Two saviours for the price of one."

I smirk. I feel like telling her to watch it: you should never take the piss out of people's religious beliefs, not in this part of the world. But this, I have learned, is Sam's language. Even when she isn't facing a deadline, she remains a journalist with a talent for catchy turns of phrase – and for cynicism.

In the moments of quiet, Sam seems to read that she may have been too quick to poke fun. "Sorry, Nabil. I don't mean to sound sarcastic. I told you I'm not a religious person. I think journalism has become my religion." She smiles so warmly, with such self-deprecation, that I have to smile back. "Are these places holy for you? Do you believe in the Mahdi?"

I turn on the radio. "No comment."

"Nabil!" She turns the radio off. The reception is terrible here anyway. "That's not fair."

"Why not fair?"

"We were having a serious discussion," Sam says.

"Were we? I thought you were finding it quite funny."

"I wasn't, really. I'm sorry," she says. "Really, please. It's just, I don't know, you do this job for long enough, and you start to become cynical about everything: every government, every leader, every system which tries to control people's lives. I guess I end up just dismissing religion, particularly in the Middle East, as a form of oppression. If you don't mind me saying."

"Say whatever you want."

"After what I saw in Afghanistan under the Taliban…"

"That's another story," I say. "Afghanistan's not even the Middle East."

"You're right."

The road has cleared up again, and somehow, this puts me at ease. "To me, it's complicated. My father doesn't believe in much of anything but the god of medicine. But he strongly identifies with being a Sunni, whether he admits it or not. My mother doesn't believe in asserting sectarian identity because she thinks this is bad for the *ummah*, that is, for the entire community of Muslims around the world. But she is a spiritual person and her beliefs and practices are very Shi'i."

"Yeah? Is there a big difference?"

"There are many differences. I don't know if any of them are so great. I'll tell you more about it later, if you want. Shi'ites love to visit tombs and graves of holy men. There is a belief that these visits can help you and protect you. Remember how Mum was on about us stopping in Samarra?"

"Did you promise her we would?"

"No, no. There are no promises in anything."

I don't say that it's not just Mum, that I also have a dream of taking Sam there. In my mind I've had an outrageous image for days, with me leading Sam by the hand until we start laughing and running up the wide, sloped stairs of the Malwiya minaret, just like we did in that stairwell but this time flying up instead of down, high above and far away from everything and everyone that could ever hurt us, a little closer to heaven.

58

Flying

I MUST HAVE got lost in the clouds somewhere at the top of the tower, where I have not been since I was perhaps fifteen, for Sam seems to have grown tired of trying to pull my theology out of me.

She lifts her index finger and pushes the small *khamsa* swinging from the rearview mirror, a bright blue bead dangling from each of its fingertips. "Why does everyone here hang these things from their rearview mirrors?"

"Oh that? I don't know, for good luck." I take a hand off the wheel to turn the *khamsa* towards me. "See, it says *'mashallah'* on it. Literally, it means 'God has willed it.' But we also say *mashallah* when we get good news. And when you hang it in your car, it's as if to say, 'May God prevent anything bad from happening here.' It's also supposed to stop you from catching the evil eye. A lot for one word, yes? My mother must have hung this here. My father doesn't believe in these things."

Sam swings it again. "It's cute. What do you mean, believe in it? Because it's like a good-luck charm?"

"Yeah, my father thinks these things are superstitious. Mum was always putting one of these things up in his car, and he would take it down, or put it away in the glove compartment. It's like a joke between them."

Sam smiles. "But why is a hand supposed to be good luck?"

"Well, this is known as *Id Fatima,* the hand of Fatima, who was the Prophet Mohammed's youngest daughter from his first wife, Khadijah. There are many beautiful stories about Fatima. She is supposed to symbolize strength and protection, but also abundance and patience. And heroism." I take a closer look at the hand with its fingers pointing down, realizing that it's fairly new because I remember there having been an older one here, with some prayer written on it, whereas this one just says *mashallah.* "People also call it *khamsa* because of the five fingers. You know, *khamis* is five."

"Right." Sam slips a hand towards her feet, and comes back with her open notebook. She jots down a few lines without saying anything.

"Are you interviewing *me* now?"

She clicks her tongue no, just like an Iraqi. "It just helps me remember things."

"Also, five is a very special number in Islam. We pray five times a day. Well, not me, maybe, but I should. I mean, I would like to."

Sam gives me the briefest of smiles and keeps writing.

"Also, we have the five pillars – starting with the declaration of faith, you probably have heard of this one, the *shahada.*" I count the remaining ones out on my hand, opening a finger for each one. "Then *sallih,* prayer, *zakat,* giving charity, *sawm,* fasting, and *hajj,* the pilgrimage to Mecca."

"Do you do any of that?"

In my mind I see Baba's doubting face. "Some of them. I

would like to make *hajj* someday. Ah, and also many people, particularly Shi'ites, say the most important figures in Islam are five: the Prophet Mohammed, Fatima, Ali, Hassan, and Hussein."

Sam writes this down, too. When she sees me looking at her, she seems amused. "It's just interesting to me, that's all. Hey, keep your eyes on the road!"

I swerve in time to avoid some rubble that could have done a bit of damage to the underbelly of the car. "Sorry. Anyway, I can find out more for you sometime, if you want."

She winces. Sometime, as if I can just show up at the Hamra in a few days and find she is still there, waiting for me.

Sam cannot stand the quiet for long, I can see, and I am beginning to wonder: is this typical of women, of Americans, or just Sam? She flips through Baba's collection of tapes below the dashboard, one plastic clink after another. "Can I put one of these in?"

"My father has very old-fashioned taste in music. But go ahead."

She slides a tape into the deck. Of course, who will my father have in the car but Oum Kalthoum? Along with Munir Bashir and Ahmed Mukhtar, that is, the great oud musicians, who as a threesome make a complete music library, in his opinion.

"Is that a man or a woman?"

"You can't tell? This is Oum Kalthoum. Haven't you heard of her?"

Sam looks sheepish. "Uh, no. I don't think so. Is that the famous Lebanese woman?"

"No, you're thinking of Fairuz, maybe. Or a young one like Asala Nasri? Actually she's Syrian. There's also a Maya Nasri whom I like very much, and she's Lebanese. There are so many famous Lebanese singers now. Do you know which one you're thinking of?"

Sam's cheeks round up like two apricots. "I have to admit I really don't know Arabic music."

"Well, I don't like Oum Kalthoum that much, but she is probably the most famous singer in all of the Arab world. She's Egyptian. You can hear it in her accent." I turn it up a little bit. "Can you hear it?"

"The accent? You mean as opposed to an Iraqi accent?" She shakes her head.

"Actually, this is one of the few Oum Kalthoum songs I really do like. It's called '*Inta Omri*'. You are my life. More than life. *Omr* means the length of a person's life – the days and years. We use this term to ask how old someone is. But if you say *inta omri*, it means you are my everything – all of my days are about you. It's like the way a man will call the woman he loves *hayati*. It's saying, you are my life."

Sam bends forwards. I suddenly wonder if, when a woman is wearing *hejab*, her hearing is impaired by her ears being covered by cloth. "What's she saying?"

Illi shouftouh qabli ma tshoufak a'inaih…Omri dhayea' yehsibouh izay a'alaya?

Whatever I saw before my eyes saw you was a wasted life. How could they consider that part of my life?

Inta Omri illi ibtada b'nourak sabahouh.

You are my life which starts its dawn with your light.

"It's so…poetic," Sam offers.

"It kind of goes on like that. It's a love song, a very long one."

"I wish I'd learned Arabic instead of French."

"I don't understand. Americans only have room in their heads for one foreign language?"

"Apparently," she says, laughing at herself and glancing in the side mirror. "Come on," Sam teases. "Your translating duties aren't over yet, Mr al-Amari. Tell me some more."

"Of this song? Let me listen."

Ad eyh min omri qablak ray w a'ada...Ya habibi ad eyh min omri raah.

How much of my life before you was lost. It is a wasted past, my love.

Wala shaf el-qalb qablak farhah wahdah...wala dak fi el-dounya ghair ta'am el-jiraah.

My heart never saw happiness before you.

My heart never saw anything in life other than the taste of pain and suffering.

I clear my throat. "It must seem a bit uh, what's that word, melodramatic, for you."

"No, it's lovely," Sam says. "It's like an ode."

Ibtadait bilwaqti bas ahib omri. Ibtadait bilwaqti akhaf la il-omri yijri.

I started only now to love my life.

And started to worry that the love of my life would run away from me.

Sam closes her eyes and leans back into the headrest.

"There's a long instrumental part now," I explain. "But the lyrics come back again."

"Hmm. Nabil, I want to take you to this great restaurant in Irbil," she says. "It's actually at a really beautiful hotel called the Chwar Chra. It's set on this gorgeous rolling lawn like the reception ground of some big banana plantation. You've got to see it. The food is amazing. Maybe we could even stay there. Unless you know of another place to stay."

I try to imagine what Kurdish food will taste like, but I can't conjure a flavour for it in my mouth. But in my head I imagine the meat of animals we never eat. Camels. Buffalo. Maybe even horse, which is probably not *hallal*. What do I know about Kurds anyway? Only that they're not Arab and that they want their own homeland, and that the goal of every Arab, Turk and Iranian is to stop that from happening. From the month she spent with the Kurds, before the war started, Sam probably understands more about them than I do.

"I'm not sure if we will go through Irbil," I say. "We can go through Mosul and then straight on towards Dohuk. It's shorter, for one thing." The truth is that I've been thinking that if, by chance, we found ourselves ahead of schedule, we could take a detour to Lake Dukan. Baba told me he took us there as children, but I don't really remember it. It's very enchanting, Baba said, and winked, while my mother packed in the food we'd nearly forgotten to put into the car. With that, we could have a nice picnic.

"Really? Oh, I was so excited about going to Irbil once more," she says.

"We'll see," I say, and realize that I like the feeling of being in charge, the captain of a small but important ship. Safin said going through Mosul is dangerous, but Baba wasn't so sure. Maybe there's just a part of me that doesn't want to go to Irbil, the city that turned on Saddam so many times in an effort to break away from the rest of Iraq. From the real Iraqis – the Arabs. Wouldn't Sam want to look up Rizgar's family, and what if the – and *Allah!* What a stunning pinging whizzing through the car and a crackling and shattering and too much air whipping and I think God, is it possible, *mu ma'qul!* It can't be!

But it can be and it must be. Someone is shooting at Baba's car and Sam is shouting *Jesus!* and holding on to the dashboard and *what the hell's happening?* and we're swerving now even though I know my hands are securely on the wheel and we're all over the road and oh my God help us and Sam is shouting *Jesus, Nabil, pull over* and I say *I think we're hit* and she says *pull the fuck over* and I can't tell her that something is pulling *us* and I can't control it and then we skid and fly into the air like we're weightless and then a harsh, metallic jangle and tinkling showers and sliding and *Allah Yihmina* God protect us in the skid that won't stop, can't stop, until slowly, it's over and we do.

I think I have been thrown on to Sam's body.

I can't see anything. No one is shouting or screaming anymore. Only the sound of glass falling like the drizzle of rain and Oum Kalthoum.

Hat a'inaik tisrah fi dounyethoum a'ineyyah. Hat eidak tiryah lil-moustahm eidaiyah.

Bring your eyes close so that my eyes can get lost in the life of your eyes.

Bring your hands so that my hands will rest in the touch of your hands.

The hands reach inside the car, many of them, pulling me out through the glass of the back window. And they're carrying me and I'm saying no, I'm fine, you have to get her out, you have to get Sam. And they say they're trying, and besides that I have a bleeding head and I should let them take me, but I can stand and

I move back to the car and I am starting to blubber and telling them to get Sam out. And the men start to lift the car from the side it's lying on, but it's so heavy and our old family junk is scattered everywhere and they're having a hard time, and instead they go into the car through the front windscreen since it's gone anyway and they work on lifting out Sam. And they're all shouting and moving and then I hear Sam moan, a sound of pain like I've never heard before, and now she's crying that no one should touch her and I know it's my job to tell her that we have to, but just the sound of her being hurt has put tears in my own eyes and I'm hoping I won't lose it completely in front of all these strangers in long robes.

"Just breathe, Sam. Take in a slow breath like you do when you're angry and let it out slowly." I know she's listening because she tries, but her breathing is short and pained instead, with an occasional *uh!* like someone who was suddenly surprised, over and over again.

They pull her out of the car, her body looking like no part of it is moving, and as they do I can hear her taking quick short breaths every few seconds, and I want to help her but the other men are holding me up. Holding me back. As they lift her, the pillow falls towards her feet and then out of the bottom of her jupeh altogether. As they carry her I see her face which is as beautiful as the day I met her, except that when she opens her mouth to try to talk, there's a film of blood all over her teeth and on her front lip, and then I feel the nausea rising in me like a wave and floating over me, and I won't now, I can't let it…

59

Floating

THE CEILING HAS a very beautiful lamp hanging from it, swinging by just a few centimetres in either direction. And that's when I realize that I've been out of it, like that first day when I met Sam. I look around and then move to sit up, and see the assembly of men, about ten of them in tribal dress and very similar facial features, staring back at me. One of them sitting next to me leans over me and puts his hand firmly on my shoulder, telling me I should rest. I start to search in a panic and then realize Sam is here, lying to my right, with pillows surrounding her head.

"Is she all right?"

"She's conscious," the man above me says. "But having trouble breathing. I think maybe she broke something," he says, pointing to his stomach and drawing a circle, "inside."

My head flies with fear. Internal bleeding? She might be dying. Baba would know what to do. "She has to get to a hospital immediately. In Baghdad—"

"We know. We have already called the army."

"The Iraqi army?"

He frowns and puts his hand on my forehead. "You should rest more. Mahfouz, bring him some water." I lay back, open and close my eyes several times, squeezing them shut to cut out the light, then letting it in again. Maybe it's another nightmare – one of my bizarre daydreams. If I force my eyes open again, I'll wake up and see it didn't happen.

Open, close, open. Still here, on the floor of someone's home in Samarra.

"…like there's any Iraqi army left." One of them sniggers at the other's comment. "He must have had a good bang in the head."

"Maybe that's why he passed out. You should have a doctor look at him, too."

"Him, he's fine. He was probably just upset to see his ladyfriend injured."

My head is swirling. I need to sit up, to take charge. I think I can do it. I roll on to my side and let some invisible force yank me upright, so at least I'm sitting up. They seem surprised to see me up again. I scan the room and count twelve of them, plus two women in *abaya*, tending to Sam. She is conscious, but seems out of it, a bit blank. Maybe she is in shock.

"Sam?" I turn to her. "Are you okay? Sam?"

She doesn't answer, but her eyes search around for my voice. Her throat passes a small, broken moan.

"Don't make her try to move her neck," one of them says. "It might be broken. They're sending a helicopter for her."

I lean over her, so that my face is above hers, directly above her eyes. "Sam, I'm here." Her eyes float up and focus on mine. Her irises are a muddier brown now, less golden than usual.

"My body hurts," she whispers.

"Which part hurts?"

She moves a fraction, as if she is trying to shift, and grimaces. "Everything," she creaks. "I, I can't take deep breaths." I notice that her mouth isn't bloody anymore, though her lip is a little swollen. Maybe the women rinsed it out for her. Maybe she isn't bleeding from inside. Maybe her teeth just hit against her mouth when we crashed.

"They said help is on the way, Sam. They called the American army. They're sending a helicopter to bring you to a hospital." I put my hand to her forehead, which feels hot, and pull out the *dambab* so I can unwind part of the scarf and let in some fresh air, ignoring a whisper of *haram*, shame, from one of the men.

How could God let Sam die? Take her away right before my eyes, like Noor? Please, don't let me lose her, too.

I turn to face the men sitting on a row of long floor cushions, staring as if they'd never seen such a scene in their lives and I'm suddenly aware of a pain in my right shoulder. I use the rest of my body to move me instead. "How soon are they going to be here, the medical people?"

"They said about fifteen minutes," says one in the middle of the group, who has coal-black eyes and what may be the most dignified grey beard I have ever seen. If I could have grown a beard like that, surely Baba wouldn't have disapproved. I can see from his gold-trimmed black robe that he must be a sheikh. The men to either side might be twins, perhaps twenty or twenty-five years younger – at most – than the man in the middle, surely their father. "I asked them to come right away. I told them we had an American woman here, a civilian, and they said they would hurry."

"How did you call them?"

The man smiles with a world of wisdom in his face, as if he could provide the answers to almost anything I'd ask. "We have our own mode of communications with the Americans."

"Do you have a Thuraya here? A satellite phone?"

He clears his throat. "Yes, we do." I begin thinking of all the people I should probably call – my parents, Sam's editors. But my parents – how would I call them? Sam said that the Thuraya phone couldn't make calls to landlines inside Iraq, because the landline system is totally out of order. They must take me back to the car at least to get Sam's bag with her most important things: camera, phone, computer, notebooks. I'm sure they would let me use their phone, if I knew a number to call. They have been very kind, so far. Who are they, anyway? And who do they think we are?

"May I ask your name, young man? Where were you and this American woman driving to?"

I look at him, and then my eyes trail across the nearly-matching faces, varied only in age, facial hair and slight differences in pigment. A receiving line, a tribal court. When my eyes meet his again, he stands up, thanking everyone for coming to help wish our unfortunate visitors well, and begins to give each of them farewell kisses. I can't stand them staring at me, and so I turn my back and wait for them to leave the room. Sam emits a half-moan and calls my name. A tear runs from her right eye, heading straight for her ear. I catch the tear before it gets far, wiping at it with my thumb.

When most of the extended tribal court is gone, the sheikh chooses a seat closer to me. His two look-a-like sons follow, flanking him like bodyguards.

"Who are you?"

Hadn't I planned for this all along? A story at the ready for any situation. Sunni, Shi'ite, Kurd, foreign, local – we would have our bases covered. Unless we happened to get stopped by a Turkoman, a Christian, or a Yezidi, which wasn't terribly likely –

or terribly worrisome – there was no community we didn't have connections with, names to throw around, if we ran into a situation like this. *Like this?* What in the world could be like this?

For Sunnis, Sheikh Faddel el-Duleimy, and maybe Uncle Zaki, Saleh's father. For Shi'ites, the name of my mother's relatives in Al-Kut. For Kurds, the letter, tucked safely into the inside pocket of my overnight bag. *My bag!* And Sam's! Did they take anything out of the car?

"Did you find, did you take any of the bags which were—"

"We took two small ones," says one of the sons. "There was too much so we had to leave the rest. It's all upstairs." His voice is deeper than his father's. It suddenly occurs to me that we're downstairs, in their basement. Why had I not noticed it earlier? Was I so out of it when they carried us inside? My head swirls with a wave of nausea, my shoulder throbs.

"Why are we waiting downstairs?" My voice sounds shaky. I wonder if they notice.

"It's for your safety," the sheikh says. "We don't know who shot at you and perhaps it's possible they will try to come and finish the job. It's better this way. If anyone comes looking, they won't find you. Not many houses here have basements, so this is your best protection. That and your blessing from God," he says, putting a hand over his heart. He turns to the son who has been quieter. "Ask Maysoun to make tea, won't you?" The son pulls himself up reluctantly, his eyes still on me. "So you are from Baghdad?" the son asks. "Which family?"

Fast fast fast. Hesitate and die, one of Sam's colleagues at the Hamra had taped to his laptop. "The Duleimy family. I mean, I am from Baghdad, but the larger family is from Fallujah and Ramadi. Do you know Sheikh Faddel, my cousin?"

I see a sheen of scepticism in his eye.

"This woman is an aid worker, a doctor who was sent here to help in the hospitals," I say. "I was trying to take her to visit some clinics in the north where there is a great shortage of medical staff."

"But then why was your car loaded with household goods as if you were moving to somewhere?"

"Hassan," the father says, lifting a hand like a scolding motion: Go easy.

"And if you are from the Duleimy family, what are you doing carrying around a letter like *this*?"

"Hassan! I said no."

Hassan unfolds a white piece of paper. Across it, three creases and Safin's handwriting. My mind is screeching as he pulls it open to reveal the rectangle of incriminating evidence, held up before my face, Baba's deliberate insurance policy turned into a death sentence before my eyes.

Too many words rushing to my mouth, and not enough air and space to get them out. My lips moving, but no sound passes over them.

"Well?"

They know they have me cornered. Maybe they didn't really call the army for help after all. Maybe they'll leave Sam here to die and then they'll kill me, too.

The sheikh's head shakes with a shortening of patience, laced with mercy. "Do not let my son frighten you," he says.

Hassan frowns, lowers the letter. Sets it down next to him.

"I'm sure there's an explanation for all of this," the sheikh says.

"Why don't we start again. So you must know by now that

you're in the south of Samarra and that you've been fortunate enough to come under the protection of the Albu Baz tribe. You are our guest, and especially as you are in distress, we will take good care of you." His voice is matter-of-fact and calm. Vaguely kind, even. "Would you be so good as to tell us who you are?"

"The Albu Baz?"

"That's right. I am Sheikh Hikmet Mumtaz al-Baz, and this is my son, Hassan Mumtaz." Hassan forces his lips into a smile, clearly annoyed at his father's exceeding generosity. "You may call me Sheikh Mumtaz. Who are you? And who is the lady?"

I look down at Sam, who appears to have drifted off to sleep with her eyes half open. Isn't that dangerous? Should I wake her up? I put my hand to her cheek.

"My daughter gave your ladyfriend some strong pain pills because she was suffering," Sheikh Mumtaz says. "Her husband is our local pharmacist. It may make her sleepy, but it is nothing to worry about. She will suffer less."

I have to dam up the tears flooding into my eyes and nose, send them back to where they came from. "She isn't my ladyfriend. She is my boss, actually. I am her translator."

"For?" Hassan leans forwards. "The Americans? CIA?"

"No," I say. "Nothing like that. She works for a newspaper in America. I am her translator."

"How can you know?" Hassan snaps. Again, his father holds a hand in front of Hassan, the way a driver braking hard protects a passenger next to him.

"I know. I trust her. We've worked together for a long time."

"Well, then. Sorry," Sheikh Mumtaz says. The tea arrives, held aloft on the hands of a ten-year-old child. Sorry for stopping you, does he mean, or sorry for my son's behaviour? The young boy places a steaming cup in front of me, then gives one to each of the men. The glass burns my hands a little, and then my lips, but I am glad for it, glad for anything to buy time to think.

Sheikh Mumtaz. If you wrote an English fairytale about him, he'd be named Lord Excellent. What did Sam say that day when Sheikh Faddel asked who she was working for? *I'm for the truth.* Just tell the truth.

And I do, and it starts to spill out, most of it, anyway, the parts that seem relevant. Trying to escape some people who may or may not be trying to kill us…forged documents…just trying to get to the truth…trying to get Sam to the border safely…my father asking for the letter, with Safin's help, just as precaution, like a talisman, a hand of Fatima, a *mashallah khamsa*. Just in case. It seemed like a good precaution at the time. That's the trouble with life. You have to prepare, have to make provisions, just in case. In case of an accident. A catastrophe. A misguided bullet. But how do you know which accident to make provisions for?

Sheikh Mumtaz takes the letter in his hand. Smiles. Looks at me. "Did you really think you would be able to pass for a Duleimy?" I can hear a helicopter overhead. He folds the paper up again. "You might want to keep this," he says, "just in case." He hands it back with pale fingers that seem unusually long and delicate, like an angel's.

I decide to come clean, or virtually clean, with Sheikh Mumtaz: all the important points of the story. I repeat for him a *hadith* I learned from my mother: No man is true in the truest sense of the word but he who is true in word, in deed and in thought. "That is what our Prophet Mohammed, Peace Be Upon Him, wanted us to strive for, I believe."

Sheikh Mumtaz seems satisfied. I also notice the slightest smile on Sam's face. But she is probably lost in her own painkiller dream, and hopefully, not feeling too much.

One of the young boys appears at the door. "They're coming!" he yells excitedly. "We can hear them already."

I jump up, worried that they will miss us somehow. "We must start moving her up."

"Not at all. The medical team should come to get her and put her on a stretcher. That will be better." Sam's eyes open and look up at the ceiling, and then search for me.

"My father is right," says Hassan. "It's probably worse if we move her any more than we already did." Sheikh Mumtaz stands and Hassan follows, as does the other brother who never said a word.

"I'll take the boys out to flag down the helicopter and find a safe place to land," Sheikh Mumtaz says. "You can just wait here with her." He places his hand on my shoulder and I am thankful for it. I can hear the fluttering of it now, the helicopter propellers whirring like desperate hearts beating out of sync, and the sound of the men hurrying up the stairs.

I move closer to Sam, hovering over her so she can see me. I think this is the closest to floating above Sam as I will ever be.

"Sam?" I lean in closer. "I want you to stay as still as possible and be brave. They will take care of you and everything will be all right."

She blinks, more of a wince, says nothing. I wait, gazing at her, and suddenly fat tears well up in my eyes. I blink and a tear spills on to her face. How embarrassing. *Tafil-baka,* I hear Bassem's bullying voice call. *Tafil-baka.* Cry-baby.

"I love you." I cough it out, almost blubbering. How could I let her see me like this? She's the one who's injured, who has the right to cry. When her eyes close again, tears run towards her ears. With her eyes shut, she can see everything now – all my weaknesses. I wipe the tears on her face with my sleeve.

"I know," she says.

I say nothing, frozen.

"Kiss me once more."

"What?"

"Kiss me again. Just a little."

And my mouth moves over the curve of hers, first hovering and then, the pleasure of my lips meeting hers, just a brush of pink skin on skin, a softness, a sweetness. Blood and love and tears. Her mouth open, ever-so-slightly, to mine.

I stop and pull away, afraid I could hurt her. I kiss her forehead instead, then put my lips to her ear. "You'll be okay, Sam. *Inshallah*. I know you will. I know you'll come back."

"I'm sorry about everything, Nabil. Your father's car—"

"Don't even think about that now."

"Would you tell him sorry, too? I feel bad that—" she gasps for more air. "And can you call Miles to tell him what happened?"

"Shh," I say, smoothing back the hair on her forehead, and as I hear them rushing down the stairs, I kiss each of her eyes. "*Ayouni*," I whisper.

There are several soldiers wearing white armbands and red crosses standing over us, and they pull me aside as if I were a child. They lay down a stretcher, and Sam cries out once as they lift her. I follow them up the stairs, and as we rush through a huge reception room on the ground floor I see two bags from our car. One is mine, and the other is a duffle bag stuffed with the food Mum made. No sight of Sam's bag with all her equipment.

628

Outside, a small crowd circles likes a football scrum, the youth of the Albu Baz tribe gathered around to watch, the men keeping them back, the women peeking out from doorways and windows, the children jumping in the excitement, shouting to the soldiers, "Hallo, Mista, hallo. What yo name? I lav yoo," with their hair whipping in the wind kicked up by the helicopter. The soldier who appears to be the head of the medical crew checks Sam's US passport, which she'd been wearing in a moneybelt around her waist. And if she were an Iraqi? If it were Amal? What would they do then? Is there something that they'll do at a hospital in Europe or America that is so different from what they would do at Al-Kindi?

I keep trying to speak to the soldier in charge, but he ignores me. Perhaps he can't hear me with all the noise, or perhaps the growing crowd around the helicopter feels threatening to him. I put a hand on his arm, he yanks it away and pushes me with both arms, and I stumble backwards. "I just want to tell you that I'm with her. I'm working with her. I'm her…fixer."

"Good for you!" he yells into the whirlpool of dust. "But we need to get going, so if you want to fix something you'd better help clear this crowd out so we can take off."

"I think I should go with her!" I shout back. "She shouldn't be alone."

He looks at me like I'm barking mad, and tells the other soldiers to start pushing the crowd back, with force if necessary. He turns back to me. "Afraid not, partner. We're not authorized to bring Iraqis with us." The soldiers succeed in widening the circumference by a few metres. Some of the tribesmen, armed with Kalashnikovs and AK-47s that double as batons, help push it further. As if suddenly regretting his gruffness, the soldier in charge comes back over to me. "You can ask after her at Ramstein Airbase in Germay," he says. "She'll be in good hands there."

The circle stretches wider, the groan grows louder, the propellers disappear into a blur. A mission to save Sam is born, defying gravity and mischievous boys, who leap up to catch a ride on the landing skids before being yanked down by older brothers. We watch them lift into the sky, the children waving, the dust-cloud thickening, the noise deafening. I feel it coming, that sensation as if I am losing my balance. I press my hand into my forehead to try to make it stop.

Inside, Sheikh Mumtaz and Hassan force me to drink a third cup of tea and a bowl of vegetable soup made by the lady of the house, whom I've not met.

"Are you sure you want to go back now?" Sheikh Mumtaz asks again.

I sip the tea, of which I've had more than enough, wishing I could find a way to dump it without their noticing. My hands are shaking, probably from having had too much of it. Too much of other things as well. "Yes, I should go home."

"But you passed out," he insists. "Maybe you are not feeling well because of the accident. And the shock of your ladyfriend being injured. Maybe you should rest here."

"I'm fine," I say. "I always pass out."

"Always?" Sheikh Mumtaz seems baffled.

"Not always. Just at inappropriate times." I smile to show it is a joke, but he doesn't smile back. "It's a problem I have."

"I see," he says. "So for you this is a natural response to such a terrible event."

"I suppose you could say that."

"Rest for now," he says. "When you're sure you feel up to travelling, Hassan will drive you back to Baghdad."

"There's no chance I can take my father's car?"

Hassan laughs. "The one we found you in back there?"

"Stop," Sheikh Mumtaz whispers angrily, "can't you see he's confused? Let him rest."

And because they insist, I do, laying out on the long floor cushions and folding my hands over my stomach, hardly able to listen to the last thing the Sheikh says.

Sam and I are running up the steps of the Malwiya, laughing, out of breath, and she keeps trying to run away from me, and when I catch up and try to grab her, I almost push her over the unprotected edge. How could I be so careless?

And then I wake up with a rush of fear, sitting up to find a young teenage boy watching me, and running off as soon as I am up. "Baba?" he calls. "Baba! He's awake." Sheikh Mumtaz appears at the door to what I presume is the rest of the house, its private quarters, and Hassan follows.

It all comes back to me, the tumbling, the tinkling of glass over our heads. I wonder if Sam is already safely in Germany. From the light outside, I can see it's early morning. I can hardly believe I've been sleeping since yesterday. Maybe they put a drug in my tea. "I'm sorry," I say. "I must get back home."

"It's very early," Sheikh Mumtaz says. "You should have a little more rest."

"Please. I must contact my family. Please take me home."

"They don't have a Thuraya phone you can call?" He sits down across from me, but Hassan remains standing.

"No," I say. "No one I know in Baghdad has one, except for

foreigners." Then again, Mustapha had one, and Technical Ali must have, too. "Or maybe some of the politicians. And the criminals."

"Do you find it necessary to differentiate?"

I smile at his joke. Until now, he didn't seem at all like the cynical type. "My parents only have a landline."

He clucks. "That won't do. Thurayas can't call those."

"You must have good contacts with the military that you were able to get them to come here so quickly."

"I believe in remaining on good terms with everyone. We are not strong enough now to fight the Americans, and we do not want to see more bloodshed, so we try to be co-operative with them and to see what they will do next. I keep asking them what their plan is now, and even the most high-ranking generals I've met say they can't tell me, because they haven't seen the plan either."

"Because there is no plan," Hassan huffs, leaning a hand on the wall. "The plan is to control us. Why do you think they're taking this American woman to Germany? Almost sixty years since the end of that war, and the Americans still have their bases there!"

"Shh…" Sheikh Mumtaz says, closing his eyes. He seems to have much less interest in anything his son says than I do. "Do you want to take our friend back to Baghdad, or should I send your brother?"

"I will," Hassan says assertively.

"Then please wait," his father says, looking at me rather than Hassan. "Be patient and persevering, for God is with those who patiently persevere."

"The second sura," I say.

Sheikh Mumtaz nods. "Our visitor is obviously well-versed in the Holy Koran."

The words soothe me. I catch Hassan's eyes roll. Perhaps he's heard his father's religious quotations too many times before. "Let me know when you want me to drive him," he says, and walks out.

"You must forgive my son," Sheikh Mumtaz says. "He is young and impatient. He doesn't like the fact I have chosen co-operation over conflict. He would prefer to be like the Al-Sud tribe, who are probably, by the way, the people who shot at your car and ran you off the road."

"Really? But why?"

Sheikh Mumtaz looks over to his *sheesha* pipe sitting in the corner. "Do you smoke?"

"Occasionally," I say, holding up my hand. "I don't think I could right now."

"That's fine. You are invited to come and enjoy with us some other time. What I wanted to say is that people have different ways they like to smoke. Some like cigarettes because it is a quick rush, and easy to arrange, you just put it in your mouth and light it up. Instant pleasure."

"For some people."

"Yes. And some people, like me, would rather prepare and smoke *sheesha*. It's a lot slower and requires much more maintenance. You must fill the bowl with water, keep the pipes clean, stoke the coals gently and wait for them to heat the tobacco. And then, even the process of enjoying it is much slower. It is not a smoke for a man in a hurry."

It's true. On the few occasions I've had any with friends at university, it seemed to be an hours-long affair, and I sometimes found myself wishing I was home, reading a book.

"Ultimately, *sheesha* is much healthier than cigarettes. You don't have people getting cancer from smoking nargila once, twice a week. It is a smoke for solving problems, not making rash decisions. Do you see the difference?"

"Yes."

"So this is a lot like the difference between tribes, like ours and the Al-Sud. Our brothers in the Al-Sud – and you should know, they are much larger in number than us – they are cigarette smokers. They have chosen to resist the Americans with violence and more violence. Sheikh Talal is their chief and he thinks that attacking all foreign forces in Iraq is the only answer to the occupation. He is building a whole tribe of people who say they are going to be the new resistance, to chase the 'infidels' out." His dismissive frown says what he thinks of this plan.

"We think otherwise," he says. "We will invite the Americans to sit and drink tea with us. We will listen to what they have to say. We will smoke our *sheesha* and wait. And then we will decide. Do you understand what I mean?"

"I think I do."

"Good."

I stand and he stands with me. "I don't know how I will ever repay you for all you have done," I say.

"Be a *sheesha* smoker," he says, putting an arm around my shoulders and giving them a manly squeeze.

I don't remember what happened after this, but it is now clear to me that I must have passed out once more. When I come to I find myself lying on the floor again, with the sheikh nearby. "Don't worry," he says, "we're bringing a local doctor to have a look at you."

"Did I – faint?"

"Something like that. One minute you were okay, then your eyes fluttered, and well…" He makes a gesture with his hand, upright, and then falling to horizontal.

I suddenly am aware of the pain in my shoulder again. I try to move it in a circle but it sends out a horrible shock. "I think maybe I hurt my shoulder when the car flipped over," I say. "I'm sure it's nothing serious."

"Still, if you're injured, you shouldn't travel. The doctor will see you. Stay and recuperate here for a few days."

"I should really get home," I say, though the thought of rushing back to Baghdad to tell my family that we never made it past Samarra, and that the family car is gone, fills me with dread. What will Baba think?

The doctor who comes doesn't look like a doctor to me. He isn't dressed in a white lab coat like my father when he's at the hospital, and his huge, intense eyes, set in a face full of wrinkles, make him look more like a fortune-teller than a physician. He examines me and concludes that my shoulder has been dislocated. "This will hurt a little," he says, and manipulates my arm and shoulder with a force and swiftness that leaves me aghast. I can hear the pop of the bone returning to its socket. "Fixed," the doctor declares. I feel woozy, but being conscious of it helps to stop me from going under again. He tries to make a sling for my arm out of the *ghutra* he was wearing on his head until a minute ago. He shakes his head no and takes the cloth off. "These don't really do much anyway. Just take it easy and get a lot of rest."

Sheikh Mumtaz, sitting on a chair in the corner, concurs. "Doctor's orders. You rest here a while."

"Actually, it's probably going to hurt more for the next few hours, just from the shock of it," the doctor predicts. He reaches into his breast pocket and pulls out some tablets in a miniature envelope. "Take two of these painkillers now, then again in four hours."

I spill some into my hand and eye them suspiciously. I don't see a name on them. "That's not necessary," I say. "I'll be fine."

"Just take one, then," he says. "Don't worry."

Every time someone has told me not to worry in the last week, I wonder if I should have worried more, not less. But what does Sheikh Mumtaz and his doctor friend have to gain by drugging me? Nothing I can fathom. And the pain in my shoulder is more unbearable by the minute.

In and out. Awake and asleep. A kind of torpor in-between. I awoke at some point having had a dream about arguing with Sam over translations, like we did in our first days working together. Now, as I lay here in the middle of the night, I find myself trying to tell Sam that there's no easy way to translate fixing. It's impossible to find just the right word for "fixing" in Arabic. There is *islah*, but that's more commonly used as reform. We also have the word *thabbata*, which could be said to be fixing. There is also *inqadh*, which is either saving or salvation. There is *shifa*, which means healing. And then there is *i'ada* and *jadada*, which are like restore and renew. I'm not even sure now if that's what we argued about in the dream, or if that's just me continuing the conversation. I just know that I can't think of one word in Arabic to fit everything that I want the fixing to be, or which describes what my job was supposed to have been.

I wake up feeling confused, but better. My shoulder is tender, but not so painful. I'm not sure now if I saw the doctor today or yesterday, if it's already tomorrow. I go to my wallet, where I find Sam's business card. It seems humbler now, having lost its hard edges. On it, I notice a number at the newspaper office in Washington. I promised her I'd call Miles.

When Sheikh Mumtaz comes down to check on me, I tell him I'm better, and that I must leave now. He says it's very late, but I can go with his son Hassan in the morning. In the meantime, I ask, could I use his Thuraya to make a call to America, to reach my ladyfriend's employer? Of course, he says, and leads me upstairs and into the courtyard of their home, where the reception is good and the night sky is a riot of stars.

"Tribune."

"Oh, I'd, could I speak to Mr Miles, please?"

"Please hold." Classical music at the other end, warped by the odd, distorted quality of the satellite call. "Sorry, no listing for a Mr Miles here."

"Oh, I meant, Miles, the international editor? Miles is his first name."

More music. "You mean Miles Crowe. One moment." Another few bars of Bach, or someone who sounds like Bach, and then, that voice.

"Crowe," the voice declares in a syllable.

It takes me a moment to find mine.

"Hello? Someone there?"

"This is Nabil al-Amari. I've been working with Samara Katchens here in Iraq."

"Yes, Nabil! We know all about you."

"Sam wanted me to call because we were…in an accident. The US army came to get her and took her to a hospital in Germany."

"Yes, yes, we know all about it. She's going to be transferred to a hospital here in Washington by the end of the week, we think."

"So she's okay?"

"She's in a stable condition," he says. "She broke a few ribs and they're probably going to do surgery for a torn spleen before flying her back here."

"I see." I try to remember where the spleen sits and how it could tear.

"We know you did all you could to help her. And we really appreciate the work you've been doing there for us. In fact, this isn't such a good time to talk because we're on deadline, but if you call me again tomorrow, a little earlier, we can talk about your continuing to work with us. With one of our other correspondents."

"Did the story run? About the Jackson documents?"

"The story? Yes, yes. Yesterday. Highest number of hits we've ever had in a single day."

"Sorry? Come again?"

"I mean, the web traffic to the *Tribune* site because of the story. Look, Nabil, I wish I could talk more, but I gotta move a story. And listen, be careful over there. Our main priority is making sure our staff are staying safe, and that includes our fixers and drivers."

60

Staying

IN THE CAR, Hassan asks me if I'd prefer to take a back road, which might be safer.

"Actually, I want to see what condition my father's car is in."

Hassan smirks. "I doubt it's still there, but we can see."

He's wrong, and at the same time right. The car, or what remains of it, is lying on its side about twenty-five feet from the road.

"I'm sure I could get it fixed. It can be towed to a garage, can't it?" What could I possibly tell Baba? That it was stolen at gunpoint? That would be better than telling him I crashed it, gunshots or no.

He clicks his tongue. "It's totally destroyed. Can't you see they've already picked it clean? Fine, I'll pull up so you can see it," he says, veering off the pavement and on to that flat, soil-less earth that covers this part of our country, half sand and half rock, a little bit of the moon right here on earth.

All is silent except for the crunch of our feet on arid ground as we approach the car. "Look," says Hassan. "They've already taken the engine and the two tyres that didn't get shot. Here," he says, poking his head inside. "They even ripped out the leather seats and the wooden parts around the dashboard, anything of value. And the body – it's like an old tin can now." He swishes something around in his mouth, perhaps a wad of tobacco chew.

There is no exaggeration in Hassan's description. My father's car is a skeleton, the flesh and blood of its insides already gone. I stick my head inside to find a hollowness, like the feeling of walking into an abandoned building you once knew well. The looters – I wonder if they are the same as the shooters? – have indeed removed almost the entire interior of the car. On the floor is a mess of papers and junk that would have been in the glove compartment, which is no longer there. I sift through the papers, checking to see if there is something important. Baba's car registration, for example.

Nothing. Nothing but old receipts, dead pens, an insurance bill he must have intended to pay at some point. Bits of the food my mother had sent with us. Shreds of fabric and lots of glass and a few bullet casings. And, somewhere in the mess of trash, the *mashallah khamsa*.

How did they miss this one? Or did they deem it worthless – a *mashallah khamsa* that failed to bring its passengers good luck? Perhaps they left it on purpose.

The sound of banging on the roof startles me and makes me bang my head as I move to stand.

"*Y'alla!*" It's Hassan, his arm resting on the roof. "Satisfied? Let's go."

Behind the wheel, he puts his foot down and flies past other cars – I assume to get out of town quickly. After a few miles he slows down.

"There was nothing you could do."

"My father'll kill me."

"Your father should kill *them*. He'll be glad you're alive. You both could have died in a wreck like that. Did you see those bullet holes in the back of the car? How is it that they didn't succeed in shooting either one of you?"

"Who are they? The Al Sud tribe?"

"Is that what my father told you? Who knows. The Al Sud tribe has 30,000 people in Samarra. You may as well have been nearly killed in Sadr City and said 'the Shi'ites did it.'"

That's also possible, I want to say. What if Ali did follow us? What if he knows I got out? My head vacillates with other worries. I'll tell Baba what happened, but somehow, he'll think it was my fault.

"It would have been better if they had killed me."

Hassan scoffs with amusement more than surprise. "Don't speak nonsense." He glances at me and trains his eyes back on the road. "You're still in shock. What a mess back there, sending off your ladyfriend like that, in so much pain. What could you do?"

Nothing, I want to say. As usual, nothing. And then the tears fill my eyes, and I feel like I might just not bother stopping them. I can feel that salty-sea taste underneath my top lip, where my moustache should be. Should be. If I were letting myself be an Arab. If I weren't trying to be a Westerner. If I wasn't trying all the time to please Sam. To please someone.

Let them fall, anyway. I turn towards the window, wipe them away with my hand, wishing that the tears would fall only out of my right eye, and not from my left.

I can feel him checking me over, watching me cry. So this is how city boys are, I want him to say. Go on, say it. But he says nothing, nothing at all, and for that I want to thank him more than anything. And so we roll silently back to Baghdad, quiet but for my periodic sniffling, and his sucking at the bits in his teeth with a *tsk tsk.*

I consider asking Hassan to drop me off somewhere else. Maybe at Saleh's. He never should have sent us to Mustapha's in the first place. He should know what a disaster he got us into with his tips and leads. Or maybe I should go to the Hamra, to tell Joon and Marcus or some *Tribune* reporter what happened to Sam.

Instead, I ask to be dropped off at the school. This way, he won't know where I live. Why that matters at this point, I don't even know. But maybe it will mean trouble for me, for my family. Maybe men from the Al Sud tribe will have followed us, and when they're looking for people who work with the Americans, they'll come after me.

It's only 2 o'clock, but the school is already locked up for the day. They are now having three hours of class, I understand, and ending by 11 a.m., so students can get home before the spate of afternoon bombings.

"Here?" he asks, looking up at the building with its stately design, perched somewhat higher up than the average school. "They won't be open now."

"I know," I say. "I have to pick something up, though. I'm a teacher here. I have a key."

He shrugs and reaches out his right hand, and places it in mine with a little bit of a slap, with much more levity than I feel in my heart. Then he pulls me close to him and gives me a hug. I seem to be like a doll in his hands, falling into him with no resistance at all. "Take care, brother," he says. "Like my father says, God is forgiving."

I nod into his shoulder. Forgiving of what? Does he think

I've done wrong? Does he think I should somehow feel responsible?

"Thank you for your help. I hope someday I can repay you," I say.

"You already did," he says. "You allowed my father to show all our brothers and cousins that not all of the Americans are horrible people, and not all of the Iraqis working with them are, either. And I think that's what he's been trying to tell us all along."

We pat each other on the back and I leave the car, deposited into the hot afternoon air. I suddenly feel a dizzy dread. I wish I'd told him to drive me somewhere else, like Najaf, where I could pray for Sam, and be surrounded by crowds of people I don't know, and not have to go home for quite some time.

I can't expect the building to be open, and despite what I told Hassan, I haven't carried the key to it in weeks. I lean my head against the window and look in, the darkness of the hallway ahead like a cavity beginning to rot around the edges.

I begin the walk home, trying to pretend nothing is wrong, trying to walk that walk like any man from Babel or Adel, Zayouna or Ummal. As I walk I can feel it, this strange thing pulsing in my body, a shaking, a feeling of shivering in the cold even though it is hot. I lift one of my hands and see it is trembling. I shake them both, shake them hard like you do after washing in a sink where there is no towel. Shed it, shake it off. But don't cry, Nabil, for the love of God, don't you let people on the street see you crying.

A poem, a poem will keep me focused. Especially an air-typed poem, which will give my fingers something to do, instead of shaking. There is one I love by the Persian poet Hafez, about the girl in red who was lost.

She's gone underground.
She is red and disreputable.
If you find her, please bring her to Hafez's house.

If you find Sam, please send her back to me.

Up Damascus Street, the shops are mostly shuttered but a few still open, their metal shutters pulled down to knee-height, so that it isn't so easy to do a quick grab and run. Please bring her back to me.

Oh, Nabil. Silly. She's never coming back. You had to know that all along. You had to know that for all the times she told you how much she cared about this country, that she was never, ever, going to be here for good. How did that American pop song go, the one that Christian guy at the CD shop on Arasat Street introduced me to when I was at university? *She's got her ticket, think she's going to use it, think she's going to fly away.*

That's it. Tracy Chapman, the one with the dreadlocks. *She knows where her ticket takes her, she will find her place in the sun.* Her ticket out of here was always in her hand; it only depended on which day she chose to use it. She was always going to fly away, Nabil, always. And still my hands can't stop their shaking, so much so that my air-typewriter is now far out of reach.

61

Shaking

I WALK IN to find Mum wrapping a large dish. When she sees me, it slips from her hands, hits the floor and breaks into pieces. Only now do I see that it's one of her favourites, the one on which she always served her *tabeet* and sometimes a small *masghouf.*

Amal's face is blanched white. She blinks at the pieces, but then keeps moving, wrapping dishes with newspaper and placing them in a cardboard box on the kitchen table. Baba is sitting in his armchair. On the footstool sits a small suitcase, which he's loading up with some of his medical reference books.

For a moment, I can't find my voice. And then, when I do, my mouth feels as dry as the Ad-Dibdibah Desert. "What's going on here?"

Mum rushes over and throws her arms around me. "*Al-Hamdulilah.* You came home. That's all that matters."

I hug her back and then let her go. But Baba and Amal haven't budged – they're still doing what they were doing when I walked in a minute ago. Amal is moving like a zombie. Baba glares at me with glassy eyes.

"Mama? Mum, what's going on here?" my voice cracks.

"Can't you see?" Baba says, in that tone that says I should know better than to ask. "We're leaving. What did you think would happen? You left a mess for us when you ran off with that woman."

I am stunned. That woman! This from my father who had said to Sam, You are like a daughter now.

"And you didn't even call us to let us know you were okay," Amal adds.

"How was I supposed to…do you have any idea what I've been…" I can't seem to finish sentences. "What mess?"

"The mess that brought a couple of gunmen here looking for you and for her, threatening to kill the whole lot of us if we didn't tell them where you were, or to pay your 'debts'."

"Oh no. Oh no. That's the, that's the people I told you about. You said you didn't think they would find us. You said they sounded like amateurs."

"Did I say that? Well, I guess I was wrong." Baba rearranges the suitcase contents, taking a few tomes out. "They said you owe them $10,000 and that you promised to pay them by Monday. Well, three days went by, and they came to collect."

I feel the heat rising in my body, sitting on my chest and moving straight to my head. "It's not his fault, Amjad," Mum says. "Don't blame him. Let him have a rest and a glass of tea."

"Woman, we don't have time for drinking tea. We're leaving this house in forty-eight hours! Everything of value is coming with us or going into storage, or you can just forget about ever seeing it again."

"Don't you snap at me," she retorts, returning to the broken plate and collecting the pieces. "Maybe we can fix this."

"Wait, Baba, tell me what happened. Who came? What did they want?"

"They wanted $10,000, I said I didn't have it. They said they'd settle for seven. I told them I could get them five, if they gave me another few days." He takes two books out, frowns at them, and puts them on the sofa. "They came back the next night and left a note under the front door. So I got them the five. And they might still be back for more."

"You gave them $5,000?"

"What else could I do, do I have my own militia?" Baba stands and walks over to the mantle clock. He looks at it, sighs, and takes it down gingerly, as if it were a baby. "Now how do we pack this so it doesn't break?"

"Baba—"

"You know, your mother's right, it probably isn't your fault, because it's happening to several other families I know. Extortion. Once they know you have money, they'll keep coming back for more. The Mutlak family had their grandson kidnapped, and the people who took him demanded $20,000. What could they do? They had the money and they paid it." He raises his eyebrows. "Now they're in Syria."

"Couldn't you…go to anyone for help?"

"To whom? The police? As if we still had a police force." He brings the clock to the table and takes up some of the newspaper Amal was using to wrap dishes. "We'll go broke like this. The hospital is falling apart. There's a shortage of medicines, not enough electricity. I lost a patient last week because the cardiology unit had no electricity. Do you know, a man came and killed Dr Hamza on Tuesday because he failed to save the man's brother? Shot him in the head, in cold blood, as he was getting out of his car. There isn't even someone to report it to! The Americans say they're going to rebuild the police force after they've finished disbanding the old one, but it'll take a year. A year! Well, thanks very much, but that's not good enough. Who can live like this?"

Mum brings the tea to me, her hands jittery. "Sit and drink," she says. But the sofa is full of things they're packing, and save for Baba's armchair, there's nowhere to sit. Instead, I find myself sinking towards the floor and finding a place there.

"Your mother doesn't sleep. Your sister sits around all day with her mind going to waste. We're leaving."

"To where, Baba?"

He shrugs. "First, to Jordan. Then I suppose we'll try to get to France to be with Ziad. Or maybe I'll contact one of my old colleagues from Birmingham." He hesitates. "What about you?"

"Me?"

"Where do you want to go?"

I think about this for a minute, trying to imagine a new life in France, or in England. Then I try to picture Washington, or New York, or wherever Sam is now. The truth is that none of them seems right.

"I don't really want to go anywhere."

"No one wants to. But when you *have* to."

"I don't know, Baba. I think I might want to stay here. There's a lot of important events to report. A lot of journalists could use my help. Or maybe I'll go to work for an Iraqi paper, like you said I should."

Amal suddenly emerges from her torpor. "Is Nabil allowed to stay? That's not fair."

My mother's jaw drops. She shakes her head and looks to my father. Baba watches me, waiting for my reaction. "Nabil is twenty-eight years old. He's a grown man. He can do whatever he wants. The rest of his life isn't pending our permission."

Later tonight, I will explain everything. I'll tell them what happened, and they'll understand. They won't be angry anymore – at least not at me. But for now, in my room, I sit at the typewriter. Now, like Sam, I have a story that matters. I'll do all the research necessary for the profile on Ali that Sam still wants to write. I'll get it to her in America, somehow. Or maybe I'll publish it here, under a pseudonym. Maybe I'll compose a new collection of poetry that will capture what's happening in Iraq, the tragedy that would cause a family like mine to leave.

But instead I sit in front of the blank paper, my fingers hovering over the keys, unable to produce a single sentence.

62

Hovering

TODAY IS THE *Arbaain* for Noor. That means it has been forty days since Noor left this world, and forty days since Sam came into it – into my little corner of the world, anyway. Forty days since the bullet came and sucked one person out of my life and injected a new person into it. It is in this little corner that you find me on the 18th of May 2003, or the 17th of Rabi al-Awaal in the year 1424, once again in Hurriyah, whose name, oddly enough, means freedom. I wonder if any of us has a clue as to what freedom actually looks like. I only know they were supposed to free Iraq, but it seems Iraq has made captives and refugees of us all.

As we line ourselves up inside the mosque, Baba and me alongside all the men in Noor's family, something in me feels relief as much as grief. My family leaves Baghdad tomorrow, but Baba says not to tell a soul. Us being here, he says, is a good deed he wants to do before he goes. Everyone is ready to say their final goodbyes, to wave Noor on like a departing guest one last time, and then shut the gate. And then lock it. The words and the movements are our sad and wonderful blur of life and death. Sad because of why we're here, wonderful because it forces us together, and I, for these forty days, haven't felt a sense of being together with anyone. Anyone Iraqi.

Mum says it isn't a coincidence that we were stopped in Samarra, that Sam was taken away from me there. She was pursued, went down, and then flew off into the sky. Mum thinks it's a sign. After all, the twelfth Hidden Iman disappeared from a cellar in the Al-Askari Mosque in Samarra, it is believed. My mother would like to believe that the Mahdi is coming soon, and so any unusual occurrence in his hometown might be an omen. I would like to believe in something.

Salat az-zuhr, the noonday prayer. Four *rakat*, four cycles of sacred speech and movement, and each of them silent. Some of the men mouth the words without speaking them aloud, some just think them in their minds. Feet slightly apart, hands to our ears with palms facing forwards, a calling, a receiving. It intones like an orchestra. "God is greatest," we speak, almost in unison. I close my eyes to stop myself from looking at Baba, to see what he is doing, to see if he is saying something. If he is praying, too.

In the first bend to the floor my head feels full and hot, and by the second, washed out, clean, like something bathed at the seashore. It is good to rest my forehead against the cool tiles of the mosque floor, and only when I realize that I'm letting myself linger too long, out of sync, can I pull up again. When I prayed in the Shi'ite mosques with my mother, there was always a *turba*, a baked pottery tile to lay our foreheads on as we made *ruku*, as we bowed our heads down – a symbol of really touching our heads to the earth. Does it matter if you touch carpet and marble instead? Wouldn't God be pleased just the same?

Standing again. We turn out our hands and close them over our chests. The imam makes his case. *Sami'a a-Llahu liman hamidah.* God listens to those who praise him. The others respond. *Rabbana wa laka-l-hamd.* Our Lord, and to Thee belongs praise.

Sujud, prostrating myself on the ground. My body feels stretched out, spent, ready to stay here. *Subhana Rabbiya-l-Alla.* Glory to my God the Most High. The third, and then a fourth. Sitting again, my eyes half open to watch Noor's brother for direction, and my mind drifts.

During the taxi ride here, I gave my father more of the details of how his car had been written-off. About Sheikh Mumtaz, about Sam's broken ribs and torn spleen. I didn't even remember that there was such a thing as a spleen, I said. Baba said of course there is, Nabil, didn't you pay any attention to anything when you took biology? He must have forgotten that I had almost failed on account of my squeamishness, on account of the fainting. He doesn't know that I used to juggle the teacher's words and invert them, make derivatives of them and add suffixes or prefixes until nothing made sense, so that I could pretend he was speaking some language I couldn't understand. I imagined myself a visitor in a foreign country, pretended I was an anthropologist in the field, studying the ways of the local people. Maybe I have always wanted to be somewhere I don't belong, grappling with a foreign language that I would intuit over time. To be forever ten years old and discovering some new tongue and opening the possibility of never having to go home. Maybe I still want to be somewhere that is not here.

Stupid words fill my head, rhymes like the ones that young American photographer was making up one day while we were waiting for an American press conference at the Convention Centre to start. Back when the very sight of *them* running *our* government from within was one of the most shocking things I had ever seen. *Qabil*. Before the story, before Sam.

*Torn spleen, beauty queen, ugly stories made pristine…*what did they call that thing black Americans do when they put their poetry to a beat? Rap music. Maybe because it feels like it's rapping you in the head. But I like that it involves improvisation, sort of like a *maqam*.

Sam said she thought it was a duty to come here and report. Not a duty to her country, but to the truth. I wonder if that's only half the truth. Maybe she, too, likes to be in places where she doesn't belong.

My mind is swirling and I know I have lost where I am supposed to be. I realize that the imam must have been talking about Noor because everybody is saying, *Rahim-ha, rahim-ha.* God be merciful to her. The imam's voice sounds like the violin Ziad had learned to play, but not entirely well: melancholy, haunting, slightly out of key.

The imam doesn't stop for my lack of attention. "Ali said: Every day an Angel of Heaven cries: 'O people there below! Produce offspring to die; build to be destroyed; gather ye together to depart!'"

Miles said Sam would be just fine. A torn spleen, broken ribs, going home soon. Nothing fatal. I think of Sam's lovely body, the bones holding it up somehow broken, and not easily fixed. No real treatment for that other than rest and time, Baba told me when I explained what happened. Not fixable, and somehow, my fault. If only I could have protected her. If only she could have landed on me in the car, instead of the other way around.

And so I remain here, unscathed. Only scarred. From the

corner of my eye, in the outer ring of the mosque, behind the columns where the women sit, I catch a bright face. Noor's? I could swear it is. I turn to see it, but it's gone, dissolved into the face of someone who cannot yet be fourteen. Somebody else's light.

At Noor's house, the meat of a large lamb slaughtered in honour of her *Arbaain* lies on the table. Another lamb's meat is passed out to the poor in a nearby neighbourhood. I don't have an appetite but Baba pushes me, and I manage to eat some *quuzi*, the whole animal stuffed with rice and almonds and raisins. A dish I used to love.

What would Sam think if she saw this feast on a day of mourning? I wonder if her people, Christians or Jews, whatever they are, prepare all this food when they are thinking about someone who has died. It seems like the least appropriate moment to eat. And yet, this is the way we honour our dead – by showing how thankful we are that we are alive. By making sure the people around us will not go hungry.

Halfway through our taxi ride home, Baba breaks the silence.

"While you were gone, Cousin Saleh stopped by," he says, speaking in a whisper, as if the driver might eavesdrop. "He wondered where you were and why you stopped coming."

"What did you tell him?"

"That you were on an out-of-town trip. That I didn't know more." Baba stares out of the window at the Ministry of Defence, riddled with blackened craters caused by US missile strikes at the start of the war in March. The building, with its high, sloping sides leading to a flat plateau, looks like it was meant to recall the age of the ziggurat, when our ancestors thought a temple built this way could connect heaven and earth. Baba looks at the ravaged building as if noticing it for the first time, though I know he's passed this way before. Being a passenger sometimes forces you to see more than you do as a driver.

"Maybe you should stay with Saleh," Baba says. "You shouldn't stay in the house on your own."

"I don't know, Baba. I'm not sure Saleh was such a great help after all."

"No?" he asks, lowering his eyelids as if he senses that this is an understatement.

"No."

"Oh, and he says his wife is pregnant."

"*Mashallah*. That's good news."

"I'd like to see you start a family." He senses the imposition. "Eventually, I mean. Anyway, I don't think you should stay in the house alone."

"Oh, I'll be fine. I'll figure something out. If you're really worried, I can stay with Wa'el next door."

"I don't worry. I plan."

"Are you really leaving tomorrow?"

Baba pushes out his bottom lip. "Well, I might put it off a day or two, just to make a few arrangements. Put things in storage. I need to finalize things with a driver. But we are leaving, Nabil. Are you sure you want to stay?"

"I'm sure," I say. My fingers twitch to type out a fuller, more complex response. Instead, I look him in the eye as I never have before. "I'm absolutely sure."

"That's what I'd hoped you'd say."

At home, I head straight for my room. I can feel Amal following me there, hovering at the door. I invite her in and ask her to close the door after her.

I lie back on the bed. She shows me the sea-green sweater she is knitting, a look-alike of an English prep-school jumper, in miniature. She says it's for Ziad's son, who will be two years old soon. Harun, our nephew, my parents' first grandchild. We have yet to lay eyes on him. A funny name, choosing Harun. Harun al-Rashid, who died in the year 809, was Baghdad's most famous rebuilder. He, if anyone, was the great fixer of Baghdad. Maybe our little Harun will come home some day to build us up again. Sometimes it feels that it will take that long, a quarter of a century at least, to imagine a time when we will be rebuilt.

It can be very cold in France in the winter, Amal reminds me, as if she knows this from first-hand experience. This being late May, and already the thermometer inching towards 40-degrees Celsius, I cannot muster much sympathy for them. It'll be a nice colour for Harun, I tell her. In the pictures they sent, he appears to take after his mother, who has green eyes.

"Nabil, did you ever ask her if she would marry you?"

I glare at her a moment, then up at the ceiling. "You know I didn't."

"I don't mean Noor. I mean Sam."

"What? No." I can't figure out how my sister seems to look past my clothing and flesh and bones, directly into my brain. "Of course not."

"Didn't you think of it?"

No answer. My eyes on the window. Anything to avoid looking at her, letting her see any more than she already does.

"Well I think you should have. You obviously love her," she

shrugs. "Maybe she loves you, too. How many times in a lifetime do you think that happens? You should have at least told her."

I take my desk chair and sit on it backwards, the way I'd once seen Sam do while we were in her suiteroom at the Hamra. It seemed terribly unfeminine to me, and at the same time, kind of sexy. I rest my elbows on the edge of the chair, my hands on them, the way Sam did. I watch my sister's face, the eagerness in it masking the pale hue she has developed since she stopped going out, since the first bombs fell on Baghdad – in *this* war, that is. Since our lives were transformed into something else entirely.

"Don't ask me anymore about Sam. This is a day for thinking about Noor."

"But you're thinking about Sam as much as you are about Noor. Maybe more."

"How do you know what I'm thinking? There's no one in the whole world who knows what it feels like to be in my shoes today."

"Tell me, then. You can tell *me*. I promise I won't tell Baba and Mum."

"Sure you won't. You think I don't know that they send you in here to check on me?"

Amal's eyes betray a sense of guilt. "What do you expect from them? They're just worried about you. Mum is so sad about what happened to Sam. And considering Baba's car, I think—"

"Amal," I say, cutting her off. I feel a slicing in my stomach, the sound of the glass showering over our heads. "I'm going to pay him back for that. I've saved up a lot."

"Good luck getting it out of the bank."

"It's all in cash, from working with Sam. I have enough to

buy him a used car today, but he said it's better that they hire a driver to take the three of you to the border, because you wouldn't be allowed to take the car into Jordan anyway."

"That's not the point," she says.

"I know."

"You should go and talk to them. You should be with them now."

I shake my head. "Later maybe, before you leave."

Amal carries on but I find myself tuning her out, like a radio losing reception. I have no energy left in me for giving comfort, nor for receiving it. As much as I love them, Amal and my parents, I want them all to go away. I'm glad they're leaving. Maybe I am responsible for that, maybe Sam is. Maybe George Bush is. Maybe all of America. Maybe Saddam. It hardly matters. Most importantly, they'll be safer elsewhere.

The helicopter in my mind is taking off again, and this time, I jump on the landing skids, too. Get carried away along with Sam. It would be terrible of me to tell Amal to leave me now, but that's exactly what I want.

Instead, I'll go where she can't: out. I hold my hands out to hug her, and she falls into me. There is nothing in the world like a little sister's love, one of the few kinds of love that comes without condition, without a price, and, if you are as lucky as I am, without the pain of almost every other. I rock her in my arms, the most beautiful moment of my day.

"I'm going out for a while. Tell them not to worry."

Amal pulls away from me. "Where? Where are you going now?"

"I don't know. For a walk."

"You can't just go walking around town, Nabil. That's crazy."

No, *you* can't just go walking around, I want to say, because no father in his right mind lets a pretty young daughter out on to the street anymore. But just an average man like me? It hardly matters. "I do it all the time. I walk closer to town to get a cab to work." I say *walk* and not *walked*, as though I will get up tomorrow and do what I used to do. As though I have any idea what I'm supposed to do with my life tomorrow.

"Can I go with you, then? I want to see the city once more before I leave."

Her hopeful face makes me want to cry. "Not now, Amal. When you come back."

Her head rolls back with disappointment, the remnants of her girlishness snapped into place by her growing womanhood, which decides that she is not going to cry. Instead, she picks up the half-knitted sweater she had set down, which looks like it is unravelling more than it is being put together. "Just don't do anything foolish, and don't stay out late," says my fourteen-year-old parent, "And don't take any unnecessary risks," she calls as I leave the room, her hands moving the long needles quickly, as if her time were precious.

The long walk is good for me. What does it matter if I walk for miles, from Yarmouk Street down to Jinoub, all the way south though Qadisiya, into Tamim and Maarifa. It feels better just to move, to keep putting one foot in front of the other until my soles are almost numb. It is only now, when I get to Jazair, where I know I can find some place to get close to the river, that I feel the throbbing in my thighs, the pain of pushing too hard for too long, of pretending to be unable to feel anything. My shoulder, too, is sore, though much less so than yesterday.

Everyone says you should avoid the river these days. The Americans control everything along the Tigris now, because how can you control Baghdad if you don't hold the river in your hands? Many people stay away, because if a soldier thinks you look suspicious even for a moment, they say, he will shoot you dead and never hear a word of complaint about it. But there are still fishermen who come here regularly, whether early in the morning or late in the afternoon, the cooler parts of the day, to fish out a fresh catch of *simmich* from the murky brown water. If you're not sure your family will eat dinner, you will fish despite the fear of not coming home again.

Of several fishermen on the bank, I see an older man who has more than one pole with him. I ask him if I can borrow one for a while, and I hold out a few dinars in my hand. The fisherman waves away my offer and readily hands me his extra pole, scratched and burnished as though Abraham himself might have used it. Maybe he, our forefather, fished just like this in Ur, south of here, on the other river that demarcated what we were from what we were not. Between here, the Tigris, and there, the Euphrates, we became a Mesopotamian people, probably the world's first civilization. We built cities and languages and towers. Wrote tales of Gilgamesh and codes of Hammurabi. Founded mathematics. Forged religions. Hosted prophets. Discovered God, or let God discover us. No defeat from afar can take that away from us, can shame us from the love and pride for Iraq that we carry in our hearts.

I move down the sloping stones, closer to the river. From here I can see the silhouette of the statue of Scheherazade, just a little further down the bank. Maybe instead of trying to tell Sam about the hand of Fatima, I should have told her about the mind of

Scheherazade. She saved her life from a murderous king by her ability to tell him a new story every night. Until then, the king had a habit of marrying a beautiful woman every day, enjoying her for the night, and then having her beheaded in the morning, sure she had betrayed him. Through her great knowledge of history and literature, through her ability to weave stories together, Scheherazade told the king enchanting tales that kept him on tenterhooks each night until it was almost daybreak. After a thousand nights of this, he fell in love with her and made her queen. The writer Ibn al-Nadim mentions it as already having been famous in his tenth-century catalogue of books in Baghdad. So we have known for at least a thousand years that a storyteller – a female one, at that – can change the course of history.

Our stories are our strength. They have the power to keep us alive.

The odd thing about the bend in the Tigris in this part of Baghdad is that it is sometimes hard to tell which way the river is flowing. Logic says it must be moving downstream, but right now, I am quite sure it is flowing up. Sometimes you must simply trust that things will flow exactly as they are meant to, and when they don't seem to flow in ways that make sense, to believe that the hand of God is behind it. *Al Mu'eed* – the seventy-fifth of God's ninety-nine names – is the Restorer. Though I hope it is not blasphemy to say so, I should like to create the hundredth: the Fixer.

I tie my bait with a flimsy knot that I know will never hold. I like the liberating feeling of the *khamsa* as it flies off my pole, waving to me just before it hits the water.

Nihaya — The End

Acknowledgements

This book is dedicated to the memory of all the fixers, journalists and truth-seekers who lost their lives trying to tell the story in Iraq, in particular the friends and colleagues I lost: Alan Enwiyah, Mazen Dana, Marla Ruzicka, and Elizabeth Neuffer. This book stands in memory of Anthony Shadid and Marie Colvin, two journalists I greatly admired, who lost their lives in Syria in February 2012. Lastly, this story is in memory of Nadia al-Janaby – a woman I never met – who was killed in Baghdad in April 2003.

The people who most influenced this book are those who quickly became more friend than fixer, and who have remained in my life long after the story was over. For that, I am deeply grateful to Alia al-Janaby in Baghdad, Rizgar Hama Salih in Iraqi Kurdistan, Lutfullah Mashal in Kabul, and Nuha Musleh in Ramallah. Many other interpreters and fixers I've worked with over the years have left an impression on me, and they too have contributed to the birth of this book, albeit unwittingly. Many of them already were or became leading journalists in their own right. These include Safwat al-Kahlout, Saud Abu Ramadan and Mohammed Dawwas in Gaza; Samir Zeidan in Bethlehem; Khieu Kola in Phnom Penh; Gedsiri Suhartono in Jakarta; Kim

Ghattas in Beirut; Said al-Enizi in Kuwait City; Sherine Bayoumi in Cairo; Jinna Park in Seoul; Hana Kusumoto in Tokyo; and Ellen Tordesillas in Manilla.

I want to thank the book's first readers, to whom I will be eternally indebted for their incisive critique and encouragement: Alia al-Janaby, Wayne Johnson, Tania Hershman, Shana Tabak, Monique Taylor, Andrew Tertes, and Alys Yablon Wylen. Aloma Halter's wonderful literary eye played a particularly important role in the editing process. Mussab Aljarrah was gracious with his time in reviewing my usage of Arabic as spoken in Iraq. I'm also grateful to the members of the Jerusalem Writers' Circle – Nadia Jacobson, Karen Marron, Anna Melman, Sarit Nagus, Debora Siegel and Batnadiv Weinberg – who provided helpful feedback and comraderie. Finally, Martine Halban's brilliant insights and Judy Stewart's thoughtful editing have been indispensable in preparing this book for publication.

A good fixer leads you down new pathways and opens your eyes to things you didn't notice. In that definition, my most important fixers have been my teachers and tutors. I am deeply grateful for gifted teachers who, because of their wisdom in the world of writing and in life itself, have made this book possible.

In chronological order, they are: Sandy Rosenberg Cavanagh, Robin Reisig, Joshua Friedman, Sandy Padwe, Aryeh and Sandra Ben David, Diane Greenberg, and Dina Wyshogrod. Special thanks go to Wayne Johnshon at the Iowa Writers' Workshop and Robert Eversz at the summer writer's workshop in Prague. I am also grateful to the teachers who opened my eyes and ears to the beauty of Arabic: Moin Halloun, Omar Othman, Nasra Dahdal and Anwar Ben Badis.

I deeply appreciate the many friends and colleagues – writers, editors, and other literary soulmates – who have shared this journey and reminded me why we were on it: Ayla Peggy Adler, Tara Bahrampour, Scott Baldauf, Warren Bass, Faye Bowers, Yisrael Campbell, Jeff Eckhoff, Mona Elthahawy, Ruth Andrew Ellenson, David Erlich, Kourosh Karimkhany, Laura King, Judy Klitsner, Dina Kraft, Jonathan Ferziger, Linda Gradstein, David B. Green, Orly Halpern, Leah Harrison-Singer, Roger Hercz, Deborah Horan, Tovah Lazaroff, Quil Lawrence, Ben Lynfield, Naomi Michlin, Julie Meslin, Matt Rees, Rachel Stassen-Berger, Sam Thrope, Yael Unterman, and Molly Weingrod. Friends I worked alongside during my trips to Iraq and Afghanistan merit special mention: Adnan Nidawi, Stephen Farrell, Farnaz Fassihi, Bay Fang, Ivan Watson, Dafna Linzer, Borzou Daragahi, Larry Kaplow, Scott Peterson and Liz Sly. Thoughts of appreciation go to Mallory Serebrin-Jacobs and Shoshana Gugenheim, because I watched them continue to create art even after they created life.

I want to thank those who offered me a place to write as I worked on this book. The Mossers, the Ben Davids, and the Dempseys have all given me quiet, comfortable spaces to write, as did Rhonda Adessky and Jay Kaplan, Laura King, Elaine Markson, Ruthi Soudack, and Daniela Yanai. There will always be a special place in my heart for the Al-Janaby family in Baghdad, who opened their home to me and made this book possible.

I feel deep gratitude towards my parents, my siblings Craig and Ilana, and my extended family, all of whom have been supportive and understanding of the gypsy life I led for so many years. And finally, to ND, the love of my life, the fixer of many broken things, and the father of our two little lights, Eli and Zahara.

665